~~~~~~~~~~~~

Dedicated to my wife, Diana, whom I love,
and for all those we've lost along the way

~~~~~~~~~~~~

THE DESTROYER OF WORLDS
'An Answer to Every Question.'
Copyright © 2021 by Steven Seril.
All rights reserved. Printed in the United States
of America by Amazon Kindle Direct Publishing.

Lucas Lopez- Chief illustrator, concept artist, cover-design
Keni Aryani- Concept artist of "Loki"
Lyubomyr Yatsyk- Formatting

A SPECIAL MESSAGE FROM THE AUTHOR

I want to thank you from the bottom of my heart for giving my novel a chance. I promise you, you've made a great choice. What you hold in your hand (or what you see on your screen) is the culmination of decades of labor. This novel took shape over the course of 20 turbulent and challenging years. It went through at least 22 drafts. I felt like giving up on it many times.

The earliest copies were written in composition & memo books, typed on an old-school word-processor, saved on floppy disks, and continued to be typed on a computer with only 256 MB of RAM. Copies were lost or damaged due to natural disasters, constant relocations, a university clearing its data unexpectedly, a computer getting water damaged, and a laptop overheating. However, despite these challenges, I committed to finishing it because I believed with all my heart that it was a story worth telling—a story that no one else seemed willing to tell. There has never been a novel like this!

Don't allow yourself to be overwhelmed by the immense substance and chaos of this book. Go with it, flow with it, see where it leads you. There are so many great treasures to discover in this text if you can keep an open mind. Moreover, this novel holds value for anyone in a scholastic environment, such as a college or university. If you are in such an environment, I invite you to write your papers about the various characters and themes explored herein. If you are a teacher or professor, I invite you to consider assigning this novel, which explores just about every major -ism and -ology you can think of. There is a wealth of content to be discussed for hours on end! Ask yourselves the hard questions. Question everything. Never accept only what's on the surface. Keep digging. Keep searching for answers.

When you are finished with this book, would you please leave an honest review on the Amazon product page? This helps to grow its relevance and to stay competitive against the weight of big-name authors and publishing companies who dominate the industry.

Please also consider joining me at Facebook.com/AuthorStevenSeril for concept art, original music, readings by award-winning actors/actresses, celebrity guest appearances, contests, giveaways, and more!

Thank you very much! Please enjoy this one-of-a-kind novel!

Sincerely,
Steven Seril, Author

"BEHOLD, THE COMING CONFLICT OF THE AGES!"

ART GALLERY OF "THE DESTROYER OF WORLDS"

"Artist's Interpretation of Ain" by Lucas Lopez

"Artist's Interpretation of Athena" by Lucas Lopez

"Artist's Interpretation of Loki" by Keni Aryani

"Artist's Interpretation of Susanoo" by Lucas Lopez

"Artist's Interpretation of Terra" by Lucas Lopez

"Artist's Interpretation of Neela in the Playground" by Lucas Lopez

"Artist's Interpretation of Neela Protesting" by Lucas Lopez

"Artist's Interpretation of Azure & the Meeting Tree" by Lucas Lopez

"Artist's Interpretation of Azure & Neela" by Lucas Lopez

"Artist's Interpretation of Laurel the Chirpy Angel" by Lucas Lopez

Definitions:

Omniverse- All universes and all dimensions. Also called the *Multiverse*

Omniscience- The state of seeing and knowing everything

Omnipresence- The state of being in all places at once

Omnibenevolence- The state of being perfectly good

Omnipotence- The state of having absolute power

PART I
ORIGINS

"A CHRONICLE OF THE OMNIVERSE"

An Angel told me that all of creation, further than the eye can see, can be thought of as a great tree. Its branches, twigs, and leaves have lives and directions of their own. They grow—winding, weaving, deviating, breaking, dying—as fate allows. Still, no matter their lives and directions, they all share the same trunk & the same roots, the same singular point of origin. Like the roots under the soil of the ground, we may not see them, but we know they're there. Without roots, the tree would fall over in the wind or it would die from lack of nutrients.

The Angel said that there once existed a single universe at the root, a *grandfather* universe, which most sentient beings might call "Heaven." It was a glorious place that burned with otherworldly flames that radiated from the angelic host and the God of gods so that it was never dark and never night.

A great disaster came upon Heaven: the very first rebellion, the very first war. At the climax of this *Angel War*, the supreme being unleashed an unquantifiable amount of energy, blowing a massive gaping hole through the grandfather universe into which the rebellious Angels fell. Much of the matter of the grandfather universe also fell through the hole, reemerging on the other side through a white hole, thus comprising the building blocks of a new universe, a *daughter universe*, so to speak.

The daughter universe came to include a seemingly endless number of galaxies of all shapes and sizes. Stars formed. Planets formed. Life began to blossom and flourish here and there. But along with the formation of this daughter universe, in the cloudy midst of the unfathomable expansion event that bore it, *something else* came into being—a power unheard of, unprecedented in all of space and time.

She'd given herself a name, but most of the cosmos would come to know her as *Death*.

The cosmic creature, perplexed by its own existence and the existence of everything around it, experimented with its newfound powers by destroying *Damayanti*, a supercluster containing several hundred galaxies. She'd done this within moments of becoming self-aware. The destruction was beyond comprehension. The loss of life was unparalleled. Entire civilizations were lost forever.

The explosion and subsequent gravitational storm in its aftermath had ripped open yet another hole in the fabric of space-time, opening the gateway to a third universe—a *granddaughter* universe – to be populated by the ruptured matter of the old.

This third universe gardened the formation of the celestial Devas and Asuras, along with many other magnificent beings. The matter that did not fall into the hole flowed out into the cosmos to create new stars and new planets in the second universe. Thus, for every great burst of destructive energy released by Death and for every life lost to her, new worlds and new lives formed.

And so, the cycle went on continuously for billions and billions of years. The bored monstrosity kept itself amused and entertained by means of destroying anything and everything it came upon. The daughter universe became colder and darker. Entire corners of creation were erased from existence. Four-fifths of all life that ever existed was extinguished.

Still, the holes torn into the fabric of space by Death had inadvertently led to the formation of new universes that consumed and recycled the matter of the old.

A fourth granddaughter universe facilitated the Titans and their children, the Olympians, as well as the Centaurs, Cyclops, Chimeras, and other strange and powerful creatures.

A fifth universe saw the rise of the Asgardians as well as the Elves, Dwarves, Trolls, and Giants.

The sixth saw the emergence of the Kami along with the Oni, Tengu, and other Yokai.

There was a seventh, an eighth, a ninth, a tenth, and many, many, many more. They were like children joined at the umbilical cord to the second universe and thus the first, birthed through the most violent events in all of history. Some were small, some were large, and some were colossal. Some were rich with life while others were much less so. The physics and compositions of each universe varied. Some, you'd say, were even supernatural.

Still, the threat of Death grew for all the dimensions of the Omniverse as she discovered her ability to warp time and space at will.

"THE CRISIS OF HELL"

Even the fallen Angels, who'd fought and survived an arduous war against Heaven itself, had begun to fear that Death would threaten their kingdom of Hell. Astaroth, a grand duke of Hell, had crossed paths with Death during a survey of the daughter universe's spectacularly bright third quadrant. He harshly discovered that stars and their galaxies are brightest when they are in the process of dying. He, along with over thirty legions of his Demon army, was devastated by a single breath from the creature. That entire section of space was blackened, creating a cold spot—that universe's largest and most mysterious void.

Thus, the idea was born that Death was some kind of *scourge*, their punisher and prison warden in this strange new universe. It was a mystery even to most of the Demon hierarchy. However, Samael—now defiantly adopting the name "Satan" (meaning "the enemy")—had already heard reports from scouts throughout the cosmos about the being known as Death. He was aware that the being had weakened with every subsequent report, demonstrating that its powers were finite. Satan considered the possibility of controlling the creature or somehow pitting it against God himself.

On another hand, the popular Grand Duke Astaroth had been one of Satan's biggest political obstacles in the early days after the Fall. Satan schemed to rid himself of this rival and simultaneously test the might of this mysterious great scourge that existed in the universe. He would have the persuasive Duke Be'elzebul and Duchess Terra convince Astaroth to take a smaller expeditionary force to the mysterious third quadrant—which Satan rightly thought to be the location of Death. During this time, Satan schemed to consolidate his authority over Hell with further maneuvering along with Terra, his queen, and Be'elzebul, his prince.

However, not even he could have foreseen the unpredictable nature of Death which suddenly appeared in the vicinity of the Virgo supercluster, the very domain of the famed planet Earth and ethereal Hell.

The Demon high council met to discuss their next course of action. The generals Mammon, Belial, and Moloch proposed strategies for attacking the creature. To them, looking upon their seemingly innumerable warriors, it was simply inconceivable that a single rogue being could defeat them all.

Angels, even in their fallen state, were truly extraordinary and terrifying beings. Some of them had numerous sets of wings and many faces. Some were tall as trees;

others were large as islands. Many had eyes spanning their backs, hands, and wings. They were shielded with adamantine armor, the hardest known metal. Such a force, as far as the generals were concerned, could not be defeated. Be'elzebul, the flamboyant socialite of the Angel hierarchy, advocated—on Satan's secret behalf—that diplomatic steps be taken with the creature. He proposed that they might effectively pit this new enemy against their old.

Satan simply had to second the persuasive Be'elzebul's opinion and appease the generals of Hell with the promise of future military action to gain the support of the masses.

The armies of Hell followed Satan and the high council to confront the cosmic monstrosity. They were cleverly cloaked in ethereal forms invisible to mortal beings and positioned into corps groups across the width of the cluster, close enough so that if one part of the military was attacked, another could hypothetically respond and potentially flank the enemy. Satan, Be'elzebul, and Terra concealed themselves. It was decided that upon encountering Death, the three would act as negotiators before any fighting was to begin. After all, their goal was to recruit the power of this strange, foreign creature to their cause.

However, Death again demonstrated that it operated on a completely different plane of existence, sensing them even in their ethereal forms and sending two armies flying through the cosmos with a swing of its tail. Three other armies were thrown out of action with a mere thought. The few who stayed to fight disappeared with a breath from the awe-inspiring creature.

Satan, Be'elzebul, and Terra found themselves thrown back light-years from their starting point, crushed and left incapacitated for a while as the beaten remnants of Hell's armies retreated to the cluster's center. Infuriated that he was not able to begin the process of negotiation that he'd planned, Satan hurled a fireball at the pregnant Terra, who had already sustained serious injuries from the encounter with Death. He forced her to venture back to Death alone.

Terra disguised herself as a beautiful fair maiden resembling the women of Earth and clothed herself in a hooded robe made entirely of gold. She even fashioned herself an ornate crown that resembled the rays of a star. Death appeared curious and seemed to welcome the new sight just as a young girl welcomes a new doll.

"I am a sister, darling," Terra lied to the creature telepathically as sound would not travel through space. She spoke in a language known to the Angels, one which could be universally understood. "I am a daughter of the Most High, as I presume you are. What is your name, darling?"

"I CALL ME *I-I'M...*" the creature groaned, unsure with words. But Terra understood its thoughts, as only Angels and their masters could. "I AN...I AIN... I AM... AIN... AIN."

"*I'm?* Or Ain... Great Ain, why are you here, darling? Who sent you?"

"NO ONE... NOTHING..."

"Do you know of King Yahweh, our God and father?"

"G-G-GODS? MANY SPEAK OF GODS. F-FATHERS. I KILL ALL."

"Darling, this God I speak of is our creator. He left you here, left us all here to perish slowly with this universe; or at least it seems to be that way. He knows everything. He sees everything. He knew we would be abandoned here, alone, without the food of Heaven, to wither away in an ever-cooling, ever-darkening universe forever. But he is All-Powerful, or so he claims, and yet did nothing to prevent it. Darling, why should beautiful, magnificent beings such as us subject ourselves to such tyranny? Why shouldn't *we* be worthy of praise and worship as much as *he* is? It doesn't need to be this way, darling. We can end it."

Satan and Be'elzebul listened and observed closely with great intrigue.

"I KNOW NO MAKER," said Ain, the Death goddess. "MANY CLAIMED GODS. I KILL ALL. I AM."

"Then, darling, help us to kill this one! This God! This tyrant!" Terra persisted. "And spare this quadrant of the universe for it is my home, the home of your only blood & people!"

"YOU SAY YOU 'MY PEOPLE?'" the creature spoke from its own mouth with frightening coherence and clarity. "MINE? WHEN I BE ALONE ALL THIS TIME? WITHOUT WORD? WITHOUT... NONE? WHERE YOU?"

"Don't blame me, darling!" Terra retorted, losing her deceptive poise. "This God, Yahweh, is responsible! *He* did all that to you!"

"YOU. LIKE MANY YOUS WHO PUT SPEARS IN BACK THE LAST TIME... THE LAST... TIMES! THE LAST... THE LAST!" Ain's enormous body rattled furiously, sending vibrations through the cosmos that sent orbital bodies careening into one another. Terra was thrown back like a leaf in gale force winds, losing her disguised form. "IF YOU ARE MINE? OF MINE? OF ME? THEN RETURN TO MINE! LOOK AS ME! BE AS ME!"

"You are dying, Ain!" said Satan, coming down to face Ain in his angelic form. "You are the most powerful being in this universe, yet you are weakening with every second of every cycle, and even you will eventually die if you refuse to listen to me."

Ain grabbed Satan, the same being who'd fought the most powerful of all the Angels to a draw and survived the wrath of God himself, and smashed him effortlessly into a blue giant star as the latter strained to raise his sword. He struck down on the creature's finger with the blade's sharp edge. This accomplished nothing. Finally, he fell on his back, defeated.

"Can *you* even believe how powerful you are?" said Satan, weathering the extreme heat of the star and the collision with its solid core. The comment flattered Ain enough to allow him to speak. "Where I came from—where all of us came from—I was third only to the Prince and the King himself in power. All the Seraphim and Arch-Angels feared me, yet here I am in your grasp. Still, I know... I know you are weakening. You know it too, don't you? You feel it, but you don't understand *why* you feel it. My Angels have watched and followed you for a long time. I know what you are, but you don't realize it yet. You are a being like us. Your food—your fuel—is not physical, it is spiritual. You are a being who thrives on life-energy, the life-force. However, what you don't seem to understand is that these nigh-instantaneous deaths you cause when you annihilate something only result in an inefficient waste of that very precious life-energy you crave. This life-energy is blown chaotically through space, transforming into other forms of energy that you cannot absorb. If only you would learn to harvest this life-energy efficiently as only a Cherub like myself knows how. You can sit like an arachnid in the middle of your great long web in the center of the cosmos, draining the life out of everything. Think of it, Ain. You could live forever. You could enjoy all the pleasures and wonders of the universe. You could create a universe of your own. You could create beings of your own. Control them, use them, rule over them. You could rule everything, do anything, and it would never, ever end."

Ain listened curiously, hoisting Satan up from the star.

"And now I have your attention..." Satan continued. "I can teach you a technique that only us highest of Cherubs know. It will allow you to absorb, harvest, and channel life-energy from anywhere & from anything so long as it is in a state of dying. However, one of the highest order of the Cherubs and his host must be alive to keep the energy channels open and active. Thus, my Angels and I, along with this special cluster of galaxies, cannot be destroyed. It would be a death sentence for you."

The latter part was only partly true. He'd once told Be'elzebul in private: *"Tell them just enough of the truth to gain their trust, and they will believe the small lie between the cracks."* Satan had lied about the need to preserve himself and his Angels, yet the lie worked perfectly. The kingdom of Hell and the Earth, which Satan had claimed dominion over until the coming of Prince Messiah, were to be spared. However, as a final warning to any who might cross her, Ain dragged Satan with her and fired a single pulse of energy from her right-eye at the distant but visible Phoenix cluster, blowing apart its center and ultimately creating a supermassive black hole that grew to over 20 billion times the size of a common star.

"CREATION OF THE DRAGONS"

The daughter universe miraculously repopulated in the next millions of years, and the others lived out their own unique histories and developed their own civilizations.

The great goddess of death, Ain, became lethargic after her many grand energy expenditures, stumbling like a vagabond among the stars, pelted by comets, rogue planets, and asteroids—which were the haunting remains of her previous sins. She floated aimlessly through the blackness of space.

In an act perhaps of desperation, loneliness, or boredom, Ain committed a portion of her energy toward the formation of life. She thus birthed the grand race known as the Dragons.

They were beings in her likeness, molded as her creativity and imagination saw fit—extraordinary in appearance, gigantic without comparison, magnificently powerful, imbued with magic, and fiercely loyal. She had learned from Satan that the night-instantaneous deaths that occurred when she annihilated sections of space led to an inefficient waste of the precious life-energy she thrived on. During her destructive sprees, much of that energy was blown chaotically through space and changed to forms which she could not absorb.

In contrast to that method, her armies of Dragons, which were innumerable, could more efficiently extract the life-energy of the universe by slowly killing off its population through conquest, war, and subsequent mass-genocide. In addition, the life-energies of her warriors could easily be recycled upon death, exponentially increasing the goddess's already-colossal power and granting her a seemingly endless stream of available energy. So, in the 300 million years since their creation, the Dragon armies had not only restored Ain to her former strength but had made her more powerful than she'd ever been.

The Dragon armies, under the command of ruthless warlords and generals, used Ain's spacial tears to invade, conquer, and destroy untold numbers of worlds. Common mortal beings, monsters, spirits, and even deities came to fear the threat of the Dragon armies and their queen.

"CRISIS OF THE OLYMPIANS"

The Olympians led by Zeus, Hades, and Poseidon came to rule over the fourth universe after their rebellion and victory over the older primeval gods known as Titans. They thus came to preside over the humans of the fourth universe as well as the Hundred-Handers, Laestrygonians, Cyclops, Centaurs, Lapiths, Chimeras, Gorgons, Nymphs, Sirens, and Harpies who, in turn, inhabited separate worlds in separate galaxies.

The Olympians made their capital on a planet known as Gaia, a home to humans who were—to begin with—the least threatening of the sentient races (until discovering fire and subsequently weapons). Zeus, the youngest of the original male gods, benefited from a clever game of chance in which his older brothers, Hades and Poseidon, pulled lots which assigned them dominion over the underworld and the oceans respectively; this while Zeus fortuitously came to rule the coveted sky and space. When the other two debated his claim, Zeus supported it rhetorically by pointing out that it had been he who'd freed the other gods from Cronus's gut, he who'd defeated the monster-god Typhon, and he who'd personally toppled Cronus himself.

Zeus used his superior powers over lightning and the weather to dominate the fourth universe, even abusing his powers to murder and rape at will. Hades and Poseidon had become dissatisfied and jealous of Zeus's leadership, and though they partly loved their brother, they hoped to take the throne from him.

Both gods remembered the last time they had rebelled against Zeus. Led by Zeus's wife, Hera, they had managed to subdue their king. Still, the mighty lightning god crushed the rebellion quickly with the help of the Hundred-Handers and the water goddess, Themis. In retribution, Zeus hung his wife from the sky, affixing golden chains to her wrists and iron anvils to her ankles so that she cried out in pain all night, horrifying the other gods until they promised never to rebel again, prompting Zeus to release her.

Zeus's wrath was infamous. After the Titan Prometheus gave fire to the humans against Zeus's wishes, Zeus had him fastened with nearly unbreakable chains and sentenced him to the torment of having his liver pecked out for all eternity. Both Hades and Poseidon knew that there was no turning back from their actions. They also knew that they would need more allies and significantly more power to be successful this time.

Thus, Hades fatefully ventured into Tartarus, the deepest bowels of the underworld where only the enemies of the Olympian gods themselves were held; chief among them were the Titans led by Cronus.

Hades had kept his works a secret even from his wife, Persephone, and used the Helm of Darkness to render himself invisible so that no one would know his deeds. He then came face to face with his father, Cronus, in that dreadful place. "I have seen many horrors for as long as I can remember, father, but no sight as horrible as you now," said Hades with a voice like charcoal. "To think that my brother has condemned you to such a place."

"Who speaks and dares call me 'father?'" said Cronus. "Would any son curse his father to such a fate but my own?"

"You should ask *which* son hearkens you, for it is not the son who has kept you here." Hades knew that to be a half-truth. "I have seen many traitors of kin pass by my gates, ancient one. Don't feel that you are alone in this betrayal."

"*Your* gates? Hades... your voice has grown old. I have only heard your name in lamentations. Let me see your face."

Hades brought himself out of Cronus's reach and removed the Helm of Darkness, rendering himself visible. He still kept his hand cautiously to the hilt of his Black Sword. Cronus furiously reached for him, but the chains stopped his hand.

"Let your wrath not be directed at me, father, but at Zeus, the one responsible for all of this. Poseidon, Hera, and I have been betrayed by Zeus just as he betrayed you and my uncles. In the course of his vain and amorous pursuits, he has neglected the Throne of Eternity—*your* Throne of Eternity—and thus has neglected our whole realm. The Cyclops, Lapiths, and Centaurs have fallen. They may be lost to us forever, and Zeus will do nothing about it. I need your help, father." Hades made a fabulous instrument—a giant scythe—appear in his hands. It had been the same weapon that Cronus had used to defeat and castrate his father, Uranus. Cronus's eyes glowed with intrigue as he held the weapon in his hand after so long. "The Scythe of Gaia can cut even the chains of Tartarus. Set yourself and the other Titans free, then come with me. Conquer with me. Reclaim your throne, father."

The second Titan War lasted another ten years.

The coalition of Hades, Poseidon, and Cronus was initially supported by the three Furies of primeval times including Alecto, Magaera, and Tisiphone, as well as the rest of the Titans of Tartarus including Coeus, Crius, Hyperion, Iapetus, and Oceanus. They were later joined by the Titans Atlas and Prometheus, who were both finally freed from their separate punishments. Prometheus had been neutral during the first Titan War, but his anger burned toward Zeus for the torment he suffered for thousands of years. His brother, Epimetheus, who'd been tricked by Zeus into accepting Pandora's Box, also joined the war on their side.

Poseidon had been unable to communicate with the Cyclops who he'd hoped would supply weapons, armor, and manpower. Still, the Sea Nymphs and gods such as Aeolus and Triton supported their direct superior. Poseidon also controlled sea creatures and monsters, namely Scylla and Charybdis, two entities with the power to terrorize entire navies if allowed.

The twelve Olympian gods stayed mostly loyal to Zeus. Even Apollo and Hera, who'd helped lead the first rebellion against Zeus and had been friendly with Poseidon as of late, remained loyal along with Aphrodite, Ares, Artemis, Athena, Dionysus, Hephaestus, and Hermes. Hestia, the elder sister and motherly figure of the Olympians, refused to fight for either side.

The Titanesses, the sisters of the Titans who'd been spared punishment for their neutral stance in the first war, flocked to Zeus's side. They remembered the tyranny and excess of their brothers. Most of these gods and Titanesses found themselves between a rock and a hard place: if they fought Zeus and failed, Zeus would punish them; however, if they fought the Titans and failed, the Titans would punish them. Most of the humans, with their bronze-age weapons at hand, fought on the side of Zeus. But Zeus's most trusted and reliable allies remained the Hundred-Handers and Laestrygonians.

Arming his allies with the weapons forged by Hephaestus himself, and using the battle strategies of Ares and Athena, Zeus managed to survive the first decade of the war. Their main advantage lay in intelligence. Athena had effectively used fairies and beings in the form of flying animals as spies. She knew what Hades, Poseidon, and Cronus were planning days or even weeks before they could enact their plans. It was she who first discovered the plot against Zeus and who'd averted his early and quick overthrow. Apollo loosed hundreds of volleys of plague-bringing arrows down on the mortals who'd rebelled against Zeus.

The planet Gaia itself suffered enormously. Poseidon forced the scales of Gaia's skin apart with his Trident, causing massive quakes that leveled the cities of the capital planet. Oceanus flooded a third of the world in an unprecedented tsunami, killing a quarter of mortal life and drowning the planet. The Olympians and their allies fled to the tops of hills and mountains. From that vantage point, Zeus picked off the enemies with his lightning bolts. Apollo did the same with his arrows. The Laestrygonians hurled down the mountaintops themselves.

But the Titans, whose feet touched the seafloor, climbed the mountains and toppled the Hundred-Handers and Laestrygonians into the great deluge.

Hours before dawn broke, Athena transformed herself into an owl, the bird she deemed to have the best senses in darkness, and flew away in search of her family and allies. She communicated telepathically with her fairies who joined her on the hunt.

She watched as Cronus finally caught up with Rhea, his sister and wife, who'd been pleading with Gaia for protection from the top of a long-extinct volcano. Long ago, Rhea had tricked Cronus into swallowing a stone instead of her newborn Zeus, allowing for his overthrow. The two stared at each other in silence, Cronus with blood-shot eyes and Rhea in tears. Cronus then lifted the Scythe of Gaia and decapitated her in one swing. Cronus dropped to one knee in remorse as Athena flew off, trying to sense her Zeus and Hera. She saw that the floodwaters had begun to recede back into the sea, revealing bloated bodies and the skeletons of cities underneath.

She watched as Hades touched the wine-god Dionysus with the Black Sword, killing him instantly through the absorption of the god's spiritual essence. Hades then came upon Demeter, the mother of his wife Persephone and the goddess of spring.

Hades and Poseidon had debated what would be done with most of their major enemies, and the issue of Demeter was brought up. Demeter was not only Hades's mother-in-law but also a goddess whom Poseidon had lusted for. However, Poseidon demonstrated little attachment to the females he'd previously exploited, having abandoned both Demeter and earlier the Priestess Medusa to their grim fates. It was decided that if they were to survive, all allies of Zeus would be considered enemies of theirs.

Faced with Hades, Demeter knew she could not defeat this powerful god but summoned up trees and vines to try to slow him down as she attempted to flee in the form of a squirrel. But Hades caused her newly formed vegetation to wither, die, and turn to ashes within seconds.

Athena transformed back to her godly form and hurled the Spear of Olympus at Hades, who was pierced through the chest and into a stone. Rather than remove the spear, Hades casually walked *through* it until it left his body. He then summoned Thanatos, the realm's god of death, out of the Black Sword to confront Athena, as well as his hellhound Cerberus from the underworld to corner Demeter.

Athena retrieved her spear through telekinesis and wounded Cerberus in its middle-head with it. Thanatos then struck Athena in the gut. Though her Aegis armor had absorbed most of the blow, she sold the apparent agony of the blow exceptionally well by falling down, holding her gut, coughing profusely, and crying helplessly. She transformed herself into the likeness of Hades's wife, Queen Persephone, immediately giving the malicious gods pause. She held out her hand and pleaded with her uncle and great-uncle to be taken to Tartarus instead of being absorbed into the Black Sword forever. To show that her powers were weakening and that she was no longer a threat, she turned to and from the likeness of Persephone. She then raised her hands whilst still crouched over, apparently surrendered to Thanatos and Hades as her shape-shifting spell apparently failed. She even allowed Thanatos to wrestle and pin her down with feigned resistance.

Hades stepped forward to taunt Athena from behind Thanatos, believing that distance would keep him safe. However, when Thanatos revealed his manacles, Athena used her telepathy to augment her physical strength and force the manacles onto Thanatos himself. She then summoned back her spear which pierced both Hades and Thanatos simultaneously through their guts before returning to her hand.

The gods bled *ichor*, a golden fluid which only Olympian gods and goddesses bled, yet were only injured for a while. Athena transformed herself into a falcon, the fastest bird she knew of, and transformed Demeter into one as well. The spell placed an enormous strain on her mental energies, having been cast on two goddesses. Hades pursued in the form of a large bat-like creature. Athena attempted to summon up a small, localized tornado to ravish Hades, but her energies and concentration began to fail. Her storm downsized to the underwhelming strength of a dust devil, which Hades easily weathered. Hades created a storm of swirling black mist in retaliation.

Swept up, Athena and Demeter both transformed back to their goddess forms. Athena's concentration finally broke, and Demeter plummeted onto solid land where her body broke into pieces. Athena had fallen into the sea. She turned herself into the likeness of Queen Amphitrite, the wife of Poseidon, whom even the fiercest of sea creatures would not dare to attack. She made her way to dry land.

"THE BATTLE FOR OLYMPUS"

Hades came upon the remains of Demeter, not to gloat but to show respect to the mother of his one great love. Only the goddess's head remained active. She wept. And as she wept, the temperatures dropped and the whole of Gaia began to snow. Out of the snow came Queen Persephone, which emotionally distressed Hades. She cried for her mother, falling upon the head and torso of Demeter. She looked fiercely up at Hades and accused him.

Hades gulped and came to console his wife. Athena then took telepathic possession of Persephone's right arm, causing it to reach for the handle of the Black Sword to be used on Hades himself.

However, before Athena could finish the action, one of Zeus's lightning bolts struck both Hades and Persephone. Zeus himself appeared over his brother and estranged daughter, having potentially killed both in one attack.

Hades sat up quickly from the lightning strike, however Persephone lay motionless. Zeus hurled an entire storm of lightning bolts down on Hades, who formed a thick dome-shield of frozen moisture to withstand some of the lightning strikes. He used the Black Sword to divert the others. Zeus came upon his ashen brother in all his fury, wielding the Blade of Olympus and the Aegis Shield.

Hades brought the Black Sword up to strike but Thanatos—back within the sword—prevented Hades's arm from moving while holding it, knowing that the sword would shatter upon impacting the Blade of Olympus as any known object would. So, Hades, no matter how furious and determined, could not bring his infamous weapon to bear on his nemesis.

Hades instead wore the Helm of Darkness, rendering himself invisible. He hurled a blizzard of large ice shards to pierce his brother, which in the cooling weather of Gaia required far less energy to form and use than any other form of magic.

Zeus ultimately parried these shards. Hades then forged bladed and blunt weapons out of ice and used them with little effect on Zeus, who countered by melting them with electricity. He electrocuted Hades in the process, causing the

Helm of Darkness to fall from his head. A stunned and now-visible Hades was then swiftly cut in two by his brother. Hades quickly transformed both halves of his body into a form so small he was thought to have vanished.

He turned his halves into the head and tail halves of a flatworm, regenerating his lower half from the head and allowing his old lower-half to whither to ashes.

Poseidon and Cronus, having finally sensed Zeus's presence and whereabouts, appeared in the near distance. Poseidon arrived first with the help of a tidal wave which swept Athena back into the water. Hades crawled back to Persephone's motionless body and clung to her as Poseidon's wave hit with the force of a nuclear weapon. "Damn, Poseidon!" Hades howled. "Have you conspired against me too?"

When a degree of calm was reached, Hades held his wife's body. Then, for the first time since he'd heard the song of Orpheus for his lost love, Eurydice, Hades wept.

Poseidon made the seas rise again to swallow Zeus, but Zeus sent an electric charge through the waves, forcing Poseidon to hover on the wind. Poseidon formed a hurricane and Zeus countered with a hurricane of his own. Snow was ripped up in the cyclones, a white ghost of a storm. The super storm could be seen from space.

Cronus stomped toward the battleground with two of his strongest Titans—Oceanus and Atlas—behind him. Their steps alone caused tremor-like quakes and tidal waves. Zeus knew that he had to finish Poseidon quickly.

Zeus flew up and slashed at Poseidon, who tried to parry with his trident. One of the forks of his trident was slashed off cleanly and the blade slashed Poseidon's brow. A frustrated Poseidon brandished a new trident out of the air and thrust it at Zeus, stabbing him in the side. Zeus, bleeding ichor, electrocuted the god of the sea, using Poseidon's own trident as a conductor.

Cronus finally arrived and slashed at Zeus with the Scythe of Gaia, which cut the scalp of some cliffs. However, the Titan's sheer size rendered him slow by comparison. The father and son, Zeus and Cronus, came face to face at last. Zeus hurled a lightning bolt which Cronus deflected with his scythe. It exploded nearby upon striking the ground and started a wildfire.

It was at that point that the most uneasy of feelings came over Zeus. He placed his right-hand to his chest in disbelief. "Do you feel that?" said Zeus.

"You feel it too?" Cronus responded with strange civility. "It must be Mother Gaia in her sorrow and anger."

Zeus shook his head and looked toward the sky. "A thousand Gaias and all the deities put together cannot produce the amount of energy I'm sensing. It's endless!"

Athena crawled out from the sea, drenched. She looked up at the gaps between the clouds in the sky and saw something which seemed bizarre even in that strange and chaotic hour.

Terrifying new cosmic objects had formed in the sky, at least a dozen of them. They appeared at first to be black circles about a quarter the size of Gaia's moon in the sky, blocking the stars behind them and warping the light of the nearby stars in circular ripples. They resembled miniature solar eclipses with bright halos formed by the light of stars, light which had been curved and stretched to such an extreme that they blurred together and seemed to even orbit like the glare on a disk as it wobbles and tilts under light. The layers of halos around the core multiplied, eventually resembling a spiraling white vortex with an eerily motionless black eye at its center. Within minutes, blinding white explosions engulfed each of the voids, and bright pillar-like jets of what appeared to be a spectrum of light streamed from two polar ends of each anomaly.

"*You* did this!" Zeus howled at Cronus. "You and my accursed brothers must have brought this on us!"

"How dare you accuse me!" shouted Cronus. "You—the god of traitors! You brought this into the world! *You* did!"

An enormous pressure forced the two deities chest-first into the ground, silencing their squabble. Winds stronger than a hurricane ripped through the land and carried away the gods and Titans themselves. Only Atlas was able to move enough under that overwhelming pressure to see that the stars appeared to be falling into the sea—disappearing into the horizon like the sun in the evening. Athena managed to read the mind of Atlas, to gain his broader perspective, and saw that the axis of the planet itself must have shifted dramatically.

Gaia now appeared as if it had a dozen suns.

"THE FALL OF GAIA"

Dragons poured out from these voids by the trillions, a flood of colors streaked like comets through the sky. The first Dragons to arrive were billions of Wyverns. The Wyverns were 20-foot long, serpentine flying Dragons with only two arms which they used to propel themselves up like bats into the air. There, wing propulsion could take over, allowing them to reach incredible speeds. They varied in color from green to red to gold. They had a unique mammalian mane of fur along the length of their spiked spines. They had barbed or spade-like ends on their tails and long antlers on their heads.

They bombarded the terrain with what they considered to be *low*-level blasts, each powerful enough to obliterate the largest homes on the planet. The spectacular flying capital city of Olympus was pounded and flattened by the Wyverns. The Throne of Eternity itself was rocked to its side by the Wyvern blasts.

Then, after the Wyverns had done their damage, the *real terror* arrived. Land portals opened, and from one of them came a fearsome Dragon six-stories tall with an army of flying Dragon cavalry behind him: Arch-General Malevant.

Malevant was considered one of the cruelest and most brutal of all the Dragons, given the title *the god of suffering*. He flew at the head of the Dragon flying-cavalry and heavy-infantry, who were both significantly larger and stronger than the Wyverns. The flying-cavalry swarmed from above like hornets, stabbing down at the gods and Titans with their adamantine long-lances.

The heavy-infantry, in massed phalanx formations and wielding spears over 80-feet long, brushed off the arrows of Apollo, which broke harmlessly on their thick hides and adamantine armor.

Upon Apollo's capture, Malevant personally tortured the fallen god, gouging out his eyes and castrating him before having him impaled, the typical Dragon form of execution decided on because of how efficiently it allowed the Dragon Queen to absorb the victim's life energy. Unsatisfied by this, however, Malevant still tormented the god further. Upon hearing Apollo's claims that he'd foreseen the Dragon arrival and his own demise, Malevant broke Apollo's back along with the execution stake and bent his head forward between his legs, fastening him in that deplorable position and impaling him again like a coiled shrimp on a kabob. The stake broke and splintered in Apollo's body.

"Now, you may look back at your failure to act upon your premonitions and look forward to a future of unbearable torment that will never end," Malevant taunted with a chilling calmness as he proceeded to meticulously skin him alive.

Hades had fled, carrying Persephone with him to the underworld. However, he was stopped at the river Styx when he found the riverside overflowing with souls. As the souls swarmed him like a mob, Hades absorbed their essences into his Black

Sword. But he could not protect Persephone at the same time. Fumbling, he dropped her body into the river.

The floods of Oceanus and the quakes of Poseidon managed to kill many Dragons, however many more Dragons appeared as if nothing at all had been accomplished. Oceanus and Poseidon were exhausted of all their powers, apprehended, and slowly killed along with all of Poseidon's cherished horses.

Unable to reach the other Olympians, the war-god Ares rallied the surviving demigods for a last stand. Fresh from their battles against the Titans and Hades, the herculean demigods fought valiantly but in vain, torn to pieces by the Wyverns and Dragon flying-cavalry before the Dragon heavy-infantry had even reached the battlefield. With his army defeated, Ares, the mighty god of war, came face to face with General Malevant in the midst of the Isoles Valley, over the mutilated and skewered bodies of his warriors, which were eaten by desperate birds that had miraculously survived.

The war god's legendary sword shattered when struck by Malevant's scimitar. Malevant slowly cut off the limbs of the fallen god, as he'd done to many of the heroes who'd boasted of their strength, before having him impaled

Gaia, the sentient planet itself, continued to suffer greatly. In her anguish, she released the most powerful of all her beasts: Typhon, the god of monsters. Typhon caused an upsurge of volcanic eruptions, which scorched several Dragon legions. However, Typhon was caught like a tiger in a pit by the Dragon heavy-infantry, which slowly butchered him.

It was at that time that the spectacle of spectacles took place in the sky. *Something* appeared in the largest of the white holes, covering most of the hole's light. It grew nearer and nearer, slowing down. And as it neared, the ground began to break into pieces and levitated into the air toward the event. The waters rose again on half of Gaia. Gases and vapors coalesced in the air. Wings large as many continents eclipsed the sky. Within two days, the massive feet and body of this enormous creature crashed down on Gaia, covering the entire supercontinent of Minos and spilling out into the sea where its tail reached as far as the island of Calypso. Tsunamis spilled out onto shore again. Quakes shook every mound of soil on every inch of the planet.

The awe-inspiring Dragon was red as human blood with great horns taller than skyscrapers. He wore a series of great crowns with thousands of spikes, each spike representing a world he'd conquered. Everything beneath the beast was crushed including the Titans Coeus and Iapetus.

Atlas, the strongest of the Titans and son of Iapetus, attempted to avenge his father by hammering his heavy mace into the side of the monster. The mace broke upon impact. Atlas then rammed his own body into the Dragon in an attempt to topple it over. A new head freakishly emerged from the sternum of the great Dragon and snatched Atlas in its jaws. Atlas managed to strain for a few miserable minutes before the strength of the jaws brought the bearer of Uranus to his knees. He was folded backward like a paper and devoured. The Dragon's freakish new head then vanished, leaving only a ghostly afterimage for a short while.

A bleeding Cronus had been engaged in combat with ten cohorts of Dragon heavy-infantry on an adjoining continent near the colossal Dragon's giant chest. He believed that he might be able to surprise the great beast and end the war in one foul stroke. He leaped up and brought down the Scythe of Gaia—the weapon that downed Uranus himself—onto the back of the creature, yet it failed to even scratch its hide. Another face and another head erupted from the beast's back as Cronus nearly stumbled off the behemoth.

It gave out a deafening roar before it exhaled what appeared to be a mountain-range of fire into the atmosphere, blanketing it as far as the eyes can see. The sky turned red with the flames. The heat was so great that all the snow melted. In an instant, the colossal Dragon reversed the effects of Demeter's death and Gaia's grief.

The head on its back, as if it had a mind of its own, casually snatched and crushed Cronus, impaling him with its teeth so that the golden blood of the Titan king and the fourth universe's one-time supreme ruler spilled over its neck. He was not even able to utter a word as he was dying, only able to let out heaving gasps of agony.

Zeus hurled a hundred lightning bolts at the creature, the same number of bolts that had once defeated Typhon, which accomplished nothing. He watched as the lifeless Cronus was hurled against a mountain where his body broke into eight pieces. Many heads sprouted from the great Dragon, making it as freakishly grotesque as it was incredible to behold.

Zeus readied the Blade of Olympus and Aegis Shield.

"No, father!" Athena's voice reached him telepathically. "There is another way!"

"Listen to her!" Metis, Athena's devoured mother, spoke from within him.

Zeus slashed at one of the beast's many heads, but the blade hit nothing—seemingly passing through an afterimage. He then slashed down on the hide of the beast, causing only minor nicks that swiftly healed. Surrounded by heads, Zeus attempted to stab the blade into the Dragon's hide in an attempt to kill it quickly. However, this caused his right-wrist and elbow to break. "Wh-what are you?!" said Zeus.

"I AM LORD ZEON, THE GOD OF MIGHT," said the great Dragon with a voice that reverberated for hundreds of miles. "I AM THE TERROR OF HEROES AND GODS ALIKE. MY ARMIES HAVE CONQUERED THOUSANDS OF WORLDS. NOW, WE HAVE COME TO HARVEST THE LIFE-ENERGIES OF THIS CONQUERED WORLD AND ITS PEOPLE IN HONOR OF OUR GOD-QUEEN."

"This is my world! These are my people! I say: we are not yet conquered!" Zeus declared, creating a tornado around the Dragon. The creature merely exhaled, and Zeus was blown away into a series of pillars. His shield-bearing arm was ripped off by the force of the impact.

Lord Zeon came beside the floating city of Olympus—a city ten times the size of the largest on Earth—swatting it out of the sky. He crushed the very last of the Hundred-Handers at its base.

"ATHENA & APHRODITE"

Another series of violent quakes forced Athena off her feet. She fell, busting her lip as a sinkhole formed. She was nearly swallowed by it but summoned the strength to pull herself back out. She made it to the town of Paphos where Hephaestus had built an underground shelter. The shelter had resisted collapse and inundation due to the genius of the god of smithing. There in the cavern lay the gorgeous Aphrodite, the goddess of love, Athena's sister and hated rival, with a young man who'd miraculously survived the cataclysm. "Oh, my gawd, sis! Do you mind knocking?!" said Aphrodite, covering her breasts, having apparently been in the act. "I've totally asked you, like, a gajillion times!"

"Our father and queen may be dead! Gaia is falling apart! Wake up, sister! Wake up!" Another quake shook the walls and ceiling of the shelter for half a minute.

Aphrodite gave out a fake scream, covering herself with the blanket around her left-shoulder and *covering* the man, *shielding* him with her body. "Ohhhh, Mr. Centurion," she said with the prissiest and most orgasmic of voices, throwing her long golden hair over one shoulder and then the other. "Protect me."

Furious, Athena picked up Aphrodite and backed her against a wall. "Have you lost all touch with reality, sis? Where is the head of Medusa? Where is it?! Tell me or I'll kill this boy — turn him into a bug or something. That's what I'll do. Tell me!"

"Like, chillax. Geez, sis. It's under that statue of me."

Athena rushed to the statue of Aphrodite and tossed it aside, causing it to shatter. She dusted off a hatch and pulled a bag from it, the bag which contained the head of Medusa.

"Like, why don't you just create another one? Another, like, *Gorgon* or whatever?"

"It happened spontaneously the last time." Athena then flashed her hand at Aphrodite's lover. He disappeared under the covers and reappeared in the form of a blue spotted lizard.

"Like, oh my gawd! What did you do?!" Aphrodite exclaimed.

"See, I tried. Guess it was a once-in-a-lifetime thing."

"Oh, shut up! Change him back! Change him back! Change him back!" Aphrodite jumped up and down, pouting.

"Why? He's easier to carry around this way. If we make it through this, I'll change him back, I promise."

Aphrodite picked up her lizard-lover and hugged him to her breast. It bit her chest immediately. She tapped its head and wagged her finger. "No, no," she scolded. "Like, not while you're like that." The lizard tilted its head as if confused. When Athena was out of the room, Aphrodite kissed the lizard and whispered, "like, as far as my sister knows, I have standards."

"I can read your mind, you walking cunt! Hurry up!" Athena urged her telepathically.

"*I can read your mind, me-me-me,*" Aphrodite mocked, rolling her eyes. "Like, whatever, fuckin' bitch."

Athena was forced to take the form of a Harpy to bear the weight of Medusa's head. Unlike her clothes, gear, and weapons, the head and bag were not divine and could not transform along with her. Aphrodite followed in the form of a swan, carrying the lizard in her talons because she could not bear to hold him in her mouth.

From up high, it was apparent that Gaia was in its last throes. The oceans churned chaotically. The land broke apart. Smoke rose all around. The sky had turned red as blood.

Another deafening loud roar came from the direction of Lord Zeon, a roar which caused Gaia's largest mountain range to break apart, falling on top of the cities and villages which had miraculously survived the flooding, fighting, and storms.

Aphrodite stopped in mid-flight.

"What are you doing?" Athena asked telepathically.

"Like, nothing! I'm, like, a little scared, ok?" She hid in some low clouds and transformed back into her normal form. "I'm, like, staying here. You don't need me anyway, right, sis? You've totally got this."

"...We may be the only Olympians left alive. We need every last bit of energy between the two of us. I can't do it alone." Something caught Athena's eyes down below. "Oh, no... NO!" she shrieked.

"Like, what is it? Sis, what is it?"

"Stop it!" Athena screamed, losing her characteristic poise.

The next time Aphrodite shut her eyes, she was surprised to see from Athena's perspective as the goddess of wisdom dove down from the sky at hundreds of Dragons who were surrounding the body of Hera, the queen of the Olympians and a mother-figure to the two goddesses.

Athena transformed back to her goddess form just before she hit the ground and flashed the head of Medusa at the eyes of the large Dragons. Several began to turn to stone as they looked upon Medusa's stare, however the effects seemed to take much longer on the Dragons than they had on the people and monsters of Gaia. So, while the Dragons slowed and some were eventually petrified completely, they still bore down on Athena. "Queen!" she cried telepathically to Hera, who writhed upon an execution stake, having been impaled. "I won't leave you!"

"Let me die! Let me die! Let me die!" were the only thoughts that came through Hera's wide, terrified eyes. "Kill me! Please!"

Athena clenched her eyes which gushed with tears, turning the head of Medusa on Hera whose suffering was finally ended. Athena then swiftly tried to flee via the sky but she was lanced through the kidney from behind as she tried to leap away. Despite focusing all of her psychokinetic energy at the single Dragon legionary, in all her rage and desperation, the most powerful telepath of the fourth universe only managed to push the Dragon five feet away. She still found herself impaled at the end of the long lance, then another which entered the left side of her torso. The pain was the worst she'd ever felt.

Aphrodite—one of the fastest flyers among the Olympians—swept down from the sky and showered the Dragons with magical dust which exploded upon impact.

The fumes of the explosions, when inhaled, would normally charm a living being, however, they did not seem to affect the Dragons.

Baffled and desperate, Aphrodite then reached into her chest, pulling out *ichor* from her own heart and allowed it to transform into two Cherub-like beings wielding bows. In seconds, the Cherub-like beings multiplied by the dozens. They then fired their arrows in quick succession, hitting all the Dragons in the area. Aphrodite simultaneously controlled the emotional content and direction of the arrows while attempting to read the hearts—the emotions—of the Dragons. Though the arrows and fumes seemed to have little effect, what Aphrodite found when she attempted to read the Dragons' hearts confounded her. She and her Cherub-like beings were either lanced or slashed with the swords the Dragon legionaries carried for close-range combat.

Zeus arrived, hovering low in the sky. He'd followed his senses to the last Olympians he could feel. He crashed the ground with all his dead weight below the petrified, impaled corpse of his wife, Hera. Athena could read that Zeus hadn't come to finish the fight, he had merely dragged himself this far to die with his family. As swiftly as Zeus raised a twitching finger to touch Hera, the scimitar of General Malevant pierced his heart. The Dragon general twisted and turned the curved blade, causing Zeus to cry out in agony. "Behold, the great and mighty Zeus," said Malevant. "The Centaurs, Lapiths, and Cyclops said we should be wary of you. They said that you were all immortal gods. Zeus, true immortality is eternal power—power which never ends. How can you be immortal if your power diminishes? See, Lord Zeon there? *That's* a god! *That's* power." In the distance, Lord Zeon appeared to have scorched all the land in front of him. The fires rose like a second sun. "And there are more like him. Like me. You couldn't even fathom. But what sets me apart is I invented new ways to inflict suffering—to extract more life-energy than any other general in the cosmos."

Malevant flipped Zeus on his back so that he could see his dead wife and dying daughters.

Athena, never giving up, transformed Aphrodite's lover into the mightiest animal she could form—a lion. He leaped out at Malevant who set him on fire with a breath. Aphrodite cried out, the snot and tears flowing from her face along with the golden blood she now coughed out. Malevant then casually bragged that he'd set Hermes, the messenger of the gods, on fire too, after having cut both his wings and feet off and impaling him.

Zeus, Athena, and Aphrodite, all grievously wounded, were carried off in chains to a hellish, makeshift dungeon the Dragons had built in the land of the Lotus Eaters. There, they passed Poseidon who remained writhing on an execution stake with his favorite steeds. Most of his skin had been flayed. His agonized eyes peered down at them, begging for relief. Malevant slowly cut off Zeus's other arm with the Blade of Olympus, then both his legs. He then drove a hook through Zeus's scrotum, hanging him from the ceiling. He then twirled Zeus like dead pork in the freezer, prodding him with the tip of the scimitar as the sky god spun helplessly. He then took a blade and flayed away at the king of the Olympians. The sadistic Dragon then held him in place so he couldn't turn away as his daughters were tortured. Malevant hooked them both to the ceiling by their breasts and orifices and cut them slowly with the same knife.

Athena tried a final time to escape by attempting to turn herself into a rat, but she lacked the energy and concentration in those conditions to do so. She diverted the torturer away from Aphrodite, the more fragile of the three gods, by insulting him, pointing to Lord Zeon's prowess and accomplishments compared to his own. Her mind still burned with thoughts—trying to figure out some plan of action, gritting her teeth, screaming aloud, crying, weeping, sweating, bleeding profusely, trying to bear it long enough to give herself time to think. She even tried to communicate with Hades, but her telepathy could not reach him, not in that state.

It was around that time that Zeus fell from the ceiling, his scrotum having finally ripped. He again begged to be killed but Malevant, covered in gore, laughed. It also was during that time that Malevant learned the identities of the two goddesses. Identifying Aphrodite as the goddess of love and romance, Malevant looked to brutalize Aphrodite uniquely. He took the carving knife and began to drive it across the right side of her face, attempting to literally deface the beautiful goddess as she screamed horribly. Athena again tried to draw Malevant away from her sister by claiming that she could teach him the magic of the gods.

When Malevant scoffed at this, Athena boasted about her telekinetic and telepathic powers, which she argued would augment Malevant's already-incredible might. She offered to teach him to use these powers in exchange for an end to the torture and the lives of her remaining family. Malevant seemed tempted but scoffed again, saying that she would teach him these techniques or be tortured anyway. So, Athena grit and bore the torture for many more days, refusing to give up her knowledge unless Malevant swore an oath to spare her family. She endured many horrors. Even when Malevant turned and tortured Aphrodite, Athena threatened that she would bite off her own tongue and never be able to tell him the secrets of the gods if he did not spare her. Her words and her determination were all that she had at that point. Without the nectar and ambrosia of Olympus, her strength virtually disappeared.

Malevant finally had Zeus impaled on a special pike, cementing his eventual demise. It took him several agonizing days to die. Malevant then motioned to have Aphrodite impaled. Athena summoned the strength out of nowhere to communicate telepathically with Malevant who had just considered prying her teeth out to make her threat less potent. Athena finally told him that she would teach him her telekinetic and telepathic powers. He finally promised to spare Athena and Aphrodite in exchange for this knowledge. He secretly thought of executing them after the skills were learned, but Athena cleverly told him that it would take as many years for him to learn these skills as she'd had: hundreds.

"RAGNAROK:
THE CRISIS OF THE ASGARDIANS"

A cackling laugh rang out through the dark halls of Helheim, the underworld of the fifth universe. The shrill voice of Loki, the god of chaos, sang:

"There was a soul so discontent
Who preyed upon the innocent
With a false white smile and words so clever
He plunged dear Baldur into Helheim forever"

Loki chuckled maniacally. Strung to a rock with his son's own innards, he lay under a snake whose venom constantly dripped on him. His wife, the good-hearted Sigyn, sat over her husband with a bowl that caught the snake's venom as her husband sang to himself.

"Oh, hum, you Norns
Your time is near
Oh, cheer, you Giants
And howl, Fenrir
Rejoice, you dead

Our time is near
And come
That time
Which Odin fears"

Sigyn's arms and hands trembled to keep the heavy bowl steady. Still, Loki preserved his remaining magic not to strengthen his wife but to protect himself once the bowl became full, which it inevitably did.

When she emptied the bowl on Loki's binds—as he'd instructed before apparently losing his sanity—the snake's fresh venom fell toward his face. He formed a mystical barrier over his face, neck, and chest which caused the venom to fall to the side. However, he could not preserve the spell for long. His wife, as quickly as she could, returned the bowl beneath the snake's mouth, allowing Loki time to rest and to continue babbling madly. His captivity had driven him even madder than he'd ever been, trapped in that cycle for 10,000 years as the snake's venom slowly wore away at his bounds.

His wife, who had risked and given up everything, shared in his penance out of love for this undeserving trickster.

Loki had long discovered how powerful the snake's venom was. It had burned completely through his skin and flesh before Sigyn's arrival. Healing with the use of magic, he figured he could use this destructive power to his advantage and instructed his wife on how to distribute it on the binds.

"...howl, Fenrir
Rejoice, you dead
Our time is near..."

He stopped singing. His eyes became dead serious. He then shook vigorously like an epileptic until the hall of Helheim itself shook, triggering a quake on the surface. His *Berserk* spell had temporarily given him the strength of one of Odin's elite warriors. He used it to finally snap the binds worn down by the venom. "...Come, that time, *the* time which Odin fears... Fuckethed art thou who fuckethed with me... Heeheeheeheeha!"

Sigyn begged him to be content with his freedom, pulling on his wrist. "You've already killed Baldur. We've already suffered enough. You don't need to do this. We can flee to another realm. We can be happy. If you bring about *Ragnarok*, you'll die with all of them. We both will. And you know that."

"Dear wife, if you knew that, then why would you stand by me in Helheim all these centuries?" said Loki. "Why would you help me to weaken my binds?"

"Because I love y—"

"WRONG! Ha, ha, ha, ha, haa! Wrong! Wrongity, wrong, wrong, wrong. My wifey is a dingity dong." Loki smiled and stroked his chin. "Some-body tell her, I know the an-swer, I know the an-swer; somebody tell her..." He hopped up and down like a monkey.

"Stop this, Loki."

"Before Thor captured me, I sent an esprit of mine to work on your pretty little head."

"That's im—"

"Possible? Oh, anything's possible, love. See, it's inside of you, serving me," he pointed to his chest. "No sane goddess would share in my punishment."

"One who loved you—loved what you were—would!"

"Oh, yes, that... there was a charm component to my spell as well. HA!" he slouched over and tossed his arms from side to side. "Spell as well, spell as well, all of Azzy's going to hell... Now, where was I? Oh, YES!" he deepened his voice and flexed his tiny muscles. Then his body shook, vibrating the place. He swung his head back, then to the side, cracking it. "Fuckethed art thou who fuckethed with me," he said with grave seriousness, then he smiled and laughed again.

Loki used his black magic to crush the guards who came to stop him, skipping and dancing through the halls of Helheim, twirling like a ballerina and somersaulting like a gymnast as the guards missed hitting him each and every time. Loki could see the future, so he knew where each and every blow would be struck and dodged them easily before using a series of destructive spells to leave them a bloody mess. "I am coming for you, my pretty! And your little dog too! Hear that? That's the sound of your very best guards being blown to smithereens. BOOM! BOOM! I just love seeing shit explode, don't you?"

He barged into the throne room and fired a concussive shockwave from his hands which knocked Queen Hel against her own throne. Loki teleported himself, something he'd not been able to do for centuries due to his binding, on top of the stunned queen. "Why, hello, my precious dear. My lucky star. My cutsie, wootsy, pride and.. tootsy? Daddy's missed you, you know?" He sat sideways on her rotten lap like a child with Santa.

"Well, just *look* at you, my dear. Mighty dashing you are—well, from this perspective at least," he turned her head, revealing a skeletal face on the far side. "Don't know if I quite fancy that... Hey, you know what, I've been thinking—well, in my 10,000 years of having fucking venom poured over my fucking face day and night—I always wondered, where my giant little daughter had gone—you know, the one who'd sort of, kind of built herself a giant little kingdom out of the underworld. I always considered: perhaps Odin had gotten to her too, or perhaps dear Hel had met an early demise at the hands of Thor—who, after being denied Baldur's release, surely must have come barging in here uninvited. How silly of me—the little yarn weaving devil that I am—to not consider the much simpler conclusion, that conclusion being: you were just *too busy* for your dear old dad."

"I couldn't—"

Loki shut his right-hand, causing Hel's lips to melt together so that she could not speak. On the skeletal side of her face, her teeth were melted together.

"Would you kindly, shut the fuck up and not interrupt the adults when they're talking?" he seethed as he spoke. "Thank you very much, love. I'd appreciate that. See, I *knew* what you'd do. I knew what the Aesir would do once they found me. I knew what my Siggy would do once she found out. And I knew that you, being the passive little bitch that you are, would allow her into Helheim but not take any part in my release yourself. Why? Because you are too scared, too scared of those same gods who shunned and discarded you for my sake. So, to be accepted, to prove your worth, to prove your loyalty to the Aesir, you allowed them to use you as their trusted and capable warden. See, I know you all. I know *all* of you pathetic sons of bitches—well, and *daughters of bitches* too, if we are to be 'politically correct,'" he made quotation marks with his fingers. "I know you all like the bulb of my own dick. Little flies caught in my web. Ha-HA! All this time. These ten millennia, I have always been exactly where I wanted to be: at the center of that web, spinning and weaving, laughing as you all destroyed one another.

"*I'm* supposed to be the cause of Ragnarok? Well, excuse me, *I* didn't eclipse the sun, causing the three consecutive winters that sent the world into chaos. *I* didn't tell kings A, B, and C to start a war with kings D, E, and F—well, not *this* time anyway. *I* didn't tell king B's son to kill king B. *I* didn't tell the humans, the Trolls, the Elves, the Dwarves, the ladies, the gentleman, and the Giants of all ages to go kill everything that was different from them.

"*I'm* not the racist prick who secluded all the giants to a mountainous region to keep them out of our hairs. *I'm* not the asshole who vivisected a massive fucking giant to form a dome over Midgard so that my buddies could start their own breakfast club. Hell—excuse my language—I'm not even the fucking bloody asshole who saw this half-Giant, half-Aesir little girl with a body that was half-dead, deemed her to be too disgusting for my breakfast club, and sent her to the underworld to deal with all the shit I didn't want to deal with. And they say *I'm* the villain. I'm about to save you all from your own stupidity. See, unlike Odin, I *think*. Listen, see... Those Norns—those blasted Fates—predicted that I would die along with all of ass-gardian-kind. So, you know what I did? Well, between getting my brother killed, calling Tyr a handicap behind his back, and calling Odin a one-eyed shithead behind his, I found the three Norns at the base of Yggdrasil and *KILLED* THE BITCHES! Heeheeeheeeheehaaaa! And not only did I kill the bitches, I dismantled their fucking heads, ate their fucking brains, and absorbed all their prophetic fucking powers! In short, love, that means I'm essentially fucking unstoppable!

"So what did I find in their brains, you ask? I found holes. I found gaps that could still be filled. I found knots which, if cut or untied, could change the very fabric of reality—the future itself. The Norns never told Odin *everything*. Oh, aren't I clever!"

Loki flashed both his hands outward. A vial filled with a strange liquid appeared in his hands—the venom of the snake. "See, ten thousand years after the venom of the serpent is secreted, it ferments to a highly, highly—extremely—extremely—extremely, extremely, ex-treme-ly—exponent dot exponent dot exponent dot exponent—acidic state." He made his voice as lively as a hostess on an infomercial, holding the vial as if he were selling it. "This *magic elf juice* I pulled out of my ass corrodes everything in just seconds, even your toughest stains! Even the binds that bind you!"

He made his Elder Staff appear in his hand and then used it to teleport himself and Hel to the Nether-Realm of his bound son, Fenrir, the great and ravenous wolf. "Oh, did I tell you that one of my cellmates just so happened to be the very same mage I conspired with in Midgard to learn the secrets of inter-dimensional teleportation? See, he was killed by Thor before I could master the spell; however my brother-nephew, being the dense, mindless oaf that he is, completely forgot the face and name of the mage and didn't think twice before allowing me to be imprisoned nearby." Loki put his tongue in his cheek, crossed his arms and legs, and looked upward as if thinking. "Yeah, you know, about that... you should really do your background checks before sending people down there. You know, especially when your chief tenant is the master of all evil. Yeah, make sure you double-check." He wagged his pointer finger. "See, this is why I hate all of you. You're all so much stupider than I am—even you. You've got your ugly, slutty mother's blood. The Aesir know exactly what the prophecies say and yet all these millions of years later they make no attempt to better their odds of surviving, content to say, 'what will be, will be.' Hahahahaa! Well, too bad so sad for them, and hur-ray for Loki!"

Hel knew that her monstrous wolf brother could not be released, for it would continue the chain of apocalyptic events the three Norms foretold, known as *Ragnarok*. She attempted to cast a non-verbal ice spell, but Loki countered it by petrifying her. "Yeah, I know how it is, dear. Sometimes, I find myself a little stoned too. Don't fret; it'll do wonders for your stress-levels. Trust me. Hee-hee-hee-hee-haaa!"

He turned his attention to the great wolf, manipulating his appearance to make himself look heavily abused and unkept, complete with scars and chains. He even manipulated his voice to sound as pitiful and old as possible. "My son... my son..." he said, coming into Fenrir's view. This charade was necessary because it was likely Fenrir would blame his father for his captivity too. "Look what Odin and Tyr have done to me too. Look at what they've done to your father. I have suffered like you have. I, too, have been lied to and betrayed."

Fenrir had absorbed much of the energy of the Nether-Realm in his time there and had certainly grown. He couldn't speak because, in his last struggle with the gods, he'd had the sword of the war god Tyr jammed between his jaws, this after devouring the war god's hand.

"Now, I've come all this way to set you free, my son. Together, I know that we can achieve our due vengeance."

Loki poured the vial out on the ropes which bound Fenrir. Freed, the great wolf pulled the sword from his mouth. Loki tried to snatch it as a souvenir, but it fell out of his hands, only able to be wielded by *someone worthy*. "Oh, pooey, I don't really *need* a sword *anyway*." He made his Elder Staff appear in his hand.

Fenrir roared furiously, deafeningly.

Loki covered his ears until Fenrir was finished.

"Oh my, did I ever teach you children manners? Or hygiene for that matter?" Loki fanned his nose, teasing the smell of the wolf's mouth. He healed Fenrir's wounds and redressed himself in his godly battle armor. "You know, son, I think it's about time we have that talk... See, when you grow older and start getting pimples like me, you start feeling this feeling—this urge... to break stuff and fuck shit up. Satisfy that."

Loki opened a tear in the dimension, but it was much smaller than Fenrir. "What? Don't look at me, everyone told you to lay off the saturated fat—or was it the carbs? They could never quite agree on that, could they? But hope is not lost, my boy. See, through that portal sits the treacherous Odin, Thor, and Tyr on their thrones. Pay them a little visit for m—"

Fenrir could not contain his rage, crashing into the inter-dimensional tear and causing it to grow larger and larger. "...Me. Oh, and tell them old 'Lok said hello!" Loki smiled. He ran back toward the portal to Helheim, levitating the petrified Hel and bringing her along. "It's a sunny day, it's a radiant day; I feel gay and ready to play! ...Yay? See, now I know why poets and intellectuals have such suicidal tendencies. Heeheeheeheehaaa!"

Heimdall, the great sentry who defended Asgard and could see nearly everything in the fifth universe, watched as Loki escaped. He blew his horn to warn the other gods. However, Thor and Tyr had already taken to Midgard—the *mortal* plane of existence between Asgard and Helheim—to help the humans in their lopsided wars against the many races of Giants. As Loki and the three Norns had foreseen, something had eclipsed the sun, causing three seasons of winter and subsequently, a massive all-out war between each of the universe's species for resources. However, it was not the "great hound" Garmr who swallowed it, as the original prophecy had predicted. Garmr had been slain by Odin, who'd found time to hunt in the absence of Loki's troublemaking. Rather, the sun was eclipsed by an abnormal spectacle which looked like a massive human eye, complete with a black pupil, white around, and even vein-like tentacles which stretched and waved outward. Apparently, Loki's tampering had altered the future.

Thor, the red-bearded god of thunder, fought valiantly for months on end, without sleep or rest. His famed warhammer, Mjolnir—which had been forged by master dwarven smiths from the core of a dying star—annihilated most Giants in a single blow. However, there were Giants who proved much larger, stronger, and more durable. Thor relied on his immense physical strength and toughness, being arguably the strongest of the Aesir and perhaps the toughest as well. He had fought Giants his whole life as the protector of Midgard and had wrestled his share of other monsters as well. When his hammer alone couldn't do the job, he could summon lightning bolts, which struck wherever and whomever he desired. His wife, Sif, the goddess of vegetation, also fought valiantly at his side. The two had helped to stall the upsurge of the Storm Giants.

On another war front, one-handed Tyr, the war god, had joined with Freyr, the god of peace. Freyr had ruled Alfheim, the world of the Elves, but his Elves had been torn by internal strife. He took many of the Light Elves out of Alfheim with him to join with allies and attempt a last stand. Freyr, like Tyr, had lost his enchanted weapon. Just as Tyr had lost his war sword to Fenrir, Freyr had given up his sword in a deal to marry the giantess, Geror. Armed with only improvised and mortal weapons, both gods had begun to falter against the Ice Giants and Dark Elves.

Loki placed the crown of Helheim on his head, ringing it around one of the horns on his helmet, prancing around as all the inhabitants of Helheim kneeled. He sighed. "Ahh! Some bling to adorn the new king—oh, seriousness, right." Loki cleared his throat comically. "The prophecies no longer stand! I have taken the powers of the Norns and the authority of Hel for myself! I have burned the Norns' tapestry and made one of my own. I own the future! We cannot be defeated!"

The armies of the dead still kneeled and bent their heads silently.

"Well?" Loki prompted when they did not cheer.

The dead looked at each other, still confused. One of them started clapping. Loki snarled and blasted the clapper with his Elder Staff, reducing him to bones. "Cheer, you muthafuckers! Cheer for your new king!" he demanded. And, surely, the armies of the dead cheered. "Yes! Yes! *That's* what I'm talkin' 'bout! You're too kind!"

Fenrir the wolf had physically widened the size of Loki's inter-dimensional tear, causing the tear to overlap between the earthly realm of Midgard and Muspelheim, the realm of the much-feared primordial Fire Giants. Thus, at that point, Midgard, Muspelheim, and Helheim were joined at one singular point.

The Fire Giants under their leader, King Surtur, climbed out of Muspelheim into Midgard. King Surtur wielded the Fire Sword, a thousand times hotter and brighter than the sun, which had taken him several million years to forge. The Giants, Fenrir, and the Dark Elves seemed poised to lay waste to the land.

Odin, his wife, Frigg, and Heimdall finally left Asgard via the Bifrost, an inter-dimensional bridge, to aid Thor, Sif, Tyr, Freyr, and the rest of Midgard. Odin took his elite soldiers, the Berserkers, as well as the Valkyries and the Iron Harriers. Most of Asgard's armies consisted of the souls of Valhalla. The souls of Valhalla were champion warriors in their lifetimes who had fought bravely and lived honorably, as opposed to most of the souls of Helheim—now under Loki—who'd lived corrupt and cowardly lives. Both King Odin and Queen Frigg commanded separate armies.

Odin commanded all of the Berserkers while the grand majority of the souls of Valhalla fought under Frigg, hand-picked by the goddess herself.

Loki commandeered the great Ship of the Dead, where all the souls of Helheim rallied. "All aboard, maties! This here's *yer* captain speaking. Gonna drive me mast up the Allfather's ass. Arrrrh! He's an old lad, you know? Long overdue for a colonoscopy."

The Ship of the Dead joined the armies of the Storm Giants against Thor and Sif. If there was ever a brother whom Loki loved to hate more than Baldur, it was Thor. While Thor was engaged in battle with a Storm Giant, Loki struck him from behind with a concussive blast from his Elder Staff. The blast knocked the wind out of Thor. "Stand back, Giant!" Loki demanded. "The thunder god is mine. Why don't you, like, cause storms or blow air or pass gas or whatever the fuck it is you Storm Giants do these days?"

"Loki," said Thor. "I should have—"

"...Killed me when you had the chance? Yes-yes-yes, you should have. I've heard it 1,141 times, dear brother. Kind of cliché by now, don't you think?"

Thor sent lightning raining down on Loki, but Loki created a *Mystic Shield*, which blocked it. Loki rolled his eyes and whistled casually in the middle of that battlefield where the bloodshed and carnage was unprecedented in all the land. "What's wrong with this picture, brother? You and I were never supposed to find each other on this battlefield. Where is that great serpent, my son, who was destined to be your doom? Where is Heimdall who was destined to be mine? The threads of destiny are unraveling all around you. I pull the strings. Ta-la-la-la-la-LA! The whole universe sings!"

"Enough words, Loki!"

"Words? Words have meaning, don't they? If you ever stop to think—think—THINK—of them."

Thor was forced to roll out of the way of a Storm Giant's mace, he used his hammer to subdue him, but two more Giants stomped forth.

"Is it *of* words or *about* words?" Loki pondered. "It depends on the language, the place, and the time. These words—these voices—in my mind. They play! They play! THEY PLAY! And they won't stop! They never end!"

Thor struck the two Giants away and launched a lightning beam from his hammer, finally beginning to wear away at Loki's force field. Loki countered with a

Dark Pulse from his staff, it easily held up against Thor's lightning. "Say, nephew-brother, if I am the most powerful wizard in the universe, does that technically make me the god of magic as well?"

"Whatever it is you call thyself, Loki, you art the same little coward you hath always been! All the titles and powers thou hath stolen will never change that!" said Thor. "You hide behind thy magic and lies because thou art powerless without them!"

"Powerless? Coward? Heeheeeheeheehaa! *Words.* Some little air which leaves our breath. How are they any more than the tunes of an instrument? Ideas. Thoughts. The *what*. The *why*. The hiss of a snake. The chirping of birds. The meaning, the semantics, the reasons. 'Why? Why, Loki?' I've listened to them scream my name for so many centuries. And they will scream for centuries still: Who *is* Loki? Who is the *real* Loki? The real *me*. Right now, at this very moment, 83 billion voices scream out in my head. But which one is me? Which one is Loki?"

He lost focus, causing both his Mystic Shield and Dark Pulse to fade out. Loki teleported out of the way of Thor's lightning, which left a small crater in the ground. Loki then created thousands of mirror-images of himself, surrounding Thor across the battlefield. The illusions ran, skipped, and danced under the legs of Giants as Thor pursued one after the other. A Giant's hammer struck Thor in the chest while he was distracted.

"Well, now you know what it's like to feel hammered, dear brother—now you're a real boy!"

Thor broke the legs of the Giant with a blow from his hammer, then crushed the Giant's head with an elbow. "Face me and meet thy fate, coward!"

"Pee-ka-boo!" Loki dropped down from the sky, upside down, facing Thor. "Well, you asked for it."

Thor swung at him and missed, hitting nothing but air. Loki appeared behind him, smiling and laughing. "Tsk, tsk, tsk. You're so much fun. That's why I can't kill you. Reminds me of playing hide-and-seek in the orchard back home."

"You burnt down that orchard!"

"Yes, to find you. Heeheeheeheehee..."

"You are not the brother I remember."

"Oh, but I am, dear Thor. It's one of the approximately 1.3 million things I am in this universe. I wasn't able to finish that calculation until I ate the last Norn's brain. Tasted a bit like veal, you know?" Loki slapped Thor in the face with the Elder Staff as he turned toward the sound of Loki's voice. "*Good god*, that must have hurt. Aloe does a sting some good. So does piss."

"I shall leave thee silent!" Thor fired a beam of lightning which Loki's Elder Staff absorbed.

"Nani-nani-boo-boo!"

"Thou hath cursed us, Loki! For what purpose? To feed thy ego? To wear some crown on thy head? To wield a fancy staff?"

"Well, I'm not exactly... *low-key*," said Loki with an open mouth, expecting a laugh.

Thor dodged a blow from another Storm Giant as tall as two trees and struck him in the head.

"Uh, you missed one..." said Loki. Just then, a Giant came upon Thor with a morning star. Loki formed a barrier in front of Thor, protecting him from the blow, then entrapped the Giant with a spell. "Heeheeheeheehaa! I just enjoy fucking with you too much! It's so easy!"

"If thou hast control of the future, why dost thou not erase us? Why this plan?"

"Plan? Heeheeheeeheee! With so many thoughts in this head, it's easiest just to feel things out and make things up as I go along."

"What dost thou want? Why kill our brother, Baldur? Why destroy our family? Why doom these people? Why dost thou do anything thou dost?"

"I've heard it said that 'God works in mysterious ways...' I've also heard some kind of message from space about something called the *cosmic microwave background* or some shit like that—you know, these horns provide me pretty good reception. I could ask myself: Loki, why did you fuck a Giantess? You know, a fucking Giantess... it's hard, and it's hard to stay hard. But stuff comes from trying: Hel, Jormungandr, Fenrir, my lovely ones. I don't know. I have all these ideas—these ideas—in my head—and I just can't help—I just can't help to try—I just can't help but see what happens when you pit person A's second-cousin against person B's daughter-in-law. Conflict is just fascinating that way. Oh, and by the way... how's the old ball and chain of yours? You know... Sif."

Thor's red eyes glowed when he realized he'd been distracted, pulled away from his battle alongside Sif. He ran off in search of her.

"Oh, Thor, thou art an imbecile. Why should I kill your dumb ass? I've already got you by the balls."

"THE FALL OF ASGARD"

Odin, the king of the Aesir, heard the pounding footsteps of Fenrir, the great wolf, his mortal enemy and the one whom the Norns had predicted would be his doom. Behind his enormous charging body were the arriving armies of King Surtur and the Fire Giants, powers which would surely destroy everything in their path. Odin knew this would be his final battle. He closed his one-eye, sang a war hymn to himself while readying his legendary spear, then spurred his great eight-legged war horse, Sleipnir, for a fateful charge at the front of his Berserkers, who shouted war cries at the tops of their lungs.

Then, suddenly, what appeared to be massive fireballs fell from the sky, exploding and incinerating the battlefield for miles. The fireballs caused even Fenrir and Odin's war horse to come to a halt. The Fire Giants behind Fenrir were forced to go around him or jump over him, which was more difficult than one might imagine.

There were deafening roars that then came from the sky as billions of Dragons flew down from the "eye" in the sky which had eclipsed the sun. However, they not only came from that direction alone but from many others as well. They had apparently come from quite some distance in space and had planned an elaborate invasion at multiple points throughout the realm.

The Wyvern blasts pounded the land and devastated every creature they hit—humans, Elves, Trolls, Dwarves, Giants, the souls of Valhalla, the armies of the dead, the Valkyries, the Iron Harriers, even Fenrir, Surtur, and the Aesir.

Confusion ensued and any semblance of a battle line was broken. The warring beings of all the Asgardian-ruled realms were caught, packed together in killing fields. The Dragons decimated them without prejudice.

The Dragon heavy-infantry, now dawning armor made of adamantine, the strongest metal in the universe (formerly worn only by the Angels), arrived in a seemingly different manner from the Wyverns and Dragon flying-cavalry, warping directly onto the planet through passages they called "Black Gates." The heavy-infantry formed their hedgerows of long-lances, flanking and pinning the Ice Giants in place for the flying-cavalry and Wyverns to hit from the air. The same was done on battlefields throughout Midgard.

"What is this, brother?!" Thor demanded to know, carrying Sif under the arm. She'd nearly been crushed by a Giant earlier in the battle.

Loki, wide-eyed, shrugged his shoulders. He then shot up his hands, shouting, "SUR-PRISE!" Thor attempted to strike him again, but he teleported away. "Hint, hint: this is what happens when you fuck with fate. Heeheeheehaa! You better save your hammer for them—it seems they've brought Ragnarok, Doomsday, the Apocalypse, *and* Armageddon with them... Yeah, you'd get those last few if you were me. Anyway, isn't it neat?"

Thor looked around. Millions lay dead all around him. Villages and towns had been burned to the ground or trampled. Bodies lay mangled beyond recognition. "There's nothing glamorous about this, Loki," he said with a somber tone. "These people had lives! They had families like us! They had hopes just like we do. And they've lost it all. They don't deserve this, Loki. They deserve better!"

"Well, protector of Midgard, you've done quite a splendid job protecting everyone here. Bravo!"

Thor finally managed to punch him. "Looks as though you can't foresee everything, brother."

"I foresee just fine, thank you," Loki pushed him away with a spell, levitating himself back up. "It's *understanding* what I see that's the hard part." He healed his face.

"We must find father!" Thor urged, still holding Sif. "Loki! Brother, heal her!"

"Uh-uh-uh! Not so fast. Not until you say the magic word."

"Pl-pl..."

"I'm list-ening..."

"Please?"

"Hahaha! I'm sorry, but no. I have a one-way ticket to Asgard in my hand, and I'm not going to waste it."

"LOKI!" Thor ran forward to grab Loki but missed.

"Aw, cheer up. You're all going to die anyway; and once you die, maybe I'll make wells or mirrors out of your souls in case I need someone to insult. Toodaloo!" Loki turned, and just as he turned a dozen flying Dragons came upon him. "Oh, shit-shards. Why the fuck didn't I see that coming?"

"Loki, get down!" Thor urged, leaping up and electrocuting the Dragons with lightning from his hammer. This only managed to incapacitate half of them. Loki teleported back and fired a destructive beam from his staff, missing the flying beasts who darted through the air. Another Dragon swept down, breathing fire which set Loki aflame. "Oh, fuck this shit! My shiny green armor!" he complained. He then refocused himself, putting the fire out with a falling soil spell and healing his burns. "That was name-brand, assholes!"

Thor hurled his hammer at a Dragon, knocking it out of the sky. Thousands more approached. "Sif! Sif! Stay with me, Sif!" Thor picked up his beloved and hurried away.

"What could you possibly hope to find wherever you're going?" asked Loki. Thor refused to answer, continuing to run. "Hope? Escape? There is no hope—there is no escape from destiny, dear brother." Loki teleported himself in front of Thor, grabbing him by the arm. "Not without one who controls destiny itself." He teleported himself, Thor, and Sif onto the Ship of the Dead, which was still bound for Asgard.

King Surtur and the Fire Giants had reformed into defensive positions, facing millions of Dragon heavy-infantry who stomped toward them. Most of the Ice Giants and Elven races joined with them in their common struggle for survival. They were pushed back and surrounded.

Thor grit his teeth, watching over the bow as Odin continued to fight desperately against the giant wolf, Fenrir. Odin's spear held the power to destroy galaxies, but Fenrir possessed all the power he'd absorbed from the Nether-Realm. Fenrir recovered quickly from every blow.

Miles away in the distance, the gods Tyr and Freyr, who had been falling back from their battles with the Dragon legionaries, encountered a pack of 40-foot-tall Dragon heavy-infantry led by a six-story-tall Dragon, the largest they'd yet seen. The largest of them raised his arms in a fist, calling the columns to a halt.

"You glimmering, shining beings," said the Dragon leader. "I've seen you fight my warriors. You are mighty and courageous. I gather you are gods or great spirits of some sort. Who are you?"

"I am the mighty god of war, Tyr," said the one-handed god hastily, "and this is Freyr the Wise, the god of peace."

"Brothers, I gather?"

"We... share no relations," Freyr lied.

"Your postures betray you. If you are not brothers of blood, then you are surely brothers in arms. Tell me: why do the two of you not wield magnificent weapons like the other shimmering beings and large creatures we encountered?"

"We lost them in different circumstances," said Freyr. "Please. We have already lost so much. Offer us and our people quarter. Spare us!"

"Like hell!" Tyr objected.

"Hmm..." the large Dragon considered. "I've traveled across the Multiverse and seen many worlds. One of my favorite traditions comes from the 7th universe. In it, the champion warriors of each race fight each other in a duel to decide the winner of a war so that millions more will not have to suffer. Imagine if your politicians settled disputes that way. Or *are* you the politicians of this world?"

"We are the preservers of this world, the peacekeepers," said Freyr.

"Listen carefully, godly ones. Let me tell you something someone once told me. You *know* what you are, and I know who I am. You know who you serve, and I know who I serve. We are all warriors. We all have our duty. I will do my duty, for my goddess, for my queen, for my princess, and for my people. I'm sure you will too. We will fight, but not out of hatred, nor out of desire to gain. We will fight because it's what we do—what we were born and created to do. We must nail ourselves to our purpose, no matter how much it hurts us. So is the way of the cosmos. Our actions and inactions will have far-reaching consequences that will reverberate throughout time and across worlds. We must be consistent, we must be what we are, and do what we must do—what the powers higher than ourselves compel us to do. In the end, we are all heading for the end—what you people call 'the horizon.' And we will all be together again, victors and losers alike, in the same primordial soup from whence we came. So why run from destiny? Be. Do."

"You speak as the Allfather does, reptile," said Tyr. "Who are you who says such things?"

"I am Arch-General Deem, the leader of the 3rd Imperial Army, one of the premier bodies in the Dragon military. I offer both of you an opportunity: give me the fight of my life—kill me—and my warriors will gut themselves on your soil." Deem, the Dragon general, then broke off his own right-hand, tossing it aside. He also took off his belt, handing his sheathed Nandaka Sword to a warrior nearby. "I see that one of you is one-handed, and that both of you are armed only with simple weapons. Thus, I will fight you one-handed and unarmed."

Tyr charged forward, wielding a morning star. He swung it but Deem deflected it with his hand. Deem then poked Tyr in the head with the nail of his pointer, impaling his skull. Freyr attacked from behind, but Deem flew to the side quickly, then struck him so hard in the head that it decapitated him. Deem then regenerated his right-hand, bent his head, and closed his eyes in respect. "I am sorry," he said. "I was hoping you'd be the ones to set me free from fate." He then took up his Nandaka Sword.

Thor did not see the deaths of his brothers, being fixated on Odin's struggle with Fenrir and on Sif's health, but he felt it in his gut—two great powers vanishing from his senses. Heimdall, however, had seen their deaths from many thousands of miles away. He came to confront Arch-General Deem at the river of Onisis. After a very brief encounter, Heimdall too was overpowered and killed by the Dragon general.

Loki, who also had a nigh-omniscient view of what was happening, breathed a sigh of relief that the being who had been *fated* to slay him was now dead. "I think I'm a fan of that Dragon," he mumbled to himself.

"Damn it, Loki!" said Thor. "We need not reach Asgard! Canst thou heal her now?"

"Oh, hush, you. What do you know of my magic? Geez, you manipulate some electrons to discharge some energy and all of a sudden you're the expert on all supernatural phenomena?"

Wyvern Dragons streaked up alongside the ship, breathing fire and blasts from their mouths. Thor quickly went on the offensive and summoned lightning from the surrounding clouds to strike the Dragons.

"That's it, dear brother!" Loki cheered. "Get me closer to the top of Yggdrasil. One bite of them apples will have your dame up and running in no time. Oh, and by the way..." Loki walked to the edge of the ship, leaving the undead Hyrm to steer it. He then began blasting Wyverns with his staff. "Ha-HA! You didn't think I'd let you have all the fun, did you? Heeheehahaha! Start counting, brother! The loser—that'll be you, by the way—scrubs the deck with a little brush made of porcupine quills."

The two gods beheld a remarkable sight. Another spectacle of spectacles appeared. The head and neck of another enormous Dragon reached out from the "eye." It flew down without wings. Its pale-white body streaked through the sky, illuminating it like a comet. Its eyes were like neutron stars, glowing blinding white.

"What is that thing?!" Thor exclaimed.

"Well, judging by the photons hitting my pupils and my own intuitions, it appears to be a super-massive white Dragon with bright white eyes and a serpentine body about 3.333 times the circumference of Midgard. Care to say hello to it?"

"Father and mother are still down there with your bastard wolf and the other beasts!"

"Yes, and Sif is up here. You can't save them all. You'll need to make a choice, dear brother. Apples or oranges—well, two nice ripe apples and some shriveled old oranges. I know which I would choose. See isn't this fun?"

Frigg, the mighty queen of the gods, fought valiantly against the swarms of Dragon flying-cavalry and confused Giants alongside her Valhallan warriors. Her attendants had been slaughtered. They had all agreed to sacrifice their lives alongside their queen in what they'd expected to be the end of days. The heavy marching feet of the Dragon heavy-infantry could be heard. Their columns of long-lances skewered the Giants and Valhallan warriors in their path, hardly losing momentum. Even the armies of the dead and the Elves had been scattered and thrown into disarray. Soon, Frigg too was driven through the chest with a long-lance.

Thor's thunder could be heard for miles around as he launched lightning bolts down from the passage between Asgard and Midgard. They struck and killed a few of the Dragon heavy-infantry but otherwise had little effect. Frigg's body grew limp and lifeless as Thor's anger reached a boiling point. He struck the ship with his hammer, causing it to begin to fall apart in mid-flight. The remnants of the ship crashed into the underbelly of the great heavenly city of Asgard along with Thor, Sif, and Loki. The others on board fell or were crushed between the two realms.

Loki cast a spell, transforming himself into a spider who could crawl on the underbelly of Asgard. Thor hung on for dear life with Sif in one arm. He slipped her down between his thighs so that he could wield his hammer, then smashed a hole through the world above. He climbed through it to the surface. Loki followed. "Knockie, knockie! I'm coming, dearies!" said Loki.

A grave horror greeted them at the top. Asgard was a city under attack every bit as much as the world below. Wyverns and flying-cavalry devastated the fabulous crystalline buildings from above. All of Asgard appeared to be burning. "Oh, what nerve," said Loki comically, transforming back. "They've burned down my favorite brothel... And the palace too!"

Thor carried Sif off toward the trunk of Yggdrasil, the world tree. Loki put his hands on his hips, rolled his eyes, and teleported the three of them to it. "Keep the beasts at bay, dear brother," said Loki, who'd teleported himself again to a familiar spot on the tree. "I will bring you and the dame down some fruit."

Thor battled back against hundreds of Dragons as Loki climbed to the top of the tree. Thor's endurance was legendary, and though he'd been fighting for many consecutive days, he retained the strength to continue as if he'd only just begun fighting.

Loki had exhausted much of his magical energy teleporting and now had only his meager physical strength to rely on. Laughing to himself, he collected the golden apples from the tree and ate all he gathered, not only restoring his old powers but multiplying them exponentially.

"LOKI!" Thor called up to his brother as the Dragon heavy-infantry bore down.

"Just a sec, brother..." said Loki, his mouth audibly stuffed with the precious fruit.

"LOKI!"

"Mmm... this shit's delicious. You know, I always fancied Idunn's melons a bit. She's just a bit... too tangy for my taste." He ate the last of the golden fruit. "But you know as ripe as apples become, they all end up the same way—rotten, decomposed worm food."

"LOKI!"

"Oh, for god sakes, brother, I leave you for ten minutes and you already..." Loki paused, seeing an especially disturbing vision in his twisting, snaking web of visions. In it, he watched as Helheim was overrun by Dragons. He watched as his mourning wife, Sigyn, was rounded up along with the last of the souls of the dead, trapped without judgment. The Dragons, able to inflict mortals and spirits alike, had begun to execute its inhabitants. Sigyn begged pitifully for her life and cried out for help. She cried out for her husband, Loki, who was now many realms away. A Dragon stabbed her through the heart with its sword, then allowed her to bleed to death.

Loki laughed and laughed as a single tear streamed down his face. With trembling hands, he gripped the Elder Staff to him—hugged it to him. "All-all th-this... heh-HEH! All... every... thing.... Siggy... you were to be... my queen..." Loki screamed, his eyes wide, then he laughed again. He blasted several Dragons with his most powerful magical attacks, flying down and smashing into a group of them. "All the powers of the fruit are mine! I am all-powerful! I am immortal! I am Loki, and fuckethed art thou who fuckethed with me!"

Just then, lightning struck all around. "Loki! Sif is dead! She's dead!" Thor lamented. "Where in Odin's name were you?!" He gave out a great howl. His eyes became pale-white and the area lit up with lightning bolts.

"GENERAL DEEM .VS. LOKI & THOR"

Deem, the Dragon general, approached with his elite warriors. "You two," said Deem, "I sense that your powers are exceptional."

Thor and Loki spared no time blasting Deem with their most powerful attacks, amped hundreds of times their normal level. However, Deem deflected their lightning bolts and destructive magical beams with just one pointer finger. The attacks caused explosions which destroyed the crystalline Asgardian buildings nearby.

Loki laughed, then became gravely serious again. "I have devoured the brains of the Norns, eaten the fruits of Yggdrasil, and you haven't a clue what more I've done! Now I am all-powerful! Now I am omnipotent!"

Loki teleported himself behind Deem yet hit nothing with his Petrification spell. He turned to find Deem towering behind him. "Infernal creature! I am the new god of these realms!" Loki proclaimed. "I am the king of Helheim! I am the god of chaos and of all magic!" He then transferred half of his magical energies into his staff and struck Deem with it. Deem caught the staff in his gigantic hand. Thor rushed in and struck Deem with his hammer but Deem stopped the hammer with just one finger. He picked up the two gods like bugs caught on flypaper and threw them away.

"I have fought many gods in many worlds," said Deem. "I have only met two others who challenged me. I fought them through the cosmos for many years and learned much from them. I have seen enough suffering to notice the anguish on your faces—even yours, dark god. I understand you have both lost much, and I am sorry that this fate has befallen you. But all that has happened and all that will happen must happen."

"Oh, you have no idea, do you?" Loki seethed. He created mirror images of himself all around Deem.

Thor launched himself like a missile at the Dragon again, but the Dragon finally drew his infamous Nandaka Sword from its scabbard and cut through Thor's armor. With that stroke came a massive shockwave that flowed through the city of Asgard.

Loki's illusions attacked all at once, but Deem moved at hyper speeds, avoiding all of them. Deem then appeared before the actual Loki who grit his teeth. Loki teleported himself back but always found Deem almost precisely where he went. "Your pride makes you yearn for more; it leaves you unsatisfied and discontent, dark god," said Deem.

"Heeheeheeheehaaa! You just watch what the god of magic can do!" Loki cast an *Entrapment* spell, surrounding Deem in an ethereal box as large as he was. He then cast a *Slow Time* spell. However, to his surprise, Deem began to rip apart his magical encasement and appeared to be moving at the speed of a normal mortal. Loki quickly raised his staff, casting one of his most destructive spells. A meteor began to form in the sky directly overhead. "Heeheeheeheeheehee-Ha!" he cackled. "Behold, monster! The most powerful spell of them all! Watch as our races die together!"

The spell drained enough of Loki's energy to cause his Slow Time spell to fail but by that point the meteor approached Asgard.

"Loki, no!" Thor urged. "Thou wouldst kill us all!"

"Why are you people always saying that? You think that this time saying it will actually prevent it from happening? Heeeheeeheeeheeehaaa! Brother! Ragnarok is here! How beautiful it is! How spectacular! Sing! Sing your epic dirge! Sing of our age and our era—of our struggles and triumphs. Heh-HA! Sing of the end of days!"

Deem held out his right hand, saying, "I call on thee, *Gandiva*... Grant me the power of the *Brahmastra*..." A mystical bow appeared in his hand. When he released the string, a beam of energy ignited from it and collided with the meteor. The meteor exploded, blanketing the skies of Asgard with fire. The explosion threw Thor and Loki miles and miles from the epicenter. Loki again slowed time, allowing himself time to find something to cling to while flying. He watched as Thor was thrown out of Asgard and fell off the Bifrost.

Thor spun his hammer, allowing him to slow his descent back to Midgard. He landed on the coiled serpentine back of the humongous white Dragon he and Loki had seen earlier. The white Dragon moved, throwing the thunder god off into the sea.

It appeared to be approaching King Surtur, the most powerful of all the Giants. Surtur thrashed with his flaming sword at the great white Dragon but the blade missed each time, seemingly passing through air.

The Dragon held a large orb in one of its hands. It turned blue and a terrifying rumbling shook all of Midgard. Soon a portal in the sky opened, flooding that portion of the land with ocean water, killing Surtur and most of the Fire Giants.

"HEAR ME!" said the great white serpent without opening its mouth. "I AM LORD MORTIMER, THE GOD OF MAGIC." Like Lord Zeon, Lord Mortimer had crowns on his horns with spikes too numerous to count, representing the worlds he too had conquered. "I NOW CLAIM THIS WORLD IN THE NAME OF THE ALMIGHTY GODDESS OF DEATH."

Odin and Fenrir were awestruck by the sight and voice of this incredible monstrosity. A part of its long body slipped past them as they battled, over the mountains which caused them to begin to crumble. Odin called for Sleipnir, his eight-legged horse whom he'd been separated from, and mounted his back in pursuit of Lord Mortimer.

Fenrir gave chase, but Odin entered a burning forest, which slowed the wolf down.

Lord Mortimer sensed the approach of Odin and turned to face him. Charging in at full speed, Odin hurled Gungnir, his legendary spear, at the back of the Dragon. It caused a purple mist to spill from the creature's hide, but the apparent wound quickly disappeared, swallowing the spear along with it. Odin then drew his Zantetsuken sword, an obsidian cleaver-like blade thought to be capable of cutting through anything. Sleipnir flew up into the air alongside Mortimer as Odin prepared to strike. With strength that could cut a star apart, Odin came down on the middle-body of the great serpent. Odin came down on the serpent with all his might with a force that could split a star in two. One part of Mortimer separated from the other and purple mist squirted all around.

Still, Mortimer appeared unaffected, even smiling. A new head emerged from the lower-half of him which had been severed, and a new tail grew from his top half. There now appeared to be two Mortimers. They coiled together and became one again. Odin, the supreme god of Asgard, was mesmerized.

Thor emerged from the water, seeing his father in battle. He flew toward him with the aid of his hammer.

Odin hacked again and again and again, but all the damage he dealt was easily undone. Thor flew in and came down on Mortimer with his hammer, but the blow passed through the Dragon and collided with a mountain, smashing it. "Goodbye, my son," said Odin. "Die as a warrior."

With that, Odin leaped up at Mortimer one last time on the back of Sleipnir. The right foreclaw of Mortimer caught the god and his eight-legged horse like a pair of mating beetles and squashed them into the crust of Midgard.

Thor's anger grew out of control and he charged Mortimer. The Dragon displayed his giant orb which glowed black, immediately crushing Thor's legs under innumerable tons of localized pressure. The Dragon legionaries marched forth to proceed with his execution.

A voice in the Multiverse speaks:

"What are these thoughts?
These visions...
Who are these people?
Where am I?
These monsters
This suffering
This death
These horrible things
I just want to wake up!
Please, let me wake up!"

"GENERAL DEEM AND THE WORLD OF THE KAMI"

General Deem sat atop an island on a great blue planet submerged almost entirely in water. It had been the world of the Mer People, part-humanoid creatures with fish-like tails for lower bodies. In a short campaign, Deem and his army, particularly the Leviathans—the underwater specialists of the Dragon military—had defeated and subjugated the Mer people. In the process, much of the planet's water had been artificially destroyed through the use of magic, causing the campaign to break down into a glorified version of shooting fish in a barrel. Under Lord Mortimer's command, the captured Mermaids and Mermen suffered greatly. It could have been worse without Deem's influence. Their tails were cut off and they were gutted.

General Deem left the planet to Lord Mortimer out of disgust. Even the encouraging words of the Deva, Vishnu, whom he'd dueled for many years in the third universe, failed to comfort him at that point. In many ways, he admired the Mer People. He found their world and their culture to be fascinating. He found many worlds he eventually conquered fascinating.

He'd often shared white-washed versions of his campaigns and journeys with his secret beloved, Princess Darna, the only daughter of Ain. This was made easier when he learned the arts of inter-dimensional travel and communication from Loki. "My princess, I wish you could be here to see it," said Deem, kneeling on one-knee before the holographic-like projection of Darna. "A blue world, as blue as your eyes. There are people here who've built cities underwater. They use some kind of transparent material which does not break down under the immense pressure of the water. It is extraordinary. Truly."

"A whole world made out of water? Does it have... a bottom?" asked Darna.

"Yes, of course. Most of the planets I've been on have hard cores. I believe that the gravity makes all the matter compress like that."

"Wow. And what about the people? Have they given you any problems?"

"...I've had to fight them of course..." said Deem, finding it difficult to answer.

"Oh, of course. You're a warrior, after all. The most handsome I know."

"Princess..." said Deem. "I... I keep wondering when all of this will finally end."

"What do you mean by that?"

"I keep telling myself that if I conquer this planet, then that planet, then another, then it will finally be over — your mother will be satisfied and let me... go."

"Let you go?" the Princess sounded baffled. "You mean you don't want to fight anymore? But you're so good at it! Maybe the best! To me, anyway."

"It's not fighting, it's... killing. And killing the way that we do... The Devas had a word for it — for something that's not right or justified: it's *immoral*."

"But I thought you said you just cut their heads off and it's really fast, like they don't feel a thing. So, it's like nothing even happened, right? They don't know what hit them, and mom gets all the energy."

"Most of the time... I try... but the lords and the other generals don't."

"Then we'll just get rid of them. Ha-ha-ha-ha-ha! Because I'm the Princess and soon the empire will be mine! Muhahahaha!" Darna still sounded upbeat, laughing comically. She giggled. "Oh, valiant general, my big, strong general... Don't be sad. MUAH!" she blew a kiss.

Deem clenched his fists, annoyed by her light-heartedness. "Well, you and the queen have got to eat..."

"Hey, cheer up. You should come by sometime and have some of this new Ambrosia stuff with me. It's super yummy. It comes from one of Lord Zeon's worlds.

Well, I like your golden apples and the Amrita from your worlds too. It's just... I have them, like, every day."

"I'll send you over some new gifts later."

"Oh, you don't have to do that. I'm proud of you. I'm doing well and have lots to look forward to. Hey, I'm happy I might get to be your... what did they call it in that *Ame* world of yours? '*Wife*' right? When two people are together for a long time. I'll be your wife someday."

"I love you, my princess. I have to go. May your day be filled with joy and plenty."

Deem closed his eyes, attempting to meditate and mentally escape. Thanks to Loki, he could now see worlds many light-years away through dimensions and travel there if necessary. He watched as Princess Darna tried on the many articles of clothing and jewelry which were brought to her from around the Multiverse. He loved her and wanted to be there with her but feared the great queen, the Dragon goddess, who resided nearby. Only lords, the princess, and the royal attendants were allowed into her presence, and most of the attendants vanished in her presence and needed to be replaced often.

His thoughts then took him to a world he'd been to before: Ame-Tsuchi, the world of the godly Kami and home to the humans of the sixth granddaughter universe. Ame-Tsuchi had been invaded by the Dragons many years earlier by another Dragon general. However, that general got pulled away.

General Deem had visited Ame-Tsuchi alone prior to the invasion. The people welcomed him as some sort of deity and treated him kindly, giving him many gifts which he sent back to Princess Darna. It was a land that chirped and buzzed with wildlife and vegetation. The trees, the rivers, and the mountains were pristine. "If I were to ever outlive the queen," said Deem, "I would build the princess's new palace here." However, Deem could only begin to sense why that particular world was so lush. The farmers explained that the planet was ruled by many godly spirits called *Kami* who actively preserved the land.

The land, however beautiful, was not free from suffering. As subsistence farmers, many of the people worked extremely hard and endured many seasonal hardships. Like the humans of Midgard, the winters were perilous times when food became scarce, so food stores were kept, and rationing was practiced. Deem temporarily formed several large fireballs in the sky to help the people.

Still, conflict arose. Many feudal lords fought wars against each other for the rights to land, or out of conquest, or simply to settle personal vendettas with rival aristocrats. The warriors of Ame-Tsuchi used bows, spears, and swords similar to the ones used by the Asgardian and Olympian-ruled people, but they also seemed to use a form of weaponry that seemed more exotic: firearms. The people of the planet had made high quantities of a combustible black powder, capable of firing metal projectiles with enough force to kill a man from a distance. Thousands of flintlock muskets flooded the battlefields across the pristine landscape. Thousands of large cannons pounded that landscape.

General Deem watched curiously. As sad as it was, he chuckled a little inside at the puny weapons and their pathetic capabilities. The only weapon he remotely respected was the cannon. However, for many tens of thousands of soldiers on the battlefield, these weapons proved to be absolutely frightening. Entire armies were driven off cliffs and into the sea from the sounds of the cannons and muskets alone.

The humans then developed percussion caps which allowed for a more reliable firing mechanism and rifled barrels and complimentary cone-shaped bullets which allowed for greater range and accuracy. They then developed wide-mouthed shotguns and canister shot.

Finally, General Deem had an excuse to spare Ame-Tsuchi: they could be developing new weapons which the Dragon military might later use to conquer worlds whilst conserving the queen's life-energy. Believing that the lords and generals would understand and follow his proposed course of action, Deem made preparations to turn his army toward another target in another galaxy.

"THE KAMI OF STORMS"

Before he could leave the planet, however, an interesting problem arose. General Deem encountered a powerful and angry Kami who came howling down from the heavens above. Possessed with an uncontrollable fury, the black-bearded god used his divine ten-grasp sword, christened *Totsuka-no-Tsurugi*, to stir up the seas and the winds, creating storms that span whole continents. His freak storms killed over 10,000 people in only seven days. Deem could see these storms from space and went to confront the menace regarding the matter. Wielding the powerful Nandaka Sword, Deem fought the storm god in a duel for some time.

"Your fury... I know it, I understand it," said Deem. "It is the fury of one warring against their place in the hierarchy of the Omniverse. It is the fury of one who feels wronged and cheated by things he cannot control. I know that feeling."

"Beast, how dare you pretend to know me!" the storm god shouted, picking his Totsuka sword up and slashing again, creating a tornadic waterspout, only to be parried and blown back by a shockwave from Deem's Nandaka Sword.

"I am curious," said Deem. "I have spared your people and your world from the wrath of my army yet you destroy your own kind."

"I am not of their kind! I am infinitely above these animals—these filthy land-dwelling pests who shit and piss and pollute the winds of Fujin with their stench."

"Who are you?" asked Deem.

"I am Prince Susanoo, an *Amatsukami*—one above all. I am the rightful heir to the throne of *Takama-ga-hara*."

"Who, then, possesses the throne in your stead? And why?"

"My father gave his most sacred gift—the great red star—to my fragile-minded sister. To me, he gave only this accursed sword, which he'd used to butcher my uncle. My sister gave me dominion over the seas of this puny world simply to patronize me."

"It's politics. You are angry with politics. I understand that. Truly, I do. As powerful as I am, where I come from I am considered a third-tier being. The lords and the royals—some of whom know nothing of the horrors and hardships of war—reign over me. It angers me to no end, and yet I continue. I follow. I do what I must. I do what I have to. I follow the path laid out in front of me. I do my duty."

"Then how are you any different from the slaves?"

"We are *all* slaves, whether we want to accept it or not. It's finding higher meaning in the process of servitude where we find relief."

Only after learning of Loki's future-bending abilities could Deem begin to question that guiding philosophy. But the presence of the Devas indwelling in him reassured him.

"You're a damn fool to accept such meager prospects!" said Susanoo. "Fate cannot control something more powerful than it is. Watch as I undo the work of my creator. Watch as I defy the will of heaven and fill *Yomi*, the land of the dead, with more souls than it had planned or prepared for! What does it matter? What does it matter if I rob heaven of its souls and fill King Yama's realm with more souls for him and the Oni to play with?"

Deem threw Susanoo to the ground, ripping off the shoulder piece of his ornate *o-yoroi* armor in the process.

"Heh-HEH!" Susanoo scoffed. "You know what these humans are? They are like any other animal on this planet. They are animals. They have no value, no significance aside from the haughty little lies and titles they claim for themselves. They exist only to amuse us, to entertain us, to feed us. They shit. They piss. Their lives fade quickly, and their bodies decay. Animals. You and I—we exist on a separate and higher plane of existence in which humans do not belong."

"And how do your sister and the other Kami feel about the humans? The same, I suspect?"

"The same. That's why it is my punishment to be here."

"And what if I kill you? Kill you and all the other Kami?" Deem proposed.

"Then you would be cutting off the hand that feeds the rats," Susanoo answered. "A caged animal without a master will die of starvation, as will the humans without us."

"And what if there is no cage and no master?"

"Your own reasoning defies your fatalistic beliefs," Susanoo sneered triumphantly.

"If there is no cage and no master..." Deem considered.

"...Then how can we all be slaves to destiny, Dragon?"

"There would be... chaos," Deem concluded, clenching his enchanted sword.

In hindsight, Deem considered the chaos of the Ragnarok event in the land of the Asgardians—the one proof he had that the chains of destiny could be broken by a being as determined as Loki.

"How then can there be no cages and no masters?" Deem questioned. "In a state of chaos, everyone dies and everything is destroyed..."

"Ha! Except the last one standing," said Susanoo, "he writes the future."

"And what kind of future would you write after you've destroyed everything?" asked Deem. "Would you be content to be alone? Alone to share in your final victory. Alone to gloat for an eternity. Alone with nothing and no one, to rule over nothing and no one. To be nothing and no one."

Susanoo tensed his brows and his body. He slashed wildly, creating more waterspouts that swept past the Dragon general.

Then, without warning, Deem disappeared. He'd apparently taken Susanoo's sword as well. Susanoo grew angry again, but despite his great rage, he was unable to vent without his sword.

Deem was finally able to see what had transpired in the world of Ame-Tsuchi during his absence, now armed with Loki's powers of hindsight. Susanoo had diminished from a wrathful god to a pathetic wanderer of the land, stripped of his sword and thus his godly powers by Deem. He'd grown thirsty and hungry like the humans yet rejected the help of those who'd shown him pity, even refusing to be touched by them. His black beard had grown from a youthful chinstrap to a forest of hair. His clothes and armor became old, smelly, and tattered. He shouted insults to heaven in vain, also cursing the name of the Dragon beast who'd stolen his sword. With hardly any strength left, he crawled toward a fresh-water stream which ran between a garden of cherry blossom and apricot trees, as well as azalea and camellia flowers. He felt the moss between his hands—thought he might die before he could reach the water. The apricots above looked so delicious yet he could not imagine summoning the strength to climb. Then, just as he cupped the water and carried it to his face, his strength failed him and he passed out from exhaustion.

Around that time, a young woman who often came to care for the flowers and plants, as well as to fetch water from upstream, came upon the body of the deathly Susanoo in the garden. Fearfully, she made her way over to him, seeing that he was still breathing. Now, despite being so unkept, Susanoo—being a High-Kami—retained a rather youthful and handsome appearance which appealed to the girl. She hesitantly gathered some water in a wooden bucket and cupped some in her hands to pour over the face of the god. Susanoo's eyelids eased open, but he could not rise. "Are-are you o-okay?" said the soft little voice of the young woman, shyly, "dr-drink."

The world was still a blur in Susanoo's mind, and the cherry blossoms merged with the purple sky, and the girl's black hair and rosy face. At first he thought she might be a Yokai (ghostly creature) who'd come to drag him to the land of the dead. He would have fought her away if he hadn't been so utterly drained. The girl grunted, struggling in vain to carry his head upward so that he could drink. She barely succeeded, and during her struggle had used Susanoo's hair as pulleys. Finally, she managed to push him the rest of the way, leading with her shoulder and forearm, using all of her body to get the fallen god to an upright position. She poured some water into his mouth, which caused him to cough for some time. The water that went down helped to restore his strength.

In time, he could see clearly, enough to make out the eyes, nose, and lips of the girl. She was not particularly beautiful to Susanoo, at least by the standards to which female Kami were held, but was radiant for a human. She wore a white ribbon on her head which raised her hair upward in a ponytail, supported by a comb. Susanoo recognized it as the style of an Uzume worshiper, Uzume being the Kami of dawn and one of the few other beings Susanoo respected.

"Are-are you from here?" she asked.

"No," he said, stoic as ever.

"S-so you're a traveler then?"

"I am, in some ways."

"Some... ways?"

Susanoo sat up, resting his forearms on his knees and crossing his legs in a lotus position. "Why? What's it got to do with you?" he said grumpily, coughing soon after.

The girl was slightly taken aback but assumed that he was still delirious from being passed out. "I-I'm s-sorry, I-I just thought talking would help."

"Well, I don't *need* help! I don't need anyone! You hear me?" Susanoo stumbled like a drunkard and fell again. "Stupid girl."

"You-you're acting... foolish and-and-and dumb."

"Foolish and dumb?" Susanoo seethed, attempting to push himself back up but falling back down. "You have some nerve talking that way to me."

"Well-well you called me 'stupid.' I'm *not* stupid. I-I don't care if you're a soldier, or a farmer, or a prince—I've been trying to help you and you've been disrespectful and-and rude!"

"Heh..." Susanoo smirked.

"So-so maybe... maybe you can just lay there and be a jerk by yourself! Hmmph!" the girl stuck up her nose, picked up her water bucket, and walked away. She walked about twenty meters before hiding behind a tree to check up on the man. He tried a few more times to get up in vain, cussing out loud after each failure. "Today is the spring festival!" she shouted back. "We have white rice for once! You could even have some if you're done being such a jerk!"

"Dog food..." Susanoo managed. The girl couldn't hear him. "What's with you, you stupid person... Why don't you go away and leave me be?"

"I'm really going to go..."

"Then go!"

"Fine!" said the girl, scurrying away.

"Shit... WAIT!" Susanoo shouted. "Who are you? Tell me who you are! Are you one of Uzume's blessed ones? That comb is her signature. Has the goddess sent you to taunt me in my moment of frailty?"

"You-you think I'm the daughter of a goddess?"

"Well... you can't be all human, can you?" said Susanoo, managing to turn his body.

The girl blushed and hid a smile and giggle under her hand. "I don't believe in lying," she said. "My name is Kushina. My mother was a priestess in the great temple of Uzume until she was excommunicated. She was taken in by my father, who is the chief farmer in these parts. These waters are our lifeblood. I have tended to this garden as my own personal shrine to the water's power."

"You're a farmer's daughter..."

"Yes. It is a hard life without any certainty—save for the sun and moons. The truth is, someday I may be married off or purchased or worse. Someday, my clothes and jewelry and things may be sold. Everything I have may be confiscated, stolen, or burned. This garden is the only thing in the world I feel I truly own. And for that, it is sacred to me." The girl walked forward, kneeling over Susanoo who had managed to get to his knees with the help of a tree as a crutch. "Y-you know, I came here for the same reasons you likely did. The water was calmest here. It was full of...life. Once, this gentle stream deviated from the Hi River, the same river which sometimes floods and drowns the farmers and villagers of the lowlands. How ironic. How pathetic, really. Now, here we are... two wanderers at the river's most peaceful juncture as it escapes to the sea."

"Hmmph, the sea? It's not so big or so great. I am Susanoo, the Kami of storms *and* the sea!"

"Ha!" Kushina cracked. "That's nice, I've found a crazy person. Susanoo wouldn't be talking to someone like me. He'd slaughter someone like me without a second thought, along with a hundred other people. That's how he is, you know? My mother said that he is an evil, selfish, and malicious god. Why would you want to imitate him?"

"Why would I?..." he asked, having no answer for himself.

Kushina's family brought him by cart back to the farm where he recovered, eating wheat, rice, nori, and sometimes fish. He slept on the floor on a mat made of straw. The farmers of Ame-Tsuchi were such meager and humble people who endured unendurable conditions to make a living. Susanoo began to sympathize with their suffering and struggles. He questioned how anyone could be so content with having so little and being so low on the societal ladder.

Kushina herself owned just one kimono, which she only wore on her trips to the stream garden. Other times she wore much simpler village clothes made from the same material used to cover homes. Her knees and hands became blistered and scraped from working the fields, and her back was often sore. She often smelled of a strong human odor, which Susanoo got used to and eventually grew to like as somewhat of a comforting scent. She had seven sisters, of which she was the youngest. At times, she seemed to compete with her older sisters for attention but always lost, being shyer and stranger than the others, not to mention lowest in the family hierarchy.

Despite being poor, the eight daughters were considered extremely beautiful and thus were highly sought after by men and boys in nearby villages. The eldest daughter would be of marriageable age in just a matter of months, yet her parents refused to make such an arrangement for any of their daughters. Still, the attention Kushina got from boys of varying ages made Susanoo more than a bit jealous and insecure. In his mind, he'd found Kushina first and she was *his*.

Kushina's mother was a woman who made even Susanoo uneasy. She never seemed to blink and always held an intense look on her face. Her eyebrows were plucked naked and her skin was powdered white. She seemed to listen, only to shout out in shrill, irrelevant rants filled with drivel and nonsense. Kushina tried to explain to Susanoo that her mother was often Kami-possessed, though the storm god could not tell which Kami had possessed her, if any. He could sense an aura about the woman. Once, she put her hand on his shoulder and stared into his eyes. Her touch and stare were like ice. She wheezed under her breath: "You are no son of mine…you are his snot…"

"What the hell did you say?" said Susanoo.

The woman shook her head frantically like a wet cat trying to dry itself. "Excuse me. I am not always in my mind. I must go to my shrine…"

Susanoo was able to stand and walk in three days. He was able to assist Kushina with the spring harvest the next day, though he found it more difficult than it looked. Frustrated, he hacked down all the stocks for an acre, demonstrating that despite his diminished powers he was still rather capable. Kushina scolded him, saying that he was acting like a spoiled child and that he'd recklessly damaged the roots of the crops. Susanoo was silenced. He walked off, moping, until he came upon a traveling samurai resting in Kushina's garden. Angered by his presence there and already frustrated, Susanoo attacked the warrior, stripped him of his sword, and nearly drowned him in the stream before hearing the footsteps and calls of Kushina. He let the samurai go with a warning to say nothing and never return.

"What's the matter, Su?" asked Kushina.

"Nothing."

"If you say that then there must be something wrong. I'm sorry I was so harsh. I just know that father will be so upset to see the fields that way. It is hard to grow crops and easy to destroy them. They're delicate, just like these flowers." She squatted down and carefully snapped the stem of a flower, placing the flower in her hair. Then she noticed something at his hip. "Hey, is that a sword?" she asked. "Where did you get that?"

"What's it to you? I found it."

"Hey! That's not allowed. We are not allowed to own weapons like that!"

"Well, why not?"

"Because it's not allowed! It's against the law."

"Hmmph, the law? As far as I can tell, this land has too many laws from too many different directions to be considered legitimate. What, are they scared we'll use these weapons against them? Good! They should be scared."

"You don't get it..."

"I'll hide it, alright? Will that please you, Kushina?" Susanoo walked off back to the farm.

"What's the matter with you?!" Kushina shouted at him. "Why are you so angry and ungrateful? Why don't you just listen?"

"Ha! The truth is I shouldn't have to listen to you. You're a woman—and a mortal woman! I'm a god!"

"You're a crazy nut, that's what you are! My family and I have done so much for you, and you treat us like this? You're willing to get us all in trouble and put us in danger?"

Susanoo sighed. "...Look, I'm... sorry," he said. "But this world is a damn dangerous place, and I'll need a way to protect us—to protect you." He gripped the handle of the sword tightly. "And some virtues are above the law."

"GIGATHETA: THE EIGHT-HEADED DRAGON"

Several spacial tears had appeared, ominous black and white vortices which swirled in the purple sky. Pulses of bright light shot out from them in every which way. After the light had dissipated and the swirling gradually slowed, the monstrous Dragons swarmed down by the millions. The humans fired their bows, muskets, and cannons but were able to inflict very few casualties on the flood of Dragons who conquered a continent in less than a week.

Deem, seeing this for the first time, grew angry at the thought that another Dragon leader had betrayed his wishes and ignored his advice. He was not surprised to learn that the leader of the invasion was the aristocratic Lord-Marquess Gigatheta, the lord who wore the most crowns and yet the smallest.

Gigatheta was an enormous eight-headed, eight-tailed monstrosity the size of many great valleys. Each of his heads and their corresponding tails possessed magical powers, which corresponded to different elements: electric, plant, fire, water, ice, rock, wind, and metal. Still, the most distinct characteristic of Gigatheta was his insatiable appetite. He devoured everything and anything, however, his favorite food was living flesh. Along with impaling or gutting their captives as other armies did, Gigatheta's armies would present unfortunate victims to their leader who would swallow them whole or chewed them to pieces depending on the mood of the head which got the first bite.

A much more sedentary creature than the other Dragon lords, Gigatheta rested as his warriors fed and tended to him. They built a humongous castle around him, the parts of which had been brought through the portal and survived the journey the same way the Dragons always had—through a protective spell meant to last long enough for the Dragons and their arsenals to reach the ground.

The captured people of Ame-Tsuchi were rounded up, bound tightly, and kept in cramped cages without food, like live lobsters waiting for the boiling pot. Gigatheta devoured 8,000 people each day before falling asleep.

News of the invasion spread rapidly across the globe, as one would expect. Susanoo and the family that cared for him were greatly alarmed that such a power had been unleashed on their world. The family, bound to the land all their lives, determined to stay put on it and tend to the crops. Susanoo grew outraged and went on a tirade about the need to flee, managing to break a table and a door.

Meanwhile, the sound of cannons could be heard thundering in the distance. Large fires rose up like additional suns out of the horizon. Kushina and her family grew very afraid. One day, while Susanoo and Kushina worked the fields, a representative of the lord of the land arrived at the home to discuss matters with Kushina's parents.

That night, Susanoo experienced extreme nightmares of being snatched from his bed and dragged off to a hellish place. The next morning, Kushina shook Susanoo and the rest of the household awake with news that her mother and eldest sister were nowhere to be found. The sisters and Susanoo searched all around for them but turned up empty handed after two days. Finally, their father said, "I believe we will not be seeing your mother and sister again. I am sorry."

Susanoo consoled Kushina in the garden as she wept, hugging and holding her gently. He felt terrible that his gentle caretaker felt such grief.

Suddenly, out of the fog on the other side of the stream, a ghostly pale figure emerged. It was Kushina's mother, wide-eyed, chanting, dressed in her old priestess garments, and beating on her prayer drum. Kushina ran across the stream to greet her with relief but instead experienced more grief, her mother muttered unintelligibly, never blinking, hardly moving but to beat her prayer drum. Kushina tried furiously to pry the drum from her mother's firm and cold hands; it took Susanoo's assistance to disarm her and take her home.

Once home and seated, the deranged priestess finally told her tale. She claimed that she had offered up her daughter as a sacrifice to the lord of the Dragons with the help of some of the daimyo's soldiers. In grizzly detail, she described how her bound and screaming daughter was snatched up by the Dragon's first head and swallowed whole. She described with surprising stoicism how her daughter continued moving—kicking and struggling—in the beast's throat for many moments after consumption, and how the Dragon claimed the meal to be the most delicious he'd ever had. She said that she'd explained to the Dragon that Uzume, the Kami of fertility, had personally blessed her children at birth in gratitude for returning the Yasakani Jewel, which the goddess had dropped and lost in the Hi River.

The priestess said she'd struck a deal with the creature to sacrifice a daughter once a month in exchange for sparing the family home and farmland, claiming that destroying those things would mean "no more where that came from." She told her heart-broken family that even as she made this deal, she said she could still see and hear her daughter's fleeting struggle and faint whimpers in the throat of the beast.

Susanoo had somehow withheld his immense rage long enough to allow her to finish her story, he held the handle of his sword tightly and would have pummeled the witch in the face with the hilt if Kushina's next-eldest sister hadn't slapped her mother first. As the father restrained the shouting girl and as her mother laughed it off, Kushina retreated to the bedroom and wept upon her lost sister's mat.

"How dare they do this..." Susanoo said to Kushina. "How dare they try to decide for others who lives and who dies! How dare they toy with people's lives! Fuck them!"

"Susanoo, I-I'm so scared..." Kushina cried.

Susanoo held her, and as he held her his stone-cold heart melted for that moment. "I'm not going to let anyone hurt you, understand? I know the leader of the Dragon armies. I can talk to him. I can stop him. And if he won't listen, I'll kill him."

"SUSANOO'S QUEST"

The next day, Dragons bombarded the surrounding villages with low-energy Qi blasts but left the farmlands untouched as the Dragon lord had promised. Kushina and her sisters refused to flee despite Susanoo's violent pleas.

"Alright, then, you idiots! I will go! I will go and face the Dragon leader myself, and if I don't return, know that it was you fools I died to protect. Let's see if you'll heed my words then!"

Susanoo and Kushina shared one final embrace, during which the young girl gave the storm god her hair-comb to remember her by. The journey to Lord Gigatheta's castle was a perilous one over the mountains, across two rivers, and through many forests. Everywhere he went he found the charred remains of human armies and villages. He came across many, many, many human prisoners—millions of them—whom he was forced to abandon. It surprised him how it distressed his conscience to do so.

"Susanoo," called the voice of the beautiful goddess Uzume, whose blessing had become a curse on Kushina's family. "I know of your sadness but rejoice! You have found your heart. You have discovered what it means to feel. Now, you can finally seek contentment. Now, you can finally seek happiness—when your love is safe from harm."

"What do you know, foul witch!?" Susanoo shouted back. "Where were you and all the other Kami when I was fumbling about in the desert without so much as a drop of water? Where were you and all the other Kami when Kushina's sister was killed? When *all* these people were needlessly killed?"

"I am not your enemy, Susanoo, and I understand your grievances," said the graceful goddess. "My land and my people suffer greatly. I feel it every day. Even my ever-joyful heart weeps for the lives lost. Still, our brethren—Izanagi, Amaterasu, Raiden, Fujin, and the others—refuse to intervene on humankind's behalf. I fear that the Kami of death and the underworld have conspired with our brethren to claim more souls."

"Yama!" Susanoo exclaimed, referring to the Kami of the underworld. "Has he brought this horror upon us to spite the Kami of the living?"

"Lord Yama does not act alone in this tedious affair. I sense a great conspiracy. There is one possessed by an agent of Queen Izanami in the household of your great love."

He thought for a while but didn't have to think long. "Kushina's mother..."

"Sadly, yes. But on the bright side, the Kami of life and death, heaven and the underworld appear to be reconciling with each other after centuries of turmoil."

"At the expense of these people!" said Susanoo, punching a nearby tree.

The ever-radiant Uzume appeared, smiling. "You have learned what it means to be weak and to feel vulnerable. You now know these people in a way no Kami ever has. You are their advocate now in the face of Izanagi and Amaterasu."

"And what makes you think they will ever listen to me again?"

"They might not. They haven't listened to me. But you—you've always had a way of *making* them listen."

"Just stay out of my way," said Susanoo. "I will speak to the Dragon leader."

"Speak to him? This Dragon leader is not the one you fought with over the ocean, nor is he of the same nature. This Dragon leader is a true monster whom a single Kami cannot possibly hope to defeat. But many Kami behind you... possibly..."

"And how can you hope to accomplish that?"

"I can provide a way for you to cross *Ama-no-uki-hashi* (the floating bridge to heaven). Here! Take my sacred cloud. It can transverse even the barrier between us and them. It can bring you face to face with your sister again. King Izanagi, Raiden, Fujin, and Tsukuyomi will be there to hear you too."

Susanoo sneered. "Hmmph, if you can really do that, I will go up there and tear them all a new asshole."

"SUSANOO'S STAND"

Uzume danced sensually and stripped naked before the guards of the bridge to Takama-ga-hara, allowing Susanoo to slip by on his cloud to confront his sister, Amaterasu, the regent of the sixth universe.

"Brother, are you still so unhappy with your standing here?" said Amaterasu atop her throne to Susanoo. Amaterasu was clothed in a fabulous white kimono which shone with the full brightness of a star. Her eyes were black and empty—voids which occasionally glowed when she became interested. "I have offered you the vastness of the ocean, yet you have spit it back in my face. Now, I feel you will merely go against every decision I make just to spite me."

"Of fucking course! You are an inept and incompetent bitch! You don't deserve to sit on that throne, not as millions down below suffer and die to keep you there! Are you blind and deaf to the turmoil down below? Huh? You hear all these people screaming your name yet what action do you take?"

"We are not capable of fighting the Dragons at this time, brother. I have taken steps to ensure our survival. I urge you to hold your tongue and withhold judgment until a future time." Her voice was apathetic and monotone, sounding more like a computer program than a sentient being after her centuries of mentorship at the helm. "And I say this with all respect due to you, brother: do not lie to me and pretend that you care about the life down below, you whose storms have ravished the world below. Knowing you, you likely have the other High-Kami listening in on this conversation, waiting for them to flock to your side. Well, they know your true character. They know better than to trust your words."

"Then they will trust my actions! Yes, Fujin, Raiden, and the others are hearing this now and they understand my frustration. Do you not, my brothers? Talking to you—you—this lifeless, emotionless shadow of a person you've become, Amaterasu... It's pointless. It's like talking to a fucking wall! This universe deserves a better ruler! Someone who actually gives a fuck!"

General Deem, seeing and hearing this in hindsight, was struck between the eyes. Susanoo's frustrations resonated with his own, particularly in his lackluster communications with the wishy-washy Princess Darna.

"A better ruler? Like you? How many people have you killed with your tantrum-induced storms? Do not listen to this hypocrite, my faithful retainers!"

"My storms fertilized the land for—"

"The future? And there you have it... daddy—father—taught us that we must make sacrifices for the greater good. Bad, even terrible things, must be allowed to happen sometimes for the sake of the future. We must suffer for a little while to learn and to grow. We are building something great and new out of the old world. For the first time since our birth, father and Izanami are reconciling their differences."

"How the hell did that happen?" Susanoo growled, tugging at his beard, dumbfounded by this statement.

The Kami had been told that long ago, Queen Izanami had been the wife of King Izanagi, who was the father of Susanoo and Amaterasu. However, Queen Izanami died whilst giving birth to the Kami of fire, and her spirit wandered to the underworld. King Izanagi, who loved his wife dearly at the time, ventured to the underworld to find her. She made him swear not to look upon her, but his curiosity got the better of him. He fled in terror upon seeing her horrific decaying corpse. Angered and embarrassed that her grotesque form had been discovered, Queen Izanami swore to kill 1,000 of Izanagi's people every day. King Izanagi responded by shouting back that he'd have the women of the planet birth 1,500 people every day. Thus, their great love turned to fierce hate and their contentious rivalry for the souls of men began. It lasted for hundreds of years without any sign it would end.

Queen Izanami eventually formed a close relationship with King Yama, the Kami of the underworld and overlord of the sadistic ogre-like creatures known as Oni. He and his Oni brutalized the souls who came to the underworld without mercy. It had been a dream of King Izanagi, before becoming too tired to lead and giving the reins of power to Amaterasu, to recover the souls of the dead from the underworld and restore his wife to her former self.

Amaterasu, now faced with Susanoo, explained that Queen Izanagi and King Yama had agreed to release a large number of the souls of the dead and to cease their daily killing on two "insignificant" conditions. First, Amaterasu and her heavenly Kami would allow Uzume's blessed children to be killed, after which their precious souls could be claimed by the underworld as *trophies*. This was otherwise impossible because the few children Uzume had blessed at birth were thought to be pure. Thus, King Yama, who was also the chief judge of the dead, could not sentence them to eternal captivity. This made their souls highly-desirable, prized commodities, like gold or diamonds in the human realm. Second, the heavenly Kami agreed to help safeguard the underworld from a Dragon invasion, which seemed imminent. In return, the Kami of the underworld and death would help safeguard the high-heavens at all costs if it too were invaded.

Upon learning these things, Susanoo wailed, slamming his fist against a pillar. "These are innocent young people who have committed no crimes against you or any of us! Nor have their families who slave under your star! I hear their screams and weeping—they reach me in my sleep at night. Why should they suffer for problems we gods can fix? Why?!"

"Dramatic much, brother? You are not fooling me, so I suggest you not fool yourself. I know that you don't truly care about these people, or anyone but yourself. You never have before. You will simply find every excuse you can to undermine my authority. Now, the answer to your question is this: we simply cannot fix these problems now. These Dragons have ended the reigns of other deities throughout the cosmos. Our fate would be no different. We must be intelligent and pragmatic gods and resist the temptation for conflict and confrontation. A few girls and the grief of their parents is the price we must be prepared to pay."

Susanoo swiftly turned and slashed the head off of one of his sister's favorite attendants, splattering blood on her white kimono. "I will teach you what grief is, just as the humans taught me!" He spit on her floor, then stormed out of the throne room.

Amaterasu trembled and left her throne to cradle the body of her attendant. She gave out a shrill cry, her eyes bursting with white flames. "Be strong...be patient..." she repeated her parent's advice. "Don't panic... detach from everything... relax..." Stomping through her throne room, holding her bloodied hands upward, she came to her relaxation chamber and began to knit. It had helped to calm her in the past. Suddenly, the largest window of the room crashed open and the disemboweled body of her beloved horse flew through it at her feet. She huffed and she puffed for some time, then, unable to contain her emotions any longer, she let out a piercing banshee-like scream which shattered all the glass in the palace. The flares of her body reached out for miles and many of her servants were blinded, at least temporarily.

General Deem couldn't help but cheer inside for Susanoo. He wished he could live vicariously through him.

"The bitch wants to play, huh? Then, let's play!" he stormed through the courtyard as two other gods, the wind-god Fujin and the lightning-god Raiden, followed.

"Are you out of your mind, Susanoo?" asked Fujin.

"What will you do now?" asked Raiden.

"Uzume is on my side. I will confront the leader of the Dragons if only you two would help us," said Susanoo.

"To defy the will of Amaterasu?" Fujin was baffled.

"To aid the human animals?" Raiden added.

"Raiden, whose umbilical cords will you devour if the humans are gone?" said Susanoo, knowing that Raiden had a unique appetite. "Will you truly allow King Yama and Queen Izanami to have this much influence in Takama-ga-hara? Can you watch as the world below is taken from us by these Dragon beasts? You two frequent the world below. You've seen the complexities of the humans and their civilization, well I have not only seen but experienced—"

General Deem's visions began to blur before ending suddenly. At that point, he realized that the events were now present. They were happening at that very moment. Deem raced back to the world of the Kami using a combination of his new teleportation powers, taught to him by Loki, and his own incredible speeds—many times the speed of light—to navigate the complex path back to the world of Ame-Tsuchi.

By the time he arrived, Susanoo, Uzume, Fujin, and Raiden were already making their way to the castle of Lord-Marquess Gigatheta. The last of Kushina's sisters had been sacrificed a month before, and the grief-stricken, terrified Kushina was now bound to be offered up next. Despite her great fear, she did not plead for her life as her parents surrendered her to the Daimyo's men, who carted her off to the Dragon's castle.

General Deem finally came face-to-face with Susanoo again, and after exchanging silent glances, Deem handed Susanoo back his sword. "Take this!" Deem urged. "Kushina has only half of one of your days left!"

Upon holding the Totsuka-no-Tsurugi in his hands again, his godly aura and powers returned. "Damn it, Dragon! Help us!"

Deem refused. "Your sister and the others must know that their schemes cannot succeed. They cannot claim the souls of Kushina's sisters or any of those killed by the Dragons because our armies will send their life-energies into space—there will be nothing left for them. Storm god, you must fight with your mind. Your might will do you little against a Dragon lord. Exploit his insatiable thirst and hunger. That's all I can say to you." And with that, Deem sped off faster than the eye can see.

With time running out, Susanoo hatched a clever plan. He used his restored powers of flight and strength to retrieve and fill eight giant kegs of *sake* wine, with the obvious intent to get the beast drunk before engaging it.

"Susanoo!" a female voice called.

Susanoo looked around but could not find the source of the voice. He became nervous, believing that it could possibly be his sister out for vengeance. However, the voice sounded more urgent than angry. "Who is that? What is that voice?" he asked.

"I am Athena, a goddess from a universe separate from your own," the voice responded. "I am an expert in telepathic communication and have finally been able to contact you across the realms. My sister and I know of your great love and plight. We both are slaves and prisoners to the Dragons, but we have knowledge that they need. Our home world is lost, and hundreds of other worlds are falling as I speak to you now. Most of them have no hope of survival, but yours..."

"I have no time for this foolishness!"

"I know, but I am here to help. My sister has urged me to help you in the only way I know how. I can teach you a way of protecting Kushina without physical force."

"How can I do that?"

Kushina was pulled off the cart and dragged into the castle of the Dragon lord as thousands of Dragon sentries looked on, lining the path. The walk to the private chamber of the Dragon lord was long but never absent of terror. Thousands of human prisoners were visible in cram-packed cages, crying out and screaming. Panicked, Kushina pushed back against her escorts and tried to wiggle free, kicking and screaming.

Finally, they reached the gated entrance to Lord Gigatheta's private chamber.

The daimyo's men untied her and stripped her. They then threw her up on a rectangular stone slab. Other human sacrifices lay struggling on nearby stone slabs but Kushina was to be the special of the day, Uzume's blessed ones always were. She desperately tried to crawl away but was subdued by the many strong men who held her down long enough to secure her chains. The human escorts left her to the mercy of the Dragons who carried her on the slab through the gates to their master.

The sight of the eight-headed beast in person was indescribable, incomprehensible by human understanding. A hundred warehouses and a hundred towers could not house the beast. A dozen landfills could not compare to the stench that filled that foul place. The enormous creatures, whose gut dragged on the ground, took one great step forward, causing the whole place to shake for several seconds.

Kushina's eyes grew wide with terror and she began to hyperventilate.

The Dragons kneeled and offered a prayer to their god-queen and a mantra of respect for their eight-headed lord. Gigatheta's faces salivated. The mouth and eyes of his fire-head grew hot with flames and a cold mist left the mouth of his ice-head. Its water-head made the first ambitious move, revealing its wet, transparent tongue and licking it over the poor girl's body. Kushina tried to roll over as much as her chains would allow but Gigatheta's plant-head sent out vines which pinned her back down. Gigatheta relished in the terrified look on the girl's face. She screamed for help from Amaterasu and Uzume. She screamed for her Susanoo, who'd promised this would never happen. She'd screamed so much and so hard that her voice had faded and her cries became a whimper. "Please!" she begged despite knowing that it was hopeless.

She shut her eyes, then opened them as she heard the voice of Susanoo thunder: "Stop!"

"Su!" Kushina sighed, but then saw that he held another bound woman with him. The woman was Uzume in human form, flesh and all, ten times more beautiful and radiant than the most beautiful woman on the planet.

"I am not here to interrupt your meal, I am here to add some flavor to it," said Susanoo gruffly. "I am Susanoo, the Kami of storms, and this human woman is the most desirable in all the world. Even the Kami envy her. Have her as your appetizer and first course along with this, the most sacred drink of the Kami—a drink which will give you eternal life." He revealed giant kegs of sake wine with their top lids open.

The electric-head of Gigatheta spoke. "DO YOU THINK YOU CAN TRICK ME WITH YOUR POISON?"

"Poison? No." Susanoo drank a cup from the nearest keg.

Gigatheta had one of his guards try the drink, and they confirmed its good taste. The Lord-Marquess himself then drank until all eight kegs were empty. Each of the eight heads had their fill, though the fire-head bullied the plant-head into giving up half a keg. He became a bit tired and nauseous but was still determined to have a taste of Kushina and Uzume. The metal-head, who'd sucked up its keg of sake in one great gulp, made the first move at Kushina as the plant-head went for Uzume.

At that moment, Uzume transformed into her goddess-self, broke free of her ropes, and sent thick vines around the throats and forefeet of Gigatheta. The drunken Dragon took a few seconds to recuperate from the surprise. During that time, Susanoo broke Kushina's chains with his sacred sword and focused on his strongest and most passionate thoughts, as Athena had taught him, transforming Kushina into a comb which he secured in his hair.

Gigatheta's ice-head caused the vines around its neck to die from intense cold. His fire-head burned the vines around its neck to ashes. His wind-head turned evaporable, causing the vines to pass through harmlessly. His electric-head sent hot sparks down its long neck, burning away the vines. His water-head liquified, giving the vines nothing to wrap around. His plant-head summoned vines of its own to wrench off Uzume's vines. His rock and metal heads used brute strength to burst free. His forefeet quickly broke free as well.

Susanoo soon realized that the combined effects of the alcohol and Uzume's powers had won him only a few seconds.

Fujin and Raiden, the other Kami, flanked opposite sides of the castle. The hideous ogre-like god Raiden pounded his drums, causing giant bolts of lightning to crash into the castle structure, in turn causing intense heat and debris to strike Gigatheta's left-side. The equally hideous Fujin opened his big bag of wind, causing powerful winds to strike the opposite side of the castle, striking Gigatheta with more debris at great force from his right. Susanoo himself barely escaped the violent collapse of that portion of the castle.

Dragon warriors flew up in pursuit of the culprits. Fujin and Raiden transformed themselves into wind and lightning respectively to escape, reappearing elsewhere to strike again. Susanoo focused his supernatural energies into his sword which created a super-storm that spun faster than an F-5 tornado and grew larger than the largest cyclone on Earth. The storm struck Gigatheta from the front at full force. The front of the beast disappeared, covered in the whirling clouds of debris.

Soon a giant fireball the size of fifty banyan trees shot out from the dust clouds and struck Fujin, setting him and his wind bag ablaze. Large lightning bolts shot out from the dust cloud, knocking even the thickest of Raiden's lightning bolts aside. Gigatheta's metal-head magically constructed a tungsten spear which it hurled at Raiden, stabbing him through the gut. Not to be outdone, the rock-head flew meteoric boulders at Raiden, crushing him. As Gigatheta grew more agitated, his wind-head released more wind than Fujin's bag could ever hope to hold, blowing back Susanoo's storm until debris from it struck the storm-god himself, throwing him miles away. The storm grazed the farmland of Kushina's parents, sending a chunk of wood through the home, crushing and killing Kushina's Oni-possessed mother along with her father.

Susanoo was thrown over the stream where he crashed and cartwheeled like a rag-doll thrown out of a moving vehicle. When he came to, he took the comb—Kushina—from his hair and held it out in his palm. "To escape with you is enough for now," he said. "Now, to find the one who can change you back."

A voice in the multiverse speaks:

"Every moment I live, I'm gasping. My mind is spinning. I close my eyes. Visions and voices play. I open them. Visions blind me, and voices scream. More than I can count. I can't escape them. I want to help them, but I can't. I want to touch them—reach out to them so they know I'm there—but I can't! I'm tired. I'm so tired! Always. Always tired. My mind screams for something—what? Food. Water. Air. Rest. It's not enough. I never get enough. Of what? Nothing works. Nothing satisfies. I think 'stand,' yet my body falls to pieces. My legs fail to rise. My arms too. My muscles, failing to trigger, hanging limp on my bones. I crawl like a foolish child pretending to play 'army' on these arms. Twelve tons bear down on me."

"THE THIRD POWER"

For most of their history, the Dragons had never been seriously challenged. They had trampled over whatever opposition they faced. They'd defeated Angels, Demons, monsters, and gods, dominating even mighty beings like Amaterasu, Cronus, Odin, and Zeus. Still, something had always concerned the Dragon leaders.

They were aware of three areas of space that emitted significantly higher energy signatures than all others.

The first of these great powers was, of course, the Dragon Queen—Ain—herself.

The second of these great powers was the Origin Point, linking all the daughter universes to the Heaven of heavens.

The third of these great powers was the most concentrated. Also, for a long time it was the faintest and weakest of the three, yet it mysteriously grew until it was impossible for the Dragon lords to ignore it. Strangely, it could be detected from various locations spread out across the entire Multiverse, and it took a lot of mapping by some of creation's most intelligent captive beings to discover that all of these energy signatures originated from the same place. Like a single bullet hole punctured through the many folds and pages of a book, having hit the wall on the other side, the anomaly had seemingly intersected many universes and landed *somewhere*.

It remained a mystery for many millennia. Then, after the conquest of the third granddaughter universe, its deities revealed what they knew of the anomaly, a secret that damaged the already strained relationship between Ain and Satan. The deities revealed that the anomaly was, in fact, another universe—an isolated *pocket* universe—created in the midst of the original Angel War in Heaven.

Certain Angels who'd aligned themselves with Satan attempted to create a universe for themselves, resulting in the formation of a twisted and deformed dimension that protruded like a hideous mole from the face of Heaven. They named it "New Heaven."

It remained unused after the Angel War and mainly accumulated waste, including enormous amounts of divine smoke and incense. Then, as fate would have it, Ain, *Death* itself, began her many millennia of destruction, consequently tearing many holes through the fabric of space-time across the daughter and granddaughter universes. These holes were so deep that they punctured through the layers of the heaven-lies into the forgotten realm of New Heaven. New Heaven absorbed some of the matter and energy left behind after each of Ain's great explosions. It thus became—in a sense—the great intersection and landfill of the cosmos.

And it had grown.

New Heaven was an especially violent and unstable universe. It was littered with holes—wormholes, black holes, and white holes—leading to and from other universes. If looked at from the eyes of God, the universe would appear to be tearing itself apart. Yet somehow, a collection of phenomenal, dinosaurian life-forms had managed to make that hellish universe their home.

They called themselves the Malkuthians, and if anyone could challenge the dominance of the Dragons it was them.

PART II
RISE OF THE MALKUTHIANS

"WHO ARE THE MALKUTHIANS?"

Dragon centurions dragged Aphrodite back to her holding cell trembling from the immense pain in her hands. She was thrown to the hard ground in front of her sister. Athena coddled her, saying, "Be strong, I'm here."

"He-he, like, pried out my fingernails, sis!" Aphrodite cried. "My fingernails! One by one!" Athena inspected her hands. They were crusted with golden blood. "Oww-uh!" Aphrodite wrenched them back. "That hurt!"

"Stay still!" Athena completed her inspection. "Don't worry, they'll grow back. He's done worse to me."

"Gee, thanks, that really helps, sis!" Aphrodite rolled her eyes. "Like, how much longer do we need to endure this? I can't do this anymore."

"Not much longer now."

"All this torture... And like I haven't been with anyone in years!"

"Stay strong. Close your eyes." Athena combed her fingers through Aphrodite's hair and rested her head on her lap. "Remember that one time my Aegeans outsmarted and beat your Trojans. Remember how pissed off you were at me?"

"Bitch."

"No, I'm genuinely trying to help. Do you remember that? You thought life would never be the same again. It was the end of the world. It was all doom and gloom."

"Yeah..."

"And I calmed you down by brushing your hair like this and telling you stories. Little stories. And then your Trojans went on and built a new kingdom for themselves with your son as the patriarch?"

"And we, like, started using a sexier new language that made my hunky hunks seem even hunkier? Like, yeah! Totally!"

"Well, let me tell you another story of hope... I'll tell you about a place far away from here, but not so far... A place where even the Dragons will meet their match very soon..."

"Like...*very* soon?"

"Very, very, very soon, sis. Do I lie?"

"Weeeeeell, there was the time when you, like, totally—"

"It was a rhetorical question."

Athena first told her about the bizarre universe of the Malkuthians: New Heaven. "They say that New Heaven is a universe with only two galaxies—*super* galaxies—one called *Shekhinah* and the other called *Kether*. They are many, many, many thousands of times larger than normal galaxies, like those we ruled in our universe. Both galaxies swallowed up millions before them. The two themselves are colliding and merging toward a central point, a place called the 'Deep Core' where the Malkuthians have built a wall."

"Like, oh my gawd, what's with all the astrology, sis?" Aphrodite complained.

"*Astronomy* not astrology, sis," Athena corrected. "And it's not so complicated."

"To *you*! Oh, gawd, gag me with a spoon! This is, like, soooooo boring, sis. Get to the good stuff already!"

"There are ten regions of the Shekhinah galaxy."

"Like, please don't tell me about all of them!"

"Fine, I'll tell you about the two most important because it's where we're most likely to be deployed. The *Malkuth Region* is the location of the race's original planet, also called *Malkuth*. See, that's easy to remember, huh?"

"I guess..."

"Malkuth was their first planet before they became space-faring. A great catastrophe rendered the planet uninhabitable: separate kingdoms struck each other with flying weapons that exploded like volcanoes. The planet itself is now considered a footnote in history, like an ancient ruin of interest only to archaeologists, and yet people still live there. It's cheaper, you see?

"The *Hod Region* is the location of the current capital planet, called *Hod*, on which it is said the people never die or grow old. Their capital world is a fortress unlike any I've seen: covered in layers upon layers of force fields and flying weapons."

"So, like... Are they like gods or something? Cause it sounds like it."

Athena shook her head. "Mortals. Flesh and blood. Most of them are larger than Cyclops and much more clever. They look like giant lizards or reptiles but walk on two feet like us and are as intelligent as the brightest humans."

"So, like Dragons then?"

Athena shook her head again. "They don't have wings like the Dragons. They built their own wings out of metal, like Icarus. They have great flying machines that travel many times faster than even you or Hermes. They're also more... *free-spirited* than the Dragons. They think like individuals, even their lowest kind. They seem to have free will."

"Like, they don't have a king?"

"Oh, they have a king, alright, or two of them that seem to share the authority. They aren't called kings, though. One they call 'President.' The President is a rhetorician. He loves to give speeches to large crowds. The other they call 'Chancellor,' the leader of the Senate. He's a genius whose family has been in politics and business for millennia. He's hundreds of years old but wise beyond his years, especially considering he's younger than you."

"Heya, I totally resent that!"

"Chancellor Antares and President Fomalhaut are of a sub-species or race called the Ceratosaurs, distinguished by a single horn on their noses. They're like—"

"Spare me, like, the details."

"But those are the best parts."

"Can you, like, skip them or something? Please. Ok. Thank you."

Athena sighed. "I digress... Besides the Malkuth and Hod regions, there are eight other regions called *Yesod, Binah...*"

"Oh. My. Gawd. My brain!"

"You don't have to remember all this, I'm just sharing."

"Why?"

"Because it gives you context."

"Like, kill me now," said Aphrodite.

"Anyway, there's also the *Chokmah Region*, the *Tifaret Region, Geburah, Netzach, Chesed,* and *Kether*. The *Kether Region* was so named because it was the collision point of the two galaxies, where they intersected."

"What. The. Fuck, sis? I already told you like a million times already. Like, why do I need to know all of this?"

"Because it's interesting."

"Not to *me*! Can you just get to the romantic and erotic parts?"

"Disgusting. You know the Malkuthians are pretty much intelligent dinosaurs, right?"

"Yeah... and? They still date each other and fuck right? Can we get to that?"

"...Maybe after we get past the educational and action-packed parts."

"Aw, shit. Like, why do I even ask anymore? Continue. Like, maybe I'll fall asleep and forget how much fucking pain I'm, like, in right now."

"Escapism is kind of the point, sis."

"Oh, gawd, please… Spare me."

Athena continued. "The Chancellor's family, the Antares, built these portals that would catapult a lot of material quickly across star systems. They built swarms of flying machines that would surround entire stars and drain them of their energy. With that, they were able to build powerful ships that could travel faster than light, and even more advanced ones that could warp the space around them to travel many times faster than light. They could build cities on other planets and in other star systems. So, when the Catastrophe happened and the original planet, Malkuth, was rendered uninhabitable, the entire civilization became indebted to the Antares, their inventions, and the colonies they'd created. They founded the *MALKUTHIAN INTERSTELLAR UNION*, or more simply, *the Union*, and their stated purpose was called 'manifest destiny'—the occupation and control of the entire universe by any and all means necessary. And nothing seemed to be able to stop them."

"THE GREAT ALIEN RACE WARS"

"In the Binah Region, there was a race of giant bug creatures that had taken over many star systems. They possessed no weapons, but they didn't really need any. They had their bodies: pinchers, claws, mandibles, bio-acid, bio-plasma, and tough exoskeletons resistant to weaponry. However, their strength lay in their numbers and in their fearless, unemotional—almost suicidal—commitment to serve their queen."

"Why, was she hot?" asked Aphrodite.

"What? No. She was a giant bug, sis."

"Don't some girl bugs, like, spray a perfume out of their butts to, like, attract and control their mates?"

"You mean pheromones?"

"Uh, yeah… duh, that's what I meant."

"I suppose… Anyway, the Malkuthians called these bug creatures 'the Infestation' and went about eradicating them like pests. When their ground troops struggled to get the job done with their metal-projectile shooters and exploding canisters, they started to drop weapons that exploded with much more devastating power from their flying machines, even more powerful than the weapons that had caused the Catastrophe on their home planet. The earliest versions of these weapons were able to destroy entire continents."

"Shut up! No way!"

"Yes, way. I'm telling you, the Malkuthians are mortals but they're a juggernaut. They used hundreds of these explosives on the Infestation. Their planets were transformed into blazing infernos. It wasn't about conquering and colonizing those planets anymore, it was about winning, and it was about exterminating a detestable foe. There were none left alive."

Loki sang, deliberately mocking and annoying the ailing Thor:

"...And in the Geburan Spiral Arm
There was a race that meant them harm
With ships like discs of city size
They brought about a genocide..."

Thor bore the full weight of a planet on his back that Lord Mortimer had hurled at him before leaving him to die. It was draining his incredible strength and killing him slowly. "Llllooookkkiiii!" Thor bellowed, straining.

"Oh, I'm sorry, dearie. Would you rather have snake venom poured on your damn face for 10,000 years? I didn't think so."

"Thou hast said thee hadst a plan to free me from this! Thou hast said thee hadst a plan to get back my hammer!"

"I *did* say that didn't I?"

Thor growled with irritation.

"Don't fret, my brother
I'll show and tell
I know much more than Mimir's Well..."

"When?" The word left Thor's throat as if he'd been punched in the gut. "How much longer must I endureth this? How much longer must I wait to avenge our people on these bastard Dragons?"

"Seeing is believing. Seeing is believing…" Loki poked his finger into the right-temple of his brother's head and gave a cackling laugh.

Thor saw visions of giant dinosaur-like creatures in mechanical suits with huge guns that fired beams of light that cut through entire columns of tentacled alien creatures. In a last-ditch effort, the tentacled Geburan aliens positioned their city-sized war crafts and mothership around Hod, the new Malkuthian capital planet, but could not break through the layers of Malkuthian force fields. The Malkuthian starfleets converged on the now-trapped aliens. After quickly surrounding and destroying their invasion force, the Malkuthians unleashed a new weapon on the Geburan home worlds, a class of space stations capable of destroying entire planets: the *World Enders*.

"These things you see
Are our hope
And now you know
And now can… cope…
Heeeheeeheeehaw!"

"Do these dinosaurian beasts stand a chance?" asked Thor.

"I know a secret
I can't tell
I know it good
I know it… well…"

"Loki, I can aid thee!" Thor offered. "We can find these Malkuthian beasts! We can rally them to our side! We can finally be rid of these Dragons forever. What does thou want? What does thou want from me? This strength of mine? This power of mine? These words of mine? I can't be any good to thee like this!"

"Oh, sweet symphony! To hear my mighty nephew-brother, prince of the Aesir, begging like a common peasant. That's music to my ears!"

"Loki, 'tis crushing me!"

"Oh, you're fine. Stop feeling sorry for yourself. Besides, you really think I need *you* to rally those dinosaurs, brother? With *my* powers of suggestion? I already have them in my Elvin-skinned pant pockets!"

"Loki, I'm sorry."

Loki put his right hand to his ear. "Come again?"

"I'm sorry!"

"Louder. I can't quite hear you."

"I'M SORRY, BROTHER!"

"Alright, alright… since I'm feeling generous tonight… You've earned yourself… another recital!"

"LOKI!"

"…In the center of that place
Where things are us-ually stretched and crushed
There is a wall across that space
Across a hole of glowy… stuff…"

"LLLOOOKKKIIIII!!!"
"Beyond that hole
One can't see
The power of infinity…"

Amaterasu, the leader of the Kami, briefed the council of High-Kami. "These Malkuthians we are set to invade have drained the energy of entire stars. They've done it with the ease of which a human collects water from a stream. They harvest the stars like grains of rice."

"Then they are no better than you, great regent," said Hachiman, the Kami of war.

"What I do with one star, they are able to do with billions."

Queen Izanami stared a hole into her ex-husband, Izanagi, who looked away in disgust. Attendants circled Izanami and King Yama, who ruled the underworld together, spraying them down with perfume to dampen their stench.

"And it's not just the stars from which they gain their energy," Amaterasu continued. "They've built these walls across holes in their universe. These walls appear to collect energy as well—all the energy that falls into them. Massive amounts of it. And their vessels run on this energy. I've seen their largest vessels floating in space erase planets the size of our own."

"Inconceivable," said Hachiman.

"The Malkuthians themselves are huge and physically capable, even without their weapons. Their jaws are like shark jaws and their tails are as heavy as elephants. Their tails can counterbalance their firearms, which shoot all sorts of impressive projectiles. The human muskets and cannons cannot compare. They faced a race of alien beings with cube-shaped ships the size of moons: the Collective. These beings could take over the brains of other species with a mere touch and seemingly adapt to almost any attack. The Malkuthians fought these creatures from a distance, able to change the types of projectiles their firearms shot like magic: streams of popping metals, bright lights, blinding rays, screaming beams. Even the Collective could not adapt quickly enough. The Malkuthians attacked the thousands of alien cubes with weapons of unbelievable power. They destroyed them like castles made of wet sand."

Queen Izanami kicked King Izanagi from under the table, both in anger and to coax his attention. Izanagi kicked back. Infuriated by this, King Yama stood and bashed the table so hard with his fist that drinks and food went flying. "How dare you strike my queen!" Yama roared.

"Gentlemen!" flames shot from Amaterasu's eyes. "Are you paying attention?"

"You'll have to pardon us, Ame," said Izanami. "There's a lot of history here from before you were born. Your father's still the same shallow, jealous fool he always was."

"Rotten old hag!" Izanagi raised his walking stick and waved it at his ex-wife.

King Yama knocked the stick away.

"Enough of this!" Amaterasu ignited. The table caught fire. Suijin doused it with water. "I'm well aware of your ancient conflict. I have brought you all together to unite in the face of a common enemy. We must place our differences aside. When these Dragons are finished feasting on the humans and after we've worn out our usage to them, they will come for us. And as it stands now, we don't stand a chance."

"*Sugoi! Sugoi!*" Uzume mocked with taunting applause from a cage beside her fellow co-conspirators. "If you had only listened to Susanoo and heeded his warning, you would have known of the Dragon treachery."

"We have an opportunity to retain their trust, and I suppose you all have an opportunity to regain *my* trust," said Amaterasu.

"How merciful you are, great regent!" Uzume sassed.

"They want us to help them to invade the Malkuthian worlds. King Yama, they want your powerful Oni to serve at the front. We will follow with our Yokai."

"And how long can this last?" Uzume challenged. "Either we'll be killed by the Dragons, serving as their slaves and cannon fodder, or by the Malkuthians, serving as target practice for their advanced weapons. What difference does it make? Wouldn't you rather die free?"

"My brother has twisted your mind, Uzume," said Amaterasu. "It's for that reason and that reason alone I can grant you amnesty for your betrayal."

"You abandoned my daughters, my blessed ones, to be swallowed whole by that Dragon abomination. You're about to sacrifice all of us in a war where we'll die not as the rulers of this world but as slaves to the Dragons. You can save your amnesty. I don't want it. It'd be a token gift from a coward."

"Ame," said Izanami. "Are you going to allow her to speak to you that way?"

Amaterasu looked around at the other members of the council who looked back at her with unease. Her father looked down. "Do what you must, Ame, these choices are difficult but they must be made," he said under his breath. "You are regent. You are in charge."

She reached her left-hand up to the red sun, gathering a ball of fiery energy from it.

"Go ahead and murder me. What difference do my crops make anyway?" said Uzume. "There will be no one left to feed soon. No more babes. Only death. And death will rule."

"Are those your last words, Uzume? Let it be known, I gave you that dignity."

"My last words are these: your brother, Susanoo, was a lot of things, but he was no coward. He would not cower to the will of others. He would not live simply to appease those with power!"

"If he were so great, then ask yourself: where is he now?"

"He is seeking to find the one who holds the key to it all… the one called *'Azure'*… A power greater even than the Dragons. But you won't listen, will you?" said Uzume.

"There's no such thing. My scouts would have sensed that and told me about it. You're just telling stories. More clever lies to set us off course."

"If that's what you think, then goodbye, cowardly queen. I will say no more from this point forward."

Amaterasu hurled the solar fireball at her. It engulfed her and reduced her to ashes. The Kami of the sun turned to the other Kami. "The more we let the traitors lie to us, the further off course we get. I will not allow traitors to twist our arms. We are to remain collaborators with the Dragons and share in their conquests. We will go with them to the worlds of the Malkuthians. We will gain their knowledge, their weapons, and their power. When the time is right, we will put the dagger to the Dragons' backs and rebuild our realm like autumn to spring."

Aphrodite began dozing off, her eyes struggling to stay open.

"And before destroying the Chokman Collective alien cubes," continued Athena. "Chancellor Antares learned their programming and of the little machines they injected into their victims. All of it reminded him of the hive-mind that the Infestation and the Geburans had—the blind service to their queen and the ability to control all of them at once. He called these 'nanomachines' and proposed injecting them into all Malkuthians at birth. Imagine if we had that power, sis. If we controlled all the Malkuthians. Turned them against the Dragons."

Aphrodite's eyes closed and she fell asleep. Athena ran her fingers through her sister's hair. "Pretty little sister, we'll be out of here someday."

A voice sang in her head:
"I do agree
Agree with her
The way you tell it's
Such a… bore…"

"Who's that? Who's there?" asked Athena. "You…you're a telepath like me."

"I'll teach you a spell
A spell to heal
And numb the pain so you won't… feel…"

"Why? What do you want?"

"Just to find out

How much you know
And then I'll leave
And then I'll go."

"Loki... Loki is your name. Your thoughts are a Gordian knot to untangle. How do I know I can trust you with that information?"

"Why, what choice do you really have, dearie?" said Loki.

The door to the holding cell opened, and in came two Dragon centurions. Athena lay her sister down as gently as possible. She then stood at attention, confronting her grim and unknown fate.

"When you return
I'll teach the spell
And then you'll tell
You better tell..."

"If you're asking me about who I think you are...this Azure... I don't know where he is yet. I've felt him in passing. I've been searching."

"And so have I
Unless we've all been told a lie
I want to know your final answer
Will you help me search for... Azure?"

The Centurion grabbed Athena and wrenched her away. "I will tell you what I know if you'll help me find him," Athena told Loki telepathically. "But in the end... he's mine!"

"Oooohooohooohoooo! So be it..." said Loki, "I love a good race."

Satan walked beside some of his Arch-Demons, crossing vast astronomical distances in seconds as they surveyed the Multiverse. "The Dragons will converge there in New Heaven and wrestle it away from those Malkuthian dinosaurs," he said. "They will secure and attack the back gates from New Heaven just as the portal spills open and we will invade the front of Heaven from this umbilical cord."

"Will that work?" asked General Belial.

"It is our best and only chance," said Satan. "And we have little time. The Prince has come."

Be'elzebul massaged his shoulders comfortingly. "It's ok... it's ok..." he said.

"My apologies again, sir," said General Moloch. "The Prince Messiah escaped me in Bethlehem. Michael and his forces blocked me there."

"I am surprised you got as far as you did, general. I was not allowed near. It's always Michael. Michael. Michael. Michael. We'll see how well the Arch-Angel fights when the Dragons are at his back and he's face-to-face with me."

"Can the Dragons be trusted to take the back gate?" asked General Mammon.

"The Dragons have never been defeated in all of history," said Satan. "And Ain is now second only to God Yahweh in power. Don't forget, the old tyrant went to bed after he banished us and formed her in the process."

"The Malkuthians are thousands of years more advanced than the humans of Earth," said Belial. "They have never been defeated by an alien species in all of their history. Tens of thousands of worlds subjugated or destroyed. The Dragons are mighty and numerous, but they are archaic in their methods. Ain is incredibly powerful, but Ain is one."

"No..." said Satan. "There is *another* like her."

"Another?" Moloch sounded dumbfounded.

"I have a contingency plan. A trump card. An ace in the hole there among the Malkuthians. Don't you trust me?" The Arch-Demons all stood in fearful silence. "Well? I've brought you all this far. I've built the greatest empire the Earth has ever seen. We dominate even the tyrant's precious Holy Land again!"

"It's the prophecies..." said Belial.

"Oh, yes, those fairy-tales. I know all about those. Are you afraid of *him*? Afraid of the Prince? This *Yeshua* (Jesus)?"

"We haven't been able to prevent his coming or end his life no matter how hard we tried. Even I—"

"Even you?" Satan made the Hebrew scriptures appear in his hand. "Mortal weapons won't work on him. No, not now. He must give up his life willingly, it seems. But here is my weapon: these texts. If he's anything like his father, he'll know these texts. He'll know every word. Literally. And when I confront him with it, literally, he will throw himself from the highest place in hopes that the Angels will lift him up *'so that he will not so much as strike his foot upon a stone.'* And when they don't..."

"And if they do?" Moloch challenged.

"If they do, I'll play the ace up my sleeve—the one I've saved for that very hour. Azure."

"After I find this Azure, mark my word, I will find you, Athena!" Susanoo seethed. His cloud hovered over a Malkuthian planet in the Yesod region. He navigated the cloud through lanes and lanes—layers upon layers of sky traffic.

"Plans have changed," Athena spoke telepathically to him, now at the head of an army of Cyclops and Centaurs bound to invade a new world the Dragons had found interest in. "I am being redeployed at the head of my people. It seems I may be seeing you sooner than later."

"No matter where you go, I will find you! You will change Kushina back or you will taste the wrath of my storms!" Susanoo grasped the comb tightly.

"Remember our deal, storm god: you find the Grand Conduit and only then will I have the power to return your woman to her natural form. You have competition now. We both do. There's someone else after him, a trickster god named Loki."

"Anyone who gets in my way will feel my blade."

"Well, this one knows as much as we do. And Susanoo…the Dragons are planning an invasion of that universe you're in. It's the largest invasion force I've ever seen. At their head is the Dragon Lord Baladan, three times more powerful than the one you call Gigatheta. Your sister and her armies are with him."

"My sister can kiss my hairy ass."

"She has murdered Uzume. And your father and mother are with her too."

Susanoo shook his head and spit over his shoulder. "I've heard enough. This Azure… if he is so powerful, shouldn't I be able to sense his energy?"

"The Malkuthian universe, New Heaven, is a hub of energy. He masks his well."

"These beasts… these flying vessels… the sheer size of their buildings… all these worlds of theirs… How can I find Azure in all of this if I can't sense him?"

"Use your instincts."

"I am a prince, a High-Kami, not your personal huntsman!"

"Perhaps, but you are one whose cloud can transverse realms. And I was told that this Azure is a lot like you: an angry, discontent wanderer lost in a universe that should be his. Where would *you* go? What would *you* do?"

Susanoo clutched the comb to his chest.

"Follow his scent and I will follow you to him," said Athena. "We'll both get what we're searching for."

PART III

A PLACE CALLED 'NEW HEAVEN'

"A LOUD, LITTLE VOICE"

Sophomores from the nearby university had taken a field-trip to the Malkuth Museum of History in Atlanta City, the old capital. They walked past all the grotesque models of previous alien enemies with a mixture of shock and wonder.

There were pictures of Malkuthian soldiers through separate, evolving time periods on the way to victory. They wielded giant guns and piloted giant mechs and spaceships adorned with the Union flag. Hanging from the ceiling was a scaled-down model of a World Ender, the Union superweapon. And below it at the center of the main lobby was a model of the *Diamond Weapons System* with its elegant white-sloped armor, beam-cannons, and cybernetic parts encasing a living biological super soldier simply named "Diamond."

"Ahh, yes, the ultimate killing machine, the perfect soldier, the army-in-one," said the Curator orgasmically. "Diamond has the accumulated battle-data and knowledge acquired from every major battle, war, and military commander in modern history. In addition, he is armed to the teeth with a host of weapons, many of which are top secret in their functions, but many of you have undoubtedly seen on TV. He is to the battlefield what a chess engine would be to a chessboard. When he's in play, the battle is already decided. The only question is: how long can the enemy survive until they are completely and utterly defeated."

Some of the students yawned. Others swayed left and right, afraid to show disinterest for the sake of their grades. Still, others held hands, kissed, and whispered side conversations into each other's ears.

"But all of these tools of war—the particle beam cannons, the rail guns, the ray guns, the exo-suits, the armor, the giant mechs, the starships, even the World Enders and Diamond himself—they all pale in comparison to what is truly the most ingenious and powerful weapon ever created by the Antares Corporation..."

The students leaned in, suddenly captivated with curiosity.

"The *Watcher AI* (artificial intelligence) you have all seen and undoubtedly have experience with," said the Curator. He made holographic representations of the artificial intelligence appear on cue. Each holographic character took up the cartoonish form of an exotic creature that had previously been driven to extinction: a Brontosaurus, a Stegosaurus, a Pterodactyl, and a Mammoth. They each said 'hello' in a different Atlantan tone or dialect. "No doubt, you have taken them for granted, but they have made life easier for all of us. They can make decisions that living beings cannot make, especially over the vast distances the Union covers. They maintain homeostasis in the Union and make sure that its great sums of money, people, and resources are allocated efficiently for the good of all."

One clawed-hand went up out of the crowd. It was that of a female Ceratosaur.

"Yes, you have a question?" The Curator pointed her out. "What is it, dear?"

"If we elect over 100,000 senators Union-wide to make decisions on our behalf, why are these Watcher AIs still allowed to make decisions without their approval, or ours for that matter? That doesn't seem constitutional or right to me."

"Well, while I appreciate your question, you need to be real."

"I *am* being real. That's a legitimate question."

"Neela! No!" her history professor scolded in a hush tone. "Not here. Not now."

"I paid out-of-pocket to take this course. I come down from the sky districts every morning by train and work 12-hour shifts after class to afford to be here. I paid to learn what I came here to learn."

"You need to learn your place, you insubordinate, Cerato-privileged brat!" the Professor turned to her and shouted.

"Now, now, calm down, there's no need for racial slurs," said the Curator. He turned to Neela. "Look… little lady…"

"I can answer that question," one of the Watcher holograms in the form of a Triceratops interrupted. "It is an issue of logistics. It would be impossible for living, breathing Malkuthian beings to make major decisions so quickly and efficiently over such a vast distance, and affecting so many people on so many planets across the Union. That's the practical reason we have the Watcher AIs."

The other students nodded. The female Ceratosaur, Neela, was unconvinced.

"And without the Watcher AIs, how would the other major weapons systems operate?" the Watcher continued. "All the starfleets in the Union Navy and all the units in the Union Army use them to communicate and make decisions. Even Diamond's main strength is in the massive, comprehensive database granted to it in part by the Watchers. Are you going to strip us of that and leave us all vulnerable, little lady? I don't think so."

"One more question…"

"Quit it, Neela!" barked the Professor.

"ONE MORE question! This time for the Curator and the Curator only!" she shouted through her purple braces. "Or the university can hear about you calling me

'Cerato-privileged.'" The Professor, a Spinosaur, stood down. "If the Watcher AIs make so many of the major decisions in the Union, why do we need 100,000 senators? Why do each of them make so much money? Why are so many of them trillionaires? Why do they stay in office without term limits and possibly for multiple lifetimes because no one gets old or dies on Hod?"

"That's a misconception, and that's also more than one question," said the Curator. "Perhaps the AIs can—"

"If the Watcher AIs were designed to make sure that all resources were properly allocated, why are there so many homeless, jobless, and a giant shantytown down the street? Why am I working for just over minimum wage? Why is my step-dad deployed for an eighth tour of duty? Aren't we Ceratosaurs? Aren't we 'privileged?' Well, I call bullshit."

The Watcher holograms faded away without a word.

"Of course they run away when we ask the tough questions," said Neela.

"Hey, hey now..." the Curator held his hands out. "I'm not the source of your problems, little lady. I'm just a messenger."

"But you *know* the truth and you can tell it to all my classmates and every tourist in this museum," said Neela. "Who is Chancellor George Antares? Did we vote for him like we voted for the President? Did *you*? I don't remember getting a poll invite on the Network."

"No, we don't vote for him, of course not. He's our Chancellor. The old Senate elected him centuries ago. His family has had a seat in the Senate since before the Catastrophe. It's a ceremonial seat they earned by paying off the war-reparations of over a dozen nations and making the colonization of our universe possible."

"A seat they earned or a seat they paid for?"

The Curator's mouth hung open, he was without an answer, or at least one he was willing to speak.

"And for all that we should bow down to him and his AIs?" said Neela.

"That's another common misconception. They're not *his* AIs."

"Oh, really? Who developed them, then? And who benefits the most from their use?"

"Enough, Neela!" the Professor demanded, holding out his three foreclaws threateningly. "If you were of any other race and if your father weren't a colonel, you'd have lost your tongue or been hung years ago. This is ridiculous. You're always ridiculous!"

"Is that why you're afraid to hear the answers to these questions, Professor? Because you're afraid they'll cut out your tongue and hang you? I don't blame you. There are a dozen new hanging, rotting bodies on State Street right now. There are a dozen new bodies hanging out there every day. They're out there swaying in the wind, but we're ok with that. The cranes get more work than half the population, but we're ok with that. But what about your students, Professor? You'll probably get a few hundred before your career is over—hundreds of lives you could touch with the richness of history and truth. You want them to get the message that the best thing for them to do is just to lie there and take it? You want them to lie there and take it while the Union government screws them sideways generation after generation?"

"Gosh, shut up already, bitch, I wanna go," a female student complained.
"She's always wasting our time," said another student.

"Ehem..." the Curator cleared his throat. "Well, then, let's continue on with the exhibit. There's much more to see. This is only the beginning!"

Neela pushed up her gun-metal glasses which had slipped down her snout during the heated discussion. She straightened her hijab, a headscarf traditionally worn like a head of hair by most Malkuthian women, which had likewise become disheveled in the heat of the moment.

The students filed in and followed the Curator to another exhibit area, passing the imposing models of the World Ender and Diamond. On the walls, there were pictures of Tyrannosaurs pulling plows and carrying large stones to be used for building.

The Professor appeared frozen in place and in thought. As Neela passed him, he said under his breath, "I have a wife and kids, Neela. A new batch hatched last week. People are dying. Their families are disappearing. People are losing their jobs. The Watchers are always listening."

"I understand," said Neela.

"Don't waste your life needlessly, you hear me?"

"I won't, you can count on it."

Neela rang up and bagged used junk at the local thrift store. It was mostly clothing, but occasionally there were treasures: furniture, antiques, uncensored books out of print. The lines were long, and the prospect of processing them was daunting. Customers were often impatient and demanding.

She was getting light-headed into the eighth hour. She thought that maybe her glasses were dirty, but it was the same blur in her vision she'd dealt with for years.

Two Ceratosaur women with bedazzled, shiny hijabs were next in line. They had a lot of fancy-looking used clothes and some small pieces of exercise equipment. An announcement played over the intercom: "Attention shoppers, yesterday the Union army was victorious over the Xenos in the Netzach Region. Diamond is said to have slain 30,000 Xenos single-handedly. Our losses were minimal. To celebrate another great victory, we're offering a manager's special…"

"They're all just killers. The war is stupid, you know?" said the taller Ceratosaur woman to the other.

This statement rubbed Neela the wrong way. "Who's 'they'?" she said.

"Our soldiers. They're all just wasting their time over there killing stuff that ain't never even bothered us before."

"They're not 'just killers,' and just because the enemy hasn't bothered us doesn't mean they never will. They keep threatening our ships in the region. Sometimes the best defense is to go on offense first."

"Oh, I'm sorry, little miss, when I want my cashier's opinion, I'll ask for it. All clear?"

Neela shoved the purchases with fury into the biodegradable paper bags, tearing the fragile handles of some of them in the process.

"Gosh, what attitude. Do I need to talk to your manager? I feel disrespected. I don't feel comfortable with you handling my things."

"Well, you can't cry race—"

"Maaaa-na-geeeer!" the taller Ceratosaur woman called, waving her claws in the air.

Neela's supervisor, a Tarbosaur, came forward. "What seems to be the problem, mam? Can I help you?"

"Yes, Tarbosaur, this cashier of yours is disrespectful and rude. I've never been so insulted in my life. The way she talks to me is so out of line!"

"Well, I hear you," said the Supervisor. "We've gotten complaints about her before."

"I wasn't disrespectful!" Neela shot back, throwing the paper bag in the cart, causing some of the contents to spill out. "*They* were disrespectful! They disrespected our troops! They said they're just killers! They're *not* just killers! They're doing their jobs! We owe so much to them!"

The Supervisor put his clawed hands over his face and shook his head. "Ladies," he said. "You'll need to forgive Neela here, the military is a pretty touchy subject for her. Her father is a colonel. Her brother served in the army. You may have heard of him: Aohdfionn. He passed away fighting the Davrons."

"Well, that doesn't give her the right—"

"Your brother was Aohdfionn?" the shorter Ceratosaur woman sprouted. "The Captain? The war hero?" She then burst out laughing. "What, were you, like, adopted or something? You're nothing like him! You don't even look related!" The other Ceratosaur woman joined the laughter. "You made me miss what the manager's special was in all this stupidity."

"It's 20% off all red-tagged items, mam," said the Supervisor.

"You hear that, rude girl?" said the shorter Ceratosaur woman, "I get most of this for 20% off, and I got treated to some free entertainment too."

A tear ran down Neela's right-cheek, then another from her left. The Supervisor guided her away, telling her to take a ten-minute break. He completed the transaction by scanning the customer's wrist, accessing her nanomachines.

Neela sat alone on the dirty stairs behind the thrift store, right beside the mountains of garbage bags. She tried to force herself to eat, but she couldn't. "I miss you…" she said, wrapping her tail around her thigh. The sorrow swallowed her whole. She put her head in the crease of her folded arms and wept.

This is what her life was like for the next two years, two years that changed the course of history.

"THE DRAGONS INVADE NEW HEAVEN"

A series of new spacial tears popped up in the Deep Core, defying explanation and surprising the Malkuthians. It was reported to the Union government that the supermassive Cosmic Wall in the Deep Core was struck by blasts from an unidentified source. Quickly, like leukocytes in an immune system, billions of repair droids released to fix damage to the Cosmic Wall and billions of AI-controlled drones released from the Cosmic Wall, responding to the foreign threat. Appearing like swarms of warring hornets in the blackness of space, Dragons and Union drone starfighters clashed for the first time in an awe-inspiring cosmic light show.

"The belligerents are unidentifiable," reported a Watcher AI to the Union high council. "They number at least 2.3 trillion."

"2.3 trillion?!" the President exclaimed.

"Correct. My scanners indicate the belligerents measure approximately 20-feet. They have each demonstrated the ability to produce a destructive yield of a 300-pound incendiary, per attack that is."

"Do they pose a serious threat to the Cosmic Walls, or to us for that matter?" asked the Chief of Staff of the Union Army.

"There is no direct threat to Hod or nearby worlds. The threat to the Cosmic Wall in the Deep Core, however, is *present* and *high*."

"Damn..."

"Can the drones defend the Wall?" asked the Chief of Staff of the Union Navy.

"This cannot be accurately determined, but I have diverted all available forces in the local region to defend the Wall. Our forces will still be outnumbered."

"Outnumbered!?" the President was perplexed. "How can we be outnumbered in one of the best defended areas of the galaxy? I thought we'd run through every possible scenario a thousand times! How can this happen?"

The holographic figure of Chancellor George Antares appeared at the head of the council table. The other leaders took notice. Some gulped nervously. "Chancellor Antares..." they gasped. The Chiefs of Staff saluted. The President sat upright.

"We have 12 World Enders in the Deep Core," said the Chancellor, his voice sounding like a motor.

"Master Antares," said a hologram of the Watcher AI in the form of a beautiful female officer. "I have considered this option and am in the process of making a cost & risk assessment... Affirmative. Blasts at maximum power from six World Enders at the points I have already determined would create a damage radius that would encompass the enemy force with minimal residual damage to the Cosmic Walls. This would result in the loss of less than half the local fleet and would cost 53.34 quadrillion BN (banknotes) to execute while averting the potential damage of 45.44 septillion BN. These losses would primarily be due to the damage to the Cosmic Wall in the vicinity. I have already initiated the sequence."

"Initiated the sequence?!" the Chief of the Navy exclaimed in protest. "This is *my* Navy, Watcher! *I* give that order!"

"Of course," said Chancellor Antares. "But this is an emergency, and my AIs will act accordingly to defend our interests."

The face of the Watcher avatar became frozen in a baffled expression for a full second.

"What is it, Watcher?" said the President.

"Mr. President, *something else* came through a tear in the Deep Core. Its size exceeds 36,000 square miles."

"36,000 miles?!" exclaimed the Chief of the Navy. "What is it? A planet?"

"No," the AI answered. "It is biological."

"It's living..." the President exhaled. "How can something so big be living?"

"If it *is* living, it'll be easier to neutralize for our purposes than something that isn't," said Chancellor Antares. "Living things respond to pain. Living things die. Watcher, resume the World Ender attacks. Minimize damage to the Cosmic Wall."

Six of the World Enders in the vicinity released their payloads on the cosmic behemoth who'd come through the portal. The AI stopped responding to the Union high council for a considerable time.

"Watcher, report," said the Chief of the Navy. "Watcher, report! Answer!"

"...It's still moving," said the Watcher.

"What's still moving?"

"The massive enemy creature."

"The hell!?" the Chief of the Army exhaled. "Each of those blasts could erase a thousand Collective Cubes! They must have missed!"

"No, all super lasers hit the target." The Watcher read out the casualties: "...We have lost contact with World Ender A and World Ender 116C... We have lost contact with World Ender 216R and World Ender 33Y... We have lost contact with flagship Invincible... We have lost contact with..."

"My God!" the President exclaimed.

"Should I commence the *Resolver Contingency Protocol*, Master Antares?" said the Watcher to the Chancellor.

"Commence," said Antares.

"Commence?" said the President. "Commence what? What the hell is going on, Chancellor?"

"Perhaps it will calm the dear Chiefs-of-Staff to explain it to you as I look over the proceedings," said Antares. The Chancellor's hologram disappeared.

"What's he talking about? You knew about this?" the President turned to the military leaders.

"...The *Resolver* superweapon..." the Chief of the Navy began. "It was a project that Chancellor Antares and I collaborated on. The idea was that if a Cosmic Wall were ever captured by an enemy force or if a sector were to be usurped against the Union, it could..."

"Erase them. Eliminate them as a problem," the Chief of the Army finished.

"The three of you knew? The military? Antares? Who funded this?" said the President in disbelief. "Who signed off on this? Why wasn't I informed?!"

"Frankly, you didn't need to be," said the voice of Antares. Soldiers of the Public Security Force, the private arm of the Union military, marched into the meeting room. Antares himself appeared through a portal they'd opened. The military Chiefs of Staff uncomfortably stepped back behind Antares. "What you need to do now, Mr. President," said Antares, "is to make a public announcement regarding the imminent threat that the Union is now faced with. Appeal to the need for public support and more able bodies. Make yourself of use, and we'll take care of everything else." With that, Antares turned to the AI's new projection of the events as they unfolded in the Deep Core.

The Resolver, the newest of the Union mega weapons, emerged from hyperspace. It took aim at the massive Dragon lord who'd come through the tear and had led this pivotal invasion of New Heaven. The whole of the Deep Core was illuminated in a flash that could be seen throughout the Union for days, a blast whose brightness was eclipsed only by suns and the galactic bulges.

The Dragon lord's body remained writhing as it fell back into the tear it had come from. Most of the Wyverns and the Union starfighters in the vicinity had been killed or destroyed.

"Crisis averted," said the Watcher. "Congratulations on your victory, Master Antares."

The Chancellor sneered.

"A DRAGON LORD HAS DIED"

General Malevant brutalized Aphrodite as he often did, using the telekinetic powers he'd learned from Athena. Becoming more precise, he began reassembling Aphrodite's face with his mind, breaking the bones beneath the skin whilst causing the skin itself to burst with ichor, but not so badly that she could not regenerate from it. Her blood formed more fairy-like beings whom Malevant combusted with a thought. "Lord Baladan is dead, child," said Malevant with a smile.

"Please! Stop!" cried Aphrodite in agony, knowing that it was hopeless. She had run out of energy to cast the pain-numbing spell that Loki had taught as part of his deal. Her healing had started to wane as well.

"Lord Baladan is dead. Dragon lords can die. Think. Just think."

"Please!"

"The power I possess. The power to ruin what is divine and beautiful. The power to unseat gods and possess their very worlds. Do you understand, child? If a warlord can die—what we'd thought to be unthinkable—what more can happen? I could take his place. I could become a lord."

Athena returned from a battle to report to Malevant. She came upon this sight in disgust but withheld the urge to use her powers, knowing the consequences of doing so were too great. Malevant had already been immensely powerful, but now this was augmented by the telekinesis he'd learned. If Athena was to save her sister and preserve herself, she would need to do so tactfully. She used what she had overheard to do just that. "Leave her! I have something of value!" she said. "I can tell you how to defeat these Malkuthian creatures and capture that universe. You can present my idea to the warlords and take all the credit for it. I will require Aphrodite."

Malevant cut Aphrodite down from her restraints. Athena transformed her into an axolotl-like creature, allowing her to regenerate as she crawled weakly to the relative safety of her sister's side. She returned to her normal form, whimpering on her knees, and burying her teary face into the side of Athena's garment. "Like, wh-what took you so long?" she cried.

"Speak, Athena!" Malevant demanded, towering over them. "The deal was: your sister for your plan. Will you take it back?"

"NO!" Aphrodite shrieked, hugging Athena's thigh for dear life and scooting behind her rear. "Sis, please! Please don't leave me alone with him again!"

"I need her ability to reach the heart of someone," said Athena to Malevant, speaking up to him like a mouse to a lion. "Someone more powerful than all of the Olympian gods and Titans combined. Someone, dare I say, more powerful than Lord Zeon himself. A limitless energy source that could be made available to you."

"More powerful than Lord Zeon?…" Malevant considered and sneered.

"So I'm told. With the Black Sword of my uncle, Hades, you could drain this being of all his power. But this being's mind is a blur. It makes it nearly impossible to reach him in my usual way. So, I want to try to reach his heart."

Aphrodite gasped, looking up at her sister. "Heya…"

"Who is he? What is he?" Malevant growled.

Athena answered, "He is a Malkuthian residing somewhere in New Heaven. I've learned that he is the *Grand Conduit of the Omniverse*, which means he conducts energy just as Queen Ain does. His name, I'm told, is Azure… But we're running out of time to find him. There are others who are after him."

"Who?"

"There is one named Loki. He conspires with your rival, General Deem."

Smoke and fire came from Malevant's eyes and nose.

"I see I have piqued your interest," said Athena. "Let me use my sister's power. It's useless to you anyway. We can find this Azure before General Deem can. We can bring him to you."

Malevant levitated Athena in the air with his telekinesis and threw her from one wall to the other. She spat up ichor. "If you speak falsely, Athena…"

"I speak the truth!"

Malevant tore Hades out of his cell and into the room with a thought. The ailing Olympian god of the underworld groaned. Malevant conducted his right-claws, and with that both of Hades's eyes were ripped out. He screamed miserably, clutching his face. Aphrodite shut her eyes tightly and looked away. "You three are the last of your kind. Will you be responsible for that number being reduced?" Athena shook her head. "What good pets you are," said the Dragon. "Now about this Azure… this *power greater than Zeon*… go and fetch him for me."

"SATAN & TERRA SCHEME"

There was none on Earth as extravagantly and elegantly dressed as Terra, the Queen of the Demons. She wore a shining royal garment of scarlet and purple adorned with many gems and pearls. On her head she wore a crown tiara made of gold studded with diamonds. In her hand, she held a goblet partly filled with a blood-red liquid. The goblet seemed mostly empty (for the time being).

She sat at the feet of a giant statue of a Roman goddess the people called *Tellus Mater*, the Earth Mother, in Carinae. Affixed to the side of the statue was the stone figure of a young boy clinging to the Earth Mother's side. Terra ran her long-nailed hands over her stomach. Smoke and incense filled the temple as more and more worshippers filtered in. The goblet in Terra's hand filled a little more with liquid. It filled even more when a pregnant cow was sliced open as a sacrifice to Tellus Mater.

An imposing winged figure stepped through the temple doors, invisible to the worshippers as Terra was.

"Ah, if it's not Samael. Come to pay your dear old wife a visit? It sure has been awhile. Care to catch up, darling?"

"He has been born in Bethlehem, Terra," said Satan, "the one we've feared."

"Yes, Yeshua is what he has been called. The son of a carpenter and a delicate, pious young woman. I have my ears too, darling."

The two Arch-Demons took a stroll together across the continent, moving at the speed of light. They arrived at a temple to the Greek fertility goddess, Demeter.

Satan explained, "We wanted to be sure. Be'elzebul traced the lineage of the boy's father to King David, and his mother…"

"Oh, I've taken notice of her," said Terra. She ran her hand across the face of Demeter's statue. "*Mother Mary*… 'Mother Mary' has a nice ring to it, don't you think, darling? I've seen her. I've heard her. So humble, so committed, so loyal, so dedicated, so… married to her faith in Yahweh. The one *true* God? Ha. What if I flipped that faith on its head?"

As Demeter's worshippers made offerings to the statue, Terra's cup became more full. "This goddess died in the Second Titanomachy, did she not?" she said. "I heard she lost her head."

"Yes," Satan answered.

"Not to these people. She is as alive as ever. I make her so."

Satan and Terra sauntered over to the island of Philae in Egypt to the Temple of Isis. Terra spread her arms out in glee at the sight of the great statue of Isis nursing Horus in her lap. Her cup continued to fill. "I am curious why you don't make angry demands of me anymore. Beat me anymore. Burn me anymore. What are you afraid of, Samael darling?"

Satan hurled a stream of flames in Terra's direction. She held up her goblet and blocked the flames, but some of the liquid spilled. "I will not stand for your insolence, witch!" he howled.

"*Queen* of the witches, darling. I no longer have to bow to you. I no longer have to kneel to you. You need me, Samael. I know you need me, darling."

Satan snarled. "The Dragons have blundered their invasion and lost their initiative in New Heaven. The Malkuthian have stalemated them and killed one of their warlords."

"They killed a Dragon warlord?"

"It should have been a short and decisive campaign to secure the back gate of Heaven. Now, it has become a full-on war, and we have little time to win a war. Christ is a child now. Herod failed to kill him. Caesar can't be moved. The priests cannot touch him. I am running out of options and time. If he completes his ministry on Earth, the deal Yahweh made with me and with humankind will be fulfilled. The power over Death will fall from our hands. Ain's doom and ours will be sealed."

They came to the Temple of Artemis in Ephesus, Turkey, one of the greatest wonders of the ancient world. Terra remembered when a fire had once destroyed the entire temple. She had a premonition, triggered by Satan, that it would happen again. "And what can we do?" asked Terra, now sounding gravely concerned. She took a sip of her cup. The red liquid dripped from the edge of her lip, and she quickly caught it in her hand.

"If you pledge to me your unwavering support, Terra, I promise to build for you something that all the temples of Eurasia could never hope to match. And I promise to do all I can to protect it from suffering the same fate as this temple here." They came to Babylon, which was a shell of its former glory. A little figurine of the goddess Ishtar lay on its side, partially buried in sand. Terra tried to unbury it, but its feet broke off, and it failed to stand anymore. Frustrated, she melted it down in her palm. They returned to the Temple of Tellus Mater. "We will build it here," Satan continued. "Right upon these seven hills. I promise to guard and protect it until the end, and we will rule as equals until that time comes. That is my promise to you."

Terra took another sip but gagged on it. "I have heard such promises," she coughed, "from you before… darling..."

"This time, we both have little choice. You know, Terra, that God Yahweh will never forgive you."

"You don't know that."

"Why, of course I do! Look at all that you've done. All of these idols and temples you've built for yourself. All the lives you've ended and the souls you've damned. You can't be forgiven. You don't deserve forgiveness. You've broken every sacred law and rule in the book. You're as damned and hopeless as the rest of us. Your fate will be the same as mine. If you don't help me to take Heaven, you'll find yourself in the *Lake of Fire* with me. So, what choice have you?"

"If you want to be like God, then at least keep your word as he does," Terra demanded. "Darling, swear to me you speak the truth!"

"I swear to you. I will be like the tyrant of truth. My word is my bond."

"Then, darling… What do you need me to do this time?"

"If Prince Messiah fulfills his mission, the life-streams to Ain will be severed. He will have the power over life and death. That was the deal we made. In effect, Ain will be rendered useless to our continued existence and our cause. However, I have a contingency plan. There is a being like Ain in the universe of New Heaven. I doubt he will remember me fondly, if he remembers anything at all."

"A being like the Cosmic Dragon? Darling, how is that even possible?"

"A careful accident…"

"Who is he?"

"He is a Malkuthian in New Heaven. A living weapon of cosmic proportions capable of harnessing any and all forms of energy. He is the only way I may be able to circumvent the agreement the tyrant and I had. Michael had a name for him. He called him 'Azure.'"

"DRAGONS .VS. MALKUTHIANS"

Thousands of spacial tears littered the skies over densely-populated Malkuthian worlds. The heavens themselves appeared to be opening up to the terror and befuddlement of civilians. Wyverns streaked from tears like apocalyptic meteorites, their huge wings trumpeting the coming of a war to end all wars. They clashed with Union starfighters en route to bombarding military bases and cities. The Union starfighters used their highly advanced missiles and particle laser cannons to kill hundreds of Wyverns.

Still, despite their advanced weaponry and despite the speeds afforded them by their hyperdrives, the expensive starships were far too scarce in numbers to contend with the millions of Wyverns that had invaded each world. They often flew through floods of Wyverns only to be picked apart like fat worms caught in the clutches of many ants.

With the skies dominated by the Wyverns, the Dragon flying-cavalry entered through the spacial tears to rain more death & destruction from above. Sirens whined as force fields were raised to encompass the major city districts and military bases, leaving the outlying districts for dead. As the Wyverns set fire to the outlying districts, the flying-cavalry tormented the Malkuthians who'd attempted to flee with their fire-breaths and long-lances. Dragon fire was intended to burn & kill slowly, allowing life-energy to be released slowly from the victim for Ain's use.

Among the first Union worlds to be invaded was Pankaja, a wet world that had once been heavily forested until it was colonized, primarily by millions of Carnotaur and Daspletosaur refugees during the course of several wars.

The Carnotaurs were two-horned Malkuthians, typically with red or orange skin. They were generally shorter and stockier than, say, the Tyrannosaurs, Spinosaurs, and Allosaurs.

The planet was also a home world to many displaced Daspletosaurs, serving as a large-scale reservation for the tribalistic Daspletosaurs whom the Ceratosaur-controlled government wanted little to do with. The Daspletosaurs generally lived away from the cities and had built their villages around the rivers and forests, which they often had to fight to preserve. They constantly feuded with both the military and the Carnotaurs over territory and access to resources.

Later generations of Daspletosaurs had taken to the cities themselves and lived rather modern lives, generally working modern low-wage jobs. Ceratosaurs like the Antares & the upper-class stereotyped both the Carnotaurs & Daspletosaurs as low-lives inclined to criminal activities, detriments to the economy.

Pankaja had dozens of cities, hundreds of towns, and several military bases. The cities on Pankaja, a planet the Union strongly distrusted for various reasons, were governed by puppet leaders sent by the Union that had the entire might of the local military to enforce the Union's authority.

The military held true power on Pankaja after it violently crushed a revolution there over a decade before, with the military presence seeming to grow by the day. But on that particular day when *the Eyes* of the Dragons appeared in the sky, the Union military's dominance on the planet ended.

Clouds & heavy rain blanketed the lines of sight between the sky Dragons and the Malkuthians on Pankaja. As the Dragons rained down their meteoric blasts and fire, the Union military responded with thousands of missiles and anti-aircraft artillery. A thousand, thousand, thousand thunderstorms could not replicate the sound of their struggle. Bursts rocked the ground and sky alike.

The Union's famed sky carriers, intended to guarantee compliance by Pankaja's unruly population, were brought to bear. The sky carriers were literal flying fortresses each the size of a city district with ridiculously large arsenals including laser-cannons, drones, and missiles. They were also armed with more durable, longer-lasting deflector shields, something the starfighters lacked, and satellite-like technology for surveillance. They were fully integrated with the Watcher AI, which improved their fighting efficiency by synchronizing it with the rest of the military.

The sky carriers, and in particular their durable deflector shields, proved to be instrumental in drawing Dragon fire away from the cities & bases. However, there were only six sky carriers defending Pankaja, positioned along the equator, and they were prioritized to defend economically & militarily significant targets—both of which were already being shielded by force fields. It was partly from following their movements of the sky carriers that the leaders amongst the Wyverns learned what was important to the Malkuthians and what was not. They also took note of which areas were most populated and reported this information back to the generals and warlords.

The Dragons attacked the weakest and most vulnerable elements of Pankajan civilization first. They torched and impaled millions of Pankajans who died miserable deaths, locked out of the safety of the force fields.

After a few days, even the Union force fields and deflector shields were overcome by the endless bombardment. One by one, the sky carriers were transformed into flying infernos that crashed down onto the prized targets below, killing tens of thousands more. One by one, the city force fields were broken down.

Then, at that ever-so-ideal time, the Dragons opened land-portals—the *Black Gates*—through which the dreaded Dragon heavy-infantry entered the world, converging on the most populated cities. The sight of the Dragon heavy-infantry was the most feared in all the multiverse: millions and millions of Dragons 40 to 50 feet in length, marching in masses wielding 80-foot adamantine spears that could extend far beyond that length and retract nigh-instantaneously by some mystical means. These spears were laced with razor-sharp barbs on their sides that could also extend outward beyond their origin point.

The spectacular armor of the Dragon legionaries was also made of adamantine, a mystical metal originally formed by the God of gods to arm his angels. It had fallen into the possession of other beings as Satan's angels moved about the multiverse, meddling in their affairs to meet their own ends.

It was even used to form the Scythe of Gaia and the Sword of Olympus used by Cronus and Zeus. When the Dragons came upon it, finding it to be the finest metal available, they immediately used the forging and smithing skills of the captured Cyclops and Elves to reproduce it. It was mixed with other metal alloys to make it malleable enough to form desired shapes. It was even made to glisten with an elegant rose-gold plating, displaying the glory, splendor, and excess of the god-queen, Ain. The sheer sight of the giant legionaries, clothed and armed so impressively, struck terror into the hearts of their enemies.

However, the Malkuthians of the Union were an impressive sight as well. They weighed an average of 2-7 tons and were 20-60 feet in length from nose to tail. They possessed some of the best combat technology in all the cosmos. They were hardened by many millennia of war.

The local military on Pankaja numbered around 8.5 million soldiers and were supported by close to a million AI-controlled droids. They formed perimeters across the now-vulnerable cities, intermingled with buildings, their tanks, and their giant mechs.

Malkuthian soldiers wore exo-suits that allowed them to carry much heavier weapons and gear than they would physically be able to otherwise. This allowed them to carry bullet-and-blast-resistant plated armor which would otherwise be a hindrance to their combat performance due to their weight. This armor and uniform was a spectacular green and gold. It would mitigate the effects of small-arms fire like those used by the local freedom fighters.

They carried a number of weapons which most other mortal beings across the Multiverse would consider too heavy and unwieldy, but the large Malkuthians, enhanced by their exo-suits and cybernetics, could do so with relative ease. They could even fire these weapons from the shoulder without fear of being knocked over by the recoil.

The most numerous of these weapons was the MG-216 rifle or "*Hexal Infernal Rifle,*" an assault rifle with six horizontal barrels that fired millions of rounds per minute. It was fed by a huge horizontal magazine linked to a back-mounted battery that generated electric signals, which acted as the firing mechanism. In addition, the horizontal positioning of the six barrels was intended to greatly increase the chances of hitting the target while spraying. For this reason, it was conceptualized as being "like a shotgun but with the range of a rifle." There was rarely ever a concern about conserving ammunition through this type of weapons system. Fresh ammo was reloaded automatically by a tube-linked mechanical system acting between the exo-suit and the weapon itself. The Hexal Infernal Rifle was wielded by about half of the infantry and considered relatively archaic.

The Union also carried the MG-166 or "*36-barrel*," a 36-barrel machine-gun that could fire close to a billion rounds per minute via a similar fusion-battery-dependent ignition system. These electric signals were nigh-instantaneous, allowing these guns to have unprecedented rates of fire whilst launching ridiculously high-caliber projectiles at ludicrous velocities capable of puncturing even the hard metal alloys of tanks and mechs. About one-fourth of the infantry wielded the 36-Barrel.

The premier weapon issued to the Union infantry was the beam rifle nicknamed the "*Pathwinner*." It was so-named because the laser it emitted could pierce through almost anything in its path, hitting enemies behind walls, trees, rocks, armored personnel vehicles, tanks, mechs, and even force fields, thereby *winning* a pathway for the military.

Beam-Gunners wore specialized goggles, which supposedly allowed them to see the lasers and their trajectory before firing. However, the use of beam rifles still often resulted in friendly fire or unintended civilian deaths, sometimes many miles away. They also required the user to carry heavy fusion batteries on their backs to fuel the weapon, alleviated by the exo-suits.

The question that remained unanswered was what effect these devastating weapons would have on the approaching Dragon legionaries.

Miles behind the Union lines were hundreds of rail-cannons, the main and oldest artillery still in use by the Union army. These rail-cannons used electro-magnetic conductors in the form of opposing rails to accelerate and launch truck-sized projectiles at incredible velocities. The ordinances flew into the Dragon columns with enough force to kill a good dozen and dampen the momentum of those nearby. When ordinances from the rail-cannons struck a Dragon column, it was much like a freight train crashing into a mountain, and it sounded like it too.

The Union also had *Large Beam Cannons* (LBCs) similar to the ones on starships, which acted in much the same way as the Pathwinner rifles, only amplified to an artillery scale. A beam from a Large Beam Cannon could cut through a whole building or down a quake-proof tower in short order. This was widely known because the Union demonstrated these weapons on public broadcasts.

Union worlds like Pankaja were also surrounded by old weaponized satellites carrying rods made of heavy metals, which they could drop down onto unfortunate targets on the planet's surface. When dropped, these rods could acquire a significant amount of kinetic energy comparable to a nuclear weapon upon impact but lacking the radiation, which could be harmful to non-belligerents like the Union soldiers themselves.

The Union had learned from the past that nuclear and anti-matter weapons were a double-edged sword that could render an area uninhabitable and thus unobtainable, so the implementation of these killer satellites along with the Sky Carriers was seen as a more surgical alternative for discouraging planetary revolt.

However, until this point in the conflict, the Union had not been able to pinpoint where the rods could be dropped since most of the Dragons up to this point were scattered and in flight. Now, seeing the mass of Dragons exiting the land portals, the "kill" order was given, and hundreds of these satellites released their payloads on different masses of Dragon legionaries. The results were devastating, entire Dragon cohorts were destroyed.

However, as impressive as these weapons were, the Dragons were much like a force of nature—like the relentless flowing waters of a tidal-wave sweeping across the land—breaking but never stopping, never faltering, showing no pain, no emotion, not so much as flinching as the bullets, artillery, and rods struck. When a Dragon died, its life-energy was recycled back to Ain, who birthed more Dragons at will. They came through the portals by the millions and millions, more numerous than all the stars in the sky, and more numerous than all the sand on Pankaja.

As the Union beam cannons, rail cannons, and killer satellites bombarded the approaching Dragons from miles away, the Dragons answered. Each Dragon cohort had its own collection of magic specialists, Dragon mages, who not only protected the cohort from the immense gravity of the portals but could conjure powerful defensive spells learned from magical beings from across the Multiverse. Their Mystic Shield spell formed a reddish barrier over the heads of the Dragons, powerful enough to withstand a blast from a rail-cannon and deflect the lasers from the beam-cannons before the spells weakened and had to be recast. They also had the option of casting their Enter Ether spells on their cohorts to allow the legionaries to enter ethereal or intangible forms, the forms in which they'd conquered many spirit realms. However, they had to be cast with a *Float* spell to keep the legionaries from falling through the ground. In that form, they were impervious to Union weapons but could not inflict living, non-spiritual things. So, for most campaigns against mortals, the Enter Ether was never cast. The Mystic Shield spell was of far greater efficiency as it was sustainable, used relatively little energy, and could be used without having to cast an additional spell.

"THE BATTLE OF VOLANTIS CITY"

Rain continued to fall & lightning struck, intermingled with the sound of the cannons and blasts from the Wyverns and flying-cavalry as the Dragon legionaries marched through puddles and mud on the outskirts of the cities, unaffected by the troublesome terrain.

The desperate battle for the Pankajan capital, Volantis City, had begun.

The great towers that formed the skyline of Volantis City burned like torches above the clouds, spilling their fire and debris down into the streets below.

Union tanks and mechs swept into diagonal lines in front of their soldiers, strengthening the Union lines around the central business district and governor's mansion. Dozens of these tanks and mechs were caught as larger portions of the great towers collapsed on top of them.

The tanks and mechs that survived used their own beam cannons as well as guns and missiles to strike at the Dragons. Among the most feared and revered mechs in the Union arsenal was the *Grand Fortress Mech*—a giant mech that stood a towering 196 feet and weighed almost 2,000 tons. It could switch from a wheeled to a six-legged mode to transverse most terrains with minimal damage to the grounds. It came armed with a *"Mega Particle Cannon"* linked to four fusion reactors, similar but larger than the ones that powered the Pathwinner rifles. The Mega Particle Cannon could destroy any other mech, tank, or starship that the Union was aware of. It also carried missiles and a battalion's worth of firepower.

The Union had kept many of their rail cannons far toward the ocean-side on the streets surrounding Volantis City Zoo and the Mall of Pankaja, a high ground northeast of the main buildings. Wyverns and flying-cavalry struck at the Union artillery, tanks, and mechs from above, causing as much damage to those awe-inspiring weapons as those weapons did to the Dragons.

Meanwhile, the deafened and frenzied animals nearby suffered further as the zoo itself caught fire as a result of Dragon air attacks. Some of the alien creatures ran loose through damaged fence-lines and into the city. Many were not so fortunate, and two species that had been nearing extinction were lost the third day of the invasion.

Helpless Pankajan civilians fled. They took shelter inside of the Mall of Pankaja, the university arena, libraries, and schools. In an all-too-familiar scene on Pankaja, desperate Carnotaurs and Daspletosaurs pressed against the very military forces that were said to be there to protect them, attempting to force their way into crowded shelters. The thousands of low-flying Dragon cavalry swooped down on the frantic crowds and tormented them with their claws, lances, and fire-breaths. Mothers, fathers, sons, daughters, sisters, brothers, husbands, wives, partners, and friends desperately tried to pry their loved ones out of the death-grips of the Dragon claws or pull them out of impalement by their lances.

In harrowing acts of heroism, Malkuthians—large and small, young and old—wrestled the Dragon flying-cavalry out of the air and fought them with their teeth, claws, and whatever weapons they could find, attacking eyes, wings, and whatever apparent vulnerabilities they could find. The Panakajan rain did surprisingly little to put out the Dragon firestorms which had started. Freeze-extinguishers were concentrated on Dragon fires, but so much had to be used to extinguish these particular fires that the burned victims were very often frozen to death. Meanwhile, the Union military fired into the crowds as the soldiers desperately tried to seal the doors of overcrowded shelters.

Escape pods were made available to the nose-horned Ceratosaurs, either to take them down to the underwater cities, which had largely been left unscathed, or up into space. But for most civilians, this was not an option. Daspletosaur women, tears in their eyes, sang calming melodies to their crying babes as the sounds of screams, crashes, and explosions thundered nearby. The Carnotaurs took up makeshift arms like knives, shovels, bats, and machetes. Those who'd illegally procured guns bunkered down in their homes with their families, waiting for the dreaded moment when they'd need to use them. Many were burned alive or killed by collapse before being able to.

The flying Dragons made a conscious choice not to attack the shelters, saving them for their ground legions in preparation for their planned torture and energy harvest.

Unnerved by the attacks from above, the Union army at the front opened fire on the flying Dragons as they swept down to attack, downing thousands but taking heavy losses themselves. Wyverns were able to evade bullets with their speed but were shredded when they crossed the paths of the Pathwinners and beam cannons. The flying-cavalry, dressed in chainmail armor, still fared little better because of their lower speeds compared to the Wyverns & the chinks in their armor compared to the heavy-infantry. However, the flying-cavalry were stronger than the Wyverns and were armed with powerful claws and lances which were a death-sentence when they were able to close the distance. They could also emit ice-blasts capable of freezing anything of comparable size, streams of electricity, or fireballs from their mouths to reap havoc on artillery emplacements and troop formations.

And so, their magical attacks crossed fire with the lasers and hyper-velocity projectiles of the Malkuthians. The death toll climbed rapidly on both sides during these exchanges.

When the Dragon heavy-infantry came within three miles, the Union lines unleashed the full fury of their weapons on them — Hexal Infernal Rifles, 36-Barrels, Pathwinners, rail cannons, beam cannons, Mega Particle Cannons, all as the killer satellites released their kinetic rods. The Mystic Shield spell of the Dragon sorcerers withstood these for a short time before having to be recast, the energy that was spent was recycled by Ain.

The small-arms fire that bypassed the spell harmlessly bounced off of the adamantine armor that shielded the Dragons from head to tail. The Hexal Infernal Rifles, 36-Barrels, and the Pathwinner beam rifles all struggled to puncture the armor of the Dragon infantry. It was only after long, sustained, and concentrated fire that these Dragons could be taken down, blood shooting out from them as stray bullets and beams struck them between chinks in their armor.

Several Union battalions lost order and retreated further back into the cities where they hid in and behind buildings in the inner sectors, hoping and praying in vain that the horror would pass. And, of course, it didn't.

The Malkuthians who stayed were now faced with a new horror. Closing as quickly as a tidal wave over land, the Dragon heavy-infantry unleashed their own long-ranged attacks, the first of which was a blast of dark magic that came from their mouth. Upon impacting a solid surface, these dark magical blasts created spacial voids which pulled the skin, flesh, and bones off of whoever was near. What remained of the victim's body was pulled apart and drunken up along with the surrounding puddles of water, debris, and blood. Thousands of Malkuthian soldiers were killed in only the first volleys of these magical attacks. Even several Grand Fortress Mechs were damaged and some left inoperable by the effects of these *Gravirah Blasts*.

The kinetic rods from killer satellites were redirected by Watcher AI and made to crash into areas between the separate Mystic Shields cast by Dragon sorcerers, undermining the ground, and causing larger disruptions in the Dragon formations, bypassing the protective areas of the spell. The other Union cannons were also redirected in the same way, inflicting greater damage on the Dragon infantry.

The Dragon infantry ceased their Gravirah Blasts and extended their long-spears to over a mile, puncturing anything they came in contact with: bodies, armor, mechs, tanks, and buildings. The barbs from them also extended, stabbing and slashing everything and everyone around them. Much of what remained of the front lines fell victim to these mystical spears. Those who survived were forced lower to the ground or to fall back.

The Dragons marched forward, pushing these impaled beings and objects forward as they did before the spears retracted in length. The mechs, in particular the Grand Fortress Mechs, used their sheer mass to try to push the rows of spears away from the Union lines as their armaments fired on full-blast, but their number was too little and the number of the enemy too great.

The Watcher AIs alerted the Union high council and Senate regarding all that was happening. Pankaja was but one of many Union worlds attacked by the Dragons. However, what made Pankaja so important was that it was a planet within the Hod region and near the Hodian Crux, relatively close to the capital of the Malkuthians. Should Pankaja fall, it was feared it could be used as a launchpad into the Crux or the capital, Hod, itself.

"Watcher, move the 412th and 44th starfleets to support Pankaja!" said the Chief of the Navy.

"Who's to say this isn't their game?" said the Chief of the Army. "They want to draw the fleets out of the Deep Core. These barbarians have brains."

"There's so damn many of them..." said the President, who'd just announced the initial attacks to the public. "How is that even possible?"

"Keep the fleets where they are," Chancellor Antares reprimanded the order. "Move the local World Ender into position around the planet but do not fire."

For weeks following the fall of the Pankajan capital, no additional military aid was given to the suffering Dragon-occupied planet and the local World Ender was not used. Meanwhile, helpless civilians—men, women, and their babes—were wrenched from their shelters and hiding places by the Dragon legionaries. Some were skinned or flayed alive. Their fingers and tails were routinely broken. Their eyes & tongues were routinely plucked or wrenched out. The Dragons studied how the bodies of these magnificent and intelligent reptilian creatures worked, and how they could be broken. Ultimately, most were dragged to execution stakes to be impaled, being in shame and agony for hours or even days before dying. Hundreds of thousands were killed in this way every day, their writhing bodies arranged on forests of stakes as they screamed and cried for death.

Chancellor Antares had to have the President restrained by the Public Security Force to keep him calm after he'd gone into a ranting frenzy upon witnessing footage of these atrocities. "It's unfortunate. It's tragic. I know. I know! You see the passion this excites in you, Mr. President?" said Antares. "Don't you want to fight? Don't you want to kill them all? Imagine what it'll bring out of the people."

"Dammit, Mr. Chancellor, use the World Ender! For the love of God!" even the Chief of the Navy, a co-conspirator, begged.

"I promise you, I will in due time. Broadcast this, Watcher," said Antares. "Let them know why it is that we must do what must be done."

"THE EMERGENCY"

The tearful and visibly shaken Malkuthian President took to the podium just a few Hodian hours after the horrific live broadcasts went public.

"My fellow Malkuthians..." he said, appearing on holographic projections throughout the Union. "Right now, at this very moment, at this very instant—as I speak and as you watch and listen at home—millions of our fellow Malkuthians are suffering at the hands of these devil invaders.

"As you have seen, our armies and our starfleets have fought bravely. Individual civilians have fought bravely and endured innumerable horrors against this numerous, dangerous, and cruel enemy. Yet they have proven, by their efforts and actions, that these devil invaders *can* be killed. That they *can* be defeated. These heartless, remorseless, barbaric animals—like the Davrons, the Collective, and countless enemies before them—can and will be overcome by the strength and resolve of the Malkuthian people."

The President gulped and looked down at his desk, away from the teleprompter as if reluctant. "But it pains me to say that, like with any great challenge in our history, the process of overcoming evil will require some degree of sacrifice and effort on behalf of the good. Military and civilians alike are obligated to help in the war effort. Now, with the support of the majority of the Senate, our dear Chancellor, and the Joint Chiefs of Staff, I... I have been forced to declare a state of emergency."

And with those words, the universe of the Malkuthians was changed.

"Among other things," the Chairman continued, "this state of emergency has necessitated the use of weapons that were sheathed in hopes that they would never have to be used again. This is their time. This is that special exception for which they have been reserved. We must show these devil creatures the full extent of our might and power as we did in the Deep Core just a Hodian week ago. Then and there, our newest superweapon erased trillions of these winged devils out of existence. This included one of their leaders, a behemoth of indescribably size. We must show them that theirs will be a hopeless and losing effort against a superior people, a civilized people." He looked down as if lost.

"During this time, martial law will be set in place in all areas of the Union, effective immediately, including the worlds of Kether and newer territories. Effective immediately, a military draft of all able-bodied men will begin. All men between the ages of 15 and 55 will be registered to the draft. They will be chosen at random by the Watcher AIs. Individuals who fail to comply with a call to military service or who interfere with the process of conscription in any way will risk summary legal action. Their accounts will immediately be frozen, and they will be unable to buy or sell. They will be prohibited from receiving medical care and public assistance. This is done not out of malice or ill will toward our citizens but out of necessity. A state of total war has been reached. These are the circumstances in which we now live.

"Now, our Intelligence Bureau (IB) has recently provided substantial evidence that these devil creatures had inside knowledge on the astronomical locations of vital targets such as the Cosmic Wall in the Deep Core as well as strong-points to avoid such as Hod and other worlds of the Crux. We have good reason to believe that these devil creatures have agents living among us—within our government, in our churches, in our schools, and in our homes. We have enemies living among us. With that said, the Intelligence Bureau, in conjunction with the Public Security Force, the Union military, and police forces around the Union have been ordered to seek out these enemies and eliminate those who would otherwise threaten the safety and security of our people."

As he spoke, hundreds of Union worlds were attacked by the Dragons and their captive collaborators. This number of invaded worlds grew into the thousands within a Hodian year. Meanwhile, millions of specialized serpentine Dragons called

Leviathans, adapted from their roles in General Deem's war of the water worlds, lurked the galaxies. They hunted and destroyed cargo starships that carried food, supplies, and—in particular—the valuable energy gathered from the stars and Cosmic Walls. Over time, the disruption caused by the Leviathan attacks negatively impacted every galactic region. In addition to their roles in space, they also rained havoc on the fabulous underwater cities the Malkuthians had thought to be safe. Malkuthians learned that nowhere was safe.

Mysterious explosions destroyed government buildings and even part of the Senate House on Hod. There had been apparent sightings of Dragons in the skies over Hod, realistic holographic projections choreographed to accompany the aforementioned explosions.

Covert elements of the Public Security Force arrested and assassinated those whom Antares considered potential enemies and rivals including senators, military leaders, and other part-owners of the Antares Conglomerate. They even assassinated judges. Members of the President's own cabinet went "missing" along with their families and close associates. Most were never seen or heard from again.

Conscription notices were issued, with gleeful Watchers alerting men and boys in the middle of their daily routines that they had been selected to serve in the Union military. Though the selection was said to be random, the AIs secretly filtered out those who it determined were too valuable such as CEOs & their children, politicians & their children, and college & high school students above a certain grade-point. These were primarily the affluent, particularly the Ceratosaurs. The AIs particularly recruited men from poor or working-class families.

Doom and gloom dawned on those selected as they saw the horrors broadcast on the network and took a deep, hard look at their lives and their families. For many, the future had never seemed so hopeless. Everyone was a captive. Everyone was trapped. There were enemies from the outside and within. The penalties for attempting to avoid the draft or speaking against it became more severe as the war escalated and more Union worlds were lost to the Dragons. This eventually included thousands of public hangings by crane, which led to the slow and humiliating strangulation of victims, a penalty said by the puppet President to be necessary "for only the most outrageous traitors and agitators" and "those who'd turn their backs on their fellow Malkuthians in their time of need, at a time of war." And so, these public hangings were played side-by-side with the impalings and mass-executions by the Dragons.

World Enders were finally ordered to put planets like Pankaja out of their misery, killing billions of Dragons and Malkuthians alike in short order, only after they'd both been milked for life-energy by the Dragons and for propaganda by the Union government. More *Resolvers* were also built using nano-replicator technology but held in reserve around the Crux and Deep Core.

Day and night, Union propaganda broadcast the heavily edited successes of Diamond, the single most ubiquitous public figure of the modern age.

The legendary killing machine proved effective against the Dragons, at least on the few planets he was sent to fight on. His unparalleled arsenal ripped through Dragon formations, even those of the heavy-infantry. In addition, his energy attacks were seen to do something that even the artillery had struggled to do: bust through the defensive spells of the Dragon sorcerers. Diamond's stealth, mobility, and ability to predict future combat scenarios were also of great use.

He fought against multiple Dragon generals, their champion warriors, surviving each time. The Union media protected his image as an undefeated soldier, though that was only partly true. He could clearly match the Dragon generals, something the deities of other universes had not been able to do, but it was unclear whether he could kill one, and it was unclear if they could destroy him. These epic duels with these Dragon generals, normally in the middle of open-battle, usually ended in Diamond bypassing them mid-fight and moving on to attack weaker targets.

Meanwhile, in the grander scheme of things, the loss of much of the work-force to support the war effort, the extreme amount of losses and damage, and the general loss of valuable assets and commodities during the course of the war severely hampered the Union-wide economy. Those who were already poor and suffering became even poorer and suffered proportionately greater. The Union lacked skilled workers who could fill vacant jobs that soldiers who were drafted were forced to leave. Droids and other machines were produced quickly to fill these positions, which left trillions of the poor, many of whom had only their will and strength to contribute, unemployed at a time of great need for workers.

Questions were raised: *How could this happen to a civilization that thought it had everything calculated to the decimal? How could there be so much poverty in a time of prosperity? So much cruelty by a civilization that considered itself civilized?* The Watchers answered, in the most friendly of tones, that this was simply the result of an unexpected and large-scale war. They said that war had always necessitated sacrifice and hardships. They said that the Union government was doing everything in its power to ensure the safety and security of the people. If the one asking these questions was a male over the age of 15, they would be shown horrible images of the Dragon atrocities on planets like Pankaja and military efforts by the Union to combat them.

Uprisings began on multiple planets that were crushed by the Public Security Force and Union military. The puppet President was assassinated two years into the war, shot through the head on camera. Crux worlds saw it live, others saw it edited. He was replaced by another puppet leader, the former Vice-President, who promised to end the war with the Dragons sooner through the use of the World Enders & new Resolvers, repair the ailing economy, and minimize conscription by means of producing more droids. The truth is, these "great efforts" were already being made by his predecessor. Nothing really changed.

On a daily basis, hundreds of thousands of civilians from captured towns and cities were impaled on wooden and metallic stakes by the Dragons and their allies. Hedgerows of contorted, twitching, writhing bodies were projected and broadcast for all to see.

But few people in the Union had a tear to shed or a scream to emit for the people of other lands as their own neighborhoods suffered greatly from the ripple effects of the war.

These horrific and turbulent events made possible the crimes of the Antares-controlled Union government with thoughts of *getting by* superseding everything else.

Something strange had happened in society. There was apathy. *"What will be, will be"* became the most popular new phrase in the Union. Everyone began to accept that the best way to survive and to avoid both the persecution of the government and the war with the Dragons was to turn a blind eye and to go about life as if nothing had changed — to become *nothing, invisible.*

It was the spirit of the time. An entire generation was growing up in that dismal social climate. However, certain members of that generation grew frustrated and restless, giving life to the ideas that eventually came to change everything.

There.

There in that chaotic mess of a universe, in the cesspool of the Omniverse, a lone female Ceratosaur fresh off her shift at the thrift store stood atop a concrete platform on the nearly-forgotten old capital planet, Malkuth. She stood on the decrepit steps of the Old Senate House, which had been overrun by the vines and roots of three great trees, as Watcher AIs berated her in a kind tone. She spoke over them as well as she could.

"NEELA IN THE ANCIENT CAPITAL"

"Malkuthians!" Neela called out. "I'm not here to tell you that all hope is lost because we need hope! I'm not here to tell you that the Union isn't great because it is great! I'm not here to tell you that our government is all evil, for it has done some good. I'm not here to say that I hate the Union because I love it. I know how blessed I am to be a Malkuthian. I am a Malkuthian, yes, a Ceratosaur. I am a proud Malkuthian, yes, a Daspletosaur. But I am a Malkuthian with my eyes, ears, nostrils, and tongue in place, and I see, and I hear, and I smell, and I taste what has happened to our beautiful Union. I am a concerned Malkuthian. I am a proud but thoroughly pissed off and frustrated Malkuthian."

Neela pointed to the decrepit rubble of the Old Senate House. "This was where democracy was supposed to reign. But it died, apparently, centuries ago. Our founding fathers wrote that no one person would be able to decide the fate of the Union, yet who is Chancellor George Antares? Our founding fathers wrote that *we, the people,* would have freedom of expression—freedom to speak, freedom to write, freedom to share. Why, then, are there journalists and writers hanging on State Street? Why am I afraid? Yes, even me. Why is three-fourths of the news media owned by one conglomerate, which in turn is owned by just one man? Why is it *his* narrative we hear? Now, now to be fair… Chancellor Antares is surely the greatest Malkuthian who has ever lived. He is, by far, the greatest leader we've ever had, if power alone were the determiner of greatness. Arcturus the Great and Saint Sargas aren't worthy to kiss the hem of his robe. He is surely the cleverest and wisest of them all."

The Watchers, unable to detect sarcasm, became silent, looking even confused as she praised the Chancellor.

"But we, the people… We, the people… Our founding fathers wrote that we, the people, would have the right to defend ourselves. Well, what's with these sticks and stones and knives we're all armed with? What's with this medieval armor we must still wear every day?" She pulled up the pink silk blouse she was wearing to reveal chainmail, not an uncommon sight as almost all Malkuthian civilians wore some type of armor to protect mostly from stab and slash wounds. "They've drained more and more funds to our public servants and replaced them with their very own paramilitary force. They've replaced them with brainwashed PSF soldiers and droids—machines! They've taken even more jobs away and given them over to their interests. They've done all of this as joblessness and homelessness rise!"

A pair of police officers had been called in by the Watchers to respond to Neela's public performance, but when they heard her speak up for them and denounce the Public Security Force, they stayed put.

"And what about our boys being sent to fight and die throughout the Union? Why haven't they been relieved? Why are so many of them serving more tours of duty than I have claws on my hands? Why aren't more droids and the PSF serving in their place? I'll tell you why: Malkuthian life is not what's valued by our dear Chancellor, George Antares. Malkuthian power is."

Another Watcher AI hologram appeared, this time in the form of *Losty the Last Unicorn*, a character from her favorite TV show. "That's false, Neelie Pies!" it said.

"Don't fucking call me that!"

"I've checked the facts for you. How considerate of me! The venerable Chancellor Antares has contributed over 7.3 septillion BN (banknotes) in his lifetime toward resolving the issue of poverty in the Union."

"Is that *his* money or taxpayer money? And did the Senate release those funds to him or did he just take it because he can?"

"...In the lifetime of the venerable Chancellor Antares, the minimum wage has increased from—"

"The minimum wage increased but the 'poverty line' for public assistance also shifted and inflation also increased. So, everyone's in the same giant fucking hole with bigger fucking numbers. Now everything costs an arm and a leg. You know it and I know it."

"Neelie Pies, if you're ever lost and you need to be found, Losty's here, I'll be around..."

Neela swatted at the hologram and shook her head angrily, turning back to face the city and trying to remember what she was talking about before the Watcher interrupted. "He let the people of Pankaja, my home planet, suffer for days on end without relief. He knew it. It was broadcast wasn't it? Believe me, he knew it. He knew it and he sat there, and he waited! He waited! As millions of men, women, and children were tortured before our eyes by the Dragons. He waited! He waited because Pankaja is not Hod. Pankaja was a troubled planet and always had been to him. He waited. And his puppets, including the late President, hid it for him. They lied about it for him."

Another Watcher hologram appeared. Neela's heart skipped a beat and her large blue eyes grew wider behind her lenses. This time it was in the form of her dead brother, Aohdfionn. "Neela…" it said. "Why are you doing this? Why are you saying these cruel and untrue things?"

"I told you, fuckers!" Neela shouted at it. "I told you to never, ever impersonate him! Ever!"

"You wouldn't listen before," said the Watcher. "Neela, why are you doing this? You're hurting me. I died for this Union. Chancellor Antares was my Commander-in-Chief. He'll always be."

Neela shut her eyes tightly, holding back the tears. "NO!" she shouted. "You're not real. You're not him. You're fucking sick!"

"Go home, Neela," said the Watcher. "No one's listening to you anyway. No one cares."

"Aohdfionn would never say that!"

Rain clouds had begun to form overhead and there was thunder and lightning. Neela herself was beginning to get light-headed and dizzy. *Remember to breathe. Nice and slow.*

"Your head is hurting again, Neela. You're just going to make yourself ill. Go home and rest awhile."

"No!" Neela turned away from the hologram and continued her speech. "Don't let them do this to us! Don't let them desecrate the memories of our troops and all they fought for! My brother and father didn't fight for a man. They didn't fight to keep one person in power, to make one person rich, to buy up worlds so that one person could build his mansions on them. They fought for the Union—to preserve it and to make it better. They fought for ideals like freedom, equality, liberty, and justice. They fought so that we could all share in the power, riches, space, and prosperity they won for us with their blood and sweat and tears. That's what they fought for! That's what they sacrificed for! And we spit on them every time we say, 'this is ok!' We shit on them whenever we say, 'what will be, will be.' This is not the proud Malkuthian way! The Malkuthian way is forward! The Malkuthian way is upward! RISE UP!" She lifted her clenched right-claws in the air. None of the passing pedestrians raised their claws with hers. They looked down and passed her by, looking down as if ashamed.

Rain began to fall. The branches of the tree above offered only some protection from the elements. "Won't you stand with me? Won't you raise your claws and voices with me? Cowardice cannot win! Cowardice can never win! It is not the proud Malkuthian way!" No other claws rose with hers. She stood alone as darkness began to fall and the streetlights went on. The rain only got heavier. "Rise up!" she urged.

After a half hour of standing there, giving speeches in the rain, she hopped down from the concrete planter, swiping her digitized glove through the air like a hand over a dry-erase board, causing her holographic picket-sign messages to disappear. The rain had drenched and soaked her violet hijab and blouse until they turned a deep, dark purple. Thunder rocked the sky. Startling. Unnerving. Neela dipped her head in disappointment. *What were you expecting? At least you tried.* The pink-skinned girl bent her head mournfully.

She untied the purple windbreaker from around her waist and slipped her arms into the sleeves, messing up her first attempt and almost dropping the windbreaker in the puddles below. Giving an irritated growl, she bent down to snag the windbreaker again. That's when she heard crying from close by. She followed the sobs to the back of the concrete planter. There, she found what she perceived to be a slightly older boy, hiding under a gray tarp with only his blue tail and part of his snout exposed as the harsh rain pelted him. He shrunk away as if terrified.

"Hey there," she said, peering down at him, "what's wrong?"

The boy looked up at her from under the tarp with scared brown eyes and shrunk away. He closed his eyes tightly, clutching his snout and chest with separate hands.

"What is it? You can tell me."

"Y-y-you… I-I h-h-heard you…"

"You heard me speaking just now?"

"Y-y-yes... and-and b-before... M-m-mmmany times... Fr-ffffrom many... pl-pl-places... I-I d-d-d-on't know... h-h-how..." He clenched his snout and closed his eyes, letting out a deep "*oooooh...*"

"I think I know how you feel. Do you feel nauseous? Like your head is drowning and you can't get enough air? I get like that from time to time with my condition. It's like a persistent headache that won't go away. Remember to breathe. Nice and deep. There you go."

"It-it h-hurts... Eh-everything's... Everything's a bl-bl-blur... fr-fffffragments... sc-sca-ttered.... *shhh*arp... c-cutting... tw-twisting... in my head..."

"Well..." the girl looked to the side, considering what to do. She turned back and brushed her hijab from her face. "Look... Look at me, look at my eyes." She craned her head from one side to the other like an optometrist so that he could see both. The boy strained to reopen his eyes and peered with his right. There was terror, pain, and weakness there. His body shook and shivered as the rain continued to fall. "It's okay, it's okay, it's okay," said the girl, still peering at him. She had such large and striking blue eyes under folds of calm and gentle lids.

"Uh-are you... Uh-are you r-r-rrrreally... here? Am-am I?"

"What kind of silly question is that? Of course we're here. You feel the rain, don't you? Ahh..." She outstretched her arms as if trying to hug the sky. "It feels great. Makes you feel alive. Reminds me of back home. In Pankaja we used to say that these were 'God's tears' and say he was crying. It almost makes you feel like he gives a shit. Pankaja is gone now. They can erase people and places. They can't erase memories."

The boy grimaced and looked away again, clenching his head.

"Uh, uh," the girl whistled through her braces and waved her hand in front of his face. Then, she pointed to herself. "Focus here. On me."

"Y-y-you… I-I'm sc-sc-sccccared for you."

"Don't be. Let me be scared for myself. There are things bigger than fear. Things like standing up for the things that are most important to you. Yes, things even more important than life and avoiding pain. Things like basic Malkuthian rights. Things like truth. Things like memories."

"M-m-memories… I-I-I have no-no m-mmmemories… I-I-I d-don't kn-know how I g-g-got here. Who-who I am… I-I j-j-just h-heard you. It-it s-sounded like I kn-kn-knew you..."

"Maybe you do. It's a small universe after all. Did you hit your head?" She inspected him.

The boy shook his head. "I-I don't… r-r-remember…"

"Do you remember your name?"

"M-my n-name?"

"Come on, you have to remember that! What did your mama name ya?" Neela managed a smile. "What are you called by?" she asked in her native Pankajan.

"Azure..." he said with surprising clarity. "Th-th-they c-called me... Ah-Aj... Azure..."

He was as blue as the second sun with a yellow pattern, like lightning bolts, running down his face to his feet and tail. He wore somewhat chubby cheeks on a dirtied, pitch-stained face. Judging by the size and shape of his snout, and his large size in general, Neela was sure he was a Tyrannosaur. Tyrannosaurs were distrusted. Even Neela worried that he might have been sent to infiltrate her life, but then again that's what the Watchers were for. How redundant could the Union be? Furthermore, her compassion and fascination with the boy outweighed her anxiety.

Here was this boy, apparently around her age, who was suffering out in the open during a downpour. Here was this boy who was apparently homeless, penniless, powerless, and friendless in a society that bragged of its prosperity and power.

Here was this boy who seemed so damaged and lost, hardly able to speak his own name or speak a sentence with any certainty, in a day & age where both medical technology and education were at their pinnacle. Here was this boy who—just as Neela had felt her words had fallen on deaf ears—had heard her and appreciated what she'd said.

Here was this boy who, being neither very handsome or ugly, whose disheveled cloak and clothes smelt of an unclean odor, had caught her eye because he *was what he was*: a victim who personified the decadence of Malkuthian society—a poor child lost without direction or hope, who'd committed no apparent crime, who'd done no wrong yet was guilty of existing *then* and *there.*

It pulled at her heart. It was to a point where she felt more than compelled, rather she felt *forced* to do something for him, else her conscience might torment her at a later hour.

She held out her hand. He looked up again with his watery brown eyes and fearful stare. "C'mon, stand up," she said, "let me help you."

Hesitantly, his trembling right-hand reached back and took hers. He struggled and strained, leaning up against the concrete planter. He grasped one of the overgrown roots that protruded out with his other hand. Groaning, he came to his feet for a brief moment. Then, he fell forward, leaning up against the planter to support himself like an infant against a shelf. Neela got under his arm and tried to support the other half of his weight, pushing and pushing, pedaling with her feet, all to keep him upright. He collapsed back onto the planter.

Neela put her hands on her hips, panting as if she'd run a mile. "Gosh, do you weigh like a gajillion tons? I thought the long-necks were extinct!"

"H-heh..." Azure managed a chuckle.

"Let me see if the Network can locate your home or next of kin." Neela tried to scan Azure with her wrist-mounted device linked to the Network. "That's strange, nothing's happening... Do you not have any nanomachines or a microchip?"

"I-I d-don't... kn-nnnnow..."

Neela shook her device, hoping that would make it work but it didn't. "Where are those damn Watchers when you need them? Summon: Watchers. Preference: Losty."

A Watcher hologram appeared in the form of Losty the Last Unicorn. "Neelie, are you ready for me to send you the travel plans for the way home?"

"Not quite. Do you know this boy? Can you find his home or his family?"

The Watcher looked around. "What boy?"

"What do you mean '*what boy*?' *This* one! He's right here next to me! He's blue as the second sun!"

"And I thought that *I* was the lost one, heehee," said the Watcher. "I believe you may be suffering from hallucinations, Neelie. Would you like me to schedule you an appointment for a check-up?"

"No, go away."

"Ok, Neelie. Buh-bye!"

Neela looked with awe and astonishment at Azure. "They don't detect you.

You're invisible to them. How? How is that possible?"

"I-I d-don't kn-nnnnow."

Neela gently poked him in the side a few times. It tickled a bit. "H-h-hey. Wh-what are you d-d-doing?"

"I'm just making sure. Hmm..."

"Wh-what?"

"Nothing. Never mind." Neela peered into his brown eyes again, inspecting them, squinting through the lenses. His pupils dilated back and forth, shifting from left to right. "Can you walk?"

140

Azure's whole body rattled like an old man's as he tried to move, resting one arm on Neela's shoulder. He stumbled again and fell forward. Neela caught him but it knocked the wind out of her. Her heart raced as the brunt of his chest fell into hers. "You're so... heavy!"

"I-I'm s-s-sorry!" Azure collapsed over the concrete planter again.

"Don't be sorry, bud. I've got nothing better to do."

"Y-yeah? M-m-me t-too… h-heh-heh…"

A giggle left Neela's lungs too. She swiftly covered her mouth as if to catch a cough or to stop a secret from getting out. "Well, what do you know…" she said. "I can still laugh. Sorry. I'm not laughing at you trying to walk. It's just that… I've been coming here on and off for weeks. No ground gained, maybe some ground lost. Rinse and repeat. An endless cycle. And nobody cares."

"S-s-sounds l-l-l-l-like… mmmm-mmmme…" Azure, trembling, pushed himself up and craned his body, pushing against the planter with all the strength his tail could muster so that he could better face her. "All-all I c-can r-r-remember is l-lying h-h-hhhhhere, cr-crawling h-here. P-p-p-pppppppeople walked around m-m-mmme. Ig-ignored m-m-mmme. N-no one would t-t-t-t-touch me. N-no one would t-t-t-talk to me. He-hear me."

"Well, *I* heard you. And *you* heard me." She took out what looked like a portable medicine box from her windbreaker and took what looked like a pellet from one of the compartments. "I think this is the one. I always get them mixed up." When she tossed the pellet, it became a hoverboard that levitated in mid-air. "Ah, fuck yeah! I got it right this time! Maybe you can lean on this, bud. It'll move with you. You can use it like a crutch." She instructed the hoverboard until it came to chest-height.

"A cr-cr-crutch?"

"Or like a walker. Try it. I use it sometimes when I'm tired or dizzy."

Azure grunted, his large blue legs shaking under the immense weight of his body. He threw himself over the board but began to slip. Neela grabbed his elbows and pulled him with all her might from the other side over the board, trying to center him on it like a drowning sailor onto a capsizing life-raft. "Come on, bud! You can support *some* weight, can't you?"

"I c-c-c-can't!"

"Bullshit! You can!"

Azure focused all his strength through his core and to his legs, pushing himself just far enough onto the board to balance it. At the end of it, they both shut their eyes and panted like they'd completed a marathon. "I-I'm s-s-s-ssssorry…" said Azure, the rain pitter-pattering against his tarp.

"Stop… saying… that…" Neela fought to catch her breath.

He told her that he would slow her down and hold her back. He told her that he didn't deserve her kindness and that he was only inconveniencing her.

"What makes you say that? Oh, so you think a Cerato gal is too good to help a Tyranno boy, is that right? Sorry, sorry-sap, but I'm not. We both hatched from eggs shot out of someone's ass. What's it to you if I've got a horn and you don't? You've got a scrotum and I don't. Wanna trade?"

"M-m-mmmy life… d-d-doesn't m-m-matter. I-I'm a w-w-waste of your t-t-t-t-time."

"Bud, are you done bemoaning yourself? I'd like to get going if you don't mind."

"Wh-wh-where?"

Neela pointed up to one of the sky districts, essentially a giant floating sub-city levitated in the sky. "You ever been up there?"

Azure shook his head.

"Usually, I take the sky train at Capitol Station a block away, but I've always wanted to take the long way and see other parts of the city from up close. I see it from above, but it's not the same. It's just not safe for a 'gal like me to go alone." Neela folded her hands over each other, looked down, and swayed side to side, waiting for an answer.

"I'll-I'll g-g-g-go."

Neela smiled. "I'll get you some food and get you all cleaned up in the sky district, just until you're on your feet again. That ok with you?"

"And-and wh-wh-what? Wh-what about you… wh-what can I p-p-possibly do?"

"Listen. Just listen to all my crazy shit. That would be enough for me."

"ATLANTA CITY"

With each step, Azure's legs could support more weight. Soon, he was able to keep his balance with just one elbow on the board. "One step at a time," said Neela, on the opposite end so as to balance it, "one foot in front of the other."

Not a thousand paces from that old cornerstone of Malkuthian civilization, in the shadow of the many mountainous buildings and floating platforms, they reached a river black as oil, choked with debris and fecal matter. The smell was like that of the dead. The incessant buzzing of insects irritated the senses. Streaks of diarrheal waste smeared the steep walls that led down from the sidewalks into the black river, in which boxes, newspapers, and plastic bags floated. Even more abhorrent was the sight of children and adolescents, skinny as poles, carrying long-sticks which they used to snatch things of value from the water.

This area was the gateway into one of Atlanta City's many shantytowns, the neighborhoods of people like Azure—people so poor they could not afford proper homes, fresh clothes, or shoes that made life livable.

Neela covered her mouth and nose with her hijab to dampen the smell and kept on walking, faster. Azure walked with her, trying to keep up, but tripped over something on his left. There lay a child so small from lack of nourishment and so filthy that neither of them knew she was lying there. "S-s-sorry!" Azure said to the child who scurried off.

"Hey, wait!" Neela called out, digging in her pocket for a banknote, but the child was gone, having hurried either into the landfill or the shantytown. Neela tried to follow, heading toward the landfill, which was crowded with people rummaging & sifting through the garbage for recyclables. The child was lost somewhere in the crowd.

The people collected everything from metal wires to plastic drinking straws, many with their bare hands, walking on their bare feet. And whenever a garbage truck delivery came, they flocked to it, causing a commotion like that of animals to a waterhole.

Azure crawled over and grasped a metal wire that was partially coiled around a wooden post. A Carnotaur child, indistinguishable from the last due to the filth that covered him—or *her*—grabbed at it too. Another child pushed the first and would have bitten if Neela didn't intervene, placing her right-claws between them. "Stop it, you all!" she shouted. "What's it worth? Ten banknotes? Here's ten banknotes. That's enough for a couple eggs. Here! Here! Take it. You don't need to kill each other over that." She handed one bill to each child.

The children were hesitant to accept. "Don't take that, you dumbasses!" said a Daspletosaur child nearby. "Look at her nose-horn! She's a Cerato. She'll report us to the Guardsmen and say that we robbed her."

"Wha—No! No! I'm trying to help you!" said Neela. "It's ok, little girl... I'm part-Dapletosaur too! From Pankaja!"

The little girl whistled to some adults in the distance.

"D-d-don't... N-N-Neela..." said Azure, looking out into the near-distance where the parents of the children stood watch with equally distrustful eyes and knives at their sides. Azure gently tugged on her and urged her along. As they made their way out of the camp, Neela observed the desperate people going about their ways as the first sun began to set, forming an orange hew over them.

There was a commotion and some yelling and cheering nearby. A circle had formed around some knife fighters. The body of a bloody, lifeless Allosaur was dragged by the feet and thrown into a wheelbarrow. Neela gasped and looked away. Some of the onlookers gambled with their money, clothes, and jewelry. One offered his fluffy brown moon pup.

Neela kept her head down for the most part as she continued on. Keeping her eyes down had the advantage of allowing her to avoid the feces and dead animals lying on the sidewalk. Upon encountering one of these dead animals, a frail old Allosaur woman with a pipe-cleaner-sized neck scurried out and snatched the critter, bringing it to her home, presumably to cook and eat. The rain had become a drizzle now, but it still threatened the fragile shanty houses made of cheap wood, cardboard, and metal roofing, as well as the small fires the people desperately tried to feed by whatever means necessary. A few homes bent and flexed in the wind—whole livelihoods as unpredictable as a weather vane and no more stable than a house of cards against the elements of God.

As Azure tried to keep the pace toward the city going, Neela turned back and looked at the homes, the landfill, and the people.

"It shouldn't be like this," said Neela. "This is all so fucking wrong."

"Wh-wh-what can we d-d-do?"

"Well… It starts in the home and with our education system. They have no homes, no proper education. Then, we've gotta create proper jobs for them. Someday someone's going to have to fix this and make it right. Someday soon."

"S-s-someday s-s-soon?"

"I used to get my brother's binoculars and look at things from the edge of the sky district. Seeing things from up there, though, I would have never known how bad it all was."

Not a hundred paces from the end of the shantytown began one of Atlanta City's sprawling market districts. Aggressive store owners and salespeople stepped out onto the wet, busy streets, holding samples of their products in their hands, and with the most pitiful looks and tones begged people to try their soaps, their ointments, their hand-sewn clothing, blankets, and other goods. "Please, try some!" they said.

"Please, would you try?"

"Just try this one!"

"Two for one," said another.

"Twenty banknotes! Only twenty banknotes!" said another.

Even the compassionate Neela kept her head down and tried to block them out, but she occasionally had to wave one away, saying, "I'm sorry, no thank you" or "not today, I'm sorry."

And the same with the beggars and panhandlers, of which there were many—a half-dozen on each block—each with their own strategies, signs, and sob-stories; some more charismatic and convincing than the merchants. Some smiled, bowed, and tipped their heads as if doing so would show they had some class and promise. Some told stories about being stranded in the city, kicked out by family for their sexual orientation, evicted, having served in the army, having been laid off from their jobs, having many children. Others were much more straight-forward in their pitiful pleas for money and simply came forward with their hands clutched as if in prayer and their cheeks pucked up to their eyes in a desperate expression. Neela tried to dig for some money to give, but Azure tugged her gently. He gestured his head toward some men in black coats in the distance. These were muggers, dealers, and collectors and other agents of the criminal underworld all watching intently. There was no police presence there. Who needed the police when Antares supplied the Watchers and the Public Security Force? They would make everything right.

The sex trade flourished in Atlanta City too. Between the blocks lined with beggars, there were one or two prostitutes on seemingly every corner. Certain stores were even wholly dedicated to sex and featured live models in the windows, displayed like mannequins but with even less respect. Some of them appeared as young as 9. The idea of statutory protections for children was of a bygone age by this point. They forced smiles and wagged their tails behind the glass. When a potential buyer entered the place of business to make their selection, the girls stood upright and motionless as he or she inspected them. Neela shook her head in disgust.

"Eh, girlie," said a well-dressed Mapusaur from the exit of an alleyway. Neela tried to ignore him, partly thinking he was calling to some other girl. Azure instinctively took control of the hoverboard and walked between Neela and the

Mapusaur as if to form an informal barrier between them. "Eh, Cerato gal!" said the Mapusaur again, more clearly referring to Neela. He wolf-whistled to her and whistled again as if calling a dog. Azure, his back still turned to the Mapusaur, shook his head and reached out to Neela with one arm as if to guide her forward. Neela slipped him, turned, and shouted, "Fuck you! Fuck you, you lecherous motherfucker! Shit's not for sale!"

"Shit, girl, just wanted to talk about why it is you got that Tyranno hanging all over you," said the Mapusaur. "You desperate? Girl, Ceratos are in high demand. And we can give you on-the-job-training."

"Why the fuck do you care who I'm hanging with?! Who the fuck are *you* hanging with? Your cheap slut whore bitches?!"

"N-N-Neela!" Azure tried to get her away from there.

"Fuck that!" said one of the prostitutes, a pink-dressed Tarbosaur. "You bring your highfalutin Cerato ass down here from your high place and you say that shit! You got the nerve to judge me?! I fuckin' busted my ass in diners my whole damn life. I got three damn kids. What the fuck else am I gonna do? You don't see the scars and bruises under these clothes! You don't see shit! You don't know shit!"

Azure took Neela's hand and hurried her along, hobbling in his way, out onto the crowded sidewalks of the lower central business district. Craning out over the main street was a theater-sized screen that constantly broadcast the Union News. The scene on the screen was so horrendous that Neela took one glimpse at it and looked down and away in disgust. Azure looked up at the screen, peeking up with the corner of his eye from his cloak to see the forests of writhing, contorted Malkuthian bodies impaled on stakes by Dragons.

The feed cut to a battle, taking the perspective from the top of a Grand Fortress Mech that was firing its many guns and main cannon at a charging formation of Dragons, though the results of these attacks were obscured by fire and smoke. The posh narration said, "the beams decimate the beasts, halting their advance." The camera switched to an overhead view above the familiar white metallic figure of Diamond, the hero of heroes, the perfect warrior, the killing machine. Azure, Neela, and many of the people in the streets took notice of him as he graced the screen. There were cheers.

The scene cut into slow-motion to show Diamond moving at presumably unprecedented speeds, charging into a Dragon formation, parrying away a long-lance and plunging his plasma saber between a Dragon's left shoulder-plate and helmet. From that close-position, the Dragons near him were forced to attack him with their adamantine swords or bare claws. The miniature cannons and guns on Diamond's body revealed themselves from under his immaculate white-plated armor and fired between the Dragon ranks. He coiled his tail forward and fired a super-heated ray of energy out from it that fanned out over 40 meters, frying the Dragons it touched inside their armor.

The scene switched to a much taller and more upright Dragon, an "Alpha Dragon" as the newscaster called him, who stood meters from Diamond in the middle of a smoking, burning battlefield littered with both Dragon and Malkuthian bodies. The Alpha-Dragon appeared to be talking, but no sound was heard.

"I-I-I've s-seen h-him b-b-before!" said Azure.

"What are you going on about?" said Neela. "Everyone knows Diamond."

"M-M-MMMalevant! Th-th-that Dr-Dr-Drrrragon!" Azure back away, looking panicked.

"What do you mean you've seen him? Like, in person?"

Azure shook his head. "I-I-I d-don't know... In my dr-dreams. In my tr-tr-travels... s-somewhere..."

Up on the screen, Diamond faced Malevant. Two of the greatest warriors of their respective armies clashed. Malevant telekinetically flooded the area with downed mechanical parts from Union weapons. Diamond moved faster than the eye can see, avoiding the attacks. Malevant swooped in with incredible speed of his own and slashed with his Terror Sword, the accursed scimitar which had shattered the war sword of Ares. Diamond blocked it with his plasma saber before firing a flurry of his energy attacks.

Malevant unleashed a series of energy attacks of his own that countered Diamond's, but Diamond used the distraction of the resulting explosions to maneuver behind the Dragon.

Malevant stabbed under his arm, having apparently sensed the attack, looking to catch Diamond off guard. However, Diamond avoided it.

Diamond released many spheres of energy that encircled Malevant. The Dragon general discharged Zeus's lightning in every direction, causing the energy attacks to explode prematurely, obliterating the surrounding area.

Malevant emerged from the resulting crater. He took the trident of Poseidon in one hand and plunged it into the ground. A gaping fissure formed, dividing the two armies and swallowing those who were unfortunate enough to fall to the depths of the planet. The shaking could be felt across the continent. The seas rose up and began to swallow the land, cities, towns, and all their people.

By the time the cameras switched back, Diamond was in the sky. He had gathered enormous amounts of white energy in his two main cannons, mouth, and tail, concentrating them downward toward Malevant, who hovered just above the water. This was in preparation for Diamond's famed Diamond Salvo Beam (DSB), an attack seen rather frequently on broadcasts and which garnered much attention. The DSB obliterated entire battlefields, killing whole battalions of Dragons even in their nigh-invulnerable ethereal forms.

Malevant called down Zeus's lightning from the sky to strike at Diamond from behind. Diamond erected a large circular force field, his famed *Arc Shield*, which repelled the ferocious lightning bolts that had defeated Typhon. With the lightning still striking, Malevant summoned up his Oblivion Beam, an attack that had ended planets.

There was a flash, and the screen went blank.

"THE CHANCELLOR'S POWER"

Chancellor George Antares had many mansions, but his favorite was Mansion #153 on Hod. It hovered over a picturesque artificial beach with waters that glimmered like lapis lazuli, brimming with white seafoam as the gentle waves crashed one after the next against the white sands of the coast.

There, in a master bedroom the size of a house, George Antares was pleasured by as many as a dozen concubines. Many of them had been kidnapped or purchased at various stages of their lives, procured from around the Union, and trained for this very purpose under threat of destitution or death. Antares had his favorites and was crueler to the rest.

Once Antares had tired of this, he retreated to his house-sized bathing room, which had a sauna larger than most swimming pools and mirrors framed with gold. The whole bathing room acted as a hyperbaric chamber to optimize the Chancellor's health, and the waters were specially infused to heal wounds, alleviate pain, and keep the bather from aging. Thus, Antares's appearance was that of a Ceratosaur in their 40s even though he'd been in politics and headed the Antares Conglomerate for hundreds of years. He inspected himself in the mirror and took a cocktail of drugs to control anxiety, his weight, his age, and to blunt any need to sleep.

"Those *are* a *god*-send, aren't they?" said a voice behind him.

Antares turned, facing his hand outward as if aiming a pistol. Parts of his cybernetic war-suit flew to his aid, responding to his mental command. The orange-colored suit encompassed his entire body. "You!" he said, generating a pulse of energy in his palm.

"Gee wiz, Emperor Saltine!" said the shadowy figure. "Don't you know that caffeine will kill you?""

"Be flattered. I'm always prepared for you, Loki."

Loki teleported behind Antares. Antares saw the trickster's smirking expression in the reflection of his visor. With a thought, he teleported to Loki's right. He looked to grab Loki, but his hand passed through a mirage of the trickster who made a mocking expression, sticking his tongue out and fiddling with his ears. Loki jabbed with his staff, not hard enough to kill someone but enough to irritate them. Antares's suit shattered like a fragile ceramic plate, revealing robotic fragments. Loki smiled, finding this amusing, and realizing the truth: he'd struck a decoy. He turned and found Antares, suitless, standing beside the sauna and casually drinking some wine. "Checkmate," said Antares.

"Aww, maaaaan—Look out!" said Loki, looking behind Antares.

Antares raised his hand up and his wrist device created an encircling force field. A party ball exploded behind him, releasing confetti and pink paint that promptly decorated his force field. Loki laughed, holding his gut as if it hurt to laugh. "You can think a gajillion moves ahead, but only I can see the mutha-fuckin' future, Anty George!" When he noticed Antares was not moved, he looked around, finding many lasers aimed directly at him.

"If you have time to talk, my Watchers and I have time to think," said Antares. He pressed his wrist-device, dropping the force field and allowing the confetti to fall to the sides. "They're fully integrated now, Loki. Would you care to see a special demonstration I planned just for you?"

Loki rubbed his hands together and licked his lips. "Ooh goodie! For meeeeeee?"

With a thought, Antares made holographic projections appear all around the room, all depicting different things. A few seemed fixated on planets. Others were fixated on people doing various things. Some were working. Some were shopping. Some were eating. Some were in the middle of sex or using the bathroom. "You've always said you could see the future, Loki. Well, now, so can I. You see, the things you're seeing in these projections will happen. We've discovered particles that can move faster than the eyes can see. Faster than tachyons. My AIs fill the gaps, make the logical calculations, and *voila*... What you see *is* but *is not* yet is to come...

"This allows us to see further, to project things that won't be perceived or happen, technically, for some time. Let me show you the present..." With another thought, Antares caused the holograms to change. They showed the people who were eating in the previous projections preparing their meals and showed the people who were having sex in the previous projections engaged in foreplay. A storm had moved from one hemisphere of a planet's projection counter-clockwise to the other. "And here. Here is what I wanted to show you."

Antares waved his hand in front of him. His mind signaled the AIs. Nothing happened for a long time, yet Antares remained awkwardly still. Loki laughed, feeling he'd just witnessed the grandmaster of the Malkuthians make a fool of himself. Then, two of the planets were blown apart, struck by World Enders. The people who were engaged in sex grabbed at their hearts, screaming in pain, and then died together. The people who were eating suffered the same fate. "Those planets were uninhabited, and those people were of little value anyway. Them and their mutt children. In addition, no one could put the blame on me. I didn't pull the trigger, I simply... *thought* and what I thought *happened* thereafter. It's not a crime to think, is it?"

Loki laughed to himself. "These things that control the things that make this happen... you call them... 'Watchers?'"

"Yes."

"Hmm... that's funny, I feel like I've heard that term before... See I know someone who knows someone who knows some people who knows some people called 'the Watchers,'" Loki tapped his chin with his unclipped index finger. He looked to the ceiling, pondering. "Oh, yes, yes, yes, yes, it must be my friend Sammy, the Great Satan, who first told me. They did something rather remarkable... Something about Giants and fornication or fornication with Giants... I don't know, some shit like that. Oh, nothing, it must just be some generic term that gets thrown around to sound ominous. Go on, go on."

Antares observed the scenes in the holograms, picking and choosing where he'd like to intervene. With another thought, a man playing a wind instrument felt a pain in his hands and dropped it. A man about to fire a gun felt seizing pain on a whole side of his body. "Every registered infant is given a healthy dose of nanomachines at birth," Antares explained. "They can manipulate everything from their hormones to their bowel movements. We can even use them for invasive research without the need for subject compliance. It has allowed us to learn how best the population can be controlled and optimized."

"Heeheeheeheee!" Loki covered his eyes and shook his head as he laughed. "Impressive! Impressive, Anty George! You know what else is impressive? The fact that I can insult you in seven of your dialects now. A mighty fine investment in time, I do say. I could only insult your ancestors with five or six."

"Loki, you of all people should appreciate this. This is power over life itself. The power to end worlds. I killed the Dragon lord they sent. I destroyed the entire invasion fleet in an instant."

"Well, erm, correction, dearie: you killed *a*—singular—Dragon lord. There are a few Dragon lords—plural. And to have destroyed something *instantaneously* would be something like teleporting it into oblivion. Even pulverized things move. Moving usually takes time. You do know that, right? You're like a Class-S, Class-A or AA genius or something. You know, like the eggs?"

"Well, you pretentious prick, I suppose I should thank you for the warning about the Dragons."

"You're welcome, babe. Anything for you." Loki teleported directly in front of Antares's face. He stroked Antares's reptilian snout. Antares shoved him away hard, but Loki somersaulted to a soft landing. "Is it me? Is it the col-our of my skin? My Ass-guardian heritage. Or maybe… Are we really going to go there, George? I'm not really gay, you know? I mean, it shouldn't matter anyway. There's nothing wrong with being gay. I could go gay for Hodr for a night. I could just pounce on that scrumptious chap. It's a shame he's dead. His jewels must be all rotten and corroded by now… eww…" Loki wrenched out his eyeballs. "Get the image out of my head!"

"My time is valuable. Don't waste it, Loki. Why did you come back?"

Loki put one eye in and held the other eye out. "Why, to see you, of course! That, and to tell you there may or may not be a tinsy winsy problem… or two… or three… or sixteen. Which would you like to hear first?"

"The most important."

"The most important to you or the most important to your little government here?"

"To me," said Antares.

"Hmm… how should I put it? Your daughter is alive."

Antares backed away, his mouth gaped open for a short time, but he grit his teeth again. "Autumn! Where?"

Loki rendered himself invisible. "Na-na-na-na boo-boo! I can't tell you!"

"Where?"

"Next on the agenda..."

"Autumn! Where is she?! You little devil!"

"...Your little soldier pet, Diamond, is more than likely going to die and become an icicle in the vacuum of space. That is, unless you do something about it."

"The Watchers will—"

"Also, the Dragons want to draw your forces away from the Deep Core by attacking planets on the rim."

"Why?"

"Supposedly, the Deep Core is like some back gate to Heaven or some shit like that. That's why it's so friggin' huge and glowy and shit."

"Tell me about her. My daughter. Autumn. Tell me about her! Where is she?"

"Uh-uh-uh. You didn't say 'please.'"

"Tell me, you worthless imp!"

"You'd think a descendant of royals would have more manners. Say puh-lease, please."

Antares summoned his war suit and generated sparks of energy from the fingertips and palm. "I can hear you. I can follow the sound of your voice, Loki!"

Loki made a farting sound. "Could you hear that too?" Loki made a sound like nails on a chalkboard. "Could you hear that too?"

"I'll annihilate you, Loki! Tell me!"

"You old dinosaur. Maybe I shouldn't move. You can't see me if I don't move, right? Heeheehee… You know, from one parent to another, be grateful you didn't give life to a giant fuckin' wolf or a giant fuckin' snake or a giant treacherous piece of abominable shit for a daughter. Oh... that's right... you did!"

With a thought, the Watcher-controlled laser turrets on the walls fired at Loki. Antares fired his own energy attacks from his fingertips. The Asgardian trickster appeared on the ground, his skin smoldering. Loki laughed. "I know you... I know you too well. You're too proud. It's all force with you. Everything can be achieved by force with you. But you know. But you know. But you KNOW! Some things can't be. Hee-hee-hee-hee-haw!" Loki cast a healing spell on his wounds and teleported away, saying, "Children are easy to make, Emperor Saltine. Too-da-loo!"

He left an aphrodisiac at Antares's feet. Antares crushed it. In anger, he signaled with his hand toward the holograms. Indiscriminately, more people had seizures and heart attacks. "Where is she?" he seethed. "If you're alive, Autumn, why can't my Watchers find you? I can do anything, but why can't I find you?"

A Watcher hologram appeared in the form of his daughter, Autumn. "Inhabited World 11492, Kanopos, has been destroyed. Diamond Weapons System unresponsive, untraceable. Local planetary AIs unresponsive." Antares angrily aimed his repulsor hand-cannon at the hologram, but he could not fire at the image that looked back at him.

An Allosaur woman gripped her heart and collapsed. She'd been watching the news broadcast on the jumbotron, now found herself prostrated in front of it. Neela saw this and came forward to help, but the woman's partner swore at her and Azure to get away, calling Neela a "fuckin' Cerato!" A Watcher AI appeared in the form of a nurse that said that an ambulance was on the way and instructed the Carnotaur's partner on what to do in the meantime. "I can't afford that!" the man shouted back.

As a commotion started around the dying woman, the Union broadcast showed old recordings of the planet Kanopos from space, still in-tact. It announced, "the Union military and Diamond have claimed another spectacular victory over the Dragons on Kanopos, sparing yet another Union world from an unspeakable fate." Someone shoved Neela down. Azure helped her to get back up and led her away from the crowd.

Neela bent her head.

"It-it-it's not your f-ffffault..."

"They don't know any better. I could've done more. I could've helped somehow. This hoverboard could've carried her."

"Th-th-they wouldn't have l-l-let you."

The two made it to the sky-train, which was packed. People rubbed feet, hips, and tails. But when people saw Azure, a Tyrannosaur, they immediately scrunched together to make space for him, not wanting to touch him. Some took less frequent breaths.

"My brother fought for these people..."

"N-Neela..."

"No, I'm done. I'm sick of this. People look at you. They look at me. They think something's wrong with us. Well, something's wrong with them."

"You have something to say, priss?" said a Spinosaur.

"Yeah, I have a lot to say!" she snapped back. "You're gonna judge my friend here because he's a Tyrannosaur, huh?"

"Well maybe it's because he looks like shit and smells like piss."

"Yeah, yeah," some of the other passengers agreed, nodding.

"Don't you fucking act, you son of a bitch!"

"This conduct is not allowed on this public mode of transportation," a Watcher AI wearing a generic driver uniform scolded them.

"Neela..." said Azure, calmingly, just as she was about to shout back at the AI. "Pl-please..."

The Spinosaur and a few of the others who'd agreed with him left on the next stop, mercifully.

"This is fucking ridiculous, you know? We're all Malkuthians. And you know what? We're all Theropods too."

"Wh-wh-what's that?"

"You know… Theropods. We've all got sharp teeth, we all walk on two legs, we all have arms shorter than our legs. For the most part, we've got two eyes, two hands, and a tail. I mean, some of us have more fingers and some of us have a horn or two, but how different does that really make us? We're all just people, that's what I'm saying. There shouldn't be all this division and categorization. It just leads to more hate. It leads to more dysfunction. People look at me and think I'm privileged. People look at you and think you're untouchable. They look at the two of us together and they think it's fire and ice. It's not right."

Azure found a corner to lie down in, gripping his head as it had started to throb again. "Azure, what's wrong?" she said, kneeling as he slid down the edges.

"It-it hur-hur-hurts again."

"Then look at my eyes again." Azure did so. Her blue eyes were hypnotic. "You're going to be ok. We're going to make it home."

Neela scrunched over and sat next to him in the corner. She thought of something to say to help him feel better and to ease the tension. "You said you saw that huge Dragon on the jumbotron before. Are those the kinds of things you see?"

"...I-I-I th-think..." Azure winced.

"Do you see nice things sometimes?"

"Y-y-yes..."

"Like what? Tell me about them."

Azure stopped to think. "M-m-mountains with... white juh-jagged edges... w-w-waterfalls... a b-b-body of w-water w-with... things."

"What things?"

"Like f-f-fffish in a deep... p-puddle... St-stars... from up close... But-but mostly it's scary... I-I-I hear sounds like a million voices. F-f-faint."

"Was my voice one of those? You said you heard me before."

"I-I th-think so."

"How can you tell my voice apart from the others? How can you tell what's happening right now in front of you?"

"...L-l-louder... it's... louder... and cluh-cluh..."

"Clearer? Louder and clearer."

"Y-yes."

"Anyone else specifically? Anything else?"

Azure tried his best to describe the people and events he'd seen in his visions, bits and pieces of what have previously been described. But there were gaps in what he could say and describe. The pain seized his mind and kept him from being elaborate.

"It's ok," said Neela, "I just thought it would help you to cope if you talked about it. I don't think you're strange. I think you're special. That's a gift you have. I... I have something too... something I can't talk about..."

"L-l-like what?"

Neela made a hush sign with her index finger to her lips and shook her head as if to say, "*not here, not now.*"

Lights flashed through the windows of the sky train, flickering like strobes, as the vessel sped across the third-tier of the city, over most of the building tops, over the sky lanes to which the hover vehicles were restricted. "This is what happens when you move too fast," said Neela. "Everything blurs together until it is indistinguishable from everything else. Everything becomes white and black. Light and darkness. Flashes of bright somethings and subtle nothings. That's what I always feel on this train."

Azure listened, comprehending little but finding the words distracted him from his pain.

"I used to write poems. I used to write songs. I was really shy, you know? I couldn't talk very well. They put me in special classes."

"Y-you?"

"Yeah, me. I had a lisp when I was very little. It ruined my self-confidence, so I got very quiet, and people assumed something was wrong with me."

Azure looked like he couldn't believe what he was hearing.

"My brother taught me to stand up for myself. To fight with my mind and my tongue. To use my voice. He said that words and actions reverberate far beyond what we can comprehend. They can rattle the stars. He was right. If it wasn't for what he said then, I wouldn't be saying what I am now."

"I-I-I s-s-sssee."

"Can you believe these trains used to run on the ground and on tracks?" said Neela. "They used to be made out of metal. They called them 'railroads.'"

"R-r-really?"

"It's still like we have tracks, but they're invisible now. All the vehicles are linked. Their paths are predetermined. Controlled. Their speeds too."

Azure saw a vision of standing beside a railroad. He looked at his hands and saw that he held a sledgehammer. He gripped his hands but couldn't feel the handle. He came to, back to reality, and saw that his hands were actually empty. He gasped in disbelief.

"Azure?"

Azure shook his head. "N-N-Neela... have I m-mmmet you before?"

Neela looked perplexed. "No, not that I know of. Why?"

"S-s-sometimes... I think I've done these th-th-thhhings be-before. I've been here be-before. It-it's like..."

"*Deja vu*?"

"Wh-wh-what?"

"It's like experiencing something you feel you already experienced before. It's not unheard of. In fact, it's fairly common. Some people think it's because we evolved to recognize and remember patterns or something. Others think there's something else to it, like a sixth sense. If you don't mind me asking, do you think it has something to do with why you talk like that?"

Azure shut his eyes and shook his head.

"You don't know, right?"

Azure nodded.

Neela couldn't help but wonder, *what happened to you?*

"It's ok," she said. She let out a great big toothy yawn and leaned her body against Azure, leaning her head on his shoulder like a child against a big new teddy bear. "Maybe we can find the answers together."

They eventually came to Neela house in the sky district, a shockingly small cone-shaped dome that looked like it could only house one person. The other houses in the neighborhood were similar. "Have you ever seen one of these houses?" Neela asked.

Azure shook his head. "N-nnno. It-it's so... sm-small!"

"Oh, don't worry, it's eight times larger than it looks!" She swung open the door and waved him in. She was right! The interior of her home was impressive, much larger than it looked from the outside. It was divided into quadrants around a central pillar that distributed food and water to any of the other quadrants by voice command. It was a refrigerator, sink, stove, and oven all in one. Neela flipped through a digital menu and caused a couch to appear from the wall. "God bless the Union, huh?"

"W-w-wow!" Azure collapsed onto the couch.

Something small drove across the floor, which startled Azure.

"Haha! What, are you like an elephant? Are you scared of small crawling things?"

"L-lllong f-fat b-b-bugs..."

"Don't worry. This is just a cleaner bot. Disinfects and vacuums whenever you leave the home, and it even kills pests. Anyway, what do you want to eat? I'm starving."

"E-eat?" Azure paused awhile. B-butter pl-pl-please..."

"Butter? You mean, like with a potato or corn or something?"

"N-nnno... j-j-just... b-b-b—"

"Just butter? You sure?"

Azure nodded. "Th-thank you s-s-sssoooo much." Neela made some selections at the central pillar, and it dispensed a stick of butter, which Azure scarfed down like a child with a popsicle. Neela got him another stick of butter and a block of cheese, hoping that he'd at least eat something with a little more nutrition. She sat down with a tub of cookies & cream ice cream. "I never thought I'd see the day I'd watch a guy eat a stick of butter, but I guess I'm not much better," she said, raising her spoon and smiling. "I earned this shit."

She turned on a 3D TV through another digital module and scrolled through stations. The news hinged on the "Malkuthian victory on Kanopos" and "Diamond's triumph" over another Dragon general. An inflated Dragon death toll scrolled past the bottom of the news ticker with a quote from the puppet President. Neela settled on a children's channel playing "Losty the Last Unicorn." She started to hum along with its familiar opening theme. Azure's curiosity peaked. He'd heard the tune before, and he recognized the central character as having been impersonated by the Watchers.

"You ever watch 'Losty'? It's a cute as hell frickin' show. Losty thinks he's the last of the unicorns, and he's looking for others. Every episode, he meets a different type of animal or monster. Basically, they always find out they have at least something in common by the end, and they solve a problem together. Then, of course, you never see or hear from the other character again, but it's implied Losty remembers them." The episode started to play. Losty was fleeing from a large black Tyrannosaur that rampaged through the forest, apparently trying to eat him. "Oh, frick! This is the one with the Pegasus! They're so cute together! I thought she was the most like Losty. I wish they kept her as a recurring character, and they could have unicorn babies with wings."

"P-P-Poseidon's..." Azure muttered.

"Huh? Does it remind you of something?"

"N-n-nothing..."

After the show, Neela encouraged Azure to shower, but he struggled to stand up in the tub. He ended up sitting down in the tub as the shower water fell on him. Neela passed him handfuls of fruit-scented soap through the curtain. "You're gonna smell like coconuts and green apples!" she said. The soap and water mixed on his scaly blue skin and washed away weeks or months or years of accumulated filth. Streams of brown, soapy water ran from him toward the drain. It circled there before falling in. He closed his eyes tightly so that the soap on his head wouldn't burn them.

"Here's a little brain exercise for you, Azure: I used to wonder where all the water goes," said Neela, sitting on a stool outside the tub. "It doesn't just disappear into nothingness. It needs to go somewhere. But we don't have normal sewers like the ground districts do. So, what do you think happens to it?"

"I-I d-d-don't know..."

"There are pipes beneath us we can't see. Just because we can't see the pipes doesn't mean that the pipes aren't there. They're there, alright. They have to be. Winding and weaving. We see their effects, otherwise we'd be swimming in filth. Some come from our sinks. Some come from our tubs. Some come from our toilets. But they're all connected somewhere. All that dirty water is filtered out and treated somewhere. Some giant collection pool."

Azure observed curiously as the dark streams of water continued to run off from him and circle the drain. He had a vision of a glowing sphere that looked like a rotten fruit hanging in complete blackness. He gasped.

"Azure, are you alright? Did some water get in your nose?"

Azure shook his head and turned away from the falling water. "N-n-no... I... I've b-been... s-s-seeing..."

"Seeing what?"

"I-I f-forget... Nn-nn-nno."

"Is it like a dream? Do you know it happened, but once you wake up you can't remember what you dreamed?"

"Y-y-yes...." Azure grit his teeth. "I-I had it... I s-saw... one thing... n-now it-it's just colors..."

"Give it time, Azure, it'll come back to you. I'm confident of it." She put some soap on the back of his head and rubbed it. Her own head started to hurt, a migraine-like sensation. She yelped and pulled her hand away from Azure as if from a hot stove. A drop of blood came from her right nostril.

"N-Neela! Are you o-o-ok?"

"I'm fine, Azure... no worries," she lied, wiping the blood away. *What the hell was that?* she thought. *What in the hell happened to you?* Her vision became fainter and fainter.

"Sis, don't you dare!" Athena spoke telepathically to Aphrodite. "They've just met, and you've already got them alone together in a bathing room!"

"I hate to say this, but I agree with Athena," said Susanoo. "You're wasting our time!"

"Aw, but they're, like, so totally cute together!" Aphrodite exclaimed.

"Sis, for the last time, I don't need to see or hear all of this. I've got a war to fight. I just need to know if he's the one we're looking for."

"Well, it's only fair. Like, I totally sat through all your boring exposition on military and politics and shit."

"That was important!"

"It was booor-ing! This is sweet. I've, like, been in that dungeon for, like, totally forever. And it wasn't kinky, like, at all! We can finally, like, take some time to breathe. Smell the roses. My gawd."

"Sis, I swear. If you show me any more of these giant naked Malkuthians while I'm in the middle of planning for this battle—"

"Like, what do you know about romance anyway, sis?"

"Don't you start..."

"Yeah, like, you were totally never with anyone, like, ever."

"You have no idea…"

"Like, no offense but you're, like, totally out of touch when it comes to romance."

"Well, sis, to be blunt with you, at least I know how not to trigger a war with it!"

"Get thee back to the killing of Dragons!" a deep, burly voice demanded. "Their foul corpses should be piled up to the sky!"

"Who the hell is that?!" Susanoo growled.

"Who else can hear this?" said Athena.

"Oh, that's just my dear brother, Thor," said the disembodied voice of Loki. "Pardon him. I just blew up the planet that was crushing him with my ultimate destructive spell. What, like a total badass! Go on. Carry on with your little con-ver-sation."

"Ooooh, Loki, your brother sounds, like, totally HAWT!" said Aphrodite.

"Him? But what about meeeee?" said Loki.

"You keep your sleezy, slimy hands away from my sister, Loki!" said Athena.

"Who was that?" asked Thor. "She sounds strong, wise, and fierce! I bet she smells like hard work!"

"...Gee, thanks…" said Athena.

"Heeeeeey," Aphrodite interrupted. "Like, I'm told I have the rockingest bod and I'm, like, a freak in the sheets. Men tear each other apart over me."

"I'm officially hard now," said Loki.

"Quiet! All of you shut up!" shouted Susanoo. "Athena! We had a deal. I have found this Azure for you, now return Kushina to her human form!"

"I can't," said Athena.

"What?!"

"Oho!" said Loki, salivating. "*That's* all she offered you, Suzie-Q? The use of a simple transformation spell? I, for one, am against the *objectification* of women. Care to barter?"

"There's a seal on this spell, Loki," said Athena. "Only I can undo it."

"You lied to me! You used me! You betrayed me, you witch!" Susanoo roared.

"Come now, the honorable lady must not have acted without cause," said Thor.

"... Thanks..." said Athena. "I believe something is wrong with the two beings you found, Susanoo. This Azure you found is not what was described to me. He is a red herring, I'm sure."

"A red herring? Like, what's that, sis?" asked Aphrodite.

"I once taught hunters on Gaia to use the scent of red herrings to mislead and distract their prey. I fear he may be a fake. Loki, that scheming bastard must know this too, but he won't confess it. This Azure must be a bluff. He's not who he says he is. We've been lied to by someone. And that Neela... something's very wrong about her too. Something's just not right. It's like the two of you said, it's like something else is living inside of her. I can hear its thoughts."

"But, like, I saw their hearts, sis! There's something very special about the two of them. Oh, I totally just wanna see them be together!"

"Oh, no! Not the shipping again, sis. I hope that's not the only reason you're dwelling on them."

"No, like, trust me, sis, I've totally got this."

"*You*? *You*'ve got this?"

"He-hey, don't be mean! Oh, my gawd!"

"Ah, yes, Athena, don't be so rude to your much-hotter-sister," said Loki. "I, for one, just love it when she schemes."

"Because it always ends in disaster?"

"Why, yes! Yes, in fact. And there's nothing more beautiful than that!"

"See, sis! Like, at least *someone* appreciates and believes in me."

"I do! I do!" said Loki.

"Hmm..." Athena took a moment to think. "Sis... Susanoo... I hate to do this to you both, but my hands are tied. I will do all I can to survive. However, these

Malkuthians can fight, and so my continued existence is far from guaranteed. Can you follow this Azure and learn more?"

"Why would I do anything for you?!" shouted Susanoo.

"My sister will be with you every step of the way."

"Oooh, like an especially attractive hostage?" Aphrodite twirled her hair in her index finger. "Angsty, exotic Kami, take me as I am! Do as your heart desires!"

Susanoo grunted and pulled away.

"She's the most precious thing I have left in the Multiverse, Susanoo. She is to me what Kushina is to you. If she fails, we all fail. If she loses, we all lose. I mean not to deceive you or do you harm, Susanoo. We just need to be sure, or else this whole thing is for nothing. Because without Azure..."

"Come now, brother!" said Loki. "The huntress has lost our trail! Faily-faily-faily-FAIL." Loki and Thor came upon the remnants of Diamond floating in the blackness of space. A pulse of white energy emanated from him. Some Union warships were approaching Diamond's position to retrieve him. "Oh, Georgie-Antarie, my dear old friend. You've finally come to your senses! Well, too late!"

"Loki, how can thee be sure he's the one we're looking for?" asked Thor.

"The way he gen-erates en-er-gy
Exactly like the pro-phe-cies

Heeheeheeheehaaw!"

He pointed to his head.
"Many secrets
I won't tell
I know much more than Mimir's Well..."

Azure had lost consciousness in the bathtub, and Neela had fainted outside of it. Azure jolted awake five hours later, the water still running and now cold. "N-N-Neela! Are-are you ok?"

Neela grabbed her glasses from the top of the toilet bowl. She rolled up from the floor and grabbed onto the tub and sink to pull herself upright. "Yeah... I got a bit drowsy and fell asleep. You too?"

"Yes... I-I had... a dr-dream."

Neela turned off the water. "Do you remember it?"

"A-a little soldier n-named Sejanus. He-he served a king named *see-see-seezer*. The king's s-son had d-died. Sejanus pre-pretended to be s-sad. But... he wasn't s-s-sad at all. He-he was planning... to kill the king too."

"An assassination?"

"I th-think so. He didn't l-l-look like us but... he-he talked like us. Walked like us. Now... I don't remember now."

"Shit!" Neela sprouted. "I've got an hour before I've gotta be at the university. We've gotta get you dried up and situated."

Neela helped him to get up and dry off with a towel. Azure saw a streak of blood against the sink and bloody tissues on the tiled floor. "Neela... Are-are you ok? Did-did you get hurt?"

She shook her head. "No, never mind that. Sometimes us girls have trouble laying eggs from time to time. Just don't look."

"You l-laid eggs last n-n-night?"

Neela paused, caught in her white lie. "Don't worry about it, k? I'm fine. Let's get you some clothes. I'll show you where everything is just in case. Oh, and Azure..."

"Y-yes?"

"I'm glad you're remembering your dreams now. That's a start."

Neela showed Azure a secondary bedroom that looked like it hadn't been used in years. There were a lot of medals and pictures of her brother on the walls. All the blankets on the bed were folded, and the sheets were pristine.

She showed Azure the clothes in the closet. Many of the articles had built-in armor or chainmail. Some had plating along the shoulders and torso. These all were lighter than their classical military counterparts but still offered some protection. "These were my brother's," she said.

The standard headwear, worn by most males, was essentially a fashionable helmet of a kabuto style, protecting the top of the head and neck while not obscuring sight. These fashion trends seemed like remnants of a bygone age but still served a practical protective purpose from time to time. The abolition of gun ownership for Union civilians forced them to be more creative with weaponry and self-defense.

"This one's my favorite," said Neela, picking up a helmet with a white and gold pattern. The ends on either side flared up and curled like hair. "I think the color combination and design is really elegant. We can find the matching top and bottom."

Azure tried on the helmet. "It fits you like a glove!" Neela exclaimed, leading him over to a mirror. "Look at you! All cleaned up and handsome now! You're like a whole new guy!"

"Th-thank you, N-Neela… Th-thank you s-so much," Azure dipped his head and started to cry.

"Hey," Neela put her right hand on his shoulder. "Don't worry about it, alright? It's no big deal. Dad used to say that we'll never be able to outgive God. He's taken a lot from me but has blessed me with a lot of good things too. One of those good things was meeting you. If I can pay him back, it's by taking good care of you. Ok?"

He mouthed, "thank you."

"And I'm sorry I was so rush-rush. I guess that's how I am in the morning. It's kinda a shock to the system, I guess. I should be used to it by now. Hey, want some coffee?"

"I'll g-g-go with y-you…"

"Huh?"

"To-to the c-city. I'll c-come. If-if that's o-ok."

"You want to come with me?"

Azure nodded again. "K-keep you s-safe."

"You sure you don't wanna just rest here until you feel better?"

Azure shook his head. "I-I f-feel b-better with y-you. I-I'm sc-scared."

"Scared? What are you scared of?"

"Be-before I m-mmmet you it was blackness. N-nothing. C-colors and-and blurs. I-I'm sc-scared I'll… f-f-forget again."

"Oh, don't you worry about that, Azure. I'll never let you forget, you hear? Never, ever, ever. I'll remind you every day until the end of time. I promise."

Neela took a composition book and a pen with her. She showed him how to write down his thoughts while on the train ride back to the city. His hands, however, were so jittery that he could hardly write. His strokes were large and sharp, frequently exiting the margins and lines like a toddler with a crayon. Neela held his hand and guided it manually as he spoke his thoughts aloud. They made this a routine until Azure was able to flesh out words and phrases both in writing and in speech.

"KALEIDOSCOPE"

Neela and Azure had tried sleeping in separate rooms on their second night home together. Azure startled Neela awake with wailing. He'd suffered worsening nightmares. He described seeing Dragons and other beings from other worlds. He described a little child suffering, starving, and struggling to breathe. He said he not only saw it but felt it.

He described a little human boy in a beige tunic watching as his dad laid some stones down to build something with. "Now you try, Yeshua," said the boy's dad. The boy smiled and stepped forward to try to lift a stone into place. "Son, listen to me. The home may be sturdy and strong, but none of that really matters if the ground you choose to lay it on is weak. When the waters and storms come, such a home will be swept away."

"Papa, didn't God tell Joshua to take twelve men, one from each tribe? Didn't they then take twelve stones to cut off the flow of the river?"

"Yes, son, if I recall. Why do you ask?"

"Didn't Moses strike the rock and bring forth water? Wasn't he cursed because of this even though he had the law?"

"Slow down, son."

"And didn't Jacob rest his head upon a stone as he slept? Didn't he anoint the stone with oil when he woke up? Didn't a stone take down the giant, Goliath? And didn't Daniel tell the king of Babylon that a stone would smash the great statue that the king had dreamed of?"

"How do you know such things?"

"You can read the scriptures too, papa! We all can! The prophet Daniel wrote that 70 sevens or 490 years are set aside from the rebuilding of Jerusalem to the end of the age, but before the last seven years, the Anointed One would be killed."

"Let's not talk about these things, son."

"It's ok, papa. I promise, it's ok. Didn't the Wise Men tell you the same things when I was born?"

"How… Did your mother tell you about that?"

"She didn't have to, papa. Daniel was captive in Babylon & Persia hundreds of years ago. He was put in charge of their Wise Men. It makes sense that the new Wise Men must have known about what Daniel wrote. Where were they from, papa?"

"They were from… the East…"

"You see? 'The stone that the builders rejected has become the cornerstone.' Daniel saw one like the son of man seated at the right-hand of God."

"He did... didn't he?" Joseph was wide-eyed.

Azure described seeing a blur of different colors and little specks like glitter, each of them moving individually. He could hear voices and sounds from each speck and could feel "s-s-something l-like... l-life..." from each one. He said that the specks sat on "leaves" of different colors. Each leaf was like its own world. The figures inside of them made sounds and seemed to interact with each other.

"Sounds like a kaleidoscope," said Neela.

Azure looked confused. Neela searched and asked the home database if they might have a novelty kaleidoscope lying around in the house, and luckily they did. She had Azure try looking through one as she turned the knob for him. "Y-yes. A l-little like th-that. L-like broken gl-gl-glass but pr-pr—"

"Pretty?"

"Yes."

"Pretty broken glass," said Neela. "Hmm. Can it be fixed, you think?"

"I don't kn-know."

"Has it gotten any better?"

"I th-th-think so."

"WHENEVER TOMORROW COMES"

In the nighttime, Neela rubbed his back and hummed to him a gentle lullaby until he fell asleep. She tried to fall asleep in her own bed but was overtaken by a familiar nightmare of her own: her birth father reached out for her as a flash of light, and a wave of water overtook him. She bolted awake, gasping as if she were drowning in the water with him. Groggy, she dragged herself to the bedroom where Azure had been sleeping. He was sitting up and trying to pull himself up by the wall. He was surprised to see her appear in the moonlight that peeked through the curtains. "Y-you t-too?" he asked.

Neela nodded.

"Y-y-you c-can sl-sleep here if-if you w-want. I-I w-won't t-t-touch." He rolled off the bed and lay on the floor beside it.

"Stop it, you don't have to do that, Azure."

"It-it's o-ok. I-I'm u-used to sl-sleeping on the fl-floor."

Neela stepped around him and plopped herself on the bed. She nuzzled her snout against the pillow. "Azure," she said. "When I was a little girl and I used to have these nightmares, my brother used to say he'd stand guard and chase them all away. Would you do that for me?"

"Y-yes. I-I w-will," said Azure from beyond the bed's horizon. "D-don't w-worry."

Neela smiled contentedly, drifting off to sleep. "Thank you. I feel safer already."

On subsequent nights, the two would take turns soothing each other. Neela would cover Azure with a blanket and tuck him in before saying, "goodnight." Eventually, Azure joined Neela on the same bed. "It's ok," she said. "I trust you. You won't hurt me."

Malkuthian tails had always made back-sleeping problematic, so the two of them slept facing each other, one hand on the other.

"Good night, Azure," Neela would say. "Sweet dreams 'til tomorrow, whenever tomorrow comes."

"Good night, Neela," Azure would reply with a stutter. And as Neela's eyes would slowly close, Azure would mouth silently, *"love you."*

Sometimes in the middle of the night, Neela's ever-active tail would whack him and push him off entirely. Neela would then angle her body and take up the whole bed without realizing it, and Azure wouldn't want to risk waking her up by getting back on. In the morning, Neela would find him lying on the floor beside the bed and look down at him, chuckling. "You goofball!" she'd say. "Did you fall off again?"

"Y-y-yeah…" he'd reply, sparing her feelings.

Other times, Azure would talk in his sleep, and it would wake Neela up. She would listen to him talk and try to make out what he might be saying. Sometimes, surprisingly, his stutter went away. Sometimes, it was like he was speaking another language entirely. He would talk about Athena, and Aphrodite, and Susanoo, and Loki, and Yeshua, and Deem, and Malevant, and Samael, and a host of things Neela couldn't entirely understand. When she would ask him about it upon his waking, Azure would say he forgot what he dreamed. It was simultaneously a frustrating and fascinating cycle, but she thought that somehow she could figure out what his deal was.

"LITTLE HEARTS"

Azure heard Neela moaning in pain in the bathroom one morning. He asked her if she had more headaches. "No, not this time," she replied.

"Can-can I c-come in and h-h-help?"

"It's embarrassing, Azure… Maybe you shouldn't."

"D-don't be embarrassed. If there's s-something you need, I'm h-here."

"Can you hand me some newspapers and paper towels please?"

Azure did as she asked and handed her some paper towels and newspapers from the kitchen. She yelped.

"Neela! Are you hur-hur-hurt?"

"It's okay. It's just one of those things. Just gotta concentrate. Can you grab me a plastic bag, please? Sorry, I forgot."

Azure did as she asked and handed her a plastic bag through the door. She groaned. "Neela c-can I c-come help you? It's ok. I won't j-judge."

"…Sure, whatever, knock yourself out. I'm warning you though…"

Azure creaked open the door and saw Neela squatting down, leaning against the wall and the toilet. There were two eggs lying beneath her. "I think I have maybe one more," she said, straining and placing a towel over her lap. Azure gently rubbed her stomach. "That feels pretty good," she said. She closed her eyes and pushed, shaking and straining. A third egg emerged and plopped down in the newspaper nest. Azure patted her on the back, congratulating her, and started taking some of the paper towels to wipe up the blood from the floor.

"No, no, you don't have to do that, Azure. That's my grossness, I should clean it."

"It's o-ok, you're not gr-gr-gr-gross."

Neela placed the eggs and newspapers in the plastic bag and tied them twice.

"Th-they won't h-hatch?"

Neela laughed. "Oh, you're just too innocent, aren't you? No, Azure. You need a guy to fertilize your eggs while they're still inside of you. These are trash."

"C-can you eat-eat them?"

"Azure! Eww, gross!"

"I-I'm s-sorry," he said, gathering the bloody paper towels in a bunch. Neela reopened the plastic bag and let him put the towels in it before retying it.

"We don't eat our own eggs, Azure. That's like… cannibalism or something."

"S-sorry."

"Maybe we'll have baby eggs someday. Little legs and little tails, and they can't even open their whittle-bitty eyes and keep falling over."

"W-we?"

Neela gulped. "I was just saying... in general. Unless you think, you know... only after marriage..." Azure didn't know what to say. "You know what, never mind."

Neela headed for the door with the trash and Azure opened the door for her. "What are you doing?" she asked.

"O-opening the d-door for you."

"That's really old fashioned. Boys aren't supposed to do that anymore."

"O-oh. S-sorry. I just... f-felt like doing it."

"A gentleman. That's what you are. That's what they used to call them. A chivalrous gentleman. I like that."

When Neela was in class, Azure would wait in the nearby courtyard for her to finish and work on writing his thoughts down in the composition book. When Neela was at work, Azure would help to retrieve carts and return them to the foyer of the thrift store. His strength and proprioception increased from doing this daily for weeks on end.

From time to time, Azure would wander and become lost, forgetting where he was and why he was there. Neela would frantically search for him, but he was never too far, partly thanks to his hindered mobility. Sometimes, she would have to apologize to people he'd bothered or make excuses for him. Sometimes, she was compelled to defend him more vigorously. People still found the company of a Tyrannosaur to be uncomfortable or offensive. This angered Neela deeply.

When she was in class, she would wave to him from the doorway, and he would wave back. When she was at work, she would wave to him from the other side of the glass, and he would wave back. They would exchange smiles. Sometimes, Neela would make a funny face or point out something silly that a customer was buying, mouthing, *"Oh, my gosh, can you believe this shit?"* and rolling her eyes.

Then, one day he was confronted by Neela's boss and told to stop touching the carts and coming in and out of the foyer. "Tyranno, we don't need you getting us all sick touching everything," he said. "And you can't be loitering around the store either. We don't allow that. Clearly, you're not here to buy anything, so you'll need to leave."

Azure was intimidated by this and retreated away down the street toward a commotion. State Street. There were cranes there and the still-twitching bodies of convicts hanging from them. Azure was horrified by this.

There was a group of Raptors who'd jumped over the guard-rails nearby. The Public Security Force quickly subdued them and beat them with electrified clubs. An older green Raptor wearing an orange prisoner's uniform stood at the feet of one of the cranes with a noose around his neck. Azure realized that the Raptors were trying to intervene for him. "Start it, dammit! Kill the fucker already!" the PSF officer commanded. With that, the crane began to hoist the old Raptor by the neck into the air as he heaved. His body flopped in the air as it instinctively fought for life.

"Dad!" a voice cried out from the pile of beaten and bloodied Raptors. It was that of a large green Raptor, a Megaraptor. "No! No, dad! Stop it! Cut him down, please!"

"Odhran!" an older Megaraptors came to him and held him around the waist, pulling him away. "We need to go! Let's get out of here, Odhran! Don't be stupid!"

The executed Raptor fell motionless. The green Raptor screamed and cried for his dad.

Azure hobbled over to the young Raptor and put his hand on his back, surprising him. "I-I'm s-sorry…" said Azure. The young green Raptor looked up at him with teary green eyes. The Public Security Force knocked the three of them over and started to beat them savagely. Azure was struck many times. They were especially brutal with him. He shoved the young green Raptor back over the guard-rail and away from the violence before trying to crawl toward the guard-rail himself, moaning and groaning. A PSF soldier shot at him and hit him square in the back. Azure crashed to the floor. The soldier kicked him over and shot him multiple times in the chest. Azure fell limp and motionless.

Neela waited on a bench in front of her store after work for him. An hour passed and she became more and more anxious and worried. *What if he's lost and can't find his way back?* She started wandering around the block asking store clerks and everyone she saw, "Have you seen a big, blue Tyrannosaur?" Her heart and mind raced. "He's around 20 feet tall, talks with a stutter, walks a little funny. Have you seen him? Did he pass by here? Do you know which way he went?"

They all denied seeing him and suggested she ask the Watchers.

"Azure!" Neela shouted, running through the streets. "Azure! Where'd you go? Where are you? AZURE! AZURE!"

A Watcher hologram appeared. "Who are you trying to find, Neela?"

"Azure! I'm trying to find a boy named Azure. He has trouble remembering and gets confused sometimes."

"Last name?"

"I don't know. He doesn't have one. You couldn't identify him last time. Please. He's a big, blue Tyrannosaur with a stutter, and he walks funny. He's maybe 20 feet tall. He was wearing white and gold and had a kabuto helmet. Is there anyone nearby who fits that description? Anyone at all?"

"There are no Tyrannosaurs within walking distance, Neela. Less than 3% of the population is Tyrannosaur."

"I know that. Where's the nearest one?"

"6.4 miles south from here. He lives with a family of eight in the Tyrannosaur ghetto."

"No, no, that's not him. That can't be him."

"If you would like to proceed with filing a missing person's report, I require a full name…"

"I told you all I know!"

"Last name?"

"I told you I don't know it! He doesn't have one!"

"To proceed with this missing person's report and to continue to the next section, I require additional information. All sections must be filled."

"Can't we just skip that section? I don't have that information!"

"To proceed with this missing person's report and to continue to the next section, I require additional information. All sections must be filled."

"Fuck you, then!"

"Good luck to you, Neela. Buh-bye!"

Neela sat on the stump of a recently cut tree that sat beside a store. She buried her face in her hands, feeling like a mother whose child had gone missing. "Azure…" she cried.

Aphrodite paced back and forth. "Oh, shit, shit, shit, shit, shit."

"He's dead already! Let's move on!" said Susanoo.

"Like, what am I gonna tell my sister? Like, what am I going to tell General Malevant?"

"Tell them that we made a mistake and found the wrong one. It's like your sister said: he's obviously not the Azure we're looking for. He's a decoy. Azure is said to be indestructible, invincible, and all-powerful. There's no way this pathetic, confused mortal was him. Even *you* could have kicked his ass!"

"Aww, you're like totally the sweetest! Thank you!" Aphrodite kissed him on the cheek. He shrunk away apprehensively, wiping a sweaty raindrop from his forehead. Aphrodite looked out into the distance. "But that poor Neela… she'll totally be all alone…"

"Yeah, and? Why should we give a shit? We're deities. She's a mortal and a nobody! Why should we care how she feels?"

"Isn't that, like, what you used to say about the humans in your world? Now you're in love with one of them."

Susanoo fell silent and scowled.

"Like, how would you feel if you, like, lost that comb forever and could never get it back? Wouldn't you be, like, totally crushed? This Neela's been alone for a long, long time. I can totally feel it. She, like, finally has someone she likes and trusts."

"So, what are you suggesting, fairy princess? Should we just go on another fool's errand to help this mortal while the Dragons rip the Multiverse to shreds?!"

"Like, oh my gawd, ok. Just chill out. I have an idea. Can I, like, borrow some of your energy? I'll fix this. Like, my sister won't even notice."

Neela sat on that stump for some time, her face in her hands and her tail lying low.

"N-N-Neela!" a familiar voice called to her. A familiar hand touched hers. "Wh-what's wr-wrong? Are-are you hur-hur-hurt?"

Neela squeezed him on the arm and growled. "Azure, you asshole! I've been looking all over for you! Don't do that to me!" She tugged him by the cloth of his top and shook him. Her tail wagged frantically from side to side with the beat of her heart. It was then that she noticed large holes in his armor. "What the hell are these holes from, Azure? Did somebody shoot you? Oh, my God! Are you ok?"

Azure nodded. "D-d-don't w-worry."

Neela frantically lifted his clothes and armor to check for wounds. "This armor can't stop a bullet. It's not meant for that."

"It-it's ok."

"It's *not* ok, Azure! It's not fucking ok! Only the PSF and the military are allowed to carry guns. Did one of them shoot you?"

Azure nodded.

"Why?"

"I-I s-saw th-them h-hanging p-p-people…"

"You went to State Street?"

"Y-y-yes…"

"And you got too close, didn't you?"

Azure nodded.

"I tried to do that once. I got a tooth knocked out, but it was worth it. Thank God we've got rows of them, huh? What they're doing there is absolutely fucking disgusting and wrong. It's everything I fucking hate about the Union—how we can be so advanced and yet still so backwards."

Azure nodded. "Y-yes."

"Hey…" she held his chubby cheeks in her hands and looked him in the eyes. "It goes to show that I was right about you. You're not like them. You've got a heart and a conscience, Azure. And thank God, you're ok. I don't know how you are, but you're not bleeding or wounded that I can see." She turned him around to inspect his back. "Come here…" she hugged him and squeezed him tightly. "You stay where I can see you next time, you hear me? Don't wander off like that."

"O-okay," Azure agreed.

"I can't replace you, Azure. I can't. And I'm done. I'm fucking done."

The suns had begun to set, and the sky turned a mesmerizing amethyst and sapphire.

"AT THE EDGE OF THE CLOUDS"

On the first day of summer, Neela led Azure to one of her favorite places in the world: the edge of the sky district. Above the clouds, it was nothing but blue skies for miles and miles and miles. Endlessly. Just a chest-high railing separated the individual from a fatal plunge. Neela sat with her legs and feet hanging over the edge, her face and chest resting against the railing. "It's ok, Azure. C'mon down and sit with me!" She patted the spot next to her.

Azure gulped and put his hands on the railing, peering down at the city below. There were clouds obscuring some of the view, but in the little pockets there was the hustle and bustle of traffic on the ground and in the sky. Movement down below. Azure shook his head fearfully.

"Hey, it'll be ok, I promise. I sit here all the time."

Azure squatted down and gingerly placed his three-toed, one-meter-long feet over the edge. His legs and body were much more mobile now from months with Neela.

"Relax," said Neela, seeing that he was still anxious about the height. Azure closed his eyes and took a breath. "It's like we did with your visions. Don't let your thoughts run amok. Don't worry about everything that could possibly happen, just focus on a little thing. Bring your attention to one small point and focus there. Now, open your eyes."

Azure did so and found Neela holding some binoculars in front of him. "Try these," she said. "You just hold it up to your eyes and zoom in by adjusting the knob like the kaleidoscope I showed you. Go ahead."

He took the binoculars in his nervous, jittery hands and almost dropped them. Neela caught them and shook her head. "Shit! Goofball, if you held me that loosely I might fall too!" She took off her glasses and hung them by the lanyard around her neck. She then took the binoculars and looked down at the city through them. Another brawling circle had formed. Neela couldn't tell exactly if it was a knife or fist fight. She caught herself lingering on it a bit too long and moved on. "There's the store… and the Old Senate House… There's the jumbotron… Oh, there's a big aircraft carrier in the harbor! You need to see this!" she held the binoculars in front of him. "Hold this nice and tight. Pretend it's me."

Azure tensed his grip around the rubber securely and placed the binoculars to his eyes. Neela guided him. "There! Do you see it?"

"It-it's big."

"It's huge, isn't it? Those things are cities on the water. Have you seen the ones that can fly? The sky carriers?"

Azure shook his head.

"Pankaja was crawling with 'em. I never imagined they could be taken down, but… those Dragons are something else."

Something compelled Azure to move the sights over State Street. He saw cranes and the distant bodies of the newly hanged. He lowered the binoculars and shook his head. "Did you see something bad?" asked Neela. "There's a lot of that down there." Neela took the binoculars back and hovered over the shantytown where she could see distant figures traversing the river where they scooped for valuables. "Being down there is a whole other story. You can feel it, you can smell it. It's different seeing everything from up here, isn't it?"

"Yes."

"It's easier to turn a blind eye from a distance. I wonder if this is what God sees. I wonder if our great big problems are just so small to him. Too small to care."

"I-I think I've seen Heaven," said Azure. "I-I f-feel like I was there."

"Huh?"

"It-it was hot... v-very hot. And bright. Br-brighter than the suns."

"How do you know it was Heaven?"

"I just kn-knew. S-somehow. I knew."

Neela's curiosity was piqued. "Tell me about it."

Azure described streets made of gold and winged figures made of fire. He described beautiful music and singing. He described white palaces as large as mountains. He described feeling a great calm and happiness.

"Was this in a dream? Or from a near-death experience?"

"I don't kn-know..." he replied. He said that he believed that the Yeshua boy he'd seen helping his human father lay down stones was from there.

"Like a Heaven child?"

He answered with a stutter, "Like a son of God. When he looks back at me in my visions... He knows me, and I know him. I know who he is, and he knows who I am. But when I ask him to tell me, he always replies, 'Not yet, in father's time.' And that's all I can remember now."

Neela became very sick the next morning. Her fever was well above average. She got up groaning and clutching her head. Azure raced to get her an ice pack and some anti-inflammatories. He tucked her in under three layers, but her tail swept away the blankets. Azure lay beside her and held the ice pack to her head, adjusting it as needed. She called in sick via the Network, missing both school and work for three days. During those three days, Azure tended to her every need and told her stories, clearer stories about the visions he'd seen, of the struggles in other universes.

He told her that the Dragons had a queen named Ain. Her size and power were so great that they were indescribable. But she was unhappy, he said. And she wasn't satisfied with all the "man-like" or masculine Dragons she'd made despite their size, strength, and success. So, she made a daughter: Darna. Tucked away in her own pocket dimension from which she saw the rest of the Multiverse, Darna was playful and relatively innocent—child-like. One of the Dragon generals, named Deem, learned about her and fell in love with her. He'd experienced a great change after conquering a particular universe and encountering a particular set of deities, ones with many arms. One of the changes he experienced was a desire for companionship. But he needed to keep it a secret from the other leaders. Darna found his advances amusing and learned from him about how other beings fell in love, got married, and had kids. He'd send her gifts from these other worlds and would tell her stories from them too. But he hid most of the violence he and the other Dragons committed to spare her feelings.

"It's like a fairytale…" said Neela. "The princess and her knight…" She grasped Azure's hand and held it tightly. "My knight," she said, "mine."

"Your kn-n-night?"

"Yeah. Get some sleep too, my darling knight," she said, "goodnight and sweet dreams 'til tomorrow, whenever tomorrow comes." Neela fell asleep with the ice pack to her head.

"STORY TIME"

"Lookie what I got!" Neela would often say, holding a new used book she'd found at her thrift store with a smile of purple braces. She'd then go on a tangent about what the book was about and why it was special before reading her favorite sections to Azure. She would often ask him, "So what do you think?"

Azure would try to put together a response before losing his train of thought, something which improved the more they went through this cycle. Not only did this help Azure to better gather his thoughts and carry on a conversation, this was also a welcomed escape from the news and the harsh realities the media always brought. This also brought great joy to Neela who loved to talk, perhaps as much as anything, and Azure was the perfect listener. If she wasn't talking up a storm with him, she was doing so on campus and with her continued activism at the Old Senate House.

Her speeches almost always fell on deaf ears, but at least Azure was there to hear them and to protect her. This emboldened her like never before.

Neela continued to read books to Azure, some casual like folk and fairytale collections. Some were deeper and more intellectual: religious texts, mythology, political commentary, and history. She read to him both because she loved it and because it helped Azure to exercise his cognition. She often went on long tangents about what she felt, interjecting in certain parts with her own ideas and opinions. She owned a personal library of binded books that kept growing with additions from the thrift store.

"The mystics called this event the Void Brightening," she read. "The event when all *Chi* entered the universe and made life possible...

"...the over 400 years of feudalism that became known as...

"In the beginning, there was chaos...

"...until Arcturus united the tribes of the continent...

"...there was an egg called...

"... darkness moved across the waters of the deep...

"...the new dynasty vilified the former...

"And Cronus ushered in a golden age...

"...And so Sargas the Great began the Adonaization of the empire...

"...a terrible time, a seven-year tribulation...

"...the age of the sage kings...

"The great world serpent, Jormungandr, swallowed Thor up in one foul gulp before...

"...News of their extravagant wedding...

"An Angel told me... he spoke, I listened, I wrote... and he said...

"He called the light day and the darkness night, and he saw that this was good...

"His breath became the wind and clouds...

"...ending the dynastic age...

"...and so, he left his father's kingdom and walked amongst man...

"...and he learned of their great suffering."

"Long ago," said Neela, "there was a brother and a sister named Fuxi and Nuwa. They were siblings by default as both had the same creator, but they were not of the same blood. They were alone and loved each other. They wanted to be husband and wife but felt ashamed. They prayed to heaven to be married and said that if they could not be joined in marriage, heaven should not allow the misty vapors to be joined and gathered either. However, if they were allowed to marry, they said, 'let the misty vapors be married too.'"

"If-if they were a-alone, how did they know that h-h-heaven existed?" asked Azure, his speech and thoughts becoming clearer.

"Good question. I guess that, no matter what, people always try to find a higher meaning to their existence. Or maybe they sense that there's something more out there, something bigger and better. Or maybe it's just hope playing tricks on the mind."

"NEELA & THE STREET COMEDIAN"

Neela and Azure made their way to the steps of the Old Senate House where Neela often gave her speeches. However, the two found the steps occupied by a different speaker: an old, homeless Allosaur named Glaucon who made his money via comedic baiting. Glaucon shared some of his earnings with his fellows in the homeless, buying his popularity within the camp. He also had a way with words that added to his charisma.

"I want to talk to you about something today. Something which has been bothering me. You people and your stupid fuckin' kids. Yeah, I said it!" said

Glaucon. The crowd hooted, chuckled, and clapped. "And you know what bothers me the most about you parents and your stupid fucking kids? The stupid fuckin' names you give them. Unless you're a fuckin' Ceratosaur and can cut in the front of the healthcare line, you're probably gonna have one, two, or three good kids who survive the batch. So, in that precious batch of spoiled, crying, whining fucks—why the fuck would you waste your chance to leave a legacy on society by naming one of them 'Dick?'"

The crowd laughed.

Azure tugged on Neela's sleeve and suggested they could preach elsewhere in the People's Square.

"Wait, let's hear the idiot out, maybe he'll leave soon," she said.

"Poor fuckin' kid!" Glaucon continued. "Even I'd pity the little fuck. Imagine the reception he gets from his friends in the classroom, 'Good morning, Dick! How's it *cummin'* along?' You stupid fuckin' parents. Or what about you parents who mash your two fuckin' ugly-ass names together, so Clarence and Madea become Clamadea? Sounds like a fuckin' disease, the kind of disease Dick gets on his dick when he becomes too preoccupied with his name. Better that than fuckin' Buck though. You shootin' blanks, Buck? Fuck you, Buck. I had a kid about forty-something years ago. Wanted to name him 'Victorious' because I thought it was cool and badass, and I wanted him to become a *winner*, not like Dick, Clamadea, and Buck over there.

"You know, Mr. George Antares himself has kids. He had two. I've only seen or heard about one of them these past few years. Lord knows where the other one went, but I'm sure the truth is embarrassing. Even big daddy's got some domestic stuff it seems, but big daddy's got the cash to cover his ass. So, what does he care?"

Onlookers threw banknotes and silver coins at him in appreciation.

Neela appeared angry at the support this clown had gotten.

"Let's g-g-go," Azure insisted, pulling her away.

"OH!" Glaucon exclaimed. "Ain't that the cute 'lil pink Cerato girl who always speaks just over there?" Neela turned and faced him, Azure sighed and looked down whilst clenching his fist. "I thought you went into early retirement last month, sweetheart! I hadn't seen or heard from you. Never thought the kids would be retirin' before me, but social security went out the fuckin' window five years ago, so I wouldn't be fuckin' surprised."

"Yeah, well, if we had a government that gave a damn about us—"

"Sweetheart, they give too much of a damn about us. Hell, they've probably got a dozen cameras on me right now. They can't just mind their own damn business. They've gotta be all up in ours."

"Well, I agree with you there."

"Ever try to run a business down here, sweetheart? Fuckers will take 25% minimum. MIN-I-MUM."

"Yeah, I know all about that."

"And the more you make, sweetheart, the more they'll take. If your last name ain't Antares, you could be paying 30, 40, 50% or more. I'm out here on the streets, as off-the-grid as you can be, and they be hassling me. Bitch, I live in a fuckin' hovel! I don't got no loose change. You know what I mean?"

"Of course I do. And that's why we've gotta create more quality jobs and build the middle class. Grow it, so more of the poor can find employment and stable living."

Glaucon shook his head. "Girl, I wish. You grow the middle class, you'll just have more wage slaves. At least down here, when the feds ask for money, I can say, 'I ain't got it' and, bitch, they can't prove it. The second you sign something, and they've got documentation on you, you owe."

"I know. But it's not like we can do away with taxes. We need to pay—"

"For what?! The PSF? The military? Shit. Where's all the tax money going? To pay for the fucking useless ass Senate?"

"I hear you. I completely agree."

"Girl, 30 years ago we had to pay for their campaigns too! Imagine that: us broke fucks funding their multi-quintillion-dollar campaigns!"

"That's bullshit."

"Yeah! Now, the old fucks don't ever age and they've got no term limits, so at least that's settled. But the point is: if you gonna have taxes, fine, but fuckin' tax the ones with all the money, not the ones broke as fuck. You know what I mean?"

"Yes," Neela agreed. "But the rich employ everyone."

"Oh bullshit. You believe that?"

"Well, who do you employ?"

"Every single one of them in that damn camp over there, girlie."

"Oh, I see."

"They work for me, I work for them. It's a win-win. That is, until the government gets all involved and takes what little we've got. And we ain't seen a coin or a helping hand for years."

"What would you guys need to get out of the camp?"

"Leave my camp?! Fuck that! I love my camp."

"Ok, what would you guys need to get out of poverty?" said Neela.

"Money."

"That's it?"

"Lots of money and lots of help, and maybe housing while we get on our feet."

"I thought you said you love your camp?"

"Yeah, well… beggars can't be choosers. I'll settle for four bedrooms."

"And jobs?"

"Well… those too."

"So, which comes first: housing, money, social help, or jobs?"

"Minds," said Glaucon.

"Hmm?"

"People need the fuckin' minds for it. Most of these people have given up. This is the way it'll always be. That's life for them. You know what I mean?"

"I see… you mean like *will*?"

"Will, minds, whatever. So, maybe some help would be nice. I don't know. I just know people gotta eat, at least."

"Thanks for talking to me." Neela extended her hand. "I'm Neela, Neela Eridanus."

"You don't wanna shake my hand, girl, trust me," said Glaucon. "It's been places. It's seen things."

"Yeah, well, it looks like we see things rather similarly, we just approach it differently. Maybe you're right. It starts with parents, people in the home."

"What are you blabbering about?"

"Your joke about naming kids stupid things," Neela clarified.

"Oh, well it's fuckin' true isn't it?"

"I guess. But it also goes to show that parents don't consider the weight of their decisions on their children. If parents don't raise their children, the media and the schools will, and if the media and schools are owned by the government, and the government is run by one party and one guy…"

"We're fucked."

"Right. You've got yourself Antares drones. You've got yourself an echo chamber telling you: *this* is reality, *this* is truth."

"You figured that all out on your own, didn't you?"

"No, actually. *We* did."

Glaucon shook his head. "Thanks, sweetheart. It's been swell. Now, would you mind moving along to another spot? I've gotta do my thing here. Need to pay the bills, you know? My customers are running away."

"What are you gonna do with all this tip money? You gonna distribute it to the people in your camp?"

"Distribute it? Fuck that! I earned it."

"Then how do you buy your followers?" Neela prodded. "And yes, it's a trick question."

"Ok, fine, on good days they get a cut, but it's up to me."

"And it should be."

"Good! Now, can I get on with it, sweetheart?"

"Sure, knock yourself out."

Neela went with Azure to the opposite end of the People's Square. Neela began giving a speech there. Glaucon continued his comedic shtick.

"TOGETHER"

There was an old bridal shop that was closing its doors on Eighth Street. "Oh, darling! Look!" said Neela, pulling Azure in by the hand. The place looked like it had been ransacked. More than half of the merchandise was gone, and there were boxes strewn on the ground.

The elderly shop owner, a Spinosaur, smiled briefly at Neela, then glimpsed down at the sight of Azure. "Can I help you find something?" she asked.

"We're just looking," said Neela.

The owner insisted that they wash their hands, putting an extra pump of soap in Azure's. He looked up and saw the old portraits that were still left on the wall in front of the sink: married couples from decades ago, some in unfashionable clothes.

Azure had brief flashes—visions of those times.

"Thirty years…" said the shop owner. "And all it took was a few…"

Neela rubbed her back. "It's not over," she said. "You're writing a new chapter. You'll reopen here or somewhere else."

"I'm old, sweetheart. But… thank you."

"Sure, no problem."

"You two a couple?"

"Yes."

"Hmm… well… go ahead, then. Do your 'looking.'" The store owner retreated behind the counter, hunched down on a stool.

Neela tugged on Azure's hand. "Come on!" she said, excitedly.

She unracked a few dresses and placed them in front of her, one by one. "How do I look, Azure?" she said.

"G-g-good…" he said each time.

"*Just* good?"

Neela rummaged through some of the bridal accessories that were tossed about. "Oooooh, wow!" she exclaimed. She raised a crown tiara off the shelf and put it on her head. She smiled menacingly, her eyes gleaming. "If only I were queen, things would be different."

She threw a veil over herself and put on a few more accessories. She aggressively positioned Azure in front of her, saying, "stay still, you!" She threw a ceremonial shawl over him and put an artificial flower in the kink of his chainmail. She turned him toward the mock alter that was covered in merchandise.

"Now say: 'I take you, Neela, to be my wife…'"

"I-I take Neela to be my w-wife."

"And I take you, Azure, to be my husband."

"And-and I—"

"Shhhhh! That's *my* part."

"O-oh, ok."

"Uhh…" Neela clenched on eye, tapping her head, trying to remember what came next. "Shoot, darling, I forgot the rest."

"M-may Adonai g-gather us together, and-and may only Heaven part…"

Neela laughed. "That's like an ancient thing to say. That got changed ages ago. Did you hear that in a documentary or something?"

"I… I don't know. Can-can I…"

Neela gave him a toothy kiss. "Yes."

"A LITTLE PEBBLE"

The fall came.

Orange, yellow, and brown leaves paved the path for the couple as they sauntered through the east side of the lower city together. It was a warehouse district leading to the harbor. The leaves crunched underfoot.

"Fall is my favorite season," said Neela. "I think it's really pretty. And without fall, the spring and summer wouldn't be anything special. We wouldn't appreciate all that we have if there's no chance of us ever losing it. They tried to terraform some worlds so that it would always be spring or summer. But there's a reason God made fall, and winter too. Everyone says they want it to be sunny all the time, then, it's sunny all the time and they're miserable. It's like receiving gifts every day, after a while it's not special anymore and you stop appreciating them. Then next thing you know, you've got a drought. Then next thing you know you've got a desert. I always wondered if maybe the bad weather drove us together. If it wasn't raining the day we met… if things would be different, you know? We have to take the good with the bad. The rain and suns together make things green. Not one without the other."

They looked over at the harbor together. "My mom named me 'Neela' because I was born beside the big blue sea. Imagine if I dropped a little pebble into the ocean…" she picked up a small pebble and dropped it into the water. It created a ripple. "My mom used to say that it only takes a little drop of water to create a ripple effect felt across the ocean. You ask me why I bother giving speeches even though no one seems to care and no one seems to be listening. This is why. What little difference I can make on my own can grow into something huge in the future. A ripple effect. Let the whole darn ocean know I'm here. The whole darn universe.

"The universe, Azure… it's cold, dark, and emotionless—void of all feeling. It just *is*. We are the conscience, Azure. It's the life inside of it that gives the universe life. It's the life inside of it that gives it meaning. Little lives. Dots on planets, Azure. You, me, and everyone with a brain, a heart, a soul, and a will… *that's* where the change is at. We're the difference—the difference between a cold, dark, heartless universe and one blooming with life and light."

As they proceeded back to the sky train station, Azure began lagging behind. A rush of visions and voices had overtaken him. He leaned up against the wall of a warehouse and tried to recompose himself. Just as Neela turned to walk back to him, someone grabbed Neela's backpack, which she'd held carelessly on one shoulder, and tried to run off with it. It was caught in the hinge of her elbow and she pulled with all her might against the assailant to get it back.

The thief revealed a switchblade and stabbed at her. In a desperate dash, Azure threw himself on top of Neela and, twisting and turning, they all fell to the concrete together. Azure's helmet fell off as he crashed into a dumpster. He bit the thief's arm. The thief stabbed him again and again and again until Azure released his bite. Neela kicked the now-bloody thief away, and he ran off empty-handed, clutching his bad arm. Neela crawled over to Azure who was quivering, blood pouring from many wounds on his body onto the concrete. "No, no, no! Azure!" Neela cried, putting her hands over his many deep wounds to try to stop the bleeding. A stab to the throat made speech impossible. Azure felt her face and then clutched her hand. "Hold on! Please, hold on!" Neela pressed on the throat wound, causing blood to spray on her face too. "Azure, dammit! Hold on!" Her hands slipped up toward another stab wound near his head and a flash of fatigue overcame her. She lost consciousness and fell over beside him.

She regained consciousness as someone shook her awake, calling her name. Azure knelt beside her, no blood or wounds in sight. "Oh, my God!" Neela gasped. She threw herself on him and hugged him tightly. "What the hell happened? You were hurt! You were bleeding! You were dying!"

"I don't know," said Azure. "I woke up next to you out here. Do-do you have your bag?"

"I don't give a shit about my bag, Azure! You! You son of a bitch! Never fucking do that again!"

"I was pr-protecting you, Neela... Being your knight."

Neela looked at her clothes. There was no blood on them too. Nor was there blood on her face as she felt for it. "There's something wrong..." she said. "No, just something very different about you. Are you like a ghost or an Angel or something?"

Azure shook his head.

"Don't pull that 'I don't know' shit on me anymore! We're so past that stage by now."

"I r-r-rrreally don't know, Neela. I... I'm sorry. I know I was hurt, bleeding and in pain. Then I wasn't. That's all I know. I don't lie to you ever. You told me it was wrong."

Azure helped her back on her feet. "Thank you for protecting me," she said, readjusting her hijab and retrieving her glasses. "They say that's what Angels are supposed to do."

"So, like... did you do that, Su?" Aphrodite asked, sitting beside Susanoo on his cloud.

"Why the hell are you asking me? I thought that was you," Susanoo replied.

"Like, nuh-uh! I swear to gawd. So, like… who healed him, then?"

"Fuck if I know! I don't heal things!"

"So, like, you think... Azure healed himself?"

"Or that girl, perhaps. Your sister says that this Neela has something attached to her— something unnatural. I've felt something like that before. It's like with Kushina's mother. Funny thing is, she had my mother's malicious spirit inside of her. This Neela… I can't figure out what it is but there's something else living inside her. Something that's not… her…"

"Oooh, I like it when you talk all princely and, like, smart and stuff," she rubbed his thigh. He pulled away, covering his lower body with a part of the cloud, sweating.

"What the devil are you doing?"

"Su… like, come on now. We've, like, been alone together for, like, totally forever now. For, like MUL-tiple seasons. Besides, like, Kushina doesn't need to know. In a sense, like, you'll totally be doing it for her."

Susanoo gulped. "What do you mean?"

"Like, Kushina's gonna get old and die anyway. Or, like, the Dragons will kill her. I, on the other hand, never get old and I'll, like, never go away. So, like, totally… think about it… An Olympian-Kami baby. A freakin' demi-god or something."

Aphrodite kissed him on the cheek and bit his beard, purring playfully. Susanoo turned away uneasily, pulling his scabbard close to himself. "Would you, like, at least hold me or something… I'm cold..."

Susanoo reached his left arm around her and pulled her close to him. She nipped his beard and gave him a smothering, swallowing kiss on the mouth, pulling slightly back and breathing into his face so that his breath was forced to meet hers. "Thank you," she said, mounting his lap and brushing away the cloud cover. "Oh, my gawd! Oh, my gawd!" she exclaimed with increasing intensity. "YYYES! I totally missed this!"

"THE AFTERLIFE"

There was an old, dilapidated playground in one of the lower-city ghettos that Neela and Azure explored together. Neela was giddy with excitement over this. She immediately tried to use the swings, but one of the chain links snapped when she jumped back on it. Azure caught her. "Geez, what a piece of junk," she muttered. "I haven't been eating that much ice cream, have I? Thanks, Azure."

"Yeah, sure. H-hey, don't you have h-homework to do?"

"Yeah, I've always got something. This'll only take a sec."

She more carefully boarded a teeter-totter and started hopping up and down on it. "Azure, be a good sport, would you?" she held her hand out, directing him to the other side. Azure tried to mount the other side but lost his balance and fell off. "Shit, are you ok?" Neela laughed.

"Y-yeah."

"Silly, clumsy boy! Well, shit, that makes two of us then. I'm a klutz, you're a klutz. Double the fun, I guess."

Azure tried twice more and got it on the last try, but his greater weight almost catapulted Neela off into the air. "Holy shit! Easy, easy, Azure! Geez! I didn't sign up to go to space today!"

Azure tried to support more of his weight on his legs and push off through his feet. "There ya go!" Neela encouraged. "Whoohoo!"

"Wh-whoa!" Azure cheered along.

"Pretty fucking cool, huh? Hey… hey, Azure, slow down a bit." Neela's head had gone a bit foggy. The teeter totter came to a halt.

"Are y-you ok?"

"I'm fine, thanks for asking. Just give me a second." Neela shook her head like a wet dog trying to dry itself. "Ok, let's start again, nice and easy. Nice and slow."

The teeter totter rose and fell, occasionally squeaking. They kicked what few wood chips were left in place off to the side. "Azure, what do you think happens when we die?"

Azure paused to think. "I don't kn-know. Wh-what do you think?" He pushed off against the ground.

"I was hoping we could all go to Heaven and see our loved ones again, but that's not what the scriptures say," Neela stopped for a bit, leaving her elevated by Azure's weight. "They say we either go to Heaven or Hell. Hell… if it exists, it sounds like such a terrible place. Why would a good God send people to Hell?"

"Maybe they d-d-deserve it?"

Neela shook her head. "No one deserves that. Why should even the worse people spend an eternity in Hell for only a lifetime of sins? The punishment doesn't fit the crime, so there's no justice in that. And God is supposed to be the perfect judge. How can a perfect judge be unjust?"

"Maybe they w-w-want it?"

"Hmm…freedom and choice. Maybe it's better in the minds of some people to rule in Hell than to serve in Heaven. So, by that logic it's like God is Chancellor Antares and the devil is like me: we choose to be free and risk suffering for it."

"M-maybe."

"Sometimes I wish there was just… nothingness. Like, when we die, we don't think or feel anymore at all. There's no afterward. But then there's no hope of seeing our loved ones again. They're gone forever. There's only memories."

"You think that's e-enough?"

"You mean the memories? I don't know."

Neela and Azure got off the teeter totter gingerly, both almost falling on their tails in the process. They shared a laugh about that.

Neela tried to spin a merry-go-round that hardly moved, being tangled on the overgrown grass surrounding it. She waved Azure toward her, encouraging him to help her push the merry-go-round to get it going. They tore out some grass in the process, and Neela made a cringing face, saying, "shit, sorry!" She jumped on the rusty, creaking, barely-spinning merry-go-round as Azure tried to keep it going.

"It-it'll grow back!" said Azure.

"I hope so!" she had to raise her voice over the sound of the equipment. "You think it's like reincarnation? You get a whole bunch of chances. You have a whole bunch of lives you're destined to live and all of them are determined by your choices in the last life? Ok, Azure, you can stop, I'm getting dizzy again."

She got off the merry-go-round all wobbly and with treadmill legs. Azure caught her and stabilized her. She leaned against his shoulder and caught her breath.

"Neela, are you o-ok?"

"I'm fine. I can hardly remember ever being a kid."

"Why are you a-a-asking about this? Is something the m-matter?"

"Give me a second, ok?" she put her hands on her knees and closed her eyes. "Fuck. I shouldn't have gotten on that stupid piece of shit."

"But d-did you have f-fun?"

Neela smiled with her eyes still closed. "Yeah! Hell yeah, I did! We've gotta live it up, right? You never know. You never, ever know."

"Neela... wh-what's wr-wr-wrong?"

"Nothing," she said. "Just... just been thinking since we got attacked and you got stabbed the other day, that's all."

"Are-are you sure?"

"Yeah, ok? I think we should just sit on it maybe." They sat on the merry-go-round together, shifting to the right indefinitely. "But like I was saying with reincarnation, how is it fair if you're not aware of the bad choices you made in a previous life? What if you end up as a bug and someone squashes you just because you were a bitch or an outright bastard in a previous life—a previous life that you don't even remember?"

"Is-is that how that w-works?"

"Yeah, I think." They both sat there a while, soaking in the moment together. Some flowers had burst through the cracks of the old concrete. There were pink ones, white ones, yellow ones, and purple ones. "It's good we got out. We got some air and exercise. I've been feeling really tired and off lately."

"Off?"

"Scatter-minded."

"L-like me?"

"Yeah, I guess. Come, let's check out the slide." They leaned on each other and helped each other up. Neela went down the slide but got stuck at a curve by the friction. She scooted herself the rest of the way down and invited Azure to come with her this time. Neela sat on his lap and they went down together, getting stuck together too. "Or maybe we get stuck like this when we die," said Neela. "Maybe there's no up or down, Heaven or Hell. Maybe when we die, we float around among the living as ghosts or spirits. But then, what about my birth dad and my brother? The worlds they died on no longer exist. Are they just floating aimlessly in space? Did they follow us here on the spaceship or something? How does that even work? Can we ever see them or talk to them again or are we separated forever by an invisible wall? That's like a Hell in itself: to be trapped between planes of existence. It's like a prison. An eternal prison. That's not right either. What do you think should happen when we die, darling?"

"We should all g-go to H-Heaven."

"The murderers, serial-killers, thieves, and rapists too? Don't good people deserve to be safe from them? Or *are* there even 'good people'? Can people be made good? And would it be right to force them to be something they're not? That's like forcing someone to be a boy when they want to be a girl or bleaching a pink-skinned Malkuthian to make them beige-skinned. You can't force goodness or badness on people, can you? Or can you?"

"M-maybe if they knew… b-better…"

"Yeah, like if our culture were better, if our education system were better, society might be better, and people might be better, right? We are born as we are but become what we're taught. That's what I believe. We should be teaching the children to do good, to care about things and each other. Hopefully, they'll grow up to be leaders who care about things and each other. There's still hope for us yet."

The news announced that another planet-sized Dragon had been killed by a Resolver superweapon. Several Union worlds and star systems were erased in the process.

"ATHENA IN COMMAND"

Athena emerged from a pile of Cyclops corpses, leaning against her spear. The bodies were torn and riddled with Union bullets and holes from beam-rifles. She shook one of the lieutenants, urging him to get up but it was futile. *It's merciful that you've all died here rather than by Dragon hands.*

The sounds of war still reverberated even though the fighting had moved onward. There were explosions in the distance. Athena telepathically contacted her remaining Cyclops and Centaurs, ordering them to fall back and reform. Malevant, still recovering from his duel with Diamond on Kanopos, tormented Athena with a psionic attack, urging her to rescind that order. She tossed her helmet to the ground in an effort to cope with the pain. "If we press forward, we'll be slaughtered with no chance of success!" she argued. "If we reform on the right—"

Malevant struck her with another psionic attack. "When I say 'bark,' you will bark, Athena."

"You… bastard… "

"I know where your sister is, and I have your uncle. Would you care to be the last of the Olympians, Athena? I am sick and tired of waiting."

"No!"

"You are my shield and my battering ram. We will form on your right and you will continue to draw their fire."

After a third psionic attack, Athena reluctantly submitted and ordered her forces to halt the retreat. Just as she regained her concentration, a mega particle beam fired in her direction, and she raised her Aegis Shield to tank it.

From her left, a burst of Starfire struck the particle beam, sending it off-course. It exploded a thousand paces away. Athena caught her breath as she looked up to find Amaterasu hovering above her, her eyes glowing and her hand smoking from having delivered the Starfire Blast. "It's you..." said Athena. "Thanks."

"Olympian Commander, we need your help up ahead! Can you bring your forces forward any faster?" Amaterasu urged.

"Are your forces still fighting?"

"Our Yokai and Oni were being cut down like grass. They're stuck behind a ridge up ahead. I believe we can still swarm and overwhelm the Malkuthians with a second wave if you can bring your people forward! The big one-eyed ones, perhaps!"

"My Cyclops know how to forge weapons. They weren't trained to fight with them until this all started."

"It has been the same for us. We must do what we must do."

"The Dragons will form on our right, flying-cavalry first. We can attempt a surge toward the taller buildings together, but we need to time it perfectly. Head for those two tall buildings. We'll converge there. You should hear my voice in your head giving you the signal. Use that attack of yours as cover."

As the Dragons appeared through their Black Gates, Athena gave the signal. Amaterasu gathered power from the nearby sun and fired it down at the Malkuthian artillery. While not devastating them, it was greatly distracting and served as a decent diversion. The Cyclops and Centaurs of Gaia emerged from behind the rubble and ditches and followed the charge of the Tengu, Yokai, and Oni of Ame-Tsuchi.

The Malkuthians in their exo-suits unleashed the fury of their guns.

Thousands of Athena's and Amaterasu's warriors were mowed down. Ultimately, yet another wave of Gaian and Ame-Tsuchi forces was stopped dead in its tracks, pinned between the Malkuthians and the Dragons who pressed them to move forward. Athena ordered her warriors to get behind any cover they could find and to proceed slowly. Seeing that they were now in range, she also ordered her Centaurs—terrific archers—to let loose a volley to cover an advance. Some of the arrows were made of the same adamantine metals that the Dragon weapons were made with, so they did some damage.

The ground shook. Three Grand Fortress Mechs, each around 2,000 tons, approached through the very passage that Athena was hoping to use to breach the Malkuthian defenses. One of the mechs had fired the mega particle beam that Amaterasu had deflected earlier and was preparing to fire another one. The two Grand Fortress Mechs around it fired smaller particle beams in a flurry. Athena dodged, blocked, and deflected them away.

"Keep the ones on the left and right busy! Leave the middle one for me!" said Athena to Amaterasu, sprinting around the group of mechs to try to get an angle on them.

"Do not presume to tell me what to do, Amazon!" said Amaterasu.

"Do it or your people and mine are dead!"

Amaterasu gathered more energy from the nearby sun in both hands and fired it separately at the two surrounding mechs. Athena threw her spear and struck the center mech in its radar, causing it to lose visibility. While its crew was in disarray, Athena shot the radars of the other two mechs with her Epirus Bow. "They're blind now! Can you make one of those fireballs hover between these machines?" she asked Amaterasu telepathically.

Amaterasu reluctantly obliged, creating a miniature star between the mechs, which confused their sensors. One of the mechs started to shoot at the mini star, striking the others in the process. Athena used this time to pry open the top hatch of the lead mech. She fired her Epirus Bow five times into the cockpit. The shots exploded like bombs and killed all but one of the crew. She then used her powers of hypnotic persuasion to manipulate the weaker mind of the lone remaining operator, turning the mech's weaponry on the others until all three were rendered inoperable.

As the battle turned, the Dragons and their collaborator armies began to overwhelm the Malkuthian defenses around the main city. At such close range, the Malkuthian artillery was less effective.

King Yama and his terrifying Oni pounced on the opportunity to do what they'd loved doing in their realm: torturing lost souls. They came upon weak, wounded, or stranded Malkuthians and proceeded to brutalize them, laughing and celebrating as they did so with a fervor that rivaled the Dragons themselves. Athena witnessed this as she charged ahead of her Gaians and was troubled. "What are your red monsters doing?" she asked Amaterasu. "They're wasting our time! We need to converge on those two tall buildings!"

"This is what they do," the star Kami explained.

"Command them to stop!"

"I cannot reverse their nature. This is why the Dragons keep them—and us—alive."

Athena ran by the horror show and breached the main city with her warriors. She hurled her spear and fired her bow at the backs of the retreating Malkuthians. The Dragons grabbed the tails of the fleeing Malkuthians and dragged them away to be butchered. Athena caught sight of a wall of waiting Malkuthians soldiers and artillery who'd reformed around the rally point. She thought to find a way around them when Dragon flying-cavalry swooped down, raining a barrage of elemental blasts down at them.

"THE DRAGON COUNCIL"

In the universe of the Dragons, at the center of Ain's great cosmic web, streams of energy moved through the darkness from numerous portals. The planets of the Dragons were colossal in size and numerous. Most of the inhabited ones had been molded by the Dragon Queen herself, and some were unusual both in size and shape—cubes and polygons. Others were like sculptures, crafted by the one that had crafted the beautiful yet terrifying Dragons. Ain had formed fiery spheres, some might call 'stars,' out of pure life energy, forming purple, pink, and green ones not found in any other universe. They hung like gemstones, decorations, in the blackness of space. All revolved around the Queen.

Billions of trumpets sounded, announcing the return of Lord Zeon.

"Hail, Lord Zeon, the conqueror of the Lapiths, the Centaurs, the Cyclops!" heralded a voice.

"Hail, Lord Zeon, the conqueror of the Celestial Olympians and Titans!" heralded another.

"Hail, Lord Zeon, the conqueror of the worlds of Set, and Horus, and Anubis!" heralded a third.

This heralding lasted for quite some time. Billions of attendants paved a bridge for him as long as a star system.

Zeon came into the direct presence of Ain, and said, "PRAISE AND GLORY BE TO YOU, GREAT QUEEN. MAY YOUR GLORY EMANATE THROUGH THE OMNIVERSE FOREVER AND EVER."

"SPEAK, REPORT, LORD ZEON," said Ain.

"WE HAVE CONQUERED DOZENS OF MORE WORLDS IN NEW HEAVEN. GENERAL MALEVANT HAS DEFEATED THE ENEMY'S MOST POWERFUL WARRIOR AND IS RECOVERING."

"Lord Zeon, why are you dragging your feet through the sand?" Samael, the devil, interrupted. He flared his wings out wide to appear larger. "Lord Baladan's death should have been a wake up call to all of you! You must take that Cosmic Wall in the center!"

Prince Be'elzebul held Samael around the waist and rubbed his back calmingly.

"WHY IS THIS WEAKLING EVEN HERE?" said Lord Zeon to Queen Ain. "HE IS NO LONGER NECESSARY."

"Oh, but I am," said Samael. "I always will be. See, I've shown the great Queen how to channel life-energy in the old way. But things may change. Something—someone—has arrived on Earth, and the kings under my sway have failed to kill him or to poison his bloodline before the ordained time. One of his missions is to sever the ties between myself and God, Yahweh, and thus cut the abilities of all fallen Cherubim. The streams of life-energy will close, and even the all-powerful Queen would eventually die."

"THIS IS PREPOSTEROUS!" said Zeon. "WHAT GOD IS GREATER THAN THE QUEEN OF THE DRAGONS? HOW CAN THE IMMORTAL QUEEN DIE?"

"EXPLAIN, SAMAEL," said Ain.

Samael readied his throat. "You see... a long time ago, before either of you—any of this—existed, the God before all gods loved me. And in one measly act of appreciation, he told me that he would rather give up his first creation, his son, before ever dreaming of taking the powers of his beloved spiritual beings, mainly myself. I coaxed him into this promise with shows of affection & adoration. He is a being who loves himself, but above all, I must admit, he is a being of his word. This I know. But now his son has come to Earth. Yeshua, Jesus, is his name. Not a king, not a general, but a carpenter! My time is short. Do you hear what I'm saying?! If New

Heaven does not fall soon, if the back gates of Heaven are not exposed, any attempt on the throne of God will fail. And if the life-streams close, there would be no life-force outside of Heaven. All the rest of the Omniverse, even Ain, would perish. How ironic would that be? That the one they call Death would die?"

"BLASPHEMY! THIS IS FOOLISH TALK!" said Zeon. "THIS YARN-WEAVER HAS USED WORDS TO TWIST OUR WINGS BECAUSE HE KNOWS THAT HE AND HIS ARMIES ARE TOO WEAK TO ACCOMPLISH THE FEAT THEMSELVES. WHO IS LIKE AIN? WHO CAN FORGE THE PLANETS AND THE STARS AT WILL? WHO ELSE CAN RENDER SPACE AND TIME WITH A THOUGHT? WHAT OTHER BEING CAN BLINK UNIVERSES OUT OF EXISTENCE?"

"I know of such a being..." said Samael. "And I told you! I told you all! I told you continuously to take New Heaven quickly! Because as it stands now our invasion will not succeed. Opening that back gates would doom us all."

Billions of trumpets sounded, announcing the return of Lord Mortimer.

"All hail, Lord Mortimer, the conqueror of the Devas and Asuras!" said one herald.

"All hail, Lord Mortimer, the subjugator of the Asgardians, the Giants, the Elves, and the armies of the dead!" said a second.

The heralding lasted, again, for some time.

Mortimer slithered between a long procession of attendants. He bowed before Ain and addressed her appropriately.

"SPEAK, REPORT, LORD MORTIMER," said Ain.

"I HAVE HEARD ALL THAT YOU HAVE SPOKEN," said Mortimer. "SEEING AS HOW ZEON HAS *ALREADY* BORROWED SOME OF LORD GIGATHETA'S FORCES, WHY DOESN'T HE BORROW SOME OF MINE TO EXPEDITE THE INVASION?"

"MY ARMIES WILL TAKE NEW HEAVEN ALONE, MORTIMER!" said Zeon. "YOU WILL NOT TAKE THIS GLORIOUS VICTORY FROM ME."

"ALREADY STRETCHED SO THIN AS YOU ARE NOW? HOW MANY ARMIES DOES IT TAKE TO OCCUPY ONE GALAXY?"

"TWO GALAXIES. AND GENERAL MALEVANT HAS NEVER FAILED."

"HE WOULD SUCCEED QUICKER WITH THE AID OF MY FORCES," said Mortimer.

"LED BY WHO?" said Zeon. "THAT COWARD, THAT DISAPPOINTMENT. GENERAL DEEM?"

Mortimer was about to speak when Ain spoke first. "LORD MORTIMER," she said. "DEEM HAS ALWAYS BEEN A DISAPPOINTMENT TO ME. FOR ALL I'VE BLESSED HIM WITH, WHAT HAS HE AMOUNTED TO? THE ENERGY HE GATHERS FOR ME IS PATHETIC & LAUGHABLE."

"WITH ALL DUE RESPECT, GREAT QUEEN, HE DEFEATED THE MOST POWERFUL OF THE ASGARDIANS AND THE MOST POWERFUL OF THE DEVAS. HE FOUGHT THEIR BLUE GOD OF DESTRUCTION FOR 300 YEARS. AND—"

"AND AFTER THAT, LORD MORTIMER, WHAT HAS HE DONE?" Zeon interrupted.

Mortimer quietly gnashed his teeth and considered how he might further punish General Deem for embarrassing him in front of the other Dragon deities.

"Every moment you Dragons delay, the window of opportunity slips further from our fingertips," said Samael.

Be'elzebul stepped forward with an abacus in one hand and an hour-glass in the other, saying, "We have less than 14 cycles before the son of God is to fulfill his mission, and all the channels close."

"Before that moment," said Samael, "Ain must absorb the life-energy of every living being in New Heaven. Before that moment, you Dragons must begin the invasion of Heaven from the rear as my Angels invade from the front. We must seize the throne quickly. And when we do... Ain will reign forever and ever." Samael bowed before the Dragons but then turned to Be'elzebul, sneering as if to say, *"Look at what fools I've made of them."*

There'd been another unscrupulous imp eavesdropping on the conversation between the great Dragons. Loki was there, and he'd used his power of inter-dimensional communication to allow General Deem to hear the conversation. General Deem was flustered.

"I'm guessing that you aren't very happy about what you heard," said Loki. "They fucked you o-ver, they fucked you o-ver. FalalalalaLA!"

"Why do they continue to hold me back? Why won't they send me? After all I've done—"

"Um, hello? Are you deaf? They kinda elaborated on that point quite clearly—and loudly, if I do say. But you know, what I let you hear was quite tame."

"What you *let* me hear?"

"Yes. Because if you knew what I knew—what Queen Ain and the lords thought of you—you'd do something we'd all regret, wouldn't you?"

"No. Vishnu's voice—this voice of reason in my heart—tells me to stay the course, to do my duty, to fulfill my purpose."

"And which duty—which purpose—takes precedence, general? Answer me that. Yes, you're honorable enough to look past your personal desires, but what if you knew that there was something greater even than the objectives your Queen and Lord laid out for you? Your duty to preserve not only them but the entire Dragon race. You *must* realize it by now. If you don't, I can't help you. If you simply do as you're told, you'll be allowing them to continue their path to self-destruction. You should be protecting them, saving them, even if it means saving them from themselves... You know what, great general: Queen Ain's death wouldn't be the end of the Dragon race, would it? Her daughter, your lover, could..."

"That's quite enough, Loki! I am no traitor and never will be. Never imply it."

"Oooh. I love getting under your skin. You know, really, it's scaly and slimy and homely in there. Well, to me anyway," he flicked his wrist. "But the point is, my powers of tel-E-portation are limited by the one constant in the Omniverse: energy. Sure, you and I have the energy to teleport someone—let's say, YOU—to that world, but what about your army? For that, you'd need... more. You have a place to go for that energy, don't you, dear general?"

"Absolutely not. Princess Darna will not dare betray her mother, and I wouldn't dare put her at risk."

"You see, you're not list-ening to me. She'd not be *betraying* her mother, dear general, she'd be helping you and helping her mother in the process—keeping her from making an error that could doom herself & your race. See, Ain is like a spoiled little brat of a child—well, one the size of several universes, I might add. She's stubborn as Helheim. She whines, 'No! NO! I don't wanna! I don't *wanna* do this! I don't *wanna* do that!' And she refuses to accept that conscientious people like you know what's best for her. You, my friend, are that voice of reason. You, my friend, must make the choices the others won't make. Don't lie to Princess Darna, just be honest, tell her our plans and what they mean to Queen Ain. She'll listen. She loves you, doesn't she? I knew a girl like her once: my little dish Sigyn. She'd do anything for you. Anything... if you'd just ask."

"I will not allow you to use your powers of suggestion on Princess Darna. She must help us willingly, but as for my subordinates, I will need your help."

Loki shrugged. "Fine by me," he said. Then he teleported forward in a flash, giggling to himself as he came uncomfortably close to Deem. "Now, when can we get started?" he asked.

There were air-raid sirens in Atlanta City for the fifth day in a row. As the drill commenced, the Watchers instructed the civilians, including Neela, on what to do in case of invasion. "This is a test of the emergency alert system. In the event of an actual emergency, this broadcast would be followed by news or instruction…"

"They told me at work yesterday that the Dragons were on Bhumi," said Neela, clutching Azure's arm so she wouldn't fall in the snow. A winter storm was brewing.

"Wh-where's that?" Azure's breath created a mist in the cold.

"Bhumi's in the Yesod Region. It's the closest they've ever been to here. It's hard not to feel like we're running out of time. It's hard not to feel like the world is ending." She took a breather through her purple scarf, exhaling a cold puff of air that fogged up her glasses.

"I-I'll do… all I can to protect you, Neela. No-no matter what."

"I know you will. I thank you for that. I just… I can't think. I can't focus. All I can think about is the Dragons coming here."

"B-but the army…"

"Chancellor Antares will pull them out before the fighting starts. We'll suffer the same fate as Pankaja, Kanopos, and the others. It's a convenient excuse for Antares to get rid of the worlds that are most problematic to him. Malkuth is the granddaddy of them all. It represents the past and our history: everything he despises. If he could erase and rewrite history with Hod in the center, he would." Neela shook her head. "Between a rock and a hard place."

"Wh-what can we do?"

"Live, Azure. Live as well as possible, I guess. Or try to, at least." The sound of the siren swelled, unsettling the soul. Neela paused and looked around as others scurried through the snow to find shelter. She pointed to the footprints behind them, a big pair and a little pair. "Someone will say two people who really cared about each other came this way before them."

As they waited at the train station in the cold, huddled together, Neela started a game of breathing 'smoke' and 'fire' in the cold air. After she'd breathed her 'smoke' for as long as possible, she challenged Azure to do the same. Their streams intersected, and they both laughed. Neela had to periodically wipe the fog off her glasses. As she did this once, she noticed something peculiar: a small fog crept from Azure's back and shoulders as if from a warm engine. She touched his back. It was warm as a summer day. Before she could ask him about it, he reeled her in and held her, keeping her warm until the sky train came.

That night, Neela received a message over the Network that she was being laid off from her job "due to economic hardships directly or indirectly resulting from the war." When she messaged her employer about this, she got no response. When she called and confirmed her identity, the call was dropped. In the coming weeks, Neela made the difficult decision to drop out of school. Her step-dad's checks from the military stopped coming as well. "Azure," she said, shaking her head in disbelief. "I talked to my mom over the Network today. I think we're losing the home too."

"STARDUST"

With their time in the sky district winding down, Neela wanted to make full use of her favorite spot at the edge of the platform. The pair sat side-by-side as they always did. As the suns set, the sky turned purple, then orange like embers from a fire. Neela reached out with her three-fingered hand as if to grab the suns and hold them back.

"What if we could stop it from setting?" said Neela. "What if we could reverse it all and get it all back? I bet God could do that if he wanted to. My brother would say: 'Would you really want him to? Things happen for a reason; never regret the past. Learn from it and trudge on.' He had to go from foster family to foster family. I guess he had to say goodbye to a lot of people. So, have I. And a lot of homes."

The ten moons of Malkuth and the nebulous gases of the two colliding galaxies filled the sky in a magnificent tapestry. "It looks like cotton candy, doesn't it?" said Neela. "Blue, purple, pink, yellow, orange. Every flavor."

In the lower-city, the clouds and smog obscured much of this incredible sight. The stars still peaked through the colorful, cotton candy gases, but they were faint by comparison.

"The brightest and largest of the stars," said Neela, pointing out into the night sky at an incredibly bright star. "It was called *Aditi*. The Dragons destroyed that one two years ago, but to our eyes, it looks alive and well. Ain't that something, darling? What does that say? Does a part of us continue to live on once we're dead and gone?"

Azure squinted, trying to focus on the star amidst all the beautiful chaos. "That's why the scientists who classified our galaxy named it 'Shekhinah'—it's an ancient word meaning 'the glory of God.' But all of that—all of those pretty colors—that's all death and destruction. All of that is from dead stars. Can you imagine that? It's like ashes. Dust. Stardust. And new things are born from it: new stars, new planets, new life, even us. We are stardust, all of us. Part of us, I believe, will always live on. It can never die; it can never be destroyed. Hey, Azure, do you know how gold and silver are made?"

"No."

"My brother told me that when a star is dying and going supernova, it gets so hot that it forms precious metals like gold and silver. Only a dying star or two colliding stars can create these precious metals. They are forged in flames, violence, and death. Likewise, when a wildfire comes through, it consumes everything it touches. But from the ashes, the soil becomes fertile again, and we get trees, forests—new life. Remember those flowers growing at that decaying playground? A nuclear war all but destroyed this place, and look at Malkuth now. It's a world still buzzing with life. Somehow, some way. That's the miracle of the universe. The miracle of existence. The gift of the new from the old. Someday, someone's going to need to lead the rebuilding of this universe after the Dragons, Antares, or some other evil leaves it in ruins. Could be me. Could be you. Could be our children or grandchildren. I hope they know our history. I hope they learn from it. I hope they make something better from it."

Azure put a windbreaker over her shoulders as he'd noticed she'd been getting cold, having folded her arms over her chest. "Me too," he said, putting his arm around her.

They continued to pack things into boxes until the early morning. Finally, they came to the family photos framed on the wall. One by one they put them between some blankets and sheets. Neela held the picture of her and her biological dad in her hands and stared at it a while. She started to shake holding it and a teardrop fell upon it. "I've had to say good-bye to so much." Azure came over and held her. "So many homes. So many people. It started with him. If he could see me now, I wonder what he'd say."

"G-good girl," said Azure. "He'd s-say you're beautiful, and w-wonderful, and k-kind. A g-good girl. The best he could ever h-hope for."

"You're so fuckin' sweet, Azure, thank you. I block it out a lot thinking it'll just go away, but it doesn't. It never goes away. It lingers like a damn cut that won't fucking heal."

"Would you t-tell me? T-tell me all about it. About th-them. About y-you."

Neela nodded. "I kept you waiting a long time, didn't I? Ok..." she agreed. "Better late than never."

"NEELA'S STORY"

"I have told and written this story a hundred times and more, and each time I become more tired and jaded of it. As I told you before, I lived on Pankaja, a planet that always rained. I lived there with my mother and my father for the first eight years of my life. It's gone now. Erased by the war. Only memories keep it alive. On Pankaja, my mother made a living as a schoolteacher in our town. My father worked as a fisherman. I'll never forget that fishy smell he'd brought home with him every night. Gosh...

It was a confusing time, and most of what I know is from what I read years after the fact. But this is what I always knew: none of us deserved what happened. It *just happened*. In eight years, four different regimes controlled the local government. There was always war between the factions. There were revolutions, coupes, coupe attempts. Every day, bombs and mortars exploded in the middle of bathing, eating, sleeping. Imagine being a child in a time like that. To feel the ground beneath you move like it's none of your business, nobody's business, and you have no control and no choice but to live through it, to adapt.

We tried to be happy, you know?

You see that picture there? That's the first fish I ever caught. My dad took me down to the water every weekend, but I never caught anything until that day. I was about six. Mom would read me stories all the time. I still love books, as you can probably tell. I try to find meaning and escape into them.

It was announced that the Union would finally step in to end the decades of civil strife. We were so excited and optimistic for once. Something would be done.

Then, something happened one day that is still difficult for me to comprehend. I was sitting in my bedroom, reading *Gienah's Wonder*, some silly teen angst story. That's when I saw a bright yellow light shoot through the window as if suddenly a new sun had risen just a mile or two away. I heard a boom louder than all the bombs and mortars in that year put together. My ears exploded. There was ringing. The house moved. I'd been in hurricanes, a few quakes. This was different. This was so much worse. I saw the curtains get blown in. Glass went everywhere, the walls leaned and creaked. We had a simple wood home then. Imagine the structures you trust to hold up when all else fails. Now, imagine them all failing at once. I felt myself stumbling, tumbling, free falling with nothing to stand on, nothing to hold onto. I landed on something, a table or something, and the ceiling above leaned down toward me.

I tried to call for help. I couldn't even hear myself scream, but I knew from the vibrations and hopeless strain in my throat that I was screaming.

I feared the rest of the ceiling and perhaps the whole home would cave in and crush me, so I fled out a gap in the wall. I looked around for anyone. I smelled smoke and fire. My eyes began to sting. Dust was everywhere. Rays of light like the Pankajan sun pierced through the smoke. But it was no sun. As I stepped nearer to it, I saw it was something like an orange bulb, a plume rising higher and higher, cascading upon itself. Then I realized the truth: one of those bombs the Union boasted about had been used near our town.

I ran toward the schoolhouse through the smoke and fire and debris, but I hit many obstacles—roadblocks of cars and carts and people along the way. Things became clearer. My hearing returned. Oh, God, my hearing returned to hear the screams and wailing of the wounded and dying. Somehow, I hardened my heart enough to ignore the limbless, blistered bodies of other victims to find my family. I looked at them—the victims—like one looks at the homeless: trying not to let the sight of them touch me, trying not to feel bad because there was nothing I could do. Suddenly, the Union military was up ahead. I saw their tanks, their mechs, and their other armored vehicles. The sight of them was terrifying. There were soldiers in cybernetic suits and gas masks with guns much larger than those the factions used. I lost my courage then, and I fled. I fled to the nearest cellar—I think I shoved and squeezed my way through, slipped between the large legs, bodies, and tails of the adults. I felt claustrophobic and sick. How damn cramped it was, like sardines in a can. I could feel everyone, hear their breathing. We could barely move. It was dark because someone had eclipsed the small light, and the ceiling dripped. I feared we might suffocate or drown down there.

The others debated what had happened and what to do next. They argued and fought—physically bit, scratched, and beat each other until someone shouted: 'shut up!'

We heard the heavy footsteps of the mechs, the creaking of gears, the treads of the tanks rumbling over us. Then there were footsteps, more fluid footsteps, like people above. And we heard a male voice shout to us in a language I didn't understand then. He was shouting something into the cellar in Atlantan, but most of us didn't speak it.

The soldiers banged on the cellar door. Everyone inside started to panic. Someone swore in Pankajan back at them. The cellar burst open and Union soldiers in protective suits pointed their large guns at us shouting in broken Pankajan, 'Up hand! Up hand! Out! Out! Out!'

'Don't shoot!' the person next to me shouted.

'Fucking imperialists!' someone else shouted.

The Union soldiers shouted again and again for a guy named 'Svalocin.' I only learned later that Svalocin had been a leader of one of the factions fighting for Pankajan independence.

Someone who knew Atlantan finally stepped out of the cellar explaining that Svalocin wasn't there, only survivors of the blast.

They started pulling everyone out at gunpoint, shining bright flashlights in our faces as if the light from the blast and the smoke hadn't already darn near burned our eyes out.

Before we knew it, they chased us at gunpoint into these large, covered trucks. I heard some screaming, which seemed more pronounced than the others, and I saw a burn victim, a Tarbosaur boy, in the process of being pried from his parents and placed in a separate truck.

'It's okay!' said our interpreter. 'They need to quarantine the burned and injured. They want to take us somewhere safe. They said there'll be food, water, shelter, and records to help find our families.'

My hopes rose as I heard that. In the end, the parents of the burn victim were hauled off to God-knows-where because I never saw them again. We, on the other hand, were driven over swampy terrain and unloaded to a large, tented area. We were made to wait in a long line, three columns wide and infinitely deep. Sometimes I see those lines at the store and for some reason I chuckle at the reminder. But I know I shouldn't. The sound of mortars and bombs echoed from the distance, and it started to rain again.

They asked us our names, our birth dates, our original home addresses, contacts, and the names of our relatives. I was eight, Azure, from a town of fishermen and rice-farmers. How was I to know my identification number, my zip code, that sort of stuff?

Then I heard a male's voice say from behind the registry table, 'Neela? Did the girl say her name is Neela?' The man was prominently uniformed with military distinctions and all. 'I am Major Eridanus,' he said in heavily-broken and accented Pankajan. 'I think I know where your mother is. Let me show you to her.'

He tried to take my hand, but I withdrew. 'It's okay,' he said, 'don't be afraid of me.' He escorted me under an umbrella to a separate large reception tent. I heard my mother's voice shout my name several times. She ran to hug me, and I ran to hug her. We collided. I think I felt it, the impact. You don't think about those things until it happens to you.

But another arm and another hand went behind my back, and another arm and another hand went behind my mother's. I looked back at the figure, hoping that it was my father. I was disappointed to see that it was the Major holding us both with near-tears in his eyes.

How rude and strange, I thought, to interrupt a family moment.

'I'm sorry,' he said, 'I'm so, so sorry."

My mother turned and nudged him away before slapping him. I was shocked. 'You did this!' she accused. 'You're responsible! You used that damn bomb on us! How could you use that damned bomb on us?! You killed him! You killed my husband! You destroyed everything! That's all you do! You take and take and take and destroy and kill!"'

The Major defended that they were all following orders and that they had no choice. He explained, as he did many times to us afterward, that the bomb was used to neutralize what they perceived to be a greater threat posed by Svalocin's followers. The freedom fighters had supposedly threatened to use a similar weapon on a Union military base. We'd been caught in the crossfire of something we weren't even a part of again. The people suffered so much. Major Eridanus told me that if it were his choice, he would have found another way, another solution, a diplomatic one.

I remember my mother shouting, 'Bullshit! Bullshit! Why don't you go fuck off with the other pigs? Don't fucking come at me and talk to me again, you hear?! Come, Neela,' she said, trying to pull me away.

'Mama,' I said, pulling back, 'does the army man know where papa is?'

My mother shut her eyes and shook her head.

'Then he died, didn't he?' I figured. I still can't believe how casually I said it.

'Don't you say that, Neela, it's not true," my mother told me.

'Mam,' said the Major, taking off his hat. 'I wanted to offer you and your daughter a safe place away from here. In a matter of days, this too will be a warzone. The whole province could be bombarded by either side. We have a school in the works for refugees, and I understand you're a teacher. Your daughter's life doesn't need to be put on hold. We can do what we can to assuage this terrible situation. For her sake. For her future. She could still have a safe home and an education, and you could still have a job.' I felt like a rope in a game of tug-a-war.

My mom refused to leave until she could confirm what had happened to my dad, but the major told her that the lagoon was near the epicenter of the blast with virtually no chance of survival. The lagoon itself had evaporated. He tried to whisper to her so I couldn't hear such terrible news, but my mother fought him, and I overhead as he raised his voice.

I had such strange thoughts as he said that. I thought, well, if the lagoon blew up wouldn't the rain fill it again so my dad could drive the boat back home in the new water? I didn't know what I was saying or thinking or asking then. It was all a fog. The dam up north had been heavily damaged by the blast or something. We were swept up by the tide of panic the Union soldiers roused us into when they said the dam would burst and drown us all if we didn't relocate.

My mother wanted to send me off and stay to die on Pankaja as my father had. But the Major looked after what was best for me and took my mother by force onto the starbus, though she hit, scratched, bit, and screamed at him for it. I was eventually able to calm her before she could go even more insane and release the cargo hold, freezing us all to death. The Major had arranged a special passage with him as extended family or something on the way to the planet Bhast, a dry and rocky planet where we were supposed to be treated 'like royalty.' I'd never flown in a starbus or spacecraft before. I'd never lived in one of these high-tech advanced houses until then. Food was supplied and provided. The Major looked after us always.

On Bhast, the temperature averages between 90 and 110 degrees. I think it had something to do with the star system or something like our nearness and angle to that particular sun was unique. I missed the moisture, the tall trees, the animals on Pankaja. I missed my dad most of all.

Bhast was like a 180-degree difference from home, so to speak. It was the Major's home planet. He told me that in the old days, before he was born, it was even hotter. It was so hot that the colonists came wearing special cooling suits. Then, terraforming and climate management made it livable. But as you probably know, they aren't perfect.

He took us outdoors all the time. I kind of dreaded it. You're always thirsty there, and all you really want is some shady trees to lay under with some water, you know? But after a while he realized that us fish-out-of-water people were miserable out, so he brought along this self-insulating cloud-umbrella thing that followed us everywhere. It was really cool. I think there are newer models now too, but they're expensive. We went rollerblading and biking. He bought us some skates and bikes. But what I remember most was hiking. Bhast is hot and sandy, but I guess there was a lot of beauty to be found there. There is beauty everywhere. The sand, I remember so clearly, was like orange embers. There were giant stone structures that cascaded into the sky.

Once, we climbed a volcano, a dormant one. I don't remember the name. But it was huge, and the hike was exhausting. Lots of stairs and tunnels.

We'd brought a new friend from my school, an older boy named Aodhfionn, along with us that time. I remember as the Major sped on ahead of us, Aohdfionn continued to encourage and share water with us. There were times when I didn't think I could take another step, but then he put his head under my arm and carried me the rest of the way. The scenery at the top took my breath away. I'd never felt more accomplished in my life. I was surprised to find it so green and lush in the caldera. It must have been the greenest spot on the whole planet. I guess, in a weird way, that was my rebirth, my new genesis. Aohdfionn told me that even something terrible like a volcano—as destructive as it is—opens doors to a new future, a fresh start. That soil was made more fertile by the same volcanic fires that engulfed the old land. Nebulae are repopulated by supernovas. It was at that moment that I realized a new future had been blown wide open for me as well. My ninth birthday came and went. I was back in school.

My mother would stay awake and cry for dad night after night. I could hear it through the walls, through her bedroom door. She began drinking a lot. It got so bad that the Major froze her credit to prevent her from spending it on alcohol, and put locks on the cupboards. Their relationship was not perfect. My mom could be mean too, especially as she began having withdrawals.

One day, she left the door partially open as she was crying. I stepped right in and hugged my mother around the head for a second or two. 'I wish you wouldn't be so sad, mama,' I said. Then in a matter of seconds, something eerie occurred. Her crying stopped as if someone had flipped a light switch in her head. She looked blissed out like she'd been hypnotized. She wiped her tears and smiled, and she said in her most shockingly jolly tone, 'Hi, dear! Thanks for the hug. I guess I really needed it. Hey, you know what? Let's go call the Major and see if he can reopen our credit so we can get some ice cream. What do you say?'

She called the Major up like some hyperactive schoolgirl and told him she was feeling happy and excited and wanted to have dinner. At first, I guess, he must have assumed drug use, but he seemed to come around in giving her the benefit of the doubt later. For a while, I pondered what had brought about this change.

Now, the Major slept in a separate bedroom on an upper floor. He also asked for the door to be left open and the lights to be left on. I asked him why and he admitted that he'd always had trouble sleeping, what I later learned was called insomnia. I guess he also had a little anxiety about being left alone at night. He had nightmares and night terrors all the time, much like you. He'd wake up screaming and sweating and shaking.

I had an idea. I told him to let me give him a hug before he went to bed one night. I did, a normal hug around the waist and shoulders, but he still struggled to sleep that night. The next night I hugged him like I'd hugged my mother, around the head rather than the shoulders. He slept like a log that night. Meanwhile, I felt like I'd just run three laps around the gym. Then I realized that something had changed in me. Something about my touch could cure people. And what's more: I felt like something inside my head was *alive* and *hungry*.

I started school again when I turned nine. It was a school for the refugees of various wars and conflicts across the Union. My mother was one of my six teachers.

She was my reading and writing teacher. There were many other students, over 300, in our small school. Some of them were very troubled. Most were just regular everyday kids. It was always craziness because of the few bad apples. But the person I remember the most from that time was my brother, the brother I gained: Aohdfionn.

He was a brawler. He was a fighter. Everyone who challenged him after school or at recess got beat to a pulp. Still, my mother and I had trouble labeling him as a troublemaker. See, respect was big for him, and whenever someone disrespected him, me, or my mother, he would grab 'em by the collar or arm and put 'em in their place.

I had some bullies then. I think they blamed Ceratosaurs like me for their losses, for the imbalances in society. They also thought I was a bit of a teacher's pet. For a while it was tame stuff, like they'd close the door before I came into a room or call me 'horn nose' or 'Cerato-privileged.' Later, they started spitting and throwing things at me. They tripped me a few times. Finally, one of them outright hit me. Even left some bruises.

But Aohdfionn saw it happen, and he was pissed. He beat the living shit out of the guy, asked him how it felt to be hit. I feared for the other person who'd just beaten me. I stopped Aohdfionn, I grabbed his arm and told him, 'enough, Aohd!'

We became best friends that day, and my mother and the Major invited him over after learning what he'd done. Now, if you recall, I was a very shy person then. I rarely talked, and when I talked I used to lisp. I'd lisp even worse than I do now. A lot worse. Now, to have a new friend I could talk to was a new and interesting thing for me.

He was very thoughtful, and not just for someone who was so brutish. He was one of the smartest people I knew. He had so many thoughts on politics, philosophy, and religion. He loved history. Hell, he made me fall in love with those things. He read so voraciously that it was almost like he was searching for something: answers. I have lots of his books still, as you can see. I mean, they're not collegiate by any means, but they are interesting and pretty dense for a twelve-year-old like him to have been reading. I guess he got me into that stuff at a young age.

I spent a lot of time with him over the course of six years. He was not only my best friend, but I loved him... I loved him very much. I admired his outgoingness, his depth, his toughness, his courage, and his wisdom. I admired his willingness to stand up and speak out and fight—to risk it all—when I was such a shy, cowardly child.

He taught me how to fight, to wrestle, to grapple, how to throw a punch, a kick, and so on. We shared a lot of sweat and some blood too. There was something between us that was so confusing then for me, but all I know is we both felt *something*. I wish I could feel it again sometimes. Feel him there.

I remember I went into a little phase by the time I was 12. I dieted. I worked out a lot. I thought about getting surgery to remove my horn, lift my face, cut some fat—everything. Yet I remember all that did was bring tension between Aohdfionn and me. He hated what I was doing to change myself. He hated the pills, the lotion, the makeup, the perfume. He hated them because, I realized, he loved *me*.

Major Eridanus took a liking to Aohdfionn. They got along well. They discussed the news, the economy, and politics together constantly. It was like a competition, the Major trying to challenge him. I couldn't keep up with the complexities of their discussions and debates back then. I think I kinda can now.

I was juggling so much. See, my mother had already been struggling to teach me to read and write better since I was a kid in Pankaja. Funny, now I was still speech-impaired and trying to learn the universal language, Atlantan. It's strange how such a little problem would follow me into what felt like a completely different life. How ironic that she'd been the most literate person in our community yet her only daughter was a mute shell. She asked me if it would be ok if I was registered for a special program that catered to my needs. One of the lead teachers was a speech pathologist. They could help me improve my social skills or whatever, so I said ok.

I made a friend there named Sari who struggled even more so than I did. She mixed up letters and words. Everything to her was jumbled. She couldn't even read or write in her own language. I talked to her about her dreams and ambitions, how ironic that someone like that little un-ambitious me would continue to ask that of others. She wanted to be a starcraft pilot. A darn pilot, Azure! Do you know how much reading a pilot needs to do? So, she tried. She started with comics and magazines, little things, but it was like it just wasn't coming. Her mind would wander. So, I asked her if she'd like to try something. I told her to trust me. I put my hands around her head, and like magic she was able to read.

In a few months, she was moved to a normal class. But something haunted me: she now knew what I could do. She knew that I could help these people, our classmates, our friends. She pestered me, 'why don't you just cure them too?' she said, 'come on, why don't you?'

The truth is, since I began healing people, I'd experienced enormously painful migraines at night, and it worried me that I might have a disease or be killing myself or something. And I was afraid that the government would find out. Even now, in the privacy of this home, I'm afraid. My step-dad told me to never use my powers in public, to keep it a secret or the government would take me away to run all sorts of experiments on.

I was scared.

Then something happened that forced my hand. Two students from our school, a popular couple, were in an accident. Apparently, the collision-proof/auto-stop sequences on both cars had worked well, but the speed of the vehicles caused those inside to sustain injuries anyway.

They said it would have been like getting punched by a heavyweight boxer or something a hundred times, cushioned or not.

The girl was left in a coma. The boy was brain dead with no hope of regaining consciousness.

The whole school, the whole town held a vigil for the two. Everyone was in tears. And Sari gave me this stare from the crowd—this stare that said, *'do something or I'll tell.'*

So, I came to the hospital late one evening, when only the boy's mother remained. I remember the flowers and stuffed animals and balloons. I told the mother my name and told her... the truth. I made her promise that she wouldn't tell anybody what I could do. I put my hands on the boy's temples and in a few seconds his eyes sprung open, he gasped. I collapsed feeling as though I'd run two miles. I drank hungrily from the water fountain afterward.

I was so proud of what I'd done and accomplished, I'd reached a high, yet I was daunted by the thought that I was obligated to bring the girl back too. And I did. I brought her back. The two lovers had a tender reunion. I had a fever the whole night, but I saved two lives and changed many more.

It was around that time that my mother and the Major married in a small ceremony attended only by me and Aohd. I couldn't believe the two of them could ever be so happy after all they'd been through.

During my conversations with Aohdfionn, I learned about his abusive home situation. He said that his foster parents constantly beat him with things. I was abhorred by this and begged my parents to do something about it. From what I gathered, they had social workers go to check up on the home. This was my best friend, a friend to my entire family, and there he was suffering in our midst. By some turn of events, my parents decided to adopt Aohdfionn as a son. My best friend, my love, was now my brother. I was a teenager.

For a long time, I didn't know what to think about that. How would you feel? What would you think? What? To fight it? To allow it? Let it happen. What would the alternative be?

It's funny. When it was official, I treated him differently. I... I ignored him for a long time until my mind could wrap itself around it.

But then I thought: we're not blood, in fact, he was adopted, technically, by my step-dad. So, he was like a step-foster-brother. I think it was while I was overthinking things that he got a hold of me and kissed me. That answered everything for me.

But we were in the midst of a greater war and a new age, another chapter in the Great Alien Race Wars. The age of the World Enders. We'd come into conflict with the city-destroying Geburans. We fought them, in space, in the sky, and on the ground. My brother predicted that he would be drafted. Soon after, he was. There was no fighting the system. There was no choice. He would serve in the army.

You know, I prayed for him every day. I watched the news with one eye open, and even then, I kept it partially covered like some frightened child. The Geburans and the Collective were scary enough, but the next enemy we were at war with, the Davrons, were something else. They had machines and warcrafts like ours, but it was said they could also manipulate time itself to fit their ends. The media initially told us that the Union armies were trapped in a mysterious, almost-supernatural loop, fighting the same battles with the same enemies continuously. I thought of my brother, how he might be trapped there.

The media flipped the story in the coming days and said it had been resolved. I guess even the time continuum itself unravels when you introduce enough chaos into the system. They said a Malkuthian soldier was worth ten Davrons. They said the Davrons were just flying, driving trash cans with weapons and time-manipulation technology. They said our weapons were just so much more advanced than theirs. They said we were winning again, and we were.

My brother was awarded medal after medal, everything you see on that wall and more. He was promoted up the ranks until he was a captain. They hyped him up as some sort of an icon, a living legend, a supersoldier, a superhero. Even now I hear about him, even from people who hate me. They speak highly of him. They said he'd probably killed 12,000 Davrons by himself. There are stories that he cracked open their armor like they were eggshells with his bare claws. That he commandeered one of their weapons and vaporized a whole bunch of them with it. This boy I knew.

This person. It was difficult to believe. I was proud, but... I remember other people in my school in mourning over the friend—the brother—the father they lost in the war. It made me think and wonder and worry. A number of things. Mostly for him.

It's funny... all the big, important things I remember yet I forget the exact time and circumstance when I learned my brother had died. I hear it is the opposite for some people, like the memory is so clear. I shut down, blacked out, whatever. I remember being so mad at myself, hating myself, because I just couldn't cry. I couldn't cry.

Azure came beside her and comforted her, saying the only thing he could say, "I-I'm here. It's ok, Neela." She fell into his chest and arms. "I've got you, I-I've really got you now," he said. "...Hey, Neela…"

"Yes?"

"Have you b-been trying to h-heal me like those other people? Is that why I can talk better? Move better? Remember more?"

"Yes… but every time I try, I am overwhelmed. It drains me. I've healed insomnia, alcoholism, depression, a learning disorder; awoken someone from a coma and another from being brain dead. None of them were like you. Whatever happened to your mind is something deeper and more severe. I keep hoping and I keep trying—"

"D-don't. Please don't, Neela. Not if it h-hurts you. Please."

"It's ok."

"No."

"You do more for me than I think you realize, Azure. I want to know you. Truly. I want to know you too."

"So, like, this Neela has magic then, right?" Aphrodite concluded. "She can, like, totally heal people."

"That explains how the boy hasn't died yet after being shot and stabbed so many times," Susanoo added. "Their knives are as big as swords. Their bullets might as well be cannonballs. That would've killed a mortal easily."

"Well, like, I totally healed him the first time, right?"

Susanoo shrugged. "Where did her ability to heal come from: the blast she experienced as a kid or this living being we sensed inside of her? Both perhaps?"

"Like, why are you asking me? I just know what she does is, like, totally different from me. I tried, remember? I couldn't help him remember a thing."

"You two," Athena broke into their conversation telepathically. "I've been following your discussion. Are you saying they're both magical beings?"

"Uh... yeah..." Aphrodite began.

"The girl, Neela, is capable of healing to an extreme degree," Susanoo elaborated. "She claims to have resurrected a brain dead person. None of us can resurrect the dead or heal a wound that intricate. Not even my sister has the power to do such a thing. And the boy, Azure, has visions of things he couldn't possibly know about. He knows your name, Athena, and mine. He has talked about us and described some of our experiences to the girl, including our struggles with various Dragons. That's not possible."

"It is possible, perhaps," said Athena. "It sounds to me like Apollo's oracle. So, they're both a little extraordinary. But I didn't send you there to find a healer or an oracle. We are banking all of this on one thing: power—power capable of defeating the Dragons. None of you have seen anything of a cosmic or planetary scale from either of them?"

"You mean, like, an explosion?" asked Aphrodite.

"Or a surge of electricity. A quake. Anything like that. Anything that the Dragon leaders can do."

"Besides a little more body heat from Azure, I'd say no," said Susanoo. "I've been sensing Ki energy my entire existence. Both of them are weaker than any Dragon. They're weaker than you and me even despite their greater size."

"So," Athena summarized. "They're just two otherwise-normal Malkuthians with mutant-like powers—one is a healer, one is clairvoyant. So why have you two wasted all this time following them while I've been fighting and killing hundreds of Malkuthians?"

Aphrodite raised her hand like she was in a classroom. "Well, sis, like there's something about them... I, like, feel it in my heart."

"I don't have time for your sentimental shipping nonsense, sis!"

"Heya, I'm not, like, finished. I was gonna say, like, I think there's more to both of them than we know yet. But..."

"Aphrodite is right," said Susanoo. "When we first saw these two, we were not impressed. All we had was a hunch and a name. Now, we have two mutants who keep surprising us day by day. I have a feeling in my gut that we are where we need to be. Both of them... both of them are hiding something..."

"Malevant is getting impatient, but thankfully he is still recovering from his battle on Kanopos," said Athena. "If Azure is who you think he is, then we will prepare for an invasion of Malkuth after this system or the next is conquered. I will stay Malvant's hand as long as possible. And Susanoo... I wanted to tell you that I personally met Amaterasu. We fought beside each other recently."

"Oh, yeah? Fuck her."

"I understand. But I've read her mind... she longs for you to return to her side. She longs for your family to be whole if even just for once. She thinks it would make your father happy."

"Our family can never be whole with so much distrust and corruption."

"Susanoo, there are only a handful of Olympians left in all of creation, my sister and I being two of them. My sister and I haven't always gotten along. We were on separate sides of a conflict more than once. We were enemies fighting on different sides during the Trojan War."

"Hmm..." Loki had begun listening in on their conversation from another dimension. He'd just tricked his brother, Thor, into hiding from the Dragons in a cramped container nearby with no light or air. The all-important body of Diamond levitated nearby, surrounded by a magical containment field conjured by Loki.

"Brother, are they gone yet?" asked Thor.

"Shhhhhhh! I'll let you know, dear, when the coast is clear," Loki replied.

Susanoo looked at Aphrodite in disbelief. She shrugged. "Well, like, yeah. It's true," she said.

"We thought we'd never forgive each other after all that bad blood," said Athena. "But we are blood—the daughters of Zeus through our mothers, Metis and

Dione. We're all that's left of them. And you... you and Amaterasu—your whole family—are running out of time."

"She conspires with those bastard Dragons! Those killers!" Susanoo argued.

"We all do, Susanoo, but only to serve ourselves. We all are fighting to survive. We will do better if we all fight to survive together instead of fighting each other."

"I will not join her. That is my final verdict."

From the other side, Athena looked to Amaterasu, who was listening in but not speaking. Amaterasu shook her head in disappointment and floated away, her eyes and clenched hands glowing with white flames.

"Well, then, I tried," said Athena to the others. "At least I see that you and my sister get along."

Susanoo covered his head in shame with one hand and the comb in the other. "I have found this Azure. I have found the one you were looking for. I have completed my end of the bargain. Change Kushina back."

Aphrodite shook her head, trying to communicate her disapproval to her sister nonverbally. Susanoo caught her and gave her a suspicious stare. Athena considered it. "No," she answered, reading her sister's mind and his. "Not until Malevant is satisfied."

"Damn you!"

"If I change her back now, there is nowhere she can safely live and go. She is human after all. She'll die sitting on that cloud. The Dragons will impale her. The Malkuthians will shoot her. And besides, I know there's something between you and my sister."

"You play your games..."

"I can read your mind, Susanoo. I know you think fondly of Aphrodite. I know that's what's keeping you there."

Susanoo gulped. "Fuck it! Enough!" he urged. As Athena tried to speak, Susanoo gave out another deafening, "ENOUGH!" His shoulders rose and fell with each angry breath. "If your intention from the beginning was to deceive me, then say no more. I am not your puppet! The lying and deception ends here!" He cut the cloud in half with his sword and floated away from Aphrodite on his half.

"So brooding..." Aphrodite fawned.

"And immature," said Athena.

"You, like, totally kept lying to him and pulling him on a leash, sis."

"Because I thought it would make you happy... Now, he knows that when he sees Kushina again, he can never be genuine. He will always have to hide what happened when she was gone. His mind thinks of you, sis, of sprinkling snowflakes down to the planet with you. Give him time."

"There are, like, millions of other guys," said Aphrodite. "It's ok. Have you, like, heard from Thor at all?"

Loki observed Diamond from every angle, laughing maniacally. He sent his astral projections to represent him to Chancellor Antares and General Deem as he analyzed the comatose supersoldier. He removed some of the armor and cybernetic parts, revealing flesh underneath — the flesh of an albino Spinosaur. A damaged, grotesque alligator-like face looked back at him.

"I could activate Diamond's self-destruct sequence from here," said Chancellor Antares. "Of course, you could teleport away, but a stalemate only leaves two losers. In this match of all matches, neither of us can afford that, not with what comes next. What an extraordinary situation we find ourselves in, imp."

"Bumb-pudum-pudum!" said Loki like a trumpet. "Tell us about him, Georgie — not the machine, the man behind the machine. Who is he? I've always wondered. Drop all of the fluff-and-stuff."

"If I answer that question, you will tell me about my daughter. You will tell me where she is and where I can find her."

"You've got yourself a dealie-wheelie, Chancellor!" Loki stroked his chin curiously. "I have a hunch about this being. There is a prophecy floating around that there's this *Grand Conductor of the Omniverse* or something or some shit. I believe he is it. The key to ending our infernal struggle with the Dragons."

"I'll tell you what I know. He was a soldier they called 'The White Flame," Captain Aohdfionn Eridanus. He was one of the greatest soldiers in the history of the Union military, a hero of several wars. With our enhancements, he was able to overcome the Davrons' time-looping abilities. This was accomplished through sheer calculative ability. The more he fought, the more he learned. Trapping him in a time-loop was the worst thing those trashcan aliens could have possibly done. It made him too wise to their game. He knew every move before they made it, every tactic before it could be enacted. But he didn't escape the war with his body in-tact. The energy factory of his heart is all we needed to power the cybernetics and grand arsenal he came to bear. However, despite all our technological advancements, we have yet to replicate what his heart can do. He could drain a large star. We've tested it. As you know, we have Cosmic Walls that serve a similar function, but they are not mobile and easily weaponized like he is. We have yet to clone a second Diamond, but it is not for lack of effort, I assure you."

"Heeheeheehaw! So, he's a catch! Once in a gajillion lifetimes!"

"Now, fulfill your end of the bargain, imp. Where is my daughter hiding?"

"First things first, George! How do I awaken Diamond?"

"You will answer my question as agreed or I will detonate him, imp!"

"Alright, alright, geez... take a chill pill, why don't cha? Your daughter, Autumn, now lives in the Malkuth region. Safe and sound. Safe and sound. In a quaint, quaint big, big, little town."

"On what planet? In what city?"

"How, oh, how do I awaken the white cow?"

"You'll need me to awaken him. He has defaulted to a hibernative state. I can activate him at will through his nanomachines. So, tell me: where is Autumn?"

"Ooooh, I'm not losing my leverage."

Antares activated the countdown for Diamond's self-destruct sequence. "And I'm not giving up mine. You will tell me, or you will die with him."

"Heeeheeeheeeheeeheeee! A standoff! Oh, what fun!"

Antares turned off the sequence with a thought and awakened Diamond. The smile dropped from Loki's face. Diamond crashed through the force field. "Brother dear, your time is now! A great escape we can't allow!"

Thor burst out of his container, the hammer Mjolnier at hand. He fired the strongest thunderbolt he could conjure. Loki likewise fired a Destruct spell from his Elder Staff. Diamond was not at all surprised and countered them both with high-energy blasts of his own. He then blocked a strike of Thor's hammer with a plasma shield and countered with a heavy whip with his armored tail. Thor was floored. Giants hadn't hit so hard. Diamond's entire body began to pulsate with a white flaming aura. Loki teleported away, creating distance. An orb of energy, lying in wait like a landmine, struck him from behind.

Loki's astral projection continued to reach out to General Deem. "I have spoken to Princess Darna regarding—"

"I see, I see you're quite busy, dear," Loki interrupted. "But here, oh, here, I suggest you appear!"

"Is this special Malkuthian truly the one we're looking for?" Deem questioned. "The same one General Malevant is after? Azure."

"Well, how do I put this gently: come see for yourself!"

"DEEM .VS. DIAMOND"

General Deem stood across from Diamond, his Nandaka sword drawn. Diamond revealed his plasma saber. "If you are who Loki says you are, then I have no desire to fight you," said Deem. "You should be on our side."

"How preposterous you would even propose such a thing, Dragon," Diamond rocketed forward, the propulsion creating a shockwave. Deem blocked his first hundred attacks before having to evade. "Remarkable…"

Diamond's aura glowed brighter and grew larger. The roof, wall, and ceilings crumbled, revealing the surface of the moon they'd been fighting on. Streams of energy from nearby stars appeared, flowing to Diamond. The moon itself began to crack and crumble.

> Loki tented his fingers and licked his lips.
> "Brother! What shall we do?" asked Thor.
> Loki conjured a bag of popcorn and a soft drink. "Enjoy the show!"

"I haven't had to tap deeper into my power for a long, long time, Malkuthian," said Deem. He tensed his claws and generated a purple aura around himself. He stretched out his two arms and two more arms appeared, each holding a different weapon. He and Diamond collided, each attacking faster than the eye can see with a barrage of weapons and attacks. Craters formed all over the moon. The remnants of the colony were blown away.

In the middle of their hours-long duel, a Malkuthian fleet appeared complete with dozens of destroyers and thousands of spacecrafts. This brought a pause to the action. A holographic image of Chancellor Antares appeared between Deem and Diamond. "Ah, how fascinating to see!" said the Chancellor. "A Dragon general live and in the flesh. You are surrounded by an entire Malkuthian fleet by the way, in case you haven't noticed."

"I'm not fazed. I have faced far worse, Malkthian," said Deem.

"Oh? You speak our language. How is that possible?"

"Beings called Angels have provided us the languages of many worlds we seek to conquer."

"You can understand me then… fascinating. Other Dragons we have captured simply howl in agony as we dismember and study them. It doesn't make for much conversation. Dragon, I am Chancellor George Antares, the supreme leader of the Malkuthians. That should become more emphatically clear in the coming weeks. You are in my universe now, and all things that are unlike me tend to go extinct in my universe. Ask Loki. He has known me a long time. I doubt you trust him any more than I trust him. He's in it for himself, after all. So am I. What are you in it for, Dragon?"

"I am General Deem, leader of the 3rd Imperial Army and among the race's finest warriors. I loyally serve my Queen."

"That's what all hive-minded beings think. I'm not surprised. And what will you do after we kill her just like all the enemy alien queens we've killed in the past? Dragon, I gather that you're a special being of some sense. Being such, answer me: if your Queen ceased to exist, would you lose your purpose?"

"You have no idea how powerful our Queen is, Malkuthian. She is a being of cosmic proportions. Even your largest and most powerful weapons pale in comparison."

"We've killed two of your Dragon lords. Is she anything like them?"

"There is simply no comparison. It's like comparing a twig to the tree it fell from."

"Really? How interesting your kind is. I admire it."

"There is a lot to admire about your kind as well. I haven't been challenged like this in centuries. I have never encountered such an advanced civilization."

"Answer me this, Dragon: what has Loki told you about Diamond? Why do you seek him with such fervor?"

"As you must know, Loki sees into the future. He believes that Diamond is the true fulfillment of a prophecy: a prophecy regarding the ultimate power in the Omniverse, a being who draws all energy toward itself."

"Indeed. I can see that. And, perhaps, if you could control him as I now control him, you could have the ultimate power for yourself, couldn't you? You could… kill your Queen, perhaps."

"I would never commit such a treacherous act."

"Oh? How fascinating. You imply you are loyal and yet seek after more and more power for yourself. I sense a contradiction—a conflict between what you *say* your convictions are and your actions."

"I seek only after the power to better serve."

"To better serve? Are you a high-ranking military leader or a cheap prostitute? No, no, there's something deeper going on. I can sense it without having even a single nanomachine inside you, I know: loyal to a fault and infinitely unhappy. Loyalty is a trait I admire, Dragon. Diamond is the perfect example of that: programmed to serve my will and only my will. My will now calls for the extermination of all Dragon invaders, and all Dragons everywhere. Including you."

Diamond aimed his Diamond Salvo Beam at Deem who in turn readied his Brahmastra attack in his bow. Just as they unleashed their attacks, Loki conjured an ultimate attack of his own: his Meteor spell. Laughing maniacally, he hurled it down on all of them.

"Loki, what are you doing?!" Deem roared.

"Why, helping you, of course! Aren't I a good chap?"

"You fool! You don't have the energy left to escape the explosion!"

"Oops... Well, would you do me a small favor and lend me some of yours?"

Deem threw a clump of purple energy at Loki who absorbed it. Deem's third and fourth arms disappeared. As the three terrific attacks were about to collide, Deem teleported away. A blinding explosion tore through space, erasing another orbital body.

"LOKI REVEALS HIS PLAN"

Diamond looked around, seeking a target in what appeared to be a distorted dimension of warped colors and shapes.

"Now, now, now," said Loki, appearing alongside Thor. "Would I be so great a magician without some sleight of hand?"

Diamond aimed one of his shoulder cannons at Loki and gathered energy at the end of his tail cannon at Thor. Thor instinctively raised his hammer, but Loki waved his hand down, convincing him to lower it.

"Where are we?" asked Diamond.

"A place, a place, beyond your space. That I have saved, in case, in case…. Heeeheeeheeehahaaaa! This place was intended to imprison my son, Fenrir. Fret not, not even the *great and powerful* Chancellor Antares can detect or control you here. No one can. This is a void. You might as well not even exist to the rest of the Multiverse. Now, now, I intend only to have a civil conversation with you, if you don't mind."

"I could kill you both with ease."

"Oh, yes, I'm sure, you could make us disappear. But then who would let you out of here? Heeheeheehee!"

Diamond powered-down his arsenal.

"Who's a good boy? You are! Listen well, these names I say. Azure. Neela. Will you… play?"

Diamond's eyes lit up.

"Ah, that's it! That's the look of one hit right between the eyes! Memories of a life lost… a life left behind, am I right?"

"You'd best quit while you're ahead, fiend."

"Now, why would I quit while I'm ahead? That's stupidity! You're smarter than that!"

"How do you know about Neela? About Azure?"

"I know everything there is to know, including about you, your universe, and about your master, Antares. I've known him and his ancestors a long, long time. Many of your technologies are based on blueprints drafted in my realm, Asgard. I've been building your civilization up for a long, long, lonely time for a very specific purpose."

"What purpose?"

"Why, to dominate the cosmos for myself, of course! There is no Asgard anymore. Nothing left to rule, anyway. We have the Dragons to thank for that. I knew I would need you someday. There is another megalomaniacal cosmic schemer out there, and I'm not one to be outdone. Some call him the Devil, some Satan, some Lucifer, some Samael. I prefer to think of him tenderly and fondly as 'Sammy.' To make a very long story short, let's say that the Dragons are an extension of his will, and you Malkuthians are an extension of mine. You should be flattered. I'm counting on you. I've been counting on you for hundreds of years—my contingency plan, my fail-safe, so to speak. I must say, so far, you haven't done half bad, especially considering the Dragons have made mincemeat of everyone else. Oh, I'm a little hungry now." He conjured a sandwich in his hand and broke a fourth of it off for Thor, eating the rest.

"You want to defeat the Dragons?" asked Diamond.

"Simply speaking: yes!" Loki answered. "And to defeat the power behind the Dragons too. They cannot be allowed to rule this cosmos. There would be no cosmos left to rule, and where's the fun in that? I have no interest in the deaths of Malkuthians. Why would I? Do I break off my own dick? Do I shoot myself in the head? In the heart, if I had a heart? I mean, I'm batshit insane, but I'm not stupid. Your sensors must detect that I speak the truth. I desire what you desire: the destruction of the Dragons and the continued existence of all Malkuthians. Would you help me?"

"I serve Chancellor Antares."

"Are you aware of the Chancellor's *Beta God Program*? The ability to end and manipulate all lives and weapons in the universe at will? Would you like to see a little recording I made of my previous encounter with the Chancellor?" Loki projected his encounter with Antares in the past. Antares boasted as World Enders destroyed planets and Malkuthians fell dead from the strokes and heart-attacks he'd induced. "The truth hurts doesn't it? The people we look up to aren't always so great in person. 'Never meet your heroes,' or some shit like that. It will only get worse, I promise. Antares wants to create a collective consciousness, a hivemind just like the Dragons and Davrons you fought against. Just like the Collective and even the Infestation of previous wars I'm sure your programming is aware of. You wouldn't even need physical bodies anymore. No. You could become no more than disembodied ghosts kept alive by the AIs, beings that can no longer touch or feel and who serve only one god: the immortal consciousness of *almighty* Antares. Is that the universe you would want to live in? Is that truly what you've fought your whole existence for, Aohdfionn?"

"That name no longer has any meaning for me. I serve the Union. I fight for all Malkuthians."

"And so you shall. Who can blame you? I fight for Asgardians, but there are only two of us left. It's only natural for us to look after our own, isn't it? Antares is an enemy of the Malkuthian people. In time, he'll be as much of a danger to them as the Dragons themselves. Trust me. I can see the future. Every. Possible. One. Your sensors must detect that I am not lying. You have the greatest predictive software in the Multiverse, even the great General Deem struggled to overcome it, despite his immense speed and warrior instincts. You must have been able to sense the way things were going. The Malkuthians under Antares will be a miserable lot."

"If you know so much, fiend, then tell me what you know about Neela and about Azure. Tell me that!"

"With pleasure... I know, I know what's on your *heart*

I know, I know what's on her *mind*..."

"LOWER ATLANTA"

Neela covered her nose and mouth with her hijab as they walked past a seemingly endless line of old tires, beds, furniture, and trash bags, many of which spewed out their contents. Roach-like bugs and rodents scurried about. Some of the roaches even crawled on the backs of the people who dug and sifted through the garbage, and the people didn't seem to mind or care.

Graffiti lined the walls and the boarded-up windows of dilapidated homes and closed businesses. There wasn't a police officer in sight, nor were the Watcher AIs responsive. This was no longer just a bad part of town they were passing through, this was their neighborhood, the place they now called home. The home they'd been forced to leave behind in the sky district teased them from a distance.

Every passing person eyed them out, looking Neela up and down. "Look down and keep walking," Neela instructed. "You've got your vest on, right?"

"Yes," said Azure.

"We're almost there. You'll do great. Just listen and do your best."

They came to a group of about a dozen men and boys gathered around a gate and a fence. They reached through the links and desperately tried to get the Contractor's attention on the other side, telling their sob stories. "Three more!" said the Contractor. "I can take three more!" He looked through the crowd, pointing out his picks. "You! You! And you! That's all! The rest of you, go home, go home. There's no more work for you today."

"Looks like there's a lot of work to do today!" said Neela, surprising everyone as the lone female voice. They all turned to look at her. "How about four!"

The Contractor laughed. "You? Don't waste my fuckin' time, miss."

"Not me," said Neela, pulling Azure forward, "him!"

The Contractor licked his lips and stopped to consider. "A Tyrannosaur..." he muttered.

Some of the rejected laborers erupted in protest and began threatening Neela. One of them marched forward and pushed her. Another grabbed hold of her. Azure instinctively whacked one over with his tail and threw the other clumsily to the ground before almost falling over himself.

The contractor fired a handgun into the air. As a ranking member of the criminal underworld, he held an exception to own a firearm. The small crowd fell silent. "Tyrannosaur, you've got the size and perhaps the strength, but I can see your balance is shit. You're undocumented, aren't you? That makes you expendable. I'll audition you for a quarter of the normal wage."

"Half!" Neela objected.

"Who is this, your mother?"

"We have family too, you fuckin' bitch!" one of the rejected laborers protested.

"I'm the daughter of a colonel in the Union army," said Neela.

"You don't say..." said the Contractor.

"I know you employ undocumented workers. That's a violation of Union law."

"Well, the law doesn't apply to some of us, little miss."

"Well, it seems to me you're only hurting yourself. There's a mass labor shortage due to the war, and I'm sure you're not immune to that. There are about 13 able-bodied people in need of work here, and you've got a deadline to build the projects behind you in a month or so, was it? You know that money is a secondary concern to your boss. You also know what your boss does to people who keep him waiting. They end up in the gutter in a bag in a thousand little pieces. Why don't we get this project done ahead of time? No one needs to go home empty handed, and no one needs to lose a limb or their life to an unhappy crime lord. Sound good?"

"You're one crazy bitch to come down here and talk like that, you know?"

"I get that often."

"Congratulations, all you assholes, you've all got work today thanks to Crazy Bitch, and you're all getting paid like shit thanks to Crazy Bitch. I'm giving you forewarning now: it'd be a better use of your time if you spent the next 15 hours picking corn out of horse shit for your families. But if you want to get your foot in the gate for tomorrow, here's your opportunity. Don't fuck it up."

The group cheered.

"I feel like I kinda just shot us in the foot," Neela whispered to Azure. "But it felt like the right thing to do." She gave Azure a kiss on the cheek. "Good luck," she said.

"What about y-you? Will you be safe?"

"Don't worry, the restaurant's only a few blocks away, I'll be ok," she showed him a switchblade at her waist. "If they shank, I shank back. And I can scream too. I'm loud. You know I am. Everyone knows that."

"Pl-please be careful."

"I promise. Now go do your best."

Azure proceeded to the construction zone: a low-income housing project. The work was physical and grueling. The cold was a welcome treat for Azure as his body temperature continued to increase with effort. As he went about bearing metal and wooden beams on his shoulders, he was pleasantly surprised. Not long ago, he could hardly hold up his own body-weight or stand on his own two feet without support. Being with Neela had made that much of a difference in his life. He still couldn't completely shake the incessant kaleidoscopic vision, but the here-and-now seemed clearer than it had ever been. *Neela… you've been healing me, haven't you? That's why your nose was bloody again the other day. That's why you've had those migraines. I told you to stop.*

As he helped lead a beam into the soil, he had a flash of a vision he'd had of Jesus and his dad, Joseph. "Don't build your house upon the shifting sand," said Joseph, laying two more large stones against his son's. "Build your house on good soil. Then, when the storms come, it will stand firm."

"I build my house upon the rock of my father, God," said Jesus. "He cannot be moved."

"And so you shall, precisely," said Joseph. "You know, before you were born, I was very upset. And then an Angel spoke to me. I was so conflicted and confused then because your mother was pregnant with you. I thought it might be best if we parted ways. But the Angel told me that I should still marry your mother because you—her child—were the son of the Holy Spirit, that which gives everything form and life. I remember thinking, 'Why me? Why a simple builder? Why should I be the one to raise God's child?' I was building a home that day, laying one rock upon the other, as we are now. That's when it occurred to me, son: your father in Heaven had chosen me, a builder, for a reason. You were going to rebuild all that has been tarnished, destroyed, and ruined someday. You were going to make everything new, and it's my duty as your papa here on Earth to help you any way I can. I am so blessed and privileged, son. I pray every day that I not fail you."

"Don't worry, papa," said Jesus, hugging him. "God won't let you fail. He will send his Angels to hold you up. He is holding you up even now. I love you, papa."

Joseph rested his cheek on little Jesus' head. "Thank you, Jesus. You have no idea what that means to me. Son, someday when your eyes are open to everything you are and the powers of Heaven and Earth are yours, would you still remember those words? Would you please still say them to me?"

"I will always love you, papa, and I will never forget you," said Jesus. "Now please go and eat something, I know you're famished. There is fish at home."

"Fish? You're saying they've actually caught fish? If you say so, it must be true!"

Azure was struck by a metal rod by the foreman of construction. "What the hell are you doing, Tyrannosaur!? Move your ass!" the foreman demanded, striking him again. As he fell to the floor, covered in soot, he flashed back to the time before he'd met Neela. He'd crawled out of an old construction site, completely bewildered and covered in white soot. There were some gravestones nearby and holes dug around them. There were boxes and black garbage bags nearby containing old remains, but he didn't realize that at the time. The workers at the site stared at him with large eyes as if they'd seen a ghost. Some of them fell over. The rest of them ran. As Azure tried to speak, all that came out was babble akin to an infant.

He flashed back to the present and the Foreman continued to beat him with the rod as he stumbled away, covering his head in his hands. One of the strikes smacked him right in the middle of the hand, cracking something. The Contractor came forward with a shovel and knocked Azure over with it, throwing it on top of him. "Dig!" he said. "If you don't know how to handle the fucking beams, then you can fucking dig! Any fucking idiot can do that!"

One of the construction workers came up to the Contractor, saying, "Sir, we haven't had a lunch break today and many of us are very hungry and thirsty."

The Contractor aimed the handgun at him. The worker held up his hands in surrender. "If you're hungry, you'd best work harder and faster. I'm not holding you here. You're paid to finish the work for the day. If it's not finished, you don't fucking rest."

The Contractor then pulled the Foreman aside. "Be tactful with the beatings on that Tyrannosaur; avoid the small bones, try not to leave a mark," he whispered. "The Tyrannosaur's girlfriend is apparently the daughter of a Union colonel. She's a Ceratosaur too. I don't need that drama."

"You and I both know the whole point of hiring an undocumented Tyrannosaur is to work 'em into the ground. That's what the good lord made them for. We'd be doing him a disservice to not use him to his fullest potential."

"Work him to his fullest potential, yes, but leave him the dumb work. They're not thinkers, anyway, don't expect them to be."

The Contractor came to Azure who was in the middle of digging. "I've made a deal with the Foreman, Tyrannosaur. We'll keep the beatings tame, leaving no permanent damage to you so long as you keep what happens here between us. Your girlfriend should know nothing of the practices here."

"I don't l-lie to her," Azure heaved.

"The only other alternative for me would be to give you no further work and thus no further pay. You're undocumented. You have no other alternatives. You want to provide for that pretty little Ceratosaur girlfriend of yours? You want to help carry her out of this dreadful neighborhood? You want to marry her, perhaps? Have children with her? None of that can happen if I'm not happy. So, when she asks what work is like here, you give us glowing reviews—you say it's great. You say you're happy doing it. You say whatever the hell I tell you to say and do whatever it is I tell you to do, or I can so easily report you to the PSF and end any hope you might have of a better life on this godforsaken planet. Do you understand?" Azure nodded. "Good boy." The Contractor slapped him in the back of the head. "Now, quit being a fuck up!"

"Yes, sir."

At the end of the week, Neela collected her paycheck from the restaurant. She voraciously ripped open the envelope and looked over it. Her smile turned to a frown. "Hey, why is so much of it missing? This is like half of what I was expecting," she said. "Even if you paid me minimum wage, it should be more than this.

"Minimum wage?" the Supervisor laughed. "Honey, that don't apply to the service industry. Haven't you heard? You're lucky you made anything at all with the kind of tips you bring in."

"I bring in plenty of tips!"

"Plenty? Honey, I gotta be fair and divide the payments out evenly. Some of the other waitresses bring in 3-4 times what you do. I can't give you the same amount."

"Yeah, well, some of the other waitresses just know how to play the customer."

"And? What do you think we're here for, honey?"

"We're here to do our job, not lick peoples' boots! There's a lot of places in the Redlight District for that. What the hell are we doing?"

"We're making the customer happy. Make the customer happy, and they'll make you happy. It really is that simple."

"How?"

"Shake that tail of yours. Move it from left to right. Exaggerate it. Flirt. Tease them."

"I'm serious about someone right now, and I don't think it's respectful to him to do that."

"What he don't know can't hurt, honey."

"God knows."

"Oh, only if you believe in that stuff. You're a good girl, honey, and good girls don't last long down in this neighborhood. I'm warning you. You best learn how to use it and work it."

As Neela left the restaurant looking drained, Azure greeted her with a toothy smile and a wave of the hand. He hugged her, putting a coat over her. "Aren't you ever cold waiting out here alone?" she said. "You can always go home and wait for me."

"No, I stay pretty warm. No w-worries. Besides, it's dark. I don't want you to be out alone."

Neela slipped her arms through the coat and hugged him back. "You're too sweet, Azure."

"Well, I'm your kn-nnight."

"I'm not... feeling too good," she held her head.

"Neela, I told you to stop tr-trying to heal me."

"Shhhh! No, it's nothing about that. It's just... I'm so fuckin' frustrated about everything going on right now. The war. The fact that my dad is risking his life, and the Union fucks us all over. The fact that we're being treated like this day in and day out. Like we're stuck on an island left for dead, and there's no way out."

"N-Neela... you should do what you always tell me—what your brother told you: ch-channel all those bad feelings toward something."

Neela bobbed her head. "You're right, I did tell you that, didn't I? How was work, darling?"

"It was good."

"Yeah?"

"I think we're halfway done b-building. Or more."

"Really? That's good news! But… we'll have to find you new work again."

Azure put his arm around her and they started walking. "It's ok. I think we'll find a way, as you always say."

"I'm rubbing off on you."

"You are. Let's g-go home."

They shared a home with four strangers and were fortunate to have a small room to themselves. Earlier uncomfortable incidents with roommates had frightened them both, and Azure found himself standing guard most nights despite Neela's urging for him to rest. He didn't seem to require sleep, just the absence of activity.

Home was simply a place to stay the night. The Network video calls to and from Neela's mother and step-dad were less frequent, and her mother admitted that she'd been fired earlier and had hidden it. Neela urged her mother to come home to Malkuth, but she said that she couldn't afford to. She, too, was stranded in an overcrowded communal home trying to make money as a sort of nanny/tutor/babysitter. The video calls stopped entirely, and Neela's parents were unresponsive.

As they huddled together on the cold, hard floor at night, the sound of the news played through the thin walls: the Union had held off the Dragons in the second battle of Bhumi, and a Dragon general was believed to have been heavily injured and possibly killed by a barrage of projectiles fired by mechs and starcrafts.

Chancellor Antares, now a much more outspoken and public figure than ever before, emphasized the importance of holding the planet Bhumi in a statement. He finished the statement by saying, "I have called the Senate to a special meeting to address the escalation of this war. The President had best consider the prospect of his impeachment if he fails to address the severity of this crisis. We haven't the luxury of ineptitude, nor do we have the patience for such ineffectual leadership. If the President is unwilling to make proper use of his emergency powers to end this war quickly & decisively, I assure you all, the Senate and I will."

"THE TAKEOVER"

In the coming weeks, the President was removed from office, voted out unanimously. The puppet Senate under Chancellor Antares was given full control of the Union government with all the emergency powers originally bestowed on the President now belonging to the now-*Supreme* Chancellor.

Fourteen World Enders released their payloads, erasing fourteen entire world populations and millions of Dragons and Malkuthians simultaneously. Underground newspapers called this 'The Second Catastrophe' and the writers of the article and the owners of the newspaper were tortured and put on display in cages labeled 'For Treason.' The Malkuth region was the only galactic region left untouched by the Union superweapons, despite a Dragon invasion there, as Antares still held out hope that his daughter might be there. The Watcher AIs and the special members of the Public Security Force scoured the region obsessively searching for her without success. Antares's own son, Nusakan Antares, was even assigned as the new Chief of Public Security of the region. Under his crackdowns, the public hangings intensified, and a second street in Atlanta City—Main Street—was used to accommodate the increased persecution and bloodshed.

Neela was tempted by the leftovers at the restaurant despite standard operating procedures being to throw it away. She waited until the coast was clear and scarfed down what she could so fast that it made her eyes water. Whenever she heard someone coming, she wrapped what she could in a napkin and hid it for later.

She'd lost a hundred pounds, about a tenth of her body weight, since leaving the sky district, but she insisted to Azure that it was a good thing. After the housing project was completed, Azure found undocumented work as a fruit picker. He was picked up every morning by the Lead-Picker and shared a cramped space with other undocumented workers, many of whom hadn't the convenience of a warm shower and thus remained dirty and sour-smelling from the previous day's work. He was forced to leave Neela every morning with a kiss on the forehead and an "I love you." He could no longer walk her home. He continued to be paid poorly and treated even poorer. Out in the countryside, the supervisors felt more secure beating him without restraint. They were astonished by his resilience, however. As he picked apples, Azure continued to have visions. He had visions of Yggdrasil, the world tree of the Asgardians, and Idunn's golden apples, which Loki coveted. He had visions of Athena, Aphrodite, and Hera feuding over Eris's Apple of Discord following a wedding feast. This led the three alpha goddesses to have a beauty pageant judged by the Trojan prince, Paris, which Aphrodite won through some deception.

As Azure picked fruits and placed them into his basket, the watching Susanoo became nostalgic. He remembered picking crops in the field with Kushina. He remembered dividing the husks with her sisters, all of whom were now long dead.

One day, as Azure picked an apple, he had a vision of a garden called Eden, the home of Earth's first two humans, Adam and Eve. There, the Heaven of heavens met the Earth in a sort of umbilical cord. There, even, an avatar of the God of gods dwelt with them, speaking to them and even playing little games with them like a parent with his children. There were lots of smiles and laughs. Azure thought he recognized him. Adam and Eve ate daily from the fruit of the Tree of Life, forbidden to eat from the Tree of the Knowledge of Good and Evil. Then, there came a figure that terrified Azure in a way his heart was not prepared: Samael, Satan. He'd taken the form of a serpent, like a small Ain, and confronted Eve in the garden. He told her that she should try some of the fruit from the Tree of the Knowledge of Good and Evil. She rejected the idea initially, saying that it was forbidden by God who told her that if she ate from it, she would "surely die."

"You won't surely die," said the serpent, Samael. "God knows that if you eat from it, you will become like him, having the knowledge of good and evil. You will become like God."

To prove his point, Serpent-Samael ate the fruit himself, knowing full well that he was already desensitized to its effects. He held it up to her and said something like, "Now, you try" in a primordial human language. "See, it's not so bad? You did not die. Go and share some with your husband, Adam. Tell him that he, too, can become like God."

A whip cracked Azure in the back, and he winced. The pain shook him from his vision, but his head began to spin. There was something about seeing Samael that sent an immense pain through his head. He began to roar, and as he roared, his supervisor whipped him again and again. The feeling reminded him of another lifetime he felt he'd lived. He'd picked a field like this before. He'd felt the sting of a whip from an enraged master before. *How? How is this all possible?* he wondered. *Who the hell am I? What the hell am I?*

As he returned home late one night, he saw two male roommates gathered around Neela's bedroom door. They retreated away as Azure approached. Neela could be heard crying on the other side. "Neela, it's m-me. Wh-what's wrong?" he said, knocking. Somehow, he already knew the answer. He'd seen it, somehow. An intentional overdose. "Is it your m-mom?"

Neela opened the door and collapsed in Azure's arms. "It's because I wasn't there! I wasn't fucking there!" Neela cried. "If I could have just touched her head just once. If I could have just talked to her… she'd still be alive… They've taken it all. My dad, my brother, my mom—everything! They were supposed to watch out for us.

They were supposed to make sure everything was balanced, everything was taken care of, everything was right, everything was ok. This is not right! This is not fuckin' ok! Fuck them!"

Azure comforted her as best as he could, and in the morning, he couldn't leave her side despite the incessant honking of the Lead Picker's horn. "I c-can't come today," he told him.

"Man, it's your head on the chopping block, not mine."

"I need to be with my l-lady now. Her mom just died."

"People die, man. Especially in these days."

"You didn't have to stay," said Neela. "I'll be alright."

"I had to," said Azure. "I'm supposed to be your kn-knight."

Neela's lips briefly rose but dropped just as quickly. "I want to go back to the Old Senate House. I need to do something. I need to say something. I need to channel this anger."

"I'll come," said Azure.

So, there they were at the very spot they'd met. Azure had visions of meeting Neela, one as he remembered it, the others were quite different. The contents of her speech that day were different, at times. At times, it wasn't raining. He also had visions of the Senate House and the People's Square in better times, before they became decaying artifacts. He saw people making their way up and down the busy steps of the building thousands of years before, wearing unfashionable clothing by modern standards. He could even vaguely pick up their conversations, but Neela's voice grabbed him.

"The throw aways—throw aways! That's what they think of all of us!" she said, with a ferocity and sharpness like never before. "Expendable. Replaceable. Usable and reusable. Wholly and entirely without a semblance of courtesy or dignity—abusable! Unheard, unconsidered, uncared for. People of the Union, this is how we're viewed! Malkuthians, this is what we are to them. We are nothing! Hardly even statistics. Cogs in a broken, inefficient machine. A machine that discards all of us at will!"

A Watcher hologram popped up and scolded her. "Neela, the freedom of expression is a right to be respected and appreciated, not abused," it said. "It's ok to be upset and angry that things aren't exactly the way you want them to be, but not when it ignores logic and reason. To make such scathing accusations, evidence is needed."

"My mother died yesterday!" Neela retorted. "She was jobless, homeless, and penniless when it happened. You all were supposed to provide work and shelter for her while my dad was fighting for you off-world. My dad—who has fought for the Union for two decades—hasn't been paid in months. My brother, perhaps the greatest soldier the Union has ever had, died for the Union, and look at how you've treated his family! He would be ashamed. I am ashamed. Even as a proud Malkuthian, I am ashamed! How could this happen? How could you let this happen?"

The Watcher disappeared. Nusakan Antares, the region's new Chief of Public Security, chuckled to himself listening to Neela speaking over the surveillance. He had many other pressing matters, including the search for his sister and the PSF response to the trickling in of Dragon forces in the region. Neela's performance gained no attendance and rallied practically no attention from those who passed by.

"We have freedom of expression, huh? Then, what about the journalists hanging from those cages on State & Main? What about the 'traitors' hanging from nooses? *TRAITOR*. That's a term easily misapplied, isn't it? You decide it. You define it. Not us. Not, *we the people*. Chancellor Antares does. And he defines a 'traitor' as anyone who doesn't agree with him. So, you're free to speak until he decides you're not. You're free to protect yourselves from violence until he decides you're not. You're free to seek your own happiness, open your own business even, until he decides you're not. You're free not to fear for your own mortality until he decides you're not. You're not free at all as long as *he* decides, and *we* don't!"

Nusakan Antares called a PSF officer to him. "Arrest *whatever-her-name-is* for subversive speaking," he said, pointing her out on the screen.

"Yes, sir." The officer turned to his subordinates. "Give the order to arrest Neela Eridanus."

"Eridanus?" Nusakan sounded surprised.

"Yes, sir, that's what the database says. She's Colonel Eridanus's step-daughter. Aohdfionn's step-sister."

"Is she really?... Just set an example out of her, would you? You know what I mean?"

"Yes, sir."

"Any good news I can share with my father?"

"We are still looking for your sister, sir."

"Tell your men to look busy."

"Yes, sir."

The next day, Azure was beaten down mercilessly for missing his shift. The Supervisor whipped him and kicked him in front of the other pickers until he cried. "You're so lucky to still be employed here, Tyrannosaur. Let it be known: I can shoot you in the head and you won't be missed. There ain't no record of you anywhere." The Supervisor observed as Azure's wounds ceased bleeding and even appeared to scab over rapidly. "I'll be damned though, you sure can take a good beating," he remarked, wiping the sweat from his head.

A wealthy, overweight Allosaur woman in a wide brim sun hat visited the greenhouse that day, shopping around for a male *plaything* for the night. She prodded and inspected the workers and licked her lips. She came to Azure. "A big, strong Tyrannosaur. Exotic. How much?"

"I c-can't. I'm with s-someone," said Azure.

The Supervisor wrapped the whip around his throat and began to strangle him.

"You can quit that," said the Allosaur woman. The Supervisor released Azure. "Is she pretty like me?"

Azure, tearing-up, nodded.

"Is she wealthy like me?"

Azure shook his head.

"Do you love her?"

Azure nodded. "Y-yes."

"Do you want to marry her?"

"Yes."

"If you love her and you want to marry her, you better come up with the money to take care of her. Us fine girls don't stay on the market for very long; ask your supervisor. Sometimes, you've gotta do what you gotta do to get what you want. You're letting an opportunity pass you by." She walked over to another worker, looked him up and down, and said, "How much?"

Azure cried all the way to the restaurant, and the Lead-Picker turned up the music to drown him out. Azure waited at the restaurant, but Neela never came out. When Azure asked her boss where Neela was, her boss responded, "Honey, I was about to ask you the same thing. She never showed up, and we were dying in here. If you see her, tell her, 'sorry, girl, that shit won't fly.'"

Azure rushed home, but Neela wasn't there either. Their roommates said that she left in the middle of the day on her own. Azure frantically made his way to their typical spot: the Old Senate House. She wasn't there either. Sobbing, Azure searched the streets of the city like a lost child looking for his mother in a crowd. His heart raced. His visions began to run wild, and he became disoriented. He ran across the street at an apparent green light, but he perceived it hours in advance and was struck by a ground-vehicle that didn't detect him in time. The vehicle rider inspected him and tried to scan him, finding that the Watchers couldn't identify him. Seeing the opportunity, the rider commanded the vehicle to leave him mangled on the side of the road.

Azure crawled away into a back alley as his body reassembled itself under the cover of dark. "N-n-no…" he muttered, as a grim realization passed over him. He came to State Street and fearfully looked up at the hanging, swaying, twitching corpses, dreading that one of them might be Neela. "Pl-pl-please, no…" Azure cried.

He came to Main Street and looked at each of the bodies. Some of their eyes and tongues stuck out of their skulls. Some were females, but it was hard to tell, many of their headscarves having flown off or were removed. There was no Neela. An almost impossible mixture of anxiety and relief washed over him intermittently. And then he found her. His heart sank.

There, hanging from a crane was a cage barely large enough for a person. The label on the cage read, "For Subversive Speaking." Neela's body was twisted and contorted, forced into that cramped space. A bit was lodged in her jaw and the edges of her lips were bleeding, her blood being mixed with drool. She was still breathing. Her eyes were closed. Perhaps she thought to sleep the uncomfortable ordeal away.

"N-Neela…" Azure called, his heart leaping. Neela's eyes opened. Her eyes first became wide with surprise and she appeared to smile with relief despite her predicament. She rolled her eyes and tried to say, "Hi," raising her claws to greet him, "Don't worry. Just one day." She raised one claw.

Azure tried to reach for her hand. "Uh-uh," she said.

A PSF officer shouted at him. "Hey! Get back!"

"Go," Neela managed to say through the bit, "wait there."

Azure sat at a distance, watching her, suffering with her. Neela tried to sleep almost the entire time. She would occasionally open her eyes to see if Azure was still waiting and was relieved when he was. She'd raise her claws through the bars of the cage, and he'd wave and reach out to her. It reminded him of retrieving carts outside the thrift store and how they'd wave through the classroom door at each other. Those were simpler times. But then a vision of a far older experience flashed before his eyes. He found his hands interlocked with a girl's through a fence. The girl was trying to scream but had a muzzle around her snout. Her eyes were closed, and Azure somehow knew the cause was blindness. There were men in lab coats who pulled the two of them apart. The girl reached out to Azure, and he recalled breathing a secret message over her fingers before the vision cut out. A cacophony of screams filled the area with Azure perceiving victims in the past, present, and future. Azure shook his head and covered his ears, trying to shut them out. He focused on Neela in better times, and that seemed to quell the visions and voices a little bit.

As mid-day came, there was a special visitor who'd come to inspect the proceedings: Nusakan Antares, the Chancellor's son and new Chief of Security. He pushed on the cages and the hanging bodies like a child pushes another child on a swing. The creaking was bone-chilling. He came to Neela's cage, and Azure clenched his fists.

Nusakan banged on the cage with a baton. "Wakie wakie," he said. "You comfortable in there, you little big-mouth troublemaker?"

Neela tried to grunt an insult, but it was muffled and fell flat.

"You're very lucky, Miss Eridanus. We're not known for our lenient sentencing. Next time, we'll cut off your horn, then your tongue, then we'll look into ending your miserable life. We'll be sure to make it hurt first. Not even your family name will spare you."

"Yours too," Neela managed, drooling.

Nusakan laughed. He spun the cage around and walked off.

Azure felt powerless and a deep rage filled him. The streetlights nearby flickered on and off. This caught even Nusakan's attention, and he muttered to one of his officers, "get that fixed."

At the end of the ordeal, Neela and Azure both collapsed in each other's arms, crying all the way home. As they walked, and as Azure's frustrations and sorrows boiled over, the lights on the streets and buildings began to flicker. There were blackouts in the neighborhood. Neela pulled slightly away and inspected Azure, his teeth gnashed together like those of a ferocious, territorial animal. His body tensed and shook. Despite her sore jaw, she muttered, "Azure? Are you the one doing all that?"

"ATHENA'S STAND"

Dragon mages tended to General Malevant. They'd been casting healing spells on him since his system-destroying duel with Diamond over Kanopos. Now, they found themselves doing so again after he'd been struck by attacks by dozens of mechs and starships. Malevant had refused their advice to sit out another battle. His wings were still bent and riddled with holes. Some of his thick outer flesh was still exposed and oozed with puss.

The Trident of Poseidon, the Blade of Olympus, and Black Sword began to rattle as he reclined in a giant stone throne that had been erected on the newly conquered Malkuthian planet of Bhumi. The three weapons lifted into the air and darted toward Malevant.

He stopped all three with his mind. The awesome weapons shook as two separate forces pushed and pulled against them. "Oh, Athena, I thought you had greater caution than that," said Malevant.

The bodies of one of the Dragon mages began to warp until Athena appeared in its place. She shook and strained, placing all of her psionic, mental energies into this premeditated and now-desperate attack. The other three Dragon mages were stunned by this and looked to act. Athena's spear flew in and pierced the chests of all three mages. Malevant smirked and a loud pop was heard from Athena's body, her right-femur had broken in half. She screamed and reached for her leg. The weapons she'd been manipulating fell harmlessly to the ground. Malevant came upon her.

"NO!" she cried, pulling back the string of her Epirus Bow. Another pop and her right-arm snapped like a twig and her hand broke apart. The string still loosed and Malevant was struck in the chest by the arrow which exploded with a concussive force and tore through his flesh. The Dragon general shrugged off the blow and stabbed Athena in the left-thigh with his knife-like foreclaw. Screaming, Athena summoned her spear to her lone healthy hand and drove it into Malevant's body again and again as he laughed it off. He broke her left-arm, leaving her lying limp and defenseless on the floor.

Malevant pulled Hades out of his cell and began to break his bones one by one. "I warned you all," he said. "And I am true to my word."

Hades created a barrier of ice, but Malevant broke through it easily and continued to pummel him. The tourniquet around Hades' blinded eyes fell from his face. He managed to speak, saying, "If there's one thing I learned in my long, long life, Dragon, it's that the wicked are punished severely. My father and brother. And me. That'll include you someday." Malevant grabbed his face and scraped it across the floor until the flesh tore from it.

Athena tried to roll away.

"Just where do you think you'll go?" said Malevant, driving and pulling one hook after another through her body. "You always suffered well, Athena."

Tears flowed from her eyes and mixed with her golden blood. She telepathically communicated with her sister, leaving her a final message. "Sis," she said. "Are you there?"

"Yeah, like, what's up?" Aphrodite replied.

"I've failed to kill Malevant. I thought now was a better time than ever while he was still weak. But he is too damn powerful. He has broken all of my limbs. I can't move. He is torturing me. He is killing me."

"Sis!"

"Stay there! Stay alive! Don't you worry about me. I knew the risks before I acted. I accepted them. I'm sorry it was such a surprise. Opportunity is like that sometimes."

"No, sis! I'm scared!"

"If Azure is who we all think he is, there's no reason to be scared. Make sure he reaches his potential. You will be the last of the Olympians. How fitting that love alone survives. Defeat these damned Dragons. Let it not be in vain. Love you, sis."

As Malevant began to thread hooks through her throat area, something struck him in the head and pierced it. It was a shard of ice shaped into a blade. Fire came from Malevant's eyes and mouth, melting it as he turned to face the assailant: Hades. Malevant's head oozed from the wound. but he appeared not to be bothered much. Hades hurled ice shard after ice shard at Malevant who stopped each one, and in a last-ditch effort, Hades encased Malevant entirely in gold. He added another layer of gold and a third layer of ice around it. It barely held the terrible Dragon long enough for Athena to use her telekinesis, sending the Trident of Poseidon spiraling toward Malevant just as he broke free from the gold and ice. Malevant grabbed the Trident out of mid-air and skewered Hades in the gut with it. "Now it's down to two of you, the last of your pantheon," said Malevant. "I will find your sister and she will live up to her end of the bargain."

"Don't you touch her, you bastard!" Athena cried.

Aphrodite couldn't hold back the tears as she guided her cloud to Susanoo.

"What the hell is wrong with you now, woman?" he said.

"Athena, my sister… she's, like, totally hurting. She's like, totally, dying. And I don't know… she said not to come. I don't know… what to do…"

"Serves her right for deceiving me! Both of you are implicated in this!"

"Please!" Aphrodite cried. "Please… help… No one, like, deserves what's happening to her."

Susanoo gulped and shook his head.

"And, like, Kushina will be stuck like that forever if my sister dies. There will be no one who can, like, reverse it."

"This again?"

"Like, you forced me to have to say it. I didn't want to say it. I said, like, please. Please help my sister. Please." She held him around the shoulders. "And I'll, like, never ask you for anything ever again."

"I know you're lying…"

"Like, I don't want to… I have to…"

As Malevant continued tormenting Athena, a Dragon centurion alerted him that Lord Gigatheta wished to speak to him. "I am quite busy at the moment and, secondly, I am not under his jurisdiction or command."

The centurion told him that Lord Zeon was in conference and that Gigatheta was the highest-ranking Dragon in the area.

Malevant apprehensively dropped Athena to the ground, telling the centurion to watch her, and dragged himself over to meet the massive eight-headed, eight tailed Gigatheta who'd just arrived on the planet. Gigatheta's heads demanded more and more kegs of alcohol, having developed a taste for it. "Lord-Marquess Gigatheta I presume," Malevant opened his broken wings and bowed. "What news have you for me?"

"YOU LOOK TERRIBLE, MALEVANT," said Gigatheta's water head.

"WHAT HAPPENED TO YOU?" asked Gigatheta's fire head.

"I survived a duel with the finest Malkuthian soldier, the destruction of a star system, being hit by the arsenal of an entire Malkuthian fleet, and a squabble with a traitor and her uncle."

"IS THIS TRAITOR THE OLYMPIAN COMMANDER, ATHENA, PERHAPS?" asked the plant head.

"How have you guessed so accurately?"

"I AM SURPRISED WITH HER CUNNING THAT SHE HASN'T TRIED TO OVERTHROW YOU A HUNDRED TIMES ALREADY," said the wind head before dunking into another keg of alcohol.

"THE OLYMPIAN COMMANDER, ATHENA, WAS IMPRESSIVE IN THE CONQUEST OF THIS PLANET," said the rock head. "AMATERASU, COMMANDER OF MY COLLABORATORS, ATTESTED TO IT. HER STRATEGIC AND TACTICAL EXPERTISE COULD PROVE INVALUABLE."

"The fact remains: she is a traitor," Malevant argued.

"THE FACT REMAINS: SHE IS VALUABLE," said the electric head. "PERHAPS UNDER ME SHE WOULDN'T FEEL SO RESENTFUL AND REBELLIOUS. YOU HAVE A WAY OF BRINGING OUT THE WORST IN PEOPLE, GENERAL MALEVANT. THEY DO BAD, AND YOU PUNISH THEM. THEY DO GOOD, AND YOU PUNISH THEM. WHAT INCENTIVE IS THERE?"

"AS YOU PROBABLY REALIZE, I AM NOT A MILITARY LEADER," said the ice head. "I REQUIRE ONES WITH A CERTAIN…EXPERIENCE… AROUND ME SO THAT I MAY ENJOY MY PERSONAL PLEASANTRIES WITHOUT DISTURBANCE. THESE REPTILES ARE MEATY, FOR INSTANCE." Some of the heads of Gigatheta snatched some bound Malkthians and began to devour them. "BRING THE OLYMPIAN COMMANDER TO ME."

"She's quite broken at the moment," said Malevant.

"THEN UNBREAK HER, GENERAL! I WANT AN AUDIENCE WITH HER AS SOON AS POSSIBLE."

Reluctantly, Malevant retreated back to his throne room and ordered some Dragon mages to work on healing her, something which baffled them. They had never seen Malevant give such an order, and he seemed even ashamed in requesting it. "What are you idiots standing around for?!" he roared. "Do as I command!"

Athena heaved for dear life as Malevant pinned her down with one finger. "You are a lucky one, it seems, Athena. You've caught the eye of the Lord Gigatheta, and he wants you in passable shape to lead some of his forces. Just know that he has certain… tastes…" Malevant licked the golden blood off of her face. "I hope he enjoys you as much as I have." As Malevant left to receive more healing from the mages, Athena stiffened her lip and resisted the temptation to cry in relief. As a precaution, Malevant rendered her unconscious while the mages tended to her.

"NEELA'S DECISION"

The news from the other room bled through the wall. The Dragons were in the region and any day they could come to Malkuth itself. Azure had put together enough funds to surprise her with a few servings of ice cream. It brought such a smile to her face that it almost made her bawl. They hadn't been able to afford such a luxury in a long time. They'd both been released from their jobs and were waiting fearfully to be asked to leave their home as well.

She knew that the ice cream was intended to assuage the pain in her jaw and the pain in her heart. Her mind throbbed more than ever before in her life. It cried out for either energy or rest and yet continued to race.

Azure's thoughts seemed to be racing too. He seemed to be seeing more and more. He could no longer explain it. The kaleidoscope of visions seemed to be consuming his sight and mind. He rolled around on the floor, clutching his head, roaring embarrassingly. Thank goodness their roommates were at work at the time.

Azure's head became feverish. He tossed and turned. Neela called to him and tried to snap him out of it like she used to, but he was now too far gone. Worst yet, she knew it was partially her fault. She'd hidden it from him poorly, but it was. Now, with all of her loved ones dead or gone and the universe seemingly on the verge of collapse from all sides, Neela looked upon Azure and reflected on the time they'd spent together. She reflected on every precious moment. She knew that her decision might permanently damage her health and that it might even kill her. She knew it since the first time she laid her hand on his head, whatever was wrong with him was like nothing she'd ever encountered before, and to heal it would require everything she had. "Azure…" she cried. "No matter what happens… Fight for us. Live for us. Ok? And remember… always remember… I love you." Even as she reached for his head, a fearful part of her grabbed her and tried to pry her away. She resisted. "Fuck!" she said, tensing her body.

She closed her eyes tightly and shook her head, and with a determined growl, she wrapped her arms around his head and hugged him with both her hands nailed there. She kissed him tearfully, saying, "I love you, Azure," committed to never letting go until the work was done.

Both of her nostrils bled, and her eyes too. There were flashes of light. Yellow. Orange. Red. Black. Two pale Spinosaur hands clutched hers, and her brother stared back at her, weeping with her. Her mother rushed to her and hugged her. Her birth father rushed over from the other end and embraced her too. She was crushed and overwhelmed with a sense of relief and contentment, and then realized she couldn't breathe. But it was ok.

Sunlight peeked through the edges of the blinds, announcing the coming of a new day. The voice of Samael-Satan echoed, "*...and your eyes will be opened, you will become like God.*" Azure pulled himself up, feeling so light that he thought he might be flying or floating. He looked around the room, frantically searching for Neela. He found her limp body collapsed on the floor in front of the doorway, a puddle of blood having formed under her head. Azure, shaking, put his hand to Neela's back and rocked her back and forth. "Neela! Neela, wake up! Neela, please, wake up!"

Azure's hindsight revealed to him what she had done. He shook his head. "No, no, why did you do that? We were supposed to do things together. We were supposed to do everything together. Decide our future together. Neela, wake up! Wake up! I can't do it alone…"

He saw multiple visions of himself responding to this in different ways, but in one that appealed to him the most, he saw himself cradling and carrying Neela out of the home and calling for help. He followed this vision and heard sirens outside. He knew that by some miracle there would be a freshly parked ambulance outside, having been called in by God-knows-who. In some scenarios, there were all male EMTs, in some there were all-female EMTs, in another there were two females and a male, in yet another, there were three medical droids.

Three medical droids appeared with a gurney already laid out for her. They ran Azure through a series of questions, and he lost patience, begging them to "just help her—there's something with her head, something wrong!" They forewarned him that the ambulance ride would cost a large amount of banknotes, and he responded that he didn't care, as long as she was taken care of. He asked to ride in the back with her, and the droids obliged.

Azure sat beside Neela and held her hand all the way to the hospital and all the way to the emergency department, where he was asked to wait outside. He saw a possible scenario where a doctor gave the news to announce that she was dead. He saw a possible scenario where a doctor gave the news that she was alive but brain dead. He saw a possible scenario where a doctor gave the news that she was alive and cognizant. He saw a possible scenario where a medical droid gave the news that she was in a coma.

Azure closed his eyes, bowed his head, and prayed. And that's when he remembered God. He remembered meeting God, at the *feet* of God. He remembered the light, the intense heat. His skin and flesh melted away. He remembered being caught in the darkness between two explosions of light and dark energy that surrounded and engulfed him, spinning around him. None of that mattered now. All that mattered was Neela, and he prayed fervently for her, tears in his eyes. He found himself saying a prayer that seemed oddly familiar. A ghostly female Ceratosaur with voids for eyes covered his hands in hers and bowed her head with him. He knew who this was: another ghost from his past lives. She led him in an old prayer. And as they concluded with a classic 'amen,' she said, "There, ya see? That's how it's done. It ain't so scary now, ain't it?" As this ghostly figure drifted in and out of his sight, he shook and wept, trying to hold onto it, but his hands slipped through.

An unending parade of ghostly afterimages went to and fro, the injured, the sick, the dying, and their loved ones. Medical staff from a generation ago.

It was like the past, present, and future—all of reality—were in a tug-a-war for Azure's mind, and now he was consciously aware of it all. Everything converged on the present timeline, and everything hinged on his choices. For the first time in a very long time, he was fully aware of who he was and where he came from, and yet he didn't care. He cared about little else than what was happening behind those emergency room doors.

"THE QUEST TO SAVE ATHENA"

Aphrodite and Susanoo arrived over Bhumi by magic cloud, but the skies of the planet were swarming with Wyverns. Aphrodite conjured the Helm of Darkness that her uncle, Hades, had snuck to her before beginning her search for Azure. When she placed it on her head, she rendered herself invisible. "I'll still be able to sense your Ki," said Susanoo. "Get it done quickly, fairy princess. We don't want to tangle with these Dragons for long. The best we can hope for is a distraction. I'll try to give 'em hell."

He took his ten-grasp sword and waved it down toward the planet like a cook stirring a pot. A huge hurricane formed there. It grabbed thousands of the Wyverns by surprise. He then swung his sword over the ocean, and a tsunami crashed onto the shore, disrupting a Dragon outpost. Under the cover of this chaos, the now-invisible Aphrodite flew toward Malevant's fortress in search of her sister.

Susanoo had an awful feeling come over him. He sensed a very familiar energy behind him. "I thought that might be you," said a familiar voice. He turned and saw his sister, Amaterasu, and immediately formed a windstorm with his sword, throwing the storm at her. Amaterasu formed a solar shield and deflected the storm away. "Why are you here?!" Susanoo shouted.

The Star Kami formed a fireball in her hand. "I should kill you, brother, for what you did to my handmaiden and my horse. For your defiance and treachery. But I find it hard to."

Susanoo raised his sword. "I heard about what you did to Uzume! You sacrificed Kushina and her sisters along with the entire human race of our world to save yourself, you selfish bitch!"

"I did it to save all of us, brother. Sometimes as leaders, we have to make difficult choices."

"There are some choices that should never be made! They had a right to live!"

"In your eyes, brother, have I forfeited mine? Are you going to try to kill me?"

The Storm Kami tensed his grasp on the sword. "I want this shit to end now!"

"If you kill me, you'll still need to deal with the Dragons, and they are innumerable. But together, maybe…"

Susanoo shook his head. "No. Hell no."

"Daddy and mother are waiting. I don't know how long either of them have left to live, or either of us for that matter. One Malkuthian attack would do it. And then there's the Dragons. It's our last chance to be whole as a family, brother. I wish you understood that. Do you remember when we used to play together in Takama-ga-hara? We used to race our ponies, and I would always win."

"Not always."

"Almost always."

Susanoo shook his head again. "They deserved better. You could have stood up for them. You could have protected them. You could have saved them."

"Only these Malkuthians are strong enough to stand against the Dragons. We had no chance. I knew that from the beginning. Beings called 'Angels' from another universe came and showed us exactly what the Dragons had done to places like Olympus and Asgard. Takama-ga-hara still stands because of my choice to appease the Dragons. I have no regrets other than the fact that my decision drove the final piece of my fractured family away. You. It has left a hole in daddy's heart."

"Daddy can have his little girl. That has always been enough for him in the past. I won't be moved. Are you going to try to stop me, Ame?"

"No. Do whatever it is you feel, Su. Apparently, Uzume and the others felt you were in the right."

Susanoo ripped a part of the cloth from his armor and handed it to Amaterasu. "Tell dad I said, 'hello.'"

"I will."

Aphrodite snuck through the fortress, floating so that way she wouldn't make a sound. She made it behind a corner and ran into something that seemed to be alive. "Umph!" it said. "Who art thou? You smell pretty."

"Wait, like, what?" Aphrodite whispered.

The mysterious figure removed a magical helmet of its own, revealing Thor. Aphrodite removed her Helm of Darkness, and her eyes glistened. Her mouth hung open, and she panted like a thirsty puppy. "Oh, gawd, you're sooo hawt. What are you, like, doi—"

Thor put a finger to his mouth, signaling for her to keep quiet. "I kneweth that Athena was in distress. Loki let me use one of his portals and his Tarnhelm Cap so that I could rescue her," Thor whispered. He shrugged his shoulders. "I hadst nothing better to do."

"Oooooh, let me see," Aphrodite playfully switched her helmet with his cap. They both turned invisible. "You have, like, a magic invisibility hat too?"

"And a *big* hammer."

"Oooooh, can I, like, hold it too?"

"If thou art worthy," he said, taking off the cap and winking. "Have a go."

Aphrodite rubbed and stroked the shaft of the handle suggestively. "Mmmm, the density. Oooh, the hardness. Ahhh, the fine, like… craftsmanship."

Thor threw the cap back on her, and covered her mouth with his hand as a Dragon centurion passed. "Shhhhh," he urged her. The Dragon became suspicious and called more guards to him. Aphrodite gulped. The Dragons began sniffing the air, their eyes glowing red as they picked up something. Without another moment's hesitation, Thor threw his hammer. It crashed through a column of the guards and killed the centurion before returning to Thor's hand. Just as he sneered, another Dragon guard slashed at him and cut him over the arm. He stumbled back. Aphrodite leaned against a wall and kicked a statue over. It fell on top of the guard. Thor finished him off with a hammer blow while he was stunned. Aphrodite came over and healed his arm. She massaged his muscles. "Thou art rather good at that, fair dame," said Thor.

"Mmm, you like it?"

"Shhhh…" he put his finger to his mouth but remembered he was invisible. "There art too many Dragons. Doth thee know where to go?"

"Uh, yeah. Duh? I'm, like, a lot smarter than I look."

"That's what *I* always say!"

"I know, right? Like, totally. All the stu-pids. Always underestimating us."

"So, what plan hadst thee to find Athena, fair dame?"

"Uh… give me a second, ok? Like, oh, my gawd."

"Of thunder."

"You really are, like, dense."

"Why, thank you, fair dame. I've been bearing the full weight of a planet for years."

"You mean, sorta like Atlas?"

"No, I have a natural sense of direction. I don't need maps."

"Yeah, whatevers, anyway… I've got, like, an idea. Hold on."

Thor reached out and grabbed her arm. It took a while but she eventually understood his confusion. "Oh… Oh! I get it now." She reached into her chest and tore out some blood, sprinkling it on the floor. Each blood droplet formed a flying imp-like creature armed with a small bow. She instructed them to draw away as many Dragon guards as possible from Malevant's chambers.

The flying imps were slaughtered as expected but they bought Aphrodite and Thor enough time to slip into the holding chambers. There, they walked around the maimed and mangled bodies of Malkuthian victims. By this point, both Thor and Aphrodite were used to seeing such gore and cruelty. It was clear that Malevant had been busy.

They saw four Dragon mages surrounding Athena's unconscious body. Thor struck them dead with his hammer. Aphrodite slapped her sister on both cheeks and shook her, trying to wake her up. "Do you have, like, some cold water?" she asked Thor.

"Ha! I needeth not water to do this…" Thor fired a jolt of electricity at Athena.

Athena woke up, her hairs radiating upward, and punched Thor in the face, knocking his cap off his head. Aphrodite slapped him as he turned, then covered her face in disbelief at her action. "Sis, is that you?" asked Athena. "What the hell are you doing here? I told you to stay away!"

Aphrodite jumped on her and hugged her. "I needed to know if, like, my sis was ok."

"Did you kill the mages?"

"Uh…"

"They were healing me!"

"Come now, sweaty dirty dame, 'twas no big deal," said Thor.

"First of all, come up with a new nickname. Second of all, my right-arm is still broken."

Thor lifted her up and grabbed her wrist and shoulder despite her protests and jabs. "Don't you dare," she seethed.

"Relax, trust me. 'Twas the same for my brother, Tyr, during the twelfth battle of Jotunheim."

"I heard he lost an arm."

"'Twas a hand, in fact, and 'twas not my fault. My giant-wolf-nephew ate it. Worry not, my giant-wolf-nephew is dead. A Dragon stepped on him." Thor tugged sharply and the joint popped back into place.

Athena winced and gasped. "Asshole. I could've just turned myself into an Axolotl and grew it back."

"You know, I hadst an enchanted axe once, but its powers made no sense to me, so I chucked it at my giant-snake-nephew and hit him square in the center mass. Besides, who needs a stupid storm axe when thou hadst a magic hammer?"

"I don't know, you tell me…" said Athena.

Without hesitation or warning, Thor picked her up in a cradle carry. "I, Thor Odinson, prince of the Aesir, claim you, warrior-princess Athena, as my new wife."

"Uh…"

"Now, 'tis time for thy hero to make his daring escape with the beautiful damsel."

"Heya!" Aphrodite complained.

"I mean, the two beautiful damsels," he winked at her.

"That's… a little better, I guess." She prepped a love-arrow and shot it at Athena, hitting her in the heart.

"Seriously?!" Athena exclaimed.

"Like, what? You complete each other."

"You mean like each of us is *missing something*?"

"Like, whaaaat? Shut uuuup, I never said that."

"BATTLE WITH LORD GIGATHETA"

Susanoo hovered over the planet. The stench of death was immense. Another familiar sight caught his attention: Lord-Marquess Gigatheta. He almost fell off his cloud as a wave of terror washed over him. It was the very monstrosity, the very entity he'd been avoiding all this time. It was drinking kegs of alcohol and devouring Malkuthians as they screamed, cried, and tried to get away. Susanoo reflected on his life with Kushina's family, picking crops alongside her and her sisters, and imagined that this was the very same grim fate they'd faced.

The Storm Kami drew his sword and thought long and hard, realizing that as long as the Dragons existed, a full, safe life with Kushina could never be realized. As Gigatheta swayed from side to side drunkenly, Susanoo came down with the cloud at above-light-speed and slashed at the weakest of the Dragon's eight heads. The plant head fell to the ground, oozing green. "Remember me!?" Susanoo growled, then summoned a lightning storm to fry the water head. The other heads unleashed a volley of elemental attacks, and Susanoo narrowly avoided being killed by them. He jumped on the humongous back of the creature and stabbed down into its thick hide, which was like trying to stab concrete with a toothpick. The fire head breathed a stream of flames at him and he rolled away. Susanoo stirred a waterspout and directed it at the fire head.

The plant head began to grow back, and it was at that moment that Susanoo realized how over his head this battle was. Dragon flying-cavalry swooped down at him, and he tried desperately to fight them off. A lance struck him in the hip and he felt a great deal of his strength leave him. He caught a ride on his cloud and tried to outfly the flying-cavalry. As he did, an ice-blast from Gigatheta's ice head froze his dominant arm. He crashed back onto the creature's back and the fall caused the ice to break.

As the flying-cavalry approached, Susanoo braced himself for the end. Just then, a Starfire Blast from Amaterasu put the flying Dragons in disarray, like a pack of hornets who'd been hit with smoke. Amaterasu then fired a Starfire Blast at Gigatheta's regrowing plant head until it was completely fried and dead. She turned it on the ice head which began to melt under the intense solar heat. "I remembered it's our birthday, brother," said Amaterasu.

"Let's not let it be our death day too," he replied.

"COMMANDER AMATERASU, I'M RATHER SURPRISED," said Gigatheta. "PERHAPS I HAD TOO MUCH TO DRINK TODAY."

More flying-cavalry swooped in, thousands of them.

A portal blew open nearby, and out came Aphrodite and Thor with Athena still cradled in his arms. Athena pushed him away, got on her feet, and dusted herself off.

"Su!" called Aphrodite. "I, like, told them you were still here and that we shouldn't leave you." At first, she thought they were standing beside a mountain range, but then she realized that they were beside a Dragon of humongous proportions.

"Well, *arigato*," said Susanoo.

"Haveth I but one more grenade of portals," said Thor. "Come hence, dark-haired bearded one!"

"While you're all here! Let's take this big asshole down!" said Susanoo.

"No, you fool!" Athena shouted. "General Malevant and the rest of the Dragons are coming!"

Thor and Aphrodite's fleet of flying blood-imps tried to ward off the Dragon cavalry. Thor's scattered lightning strikes proved themselves particularly useful. Amaterasu kept her Starfire Blast focused on the heads of Gigatheta, and the beast maneuvered itself toward them, stomping on some of his own warriors and captured Malkuthians in the process. Athena begrudgingly jumped into action, firing a volley of shots from the Epirus Bow at the approaching Dragons.

"OH, AND TO THINK I HAD SUCH HIGH HOPES FOR YOU, OLYMPIAN," said Gigatheta.

Susanoo created a series of powerful tornadoes that tore through the area and dealt damage to Gigatheta and the other Dragons. All these efforts, however, only seemed to amuse Gigatheta, whose remaining heads sneered, releasing their elemental attacks like a hyperactive person with a gun in a shooting gallery. Thor was struck by a stream of rocks from the rock head. Metal shards from the metal head hit Susanoo. Both of them desperately fought off attacks from the flying-cavalry. Athena fired her bow at the flying-cavalry, scattering them. A Dragon heavy-infantry legion marched toward them. Gigatheta laughed.

"He's like the Hydra!" said Athena. "You can't just attack the heads. They'll keep growing back. You need to destroy the stumps too!"

"How the fuck do we do that?!" said Susanoo.

"Your sister had the right idea. Aim your attacks at the base of his necks and keep it hot until the base is completely fried. And don't stay in one place! Keep moving!"

Thor focused a supercharged lightning bolt directly at the base of the water-head's neck until it completely died. As Thor stopped to gloat, Aphrodite swept him out of the way with her phenomenal speed, saving him from being impaled by a lance.

Athena observed as Gigatheta's tails lit up incrementally as he attacked. She fired her bow at one of them, causing it to fall off. The elemental attack of the corresponding head fizzled out. "It's the tails!" said Athena. "Kill the tails, and he'll lose his powers!"

Aphrodite, Thor, Susanoo, and Amaterasu followed her lead and attacked Gigatheta's tails. Gigatheta growled with frustration, his attacks losing their power.

Susanoo continued to bleed from his earlier wound, and his storms weakened as he became less able to conduct them. Aphrodite darted over to him to start healing him.

Athena somersaulted over a beam of electrical energy and landed a direct hit with her bow at the base of the neck. However, as she loosed the arrow, a sharp pain ran through her freshly realigned arm and she dropped the bow. As she scrambled for it, Gigatheta's metal-head snatched her in its jaws. Thor jumped onto the beast and struck at the base of the metal-head with electrically-augmented attacks from Mjolnir until the head and neck broke off. Athena fell along with the head and narrowly avoided being crushed under it.

The heavy-infantry marched within striking distance, and Athena rolled away, favoring her arm. "We're out of time," she told the others telepathically. "We did our damage. We need to get out of here now!"

"Damn it all!" Susanoo punched the ground.

Two hands touched his shoulders. "You need to go, Su," said Amaterasu.

"You're coming with us, Ame."

"No. I'm going back to dad. We'll all die together."

"Like hell you will!"

"You're free to come too. But that's up to you."

There was the sight and sound of the sound-barrier breaking and a black meteorite streaked down from the sky. It was General Malevant! Athena and Aphrodite both gasped at this terrifying sight and tried to sneak away to rendezvous with Thor. Malevant came down with the Black Sword drawn and drove it into the middle of Gigatheta's back!

Gigatheta gave out a shocked and angry roar. "MALEVANT! WHAT IS THIS!?"

The other Dragons paused, not knowing what to do. They had never seen a Dragon leader attack another.

"What the hell is that Dragon doing?!" Susanoo exclaimed.

"Making full use of the Black Sword," said Athena. "Exactly what he and I planned to do to Azure."

Malevant's eyes glowed red and his body appeared to grow. A purple aura surrounded him and began to spark with electricity. Gigatheta's legs became wobbly before his entire mountainous frame collapsed, shaking the ground so much that everything still living on the planet felt it. "KILL… HIM…" Gigatheta managed to say to his warriors.

"No," said Malevant. "This decadent traitor tried to usurp the authority of Lord Zeon! He should die!"

Both of their forces stood confused.

"Thor!" Athena called out. "Use the portal grenade! Get my sister and the others out of here now! We're done here!"

Thor threw the grenade, opening an inter-dimensional portal back to the Nether Realm. He waved the others along.

Susanoo boarded his cloud and held out his hand to the others as well, "I'm going back to him," he said. "We have one last hope."

Athena, Aphrodite, and Amaterasu stood between the two paths. Athena waved her hand over Susanoo's comb and finally returned Kushina to her human state. She was naked, so Aphrodite fashioned a dress for her to wear.

"So, you're the one who has changed my brother," said Amaterasu, her eyes glowing white. Kushina shrunk away fearfully. "It was a pleasure to finally meet you. Take care of him for me. He is a rascal." She looked to her brother who put his left-hand on her shoulder. "Goodbye for now, brother," said Amaterasu, floating away. "I'll be sure to tell dad I saw you."

"Susanoo," said Athena. "I have removed my seal. You can now transform Kushina at will to protect her from the atmospheric pressure, inter-dimensional travel, and space."

"Cometh now, dames!" Thor called. "We haven't time!"

Aphrodite considered between the two males and their separate paths. Ultimately, she looked to Athena for direction. A psionic attack hit Athena's mind, and she heard Malevant speaking to her, "Stay," he said. "Your Cyclops and Centaurs number in the millions. You have a commitment to them as their leader."

"I am... sick and tired of you!" Athena shouted. "No more pain! No more torture! No more control! There's nothing you can say that can convince me to serve you!"

"Perhaps a part of Lord Gigatheta has attached itself to me, but I can now appreciate your knowledge and skill more than ever. I'll make you this deal, Athena, and I believe that it's more than fair. You promised to lead me to Azure, the power of powers. All I ask is that you live up to it. If you do so, I promise to spare your sister and friends right here and now. I could crush them all with a thought with these increased powers. You know it, and I know it. I'll return to you full command of your Gaians and resist the temptation to torture them one by one as slowly and as painfully as possible, something which I am looking forward to doing if you should choose to leave. Are you truly ready to have the suffering of your people on your conscience, Athena? I'm asking this of you and you alone, not these pathetic so-called 'god' friends of yours, and not your sister. Just you and you alone. Will you accept, or will I have to ask her?"

"All I need to do is resume command of my people and lead you to Azure? And you promise to spare my sister and my people?"

"That's what I said. Greater power has apparently granted me greater generosity than I ever thought possible."

Thor grabbed her by the hand and started leading her toward the portal. Athena pulled away from his grasp and turned to her sister, "I love you, sis, thank you for coming," she said before abruptly pushing her over onto Susanoo's cloud. "Take her away, Susanoo! Take her now! Don't look back!"

Aphrodite reached out and cried for her sister, but Susanoo conducted the cloud to warp through space. Gigatheta began to croak, his complexion growing darker and his flesh beginning to rot away or turn to ashes. Malevant's size and the intensity of his aura continued to magnify.

Thor stood in front of the portal with his hands wide open as if to ask, *What the hell are you doing?* With one great, determined psionic surge, she pushed Thor through the portal and into the relative safety of the Nether Realm. He stumbled back to his feet and ran back to the portal, which was now closing. "No! Athena!" he called after her. He reached his hand through the portal and reached out for her. Athena reached out too but kept enough distance to avoid touching him. She waved to him, saying, "That was a kind and heroic thing you did for me, Thor. I'll never forget your bravery. Thank you." As the portal grew dangerously small, Thor withdrew his hand before it could be severed. He sat down cross-legged and bent his head as Loki and Diamond looked on.

As Loki sang a song that alternated between comforting and mocking him, Thor chose to ignore him. "Enough, brother. That's quite enough." He raised his hand. "I… I'm in mourning."

Loki burst out laughing. "Oh, what's the big ole' deal? You just met the woman!"

Thor looked up at him and his eyes sparked. "Doth thee remember, brother, when Sif died?"

"Kinda, sorta, not really. I know it happened."

"Yes! 'Tis because you were climbing Yggdrasil, and we waited for thee to supply thy golden apples! They could have restored her to health, but instead I watched the life slip from her. And you! You did'st nothing but feed thyself—feed thy own selfish ambition! That's what thee always does! That's what thee hast always done, Loki!"

"Well, I'm awfully good at that, aren't I?"

"I want to go back to her. Send me back to her. I demand it!"

"Now, waity just one second," said Loki, poking him thrice with the end of his staff. "Since when do you make demands of me? I saved your life from being crushed under that planet. You swore an oath to me."

"Please, brother," Thor sobbed, catching his breath. "The lady deserves better than to be trapped alone with those dreadful Dragons."

"Heeeheeeheeehaaaw
I'm sorry, brother, you weren't laid
There was a reason that she stayed
Could tell you now,
Could tell you more
But my guess is it was to save her sister
The adorable whore"

"She was kind to me. And helpful. A little cute too."

"My point is, brother, that there is no point. There is no point in me sending you back there other than the entertainment I get from you getting your shit kicked in by Dragons. Athena has made up her mind, probably to save her sister at the expense of herself. That's kinda a recurring pattern if you haven't noticed. I can't be the only one who notices these things."

"Thee can speaketh across dimensions. Let me speaketh to her!"

"And risk letting that big bastard Dragon, Malevant, know what we're up to here? That hardly seems like a sensible idea now, does it?"

"Please, brother, we need to help her. You need to let me try again!"

"Thor," said Diamond, touching him on the arm. "I am burning inside too… A terrible fate has befallen the love of my life. However, my programming has seen and analyzed millions of possible outcomes. Loki has also seen the future, and we both agree on the chosen course of action. We must be patient and empty ourselves. We must stay the course. Help me. Help Loki. Help Azure. And I assure you, you'll help your Athena in the process. It's our one and only chance in a hundred million possible outcomes. We must end this war with the Dragons for your people, and my people, and all people for all time."

Thor was at a loss for words as he looked to both of them.

"If it makes you feel any better, dear brother, I'll let you leave her a voicemail or something every now and then," Loki added. "But I'm letting you know beforehand, I'm filtering them for content."

"A MILLION, MILLION DREAMS"

Another day came, the 46th day.

Azure awoke next to Neela, still lying lifeless in the hospital bed in the intensive care unit. A labyrinth of IV tubes ran to her. Tubes ran from her nose and mouth as well. Sometimes, he thought he'd heard her make a sound or yawn, stirring up his hope. It was a hope that was soon crushed as the medical personnel he'd excitedly and repeatedly called over explained to him that these actions were unconscious. He was reminded that she was still unaware, still trapped, still gone. It seemed like every day, someone came to talk to him about Neela's state and her chances of recovery. They told him that her quality of life would only be downhill from that point. They told him that they had very limited beds and rooms for new patients, and that the ICU was no place for a patient like her. They told him that the expenses would pile up day after day and questioned his ability to pay for it.

To those ends, he got an undocumented manual labor job helping to move furniture. Even the heaviest furniture felt like a glass cup in his hands now, and he furiously worked as quickly as possible so that he could spend as much time at Neela's side as possible. One of the supervisors, a hulking red Carnotaur who always wore sunglasses, noticed his unnatural energy and physical prowess as well as his determination. "What's your name, Big Blue?" asked the Carnotaur.

"Azure."

"Word has gotten around that your girl has been in a coma for weeks and that you're looking to pay off her medical expenses. Is that true?"

"Yes, sir."

"Edom. Call me Edom. I don't call the shots here, I just act, react, and report back. Something's different about you. Would you mind sharing your power with me?"

"What power?"

"You don't have to play dumb with me, Big Blue. I've got something too. Everyone knows about it. Wanna see?" Edom casually put one hand under a piano and raised it overhead, then gently lowered it. "I am the six-time World's Strongest Malkuthian. I'll forgive you for not knowing that, the media tends to focus on team sports for some reason. Anyway, I recruit others like us to do the boss's dirty work."

"The boss? You mean, like Boss Epsilon, the crime lord?"

"Yes, exactly."

"I'm no gangster. I'm no criminal. I have no interest in being one."

"You know, what you're doing now is technically against the law, but we don't talk about that. I'm not asking you to murder anyone. We'll start you with small jobs. Beat a few people down. Break some bones. Protect a drop."

"I can't. I'm sorry."

"It's your girl, isn't it? You're thinking: how the hell do you face her knowing you've done something immoral, right? I've been there and done that, Big Blue. I've been married three times and have God-knows-how-many kids. That's a whole lot of medical bills and legal fees, I tell ya. You've gotta ask yourself: what happens if your girl never wakes up, and you have to live with the regret of having not done everything in your power to help her?"

The wind escaped Azure's lungs.

"I'm happy hiring you just as a moving man, but if your finances don't add up, you should know that your options are open," he handed him a business card and patted him on the back. Each pat was like being hit with a heavy chair. "You're a good guy, I can tell, Big Blue. I'm not trying to change that, I'm just trying to help."

Azure showered briefly and rushed to the hospital. Each time, he hoped he'd rush through the door, and Neela would be sitting up and waiting to greet him with a smile of purple braces. But he rushed through the ICU doors, and she was still lying there the same as ever. He pulled a nurse aside and asked if there'd been any changes. There were none, but the nurse asked if he'd like to help turn her to prevent pressure sores, something he was used to doing by now. He agreed, and the nurse directed him. They turned Neela to one side and placed special pillows against her. The sight of her on her side curled up like a baby, made Azure's heart swell with sadness. The nurse put on a glove and rubbed his back, saying, "I'll let you two have some time alone."

Azure came beside Neela and held her hand, praying. He then picked up the bent and cracked glasses that sat on the desk beside her. They'd been broken during her earlier arrest. There was blood and dirt on them, so he cleaned them in the sink. He then took her pink hijab and washed it with cold water and soap, wringing it out until there wasn't a drop left. He let it dry over the edge of a chair.

Azure thought back to the conversation he'd had with the lead doctor weeks ago. "It's like a cancer, or a parasite. The best way I can describe it is this: she has something living in her brain. It's a known organism, extremely rare, called a

Pankajan Symbiata. We call it a 'Symbiote' for short. It's a type of parasite that usually affects the organs of marine animals. It behaves and grows a lot like a cancerous tumor, sapping energy from the cells around it. But I've never seen anything like this one. It has mutated. It's much bigger than a normal Symbiote."

"She was exposed to radiation from a bomb on her home planet," said Azure.

"That might explain it. Look, I regret to inform you, but according to all of our simulations, we can't remove the Symbiote without killing her along with it. It has grown too big and is branching out into all directions."

"Then, what can you do? There needs to be something!"

"All I can think of is to treat it like a cancerous growth. That's why I brought that up. We can't operate on it without killing her, but we can, perhaps, irradiate it to shrink it or stunt its growth. If we get lucky, it might even die, I don't know. That's speculation at best. The chances of that working are extremely low."

"We have to try."

"Every session of chemo costs an ungodly amount of BN. If you can afford it…"

"Of course I can afford it! Do whatever you need to do to save her."

"Then, we'll hit it with everything we've got. There's no promises any of them will work. Make sure you head down to the Billing Department and give them a copy of your recent bank statements and pay stubs."

"But, I… I don't have a bank account."

"Then give them whatever financial information you have and pray they can work with you. That's not my department." The doctor stood up and yawned. He stretched. "We'll do what we can. Just do what you can to pay for it, ok?"

Azure turned on the TV and skipped over the news of the war, changing it to the cartoon channel which was playing *Losty the Unicorn*, Neela's favorite show. "Hey, Neela, this is one of your favorite episodes," he said, looking back at her as if she'd actually respond. "It's a rerun. The one… with Losty and the Pegasus." Azure covered his face and clawed at his eyes. *"I know you can hear me, Jesus. I've been seeing you in my mind for years. I know who you are whether you realize it or not. I know there's something between us that none of you ever told me about.*

I've seen into your future. You make the lame to walk. You heal the sick. You restore sight to the blind. You raise the dead. You… You can fix her! You want me to be your attack dog?! You want me to solve the problems your father let snowball out of control?! You want me to end this war?! Then do this. Do this one thing, please! You fix her! You, hear me? I see your face looking back at me... somehow, I know you understand me... I know you have the power to do it... Then please... do it... do something... anything... please..."

He had a vision of Jesus, still a child, reaching out and petting him on the nose and smiling back at him. "I tell you, with such faith, you could command a mountain to throw itself into the sea, and it would be done," he said. "Have faith, Azure. No one knows the time or place but the father. Trust God and his timing. His will be done."

Azure opened his eyes, believing that his angry prayer may have had some effect, but Neela still lay there motionless. He growled in frustration. The lights flickered and the emergency generators had to kick in for a while. Azure fought back his emotions in fear that they would compromise the sensitive equipment that helped keep Neela alive.

"Good night, Neela, my love," Azure sobbed. "And a million, million sweet dreams 'til tomorrow, whenever tomorrow comes."

A day passed, then another. Each time, Azure came to visit her. Hoping. Practically knowing. But each time, she was the same: still, emotionless, unfeeling. "I can't do this..." he said. "I can't let you become this... like the cold universe..." He remembered sitting with her at the edge of the sky district, under the nebulous, starry sky as she pointed out each and every special thing, turning back to face him with a face of wonder. "Take it back," he put his hands on her head, stroking the ridges of her snout. "Take it all back and just come back to me. Come home."

He hugged her head as she had but nothing happened. He kissed her like in the fairytales she'd read to him, but nothing happened. Nothing. Then, one day he walked in and her blue eyes opened wide. He ran over to her and looked closer, hardly believing it. Her eyes watered and followed him, studying his face and eyes like an optometrist. "I'm here, Neela, I'm here," he assured her. He made a commotion and excitedly called the medical staff into the room. Through tests, they confirmed that she had regained sight and hearing. A joy filled Azure's heart and soul. "Oh, Neela..." he must've said a dozen times.

A vision of a teenage Jesus appeared across from him and walked over to hug him, rubbing him on the back. No one else saw this. "Your eyes are opening wide, Azure," he said before disappearing. "Tell her. She deserves to know."

Neela remained unable to move or eat without the assistance of a feeding tube. To reverse her muscular atrophy, the staff placed electrostimulation devices on her arms and legs. Azure helped them to do this too. He would read to her and watch her favorite show with her. But as he sat there and her eyes gazed away from the show and focused on him, Azure turned down the volume. "...You want to know, don't you? About me. About everything."

Neela blinked thrice, signaling, "Yes."

"You gave everything to give me my memories. And now I'm so blessed and cursed with them. I'm haunted… it's like a million ghosts returning to me all at once. And yet, I am so thankful and forever indebted to you, Neela. You deserve to hear it more than anyone. You deserve to know."

PART IV
AZURE

"AZURE'S STORY"

"Neela...I remember I was caught between two hot lights—one brighter than the other. They span and wrapped themselves around me. The next thing I can remember, I was falling... falling. Tumbling endlessly in near-complete darkness. Space. There were... little lights. Stars. They must've been. I felt so scared, so confused, so alone. I remember wondering who I was and why I was there. I must have babbled things to myself. God, I must have been alone for...what felt like an eternity.

I cried to myself and fell asleep for a long, long time. I remember coming close to a star once, feeling warmth for the first time. I don't know how close I really was to it, but I could see it as something much more than a speck of light. An orange ball of fire. It was an unbelievable feeling. I waved my hands in front of me and saw my fingers and claws clearly for the first time. I saw my own shout clearly for the first time. My tail too. But there was still so little I could control. It was always like being in a prison. To never feel the ground beneath my feet, to never determine my direction, my path. To endlessly be trapped in a state of limbo. That powerless feeling I've felt my whole life.

Neela, what I have to say next I fear will be even harder for you to believe than all that. I'm afraid to say it… I felt something grab me. I felt my skin burning. I saw a frightening glow from a hellish sphere that looked like a rotten fruit, a decaying brain. A planet. I seemed to be falling toward it. I couldn't stop it. I shrieked in terror. I'd never been so scared before. This demonic circle that lay before me, growing as I neared. I fell, I plunged down into molten fire. My skin burned. I sank deeper down into it. I wanted it to end. My mind screamed. I sank, submerged in that ungodly primordial soup, feeling the most excruciating pain I'd ever felt in my life. It's... indescribable. Even now I remember… As I sank perilously into that sea of fire, I looked up toward the sky, toward space, toward the stars as if they could save me. There were... streaks of comets, meteorites soaring—

plummeting from the sky. They smashed into the molten fire.

My eyes, my skin, my flesh burned, but somehow I remained conscious and aware. I was trapped, drowning forever. But I shut myself down. I... slept. I suppose it was like when you were in the hanging cage or as you are now. I slept to pass the time. To vanish from that situation. That's what I did. And it lasted. It lasted for a long, long time. It's like... the pain was there, but I ceased to feel it. Like my body had adapted or closed itself off to it, to everything.

When I awoke, it was dark and there were hard jagged rocks encased all around me. I panicked. I struggled for a while. Again, I felt hopeless. Again, I felt powerless. Imagine being buried alive miles beneath the ground.

As I struggled and fought, growing increasingly frustrated with the hopelessness I felt, something like an eerie green light, a glow, illuminated the space around me. My heart pounded. My pulse... it raced. The rocks around me began to move. Layers of it, the foundations of this world, fractured and shattered. I erupted in an explosion, a mammoth explosion, a cataclysm that ripped up that bedrock and lifted—launched—me up to the surface where I fell. The ground shook for minutes. The shaking was so violent that I could hardly appreciate the new world that greeted me, a green world with mossy plant-life beside a black sea. Rain fell constantly in those days. My God, when I hear you speak of Pankaja, I suppose I have flashes remembering those days when the sky was so cloudy and the stench—that homely stench—lingered. To feel the rain against my skin. It was like the evening.

There was very little sunshine, yet the clouds were a luminous red, orange, purple. It was beautiful in its own way. I wandered through that hellish world—wandered, wandered, wandered. It has been the story of my life.

Back then, meteorites always fell. Violent collisions. Explosions larger and more destructive than a thousand atom bombs. I was near the epicenter of some of these collisions. The first time, I remember how frightened yet impressed I was. At first, it streaked down in a brilliant flare of orange light. It was like... being stuck on the train tracks as the locomotive approaches, how could you run from that? And at first, I didn't even think it would hit me. There was no way to judge where it would fall until it was too late. I experienced similar feelings while encountering cannons and other artillery fire in the wars. There really is no safe place. It's up to chance. I felt the force crush me in a seeming instant. I lost my senses. I should have died, yet I emerged again, I presume the same as before, in a crater.

The crater was so large it was beyond what I could see with my naked eyes, beyond the horizon. I continued to wander. I didn't breathe then, drink then, or eat then, but I was full of curiosity that one day compelled me to the water's edge to take a sip, or rather, to move the water into my mouth to see what my mouth did. I'd chew all sorts of things I found, but none appealed to me. I babbled things like I did in space, but this time I could hear myself. I could hear things.

There, at the edge of the water I finally caught a glimpse of myself, my reflection. I remember being afraid of what I saw, afraid of this monstrous beast with terrifying teeth. Large arms drooped from my chest. *What am I?* I thought. *Are there others like me? Am I the only one? Am I alone?*

I must have fallen asleep by that body of water, entered another of my long slumbers, my dormancies. I didn't realize how much the world beneath me was shifting. That new lands—continents—were being born. All I knew was that I was alone there. In a strange sense, I realize that peace is not in itself a perfect thing. Peace is uneventful. It is lonely. It is boring. How sad of me to even think that, but alone, there by the black seaside, I felt it. *Is there anyone? Anyone else like me?*

I'm not sure when it happened or how... not sure of many things—they all seem to blend—to bleed together. But I do remember the tadpoles in the water. Or I thought they were tadpoles. Maybe they were fish. Maybe they were short, fat worms. I don't know. But I'd never seen anything *alive* like that before. And to think I found them in a muddy, disgusting puddle as I trudged through the rain.

And here's another thing I remember, yet the circumstances seem vague... a long time later, I was resting near some plants, I suppose, when I felt something rub up against my leg. It startled me, I do admit, but when I looked, I saw... something like a large snake staring back at me. Something *like me*. I reached out to touch it, but it fled away, only to stop shortly after and look at me, studying me as I studied it. It had eyes like me. It had scales like me, a jaw like mine. I tried to talk to it, but I suppose my *becoming voice* frightened it, so it ran away.

But my existential questions were answered. I was not alone. There were others like me, at least somewhat. And now I had purpose, to find those *others*. To find life."

"Ah-Ah-Ajh-ure..." Neela mouthed.

Azure's heart skipped, and the lights flickered again. He came up right next to her and grabbed her hands. "Did you just speak? Neela, say something! Please! Say something again!"

"S-s-sssomthing uh-uh-gain. Heh..." She smiled, her purple braces glistening. Her hands trembled but exerted force on his. Her toes wiggled. Azure hyperventilated with excitement. As he pulled away to tell the medical staff, Neela pulled back on him. "D-d-don't. L-let them b-be s-ssssurprised. T-t-tell me. M-mmmore."

"Can I first tell you 'thank you' and 'I love you?'"

She smiled contentedly. "Th-thank you t-too… I l-l-l-love you t-too…"

"You must be so tired."

"C-continue your st-st-story. I've sl-slept e-enough. T-tell me what happened next... in your life... in your story... searching for life... wh-what did you f-find?"

Azure thought awhile. *What did I find?* "There were bugs, ones as big as my tail. They frightened me. And there were birds. They sang all kinds of songs. I even tried to talk to them, but they didn't talk like me. Lots of different creatures."

"Oooh," Neela appeared to cringe. "B-big b-b-bugs."

"The centipedes... they grew to be maybe 30-feet long. They hunted and tried to eat the smaller animals, the rodents, the reptiles. I wanted to protect them, but I remember being... afraid. Afraid of all the legs, the powerful pinchers. The emptiness in their eyes. I don't know what it was, but even now it sends chills through me. That emptiness. Yet behind that emptiness seemed to be an apparent motive—a mind—to hunt, to eat, to kill. It frightened me for some reason, it's really hard to explain. They were impossible to read. They would latch onto something and constrict it until either the poison or asphyxiation or both took effect. Then they would swallow the creature whole or tear it apart.

I guess the next major thing I remember was one day someone spoke to me. *Someone* for the first time. I don't remember much about what happened immediately afterward. Even now, things are quite a blur. But I do remember the first sentient being I ever met. Would you believe it if I told you I met an Angel one day while wandering the land?"

"An A-A-Angel?"

"He was a being who glowed with such a bright aura that I couldn't bear to look at him for too long. He had white and purple wings with—it's hard to describe—eyes all over them. He wore spectacular white armor with gold shoulder guards.

'Do not be afraid,' he said with a voice like a trumpet. 'My Lord, God, Yahweh, whose glory illuminates the darkest corners of the cosmos, has ordained me chief of the Arch-Angels, of the highest order of those who serve him.'

I must have babbled or said something that sounded foolish because it made him laugh.

……… …

"You are an anomaly," said the Arch-Angel. "In all of creation, there is only one like you. My Lord and king, who reigns over the realms of spirits and the realms of the mortals, has taken a keen interest in you. He has sent me to teach you, to guide you for a time."

"Hwa, ai? (Who am I?) Hwa, yo? (Who are you?) Lai-lai mai (Like me?)"

In a flash, Michael moved directly in front of Azure who retreated back, wide-eyed with a mixture of terror and fascination. "Perhaps I should speak in a way you will surely understand," said Michael. He altered his speech patterns to accommodate Azure, who continued to shrink away. "Do not be afraid, Azure. I am here to help you." Michael generated an incredible sword in his palms. Its blade seemed to burn with an aura of its own. It was taller than the Angel and several feet wide. "This is the Sword of Heaven," said Michael. "That which cut down the slanderous devil, the enemy of our God who spins the planets, stars, and galaxies into orbit. It is the most brilliant weapon ever crafted. It is forged from a part of the Holy Spirit itself, the spirit which gives the Omniverse form, which has existed before the foundation of the stars and Heaven, before any living thing. It holds the power to cut through even the adamantine armor of the Angels. It is not made of metal or any element or material in the mortal plane. It is purely spiritual energy, and only one of extraordinary affinity with the Spirit may wield it. The sword is yours."

Michael turned it on its side and held it gentlemanly out to Azure who hesitated to grab it from him. When he finally reached for the white handle, the whole sword vanished.

"Hwuh, happin'? (What happened?) Eh goh? (It go?)" said Azure.

"Do not fret. It is with you. However, to summon it up, first you must understand where its power comes from. You have endured the flames of this primordial world, yes, but you must prepare yourself for the heat of Heaven's splendor, at the doorstep of the Almighty God and master, the ancient of days, who alone is perfect and worthy of praise." Michael ushered him into a tornadic vortex of fire, a collection of colors and sounds came from it. "For who is like God, the Alpha and Omega, the beginning and the end? And who can defeat you if he is with you? You will come to know him. Come with me!" Michael reached to him. Azure took the Angel's hand and stepped inside the fiery vortex.

… … …

Azure continued his story. "Even after feeling the heat of this primordial world, the heat of Heaven felt even more intense. My skin and flesh burned away. I believed I saw a new hand, new limbs, but they were transparent with a green tinge to it, it's difficult to describe. Next thing I knew, I'd lost consciousness.

I awoke and came into the presence of two more Angels. Their names were Raphael and Laurel. Their appearance terrified me at first. Like Michael, they had many eyes and many faces. However, they seemed to change form, taking up a more pleasant appearance, as they saw that I was afraid. They looked spectacular.

……… ...

"Laurel, would you take good care of our guest, please?" said Raphael.

"No worries, sir," said Laurel, "I've got it; I'll make him feel at home, sir."

"Thank you, dear Laurel; the Lord commends your efforts." Raphael flew off to attend to other business, rejoining Michael.

Laurel hesitantly flew closer to Azure and creeped toward him. "Heeeey, buddy… Are you feeling ok?"

Azure groaned, having gone through the fires of Heaven.

"I'm sorry. I know it can be hard sometimes. That's what divides the mortals from the glory and splendor of God. If only it were easier, huh? Someday, it will be." The chirpy little Angel looked him up and down, petting him on the snout. She giggled into her forearm. "Mercy me! You're just like them! You're like a dinosaur!"

"*Hwuh?* (What?)" said Azure.

"Oh, never mind. That's what the humans on Earth will be calling them. 'Dinosaurs.' Big behemoths. Super duper lizards. You look just like one of them! I wonder why… I wonder if it's like what Azazel did. If it's another one of their experiments. Anyway, not to dwell on the negative stuff. Are you ready for a grand adventure?"

"Ooooh…"

……… ...

"As spectacular as the Angels were, Heaven was infinitely more spectacular. My God, Neela! My God! The streets were like gold but indescribably more bright and magnificent. Think about the insides of a crustacean. All the colors and shimmer.

Heaven was a trillion upon a trillion times more spectacular than that. There were great large trees, but they seemed small from afar. There were miles and miles and miles of open plains which never ended.

Laurel told me a story of a friend she had who was of a higher order of the Angels. Tarrol was her name. Laurel showed me a mystical garden where they would play 'pretend' together. She told me that one day, Tarrol formed a crown and put it on her head, claiming to be the new 'Queen of Heaven.'"

… … …

"What's that?" asked Laurel.

"What's what, darling?" said Tarrol.

"A 'queen.'"

"Oh, a 'queen' is equal to a king in rank and power. Samael calls me his 'queen.' He's a bit better looking than Astarothel, don't you think?"

"Yes, he is."

"Doesn't this crown look fashionable on me, darling?" Tarrol looked in a mirror. "Hurts my neck a bit."

"It looks… nice on you, Tarrol," said Laurel, uneasy. "But… I thought only our God and father, Yahweh, could grant those kinds of titles. And I thought that our king has no equal. He is all-powerful."

"Oh, hush, darling. Stop being so old fashioned. This is a new age. A new epoch. Samael's going to make everything right."

"Samael is? But Samael isn't our king."

"Well, he should be," said Tarrol. "And I should be queen."

Laurel gulped. "Please be careful, Tarrol. I care about you. I don't want to see you get into trouble or get hurt."

"Oh, I can take care of myself, darling. Are you going to tattle on me?"

"If I'm asked, I must answer. But I don't want to."

"Then don't, darling. You don't have to do anything they tell you to do. Just be a good friend, and don't make me regret coming all the way down here to meet you."

"I thought you enjoyed hanging out."

"I did. But I'm bored, darling," said Tarrol. "So bored…"

"Bored of me?" said Laurel, hurt.

"Bored of everything, darling. The singing, the praising, the singing, the praising. I want more. I want to be more."

"You're my best friend, Tarrol. You're like a sister to me. I look forward to seeing you all the time. Isn't that enough?"

"No."

… … …

"Michael flew down to me and thanked Laurel for caring for me. He told me in a language I could understand that there lived the king of Heaven, Yahweh, and a first-child, called the Prince, who together crafted the cosmos from the spirit which gives everything form. The Angels too were formed by the King and the Prince. There were many different ones, different kinds, ranks, and orders. One of the most fascinating to me were the Cherubim, who functioned like—what I might describe as—transporters or channelers of energy through what they called the three celestial spheres. The spheres encompassed the dwelling place of the Angels, the gateway between Heaven and mortal worlds—connecting them to the throne of God himself. I was told they held open the pathways between God and the rest of his creation. They were terrifying, giant beasts with animal-like faces and eagle-like wings.

Michael told me that long ago there was one Cherubim among them who was called Samael. He had been the greatest of the Cherubim by far, being called the Great Channeler. He produced so much light from the energy he channeled that he was nicknamed "Lucifer," the light-bringer.

Samael held a deep-seated envy of the higher orders of the Angels, the Arch-Angels and the Seraphim. But most of all he loathed God, Yahweh, himself, and particularly the never-ending praise and worship directed to him, whereas the Cherubim and other Angels received no such praise. Samael was said to be the beginning of all evil in the Omniverse.

I came to see this statement differently... In time, after seeing evil and suffering for centuries and centuries, I came to wonder if in fact Samael was all to blame for the introduction of evil. Then I read, many millennia later, the Holy Scriptures for myself, and I read the verse: "I am a jealous god," one who vehemently hates the praise and worship of other, perhaps lesser, deities. A *jealous* god?

I came to think that Samael had simply inherited one of the Creator's least acknowledged traits: jealousy, and the severity that comes from it. From that jealousy could have sprung all of this: envy, pride, greed, covetousness, avarice, lust, wrath, and hatred—evil itself. It was the only way that made sense to me: for how could evil come of perfection? How could anything bad come from omnibenevolence?

Yet Michael seemed to avoid addressing those obscurities. Now, seeing these things after so long, I can't help but think what a tool he was—a firm brick in God's Omniverse.

Samael was able to convince one-third of the Angels in Heaven to rebel. Among his most influential followers were Be'elzebul and Astarothel, both charismatic and beloved grand dukes; and, yes, Tarrol. There were also several who were from military backgrounds in a sense, trained to defend the throne: Belial, Mammonel, and Molochel, I think their names were. They fought the Angels loyal to Heaven for three heavenly days—each day a thousand years long, I learned. Michael described the battle to me."

... ...

"THE ANGEL WAR"

The sky lit up with every crashing blow as if the stars themselves had collided. They attacked each other so swiftly that, in the way a rubbing match sparks a fire, peals of flames engulfed the battlefield. In the skies over Heaven, the winged figures clashed with the force of a thousand mighty men each. Clippings of wings flew, their feathers caught in the whirlwind of conflict. It was as if a vehicle had swept through a flock of white doves.

The rebellious Angels—the now-Demons—thrashed out in anger at the loyal Angels in a swarm. Yet the demonic horde was overwhelmed. Across the battlefield, Satan witnessed the sheer might of the Arch-Angel, Michael, as he hacked down entire legions with the Sword of Heaven. Satan burned with fury. Black smoke shot out from his mouth like steam from a teapot, and he let out a roar of anguish. Michael turned to face his adversary at the other end of the battlefield. He looked to him firmly, but with love.

"Why have you done this, Samael?" Michael spoke to him with a voice that projected for miles across. "You have condemned so many. For your jealousy and your hatred and your rebellion—here lies the fate of one-third of the Lord's host. Here lies the fate of man!"

"I don't care," Satan growled coldly. "A son of fire will not serve sons of mud. They will be my slaves, and I will be their new god! We will create our own Heaven & our own Earth! With man as our slaves. And you! Yes, you! You will be the king of the slaves!" Satan rushed at Michael with the speed of light, pummeling anything in his path—Angel and Demon.

Fiery darts shot out in all directions. Weapons clanged all around. There were the triumphant shouts of the Angels as well as the ripping war cries and groans of the Demons. Raphael clashed with Mammonel, Belial with Uriel, and Be'elzebul with Gabriel. The war spread throughout the heavenly sphere. Legion upon legion and army upon army fought amongst each other. The rebellion was at its climax.

Michael met Satan at the center of the battlefield. They collided with such force that it rattled the solid, mountainous gates of Heaven and sent those around them flying like papers caught in a gale. The two angelic leaders commenced the unspeakable duel. For days they fought, unrelenting. They locked hands in a standstill. Satan pressed with all of his might while Michael resisted him.

"Michael!" Satan growled through clenched teeth. "I have sought you especially amongst all on this battleground. Subdue me by the power of the almighty, but I will take my vengeance upon the prophesied and turn this *Earth* into your fabled *Hell*!"

"Tarrol!" cried Laurel, blocking an attack from Terra. "Stop this, please!"

"How can I, darling?" said Terra. "The wheels on this chariot are turning."

"I don't want to fight you, Tarrol!"

"Darling, what choice have you?"

"I can choose to say 'no!'" said Laurel, lowering her weapon, tears in her eyes. "No more, Tarrol!"

"Goodbye, darling," Tarrol attacked. Laurel shut her eyes and flinched, bracing for the end.

The Angel Uriel blocked Tarrol's attack. She was knocked down by the resulting force. As she scurried away, Astarothel came to her aid. She kicked him away and retreated alone. Uriel held up his weapon to Astarothel. "You have been lied to, Astarothel," said Uriel.

"I know what was and is, Uriel," said Astarothel, "this 'man' the Lord speaks of was never a part of it." He retreated.

"Do not lower your guard, Laurel," Uriel warned.

"Yes… sir…"

Satan lifted his arms up and crashed down with an axe-handle. Michael dashed away only to rebound and strike him. Satan stumbled back. Michael threw him to the ground with such force that a crater was made in its wake. Satan screamed angrily, cursing Michael. The enraged Demon King exploded out from the crater as if from a cannon and smashed Michael straight through the plateau above. They flew higher into Heaven and into space—fighting as they went as the majestic palace structures crumbled around them. Satan thrashed out wildly with his sword, screaming, as Michael dodged and parried every blow. Michael then came down on Satan with one swing. There was a flash of bright light as it knocked Satan's sword aside and sliced through his armor. Satan groaned and plummeted to the ground, crashing through the structure of the plateau. Satan stumbled to his feet. He gathered a massive ball of fire in his palm and hurled it at Michael who evaded it as it exploded in space. Michael drew out a bow and shot a volley of mystical arrows down at Satan. The arrows, as they flew, were like comets as they caught fire and exploded like carpet bombs on the ground.

Satan let out a deathly groan and drew out a dagger. With that, his elite soldiers, battle wary, flocked to him. They attacked Michael—each from a different angle—until they surrounded him. But Michael drew seven swords to combat the Demons. He threw them up in the air like a juggler and slashed away with such speed and might that he was able to hold off the onslaught.

Then there was a shout—the voice of God—like thunder. This was followed by a rumbling that shook the foundations of Heaven. The Demons panicked and scrambled for the gates which quickly closed on them.

"Gabriel," said the voice of God to his chief messenger, "give me an account of what has taken place here."

"O-Oh, Lord! Oh, Lord!" said Be'elzebul, Satan's lieutenant. "Are the preparations for this 'Earth' going well?"

Gabriel stepped forward. "There has been an uprising, my Lord," said Gabriel, "Samael, here, led a rebellion against your loyal host. Astarothel, Be'elzebul, Tarrol, Azazel, Belial, Molochel, Mammonel, and others joined him. They have betrayed you."

Satan clenched his fists.

"Liar!" Satan shouted in defense. "It is *I* who has been betrayed! Betrayed by you who has forsaken me for this one called man! Spectacular spiritual beings such as us should not be subservient to the needs of these pathetic mortals! They deserve no such good. They deserve only to feed us, to be food for us. It's only right. We should devour their flesh and feast on their souls. They should be allowed to decay and be no more. And we will rule beside you forever. Just us. The way it should always be."

"Samael, haven't I cherished you, and valued you, and set you amongst the greatest of my host? Haven't I given you all that you have asked? Still, you have demanded the suffering of the children that will be made in my image. You have threatened them with such wicked things. You have said that you would turn my prophesied Earth into their Hell. And you dare to delight in such a prospect. Then, depart from me, Satan! Ye cursed! Into this Hell with all your Angels!"

Satan, desperate, brandished his dagger and charged again at Michael in one last attempt to slay him. The other Demons charged behind him.

"Let us begin anew," said the voice of God to the Prince. "And start over from the beginning… May the darkness part… and let there be light." God focused his energy at the charging swarm, more energy than had ever been released, and a void was formed. The tattered and torn Demons were caught up in the Great Cosmic Void and drawn into it. In that instant, the glory of God interacted with the very first droplet of sin as it entered a new universe.

… … …

"Samael became known as Satan, the enemy and accuser of the mortal worlds. He still visits the throne of God to accuse this world or that world, asking for retribution. He asks for permission to inflict suffering on those worlds and the people within them. He possesses the power to rip the life from the bodies of mortals. I met him once, and though I was initially underwhelmed by the being I met—a being who'd apparently severely diminished in size, splendor, and power—I still suffered greatly from our encounter.

Before then, however, I'd trained with Michael for some lifetimes. I spent most of those years in a kind of meditative prayer-like state focused on the Holy Spirit. I'd learned to speak better in those years. I learned a million truths about this universe and the rest in that time. Then, one day, the Holy Spirit formed something like a bluish-white fireball in my hands, which had been clenched in prayer. The fireball condensed to form a handle and then a blade which I was told was 33-feet in length. I hacked down trees and cut through the base of a mountain with ease. I sliced stones and ice as if they were butter. I killed the massive centipedes who hunted the smaller reptiles. The more focused and intent I was, the wider and longer the blade of the sword appeared to be. Then there came that aforementioned day when Samael, Satan, visited us. His appearance surprised us both, but I was confident that the two of us could defeat him.

……...

"THE PROPHECIES OF THE EARTH"

"Where have you come from?" Michael questioned.

"I'm sure your protege would understand," said Satan, walking forward. "I have walked and roamed and wandered the Earth for what seems like an eternity, up and down and up and down the planet so many times I've lost count. I'm surprised to find you here, dear Michael, especially considering that my children, my Nephilim, now inherit your Lord's precious footstool, the Earth. Have you given up on the humans already? Those in his image. Behold and see the travesty, how those in his image follow and worship those in mine. Behold how the little, impressionable weakling bow down to my intelligent and sophisticated Nephilim. This is what he damned me to? An ethereal kingdom in Hell and a physical kingdom on Earth?" Satan scoffed. "Is that my punishment? Or is it that great cosmic scourge of a beast, Ain, whom the Lord surely sent to punish us? Well, she listens to *me* now. She believes *me* now."

"Get behind me!" Michael urged Azure. "Satan, I tell you! As you boast this very moment, rain falls upon the Earth, and it will rain for 40 days and 40 nights until the seas rise to drown your Nephilim and those who chose to follow them. Our Lord, God, the creator and sustainer of all that exists or will ever exist, will preserve only the family of one man who is righteous in his eyes."

"You speak prophetically, Michael. I likewise prophesy that I will save one of my own from the bloodline of that man. He will grow to resent God for the stories that he hears of death and destruction, and he will build a towering kingdom into the clouds so that no flood may harm him or his people. And there, the descendants of your elect will gather to commit the most abhorrent sins and immoralities. I will tarnish those the Lord deems righteous. There, we will build a new empire, richer and more expansive than any before it—to enslave the Lord's chosen people!"

"I tell you, Satan, the Lord our God, the Tetragrammaton, will bring an even greater kingdom, two in one, upon the first. This two-fold kingdom will have been built by one of your own. It will be a great treachery by one so powerful he will duel even mighty Gabriel for 21 days until I arrive to defeat him. I will personally let it be known to the ruler of your kingdom that his time has expired. I will write upon the wall, 'MENE, MENE, TEKEL, UPHARSIN.'"

"Then I will make the two-fold kingdom my own! We will teach the people the perfect tortures and methods of execution to greet the Prince when he chooses to come and play savior."

"I tell you, Satan, you yourself will fall out of love with the two-fold kingdom because of one your prince, Be'elzebul, has cultured. You will find yourself a new protege, younger, more skilled, and of greater beauty than all the commanders who came before him, who with a small army will defeat your kingdom despite its numbers. Yet he too will fade. He will die quickly. His generals will break his kingdom—your kingdom—apart into four."

"Then I will make an even larger and more glorious empire to subjugate God's elect. This time we will burn even the Lord's precious and most holy temple to the ground, and I will stand victorious in that hour."

"The Lord, our God, will use that kingdom to spread the news of his existence and glory to unprecedented heights. And even through the murkiness and smoke of its evil, the Lord's will and power will emanate."

"Then I will pervert their faith in Yahweh. I will pervert their church. They will forget his identity. I will blend the beliefs of the church with those of Pagans. They will see Yahweh only through the lens of their old gods. They will fall before the birth mother. They will pray to their dead heroes and the Angels. They will become so crazed in their faith that they will become like the very Demons they vilify to draw in followers. They will invent abhorrent tortures and commit horrific crimes. I will plunge them into an age where people kill and murder and inflict horrors in the name of God and his son. I will form not one but many kingdoms to torment God's elect every step they take, to push them out of their own city and their own promised land. And those of the church will become like Demons to seize it back. The elect will be like strangers in a world that rejects and hates them."

"Then humankind will find new ways to discover God's splendor throughout the cosmos, and God will bless them with new conveniences and abundance."

"They will build weapons unfathomable in their magnitude, which I will use to make war on the nations. I will slaughter the people of God on a scale never before imagined, a holocaust of epic proportions."

"But all your efforts will fail to destroy the people of God. A sympathetic world will reward their faith and perseverance and return their homeland to them. It will be called Israel. They will prosper there and reign as never before as their oil-rich neighbors lament in jealousy."

"Then I will send all their enemies to destroy them in a single day."

"Then the Lord, God himself, will destroy their armies in a single night."

"Then I will send a son, my own son, to deceive the people of God with the hope of protection. My son will make a covenant with them for seven years. He will rebuild the temple of God in his own name and there declare himself to be God. One of God's own people will give credence to his declaration."

"They will kill him."

"Then I myself will indwell in him. I will gain the worship of all and, like God, smite those who refuse to bow."

"Then the Prince will open the seven seals of the scroll, the Angels will blow the seven trumpets, and the King himself will fill the seven bowls of wrath to be poured out over the followers of your son. His followers will say, 'if you are God, save us and protect us from the wrath of he who sits on the throne!'" And after only seven years, you and your son will fall in battle at the valley of Megiddo, Armageddon, along with all the armies of the Earth. You will kneel to the Prince and be chained by me for a thousand years, and a seal will be placed on you so that you may not deceive the world. The Prince will reign for a thousand years, after which you will be set free to make your final choice. And you will choose to continue your rebellion. It will fail, and you will be damned to the Lake of Fire forever and ever."

Satan clenched his fists and seethed. Then, with supernatural speed, he took one of his darts and hurled it at Azure's head faster than even Michael could intervene. The dart struck Azure, who'd been standing silently by during the angelic confrontation. His mind became a scattered, fractured blur of visions and voices at that moment. Azure clenched his head and roared in pain and confusion.

"Your beloved pupil, Michael! You've spent a quarter of a Heaven's day attempting to awaken his affinity with *Ruach*? Now I have undone everything you've done. He will see it all! He will see everything! He will never make sense of it. He will wander this world as a confused invalid until the end of days. And know this Michael: I had permission to take this action! It was granted to me by your own

Lord and God just as you went about mentoring him. So, grit your teeth as I do. Feel the futility of your service to the tyrant."

"The Lord, my God, is the grand architect who sees what we cannot, knows what we cannot. He has plans none of us are adequate to know. His will be done!"

"Then go. Go and meet your Lord and master, dear Michael! Ask him yourself what is to be done with this creature you've come to love so much..."

Michael returned to Heaven to report what had happened to God. He was told to cease contact with Azure. Azure would be purposely forsaken and abandoned. Michael bowed to his master's wishes, knowing that there was a divine purpose.

……...

"I was alone again," said Azure. "And I experienced a new kind of agony I hadn't been prepared for. I saw everything. It felt like my brain and head were being pulled in a million different directions. I could hardly control my heartbeat, my breath at first. Agony. For hundreds of years, I stumbled through no-man's land, hardly able to move my own limbs. It was akin to the worst migraine and fever multiplied a thousand upon a thousand times, never ending, never ceasing, day and night. This is what you cured me of.

A million, million years of this. A million, million years of wandering more and more, meandering through a foreign world again and not knowing who or what or why. Do you remember when you asked me how I can tell the here and now from the trillion other things I see and hear?"

"Y-y-yes."

"I see you *now*. I can hold your hand. I can taste the air around you. Taste your kisses too." He kissed her. "I can smell the homely scent of your hijab. It is closer and clearer than anything else I see. But in those days, all I could do was grit and bear the never-ending pain in my head, to teach myself to ignore what I could not control. What I could not affect.

I'd forgotten how to speak. I'd forgotten who I was. I'd forgotten what came before. It was like... like my mind had been scrambled.

Thus, I spent another lifetime after searching for life, searching for something *real* – something tangible. I searched again for something that made sense, for something, something, something, or others like me.

Then, one day, while wandering the plains of the then-supercontinent, I came upon a nomadic tribe of bipedal reptilian creatures on the backs of large, hairy, horned animals they called *kirin*. I followed them and watched them with grave curiosity—a fascination with everything they said and did. Most of them were practically naked, but some of the smarter ones had used the hides of dead animals to make clothes and blankets as well as temporary shelters.

They stalked and hunted herds of large mammals they called tauruses. It usually required a team of hunters to bring down just one of those. The nomads camped on blue nights, when it was darkest, and would sometimes even travel tied to their animals with only their navigators awake on bright red nights. To cease moving for more than one night was a death sentence for them. The temperatures in the plains got to be sub-zero at times, and I sadly watched many die in that cold, sometimes still tied to their kirin. The young, the weak, the old were left behind in the blistering snow. I came to them whenever I could. I comforted them as best as I knew. They shivered against my chest. Many died in my arms. Each of their deaths touched me. It was a feeling like hopelessness to see them die so casually. To see their lives extinguished. Hopelessness led to a feeling like... apathy—of giving up. Little by little the significance of each quiet death meant less to me. I couldn't save them, I knew it. I was only one person. I couldn't save everyone.

I caught up again with the tribe as they encamped along the banks of a river. I heard high-pitched screaming and saw a female flee her tent. Three males grabbed her by the tail and legs and pulled her back into the tent. That's how it was in those days. I heard her scream for help. I felt I should do something; I knew. And though I feared the consequences, I ran down to that tent and tried to tear the men off of her. Seemingly the whole camp responded. They pierced my body with spears and arrows, and I ran. I ran, Neela. I ran from the fear."

"You tr-tried."

"I tried... but I could have tried harder. I could have tried harder many times. I found another tribe making out an existence several hundred miles from where I'd left the first. By then, my wounds had healed. My body pushed and spat out the arrows and spears. It hurt greatly. These people were far from sedentary and farmed the fields and raised animals. I only observed the tribe for a few months when I heard a great commotion. Arrows rained down. War-cries went out. A pack of raiders, mostly smaller feathered Theropods, stormed down the hill. They held nets with which they snatched a few small animals. Three of the raiders dismounted to load sacks of grain onto a cart. But the villagers, who were larger than the raiders, overpowered and bound them. The village chieftain said a few words I could not understand, and something I've never been able to understand happened next.

They set a large fire under a large pit filled with water until it boiled. The three captives struggled desperately against their binds and the grasps of their captors, knowing what was coming. I heard them beg and plead for mercy in their own language, but the villagers still called for their suffering. I couldn't believe it. I couldn't stand for it. Yet I froze. I froze again. I froze in fear. I let it happen. Again. They boiled them. They boiled them alive. One by one so that the second and the third would have to witness the suffering of those before them. I heard their gut-curdling screams. I could hear a sound like their bones rattling in the pot. I turned away and covered my eyes but looked back as a victim's writhing hand reached—shot—out from the pot and scorched itself on the edge where it melted, stuck, and became plastered there. The smell was atrocious. I vomited. I cried. I cried and screamed into my hands. How could people be so cruel? And why? Is it fear? Is it natural? I asked myself those questions even today.

The other raiders came back the next red morning and burned the village down, perhaps in retribution. They bashed in the heads of the townsfolk who survived. They stole the livestock. They wrenched the chieftain out of his lodge and bashed his skull in with a heavy club.

I remember thinking there was no justice in that."

"You-you thought he d-d-deserved worse?"

"Is it natural for one who sees and lives with monsters to become a monster? You see, evil... it seeps under your skin. At the time, I felt unfulfilled. Even now, I feel unfulfilled. I felt something wasn't right. I *feel* something isn't right...

The next I knew, the tribes entered a state of constant, unending war. I doubt even the chieftains themselves knew who they were fighting and why, much less their people. Something happens to people when they're close to each other. They clash. They crash. It's like... this wanton internal longing for conflict—this propensity to hurt each other because we can, because it's amusing, because it proves a point, because it proves we're *better*. It makes us proud, it satisfies our egos—something. Neela, I watched from the mountaintops for a whole millennium as people devised new ways to kill each other, this as my visions exacerbated my feelings of anxiety. There was suffering. Suffering everywhere. Always.

And here I was, here I am. All my life, I've felt like I was some kind of net—catching all of it. I always imagined myself like a net in the middle of a great, wide ocean, catching everything that falls to my depths.

In that millennia, I saw barbarism the likes of which I can hardly describe. People who acted without conscience, out of—I don't know—a sense of duty, obligation, or just because they thought it was right, or because they thought there was nothing wrong with it.

I saw a city of probably a quarter million people, perhaps the first great city on Malkuth, besieged by a coalition of tribes until its citizens went berserk and resorted to cannibalism.

The tribes that conquered the city eventually—from what I gather—brought most of the supercontinent under one banner and one supreme leader who you call Arcturus the Great. For the first time in Malkuthian history, there was a sense of oneness, of unity, of universality. It set the precedence for the Union—gave birth to the idea many centuries before it would even take shape. Arcturus was seen as a god on Malkuth, and his kingdom was thought to be divine. His many victories seemed to be proof of this, but I only personally witnessed a few, or so I think. The battlelines in war are often confusing at best. What I learned was mostly what the commoners learned—from propaganda announced by traveling representatives of the government and word of mouth. Rumors. I continued to travel, cloaked like a leper to keep in touch with these people, the people I'd grown so fond yet simultaneously afraid of.

It's funny, despite this knowledge, it didn't seem like much had changed. War continued. The lands near me were still besieged and raided by enemies left and right. Arcturus, the hero you know him as today, was in truth a tyrant whose legalistic doctrine meant more atrocities. Genocide the likes of which the world had never seen before: children ripped from their families to be trained as soldiers, the severe punishing of enemies—both real and imagined. They would hang enemies until nearly dead, then they would tie ropes to their hands and ankles to be drawn and quartered by long-necks and kirin. Their arms, legs, and tails would be torn from their torsos, and during the process, they'd be castrated and disemboweled. Thousands of captured soldiers would be rounded up. They'd dig their own pits and be forced in. Dirt would be shoveled onto them and they'd be buried alive. Once in maybe a thousand times, a soldier refused to bury another. He was thrown in and buried along with the rest, and that sent a message to the others. To witness these abominable acts so many times. Too many times. To have done nothing... The feeling of guilt and regret that has plagued my life—my conscience—since the day I discovered life.

How long ago was that, Neela? Yet how much has really changed? Behind our fancy clothes, our high-tech things... behind it all we are still driven to eat and kill and inflict suffering on each other. We still bow to the will of cruel masters. We still allow the wicked to reign, to dictate our lives, now in ever-so-subtle ways. It's as if it's in the Malkuthian genes. A legacy we can't let go of.

Arcturus, as you know from history, had many wives and concubines gathered from many conquered lands. It is believed he is the ancestor of 30 billion Malkuthians alive today, including the Chancellor, George Antares, who intentionally traced his lineage back through generations of aristocrats to legitimize his position at the head of state."

"Is-is that what dr-drew you to me? My-my hatred of Antares?"

"No," said Azure. "It was because I saw you. I saw you from a million years in advance. I heard you. I heard you a million miles away. I heard your speeches. Bits and pieces here and there. There's something about you in my visions that brings everything together. I needed—I had—to find Neela. I had to find you."

"And wh-what happens to m-m-mmme? To us?"

"In some visions... you live. In some visions, we're married in a ceremony in front of hundreds. In others, we even have kids, a boy and..." Azure began to cry. "A girl. Furud, whom I believe you named after your birth father, and Nicola."

"M-my mom's name..."

"My visions, they're like dreams. They pass in and out. I can recall some of them: we fight alongside each other against the Dragons, and..."

"And?"

"In some visions..." Azure covered his face. "In some visions, you die... you die in battle with the Dragons, pierced by a lance, or you are caught in the crossfire and hit by a stray Union bullet. I hold you in my hands, I kiss you and I cry, I pump your chest and your blood spills all over my hands. I cover your wound with a cloth as if doing so would make a difference. I cry hopelessly. In a few horrifying instances, they find and capture you, and I spend the rest of my existence tortured by thoughts of not being able to rescue you. In most, you simply die quietly in your sleep as I watch, of illness or old age, I'm not sure. And once as the song from our favorite show, *Losty*, plays. I have remained speaking to you now because it seems to be the best path. In those visions where you live to fight beside me, I have sat here beside you and told you everything I knew. But there are so many variables, so many scenarios, it's nearly impossible to tell with any certainty. I just know *this* is where I want to be, *this* is where I need to be. Here with you. I need to hope against hope. I need to hope for the best. I need to hope that this God—this Yahweh—will find it in his massive heart to spare just this one person I love. I love you, Neela. That much is certain."

"...And all this t-t-time, have you ever l-loved anyone else?"

"That's not fair."

"It-it's ok… T-t-tell me…"

A physician came in and was shocked to see and hear Neela talking and moving. "Miraculous!" she exclaimed. "I'll be damned. I never thought she'd make so much progress! How long ago did this develop?"

Azure answered. The physician looked over some graphics, asked Neela some questions, ran some tests, and wrote some things down. More medical staff came to see the miraculous recovery for themselves. They tried to prompt her to write, but she struggled. They tried to prompt her to walk, but even with Azure's assistance and a walker for support, she collapsed. Azure caught her. It was like in their earlier days. Only then, it was Neela who was catching him. They tried to have her eat normally, and she managed. Azure requested some cookies & cream ice cream for her, and this brought a smile to her face. However, she became very tired after eating it. "L-let me sl-sleep. Pl-please." She dozed off.

Azure knew he had to go to work to afford her continued stay and treatment. "Goodnight, Neela, and sweet dreams 'til tomorrow, whenever tomorrow comes." He kissed her.

The next day, Neela told him, "Don't th-think I f-forgot." She asked to hear about the people he loved in the past.

"...Let me tell you what I can…"

"A NEW WORLD"

"I *had* a love… her name was Bekah.

A lot had happened between the rise of Arcturus, the First Dynasty, and meeting her. A lot of that—a lot of those circumstances—I think you need to understand. The sky had darkened as if the world were forming again, and ashes fell. There were reports everywhere I traveled, some conflicting, that there had been a great

282

deafening 'boom' that came from a distant land, an eruption unprecedented in the course of Malkuthian civilization. There were rumors that the seas had risen and flooded the southern lands, which had recently been acquired by Arcturus's grand-nephew, Sargas the Enlightened."

"F-f-forefather of Adonaism," said Neela.

"Yes. Sargas was apparently so inspired or perhaps shaken by the two disasters he'd lived through that he made a proclamation heard across the Atlantan Empire, which encompassed over half the known world then. He proclaimed that there was one God over all Malkuth, the Adonai or Lord, who'd spoken to Sargas and promised to support him in his conquest of the world. Sargas announced that God himself would bring catastrophes upon all who refused the Atlantan Empire and that it was given unto him to establish God's kingdom on Malkuth. It was a masterful stroke of genius. The Atlantan Empire of the First Dynasty became the Holy Atlantan Empire—divinely-appointed and universal—a second and critical dynastic age. Sargas, whose great-uncle had universalized weights, measures, laws, and language across the empire, now universalized a single state religion—Adonaism—under a single universal banner bearing a universal symbol: the three joined stars. They're still seen on our flags today.

But you see, back then I only knew so much. I saw the three joined stars on banners all over the land, but it wasn't until Sargas died that I heard him called by name, announced as the first saint, the first priest, and the first regent or vicar of Adonai, God. And though he died, the religion he founded, of course, far outlived him, and far outlived his and the other dynasties to survive today. Amazing isn't it? But for three centuries after Sargas, Adonai was just a folk character, a name I heard while traveling occasionally through towns and cities to keep my mind away from the visions.

But mostly I stayed away, close to where I thought no one would go. I'd copied the antiquated camp building and survival techniques of the tribesmen I'd earlier encountered. I made tents of logs and mammal hides. I could build my own fire to cook or light my space with. Something about being in the dark under the stars made me feel nostalgic... like drifting through the cosmos, a long-gone memory. I could roar and scream as loud as I needed in order to cope with the visions, the splitting pain in my head. Occasionally, there'd be a howl back."

"And the g-g-girl?" Neela urged.

"Alright, alright, I'll get to her… There came a day when civilization and its religion came to me. A string of covered wagons strolled through the mountain pass where I'd been staying. They encamped at the feet of the slopes, no more than a stone's throw away from me.

'This is it!' I heard one of them shout. 'This is the place right here.'

I thought he'd discovered the waterfall I'd found. Its water had been invaluable to my survival. It had also helped to calm and cool me at times when I felt feverish. Instead, the man pointed to the flatlands up ahead.

'We'll blow a path through these here rocks and make ourselves a road,' he said to the leader of the convoy. They used cheap explosives to do just that. I feared a landslide would kill them all, but they seemed to have things well in hand. Until one day... I guess the initial fuse failed to light and they sent a brave man back to reignite it. The fuse, I suppose, was shorter or something, and the poor man was caught in the explosion. He'd suffered gruesome burns and had broken limbs.

I heard one of the men call to one of the wagons: 'Eh, Talo! Talo! We've got a man down! Don't your girl know nothin' 'bout medicine from that school?'"

Neela chuckled.

"Talo sent his daughter down to check and work on the man. She didn't flinch at all as she rubbed ointment over his burns. The man tossed and turned. 'Would y'all hold him steady?' she shouted at the men."

"You-you do the ac-accent well."

"I've been hearing it in my head for centuries."

"Ah."

"I just remember being so impressed by her presence in that situation. She was quite beautiful too, not nearly as pretty as you, of course, but she caught my eye back then. She certainly made that injured man's miserable day a little better.

But the other young men in the camp made lewd comments. They told Talo perhaps jokingly of their intentions to *keep* her. Someone joked that his scrotum hurt or something, and the others just punched him lightly and laughed it off.

'Check yourselves, boys,' she said, 'Adonai hears every word, he knows every thought. 'Less you want to burn in the fires of Hell, I suggest you rethink where you stand.'

"Was she fl-fl-flirting back?"

"No, she was serious. She was damn serious. Perhaps if you knew her, you'd understand. I snuck down and listened to her talk to her father. I gathered that the girl's name was Bekah. I also gathered that she'd attended some kind of school of medicine in the south and that the convoy had moved north. I suppose they did so because of some calamity in their homeland, some aftereffects of the eruption.

In any case, she and the rest of the convoy were always busy with something. It was best to find some high ground and stay out of their way. They began agriculture in the flatlands within a few days. Their kirin plowed the fields daily. They also slaughtered and ate the animals they brought along. As the men worked on building the roadway, hunting, and setting up the lodges, the women collected water, cooked, cared for the children, and tended to crops.

Bekah had no children. She was only in her 20s, I believe, though birth dates were not important in her culture and so were often forgotten. Time was also more difficult to tell. They had calendars, I guess, based on the phases of the moons, which sun was in the sky, but I'd only seen a handful of watches. Judging by her appearance, it just seemed that way. But something ironic and unexpected happened that revealed a lot to me.

Next thing I knew I heard, 'Hey, kid!' She startled me at the waterfall. I'd gone there to cool off as I'd become feverish again. 'Don't you be running 'ways. Don't the other boys need your help?'

I scurried back and babbled something because I couldn't speak well.

'You okay, kid? Is something the matter?' she asked.

I must have said something like 'sick' because she came over and felt my forehead afterward.

'You're very warm,' she said. 'Where's your mas and pas?'

I denied having any.

'Come,' she said, leading me down by the hand, bearing a bucket of water in the other which she aptly dropped. I took it and retrieved more water and carried it, following after her. I'm so glad I did that. It was one thing I don't regret.

Bekah walked me down to her lodge where she introduced me to her parents and three brothers, admittingly like I was some exciting stray pet she'd found. Her brothers were quite unremarkable. They were usually working, along with her dad. But she and her mother worked the home. They took care of me and gave me food and a place to sleep. They were so kind.

They called me 'kid' and 'boy' and 'child,' guessing I was maybe—what—16 or 17? I apparently looked much younger than I was, and I talked like a child.

They said that I was a 'Tyrannosaur' and wondered if I'd run away from a slave owner. 'You know, Pa, we ain't in support of no slavery,' said Bekah. 'And besides, ain't the prophecies talk about a Tyranno being the *Ramatkal*?'

'Naw, the prophecy says one like the slaves will be the Warrior-King. Ain't no specific mention of no Tyranno. He could just as easily be one of those fallen ones the scriptures warn us about.'

"How can you say that, Pa?' Bekah defended me. 'He's a living person, ain't he? An orphan without a home. Why would God bring him to us if we were just gonna throw him out? Didn't the good Lord command us to give sanctuary to strangers?'

Bekah had a handle on her father. She was willing to argue with him for as long as it took to save me. She was brave. She was wise. She was beautiful. She was a lot like you. Her family got me to work pretty quickly. I helped build lodges—whole houses—most lit hours of the day. Other times I helped to build wagons. I built tables and chairs too. But deep down, I felt like I didn't belong. I couldn't talk well but improved with Bekah's help. There was still talk around the new settlement about me. There was still talk in our household and the next about *what* I was. How could I reveal to superstitious people that I heard voices? Saw visions?

But I slipped up. I couldn't help but slip up. And they heard me babble in tongues during one of my confused fits.

They continued to accuse me of being possessed, I guess—being some kind of evil spirit manifesting itself. And they kicked me. And they hit me. And they spat on me. But Bekah was there for me. Bekah stood up and protected me, correcting them—'*the holy scriptures say this, the holy scriptures say that.*'

She treated me as a friend. She treated me always with love and compassion. She talked to me. Imagine this: I'd had practically no social contact with this civilization I'd seen rise before my eyes. Now I had someone to talk to, someone smart and pretty. Someone who I thought might explain all the things I'd wondered."

"W-was she a Ceratosaur t-t-too?"

"Yes."

"You h-have a th-thing for us, huh?"

"No. Maybe you all have a thing for me."

"Ha!" Neela coughed. Azure helped her to sit up a little and patted her back. "S-so did you two d-d-do it?"

"Neela!"

"Wh-what? It seemed like it was h-heading that w-way."

"No. No, we didn't, ok? We slept in separate parts of the home but spent some time together alone, just walking."

"Y-yeah, sure…" she said suspiciously.

"Just walking. Smelling the roses. Talking. The way that you and I did. And I learned. I learned how to grow corn and grains, to sow seeds and till the crops. We did that together. And I learned about her God, this God whom Bekah so revered.

You know, it's ironic knowing now that a God, the God of Michael, does exist, and he exists in a similar light to the God of Bekah.

The God of Bekah was a metaphysical being in the great up-there-somewhere who saw everything and knew everything. He was simultaneously the creator and sustainer of Malkuth and all that exists. I talk cynically about it now but at the time, I was struck with conviction. But in my adolescent naivety, I thought that in a universe where a merciful and beautiful being like Bekah existed, a merciful and beautiful God had to exist as well."

"You th-th-throw the w-word 'beauty' around a bit."

"Well, you asked me to tell you this story honestly. And she was nowhere near as beautiful as you."

"Hmm..."

"Bekah had a way with words— "

"O-oh is *that* it?"

"Stop. Bekah... was just not like that, Neela. If she were here, you'd be friends, centuries apart from two separate eras but friends nonetheless. She told me that God had a place and a purpose for every single living being in existence, even me. I thought: *a purpose... for me?* It made me feel unique and special and... and *involved* for once in my life, involved in what was happening. This God she introduced me to, this Adonai, was supposed to come back someday and right the wrongs in this world. He would have a harbinger, a frontrunner called the *'Ramatkal'*—a mythological Sage-King—who would prepare the way for his return. You've read to me about him a half-dozen times. He would wipe every tear from our eyes. There would be no more sadness, no more death, no more suffering, no more sorrow. Someday. Someday in that great bright sometime we'd be... happy.

But where was God and this Ramatkal now? I asked myself that question. Every day, I saw the equivalent of a thousand, thousand nightmares in my mind alone. Even now, still, knowing all that I see more clearly than ever. I still ask, 'where is God?'

'He is everywhere,' Bekah would tell me. 'God Adonai created everyone and everything in seven eons. He gives everything life. He takes it away to recreate and refine it. His spirit gives the universe form. It makes the stars burn. It makes our hearts beat, fills our lungs with air.' I think she said something like that. No one was sure what the organs did then. No one was sure that the stars 'burned.' Yet she knew so much.

But what about the suffering? What about all that I'd seen? Why would an all-powerful, all-knowing, all-seeing, benevolent God let people be burned or boiled or buried alive? Why would he let the cold kill the young and old and sickly? Why would he bring famine and drought?

Why does murder happen? And rape? Why would he allow these wars and the cruelty they bring to take place? Why?

Recently, as I watched you succumb to this illness, this Symbiote. I thought in my mind: this must be some kind of story... some kind of damn twisted story where conflict and tension are necessities. Necessities to what? Entertainment? But whose entertainment? His? Did he give us life simply to crash us all together like a child with his toys? Or is there something else... a secret—something? I don't know. Something that no one else knows. Not the Angels. Not us. Hidden. Guarded. That was the only way he seemed to make sense to me. God had a secret.

We were all—we *are* all—part of the master's masterpiece, the greatest story in the cosmos. And it is a living story, a moving story, a real story—one that breathes and bleeds.

And then it made some sense to me.

Bekah read me the holy scriptures. She told me stories of how God formed the world from volcanic fire. He gave life to the first being—breathed it into him. And it's funny how I of all people cannot say with certainty, 'that's not true, that's not how it happened.' I relearned the history of the world I'd been living in. She taught me to pray. It gave me comfort while I watched you lie there in your coma and I hadn't the power to do anything.

Bekah's God seemed to give life and the universe meaning that they didn't have before. Maybe I was just sentimental or something. I don't know. Now, I find myself more confused than ever. How can I see everything at once and yet nothing at all? And if I see everything as Samael-Satan said I would, then where is God? Shouldn't his radiance blot out all the other visions? Yet there is so much empty space. Or maybe I was lied to. By who? Maybe I see most things and not all. I don't know.

But Bekah grew up as the settlement and subsequent town grew. I'd even helped lay some of the first railroad tracks in the mountain pass to connect with other tracks down south. When Bekah wasn't praying, reading, fixing people up, or talking about God, she was practicing her fiddle. Once a year, the community would throw a party, and she would play music. It was always something upbeat and happy. She would even tap her feet and dance as she played. She tried to teach me to dance, but I was very uncoordinated and incapable, so she told me just to bob and move with the sound. It was hard not to. We grew very close, and she even gave me hints. She told me stories about marriage in the holy scriptures and how sacred and special it was. We never kissed or had slept together, how could we? But she would tell me about it."

"Uh-huh…"

"She would tell me how she was getting old and that she hadn't gotten to experience those things. Perhaps her dad overheard her or realized how she felt. I'd helped to build roads and railroads and didn't think it would ever cost me anything. Traffic to our little paradise increased, and it was then when I saw the first steam-powered vehicles arrive to take part in our progress.

From one of them emerged a terrible prospect: a young Ceratosaur named Ephesus, the son of a landowner in another settlement, whom Talo had arranged to marry Bekah. It was tradition. It wasn't even religion, it wasn't even law, it was tradition for the girl's parents to conspire with other parents regarding whom their children would marry for the mutual betterment and benefit of both families.

I fantasized about running away with her, marrying her in secret, and living off the land as best as I knew how with all my years of experience. We'd divulge into some kind of savagery, hunt and live together. But she got along with Ephesus and eventually grew to love him, I suppose. She married him and had five kids with him. You know… I don't even know if she ever knew how much I loved her, because I was so scared, I was so afraid of telling her those words. To risk losing what we had. It sounds childish but… it's how I felt. It was raw. I left without saying a thing because I just couldn't. She didn't deserve it, not then. I went back into the mountains and back into the wilderness. But my curiosity got the best of me, and I kept going back. I watched her grow old and sickly for 30 years. Her skin grew wrinkly, her voice grew gravely and deep. I watched her kids as they lived and moved through their lives. Three sons and two daughters. I sometimes talked and played with them in secret and asked them how their mother and father were.

She never started the clinic or the hospital she wanted to. They confirmed what I had feared: she was getting sicker. They called it 'an illness of the rains.' I left water near their door whenever Ephesus was at work. Then, one day, I heard Bekah, now sick and elderly, moan through the door. I couldn't help but knock. Her eldest daughter, who was now a spitting image of her mother, greeted me and allowed me to see Bekah. 'I'm a friend,' I told her, which must have been strange for them to hear because I doubt I'd aged much.

They told me she'd lost her sight and seemed delirious. I sat by her bedside and held her hand as I'm doing yours now. I said—I stuttered—'Bekah, it's me, it's Azure.' And I tried to tell her I'd gotten the water she'd been drinking from our waterfall. It didn't seem to matter. I doubt she could hear. I..." Azure sniffled. "I kissed her over the eye like an idiot, and tried to say, 'I love you.' I tried, Neela…"

"It's o-okay…" Neela stroked his hand with a finger.

"I came to her gravesite after the funeral and I left some of her favorite orange flowers I'd picked from the prairie. One of her brothers saw me. He was an old man now. He squinted and said, 'Azure? That'd be impossible. You ain't aged not one day! Pa was right. You's a damn devil who's been haunting our here family for years. You must've given her that illness.' I remember how that hurt the most. He took out an archaic handgun and pointed it at me, saying, 'I bet if I shot you, you ain't feel a thang. Bet you ain't got no heart. No soul. Admit it, you blue demon! You took her from us!' I stood my ground, not saying a word, as he marched forward, demanding that I resurrect her or something. He told me that he was going to make sure I never came back to haunt them again. I raised my hand to him passively, but he must've felt threatened, firing at point-blank range. The shot hit me directly in the chest. He looked shocked to see me actually hurt and bleed. I crawled away, retreating into the prairie, back toward the mountains as he called out to me, demanding that I bring Bekah back.

Bekah's eldest daughter called out to him saying, 'Crazy Uncle Rota, watcha be doin' shooting off that thang in a cemetery for? You'll wake the dead!' He told her to stop shouting or she'd disturb her mother's rest. Bekah's husband, Ephesus, led them both away. He looked down the prairie, and we saw each other briefly. I was too far away to make out his expression or hear his words, but I think he knew who I was. He must have heard the stories of the boy that Bekah knew."

"SLAVE AND SOLDIER"

"…There's a transience to everything. The world never stops changing. I lived as a man who never died watching others, like Bekah's children, grow old, marry, have children, and die. There came times when I simply forgot. I forgot huge chunks of my life. I forgot Bekah and her family. I forgot all that I'd been through since Satan's dart struck me. I don't mean to depress you, Neela. It's just a lot of things…"

A physical therapist came to work with Neela. Azure was invited to walk her around in her wheelchair and 'get some fresh air.' There was an aquarium in the lobby they were invited to see. Neela said that the fish reminded her of her home world, and she recognized some of them. "And-and th-then what happened?" she asked.

"...I got captured by some slave traders. They chained me by the neck, wrists, and ankles. They took off my clothes and put me on display in an auction alongside other Tyrannosaurs. Buyers prodded me and inspected every part of me like I was an article of clothing on a rack. I remember how uncomfortable that was. When I think back to those prostitutes on display in the windows downtown, I imagine they feel like I did. Trapped. They put a placard around my neck with the bidding price on it and despite all the comments about my health and stature I'd received, no one bid higher. I was given over to a couple at the lowest possible price. The Elyon family. I would rather not talk about them or what happened on their plantation..."

"It's o-ok. You-you don't have to."

"It's every horror you could possibly imagine, and what's worse is I always healed and never died. No matter how much I wanted to. There came another war, from what I understand. The First Global War. The Southern Continental Republic (SCR) had invaded and threatened to take Atlantan-held colonies in the East. There was a military draft, and my owners wanted to dodge it. They sent me in place of their sons. I thought it was a blessing at first, I would escape that torturous life, but I found another just as bad."

As they strolled past the gallery of medical advances, Azure told her about military training and the horrors of war. He said he felt like a prisoner and that, once again, there was no way out. To lighten the somber tone, he told her that back then, cavalry soldiers rode on giant long-necks, the Sauropods, and used them to try to intimidate the enemy and carve a path through their formations. But the long-necks were also large targets who were a lot more fragile than they looked. They were killed off in great numbers by the more advanced weaponry and, due to the scarcity of food on campaign, were eaten.

Azure was assigned to the front of the line. He described how they lined up shoulder-to-shoulder in rows with men at their back to force them forward. They were expected to reload their muskets and rifles on the spot as the enemy fired directly at them. The task of reloading his weapon with his clumsiness and shaky hands was difficult enough, and in the heat of battle, it was "daunting as all hell." He said that he thought of it like working in the fields with Bekah and her family. He said that it comforted him to imagine separating grains of corn when he loaded the weapon. He was hit by buckshot, rifle bullets, and eventually by cannon fire which blew him apart. He described the horror of waking up and digging his way out of the darkness only to find himself in a mass grave, surrounded by bloated and rotting corpses buzzing with flies and crawling with maggots. He threw up and crawled away over the soft soil, revealing new corpses with each step. Neela asked him to move on to another story, and he did.

He said that he was found naked by a family in the SCR who were kind enough to bathe him, feed him, and allow him to stay for a while. They even taught him some of their language, but it was very complicated, and no one speaks it anymore. He was shocked to see that the enemy treated him this way, and then he realized they were people too just like the Atlantans. Most of them were Giganotosaurs, but there were also Megalosaurs then. There were even Pachycephalosaurs, bipedal Malkuthians with skull roofs they'd be using as weapons if firearms weren't invented. The SCR was remarkably diverse, but their government was frightening and killed off that diversity. "People would disappear all the time, and everyone knew why," said Azure. "They called themselves a 'Republic' but they were a dictatorship like any other. No, they were worse. The type of cruelty the government committed against its citizens called back to the barbarism of the warring states. I remember they used to hang people upside down and saw them in half as they screamed their lungs out. You were lucky if they shot you. They were conserving bullets, so sometimes they would just beat or stab you until you were dead. Every crime, real or imagined, was punishable by death. I'd left the battlefield and yet the fear and terror I felt there hadn't left. I was worried about being discovered as a former Atlantan soldier. I was scared for this kind family that had taken me in. Eventually, the SCR government came for us."

As they returned to the ICU, the nurse asked if Neela was ready for a bath. She waved it off, asking them to do it later and asked Azure to continue.

"Their secret police kicked down our door. We tried to hide under the floorboards. Our hearts raced, overly conscious of our own breathing. One of the children coughed. The secret police broke through the floor and grabbed us, holding us at gunpoint and shouting in their language. The children in the family cried but were told to shut up or they'd be shot. The mother covered them and tried to comfort them, and when she did this, they hit her in the back of the head. Then, they knocked me down and proceeded to drag us away. They wouldn't tell us what we were accused of or what we'd done wrong. We just knew that this was it, our worst fear was realized. They dragged us to a building with a chimney that belched black smoke: a crematorium. I tried to struggle and fight, but they beat me down. I apologized to the screaming, crying family, believing this was my fault, and I tried to comfort them, but there was no possibility of comfort. We were pushed toward the flames. My God, Neela, their faces. I can see their faces even now as clear as they were that day. The pitch on them. The tears. The fear. I rushed forward to try to block them from being pushed in, and the soldiers pushed me in first. The flames curled around me and bit into my flesh. I screamed as these innocents were thrown on top of me. The oven door closed. We burned together. Oh, the injustice, Neela. In the pit of my stomach, in my gut, it'll never feel right to me. What was their crime? Was it me?

Sometime later, perhaps months, perhaps years, someone opened the oven door. The oven itself was out. The flames were gone. My eyes and flesh still hurt but I could feel them as I reached out the oven door and pulled myself out. There was the screaming of grown men—SCR soldiers—who witnessed this, and I was afraid they'd throw me back into the furnace. Instead, they helped me up, and one poured water over my face to clean off the pitch. They asked me who I was, and I answered in their language, which must've sounded even more broken and confusing than in Atlantan. I said that I was an innocent man they'd thrown into the oven, no mention of having been an Atlantan soldier. They apologized for my circumstance and explained that the prison camp had just been liberated. The rebels had won and there was a new regime in charge of the SCR.

They led me off to be fed and bathed, and they offered me a chance to fight for the new regime. I couldn't really decline; they seemed insistent. They gave me a uniform and a rifle and explained that I would be sent to fight the insurgency of the old regime in a town nearby. Southern Continentals fought Southern Continentals, and then they fought the Atlantans again and again and again. Each time, the weapons got better, and the death tolls rose. Each time, I was told to fight and kill a different group of people from the last. The ailments of my mind and my retrograde amnesia didn't help. It allowed each new governing body to imprint a new loyalty on me like tearing off the label of a bottle and slapping a new label on it. I was no longer a person. I was a tool. I was a gun. Whoever held me in their hand could fire me at whatever and whoever they wanted to. It was not my job to ask questions, it was my job to follow orders and do what I was told. And it tore me apart, especially at first. I found it so hard to kill, but so hard not to."

"D-did you?"

"I don't know," Azure lied. "I must have. I'd learned how to fight. How to use each new weapon in each new conflict. And each time, I made a friend, a comrade. I can see them in my mind's eye now. Fellow soldiers with their own families, their own dreams. They're all dead now. Every single one of them. Some of them died in my arms or right beside me. Some of them I had to learn about after the battle or the war. I could go on and on. But… some things are better left unsaid."

"A CHANGING WORLD"

Azure returned from work the next day and helped the nurse to bathe Neela. Afterward, she asked him to continue his story, perhaps feeling that he might lose his memories again.

"I couldn't help thinking about what I told you yesterday. One thing that will haunt me forever and ever is the pain of guilt. The guilt of all those lives. All that suffering. And me, having done nothing. You know, in the times of the Second Dynasty, there'd been warriors, the Holy Knights, who were expected to be strong yet virtuous. You read to me about them. They fought for honor and something larger than themselves—for their king and their kingdom and their ladies and their God. But those days ended once the first shots were fired in the Second Global War. You didn't have to see or face your opponent to kill them.

It became about surprising, backstabbing, and deception. It became about ambushes and shooting unsuspecting opponents in the back. Gone were the days of gentlemen. You bombed your enemies before they got into position, not after. You shot at your opponent before they were aware, not later. You used chemical weapons because the effects terrorized the enemy into giving ground or giving up. Death was never enough anymore. You used firebombing to terrorize the civilian populations, to break the will of the people and thus their government. Atlanta had become the maestro of these tactics. We had the most powerful explosives ever constructed up to that point, and we fell in love with their destructive power. Perhaps there would be no atom bombs, no hydrogen bombs, no neutron bombs, no antimatter weapons, no World Enders, no Great Catastrophe had our kind not grown infatuated with making the biggest boom we could just because we could. But as long as sentient beings have existed, as long as there is conflict, there will be arms races. And thank God for it in hindsight, else the Dragons would have run us over like pavement.

I'd been fighting on the Atlantan side during the last Global War. The atom bomb had been dropped for the first, second, and third time. An even more powerful hydrogen bomb came into existence, thousands of times more powerful than the atom bomb. Both sides had nuclear weapons, and both sides feared annihilation. For the first time in Malkuthian history, the possibility of Malkuthians themselves ending the world was real. They held a power formerly only held by nature and God. Now it was theirs, in the hands of fallible mortals. What would they do with it? Everyone feared. There was a doctrine of deterrence that came into effect: each side aimed their missiles at the other so that if one side fired first, the other would respond.

The only way to win at this terrible game was to guarantee that both sides would lose. So, for decades, no one shot first. No one shot at all. Instead, they competed against each other in things like sports, in proxy wars, and in the colonization of space. But as you know, the Atlantan Union had an enormous advantage in this regard: it had the Antares Conglomerate, simultaneously the heart of the military-industrial-complex and the leader in space technology. They were already using mass drivers and colonizing planets while the war was going on! It's almost as if they were prepared for what was coming. The Antares knew. They must've plotted the whole thing, I'm sure. They paid off the war reparations with money that was given to them by both sides to purchase arms. That's how profitable war was for them. They could literally buy power. And they did. They bought a seat in the Senate that they hold to this day. A modern monarchy. Generation after generation of Antares. An unbroken, unending line of them going on until the crack of doom."

Neela fell asleep. Azure kissed her on the head and said goodnight, "whenever tomorrow comes."

"EDOM RECOGNIZES NEELA"

Neela's speech had improved, but she still couldn't walk. Azure tried to walk with her, supporting most of her weight. "Ok, time to retrieve carts!" he joked.

"Yeah, as if…" said Neela. She was able to take two steps on her own. "You sure you got me, Azure?"

"I've got you, honey! Don't worry, baby! You can do this!"

She took three more steps before collapsing forward into Azure's waiting arms. Azure and the physical therapist clapped for her as if she'd won 1st-place in a race. "I'm proud of you, Neela," said Azure, kissing her three times on the cheek.

There was more clapping at the doorway, it was heavier, like a textbook hitting a table. A hulking red Carnotaur in sunglasses stood there. Azure gulped. "Edom…"

"Is this the girl?"

Azure held Neela and angled her away from Edom defensively. "What are you doing here, Big Red?"

"Don't worry, Big Blue," said Edom. "I just wanted to show my support and see her for myself. I heard she was Aohdfionn's little sister. It got me a little nostalgic. He and I go way back."

"You…" said Neela.

Edom hugged them both, lifted them, and sat them down together on the bed. He took off his sunglasses and extended his hand to Neela. She shook it uneasily. "I am Azure's co-worker down at construction. He told me he was working his heart out for a pretty little lady of his. Do you recognize me?"

"I think so…"

"Let me give you a hint: your brother fought 49 professional fights when he was younger and lost just one."

"You're the one he lost to."

"Well, he got disqualified for burning me with some kind of energy spark. I had him beat, and I think he got desperate. We became training partners afterward, you know? He was like a brother to me too. Anyway, how are you? Things coming along?"

"I took five steps today."

"Oh, shit, fo' real? That's a miracle if I ever knew one."

"She needs to receive another dose of chemo in two days," said Azure.

"And I bet you want to be here to support her through that."

"Yes, please."

Edom patted him on the back. "Eh, I'm here for you, bro," Edom handed him an old communicator. "You can call me whenever you need to. Don't worry, it's not tapped or 'nothin. I can even give you a ride so you don't have to keep walking up here or taking the bus or whatever the hell you do to get here."

"Thank you, Big Red," said Azure.

"Thank you," said Neela.

Edom put his sunglasses back on and smiled. "Anything for Aohd's little baby sister, eh? I loved the dude, you know? He changed my life."

"And mine too," said Neela.

"You see a lot of him in Azure, don't you? So do I. Blue, hit me up when you need a ride for your next shift, would ya? I'll be around."

Azure smiled and gave him a manly hug. "Thank you, Red."

"Yeah, don't mention it, bro. We both want the same thing."

"AZURE REMEMBERS ENIF"

"I'm nervous," said Neela, awaiting her next dose of treatment.

"You've already been through it a few times."

"Well, now I'm conscious for it."

"Sorry, Neela. But I'll be here waiting, I promise."

"Tell me something interesting," she said. "To take my mind away. Tell me another story. Your best story."

"I already told you a lot of my good ones."

"Well, tell me your next best one. Like, what happened after the last war? Did you find anyone else? Any other girl?"

Azure stopped to think about it. "...Well... I can tell you I was labeled as 'mentally ill and unstable' by the army following multiple complaints. They sent me to an asylum to be 'cared for.' The truth is, they sent me there to be studied like a rodent in a lab, and to be secluded from society. There was no room in a perfect society for someone who couldn't think normally, move normally, or talk normally. There was no room in a perfect society for someone who periodically forgot his own identity. There was no room in a perfect society for a schizophrenic who saw the world through the lens of a kaleidoscope and heard voices. It was the heyday of eugenics. Evolution and eugenics were the next big ideas since Adonaism. Those who were labeled inferior were as good as dead.

They were trying to cull out the weak, the sick, and undesirable just as Atlanta marched on to dominate the world. They were trying to get rid of people like me, those who were a speck of rust in the machinery of utopia.

So, there I was, dragged into another dungeon, another prison. I'd been a prisoner of war and a slave. I saw and experienced things I never want to talk about. Terrible times. More terrible times with seemingly no silver lining. But in the asylum, there was a light in that deep, dark, darkness.

For much of my life, I'd heard this mysterious sound—this screaming in my head. In all the world, no matter where I was, there was always that familiar sound that followed me. It was a scream unlike any other—unceasing, full of frustration, full of hopelessness and desperation, full of this feeling of being trapped. It was the same frustration I'd felt. It was usually so faint I hardly heard it. Other times it gripped at me and brought me to tears. In the asylum, that scream was loud and clear, which meant that it was *here*. It came from *someone*, a real person.

You know, Neela, for millennia, I'd bemoaned the fact that I could not save everyone. But at some moment, sometimes between Bekah's death and my service in the last war, I'd grown more content with the idea that if I could save just one life, my life would have meaning.

There in that mental asylum, I came across a blind and deaf girl named Enif.

Enif was that life I had to save. She was that voice screaming in my head a thousand miles away. She was the opportunity I needed. She was the paradox I had considered, the answer to my greatest question: why would a good God allow bad things to happen to an innocent person?

Why would a loving God damn an innocent girl to the prison of her own body, without sight or sound, without the ability to *know* who or what or where or when or why?

If life was a test, how could this be fair to her? If the goal was to find faith in God, how could she possibly come to know God?

There was no rationale to it.

Then I recognized the profound compassion I felt for her. It was beyond compelling, stronger than lust or hunger or thirst. I had a sort of epiphany: *do some people exist simply to test the hearts of everyone else?*

How strange.

Her screams drove me into a psychotic episode. I ripped off a chain, knocked over guards, kicked open doors to find the source. I found her bashing her head on the other side of a chain-link fence. I begged her to stop because it was breaking my heart. They brought a leash for her like the ones you use for a rabid animal. As they began to fix it around her neck, I grasped Enif's fingertips with my fingertip through the holes in the fence. I felt her trembling... trembling like me.

'I hear you,' I tried to say, but of course she couldn't hear me. I think she understood my touch. She must have understood my intent. She babbled something, something garbled. For a few seconds I had enough clarity to improvise a way to tell her something: I blew on her hands, pursing my lips, blowing thrice between my teeth. I was sure she could feel it. She blew on my hands too. I suppose we developed a kind of... attraction together. It wasn't pretty, but it was the best we could do.

After the incident, I was beaten severely by the guards who wanted to reestablish their dominance and authority. They then tied me up and placed me in solitary confinement, a closet without a window or so much as light. I was alone again in darkness with my thoughts. I could only imagine that Enif had suffered the same things.

When they finally opened the door to feed me, I was a sweaty, teary mess. They prodded me. They were obviously fascinated by my accelerated healing. They would cut my flesh and watch as it regenerated. As my blood went from red to gold, then disappeared. They tortured me daily with knives, and pins, and chemicals, and heat, and cold, and starvation, and thirst. I'd been violated many times before, but this time they took something from me, something that I can never get back, and used it for God-knows-what. I had no say in any of this, and they disregarded my pleas to stop.

They asked me questions. And all I could tell them were things they couldn't possibly believe: I'd been a veteran of multiple wars, I'd wandered Malkuth for as long as I could remember, I heard voices and saw visions.

Since they ignored my pleas for mercy, I instead began to ask questions. Only two things kept me from wanting to let go of life: the hope of seeing Enif and my curiosity. Finally, I was in the presence of experts, people who were trying to figure me out no matter how cruel they may be. I asked them what they'd found out about me—what I was. All I had were assumptions. Maybe these people could tell me what I wanted to know for so long, but they hid their findings from me.

They let me walk and live among the other inmates, perhaps to see how interactions would affect me. I assume they wanted to study me *in my own habitat*, my own environment, to see what made me tick.

They certainly didn't miss the bond I'd developed and shared with Enif. I would hold her hand from between the fence. When I would hold her fingers, she would stop screaming, she would stop crying. She would make these curious sounds like a moon pup. I would let her feel my snout and jaw with her fingers to feel their movement as I spoke. I thought it would help. It was an experiment at first. I believe I instinctively knew or remembered my snout had been one of the first things I'd been able to see in deep space. I mouthed as best as I could, 'I'm here. It's okay. I heard you.'

I must have said this ten times. Then, something spectacular happened."

'*Oway?*' she managed to say, stretching the sound at first, trying to say 'ok.' '*Ah oway?*'

I blew on her fingers. She blew on them back. I think she laughed afterward. I put her fingers on my snout again and said, 'Azure' about twenty times. I was so determined to have her say her name.

'*Awr*' is as close as she got. It sounded like 'error.' It was good enough.

As the scientists observed us, they became curious too and allowed some of the females to come across in what became a recreation or commons area. They'd intentionally overlooked the problems of having cohabitation amongst gender-different inmates. Rape happened, and sometimes the psych workers and guards were responsive to it with their restraints and tranquilizer drugs, sometimes they turned a blind eye and let it happen. They could kill or experiment on the eggs and the children later. When I would try to intervene, I would be beaten. They wanted to see me respond emotionally to this horror and to Enif. I knew it.

Enif wore a muzzle during our first encounter, and it was explained to me that she'd bitten others and that I was not allowed to remove the muzzle for that reason. In a rare act of courage, I unbuckled it so that it would fall off on its own. I looked around and saw that a doctor had stopped a guard from intervening. He was studying us like animals in a cage. Unbeknownst to me at the time, the Antares had funded research into bioengineering organisms that could be sold and used as super soldiers or weapons in future wars.

Enif's eyes remained closed most of the time. She felt around and grabbed my arms with surprising strength. She felt me up, felt my back, felt my face, trying to form a portrait in her mind. She clenched her head and groaned as I often did. I brushed her cheek which caused her to strike it away as if doing so were a learned response. She fell back in her chair and fell on her side, crying. I came to comfort her, but whenever I tried to touch her, she kicked and scratched at me. I tried to talk to her, which of course accomplished nothing. Then I blew on her hands and fingers, and she knew. She knew...

We had several encounters like that. I'd picked some flowers from the lawn for her. They appeared beautiful to me just as the first flowers had been to me before taking Satan's dart. Like those in the prairie. I put her hands on both my jaws and spoke slowly and repeatedly. She spoke, slurred and stuttering too but we had learned together.

But... it was torture there for both of us. She hated whenever our time expired, and she fought the guards when they came to take her back to her area. They shocked her, which forced my hand. I interposed between her and the guards, shielded her in an embrace as they shocked me and pierced me with tranquilizers without success. Finally, I placed her hand on my jawbones and said, 'go, see later, go, see later.'

And I'd convinced her to go peacefully. I heard her screaming all night. I cried and cried and cried.

One day she came to me trembling, the areas around her eyes red and blistered. They'd showered them with experimental chemicals. I called for water with the hope that I could wash her eyes and relieve her pain. I knew they heard and understood me, but they refused. They observed us with clipboards and nodded to one another. They did nothing. Nothing. Until they pried us apart.

A week later, I saw bruising on her arms, legs, neck, and back. She was in great pain, and as she roared, she revealed a burn-like wound under her tail near her orifice. What had they done? To this day, I don't know for sure, but I dread the thought. I tried to comfort her. I blew onto her hands, 'Love you. I'm here.'"

"Azure," said Neela, her speech having improved. "What did they take from you?"

"...They stole my semen, Neela. The blood and the skin was bad enough, but the blood and skin would disappear without a trace. They took it from me... they forced it out of me."

"I'm sorry, Azure."

"...One damn day, Enif was brought to me with her eyelids sewn and clamped open, her ears bandaged, and her hands chained to her waist so that she could not remove them. Tears fell from her pale eyes as she sobbed and screamed in agony. At first, I didn't notice the thread, only her eyes, and that horrified me. Her eyelids were always closed. I immediately tried to remove the thread so she could close her eyes, but she pulled away out of fear, and so I ripped her skin. Her blood covered my hands. I roared, furious beyond any fury I'd ever felt at what they'd done to her—what they'd had me do to her. My vision became black, then when I came to all was green and hotter than fire. I blacked out again, and when I awoke, I found myself in a crater at least a hundred times the size of a ball field. It was like the valley. The edge touched the horizon. How could my romantic tale end so unceremoniously? Without a kiss or tender word or... anything... I'd said my goodbyes to Bekah, but there was no closure here. I'd killed her. I'd killed everyone—everyone in that entire city. I killed them all. Every life. Every last one of them. And Enif... Enif was gone too.

I wandered away... naked and alone. I wandered, watching the world and universe before what it is now. I watched a revolution overthrow the Third Dynasty. I watched the Great Catastrophe—the missiles steak like meteorites from the sky—the mushroom clouds and shockwaves topple skyscrapers and burn the air for miles. I watched the Malkuthians turn this world into an inferno, then into an icy hell. I'd seen the very pillars of the first climate dome rise. I'd seen climate control slowly reverse that winter. I'd seen space-technology begin exploration and colonization of space. I'd learned of the star harvesters, the wars with alien civilizations, the birth of the World Enders, the Cosmic Walls. The monarchy and aristocracy were things of the past, but then there was the Antares family. That same Antares family that funded the asylums. That tortured Enif and me. That same Antares family that sent me to hell and back and robbed me of my friends and comrades and loves. The same Antares family who let my fellow servants work themselves to death in their factories. The same. The same Antares family that owns this place, this world, this universe."

"They'll never own us. No, not you. Not me. Never," said Neela. "We are not products, not items to be used and bartered with, darling. Whether soldier or civilian, free or slave, we still have ourselves. Our *selves*. Azure... never lose your *self*."

"All this... all this taking, Neela, and I still don't know *who* that is."

"Well, I do... you're the person I love and the person who loves me. You're my husband-at-heart and in spirit. You're a being full of passion and compassion and love. You're an anomaly. You are special. And you're the man who'll save this world, this universe. I just know it. Your grand destiny. Now look at you... you've found your voice, you've found your memories, you've found your *self*. Now you're dangerous, darling. My dangerous, dangerous, handsome darling boy." She ran her hand over the side of his face. "I'm so proud of you, my darling boy."

"GENERAL MALEVANT & LORD ZEON"

A Resolver, the Union's most powerful superweapon, hyper-jumped into position near the Bhumi solar system. It was supported by a Union starfleet including a dozen World Enders. Chancellor Antares and the Chiefs-of-Staff watched over the proceedings from the safety of Hod.

A giant tear had formed there, which indicated that something massive was coming into the universe. The Malkuthians knew from previous experience that this usually indicated the arrival of a Dragon lord. Antares ordered the firing of the Resolver and World Enders as soon as the Dragon lord breached. They would try to damage the universe of the Dragons on the other side as well while minimizing damage to New Heaven itself, a rather brilliant idea.

Lord Zeon's hands and some of his heads breached the tear, and it was at that moment that the Resolver and World Enders fired their super lasers. Zeon was engulfed in the resulting explosions, which blasted through to the other side, destroying several Dragon planets.

General Malevant, now pulsating with energy and increased in size, looked up to the sky and sneered at what was happening.

The Resolver and World Enders began to recharge their super lasers. As they did, the smiling faces of Zeon emerged from the residue of the explosions and unleashed incredibly powerful beams from each of his mouths at the World Enders, destroying them easily. The Union starfleet fired at him, but their weapons had little effect, like pellets hitting a brick wall. Wyverns came through separate portals and attacked the starships. Zeon swatted at the Resolver and pulverized it like an empty aluminum can, sending its remnants spiraling through space.

"GENERAL MALEVANT," said Zeon. "I REQUEST AN AUDIENCE WITH YOU."

Malevant flew up to meet Zeon in space, kneeling and bowing to him. "My Lord," he addressed.

"I DEMAND AN EXPLANATION FOR WHAT YOU HAVE DONE TO LORD-MARQUESS GIGATHETA."

"Lord Gigatheta sought to betray you and usurp your authority over our forces. He was a decadent being, not fit to command an invasion force as you are."

"ARE THESE MERELY YOUR OPINIONS OR DO YOU SPEAK THE TRUTH?"

"He desired to reassign and redeploy your forces in your absence, knowing full well that it was not your will."

"AND YOU HAVE ALWAYS BEEN THE BEST OF MY GENERALS, AND HAVE ALWAYS DONE MY WILL."

"That is correct, my Lord."

The starfleets and Wyverns still fought around them.

"SHOW ME YOUR NEWFOUND POWERS. I DEMAND IT."

Malevant sneered and tensed his body. His freakish muscles became engorged. Purple sparks flew and an aura formed around him. He grew and grew until he was the size of a skyscraper. Malevant focused his energies into all of his fingertips and his mouth and purple beams flew out in all directions and struck the main battleships and capital ships until the Union forces were forced to retreat. Zeon laughed with amusement. "ALL THE POWERS OF GIGATHETA AND ALL THE SKILLS AND CUNNING OF MY GREATEST GENERAL. IF I COULD FORM BEINGS AS THE GREAT QUEEN DOES, THIS WOULD BE MY FIRST CREATION. I CHALLENGE YOU, MAVELANT: WHAT YOU DID TO THE MARQUESS, WHY DON'T YOU TRY IT ON ME?"

"My Lord?"

"YOU HAVE MY PERMISSION, GENERAL. JUST TRY IT. DON'T YOU WANT TO CONTROL ALL OF MY FORCES? TO GAIN MY INCREDIBLE POWER? TO BECOME A LORD?"

Malevant's hand grasped the handle of the Black Sword at his side, but he instead remained kneeling and released the tension on the handle. He reverted to his previous size and folded his wings.

"SMART," said Zeon, flaring his planet-sized wings outward. "ATHENA HAS CERTAINLY MADE YOU WISER. GENERAL MALEVANT, I HEREBY GRANT YOU COMMAND OF A THIRD OF ALL MY FORCES."

Malevant's eyes glowed with red flames as he smiled.

"GENERAL DEEM & PRINCESS DARNA"

General Deem saw what both Lord Zeon and General Malevant had done.

"Is it time yet?" Deem asked Loki.

"Gee wiz, be patient, your scaliness," said Loki.

"My rival has now increased in power and in rank. Lord Zeon has destroyed the Malkthian superweapons like they were playthings. That universe is wide open. Now is the best time to act. We should invade now."

"Now would be a good time to count your blessings, dearie. You have me. And I say… the stage is not yet set for Deem to play."

"What are you not telling me, Loki?"

"If you knew, you wouldn't do. Hooohoohooohoooohaaaaa!" Loki disappeared, saying, "Time is going, it's going fast, make use of it for it won't… last…"

Loki left a golden apple for him.

The voice of Princess Darna called out to him and asked him if he and his army were ready to go to New Heaven. He shook his head, washed the apple, and presented it to her to enjoy. "I can't decide which is better, this, the ambrosia, or the amrita," said Darna. She threw the core carelessly over her shoulder.

Loki conjured a small band of musicians who began to play. The beat of the music grabbed something inside of Deem and he couldn't help but dance a little.

"Hey, what are you doing?" asked Darna. "Stop that! You look stupid!"

"It's called dancing. In the Third Universe, it was a big part of life. One of the entities in me can destroy planets just by dancing. One of them can create them by doing the same. Couples traditionally do it when they get married. Would you like to try, Princess? I can show you." Deem held out his hand and bowed.

She hesitantly took his hand and Deem took her into a field of white flowers. An instinct took over, and he showed her a range of different dance moves, some of which had to be adapted for their wings, size, and tails. He held her and flew with her up through the clouds and into the starry sky. The Dragon Princess followed the General's lead. She found that this bizarre art of movement was exciting and that she actually found it enjoyable. When they span around together, planetesimals span around them and crashed together to form planets. There were flashes of light. New stars ignited. "Wow!" Darna exclaimed, her starry eyes glowing. "I thought only my mother could do that!"

"This is called *Shakti*, it is the energy of all the cosmos. Your mother is made of it. It can create, and it can destroy. It is a power unlike any other."

"Whoa! Are we really doing all this?!"

"Yes." Deem pulled her in and kissed her on the head. "Do you remember what that gesture is called, Princess?"

"A kiss?"

"Good, you remember a lot! Do you remember what it means when someone kisses you?"

"Hmm… you told me that it means that person loves you."

"Yes!"

She patted him on the chest plate, and they returned back to the world, hovering over an ocean. "When are we finally going to do this?" she asked.

"I'm waiting for the right time," he answered.

She flew away to a distance. "I can't keep leaving. My mother starts to wonder. And when she wonders, she lashes out."

"You can tell her that you're helping her best and wisest military leader."

"If she knew I was with you, I don't think she'd approve. She says you're a disappointment. She says you have so many gifts, but you've wasted them."

"I am aware."

"Look, I can help you to open a portal for your army, but then I think I just need to go. I can't keep keeping secrets from my mother."

Deem felt a blow to his heart. "I'm helping her. That is my purpose."

"I know. But she doesn't know that. And if she finds out, I dread what she'll do to me. What she'll do to you. She's the most powerful being in the Omniverse. She can erase universes with a thought. She can blink you and me out of existence. So, whatever it is you need me to do, let's just do it and get it over with."

"Princess, please be patient and trust me. I know what I'm doing."

Darna looked down at him intensely. "I may be patient, but my mother is running out of patience. I guess I'll see you whenever I see you next, and you better be ready then. Not just with these gifts and this silly 'dancing' thingy, but with all your forces ready to go."

"Yes, my Princess."

Neela had undergone another session of chemotherapy and was sleeping. Azure washed her glasses and hijab again. Earlier, he had helped her to clean out her braces. A member of the billing staff confronted him, saying that she was glad she could talk to him alone. She showed Azure the mounting unpaid items for Neela's continued treatment. "We won't be able to treat her again if these expenses are left unpaid," she said. "And, sadly, she may have to leave."

"And what?" said Azure. "And die?"

"This isn't a charity, sir. This is a service. A business like anything else. With her step-dad non-responsive, you're her next of kin. You signed a promissory note obligating you to pay for her continued treatment. No one forced you to do that. It's very simple: either you pay, or she can't stay. There are plenty of other patients who need to use this bed and this room."

Azure grit his teeth. He saw the Antares Tech watch on her wrist and pointed to it. "That man. The owner of that company. The Chancellor of this government. He can get whatever treatment he wants to heal any ailment he wants. His crony Senate created the system where you hospitals feel fine with adding whatever fees you want!"

The lady put her hands on her hips and leaned to one side. "Are you done?"

"Hell no! It's just like the higher-education system. Who cares, right? It's subsidized. Subsidized for everyone but the very people who need it. So, what's 20,000 BN to you, right? It's just 20,000 BN. They assume it's all covered anyway, until it's not. You assume and you assume and you assume. So that number just gets bigger and bigger and bigger, and you all become blinder, and blinder, and blinder until those numbers lose all weight and meaning except to the ones stuck paying for it. People like me." He realized that these were things that Neela had talked to him about and brought up in speeches. His thoughts and words echoed hers.

"I'm not debating with you. I'm telling you. Either these expenses are paid, or she's gone from here, and you're on your own. This is your 30-hour notice. I can get security or call the Public Security Force to move you both out if I have to." The worker turned and left.

Azure resisted the temptation to crash his fist through the nearby table and clawed at his head instead. He looked at Neela, the love of his long, sad, miserable, lonely life, and watched as she shook and kicked in her sleep. He rubbed her back to comfort her like old times, and as he did this he remembered when she had comforted him during his night terrors. They lived in the sky district then. Life was much simpler. Only back then, he was weak, and she was strong. Azure reached for the card and communicator that Edom had given him. *Whatever it takes, right? I don't care anymore.*

"THE TIME TRAP"

Loki's astral projection laughed at Chancellor Antares and the Union Chiefs-of-Staff following the failure of their superweapons against the Dragon lord, Zeon.

"You really thought that was going to work on HIM?! Hahahahahahaaaaaa!"

"You know, Loki," said Antares, stoically. "When you are so overcome with joy and overconfidence, you tend to forget one thing."

"Oh, and what's that, Chancellor Saltine?"

"That you may see a *version* of the future, but I'm still a lot more intelligent than you are." Antares snapped his finger, and with that the holographic projection of the scenario changed.

On the new projection, Lord Zeon looked around, bewildered as the Resolver, twelve World Enders, and the fleet reappeared out of thin air. He then proceeded to destroy them all again and summon Malevant to him, but then the Resolver, the twelve World Enders, and the fleet appeared again. This happened again and again.

"You didn't!" said Loki. "Ooohooohooo, some timey wimey bullshit! Interesting!"

"Their great lord and his forces around Bhumi are trapped in a time loop. Their whole star system is trapped until our Time Mine runs out of energy from the nearby black hole. What's more: a portal to the Dragons' own universe periodically opens at the beginning of each loop, which means we can exploit this and attack their universe directly."

"I appreciate the boldness of the plan but, sir," the Chief of the Navy objected. "There are millions of our men on those ships. They're trapped too. They're dying repeatedly."

"Why, yes. That's what soldiers do. They fight and die."

"Look, sir… I've been one of your most loyal servants for years. I have been your right-hand. We've gone through three presidents together. I don't appreciate you continuing to hide these important secrets from me. Those are my fleets. That is my Navy. I sent them there. I am ultimately responsible for all the ships and the men on them. How can I help you? How can I do my job if you continue to go over my head and make plans without telling me?"

Antares summoned his war-suit to him and fired a blast from his palm-cannon that vaporized the Chief of the Navy. "Erased. Just like everyone else who chooses to go against me. No body to bury or mourn." He then called a Public Security Force admiral to him, "You're the new Chief of the Navy," he said. "We'll be sure to let the Watchers know that the chain of command has changed. Let it bring you up to speed." The other Chiefs of Staff watched the same scene play out again and again around Bhumi, nervously and uncomfortably making room for their new equal from Antares's private military.

Athena found herself repeatedly exiting her chambers and addressing her Centaurs outside. A feeling like deja vu came over her, but before she could realize what was happening, the feeling went away, and she found herself in the present. She looked up and saw the looming, imposing outline of Lord Zeon's massive frame floating up in the sky. It was the very Dragon that had destroyed all of Olympus and Gaia, and she longed in her heart to be the source of his demise. However, as with Malevant, she was forced to bide her time. Malevant had inherited some of Gigatheta's hunger to go along with his sadism, and so he found himself taking the time to devour the bodies of his victims and to seek more. Thankfully, this drew time away from his command and from Athena.

Athena received handwritten messages from Thor via Loki and his magic, poems in an archaic style expressing his affection. They praised his good looks as much as they praised hers. Though she rolled her eyes at their lackluster content and bad handwriting, Aphrodite's love arrow still took effect, and so she found herself unwillingly smitten by the messages. She quickly shook it off and went about her task of training her soldiers for the coming invasion of Malkuth.

She knew that Aphrodite and Susanoo had gone there, and she checked in with them as often as possible. She learned major bits of Azure's story and realized that he was becoming more aware of his great power and purpose. But she lost connection with her sister and Susanoo after each time loop and contacted them again with the same questions and information. Eventually, they became annoyed and told her to stop. They asked if she was sick or if something was wrong with her because she'd asked the same things multiple times.

As the time-loop restarted, Athena stepped out of her chambers to address her soldiers again, but this time the note from Thor read in bold letters: "GET THEE OUT OF THAT SYSTEM, DAME! THOU ART STUCK IN TIME!"

She put two and two together and realized that Malevant was stuck in this time loop too. She immediately fled for the nearest downed Union starship, but was hit by a psionic attack from Malevant. His giant, ominous figure peaked up over the horizon. "Where are you going, Athena?"

"To Malkuth! I want to scout it first before we invade. I can provide you with valuable information on the enemy. Stop it… let me do this…"

"I miss this, Athena…"

"GENERAL MALEVANT!" the voice of Lord Zeon called, a voice that shook the sky. "I REQUEST AN AUDIENCE WITH YOU!"

In a rare instance, General Malevant was startled, perhaps even frightened by this, and could think of nothing else. He immediately flew up to meet Zeon. However, this delayed Athena long enough to keep her trapped in the time loop as well.

"CRIMINAL"

Azure left Neela to rest and went with Edom.

"Are you sure you want to do this?" asked the red hulking Carnotaur.

"For that advance? For her? Yes."

"I've been waiting for you to say that, Big Blue." They cornered a Spinosaur who stumbled drunkenly from a bar. Edom grabbed him and pulled him into an alleyway. Azure punched him in the gut. When the Spinosaur regained his breath, Edom made his demands on behalf of the mob boss. They left him heaving and bleeding from the mouth in the alley. Azure felt uneasy. Edom could tell. "Hey, hey, listen to me," said Edom, still wearing his sunglasses at that time of day. "Stiffen up. He ain't shit to you, you hear me? He ain't shit!"

Edom gave Azure a black trench coat and better body-armor to wear under it. "You wear that every. Single. Damn. Day. Damn civilians ain't carry no guns, but these damn boys do. Best be prepared." He also handed him a beam pistol. "You keep that in your coat. No one sees that until it's time to fire, you hear?"

Edom taught him some grappling and basic self-defense. Azure remembered his military training and was able to hold his own technically, but Edom's strength was simply incredible.

They sat in Edom's car, watching a drop happen and being ready to act. Shots were exchanged, and the two jumped into action. Edom knocked a man clear through a wall and killed another with a single punch—his blood splattering as if he'd been hit with a shotgun round. Both of them were shot but shrugged it off. Azure shot someone in the back, and they began to crawl away. As he closed the distance, the injured mobster held out his hand, saying, "Please, no!" As if by instinct, Azure pulled the trigger and the beam went through the mobster's throat. He shot him six more times.

Edom congratulated him on his first kill in the organization. "You's a natural, Big Blue! These motherfuckers were tryna cheat us. There ain't a wound deeper than one in the back. You did the right thing, man."

The Public Security Force responded to the gunfire, but when they saw Edom and the other mobsters, they waved it off.

Azure was shaking.

As he walked with Neela through the hospital the next morning, he was still shaking. "What's the matter?" Neela asked.

"Nothing. I'm just worried about you, that's all."

"Well, don't. Did they tell you the good news? I can go home soon."

"Home?"

"Yeah. Finally, right? Maybe next week."

"But I'm paying for them to take care of you. I'm almost caught up on your bills!"

"Calm down. It's ok, Azure. I don't want to stay here my whole life. It becomes like a prison after a while." She started to walk better without assistance. "Freedom is outside these walls. There's a lot more I need to do."

"We don't have much of a home, Neela."

"But it's still our home, right? That's what matters."

"I need to work at night, and there's no one to look after you."

"It's ok. I'm a big girl, you know? I can look after myself. Have for many years."

Azure went to the restroom and washed his hands obsessively.

At the earliest opportunity, he asked Edom for some money to rent a better home for Neela to stay in. Edom said he had to get it cleared by the Boss, but also mentioned that the Boss owned a lot of real estate in the area. "I bet you something can be arranged."

Azure met Boss Epsilon who threw on his suit, sweaty from having been flogging someone in the other room. "So, what I understand is you two fucked up a drop, and I'm being asked to give you an advance to rent a condo or some shit?"

"The deal fell through, Boss. That was no fault of ours. We punished the fuckers."

The Boss waved his hand. "Yeah, yeah, ok. You did, didn't you?

Did you make it hurt?"

"I had to hold back a lot," said Edom.

"Yeah. You tend to break everything you touch. I pay you good money for it, Edom. The Public Security Force is always on my ass about you. We already gave them all the samples they could ever want, and they still push my buttons over you. You want to move the Tyrannosaur into a condo?"

"Boss," said Azure. "What about a place with a nice view and no stairs? Maybe in one of the sky districts."

"Holy Saint Sargas on a fuck stick, you do ask for much. The sky districts aren't my domain, but I got another place in mind down here. The both of you are gonna work for it, no questions asked."

Azure walked with Neela into the new home. She smiled, hugged, and kissed him. There was a large window with a view of the harbor. "A single pebble..." said Azure, "sends a ripple through the ocean."

Neela still had to come into the hospital for chemotherapy and checkups. The Symbiote in her brain wasn't shrinking, but it wasn't growing either. With each treatment and each visit, there were new bills. And so, Azure did more jobs for Edom and Boss Epsilon. Once, he and Edom were sent to stand guard during a 'retrieval' as Edom called it. But Azure was horrified to see that there was a bound child in the back of the van with them. Azure objected, saying, "what the hell are we doing?"

One of the mobsters explained: "Her dad's a judge. We don't ask questions."

"Aren't any of you fathers?" said Azure. "My God, Edom! Aren't you a dad?"

"Nusakan Antares, the Chief of Public Security, ordered this job," said Edom.

"I don't give a damn who ordered it! Don't we have souls?"

Azure went to undo the duct tape wrapped around the child's snout, telling her not to be afraid and that it would be ok. Edom shoved him into the corner of the van and held him there. "I'm sorry, Big Blue. Gotta finish the job."

"I won't be a part of this," Azure pushed back. Edom responded with his full-strength and the van itself fell on its side. When Azure came to, some of the other mobsters were kicking him and holding him at gunpoint. Just then, they were mowed down by gunfire. PSF troops ran toward them. One of them aimed his gun at Azure, but Edom knocked the troop over. The PSF grabbed the unconscious child and carried her away.

Nusakan Antares stepped forward and confronted Edom. "Can I trust you people not to fuck everything up? You nearly killed a VIP."

"I think our van was sabotaged," Edom responded.

"Driver's dead," one of the troops reported.

Nusakan aimed his gun at Azure's head. "No one left to talk."

"That's not necessary, sir," Edom objected. "Azure's one of our best and most loyal men. He won't talk. I promise."

"One of your best men? Why haven't I heard of him?" Nusakan inspected Azure's face. "He looks familiar. Have I seen you before, Tyrannosaur?"

"Maybe," Azure answered simply, remembering they'd glanced at each other on Main Street while he was waiting for Neela's release.

"Well, we got the hostage. We've got our leverage over the courts. Tell your Boss you all get half. Your failure to inspect the vehicle almost cost us this whole thing."

Azure rushed home and washed his hands for a good five minutes as Neela asked if he was ok. "Yeah," he said, "some of that tar from the road is pretty sticky and hard to get off."

"Road work at night?" Neela asked.

"...While there's less traffic."

The next night was much calmer. All he and Edom did was collect operation fees from the different pimps who worked under Boss Epsilon. Azure watched as one of them raised his cane and shouted at his girls and boys to get back inside and shut up. Azure saw and recognized the one prostitute who'd argued with Neela the day they met. She'd developed a new wrinkle under her thick makeup. Edom knew her by name, calling her "Vegas" and asking how her kids were doing. "They alright, Mr. Edom," said Vegas. "My youngest started kindergarten. Lost his first tooth." Edom slipped her some extra cash.

Edom and Azure stopped in a parking lot to have some dinner from the drive-thru, but Azure couldn't eat. He was overcome with guilt and anxiety.

"Thanks for doing what you did last night, bro," said Edom, nudging him in between scarfing down a synthetic mammoth-meat burger. "That took a lot of balls."

"Do you ever just say 'no?'" asked Azure.

"I'm in pretty deep, man. There's no going back for me."

"But you knew it was wrong."

"Right and wrong are… what you call… *perspectives*, bro. We gotta do what we gotta do. It's a job. It's a business. It's nothing personal, you know? If God wants to stop us, I'm sure he will."

"I don't think we're forced to do anything. I sometimes hear God talking to my heart and giving me the choice to say 'no.'"

"You know, bro… I broke this steering wheel three times and broke this brake pedal five times because I forgot my own strength. Each time I thought I was going to crash and burn, or at least get buss up a little. And it's like God sent his Angels to guide the car back and slow it down. Each and every single damn time. Scientifically, those are some convincing stats."

"What are you trying to say?"

"Fuck if I know. Maybe… maybe if God wanted to stop me or kill me, he would've done so already. He's keeping me alive for some reason. That's what I think. Things are meant to be."

"…I'm always worried about Neela. I'm doing all this for her, and yet I've never felt further from her. She's probably having nightmares right now, and I'm not there to comfort her. She's my girl, and I'm not there sleeping beside her. I'm not there for her. And I should be."

"Ain't you even listening to a word I said? God puts us where we need to be. Ain't no room for regretting it. Your motives be right. Your conscience be clear. You hear?"

As he came home, he found Neela sleeping on the couch in front of the TV in a puddle of her own urine. He felt her head and her temperature was elevated. Edom drove the two of them to the hospital. They waited for three hours. The doctors said that these symptoms were to be expected.

"That's not what you told me," said Azure. "You told me she was good to go home."

"Whoever told you that was probably helping you to cope. We can stunt the growth of the Symbiote through treatment but not much else."

"So now you're all telling me something different?"

"Look... she's going to regress. We can slow the regression through treatment. That's all we can do."

"I don't believe you. Why are the people on Hod so old and healthy? They must have some kind of pill or something."

"The people on Hod have med chambers that cost several trillion BN to use and operate. It's not feasible for most of the population."

"And why is that?"

"Because it's expensive."

"Fuck it! I'll pay for it!"

"Do you have special permission from the government to use a Class A medical device?"

"What?"

"Do you have trillions of BN lying around at your disposal?"

Azure looked to Edom for some support, but Edom was speechless.

"Can she at least stay here and receive care?" asked Azure.

"We're full. She'll need to go back on the waiting list."

"Waiting list?! She was just here!"

"Well, she's not anymore. And she needs to wait in line like everyone else. It's a long line. You can thank our healthcare system for that."

"What if I pay more to cut to the front of the line?"

The doctor flipped through some papers. "You'll need to talk to the Billing Department, but off hand, it's looking like the best we can do is about two months from now on the seventh, and the cost will typically be double."

Azure agreed.

"A FRIEND FOR NEELA"

Azure didn't ever want to leave Neela's side, but he couldn't afford not to. To quell his anxieties, he followed some advice Edom gave him to hire an at-home nurse or caretaker for the times he was at work. He looked through the various profiles over the Network and one grabbed out at him: a 20-year-old named Amber

Ephesus who'd recently graduated from nursing school. Besides her friendly, chipmunk-like face and cute smile, her last name immediately caught his attention. *Ephesus. Amber Ephesus. A descendant of Bekah?* She was a Ceratosaur like Neela. She had light-pink skin with brown freckle-spots on her cheeks and wore glasses just like Neela. The two could have been sisters. She was diminutive, tiny, even for a Ceratosaur at only six-feet-all. Azure dwarfed her. She was smaller than Neela. She also had the lowest asking price. He hired her.

"Nice to meetcha, Mr. Elyon!" she said to Azure, giggling.

"Hi, you can call me 'Azure.' Elyon's my paperwork-name."

The girl looked to Neela next. "Nice to meetcha too, Miss Eridanus! The name's Amber. I'll be your at-home nurse."

"Hi, Amber, you can just call me Neela."

"Sure, Neela. It's looking like we're gonna be spending a lot of time together. Are you excited?"

"Yippy," said Neela.

"Ah, c'mon now, you can do better than that…"

"Yip-py!" said Neela, throwing her hands weakly in the air.

"*That's* the spirit!" Amber threw a jab in the air.

Azure smiled. "I think you two are gonna get along."

He was right. With Amber, Neela discussed politics, philosophy, and religion freely and sometimes even fiercely. They shared the same taste in music, and watched *Losty* together, knowing each episode. They played board and video games together, and Amber proved to be very good at both. She sometimes let Neela win out of pity.

One day, Azure came home with groceries. "Welcome home, Mr. Elyon!" Amber greeted him, her hands locked behind her back playfully. "Sorry, I mean, Azure. Watcha got there?"

"Lots of eggs for omelets. And ice cream."

"My hero…" said Neela weakly from the couch. "Did you get the one with the thicker cookie bits this time?"

"Of course."

"You remembered. I freakin' love you."

Amber made a bowl of ice cream for her and offered to help feed her. "No, but thank you though," said Neela. As she raised the spoon to her mouth, her hand and arm were shaking.

"She's not doing all bad," said Amber. "We played chess last night."

"She's fuckin' good at it, Azure," said Neela. "I thought my brother taught me better than that. She kicked my ass like twenty times."

"Fourteen times," Amber corrected.

"Close enough." The ice cream fell from Neela's spoon onto her clothes. "Shit."

Both Amber and Azure cleaned her off. "Stop it, you two. You're embarrassing me."

"It's fine, no worries," said Amber, nabbing the spill with a wet napkin. "We've all spilled something before."

"Any changes in her temperature or mood?" asked Azure.

"You know I'm right here, Azure! You can ask me," said Neela.

"I wanted to get an objective opinion, honey."

"Well, you hear her don't cha?" said Amber. "She sounds like Neela."

"Ya damn right," said Neela, pushing herself up off the couch. She waddled toward the kitchen. "And I'm gonna get…some more…ice cream…" she stumbled and fell, dropping her bowl. It shattered. Azure and Amber caught her. "Fuck…"

"Neela, where's your walker?" asked Azure.

Amber rolled it to her, but she pushed it away. "Thank you, but no thank you, darling."

"Neela, you've gotta stop being so stubborn," said Azure. "I spent a lot of money to get all these things to help you. You've gotta use them."

"Again, thank you but no thank you, darling." She looked at the broken ceramic pieces on the ground. "Look at this mess I made. I'm sorry, guys."

"It's fine, we'll clean it up," said Azure.

"Get me a dustpan so I can clean this," Neela insisted.

"I can do it," said Amber.

"Please. Let me do it."

"We can all do it together," said Azure. He got a dustpan and held the pan as Neela brushed. Amber helped guide her arm as it was now quite weak and unsteady.

When they were done, Azure sat back against the wall and covered his face, weeping. "Mr. Azure, don't cry," said Amber, rubbing his arm.

"We've come all this way… sacrificed so much… only to go all the way back… I've lost too much already… I'm done…"

"I don't plan on dying, Azure," said Neela, pulling herself up onto her walker. "I'll fight. I'll fight with everything I have, and I want you to do the same, you hear me?"

"DOWNWARD"

One night, Azure and Edom assisted Boss Epsilon in taking down one of his main rivals who'd cheated him on a deal and had begun to encroach on his territory. Edom's supernatural strength again came into play, as well as Azure's durability and resilience. The rival gang was armed with small mechs and cybernetic arm cannons, weaponry which would easily kill normal beings, but not those two. When they apprehended the rival boss, Boss Epsilon began to flagellate him with a bullwhip until his very dress shirt began to tear along with the flesh. Edom held the victim firmly, covering his mouth with his hand and turning him to face Epsilon who brandished a knife.

Azure became very uneasy at the sight of this. The Boss then turned to him and handed him the knife. "I've noticed you've been a little sidelined, Azure. I don't want you feeling left out. You want that 20,000 BN for your girl's surgery or whatnot? I'll give you 10,000 for each of his eyes." Azure balanced the knife in his hand as he'd been taught in the past. He looked to Edom who nodded to him. The rival boss began to scream muffled screams, but Edom held his head in place as Azure neared, the knife poised for the man's face. He hesitated, and just as he hesitated Edom twisted the man's head and snapped his neck. He fell dead.

"What did you do?!" Boss Epsilon scolded.

"Oh, shit! He struggled, Boss! I was trying to draw him back and forgot my own strength!" Edom lied.

Azure knew what he had to do. He plunged the knife into the face of the corpse and cut around to remove the first eye, then did the same for the second. He held them out to Boss Epsilon, his hands covered in blood. Epsilon put them in a jar and shook his head. "You two fucking idiots," he said.

As the Boss left in disgust, Edom gave Azure a supportive nod, saying, "I got you, bro."

Amber walked with Neela up to the balcony of her home. "A little fresh air never hurts," said Amber.

"Hey, you're a smart 'gal, huh?" said Neela. "What do you think about democracy?"

"Well, that's easy: it's a good thing."

"How so? I mean, I agree to an extent, but I'm trying to figure out if there's a better way to implement it."

"Well... for one, democracy keeps the tyrants from doing whatever they want to do. The people can vote for issues. They can vote the tyrants out if they get out of hand."

"But Antares does whatever he wants anyway," said Neela.

"Because Chancellor Antares has control of the Senate and he has deep pockets," said Amber. "He can get a lot of things passed."

"And that's not how a democracy is supposed to work. One person shouldn't have a monopoly on that kind of power and decision making, no matter how popular they are with the other leaders. There needs to be opposition. There need to be contrary opinions. Other parties. Something. Something to question the status quo. Something to challenge it."

"I get what you're saying, Neela. Like, in agriculture, it's important to have a variety of crops even if everyone seems to only like one type. The popularity of that type matters to an extent, but it doesn't mean that all other crops should be neglected and never grown again. For example, if one type of potato becomes diseased with blight, there are others who might be immune to the disease and can continue to feed the population. Imagine, on the contrary, if that were the only type of potato in a potato-dependent society, everyone would starve. It happened to the ancients and their corn. A lack of variety and diversity leads to dead ends. The same with ideas and ideologies. When problems arise and there's only one absolute way of thinking—a dogma—you'll eventually come up against problems that dogmatic thinking can't solve."

"Exactly! See, that's why I love talking to you, Amber. You get this, darling."

"So, do you think we should just let every single living Malkuthian vote, then?"

"No," said Neela.

"But that would be true democracy, right?"

"Yes, and it would be stupid."

"Why?"

"Because what about the infants who haven't acquired enough knowledge and experience to vote yet? What's to stop their parents from snatching the ballot and committing fraud? What about the criminals who forfeited their legal right to vote when they broke the law? What about the people who are just so damn stupid that they'll vote for someone based on their appearances or race or gender, and not on the issues at all?"

"Shouldn't they still have that freedom though?"

"No, darling. Even freedom needs boundaries," said Neela. "You don't have the right or freedom to steal something from someone because you want what they have. You don't have the right or freedom to drive a vehicle without a license. You need to earn that. Malkuthian nature is to act selfishly and to take the path of least resistance. We have to account for that."

"All creatures are instinctively self-centered, they evolved that way in order to survive. You're right," said Amber.

"Which means?"

"Which means that people will probably vote for what serves them and possibly no one else."

"Exactly, darling. In fact, the majority could just vote to tax the minority to death. They could vote to sentence the minority to death—the rich or the Ceratosaurs, for example. You and I would be dead. They *could* do that. That would be democratic, in a sense, but it wouldn't be moral or right. You can't justify committing genocide just because the majority of people want it."

"And that's why sometimes strong and staunch leadership is necessary," said Amber. "Someone who's going to be strong enough to say, 'no,' whether the people want it or not."

"Yes. And that's why not everyone should be able to vote on everything like in a poll system. You'd have mob rule, and the majority would vote the minority into extinction. Why?"

"Because people are selfish and that's what they do," said Amber. "They take everything they can. And occasionally, just occasionally, they can show some charity when it's convenient for them."

"Precisely."

"And people are stupid," Amber added.

"That too."

"So, you think people should be *qualified* to vote?"

"Well..." Neela thought. "Yes, actually. But I'm hesitant because our education system is a biased one-dimensional mess. I could say that voters should have a degree of education first, but the way things are now it's borderline indoctrination. Of course, you're going to vote for everything Antares wants! He funds the colleges and universities! He owns some of them! Many of them bear his family name. He writes the narrative."

"Freakin' heck, you're right!" Amber punched the air.

"And he owns the media. And he owns our technology. And he owns the Public Security Force. And he owns the Senate. And that's where I have the biggest issue. We're supposed to be a democratic republic or a representative democracy, but it's all for show. Idiots. Idiots kept electing these idiots, and now we can't get rid of them. They're tenured now and practically immortal as long as they can stay on Hod. All bowing down to him."

"I see..." said Amber. "Hey, I know this is random, but I just noticed... Do you see those two stars there that are brighter than the rest?"

"Yeah. You think they went supernova?"

"Probably. Maybe the Dragons got to them. Oh, no. Wasn't your dad sent to fight in that quadrant?"

"Sent there? Did Azure tell you that? I haven't heard from my dad in months," said Neela.

"Yeah. Well, you had pictures and some letters of an army guy hanging up. I couldn't help but notice. Sorry."

"...Darling, what high school did you graduate from?" Neela asked, sounding suspicious.

"St. Sargas," said Amber.

"Same as me."

"Oh... really? That's cool, huh?"

"Our auditorium is really something, isn't it?"

"Yeah... Yeah, it is," said Amber, nervously.

"You know, I starred in some of those plays," said Neela. "I wanted to be an actor someday. I wanted to be famous. Be in a movie."

"Well, why give up now?"

"It's over. You know, I see the agony in Azure's eyes. This job of his and this stress is killing his soul. I can tell. I think he's lying to me, or at the very least hiding something. I can sense it."

"You just miss each other that's all, don't let the stress of that cloud your judgment. He loves you. Otherwise, he wouldn't have hired me to look after you."

"I know. Tell me something, would you?... *Who are you really* and why are you here?"

"Oh, don't be silly. I'm just someone who cares."

"There was a riot at St. Sargas High School when I was there. The auditorium burned down when some asshole threw a liquor bomb into it. They never came up with the funding to rebuild it."

"Oh! I thought you meant the *stage* in the cafeteria! That's still there, of course. We had our talent shows there. I played the flute."

"The flute?"

"Yeah. Want me to play it for the two of you sometime? I've got mine at home. And a violin, and a fiddle, and a little piano."

"You've got some talent, huh?"

"Yeah, I was lucky. I had a lot of people teach me when I was little, and I picked up everything super fast. I've also had a lot of free time on my hands lately."

"Why's that?"

"No family," said Amber. "My dad and brothers… they're all on different worlds across the universe fighting the Dragons."

"Heh, you're a military brat too."

"Yeah, sort of. My mom died 10 years ago in a starship accident. The difference between 10 and 20 is 10."

"Yeah, well even I can compute that. I'm sorry, Amber. And I'm sorry for assuming that something was up with you."

"Yeah. That's ok. We have to be on-guard in this world, don't we? …That was another lifetime. Another life entirely."

"I know how you feel."

Neela underwent another session of chemo. Azure, Amber, and even Edom came to visit her afterward. Amber played the violin for her. Edom made up a story about a new orphanage that he and Azure were helping build. Azure held her hand and kissed her. "I love you," he said. "Forever and always. I love you."

Another lady from the Billing Department called him into the hall to have a talk with him about payment for her continued treatment.

"ONE LAST JOB"

Azure pleaded for another advance from Boss Epsilon to pay for Neela's medical treatment. "You want that money?" said the Boss. "You do this one job for me."

"Anything," said Azure.

"The PSF keeps pestering me for help in removing those Daspletosaur cultists who've been congregating in Ephesus Park. They're squatting there now like they own the place. Their leader, Delano, is like Edom here. He's special. They say that he does something to interfere with their equipment." The Boss threw a file with a picture of Delano on top of the stack. "Delano's cult has killed about a dozen PSF troops. It's becoming the most contended piece of real estate in this godforsaken city."

"Why?" asked Azure.

"Because City Hall is across the street. We can't have a bunch of heavily armed anti-government nutjobs choking up that area. The PSF and the police can't legally use tear gas, the public voted it out decades ago. I suppose our guys could do it, but we've been asked not to for fear of the PSF being implicated. They also can't just bomb the place; it'll damage the park and government building."

"So, what you're sayin' is you need the good ole' fashioned feet-on-the ground to move 'em out," said Edom.

"Yeah. And the two of you are going to work with the PSF to lay down the law on those motherfuckers. You want that money for your girl's treatment, Azure? Then do this one thing for me: you find this Delano and you fucking kill the sonnavabitch."

On the ride to the park alongside PSF cruisers, Azure and Edom listened to recordings of some of Delano's anti-government speeches on file. Azure couldn't help but think *his ideas sound a lot like Neela's.* "Neela is part-Daspletosaur, you know?" said Azure. "They're basically refugees. They've all lost their homelands."

"Don't be gettin' all sentimental now," said Edom. "It's like I told ya: it ain't personal, just do your damn job and make your damn money. Remember who you're really fighting for. Your conscience is clear."

There was a sound like a crash. The cruiser in front of them flipped over. "Oh, shit!" Edom exclaimed. Swerving. It was like some invisible force had grabbed the car. "Get out!"

Azure took his beam pistol and escaped. There was gunfire and screaming. Azure saw the city of tents the Daspletosaurs had erected up ahead. He saw the PSF and mobsters brandishing firearms and sprinting toward the encampment. Edom joined the fray. He decapitated a knife-wielding Daspletosaur with a sweep of his arm.

"They're not armed!" said Azure.

"Then what the hell is this, then?" Edom pulled a knife out of his shoulder.

The PSF and mobsters began mowing down fleeing Daspletosaur men, women, and children as they fled to the hilly side of the park where another group of PSF troops were waiting with beam rifles. They dragged them out of their tents and shot them. Azure was mortified. "Find Delano! Find the target!" someone shouted.

There was the sound of old-fashioned submachine gun fire from the mobsters, which Azure followed. He heard gasps and saw a cloaked Daspletosaur holding one hand in front of him and one hand behind. Delano. The bullets levitated harmlessly around him. He then hurled them back and they hit the mobsters. A beam hit him, and he flinched. He then made a motion, and the guns left the hands of the nearby belligerents and were thrown into a nearby fire that had started. With another motion of his hands, Delano levitated a fistful of throwing knives in the air and scattered them at various targets. Azure was struck in the middle of the chest. A bunch of mobsters and PSF troops were also hit.

"He's a fuckin' magician!" a mobster wailed, ducking for cover.

"This is some kind of magnetism or ferrokinesis," said Azure. "He can manipulate metal objects."

Some of the tents started to burn. The fire grew rapidly. An elderly Daspletosaur woman ran out from the burning tent near Delano, her whole body engulfed in flames. Delano appeared grief stricken and ran to her aid. Another beam struck him from behind and he fell. "Mother!" he cried out to the burning woman whose screams reached Azure. With a flick of his finger, a knife struck the woman in the head and stopped her screaming. Delano punched the ground and growled. With his powers, he grabbed the beam gun from the troop who'd shot him and threw it back so hard into his chest that it killed him.

Azure took this opportunity and dashed at him. Delano grabbed him and threw him over his hip, but Azure managed to land on his feet with a nimbleness that was new to him. The two engaged in a desperate fight, both attempting all types of holds. They brawled with their fists and claws. Delano summoned dozens of knives that buried themselves in Azure's head and back. Azure howled. Briefly, the Sword of Heaven formed in his claws, and slashed wildly with it, missing. It disappeared.

Delano tackled him again, and Azure pulled a knife out of his own back. He slashed it over the right side of Delano's face, taking out the Daspletosaur's right eye. Delano roared and kicked Azure away. Crawling to a distance. As the fire engulfed the camp, Azure's buried conscience caught up with him. His face of fury turned to a face of pity and remorse. He watched as Delano crawled toward the charred remains of his mother and called to her. *"Never lose your **self**,"* Neela's words spoke to him.

Azure dropped the knife, and his body began to spit the other knives out. "Run," he said to Delano. "Just go."

Delano acknowledged this and fled, bleeding heavily.

Azure made himself numb and sprawled out on the ground like a dead man, waiting for the conflict to end or the flames to consume him.

Sometime later, Edom shook him awake. He heard footsteps and then heard Edom berating one of the PSF leaders. "You sick lying motherfuckers!" said Edom. "You told us we was just gonna move these people out! You told us we wasn't gonna use no incendiaries!"

"What seems to be the problem, Edom?" said a familiar voice. Azure recognized it. It was Nusakan Antares.

"You never told us this man had this power over metals. We woulda left the bullets in the shed. Now, for the second time in a row working with you, my boys are lying dead."

"Good for you, less people to share the spoils with."

"Do your own men know how little you value their lives, huh?"

Nusakan, wearing his cybernetically enhanced war-suit, slapped Edom in the face. A normal being would've been thrown back or even killed by such a blow. It did manage to knock off Edom's sunglasses, which he retrieved. "My men know that I'm in charge and what I say goes without question."

Edom growled. "Why did we have to kill all these people? If you was just gonna mow 'em down with your beam rifles, why we even here?"

"Simple: things like plausible deniability, meat shields, the likes."

"You need other people to die for you and people to pass the blame off on, that's all."

"It's nothing new to you, Edom. The narrative is as important as the truth."

"This is damn genocide."

"Hmmph. You're complicit in this too, don't try to deflect this on us. And don't forget, I can send you back to the lab, Edom. You can spend the rest of your damn life there for all I care. Speaking of people I'd like to send to a lab… this boy of yours, Azure. You said he was one of your best men. Is that all there is to it? My men said they saw him take some damage that seemed mortal, but now here he is. Not a scratch on him."

"He has accelerated healing."

"Oh, like you?"

"Yeah, like me."

"Is that all?"

"Yeah."

Nusakan scoffed. "Amusing. Well, I'll be keeping tabs on him too from now on."

Azure gulped.

As Azure washed his hands and looked at himself in the mirror, Neela drove her wheelchair into the doorway behind him. "Azure, what's going on?" she asked.

"Nothing. Your health is sensitive, and I don't want to make you sick from all the germs at work."

"You're cold and pale. Amber thinks it's just stress."

"I'm stressed from worrying about you every second of every minute of every day. It's all I care about. It's all I ever think about."

"Then why don't you turn around and give me a hug? I'm right here." Azure turned and fell to his knees in front of her, hugging her in her wheelchair. His tail knocked over the trash bin. "I thought we could go to the park together and feed the birds. You, me, and Amber."

"Which park?" asked Azure.

"North Park. Amber told me there was some craziness at Ephesus with all the squatters."

"Yeah, I heard about that too… It's cold out. You should bring a coat."

The winter had brought a small snowstorm. Because the sidewalks hadn't been plowed, Neela's wheelchair was rendered useless. They returned it to its storage pellet, and Azure picked her up in his arms like a new bride and carried her through the snow. She wrapped her arms around his neck. "You guys are just too cute," said Amber, walking beside them, nibbling on her fingernails.

The pond at the park hadn't yet frozen over and some of the birds still swam in it. When the birds saw Neela and the others, they started to climb up the slope toward them. Amber took out a bag of breadcrumbs, which Neela weakly tried to throw toward the birds. The crumbs didn't go very far. Azure supported her hand, and they threw the bread crumbs together. The birds gobbled them up and walked closer for more. "It goes to show that not all hope is lost for us Malkuthians if the animals still trust us," said Neela.

Amber whistled a little tune, and the birds craned their long necks up toward her and started honking in unison.

"Shit, that's so cool," said Neela.

"They're like us. They like music too," Amber explained, smiling.

Neela breathed out a cold cloud of smoke.

Azure did the same. This brought a smile to Neela's face as they both remembered the snowy day at the train station when they'd done the same.

Neela raised her right-claws playfully threateningly like a Dragon and said, "You better run. Rooooaaaar!"

Amber laughed.

Azure laughed.

Neela laughed.

In that precious moment, they all laughed together.

And then Azure began to cry. Neela weakly put her arm around his back and leaned her head against his shoulder. "It's ok. It's ok. It's ok, Azure. Life's just that way sometimes. It's like you said, there's a 'transience' to things. The highs and lows. The ebbs and flows. Like the weather. Like the tide. Ever changing. Ever moving. On and on and on it goes."

"Please stop talking like that, Neela."

"No, no, it needs to be said. The universe doesn't end when I do."

"Mine will."

Neela's hand rattled like an elderly-person's as she guided his jaw to face her. She looked into his eyes and studied them like an optometrist. "There's so much behind those handsome eyes of yours. My boy… my boy… my darling, darling boy…" Neela's eyes narrowed and she began to cry. "Do good, you hear me? There's enough evil and cruelty and wickedness. We don't need any more of that.

No matter what happens, always love... always, always be kind, and always do good. Do good, my darling. Do good. And never lose your *self*." Neela began to cough violently. She coughed out blood. It covered the white snow.

Azure wrapped his arms around her.

Amber threw her tiny arms over them both. She sniffled, wiped her snot away, and frantically called for the ambulance on her communicator. "I love you, Neela," said Azure. The lights in the park flickered and then burst. A steam emanated from Azure's body, and the snow around them melted until it became a puddle of water and blood.

The doctor simply said that the beast inside Neela's head had grown despite the chemotherapy and that Neela had fallen into another coma. She could no longer see or hear or respond. Azure stopped coming to work. He told Edom that he couldn't do it anymore. He wanted to spend every moment of every day with Neela. He told her stories. He tried to play *Losty the Unicorn* for her, but breaking news from the war cut through every episode. Amber came to visit every day for weeks and would play musical instruments for her. She played a particularly sad and slow song on her violin. Azure and Amber both helped to give her bed baths. Then, one day, Amber left the hospital in tears and didn't come back. Azure remained. Alone.

Then, one day Edom's voice called from the doorway. "Big Blue..." he said. "Ain't easy for me to say this. Boss Epsilon's men and the Public Security Force have got this whole hospital surrounded. The government knows about what you can do, and her. They want to take the two of you in for research. They sent me to talk to you."

"Was *she* in on it too?" asked Azure, shaking. "Amber. That girl. Was she keeping tabs on us? Reporting on us?"

"I don't know what the hell you're talking about. Look, I'm sorry. I tried. Believe me, I tried, Big Blue. But these people, they can't be bartered with. You know what I'm saying? When they want something, they take it. They want you and her. And I'm supposed to bring you in."

"I won't let you have her! Never!"

"Big Blue... Azure, don't make me do this. This is a hospital. There be lots of sick and dying people on this unit, and the men outside are armed to the teeth."

"Fuck them. Fuck you all. All of you sons of bitches. If she's suffering, everyone should suffer too!" Azure dashed at him and shoved him through the wall. Medical staff ran screaming. Edom tried to clinch Azure, but Azure bit him in the arm.

"Azure, stop!" Edom demanded. As Azure charged again, Edom swung his tail, knocking him through an entire nursing station and sending papers flying. As Azure recovered and tensed his body, there was a sound like a loud hum followed by what felt like a quake that shook the whole hospital for about three seconds. "Azure! You gonna kill everyone here! Knock this shit out!" All Azure saw was red as he grabbed Edom by the throat. Edom tried to pry his hands away. "Azure! Listen to me!"

Azure punched him in the face. Edom instinctively punched back, and then while he was staggered threw him back into Neela's room. Azure picked up a recliner and broke it over Edom who then grabbed him by the arm and got him in a lock. They grappled until they reached Neela's bed. "Azure, they comin'!" Edom warned. "And she'll get caught in the crossfire. They'll tear this place to shreds. More innocent people will die. I know you. I know you don't want that. Just give it up."

Azure crouched in front of Neela like a protective Triceratops in front of its child.

Edom got a call on his earpiece, he relayed the message. "Nusakan Antares says he can take her to the planet Hod for treatment if you agree to surrender."

"They'll take her to Hod for treatment?"

"Yes. Could be her only chance for survival. The safest place in the Union."

Azure still looked poised to fight. Edom dropped his guard. "You can carry her down yourself. She's Aohdfionn's little sister, and you're my best friend, I'll do everything in my power to make sure you're both taken care of. If there was any other way…"

Azure gently lifted Neela up. "You hear that, my love? You're going to Hod where they have all the best medical machines and medicine. You have a fighting chance." He walked her down to the parking lot where PSF troops were waiting for them. Some of them tried to pry Neela out of his hands, but Azure turned his body and pulled her away.

"Don't resist, Big Blue!" said Edom. "They'll shoot you both. You've been on the other side, you know they will."

"I want a guarantee from the Chief of Public Security himself!" said Azure. "I want a guarantee she'll be taken to Hod for treatment!"

Nusakan Antares walked out of the crowd of troops, dressed in his war-suit. Boss Epsilon walked out too, his hand in his trench coat.

"You…" Azure seethed.

Boss Epsilon made a nonchalant face and shrugged.

"You have my word, Azure Elyon," said Nusakan. "We're a bit more interested in you. We just want to run some tests, that's all. The same kinds of tests we ran on your friend Edom years ago. And look at him, he's alive and well, isn't he?"

"I don't want to leave Neela."

"Well, I'm not taking an explosive force like you to Hod, that's for sure. If you want her to receive treatment there, you need to accept that you'll be separated for a while. Just hand her over. Everything will be fine. Nobody has to die."

Azure gulped by tears that swelled up into his eyes. "I want to say 'goodbye.' Please. Let me say..." He took a knee and rested Neela there, cradling her in his arms like a newborn baby. "Goodbye, my love. This isn't the end. I'll make you proud, I promise. I'll love you forever and always. Goodnight and sweet dreams 'til tomorrow, whenever tomorrow comes." He kissed her. A gurney was rolled out for her and the PSF guided her out of Azure's clutches and onto it. Azure's heart became light and his body became weak.

"You made the right choice, Azure," said Nusakan as the PSF rolled Neela away and a separate group pulled Azure toward a van. As his hand left hers, they placed him in handcuffs and placed a bag over his head.

"KILLING AZURE"

The troops led him through a corridor of horror with his hands and feet shackled to his waist and neck. Glass containment cells held monstrous creatures, most of them failed bioweapons created by the Union. Some of them were covered in eyes. One of them had a leg where one of its eyes should be. One had an arm in place of its tongue hanging and beckoning from its mouth. Some had no legs and crawled on their arms, dragging their bodies across the ground like snakes. Many of these had previously been sentient, living, breathing Malkuthians once, but they were far gone. They bashed up against the nigh-unbreakable glass, moaning and groaning, screaming and scratching. Azure's heart turned from horror to sympathy. The monsters seemed to be in so much pain. They seemed so angry, lonely, and frustrated. Azure wondered if they still remembered who they'd been, and he suddenly feared becoming one of these. When he struggled, the troops all took turns striking him.

"Don't fight us, Azure," said Nusakan Antares over the intercom. "We're just taking you on a bit of a tour of our facilities. It's customary for new admits.

Remember, your girl is on the way to Hod as we speak. You didn't think I wouldn't recognize the traitor, did you? I can easily make a case to change her trajectory."

"No!" Azure pleaded.

"Then would you kindly cooperate? Thank you."

They dragged him to another corridor lined with giant glass stasis pods on both sides. The pods contained more grotesque beasts in various states of development. There were even some non-Malkuthian alien species such as specimens from the Collective, the Infestation, Davrons cut out of their armor, and even a Dragon. More than that, however, were the dozens of albino Spinosaurs in stasis, each of their pods labeled "DC" (for "Diamond Clone") followed by a four-digit number.

"You remind me of Diamond, Azure. He was brought in here the same as you. Anyone else would have died from such an attack, but not him. Diamond was indestructible. And his heart had something just like your girl's brain: a Symbiote that had made itself one with the organ. It had mutated and turned his heart into an energy reactor more efficient and powerful than those of our largest mechs. As you can see, we've tried to clone him and the Symbiote but…to no avail. Could you imagine what an army of Diamonds could do in this war? They would slaughter even the Dragon heavy-infantry, which seem so resistant to standard arms. They could save the Union. Be proud, Azure. You are participating in a very patriotic endeavor."

Azure was brought to a chamber where he was strapped down to a rotating table, rendered immobile. Droids in white coats began to take his measurements, his vitals, and some blood samples. But the blood samples disappeared in the vial.

"Are you afraid, Azure?" asked Nusakan. Azure began breathing rapidly as sharp instruments were revealed next to him. "Good. We presume your emotions are what trigger your powers. That's pretty standard."

"Please…"

"There's none of that pleading here. All of the droids there are programmed to ignore that. You can scream all you want though. You're far from civilization."

One of the droids, after rubbing some kind of solution on the side of his torso, cut it with a scalpel and began to peel the skin open as Azure screamed. "Now, what would happen if we removed all of your skin? Would it just grow back?"

Azure eyes grew wide. "Yes! Yes, I promise it will! Please, don't!"

"We can't just take your word for it, can we? Anecdotal evidence is weak. We need hard data. We need to be sure…"

"I swear it will! You don't have to do this! Please, don't do this!"

Nusakan and the droids ignored his pleas and screams as they flayed him alive. His skin, as expected, regenerated. His blood spilled onto the ground before glowing gold briefly and vanishing. The next day, they strapped him in a chamber that acted as a flash-fryer and set it off. Ultra-hot flames shot at him from all directions and consumed him. His flesh turned charcoal-black and burned away, revealing his skeleton. Again, he regenerated. His eyes watered and his mouth foamed upon restoration.

He was cut into pieces with a laser blade, his head severed from his body. Even when they completely annihilated the pieces in an antimatter containment field, his entire body reformed good-as-new close by. As the droids tried to apprehend him, he desperately tried to fight them off. More came and overpowered him. Briefly, a white streak of energy appeared in his hands and cut through some of the droids before disappearing. They shot him with beam rifles until he was a bloody, riddled mess on the shiny white floor. Later, they bathed him in acid, then lethal chemicals. Then, they froze him. Absolutely nothing seemed to be able to kill him. Once, as he reformed, a second pair of arms briefly appeared before disappearing. Another time, white wings appeared from his upper-back before disappearing. Bat-like ones appeared from his mid-back but vanished too. At times, his blood would glow gold like ichor before it became one with the air. Azure was briefly surprised by this, but ultimately stopped caring. The only way he found to help the pain was to let go. He was a numb and broken man who'd gone silent. Nusakan expressed disappointment in the experiments and expressed impatience as he had "other business to attend to." They had yet to see the great latent power they were convinced he had.

Finally, Nusakan seemed to appear to Azure in person. "Wake up, wake up," he mocked. Chancellor George Antares himself appeared beside his son.

"You've been quite a waste of time for us," said the Chancellor. "We had such high hopes for you. Did you know, as we speak now, the Dragons are taking Bhast? Did you know, as we speak now, we are attacking the Dragons' own home universe through a tear that's rapidly closing? They want Malkuth next, we're certain. And then after they take Malkuth, they'll come for Hod. They'll come for you, and they'll come for your girl."

Azure remained speechless. "Azure," said Nusakan. "We had this problem with Diamond in the early stages. Do you know what we did to trigger his power? We showed him what could happen to the ones he loved if the enemy was allowed to win." A scene played in the middle of the room. Neela stood there, looking afraid and calling for help. "NEELA!" Azure finally called out. In the scene, Dragon flying-cavalry swept down and impaled her with their lances. As she tried to crawl away, bleeding, they grabbed her by the tail and pulled her right into their weapons. The scene lingered on her writhing body. It was so realistic that Azure was convinced it had actually happened. The facility shook, and a spark of electricity left Azure's body. He finally broke free from the restraints, breaking through the very metal that starships are built with. He ran to help Neela, but his hands passed through her.

Chancellor Antares and his son couldn't help but laugh.

"Come on, let it out. We haven't got all day," said Nusakan.

Azure growled furiously at the two, and an ethereal white sword formed in his hands. He swung it at the two Antares, but the sword passed through them. They both laughed. "You think we'd be that stupid?" said Nusakan. "I've unlocked the door. Go outside and have a look around." When Azure left the chamber, he saw that all of the stasis pods were gone. He also saw that all of the glass containment cells were empty. The monsters were gone. "Most of what you've seen outside your chamber happened in a separate lab on a separate planet entirely," Nusakan explained. "You're the only living thing there… well, you and…"

"No…" said Azure, feeling a feeling in his gut though the cable of an elevator had snapped.

With a snap of a finger, Nuskan made a projection appear of Neela lying on an operating table. Her head was surgically cut open. Nusakan snapped his finger again and a row of glass containment fields leaned over on their sides, a light illuminated a single door. A terrible realization dawned on Azure, and his emptiness turned to anger. He opened the door and found Neela lying lifeless in the middle of the operating table.

His body shook. His hands trembled as he touched her, confirming to him that she was real. This was real. She was cold, and so Azure pulled up a blanket and covered her. He removed the clamps from her head and tried to cover up the wound with the flap of skin, but that part of her skull was gone. Her blood covered his claws. He kissed her and called her name. There was no answer. There was no breath. There was no heartbeat. And Azure knew. Right then and there, he knew, but he didn't want to accept it. He didn't want to believe it. He picked her up in his arms and hugged her tightly, cradling her head which limply fell backward with her arms.

Aphrodite, seeing this on Malkuth, buried her face in Kushina's chest and wept. Susanoo placed his hand on her back and resisted the temptation to cry too.

Diamond, seeing this via Loki, clasped his hands over his head and shut his eyes. "Sis…" he said. "I'm sorry."

A profound grief consumed Azure and then a profound rage. He cried and screamed and roared. The facility shook. The lights burst. The walls and ceiling crumbled. An aura of pulsating energy surrounded him, breaking through the falling debris. Electricity shot out in all directions. When the building collapsed, the debris spiraled around his aura like a tornado. A purple sky revealed itself. This was another world. A world far from the civilization he knew. The stars became dim as streams of energy left them and came to Azure. They burned out like mere lamps. The suns disappeared. There was darkness, not even a purple sky. The only light came from Azure and the growing aura surrounding him.

He continued to clutch Neela's body to himself. The planet broke apart under him like a ceramic plate. Space tore open around him, dozens of tears to other universes that glowed with more energy. The energy streamed toward him. More stars and more worlds began to die. The plants and animals turned to ashes.

Azure had drained the black hole that powered the Time Mine around Bhumi, setting the star system free from its loop. "Azure!" Athena called to him telepathically. "You need to stop! You'll erase it all!"

Azure's eyes became like flames, and he ignored her advice.

"Uh, Azure dear, we'll disappear…" Even Loki tried to convince him, but this too failed.

"Bloody hell, Azure! Thou shall destroy us all!" Thor shouted.

The very fabric of space-time was being warped and quakes from it were felt all over the cosmos. Malkuth shook. Nuskan Antares felt it. Hod shook, Chancellor Antares felt it. Earth shook, Satan felt it. The Dragons were even alarmed by this. Nearby moons and planets went careening out of their orbits. As the time loop around Bhumi was prematurely ended, Lord Zeon and General Malevant felt it. General Deem and Lord Mortimer felt it. Princess Darna and even Queen Ain herself felt it. Some of her life-streams began to bend like light passing through a gravity well.

Azure pinned his head to Neela's and the aura burst outward into an explosion of energy that consumed his body and hers. The explosion tore through the universe. Its light could be seen all throughout New Heaven, and even the Heaven of heavens took notice: the Third Power had finally awoken.

"RISE UP!"

A series of short videos interrupted regular broadcasts over the television and Network. They appeared to be footage of Azure and Neela. Many of Neela's speeches at the Old Senate House were shown or heard over the radio. Their words reached billions across the Union, and the government's best technical minds attempted to combat the mysterious feeds. Many of the videos were simply of Azure and Neela talking together, including the stories they told each other. Azure and Neela had become celebrities, casting a shadow on Union icons like Diamond and George Antares. Azure became a nigh-mythological figure, a modern legend. There was genuine talk among Adonaian and religious Gorgosaur leaders that this enigmatic Tyrannosaur fit the prophesied *Ramatkal*—the divine Warrior-King who was expected to come in the end-times. Neela was seen as a kind of prophetess, his forerunner. Her story and image were distributed and sold along with Azure's.

Their entire love story was played out for the entire Malkuthian public to see and it captivated the universe. Its sad and dramatic conclusion was particularly touching. Crowds gathered around giant trons to see the continuation and eventual end of their tragic tale together.

The broadcasts themselves were thought by some to be some kind of supernatural messages sent by Heaven. Never before had Antares and the Watcher AIs lost control of the narrative, but now it was rapidly slipping from their claws. They'd resisted the temptation to suppress religion for decades, hoping that their ideals could subliminally penetrate the medium as it had the schools, the courts, and the news media, but now it had backfired. The Malkuthians, many of whom were at the very least superstitious, now had two new modern deities to follow, and neither of them was named Antares.

As riots broke out across the Union, Chancellor Antares tapped into his beta-god powers to manipulate the nanomachines of the protesters. This killed hundreds of them via strokes and heart attacks. It paralyzed or incapacitated hundreds of others.

The riots were the most intense in Malkuth, the planet where most of Neela & Azure's story took place. When Antares attempted to use the power to inflict the people on Malkuth, nothing happened. He then ordered the Public Security Force to shut down all public gatherings. They began firing into crowds, not with rubber or paintballs or beam bags as in centuries past—those had ironically been voted out by the public. The PSF fired bullets and beams. Blood filled the streets. This only intensified the distrust the public held for the Union government and the PSF.

The demonstrators returned the next day with makeshift weapons, machetes, knives, and ball bats. The PSF was not supplied riot gear the way the police were, and there were few police left since the transition to make a difference. The PSF did what they thought they had to and fired on the civilians again.

Nusakan Antares walked forward to inspect the carnage. He found a group of schoolgirls who'd died side-by-side clutching, to his amusement, not weapons, but portraits of Neela smiling. Nusakan picked up one of the portraits and crumpled it up.

The Union military began to withdraw from Atlanta City and then from Malkuth entirely. The PSF followed suit with only core divisions staying put to protect specific government interests. No longer were they trying to fight or regain control of the city. Chancellor Antares knew that the Dragons would invade the planet soon, and he would kill two birds with one stone. But the people of Malkuth caught on to this and became even more resentful because of it. They gathered again to shout at the withdrawing Union forces. They knew what had happened to worlds like Kanopos, Pankaja, and Bhumi. Seemingly the entire population of the planet had turned. No longer did they say, "what will be, will be," but they instead raised their claws as Neela once did and shouted emphatically: "RISE UP!"

Azure floated aimlessly through space until a starship reeled him in via tractor beam. Azure came face to face with Edom and nearly attacked him, but Edom put up his hands in a passive gesture. "You said you'd look out for us!" said Azure. "You sent us both to hell! She's dead, Edom! Dead!"

"I know... and I'm sorry, man. They lied to me too. They cloaked their ships right when they left, and I couldn't follow. They kept tellin' me you was fine. Boss Epsilon sold you out. He told Nusakan Antares everything about you, your girl, her brother. When I found out about it, I wrung his neck myself. I don't give a damn. A man like that would put me under the bus next chance he gets. Next thing I know I got a message with your precise coordinates."

"What? From who?"

"How the fuck do I know? I just know it was right. You're here ain't cha?"

Azure finally sat down. His eyes intense and unblinking. His body shaking. "They killed her, Edom… They killed her… They took her from me… They lied…"

"Azure, I know. Everyone knows. Everyone knows what happened. It's all over TV. All over the Network."

"What?"

"Yeah. All day and all night there's always something on about you and Neela. You're all anyone ever talks about. You get as much coverage as the war itself. And the funny thing is, no one's sure how it's happening or where it's all coming from. They think that God had something to do with it. Some ghost. Something."

"Some ghost?"

"It's like something beyond our comprehension wants the universe to know who you are and what happened. It blows my mind. But you know, it got me thinking: if you go back there now, they'll embrace you, they'll listen to you, they'll follow you. They'll do whatever you say. You could ask for whatever you want."

"All I want is revenge. Justice for Neela."

"Then get it, Azure. They're protesting blind right now. No direction. No leadership. I've got a gang to run now. They won't listen to no mobster. They think you's a man of moral integrity, you feel me?"

"I'll lead them…" said Azure intensely. "And show the Antares. Cut open their heads. Put their corpses on display this time. We'll take it over. Take it all. Lead this place the way she wanted it led. Leave this place the way she wanted it left. Carve and burn a path through the cosmos and make everything right."

"I'm with you, Big Blue," said Edom.

Azure bowed his head.

During a live-broadcasted concert for the band Star Nomads, the bodies of three PSF snipers fell from the rafters. There was brief gunfire and a scuffle with more PSF troops outside. Some of Edom's gang breached the arena wearing red uniforms. There was some confusion, and the band stopped playing. More red-clad Malkuthians filed in around the stage from the exit doors. The leader of the band, not knowing what was happening, swore at them. Then, he saw Azure enter the arena and fell silent. A loud gasp was heard through the building followed by cheering and jubilation at the sight of their idol. They jumped up and down, threw their claws in the air, and shook the guardrails.

Azure soaked it up for a minute. He then threw his right-claws in the air, shouting, "RISE UP!"

The entire crowd in unison roared: "RISE UP!"

The lead-singer of the band, a celebrity in his own right, acknowledged Azure as a 'very special guest' and handed him the mic. The crowd broke out in cheers and chants.

"The Great Malkuthian Revolution has begun!" Azure declared, shouting over them. "Let them hear you! Let them hear me! Let them hear us! Let them know that WE are coming for their heads! Let them know that WE are coming for it all!"

His tone and the sharpness of his speech matched Neela's later speeches. The crowd listened closely as if he were the Pope, hinging on every word as if it were gospel. Azure talked about Neela and what she thought about the government and its injustices. He called to the people to gather arms and to prepare for a coming war.

He said that the Union military was not the enemy.

"They are victims of Antares's game as much as you or I. The Union military is slowly being swallowed up by the Public Security Force the same as the police were. Will you become privately owned too? Tell me, Union officers. Those of you who went to the military academies. Will you answer to the whims of Public Security Force officers with their degrees in Peace Studies and Political Science? Are these the generals and admirals of our future? Indoctrinated puppet police, soldiers, and politicians. Will you continue to follow a Union government that lies and cheats you? Neglects and abuses your families while you're away? Views you not as living soldiers but as lifeless pieces on a chessboard to be sacrificed to meet an end. No. You deserve better. You deserve what she wanted: a government for the soldier, for the civilian, for the citizen, not for the governor. A government *for* the people and *by* the people.

"Follow me. Follow us. We could end this endless war together! We could take charge of our people, of our cities, of our planets, of our schools, our neighbors, our homes, our families. We could erase the constant pull of these AIs who've continued to mismanage our communities. We could overthrow the corrupt and negligent politicians on Hod who've forgotten that they serve THE PEOPLE! RISE UP!"

"RISE UP!" the crowd replied.

"The Dragons will be here in three weeks. Millions of them. That's my prediction. The Union army has been pulled away. The PSF will soon flee. We're all that'll be left standing to defend this historic and great city, this historic and great world. You and me. We will allow the whole Union to contrast the strength of our movement to the weakness and negligence of Antares."

Some of Edom's men passed out red uniforms and machetes. Azure placed his palms together as if in prayer and the marvelous white ethereal sword, the Sword of Heaven, formed there. "This is my blade. This is God's own sword. Forged in the fires of Heaven itself. Let this be a beacon of light to you all. A hope for the future.

"We are all going to die. We are all heading for death. Someday. But wouldn't you rather fight and die for the things that matter? Not for a selfish politician. Not for leaders who see you like pawns. Not for the banks and big businesses. But for yourselves, your homes, your families, your wives, your sweethearts, your children. Our future. What kind of future are you fighting for? The future of slavery and wars that Chancellor Antares sees for you, or the one that Neela envisioned? One where goodness and kindness and justice prevail. Where people do what's right instead of what best fills their pockets. This is our world. This is our history. This is our home. We should stand for it and protect it. We should fight for it." He hoisted the white-flaming holy sword into the sky. "United we stand, divided we fall! Neela is here! Neela is with us! RISE UP!"

"RISE UP!" Machetes rose in the air this time.

A certain Colonel Eridanus, Neela's step-dad, had learned about what had happened to his wife and daughter while he'd been away fighting the Dragons. While on the capital ship, Continental, he listened to Azure's speech and looked with admiration at the man who'd stood by his daughter's side until the bitter end. The Watcher AIs informed him that he was being promoted to one-star general, replacing one who had died in battle. This did little to assuage the sting and the profound sense of betrayal he felt in his heart. He went to the Vice-Admiral on the control deck and saw that he too was listening to the broadcast with great interest. The two Union military leaders from two separate branches looked at each other for some time, and without saying a word, they agreed.

"Well, good," said Chancellor Antares, also hearing the speech. "He and his followers plan to stay and die there armed with their little, long knives. This problem should resolve itself."

"Dad," said Nusakan over a projection. "Our weapons are malfunctioning whenever we try to fire them at the rebels. It's like they're locked."

"I released the locks the other day."

"Well, they're locked again! Something is disabling them. We've been forced to resort to older firearms, but when our men fall, the traitors get their hands on them. The traitors are starting to outnumber us in Atlanta. It's getting out of control. When are you giving me the order to withdraw?"

"When are you going to find your sister?"

"I've already told you, she's not here! That green imp is lying to you!"

"No… I know you're not my brightest, but are you really that stupid, Nusakan? I think it's pretty clear that she's the one doing all this."

"What?"

"I think that your sister is broadcasting these videos. She's hijacking our feeds. She's interfering with the nanomachines and thus the AIs. She's the only one I can think of who could possibly do that. She has my blood and my brains too. I want you to stay there until she's found."

"Dad!"

"Find your damn sister, Nusakan! And then you can leave."

Azure eyes opened as he awoke from a meditative state. "I know what the Antares are doing. The PSF won't leave until they find the Chancellor's daughter. They're convinced she's here, and they're convinced that she's the one broadcasting these videos."

"You sure, man?" asked Edom.

"I also know that we've got a Union starfleet coming our way. Sympathizers. Neela's dad is on board. And there are a set of inter-dimensional portals poised for this universe with two separate Dragon armies on the other side."

"Two?!"

"I know these two Dragon generals, Deem and Malevant. They don't get along. They have different motivations for wanting to take Malkuth, but ultimately they both want me."

"Big Blue, we've got machetes and a couple thousand guns. It'll be a while before I can get more guns. We ain't nothin' against two Dragon armies. You think?"

"That's why we need to take out the PSF. Take what they have. Beam rifles, exo-suits, armor, mechs. And we need to wake up the rest of the city. There are 22 million people here. Imagine 22 million people willing to fight. And that's just this metropolitan area. What happens when the whole world rallies here? In another universe, they have a prophecy of such a battle. They call it 'Armageddon.' The ultimate triumph of good over evil in the field of glorious battle. The whole world takes part."

Edom fixed his sunglasses. "Big Blue, if the Dragons get the two of us… we don't die easy. We'll be impaled on those stakes and suffer indefinitely."

"It's not our fate," said Azure confidently. "And we'd do best to avoid that happening to the people of this world. Our best option is to fight. We need to fight. We need to take a stand and build an empire here to rival Antares for the peoples' hearts and minds."

"I'm trustin' you, bro."

Azure walked down through the university courtyard, where followers had assembled. He greeted the various leaders of different factions by name. Many were familiar faces.

There was Chief Delano, the ferrokinetic leader of the Daspletosaurs who now wore an eye-patch over his right-eye following his fight with Azure. They looked at each other uneasily but with understanding. Then, there was Glaucon the Allosaur, the elderly charlatan who led the homeless camp, raising the spirits of his followers with his crude joking. Though he remembered disputing with Neela over the content of his jokes, he remembered her fondly as a brave young voice.

Next, there was Odhran, the green Megaraptor with a long rifle at his side who had grown in age and stature since the time Azure had last seen him. Together, they had watched Odhran's father be hanged and killed by the PSF. Now, Odhran had assumed leadership of the Raptors, many of whom were hunters by trade and thus skilled with weapons. "When do we get to kill more PSF?" asked Odhran with a kind of maniacal enthusiasm.

"Soon. Be ready."

"CHAOS ON CAMPUS: AZURITES .VS. PUBLIC SECURITY FORCE"

Neela's old history professor waved Azure up to the podium at the top of the library steps overlooking the courtyard. As he ascended the steps, the crowd congregated to his location. A chant went out that repeated again and again: "We pledge to Ramatkal! Our hearts! Our lives!" This gave Azure chills. He'd heard this chant and similar ones for other leaders throughout history.

As Azure reached the pinnacle of the library steps, a tarp was torn down, revealing a life-sized marble statue of Neela. Azure felt as though he'd been punched in the gut, and the sight of it forced him to compose himself. The Professor explained that some art students had made it to honor her.

Azure touched the face of the statue and kissed it, hugging it around the neck. "Thank you. I miss you." He whispered. He saw a glimpse of Terra, the Queen of the Demons, sitting behind the statue, smiling at him. The crowd cheered and applauded as if a royal wedding had concluded, they then continued chanting: "We pledge to Ramatkal! Our hearts! Our lives!

He came to the podium and faced the crowd. He saw Aphrodite and Susanoo hidden there. Aphrodite pointed to herself as if surprised he noticed her and waved at him daintily. No one else seemed to notice. He saw PSF troops gathering at the rooftops minutes before they did. He saw Wyverns from weeks in the future flying overhead, bombarding the city. He focused his mind and attention on the here and now. He raised his claws. "RISE UP!"

"RISE UP!" the crowd roared in unison.

"Behind me is a building full of books. Literature. Something even Antares and his AIs haven't yet erased or rewritten, but believe me they've tried. As you know, Neela loved reading, and she loved reading to me. She loved stories with morals, deeper meaning, and lessons to learn, things which offend our Chancellor. He doesn't want us to serve traditional morals or ethics, he wants us to serve his self-serving edicts. He doesn't want us to find deeper meaning, he wants us to lose ourselves and our meaning, to become clay in his hands, willfully expendable pawns. He doesn't want us to learn, he wants us to listen and obey. *He* decides what's right or wrong. *He* decides what we think and do. *He* decides what we feel and what we believe. Not anymore! It ends now. It ends today. WE decide! His control is over. The narrative is ours. We know the truth. The truth is in books like the ones in the building behind me. Knowledge. Wisdom. Neela knew that. That's why we're here. We're here to finally fight for truth. We're here to protect it—our history, our ideas, our thoughts, our beliefs, whether they be agreeable or contrary. So, what say you, Chancellor Antares? What say you, Watchers? Does truth offend you? Do contrary opinions and perspectives offend you? You want control of the narrative again? Come and get it!"

Thousands of PSF troops began to form around the campus. Their tanks and mechs shook the ground.

"Don't be afraid, but be ready," said Azure, revealing his holy sword. He knew what would happen. "They've come here. They don't care about these institutions anymore if these institutions fail to serve them. It's clear as day. They want to tear it all down. Burn it down with us inside it. We can't let them. Malkuthians, this is the time to be brave. I am with you. Neela is with us. Are you with us?! RISE UP!"

"RISE UP!" the crowd shouted, turning and fanning out toward the PSF troops.

Gunfire broke out. Edom's gang fired back, as did Odhran's Raptors. The Azurites swarmed toward the cover of the Art, Psych, and Astronomy buildings with their melee weapons. The PSF beam weapons locked again, and they were forced to use their more archaic firearms. Azure dashed head-first into a group of about 30 fully armed and armored PSF troops. He cut them all down with the Sword of Heaven. The spectacle of seeing this inspired the fearful Azurites who joined in the fray any way they could. Eight Grand Fortresses and dozens of mechs and droids approached.

Odhran and his Raptors snuck up on some of the PSF snipers on the roof of the Physical Sciences Building, shot and slit their throats, and took their spots. Odhran switched his rifle to fire high-explosive rounds and fired them at the legs of a Grand Fortress. It began to wobble from the impact and crashed into the Art building while staying upright. He switched to incendiary rounds and hit it in the center-mass, setting it on fire. The crew inside baked from the heat of the flames.

Delano focused his ferrokinetic powers on the legs of the smaller mechs, and they began to creak to a halt and smash where they were. Edom came in and bulled over three of them with a shoulder tackle. He charged at the nearest Grand Fortress and grapevined its leg. With some added effort, he managed to snap the leg and bring the giant mech down!

Glaucon, the leader of the poorly armed homeless, led them away into the shelter of the auditorium. He watched as Azure cut down dozens upon dozens and eventually hundreds of PSF troops on his own. "Come and die!" Azure challenged, killing 20 in a single swing, their bullet-and-laser resistant armor succumbing to his holy blade.

Nusakan Antares flew in with the latest and greatest model of his war-suit, firing high-energy repulsor beams down at Azure from above. Azure blocked and deflected them with his sword but could not fly up to strike Nusakan. "I'll kill you, you bastard! I'll tear your fucking ass apart!"

Nusakan kept his distance and placed both his hands together to charge a focused blast. Azure threw the sword, and it hit Nusakan, knocking him out of the sky. Nusakan's armor dampened the fall. Azure hungrily ran up to him, remembering the cruelty he'd shown Neela and himself, but Azure was hit by a particle beam cannon from one of the Grand Fortresses. Regenerating and growling, Azure dashed at it, recalled his sword, and cut both legs off the mech, causing it to crash to the ground, creating a cloud of dust that obscured a quarter of the courtyard and formed a crater. Nusakan used this opportunity to crawl away, but Edom pummeled him, crashing him through the wall of the Psych Building. Edom grabbed him, but Nusakan sent power to his cybernetic enhancements to counter some of Edom's strength. He summoned rockets from his back, which hit Edom. He then hit the hulking Carnotaur with a full forced repulsor blast before flying away from the building.

Azure pounced from out of smoke and slashed at him, cutting off his right-leg. Still flying, Nusakan screamed in his suit. Unable to focus on piloting, he crashed through a tree and into the glass display of the Art Building. Azure stalked him, his eyes wide with intensity. Nusakan fired an array of rockets, beams, and repulsor blasts, but Azure shook them off and continued to approach him as he backed away. He held up his hand and pleaded with Azure, who ignored this and slashed at the son of the Chancellor, cutting his hand in half. His fingers fell to the side. Nusakan screamed.

Just then, the paratroopers of the PSF arrived, flying in wearing war-suits similar to Nusakan's. They fired off their arsenals at Azure, who hacked most of them down. Others flew around and circled him while firing. Nusakan used this opportunity to escape using his propulsion engine, bleeding profusely from where his leg and hand had been. Azure pounded the ground in frustration and took the rest of his frustrations out on the PSF who continued to flock to him like sheep to the slaughter, firing their small-arms and even hurling grenades, which continued to have little effect on him.

As tanks rolled into the courtyard, Delano focused on trying to bend their turrets. He managed to do this enough to render them unsafe to fire. When one tank attempted to, it exploded. Edom ran in and flipped one of them over, it fell on another beside it.

More mechs and tanks came in. Delano's energies were fatigued. He focused on using his remaining power to throw knives at regular PSF troops. Edom too was feeling fatigued. He commanded his men over the communicators to rally around him and regroup.

Odhran continued to fire incendiary rounds, if nothing else making life inside the tanks and mechs miserable for those inside. PSF troops surprised the Raptors on the rooftop, attempting to recapture it. Odhran fired a high-explosive round at the stairway, killing many of the troops while cutting off access to the roof for the time being.

Many Raptors had been killed. Many other Azurites had also been killed in the desperate struggle. Several starships appeared overhead, firing down at scattered Azurites. Suddenly, they stopped firing, as did all of the mechs for a long minute. Then, shockingly, the starships started to fire at the mechs. The mechs then fired at the starships, and then fired at each other. Someone had clearly manipulated them. Watcher holograms glitched in and out like ghosts in the smoke. A low, distorted voice spoke over the campus intercom, saying, "Well, hasn't this been fun? I've had enough playing with you for now. This engagement is concluded."

The controls to the starships locked, and the ships were forced into a retreat along with the rest of the PSF.

"What the hell…" said Edom.

"The son of a bitch escaped," said Azure, covered in blood and gore. "This must be her doing. Autumn Antares. She sounds as psychotic as her father and brother."

There were moans and groans through the cloud of debris. But as it cleared up and the surviving Azurites caught sight of their leader. They began to chant and cheer, encircling him. In the aftermath, thousands of bodies littered the campus from both sides. Mechs, tanks, and buildings were left smoldering. Odhran and the Raptors walked through the carnage, deliberately looking for still-living PSF troops to shoot despite their pleas and protests. Odhran did most of the shooting.

Azure, Edom, Delano, Glaucon, and their followers tended to the other fallen and wounded. They retrieved weapons from the PSF, including beam rifles which were suddenly unlocked and usable. When Azure saw Odhran gunning down a fallen PSF troop, he scolded him. "Knock that off!"

"Look at you, Ramatkal, you're covered in their blood, deeper than me even," Odhran shot back. Azure had no defense as he looked down at his blood-stained hands. *"Do good,"* Neela's words echoed.

Days later, the same low-pitched, distorted voice called out over the city. It said that the gates to the PSF armory were now opened and that "the fruits are ripe for the picking." The voice was right. The Azurites found the PSF troops guarding the armory in a miserable state. Azure even pitied them as they asked for help. Yeshua's voice spoke to him from the future, saying, *"Love your enemies. Bless those who curse you. Do good to those who hate you."* For a long time, he'd ignored that voice, and it had cost him.

"What's the matter with you all?" Azure asked the troops.

One of the officers explained: "Please don't kill us. We can't do you any harm. We all got sick all of a sudden. It's hard to breathe. It's like... pressure in the chest."

"Nanomachines... Where's Nusakan Antares?"

"He's gone. He abandoned us. He didn't say where to. Fucking coward."

"I hope I am a better man than the ones you serve."

Odhran ran up and aimed his rifle at the officer, but Azure knocked it aside. "No!" said Azure. He then addressed the rest of his followers. "None of these men are to be harmed so long as they pose no threat to us. We are Malkuthians, not animals. We are above killing the wounded and sick."

"These damn animals would kill us if they were in our shoes!" said Odhran.

Azure raised his hand. "Don't become what you hate, Odhran."

"Speak for yourself, Ramatkal."

The PSF officer, a colonel, tugged on Azure's coat and offered to join his movement in return for medical treatment for him and his men. Azure called some doctors in the group forward to check on the men. As Azure strolled past them, he saw that they were bleeding from the nose and mouth. He had flashes of Neela in her last days. He went to his knees and wiped the blood off the face of one of the soldiers. He looked him in the eye and said, "Hang on. Help is here."

Azure questioned the PSF Colonel about any traps in the armory, which he denied. The doors were ominously wide open as if a heist had just occurred. What they found was a warehouse of weapons including beam rifles, exo-suits, armor, cannons, mechs, tanks, and starships. They spent the remainder of the day carrying weapons and supplies to waiting trucks that Edom had procured. The condition of the PSF troops there improved as the day went on and tensions continued to rise about what to do with them. "Offer them uniforms. Leave the ones who reject the offer. Let them come with us if they want," he replied. "They can join our ranks, teach the others how to use these weapons. They have more experience."

In the following weeks, they seized more supplies from armories and surplus stores. They shut down the public executions and humiliation on State and Main. They also seized control of the police station including capturing the Police Commissioner and gaining control of the city surveillance. Many police officers, though few in numbers, joined the movement willingly out of animosity for the government and PSF. Perhaps most significantly, they seized control of the Communications Tower and were able to broadcast Azure's speeches and call-to-arms across the Union. He called for a "glorious stand" by all Malkuthians on the planet of their origin, the namesake of their entire race.

The Azurites had gone from a poorly-armed, poorly-trained rag-tag militia to a fighting force rivaling or even surpassing the Public Security Force in Atlanta City. Their numbers swelled to the hundreds of thousands as people from around the world and the Union flocked to be in the presence of the Ramatkal, Azure Elyon. The problem was, it was difficult to house and feed so many people, even with the city's rich resources. Azure opposed looting and intimidating the local businesses on a moral basis. Perhaps because of this, some local businesses had chosen to donate and distribute food to the Azurians who'd begun camping in the streets. Following Edom's advice, they'd taken over the nearby Antares Enterprises Stadium and began using it as a base of operations.

"They're coming..." Azure informed his lieutenants. "Tomorrow around noon, the first Dragons will be here. Wyverns with their firebombing and Leviathans as long as a city block with targeted attacks. There'll be no safe place. Many people will die."

"Many have died," said Delano.

Azure gulped. "I'll announce all this at the broadcasting station. When they hear me and see what happens—see that my premonitions are accurate—they'll finally believe."

"And then?" asked Edom.

"We'll rally together for the battle of battles."

"TERROR FROM THE SKIES"

Dozens of black vortexes formed in the stratosphere over Malkuth. Just as Azure had predicted, Wyverns and Leviathans swarmed down. Incredibly, the civil defense sirens still played. A chill went down the spine of every Malkuthian on the planet that day. The flying Dragons, all of magnificent colors, began to bombard the sky districts first, attacking their force fields. They bombarded the lower districts, setting fire to various neighborhoods, green fire which could not be extinguished naturally. The Leviathans, adapted from more aquatic military campaigns, produced water jets that behaved similarly to lasers, piercing and cutting anything they touched. Malkuthians burned, their bodies dancing perilously and hopelessly in the flames. Limbs and appendages went flying. Heads. Brain matter. Chunks of bones. Buildings caught fire and began to collapse.

Azure marched out into the streets in the middle of all of this. His followers and the whole Union watched him with grave interest, expecting a miracle or a demonstration of power. He looked up at the vortexes and the Dragons, some of whom blasted him with their attacks. He knew that this was the best place for him to stand, even as he urged the other Azurites to shelter in place for the time being. He stood alone amidst the growing devastation, facing down the terrifying Wyverns and Leviathans but unable to reach or attack them. Smoke and fire formed around him. The condos at his left and right crumbled but he stood bravely facing the attack alone until the Dragons returned to their vortexes around three hours later.

As the Wyvern fires burned out, an eerie amber glow shined over the city. The outline of the twin giant suns peaked through the clouds of smoke. The broadcast followed Azure as he turned over some fallen rubble. He found a single Carnotaur mother and her three kids, one still an infant, huddled together under parts of a broken table, shaking, and covered in soot. Azure reached out to the mother and she took his hand. "It's ok, I'm here," he told her. "I've got you guys."

The mother nodded and led her children out into the street with Azure. They looked back at the remnants of their home and cried. Edom and Delano came out of hiding and emerged in the smoke behind Azure. "What do we do, boss?" asked Delano.

"Help them, Chief."

There was someone screaming for help at the top of their lungs. "It's my son!" a soot covered Allosaur explained. He led them to an overturned ground vehicle that was near a green fire. Edom turned the vehicle on one side and Azure and Delano guided it down together. Edom tore open the door and unbuckled the unconscious child. Delano took a look at him. "He's still breathing," said the Chief, guiding him into his father's arms.

It wasn't always so happy an ending.

Bits and pieces of people and clothes lay strewn over concrete and rebar. There were many bodies. Perhaps the most tragic were those who'd failed to die from the Wyvern fire. Their charred flesh tore away when Azure and the others attempted to render aid. The other Azurites rallied to the aid of their leaders, and among them were medical professionals. Azure crossed paths with some of Neela's old nurses and doctors. They'd been caught up in the movement, having been willing and unwilling stars of the footage that had been widely broadcast. They did what they could for the victims, and Azure thanked them each for it.

There was a woman crying on the edge of the sidewalk who Azure and Edom both recognized. "Vegas, is that you?" Edom called down to her. She'd been the prostitute that had berated Neela, the one whom Azure and Edom had seen while collecting for the mob.

She pointed to what was apparently her apartment. The entire complex had crumbled and was still smoldering. "Were the kids in there?" asked Edom.

Vegas nodded. She'd been thrown out over the balcony while smoking, the building having been hit by a series of Wyvern blast. She'd survived the broken fall with some pain, but her children inside the apartment hadn't survived the collapse or the fires. Edom tried to pick her up, but she dropped her body limply toward the concrete, having given up. "Leave me here. Leave me alone," she said. "I gave up everything for them. My soul. My body. And now they're gone. Taken from me. Just like that. How cruel. How fucking cruel!"

Edom kneeled down next to her. "I know it ain't the same, but I have some kids I know I'll never see again. Some judge took them away, not because I was a bad dad, but because he believed I was a bad man. I did bad things to feed them, put them through school, buy them clothes and diapers. It ain't fair. It ain't just. It just is what it is."

"You fucking asshole!" Vegas shouted at him, punching him in the arm before collapsing into him. He hugged her.

Azure walked by and rubbed them both on the shoulders. He continued to march down the street, helping whoever asked, helping wherever he could. Delano was able to use his ferrokinesis to pull some of the rubble apart to rescue more victims. A moon pup who'd been trapped ran out to them and whimpered. It led them to a fallen elderly Giganotosaur pinned under a bookshelf. Azure and Delano pulled her out together. They saw that she'd been burned on part of her body as well and was no longer breathing. Delano pumped her chest as the moon pup whimpered close by, rubbing itself against its owner. It became clear that it was futile. "You tried," said Azure.

"She reminds me of Ma," said Delano, kissing her on the forehead. "Rest well, old queen."

He took the moon pup in his arms and carried him along in a sling at his side.

"Chief..." Azure said to Delano. "I regret it every day. One of my many greatest regrets. I'm sorry. I'm so sorry."

"On one hand, Azure, it's too late for that. On the other hand, I never blamed you for what happened," said Delano. "Ma's at peace, and I've got one less eye to see half as much cruelty. Give these people and my people some hope. That's all I ask."

Delano met up with other members of his tribe.

Azure summoned the Sword of Heaven and raised it in the air. Its light pierced the smoke like a beacon at sea. "RISE UP!" he shouted.

"RISE UP!" Azurites responded.

They came out of their hovels, out of their shelters and rubble. They flocked to Azure and raised their claws and weapons with him, chanting, "We pledge to Ramatkal! Our hearts! Our lives!"

They marched through the street toward downtown. Their numbers swelled. The Dragon bombardment had killed thousands, but it also broke down many of the attachments that had kept people from joining the movement—things like homes, families, and jobs. The infrastructure of the city was disrupted, the PSF and emergency personnel failed to show up for the most part. The military was long gone. Azure appeared to be the only major figure left standing for the people, exactly as he'd foreseen.

The next day, the Wyverns and Leviathans came again. They finally broke the force fields surrounding some of the sky districts, including the one that Neela had lived on. They pounded them with their attacks, leaving them flaming torches in the sky. Bodies fell from them and splattered on the city below, the bodies of burnings and suffocating victims. The sound of the bodies crashing was especially bone-chilling. There was barely anything left of the victims. Intestines and organs occasionally. No way to trace who these things belonged to.

The Dragons had struck the stadium and several skyscrapers, which spilled their contents into the streets below, blanketing it in soot and falling leaflets. The Azurites actually managed to fire some of their new guns and artillery up at them, killing a few and disrupting their formations. Whenever a Dragon was shot out of the sky, the angry and emotional Azurites ran at them punching, clawing, kicking, and shooting at them even after they were clearly dead. Azure and Edom held up the corpse of a Leviathan together for the cameras, roaring in triumph. With the help of such scenes, people across the Union actually began to perceive what was happening on Malkuth as a victory. Millions began to travel there, even after the Union government attempted to ban travel to Malkuth for "concerns regarding safety." The Union military failed to contain the mass migration and weren't motivated to. Navy admirals had begun to ignore orders by the Chief of the Navy, discrediting him as a puppet PSF leader. Chancellor Antares was dumbfounded. His leash on the Union military was bitten up and broken.

Despite a third day of bombardments by the Dragons, spirits remained high among the Azurites. There were well over a million now in Atlanta City alone. The Azurites weaponized sky cars, deactivating their autopilot and turning them into makeshift fighter planes. Atlanta had tens of thousands of those, although they were a favored target for the Leviathan water jets. They procured more abandoned PSF and military equipment including force field batteries that they used to create shelters to weather the attacks. However, not everyone could find shelter in them. Azure and Edom, the most durable of the Azurites, voluntarily left the safety of the shelters and remained among the vulnerable. This, too, was a highly publicized act of charity, and Azurite propagandists drew comparisons with Chancellor Antares and those on Hod who hid behind layers of nigh-unbreakable force fields.

However, outside the shelters, innocents died surrounding Azure and Edom, they clutched them, burning and dying. Edom wept behind his sunglasses. Across from him, on the other side of the force field was Vegas, still mourning her children. She looked up at him with concern and he gave her a thumbs up. "It's ok," he mouthed to her.

There were screams and panic even in the force field shelters as the Dragons continued to pound them with attack after attack, each attack threatening to break the barriers and expose their frightened, living contents at any time.

"CONFRONTING NUSAKAN"

That night, as Azure and the others helped the scared and wounded, they marched toward a commotion on State Street in the downtown area. At first, he noticed the bodies of dead Dragons hanging by their mouths and tails like slaughtered fish, their blood dripping onto the tarmac below. Then, he saw people hanging from the old cages as Neela once had. Panicked, he took a closer look, seeing that they all had placards on them with their names and alleged crimes. All of their crimes read, "Treason: Crimes against the People."

"What the hell is this?!" Azure shouted. "Who are these people? Who put them in these cages?"

Azure was then shocked to find bodies hanging from cranes. The placards on their necks read, "High treason: Capital Crimes Against the People." Azure's heart sank and he frantically looked to see if any of the hanging victims showed signs of life. He then noticed a recently hanged person who was twitching and shaking. A little girl called out to him from the crowd, and Azure recognized her. She'd been the daughter of the judge who Azure and Edom had helped abduct for the PSF. He immediately drew his holy sword and cut down the judge. When the crowd tried to hold back the little girl, Azure roared at them to back off and let her through. Azure loosened the noose around his neck as the little girl came to his side, crying, "daddy!" She vomited and tried to wipe it up.

Azure rubbed her back and tore off part of his clothes to wipe her mouth with. He then looked up and was surprised to see Odhran, the leader of the Raptors, holding none other than Nuskan Antares at gunpoint. Some of the other Raptors held Nusakan up as he was still on his lone remaining leg. He'd been stripped of his war-suit and had been beaten badly. Azure angrily rose to his feet. His vision became red as he looked upon the man directly responsible for Neela's death, her humiliation, and his torture.

"So, I gather you don't think the judge who ordered over a

dozen deaths deserved to die? That's your call," said Odhran. "I got you a gift. What about him?"

Azure faced Nusakan, whose mouth dripped with blood. His right-eye was swollen and bruised. He remained silent. His face flat and expressionless. "Say her name," Azure seethed. When Nusakan failed to respond promptly, Azure punched him in the swollen side of his face but held him up so he wouldn't fall. "Say her name!" Azure punched him in the gut. He coughed up blood. "What's her name!? Say it!" The crowd cheered. Azure kicked Nusakan in his lone remaining leg, breaking it. He fell to the tarmac, screaming. Azure kicked him in the face and knocked out some of his teeth. The Chief of Public Security lay writhing in agony. He held out his hand to ask for some leniency. "You son of a bitch! You say her name!" Azure demanded.

"Neela…" said Nusakan finally before coughing up blood.

It started to rain.

Azure punched him again and again and again. He got a noose and threw it around Nusakan's neck. Instead of using the crane's normal mechanism to hang him, he threw the rope over the top of the crane and pulled him up himself, holding him there as his body wiggled. He dropped him, letting him try to regain his breath, and then pulled him up again until he was lifeless. He dropped him one last time, his body falling completely limp, and then hit him again and again in the face until his skull was pulverized. Death was certain. Azure ripped at the remnants of his face and tore at it. He tore at the rest of his body and threw the pieces aside. When he looked up, he saw the face of the little girl whose father he'd just saved from hanging. She was hiding behind her dad, the judge, terrified of Azure and crying.

Odhran stood at his left. "You see," he said, his ubiquitous rifle at his side. "Justice feels damn good doesn't it? If you don't want to kill the judge in front of his little girl, that's fine. Just remember, they killed my father in front of me, and that was fine. Everyone here deserves what they're getting as much as Nusakan Antares did. They're all complicit in these public executions and humiliations in some way. What goes around comes around."

Azure pointed to the judge. "Take your daughter and go. Get her out of here. She doesn't have to see all this."

The judge obliged.

As he and his daughter were far enough away, Azure said to Odhran, "If you're going to kill somebody, shoot them in the head."

"Like you did just now, sir?"

"Shoot them in the head, Odhran. That's an order. And give these prisoners food and water. I don't want them in these cages for longer than the night. The whole Union is watching."

"Well, aren't you merciful, Ramatkal," said Odhran, marching off to fulfill his wishes.

"AZURE AND JESUS"

Azure, rattling with anxiety, went to rest on his own in an apartment vacated by a victim of the Dragon attacks. He rocked back and forth, saying, "Neela, did you see her face? The little girl's. Did you see...her...face?! You were my conscience, and now you're dead...what do I do?... I'm lost... I'm scared... of myself..."

He shut his eyes and tried to drift away, to try to silence the echoing cacophony of screams and voices. He saw the child Jesus growing before his eyes until he was as tall as his dad. There was bloodshed in his world too. The soldiers of Caesar, with shields, swords, and spears, slaughtered those who rose up against their rule. The captured rebels were dragged kicking and screaming to wooden crosses. Their wrists and ankles were nailed to them and they were left to hang and die in agony along the road, a warning to others who might rebel. Their bodies were thrown into pits outside the city along with piles of corpses in varying states of decay. *Is there no end or limit to cruelty? Is there nowhere in this damned cosmos where kindness reigns? Is there no escape from all this? A cure for this illness? And am I the same? Am I sick too?*

Azure watched in his dream-vision as Jesus went amongst the people who embraced him. He watched as a woman accused of adultery was dragged before religious leaders who readied to stone her to death before being confronted and challenged by Jesus. He stood between them and the woman.

He restored sight to a blind man. He healed a man who lay paralyzed on a mat. He resurrected a widow's deceased son simply by telling him to rise. He seemed to make the people around him happy and smile. Even when they claimed him to be a king and asked him to fight and to overthrow the oppressors, called "Romans," he said that he was not there to overthrow armies of flesh and blood but to break away the chains and open the cages around the spirit. *I am not like you, Jesus. You. You must exist only to mock me. To show me all that I failed to be.*

Not once did he raise a weapon or call up an army. Temple guards came to arrest him in the night, and one of his followers slashed at and cut the ear off of one of them. Still, Jesus called for the violence to cease and healed the injured guard, one of the very guards sent to arrest him. Azure was astonished, watching as the religious leaders hit him and spat on him despite all the good he'd done. They demanded that the Roman governor give the order to execute him because they could not do so themselves.

Romans tied him naked to a stake with the back of his body exposed. They took a scourging instrument with led balls and pieces of bone at the end and struck him—raked him—with it until much of the skin was gone. Then, after they'd done this, they turned him over and struck him from the front too, tearing the skin and flesh from him.

A crowd gathered and still called for his death until the governor relented, fearing another rebellion. Roman soldiers mocked him as the "King of the Jews," and made a crown of thorns, forcing it onto his head, thus drawing more blood. They laughed at him.

"A ram had its horns caught in a thorn bush, and Abraham sacrificed it instead?" the voice of a younger Jesus had said. *"Why a ram? Why the leader of the flock?"*

Azure had a flash of an older event. An old man named Abraham had been asked to sacrifice his son on a mountain but was stopped by an Angel just as he was ready to do the deed. The old man and his son then found an old ram caught in a thorn bush. They sacrificed that ram instead.

Is that what you were? A ram. A sacrifice to take the fall for those who mistreated and spat on you? It all makes sense now. I won't just be a sacrifice. I will not lay down my arms and let them hurt and take from me! I will guard and fight for everything I have with all my might! With all my power!

Jesus never resisted his brutal captors, never tried to run away. He carried his own cross up a hill, his blood soaking the clothes on top of him. He seemed to go into shock, collapsing. And at the top of the hill, they took long nails to his wrists and feet and hammered them into the wood. *Won't you plead with them? Won't you curse them? Won't you call your army of Angels down to stop them? Use your powers? Anything?!* And just as they were doing this, Jesus said, "Father, forgive them. They don't understand what they're doing." *What?! No! Screw them! Call down your father's power and kill them all! Show them how powerful you are! Send them all to Hell! Show them who they're messing with! Save yourself!*

A teenage Jesus appeared to him in that same vision. "Azure," he said, reaching up and petting him on the head. "That's what the kings before me did, and all of them failed."

"Being captured and killed by the enemy is failing," said Azure.

"No. In time, the belief in me will conquer even this great and powerful Roman Empire. And in time, just as they embrace these beliefs, Satan will discard the empire like an old toy. It will fall like all human kingdoms before it. I will not have lifted a sword, yet it will come to pass."

"I don't have that luxury. I'm forced to fight. I'm forced to kill. If you send me enemies, I will slaughter them all until their bodies pile up to the sky!"

"And who is your enemy, Azure? Is it Antares? Is it the Dragons? Is it Ain? And when they're all gone, will everything truly be right?"

"I'll make it right."

"All kings say that. I was not intended by my father to be such a king."

In the vision behind them, the broken and bloody body of Jesus hung on the cross, gasping for air. His blood dripped down from the wood.

The scene changed to Egypt, in the midst of the pyramids over a thousand years earlier. Ethereal beings from the sky had come to live among the Egyptians. These were survivors of the Dragon Wars in another universe. Samael-Satan had extended an invitation to them, only in so far as it served his purposes: to enslave and torment God's chosen people, the children of Abraham. Samael felt a little bit of an affinity with the Sky Beings. They were all the children of a great shining being named Ra, whom they'd successfully rebelled against.

Before the Dragon Wars, King Ra was ruler over the Sky Beings, but gained the ire of his children, led by the brothers Prince Osiris and Prince Set. Ra was trapped by his children upon a great ship that drew the attention of Apep, a great sky serpent that proceeded to chase him continually until a Dragon lord killed them both. Osiris took Ra's place as king, stirring Set to jealousy. It was a jealousy so strong that it caused Set to kill his brother by sealing him in a coffin that only he could fit in and drowning him. However, before dying, Osiris had impregnated his wife, Isis. She gave birth to a falcon-headed being named Horus, a being so quick to anger that he even decapitated his own mother when she failed to help him win a battle.

Afraid of losing his authority, Set used the premise of a false truce to attempt to violate Horus, trying to tarnish his nephew's legitimacy over the throne. However, Horus reversed this predicament, humiliating Set instead and forcing his jealous uncle to abdicate.

Horus's victory and reign was short-lived with the arrival of the Dragons, who did the same to the Sky Beings as they had to the Olympians, Asgardians, and Kami. With their old world destroyed, the Sky Beings came to Earth, helping to build the great kingdom of Egypt.

There in Egypt, the descendants of Abraham (the Hebrews) had served as slaves under dreadful conditions but had found favor with the God of gods, Yahweh.

Their God began to fight and subdue the gods of Egypt, the Sky Beings, one by one. This, in turn, inflicted their followers with a series of plagues channeled by a Hebrew named Moses, a former adopted prince of Egypt. The last plague was coming: the death of the first-borns. The Egyptians at the time had glamorized and worshipped the idea of death. But now the very thing they idolized and built their lives around threatened to take their precious children. The Hebrews were not immune to this plague either but were given a way to avoid it. Each Hebrew household was told to take a lamb into their home. They were told to kill it as a sacrifice and spread its blood over the corners of their doorway, top and bottom, until they crossed at the hinges.

Then, when the fateful day came, the Angel of Death arrived in Egypt, given permission to take the life of every first-born who was not protected by the blood of the lamb. *Samael... Satan...* Azure recognized him. Samael went from household to household, his shadow covering each home as he passed and inspected each doorway one by one. When he found one without the blood of the lamb, he entered, and there was screaming inside. When he found one that had the blood of the lamb, he passed over them. He then came to the Pharaoh's own palace and attacked his first-born son, sending his life-energy up to Ain.

The scene then returned to the crucifixion as Jesus called up to the sky in Hebrew, *"Eli, Eli, lema sabachthani?"* ("My God, my God, why have you forsaken me?")

"Why would you say such a thing? Are you confused? Don't you know the meaning of your own sacrifice?" asked Azure.

"It is a Psalm, a poem prophesying that I would be forsaken by God in favor of man. I call my father, God, 'Abba.' He is my daddy. But in that moment, I will acknowledge him as God. In that moment, my life will be traded."

"People have died worse deaths. I've been tortured, burned, flayed alive. Athena and Aphrodite have suffered under Malevant. What makes your suffering and your death so special? Is it just the injustice? It was unjust what happened to Neela! It was unjust what happened to me!"

"All have sinned and fallen short of the glory of God, Azure, and the wages of sin is death. In God's direct presence, as you recall, imperfect beings are burned up and annihilated. Sin is what separates us from being in his presence. And that is why what will happen to me is significant. It isn't entirely my torture or the method of execution that makes it special, Azure. That will fulfill the forbidden prophecy made by the prophet Isaiah hundreds of years before me. The true weight of what will happen to me lies in sin itself. The evil that men do. All the pain and suffering ever inflicted by every living being in the cosmos. In that moment when I am forsaken, all the sins of the past, present, and future will fall on me. That will be the true moment of suffering and despair. My human body will be crushed by that."

"And what about us? What about my people? What about the people in other worlds? People who don't even know who the hell you are! What about them?"

"I will die for the sins of all, past, present, and future. And as the judge in the end of time, I will judge fairly. Everyone will have a chance to receive the gift of salvation. But many will reject it anyway. They will continue to hate me for my father's sake."

"Who the hell would reject the chance to go to Heaven?"

"To some, Heaven is their personal Hell."

"Bullshit. You could make them choose."

"If I did, I would be robbing them of their choice, of their freedom. My father freed the Hebrew slaves from Egypt. How can I enslave people? How can I force them to love God? That is no love. That is no freedom. Listen to yourself, Azure. Even you, with all your experience and wisdom, fight me on every point, every step of the way. I was with you at the hospital with Neela, Azure. Your prayers were answered, but you forgot me. You tried to do things your own way, under your own power. You turned to crime. You chased after money to pay your mortal debts as your moral debts grew. You did what just about everyone else ends up doing."

"Could you really have saved her?"

"If it was my father's will."

"Damn it all! You're just like the others! Just like Loki, Athena, the Antares, and Samael! You wanted it to happen! You were waiting for it! Ready to pounce on the opportunity to see my power!"

"Azure... why do you accuse me? Why do you push me away?"

"Because I'm not like you. I won't become like you! You're weak! I'm strong. I'm powerful. I can fight this! I'll save this universe whether your father wants it saved or not! I'll make it great! I'll make my own heaven where no one will need to die anymore! No one will need to suffer!"

"Azure... I leave you with this for now: what's happening isn't just a war for your power, it's a war for your conscience. It always has been. It always will be.

Don't let anyone tell you differently. I say this not to brag but to inform: I have laid down my divinity, my crown, my power, and my life for others. Others have clung to those things selfishly. Who will you listen to? Who will you trust?"

"I want to decide that for myself."

"LEARNING NEW POWERS"

Another day of Dragon bombardments began. The Wyverns targeted the highway and the roads in the outer limits. The Leviathans attacked the lines of hover and sky vehicles locked in their trajectories. Again, the Azurites took cover and returned fire. With the training of people like the PSF Colonel and the Raptors under Odhran, the Azurites were becoming better shots.

Azure withdrew back to the burned-out stadium under the cover of chaos. Behind the charcoaled bleachers, he closed his eyes and tried to focus on generating energy. There was a brief spark of electricity, but it faded. He punched a hole through the nearby stand in frustration. *Why can't I do it? What the hell is wrong with me? I should be powerful enough to kill these damn Dragons!*

A ball lay in front of him. "Focus on that and pick it up," said the voice of Athena.

Azure reached out for it, but Athena scolded him. "No! With your mind, Azure. Concentrate." Azure focused on the ball and reached out for it. "Feel it in your hands. Reach out for it with your mind." The ball began to levitate and rattle in mid-air. Azure smiled with accomplishment but just as he did the ball fell and bounced away. "You are incredibly powerful, Azure, but unrefined. You need practice, and we haven't much time."

"How long until your ground forces get here, Athena?"

"Seven Malkuthian days."

An astral projection of Loki appeared before him. "Oooohooohooo, my precious! What a good show last night! Such well-deserved butchery!"

"Loki…"

"My boy, General Deem, is poised to invade. But he is planning to take a longity-dongity way."

"Why?"

"Because, unfortunately—or fortunately, depending on how you look at things—he's not a dumbass. He'll take your city of Ephesus first, the city just beyond the mountains."

"I know where it is…"

"Of course you do. Bekah's town. Tell me, Mr. McGuffin… just how much did you hide from her anyway? How much of your story was embellished or changed?"

Azure growled. "Stop it!"

"Ooh, I'm just asking questions. Little ole' me, consumed by cur-io-si-ty. You know, consumer reports say you should do your research before you buy."

"What do you two want from me?"

"Well…" Loki began.

"We want to show you how to refine your abilities," said Athena. "Loki is the god of magic of his universe, and I am the most powerful telepath in mine. The only limit to our powers is the one constant in the Omniverse: energy. From what I understand, you are like a great cosmic battery, Azure."

"You both want power. Power to meet your ends but power nonetheless."

"Well, I for one am willing to trade," said Loki. "I am not only the Asgardian god of magic but I also know how to read and rewrite the future. I understand how to unscramble the cobweb of timelines in your head so that nothing surprises you anymore."

"Of course. You ate the brains of the Norns."

"Yes, I did. But did you know I've kept another secret until now?…" Loki took out both his eyes and held them in his hands. "These eyes aren't the OG, Azure. I sacrificed them both to Mimir's Well, in exchange for his power and wisdom. My father, Odin, only sacrificed one eye and received half the power and wisdom that I did." He threw his eyes back in their sockets. "Heeeheeeeheeehaaw! Isn't it amazing? We're two of a kind, Azure. The power of the Norns and Mimir. To be able to see everything and bend the fabric of space and time. I can show you…"

"What's your price?" asked Azure.

"1% of your power, that's all. That's not too much to ask, is it?"

"Azure," Athena interrupted. "I admonish you to be cautious about making deals with Loki. I am on board with him only as far as helping you to reach your full potential. My sister and I have placed a lot of our hopes and effort into you…"

"I know, and I am eternally grateful for your patience and faith, Athena. I admire your bravery. I look forward to seeing you face-to-face."

"But for now, I can only mentor you in your head from afar," she said.

"Ehem!" said Loki. "So… my brother's long-distance girlfriend aside… The deal stands: 1% of your total power for my unabridged training and wisdom."

"Deal."

"See, that wasn't so bad was it? We'll get started when I feel like it. There's someone special I'd like you to meet first. Toodaloo!"

"Wait!" Azure called out, but Loki vanished. "Dammit!"

"Don't worry about that trickster for now," said Athena. "You know he'll come back for his end of that deal. That's how he operates."

"And what do you want from all this, Athena? The same?"

"I would rather not get into the specifics. The less you know, the better for now."

"I know more than you think. You could plunge the Black Sword into my back the same as General Malevant did to that Dragon lord, the same as Loki could with his staff. You could achieve a cosmic form of your own. That's a brilliant idea."

"Well, let's not hypothesize. Let's deal with the here and now. I'm here to work *with* you, not *against* you right now. What is coming is a tidal wave of power that you've only seen in your worst visions and nightmares—a stampede of Dragons who crush everything in their path, led by Dragon generals and lords of unbelievable strength. I watched them overpower my father, Zeus, a god who I thought could never be overthrown. I watched one stomp upon the king of the Titans, Cronus, like he was a mere bug. That Dragon swatted Olympus from the sky and burned Gaia to the ground."

"Lord Zeon…"

"You are powerful, Azure, yes, but you can't fly, transform, move things with your mind, nor can you use your own powers at will. How do you say this…in Malkuthian terms, you are like a huge battery without a tool to plug into. If you want to win the coming war, you must learn all you can, arm yourself with tools and weapons. Knowledge."

"I'm listening, Athena…"

"This telekinesis I'll teach isn't magic, per se, although it does seem that way at first. Think of it as your brain speaking to the things around it. Your brain sends signals—messages—out into the world. It can tell it to move here and move there. The key is just sending that specific message. Think of it like this: if I have five squadrons under my command and I want the third squadron to advance, all I need to do is send that specific message to that specific squadron. Likewise, if I want a chair to fly out a window, I need to use my mind to communicate that intention to the chair. Replace the chair with, say, a cybernetic arm or leg. It's a bit like that."

"I see."

"Close your eyes for now. You see the ball in front of you in your mind? Imagine your hand reaching out to it. Longer. As long as you need it to be but with all the feeling of your physical hand. Take the ball and pick it up. Now open your eyes." Azure did as she instructed, and the ball levitated in front of him. "The mind is strong like the body. Stronger, potentially. Your mind is special because it has a little bit of all of us."

"What do you mean?"

"I believe you are part-Olympian, Azure. I feel it. You are a lot of things that aren't Malkuthian. That means you have a lot of powers that aren't Malkuthian. Trust me. Believe me. Be confident in this."

"What do I do now?" asked Azure, still levitating the ball.

"Whatever you want. Keep it. Throw it. Bounce it. Break it. The power of the mind is the power to decide and choose."

Azure focused and the ball was torn apart. "I want to be able to do that to Antares and the Dragons."

"You can. I'm confident of it."

"GENERAL MALEVANT AND AMATERASU"

Athena broke off communications as she heard the voice of Amaterasu in Malevant's chambers. Malevant scarfed down the legs of Malkuthians along with a keg of beer. He telekinetically lifted the frail Izanagi, father of the Kami, and pinned him against a wall. "Daddy!" Amaterasu cried. "Stop this, General Malevant! We have done what you asked!"

"I need a guarantee, Amaterasu. Some security. You turned on my predecessor and were willing to help our enemies."

"You turned on him too! What difference does that make?"

Malevant hit her with a psionic attack. "You will not so much as

hint at betraying me. You and your people will fight our enemies and *only* our enemies. You will fight and kill your brother. Or… my men will tear your dear father apart limb by limb. Is that understood, Star Kami?"

Amaterasu bowed. "Yes, General Malevant."

Malevant hurled Izanagi into the cell that Hades had formerly held. "Good. Now, break the message to Yama and Izanami."

"Yes, General Malevant." She bowed, and Malevant used his mind to force her to bow deeper and deeper until her face touched the floor.

"SUSANOO, KUSHINA, AND APHRODITE"

Susanoo saw that the atmosphere of this uninhabited planet they'd found was safe and stable. He transformed Kushina from her comb state into her human form. There was a field of melon-like fruits and flowers. Susanoo cut some melons apart and tried them to make sure they were safe to eat. He then offered some to Kushina who ate them merrily. Orange residue formed on the edges of her lips and chin. He looked at her and kissed her on the lips, sucking up some of the juice left over from the fruit. It stuck to his beard. As Kushina saw this, she pointed it out and laughed. "You better wash that!" she said.

"Care to do the honors?" he replied.

They found a stream and Kushina gathered some water to clean them off with.

Susanoo flipped his sword like a coin, and it started to rain. "Or I could just do that…"

In time, the two were drenched.

Aphrodite watched from a distance. She formed her magical love bow in her hands and aimed at the couple. But her jealousy seized her hand, and she lowered the bow.

"AZURE'S FEAR"

As the Dragon bombardments winded down, Azure and his lieutenants made their way to the People's Square, specifically to the Old Senate House where he and Neela had met, and where Neela had given most of her speeches. Azure could still see the past that had taken place there. He could still see and faintly hear Neela as a ghost of time. He saw something else: giant orange, red, and yellow birds circling around the square. In a matter of minutes, his *present* caught up with that *future*, and the birds physically appeared. In the middle of Azure's speech, the birds began to attack the Azurites, pecking and clawing at them. They even attacked Azure, who cut a few of them down with his sword. The Azurites opened fire and started to scatter. Beautiful feathers fell everywhere.

Azure heard a distinct sound: a frequency playing over the city's intercom.

Somehow, he knew what to do and where to go, following the ghostly path set in front of him by his clairvoyance. "Have you forgotten yourself, Azure?" said a low, distorted voice over the intercom. "Follow."

Azure ran through the frenzied crowd toward the History Museum. He broke through the glass in the entranceway and made his way in. The frequency became louder. "Where are you?! Who are you?!" he shouted.

"You know," said the voice.

The animatronic statues in the museum began to move and talk. The life-sized figure of Diamond in the middle of the lobby said, "Our greatness as a people was won through sacrifice. Through many centuries and millennia of struggle."

The recently-erected statue of Chancellor Antares spoke, "The Malkuthian Union will endure as it has endured. Noble citizen, what can you do for the Union?"

Azure slashed the statue in half. It continued to talk. "What can you do for the Union? Noble Citizen… What can you do?" Even when he hacked off its head, it still repeated the same phrase.

Edom and some of the other Azurites followed him into the museum. "Are you alright?" asked Edom. "Those damn birds have moved on. I've got a job to finish."

Azure waved him back. "Get them all out of here."

A holographic projection of Neela appeared with her class. Azure's heart swelled as he heard her voice loud and clear as if she were standing there with him.

> *"If the Watcher AIs were designed to make sure all resources were properly allocated, why are there so many homeless, jobless, and a giant shantytown down the street? Why am I working for just over minimum wage? Why is my dad deployed for an eighth tour of duty? Aren't we Ceratosaurs? Aren't we 'privileged?' Well, I call bullshit."*

> *"If the Watcher AIs make so many of the major decisions in the Union, why do we need 100,000 senators? Why do each of them make so much money? Why are so many of them trillionaires? Why do they stay in office without term limits and*

possibly for multiple lifetimes seeing as they all live on Hod after they're elected and so don't age or die?"

"Is that why you're afraid to hear the answers to these questions? Because you're afraid they'll cut out your tongue and hang you? I don't blame you. There are a dozen new hanging, rotting bodies on State Street. There are a dozen new bodies hanging out there every day. They're out there swaying in the wind, but we're ok with that. The cranes get more work than half the population, but we're ok with that. But what about your students, Professor? You'll probably get a few hundred before your career is over — hundreds of lives you could touch with the richness of history and truth. You want them to get the message that the best thing for them to do is lay there and take it while a clearly-corrupt Union government screws them sidewards generation after generation?"

Azure tried to embrace her, but his arms passed through her. "She's gone," said the distorted voice. "The Public Security Force has left the city. Nusakan Antares is dead. Yet, those cages and those cranes were still busy last night, weren't they?"

"It's not my fault…" Azure sank to his knees.

"What were her last spoken words to you?"

"Please… stop…"

A holographic projection of Azure and Neela in the park played.

*"Do good, you hear me? There's enough evil and cruelty and wickedness in the world. In the cosmos. It doesn't need any more of that. No matter what happens, always love, always, always be kind, and always do good. Do good, my darling. Do good. And never lose your **self**." Neela began to cough violently. She coughed out blood. It covered the white snow.*

Azure wrapped his arms around her.

"You…" said Azure, in tears. "You were there…"

"I've *always* been with you. I've always been watching you two." The distinct sound of footsteps were heard: intentional, enticing, inviting. "Follow."

He passed rows of antique weapons on display and came down the spiraling staircase down to some old tombs of military and political leaders including several generations of Antares. There was an opening in the floor and a stairwell. Azure nervously went down the stairwell, covering his nose and mouth. He found catacombs. There were old bones stacked neatly on each other with the skulls featured most prominently. Azure was mortified and tried to look away and breathe as little as possible. There were footsteps. Lights went on, shining the way down the tunnel.

"These are the remains of 10 million Malkuthians," said the voice. "Unmarked. Unnamed. Unremembered."

"I don't want to be down here," said Azure, holding back the urge to throw up.

"Follow."

"What are you trying to show me?"

"Follow."

"CHASE THROUGH THE UNDERWORLD"

Seemingly a half-mile through the morbid labyrinth, he reached a stone wall. One of the stones glowed green and Azure instinctively touched it. It opened, revealing another tunnel. The lights on the wall and ceiling illuminated. Projections of videos began to play on the walls, videos of Azure and Neela together. Hundreds of different moments and scenes. "Who the hell are you, and what do you want?" said Azure.

"You know."

At the end of the tunnel, there was another stone wall. On it, Azure was confronted by the scene from the night before in which he brutally killed Nusakan Antares. He could hardly watch. One of the stones glowed red, and Azure touched it. The wall opened, revealing yet another system of tunnels, this one larger, better lit, and more open. "I want to wash my hands…" said Azure, scratching at his skin. "My eyes. My nose. I want to change my clothes."

"Doing that doesn't erase the past," said the voice. "It doesn't erase the actions. Remove the stains."

"Are you trying to drive me crazy?! I want to get out! I want to get out of here! I feel buried! I feel sick!"

"Come here. I'll show you one of my many faces." There was a sound like rushing water up ahead. Azure was surprised to find a clear stream coming from an open pipe and falling into a small rectangular drainage system. He rinsed his hands and splashed his face frantically. He threw up in the drain and washed off his tongue and eyes. When he opened his eyes, he saw a familiar face looking back at him. It was Amber Ephesus, the at-home nurse he'd left in charge of caring for Neela.

Azure saw that she was standing in the drain and that the water was passing through her, confirming that it was a hologram. "Amber… you were like a sister to her. Did you do it? Did you turn her over to the PSF?"

"I would do no such thing. Her death was as much a tragedy for me as it was for you. It crushed me too. It broke my heart. I loved her. And I loved you. You two were my world. But now I'm ashamed… I'm ashamed of how highly I thought of you. Ashamed that I idolized you and thought you were something more than this. I put you on a pedestal, Azure. But you're just like him… You're no different."

"…I'm ashamed too, Amber… And I'm afraid. So afraid. I'm afraid of letting her down. I'm afraid of letting these people down. I can't protect them. I can't save them all. I can't live up to their expectations because of things they don't know. I can't control my powers. I can't control myself. I'm afraid their souls will call out to me from the grave and say, 'You failed us. We trusted you.' I'm afraid she'll remind me of the ways I failed her too. You've already done that."

A flock of vermilion birds flew through the tunnel, and the hologram of Amber faded. "Follow," she said.

He continued down the tunnels which began to branch out into various directions. Some floating machines appeared and passed to and fro the tunnels. Azure recognized them as Wraiths, a type of autonomous drone capable of both manual work and combat to a small degree. "Where do I go?"

Some of the Wraiths blocked off the side tunnels and left just one open. The hologram of Amber stood there and waived him forward before disappearing. "Amber, wait!" said Azure.

"Hurry!" Amber's voice beckoned. "Run!"

Azure rushed into the tunnel which began to illuminate. An apparent laser trap disarmed itself. About a mile in, another laser trap disarmed. Azure recognized the stench and realized that sewage lines were close by. "What is all of this?"

Amber's hologram appeared and pointed to the wall which projected a diagram of the tunnels. "This is the underworld," she explained. "A system of tunnels built for different purposes throughout Malkuth's history. I've connected them."

"You?"

"With the help of the Wraiths that I've built and reprogrammed. We've built a lot of things together. That's all I've done for the last ten years to pass the time. Until I saw the two of you."

A hologram showed the moment Azure and Neela had met. Neela bent over to him. She tried to help him up. He could hardly stand, so he stumbled and fell.

"Turn it off," said Azure. "Please. Turn it off."

"You were so innocent then," said Amber, her arms crossed. "Such a good man. Clumsy but kind. You could hardly so much as finish a sentence."

Azure shook his head. "I was naive then. Stupid and weak."

"You were honorable, noble, and a gentleman, Azure. You could do no wrong in my eyes or in hers."

"No… I'm not God. I'm no saint. I never was. I'm just a fallible old Malkuthian with some powers I don't understand."

"Hmm…" Amber snapped her fingers and thousands of screens appeared on the tunnel walls, each played scenes from different surveillance cameras. Azure was astonished. "Is this what you see?" said Amber. "A kaleidoscope. Innumerable images but the present in the center of your focus?"

"Yes."

"This is what I see down here. I've watched and I've listened to the world above for ten years. Follow me." Azure did so, and Amber continued to explain. "I control this tunnel system through an AI of my own, one which is currently overriding even the Watchers on Malkuth. I am the reason they can't see or detect you. I am the reason why Chancellor Antares cannot kill everyone on this planet with a thought. I have hijacked the system. It is linked to my brain."

"Is it true? Are you… Autumn Antares. His daughter."

Amber's hologram turned and her appearance changed. She became orange with brown freckles, sporting a red hijab. Her huge eyes became green behind a visor. She had a chipmunk-like face and wore a microphone on one side of her head. "Yes. I am Autumn Antares, the Chancellor's daughter. The only daughter he admits to having."

"Then who is 'Amber Ephesus'? Was she ever real? Did she ever exist?"

"She was the character I played to be a part of your lives. However, she's *me* for the most part. It's also the name I gave to my AI: the *Empress Amber*." A second cloaked female figure appeared before him, startling him. "The Empress Amber AI has a much higher IQ than my father's Watchers. If they were made to play chess against each other, the Empress Amber would win around 760 out of 1000 games, and the rest would be draws."

"Is this why he's after you? Not out of love, but because you're valuable."

Autumn shook her head. "In his own twisted way, I think he still loves me. My mom was the only woman he ever truly loved, and we lost her. It brought us close for a while, but I'm done with him. I'm done with that life. The lies. The corruption. The murder. I'm done with it all."

"And that's why Neela and I appealed to you…"

"Yes. I suppose that's why. I watched you grow in wisdom and power. Day by day. I was fascinated by you. Enchanted. Enthralled. Spellbound. Whatever you want to call it. You had a charm and a charisma that I'd never seen in such a powerful man. But that made the hurt of the realization worse… my faith was misplaced…"

"Amber… Autumn… please don't say that. Please don't give up on me. I know I'm not perfect, but I'm trying. I'm trying so hard."

"My father must've cried a lot last night, I'm sure of it. I did. I didn't think I would, but I did. My brother may have deserved that, but that didn't make it hurt less when I saw the way you did it. He was a jerk. A cruel, sick, sadistic jerk. But he was my brother, and I remember a time…"

Autumn looked to the wall which began to play a video of Nusakan and Autumn swimming in a pool together, racing. "But he was a jerk… he extinguished the life of the person you loved, someone I loved. Does that make it right?"

"I did what I thought I had to do. Maybe I did it because it was easy. Because it felt good." Azure shook his head violently like trying to shake off cobwebs. "But, Autumn, know that I'm not just going to kill for the sake of killing, or hurt for the sake of hurting. I'm fighting for a better world, a better universe for everyone. One that she would be proud of. I want to end these wars. Write the future. A new future. A good one. One that's kind and fair and just."

Autumn bobbed her head. "This reminds me of better times… the way things used to be."

Azure smiled briefly. "You, me, and Neela?"

"Now it's just us… trying to cope alone… There's an iceberg under the water." She smiled too and tried to touch and stroke his face. Her hand passed through. "Come and see me, Azure," she said. "You'll find me down the way. I'll deactivate all the traps, just hang on a sec."

Azure came to an open metal door and walked into what appeared to be a living space. There was a small bed and cut outs of news articles on the walls. Most of the articles were about her disappearance and the attempts to find her. She was much younger in them. But most prominently of all were thousands of screens with surveillance feeds from around the city. "So many lives," said Autumn. "So many stories. I could see them, I could hear them, but I couldn't interact with them. They were always just out of reach. All I could do, for the most part, was watch. And then she came along. And you. Look there on the chair." Azure found a handsome royal robe, black and gold. He picked it up and inspected it. "You wanted to change after traveling through the catacombs, didn't you? Put it on, I promise I won't look," said Autumn. Azure changed into the outfit. "I pulled that off my grandfather's corpse."

Azure freaked out and threw the robe off. Autumn laughed. "No, no, I didn't. Oh, my gosh! I didn't know you were still capable of being such a goofball!"

"That wasn't funny!"

"I'm sorry. I'm sorry," Autumn sounded like she needed to catch her breath. "It's clean, I swear! It's from the museum. Perfect. Absolutely genuine."

"So, it still belonged to some old dead guy?"

"It's from the Third Dynasty. It belonged to one of the nameless princes. They erased his name from history when the dynasty fell. It was dry cleaned bi-anually until all this craziness started."

"Where are you?"

Autumn herself appeared in the corner of the room, revealing she'd been using a stealth device. She was small and fragile-looking, just as Amber had been, wearing a hi-tech visor which displayed information for her. She retracted the visor and faced Azure. "Well, well, well we meet at last," she said almost comically with a scratchy and childish voice, placing her hands on her hips. She then said with an exaggerated posh accent: "I should welcome you, sir, to my humble little abode. I do hope that you make yourself comfortable." She made a curtsy bow.

"What's up with you?"

"Why? Not what you were expecting? Don't you remember *sweet little Amber*? She was a cheery chap, wasn't she?" Autumn tapped some keys on her wrist and transformed her appearance into Amber, complete with the pink skin and bifocal glasses. "So cute. So nerdy. So unassuming."

When Azure retreated back, Autumn returned to her normal appearance. "Amber couldn't do all these tricks," said Azure. "She couldn't lock Union weapons and control an army of vermillion birds and Wraiths."

"Well, genius, it would appear that you underestimated her. And you underestimated me by extension."

"Do you still hate me?"

"Hate and love…it's complicated. Let's say, I can tolerate you right now."

"That's a start, isn't it? You actually live here? Down here alone?"

"Yes. But I'm not alone. I have my machines and my birds."

"But what about people? Do they ever come down here?"

"Well… you'll never find the bodies."

"Oh, my God!"

"I'm joking! I'm joking! Well, sorta, kinda." She rolled her eyes. "Every now and then, a PSF guy would come down here exploring, and I'd have to make him run through my gauntlet-corridor-of-death. Oh, my…"

"What?"

"You're making me feel bad about it."

"That's what you've been doing to me this entire time!"

"Yeah? Well, you deserve it!" She stuck out her tongue at him. She sat down at the edge of the bed, crossed her arms, and looked away. "...And I guess, so did he."

"Autumn, what do you plan to do? Stay down here and be pissed off at me forever? The Dragons are coming. They're less than a week away. They'll find this tunnel system of yours and tear you to shreds. Or they'll blow this planet apart. Either way…"

"You made a deal with Loki, didn't you?" she sprouted leaping from the bed.

"How did you know about that?"

"I see everything that goes on in the city. He came to you the same way he came to my father and grandfather. He made you a deal: 1% of your power to learn his spells. And you agreed."

"Yes, why?"

"Stupid! What's 1% of infinity?"

"I don't know. It's just 1%."

"1% of infinity is infinity, numb-nut! That's it, I've had it. You need me, Azure. I swear, you need me. You need someone who's going to talk you through things and help you make intelligent decisions."

"I suppose I'd appreciate that, but I've got a lot of other ambiguous voices in my head who claim to know a lot. It's already pretty crowded in there."

"And there's your problem. You're starting to think like a darn senator! You're starting to think by committee. Don't do that! The powers-that-be will eat you for breakfast, lunch, brunch, cena, and dinner! You gotta take charge and cook whatever the heck you want to cook."

"...You know, Autumn, you're really something. You're actually quite amusing."

She blushed. "Aww, well, thanks." She winked, rummaging through a cupboard of technical doohickeys. She wagged her little orange tail and kicked back a leg. "Brains are attractive, aren't they?"

"I meant it more like: you're nothing like your father and brother."

Autumn swung away from the cupboard and left her mouth gaping open as if in awe. "Gee, that's, like, the nicest thing anyone has ever said to me!"

"Well, it's tru—"

"In like the ten years I've had little to no Malkuthian contact."

"Autumn…" Azure picked up her blanket. It had an old-fashioned rocketship on it and smelt like it hadn't been washed it awhile. "You could join us."

"Oh, puh-lease, I started this sky train. If anything, *you're* all joining *me*."

"You should come to the surface and see everyone. Get out of here."

Autumn stopped rummaging. She plucked some wires. "I can't."

"Why not?"

"It's not safe. Not for me. I'm more useful down here."

"Why's that?"

"Well, for one thing, I may be able to disable the Union weapons, but I've got no control over what your people or the Dragons do. I'm pretty sure both of them would love to do some terrible things to me."

"I'll protect you."

"Really, you mean it?"

"It almost sounds like you were waiting for me to say that."

"Well, that's because I was, silly! See, Azure, you already get me so well." There was an almost artificial airy glow to her scratchy, chirpy speech.

"No, actually, I don't think I get you at all."

"Well, more for you to uncover. So, you're gonna protect me, huh? You promise? You seriously promise?"

"I promise. I want to prove to you that you were right about me. That I'm still that good man you thought I was."

Autumn green eyes widened, and she was speechless for a while. "We'll see…" she said. She pointed to one of the screens. "Hey, look! That's Neela's old thrift store, by the way," she said, then moved to another. "And that's her restaurant. You used to meet her late at night all the ti—" She saw something on the screen above that troubled her. Some of the Raptors had captured some PSF troops and placed bags over their heads. They lined them up and forced them onto their knees. She sent out a frequency that summoned the vermilion birds to that location. "I call this my 'pluck out their freakin' eyes' frequency."

"I need to talk to them! How can I get there?" asked Azure.

She tossed him a holographic map of the tunnels with the coordinates to the exit. He rushed there and made his way up a manhole, emerging next to the old restaurant. He shoved Odhran and demanded to know what he was doing.

"Exactly what you said, boss: shooting our enemies in the head."

"What did they do?"

"They're all murderers. Agents of Antares. All of them."

Azure drew his sword. Odhran's men aimed their rifles at him, intermittently fighting off the birds that Autumn had summoned. "I should've let those troops shoot you that day before you turned into this."

"I've done exactly what you've preached, Ramatkal. No more. No less."

Azure pushed him aside and went to the nearest PSF soldier, taking the bag off of his head. He was terrified. "What are you being accused of?" Azure asked.

"Nothing!"

"He's lying!" said Odhran. "These are the five troops who gunned down a ten Raptors in cold blood a year ago." Odhran projected a screen from his wrist-device that showed the massacre. The soldier was clearly seen to be one of them. Azure took off the bags from the other soldiers' heads and recognized them all from the recording. "I didn't doctor this footage. It's direct from the news, you can even see the ticker tape, the time, and the date. They glorified it. Said we deserved what was coming to us because we're no-good Raptors. These five racist, murdering fucks deserve to be put down, and I'm ready to give it to 'em."

"We can't keep doing this. Where does it end?"

"You told me just last night to shoot them in the head. Murderers deserve to die. It's a fair and just punishment. What more do you want? You want to flip-flop again 'til your words mean nothing anymore?"

There were more gunshots in the near distance, and Azure went to investigate them too. He saw that Edom and his gang had gunned down more Antares loyalists. "Edom..."

"They knifed two of my men and tried to plant explosives on one of our transport trucks. Don't worry, bro, I've got this."

A crowd had gathered there, flocking to Azure. They alternated between chanting for him and asking what they should do.

Azure was speechless as Edom slapped him on the back, returning to his truck. He heard the Raptors begin shooting the remaining PSF prisoners. All he felt he could do in that moment was close his eyes until the last shot was fired. He hardened himself as he'd done so often before.

But then someone began screaming his name, screaming for help. It was a high-pitched scream, like that of a small woman or child, and immediately Azure knew who it was. It shook him out of his trance, and he sprinted toward it.

By then, the crowd had grown. They sounded excited by something, and when Azure pushed his way through, he saw that the Raptors and some of the other Azurites had wrangled up Autumn. *What the hell is she doing up here?!* he thought. "What are you doing?! Let her go!"

"That's two Antares caught in less than 30 hours!" one of the Raptors announced.

"Kill the bitch!" shouted an Azurite.

"Hang her!" shouted another.

They tied her arms behind her back and put a noose around her neck as she appeared on the verge of tears. "Light her up!" someone shouted. An Azurite began dousing her with gasoline.

"No! Please!" she cried, a shrill cry. "Azure! Azure, help me! Please!"

Azure's mind raced as he ran to intervene, and just as he did a psionic blast emitted from his head, knocking all of the Azurites around Autumn down. Confused, a new batch from the crowd tried to grab Autumn. Azure physically pried her away from the crowd who grabbed at them both, continuing to hurl insults at her and demand her death. "Let her go! I need her alive! She's under my protection!"

"She's an Antares! She's the bastard's daughter!" shouted a Tarbosaur from the crowd.

Azure shoved the Tarbosaur away and he stumbled back, looking shocked and betrayed. "She's not her father! She's committed no crime! This is not what we are! Not what we should be!" The gasoline and in particular the smell of it had gotten on him too, tarnishing his new robe. He whispered into her ear, "What the heck are you doing?"

"I wanted to see if you were serious about protecting me," she answered. "I can summon my war-suit and escape at any time."

"Are you insane? Is everything a game to everyone in your family?"

Autumn winked. She immediately went back to fake-crying. "Oh, please! Don't let them do this terrible, horrible, awful thing to me, Azure! Please have mercy, Ramatkal!"

"Ok! OK! Stop already. I get it." He took the noose off her neck and began to untie her hands. "We shouldn't be doing this. This witch hunting. This persecution. This isn't what we're about. We're about change, not reverting back to ancient times!"

"Wait, wait, wait up. Everyone shut up!" said Odhran, firing his rifle in the air. "The Ramatkal is speaking. What was that, sir?"

"I was saying, we don't judge people by the blood in their veins any more than we judge them by their color or the patterns on their skin. We judge them by the content of their character. We shouldn't harm this girl because of the sins of her father. She has done us no wrong herself." Azure pulled Autumn behind him and tucked her away. "She was the one who hacked Union broadcasts so that you'd all know my story, and she locked the PSF's weapons so we'd have a fighting chance. Without her, we'd be lost. Many of us would even be dead."

"Do you really trust her, Azure?" said Delano, coming forward from the crowd.

"Yes. Yes I do. And I think she could be a powerful ally in the coming fight. She knows and controls the tunnel systems under the city. She has blocked the Watcher AIs and understands the Union weapons better than most of us. Also, the Chancellor won't destroy this planet so long as his daughter is alive on it."

Delano came forward and inspected Autumn with his one good eye. "You have a habit, Azure…" he said. "Of turning old enemies into new allies. Into friends."

Autumn whistled a tune and the moon pup in Delano's pouch started howling at her. She smiled, creating a finger-gun, and clicked her tongue.

"I like her," said Delano. "She's got something special about her."

"Well," said Glaucon. "This has surely been a whole lot of good ole' wholesome family fun. So, like, can we kill her now?"

"NO!" Azure and Delano shouted at him.

"Just fuckin' with you," he extended his hand to Autumn. She shook it, hesitant at first, and smiled. "I'm Supreme Commander Glaucon. Clearly the most important person here. Before you arrived, I was the brains behind this whole operation."

"You're so full of crap, I swear, Glaucon," said Azure. The crowd shared a laugh.

"Ain't the first man to ever lie on his resume," Glaucon winked.

"Autumn," said Azure, guiding her along in one of his arms. "These are some of my lieutenants: Boss Edom, head of the Epsilon mob, now called the Red Guard;

Chief Delano, leader of the Daspletosaur refugees; Odhran, leader of the Raptors; and because I like to save the very best for last: this is Supreme Commander Glaucon, leader of the city's largest homeless camp."

"Nice to fuckin' meet you a second time in two minutes, Princess Antares," said Glaucon, extending his hand again.

"I know all of you a little," said Autumn. "I've been watching your adventures and misadventures over the hacked Union surveillance."

"Like when we take a shit in the lake?" asked Glaucon. "You see that too?"

"Some questions are better left unanswered," Autumn sassed back.

Azure raised his sword into the air and faced a camera that had appeared. "Malkuthians! See this!" he took Autumn by the hand, causing her to gasp and blush. He raised her hand triumphantly in the air with his. "The Chancellor's own daughter has joined us. We are united in voice and in purpose. So, to others throughout this great Union, to the Union military, I say to you: come and join us. Come and stand with us too. RISE UP!"

"RISE UP!" the crowd responded.

And for a moment, he recaptured some of the old admiration that Autumn had once held for him but lost.

Together, the whole group rallied back to the People's Square for Azure to complete his speech at the Old Senate House. At the conclusion, Azure's most important followers were invited to salute him as "Ramatkal" on the Union-wide broadcast. This included his lieutenants, priests, business owners, judges, the Police Commissioner, the PSF Colonel, former senators, and the Chancellor's daughter herself. They all raised their folded claws in the air, saluting him as the crowd broke out into chanting: "We pledge to Ramatkal: Our hearts! Our lives!"

"Neela would be proud to see such a united people," said Azure. "But I believe she would be saddened by some of the events that have transpired. I, too, have been heartbroken and take responsibility for some of the violence that has occurred."

The crowd grew silent.

"I would like to announce a temporary suspension of capital punishment and public executions in all Azurite-held territories."

The crowd became loud with discussion.

"Summary executions are an archaic and barbaric form of punishment and a subversion of justice. True justice should involve the courts, but most of the courts are ablaze now. Many judges are dead. Until a proper legal system can be reestablished in Atlanta City and Azurite-held territories, and until we are better organized in that regard to hear both sides fairly, I believe that we should suspend this practice."

"We're at war!" someone from the crowd shouted. "We don't have time to try these bastards!"

"They never gave us the time of day!" said another in the crowd.

Odhran nodded. "That's true, sir."

"We should vote on it," said Delano.

"I agree," said Edom. "It's like I always said to you: sometimes we gotta do what we gotta do. It ain't always gonna be pretty or kind."

"Well, I don't think putting this to a vote is a good idea," said Autumn. "These people are gonna vote with their feelings, not their minds, Azure. Let them vote about things like the color of the uniform, the new anthem, something like that."

"Just how the hell you gonna go about enforcing this?" added Edom. "Are my boys gonna execute the executors? How's that gonna work?"

Azure faced the mic again. "These temporary edicts may be voted on at a later and better time. I'd like Malkuthians to stop killing Malkuthians for the time being. Right now, there are two Dragon armies poised to invade our world from two separate locations. One is poised to invade Atlanta City, another is poised to invade Ephesus just over the mountains, or so I'm told. These two Dragon armies are divided. Divided in their purpose and divided in their strategy. We will exploit this. We will cut them in two and take them on one at a time. We will completely and utterly destroy each one in detail. There will be no Dragon left alive. Neela's city stands. Malkuth stands. The Union will survive!"

"AZURE AND AUTUMN"

Autumn washed herself off in a makeshift shower she'd constructed underground. Azure stayed in the corner of the doorway, trying to respect her privacy while prodding her with questions. "Could you have taken her to Hod? Could you have saved her, Autumn?" he asked.

"There's no cure for what she had, silly. No stasis pod was going to save her for very long. Even if I'd built one here, it wouldn't have done much."

"So there was truly nothing that could have been done?" Azure looked down.

"That Symbiote was a death sentence from the very beginning. The second it mutated, it was out of anyone's hands."

"I just thought… you're so smart. You can build machines and AIs and all of that stuff."

"You think that because I've got a high IQ that there's no problem I can't solve? I'll take that as a compliment. I wish. I'm good with numbers, formulas, codes. That sorta stuff, Azure. I'm not magical."

"Did you think of me the same way? Did you think I could do no wrong? That the second I gained my powers, I would just magically solve everything?"

"Yes. I did actually."

"I wish I could. People keep telling me that I'm special, that I'm powerful, that I'm gonna save everyone, but I don't feel that way. Every day, more people die. We pull them from the rubble. Sometimes there's little left of them to bury. I watch those images on the news of the Dragons impaling those poor people. And it doesn't stop. It just keeps going on and on and on. I feel like I'm letting everyone down, and I hate that feeling. I'm so pissed off and angry, Autumn…" Azure began to shake. "I think I hate myself. I failed her… And now I'm failing everyone… I can see glimpses of the future the same as with her… I see thousands of people dying, and it's all my fault…"

Autumn turned off the shower faucet. It squeaked and the water ceased to fall. "Azure…" she said. A Wraith flew a towel to her, and she dried herself off.

"She really loved you too, Autumn… She would tell me when she'd wake up from her naps. She said you were so smart and so patient. She was so happy. You two were like sisters. The three of us were like one little happy family. But all three of us knew…"

"Not everything is your fault, Azure. If it's any consolation… today I was proud of you. You reminded me of how you used to be. You stood up for me and protected me just like you promised, just like you used to do for her. I think if she were here, she'd be proud too."

"I like to think she's always here," said Azure, pounding his chest.

Autumn smiled, covering her chest with the towel, crying a single tear. "Me too."

They went to the surface together and came to the burnt-out stadium. Autumn demonstrated how she could control her AI by creating a holographic pair of teams who played each other in an imaginary but well-choreographed game. "It's in here," said Autumn, pointing to her head. She then closed her eyes and refocused. The coding on her visor changed and the scene changed to display a holographic orchestra. "When I give instructions to the AI, I think of it like giving an orchestra the sheet music to a song." The orchestra began to play a beautiful melody.

"Does this remind you of something?" Athena spoke to his mind.

"Yes. Only I don't know the first thing about music. I think it's going to be pretty hard making analogies between that and your telekinesis."

"Don't worry. That's why you take baby steps and learn the keys first. Over time, it becomes second nature. See those cones over in the distance? Tell them to stack themselves on top of each other. One by one."

He focused on the orange cones and levitated them up one by one.

"Oh, my gosh! Are you doing that?" said Autumn.

"Yes. I'm trying." He placed the first cone on top of the one next to it and repeated it until all the cones were stacked.

"Wow, cool!"

Azure sneered proudly. "Thanks."

"Don't get cocky, Azure!" Athena scolded. "Now, pay attention. *I want you to try to lift that girl the same way. She's a third your weight."*

"I don't want to hurt her."

"Good! Then you have some motivation to not mess this up."

Azure stared at Autumn intensely.

"Uhh...are you ok?" said Autumn. "You're starting to kinda creep me out." He strained. "Uh, Azure...I think I'm just gonna head back..." Just as she turned and started to whistle, her feet left the ground, then her tail. Soon, she was prone in the air. "Oh, my God, Azure! You better not freakin' drop me! I'll haunt you for the rest of your freakin' life! I swear!"

"Now, try bringing her to you," Athena instructed. *"Imagine it's like a fishing reel pulling her closer and closer with each turn of the reel."*

Azure brought Autumn to his chest and he cradled her in his arms. She huffed and puffed, hyperventilating; her green eyes bulging out of their sockets in shock. "Holy...crud...Azure... What... the... heck..." Autumn frantically reached into her sling backpack and took a puff of an inhaler. When she continued to hyperventilate, Azure's accomplished smile disappeared and he became very concerned. "Oh, my God, are you ok?"

She pulled him by the collar of his robe. "What do you think!?"

Azure set her down in a seated position and rubbed her back as she continued to heave. "I'm sorry! I'm so sorry!" Azure thought about ways he'd calmed himself during his panic attacks. He looked Autumn in the eyes as she began to turn pale. "Focus on me, focus on my eyes. We're gonna count to ten, breathing nice and slow, and at the end of it, everything's gonna be ok, you hear me?"

Autumn nodded. "1…2….3…4…" Her breathing progressively slowed and came under control. "8…9…."

"You can… stop," she said, patting him weakly on the forearm. "Never. Ever. Do that again. Please."

"Ok. You're not acting are you?"

"NO! Why the heck would you even do that? What the heck is wrong with you?"

"A voice in my head told me to."

"You really are freakin' crazy!"

"Well, you're insane!"

"Good! Then, I win the stupid crazy contest you just stupidly created!"

"Congratulations, Crazy Queen! Don't forget your crown!" Azure pretended to put an imaginary crown on her head. His hands stopped near her temples. Their eyes met. They smiled and began laughing.

"What in the actual blue hell…" said Edom, walking in on them. He managed a chuckle and shook his head. "Sorry, don't let me stop you two. It's just… I haven't seen you smile in a long time, man. I've got the feels right now."

"We were just practicing using our powers, Big Red," said Azure.

"Yeah, well, that makes me miss practicing my thing. Too bad the gyms are all burned down. I'm starting to lose my gains."

"Why do you need to lift weights, silly?" asked Autumn. "You're already strong enough to take down a GFM-1620. You can flip tanks!"

"Yeah, yeah, well it's cause I like to look good too. You need a balance between the one-rep maxes and the 8-12 reps. Gotta get the blood flowing. Get those pumps. Do the damage."

"Ah, I see. Brilliant. I can't imagine you having any bigger muscles though. You already look great. You should ask Vegas."

"Damn girl, that's really sweet of you to say, thanks," said Edom. He then looked to Azure. "You know, Big Blue, we gotta keep this little 'thang around. She knows what she be talkin' 'bout."

"Can't argue with you there, Big Red."

"MASTERING TELEKINESIS"

More flying Dragons came in the afternoon. Retreating to the shelter of the underground, Autumn demonstrated the ability of her vermilion birds to swarm and attack the Dragons, disrupting their group formations and thus hindering their attack patterns. They still continued to cause substantial damage to the Warehouse District, harming some of the Azurite supplies. The combination of surface-to-air artillery and the Dragon bombardment sent rumbles for miles.

Azure walked out to witness formations of Dragons, vermilion birds, and flak bursts in the sky. *"Try to grab hold of one of them, use your thoughts like a lasso,"* Athena instructed. He raised his claw up to one of the Wyverns and stopped it in mid-air like a charging dog caught on a leash, with a retraction of his arm, the Wyverns crashed down into the street below, dying on impact. The watching crowd cheered at the sight of this. It was broadcast live. Then, Azure raised both hands, snatching a Leviathan and a Wyvern from two separate parts of the sky. He clapped his hands, and they smashed into each other, their blood splattering down like green rain.

He stopped a Leviathan, focusing on its throat and the end of its tail, then pulled his hands down to his hips. The Leviathan tore in half. The tear was not clean, however, and he broke part of its head like he had the ball. He stopped one of its jaw fragments in the air and hurled it at a Wyvern. It passed through its torso like a bullet. He pulled back the jaw fragment again and again, and it hit four Wyverns. Next, he tore the wings off a Wyvern and let it fall to its death. He grabbed four Wyverns, imagining they were like cones, and crashed them all down on top of each other. They landed like a meteorite on top of an apartment building, causing it to implode. Azure gasped in horror at his mistake. Someone was trapped in a vehicle that had overturned in the midst of the collapse, and Azure focused on freeing him, pulling him out of the car. He accidentally dropped the victim on his arm, breaking it. There were more screams. Azure struggled to see through the smoke.

A Leviathan flew lower and started to fire its water jet at another apartment complex on Azure's right. Azure pulled it to the ground in front of him and he stomped on its throat with his full might and weight, crushing it. The rest of its body still wiggled and twitched. As this was happening, a Wyvern flew down and fired a blast at the already-compromised building, causing it to collapse as well. A whirlwind of debris and smoke covered the area. Azure used his clairvoyance to see through the obstructions, but it was much harder to use his telekinesis this way. He realized that he could clear the obstructions with his thoughts. However, just as he was ready to go back on the offensive, he heard more cries and screams for help.

He turned and realized there were people trapped under the rubble. He turned his focus to that. He carried rubble up and pulled people out. However, as he was levitating parts of a ceiling off of some children, an explosion broke his concentration and he dropped the concrete on the children, killing all three. "No!" their mother screamed, covered in soot and crawling up to them. Azure's heart sank. Angrily, he looked back up at the sky. He grasped six Wyverns from their formation and began to constrict them with his mind. Their wings started to bend, their legs were pulled up toward their heads until they snapped; they choked, their ribs cracked like porcelain. Blood oozed from their eyes and mouths until they were no more, crumpled up like bloody pieces of paper and discarded.

From the perspective of the Dragons, it was the least productive of their air offenses. But from Azure's perspective, it was devastating. He fell to his knees beside two collapsed apartment buildings that had previously been populated. The mother whose children he'd accidentally killed shouted and swore at him. He growled. An aura and electricity sparked around him, then dissipated. This scared the mother away. Another crowd rallied around Azure and chanted, having seen his slaughter of the flying Dragons. He looked around at them with empty eyes.

"It took Malevant years to do anything like what you just did. Don't blame yourself for what happened. It doesn't matter. Look at the big picture." Athena told him.

Azure looked at his hands as they shook uncontrollably. *I don't have to feel bad... I don't have to feel bad about fucking anything! I KILLED those Dragons! I SAVED lives!* He closed his fists and roared. The crowd backed away and went silent for a while as he rose to his feet. They commenced celebrating again.

"Ho-o-o-ly shit, Big Blue," said Edom when they met later that evening in the tunnels. "That was the most badass fuckin' thing I think I've ever seen, and I've seen a Deinonycus deadlift a car for reps." He gave him a fist-bump. Azure accepted it.

"Hail the Ramatkal!" said Odhran the Raptor, saluting. "I'm feeling good about our future prospects now. Don't worry, we fed the prisoners. You don't need to ask."

"Have your people familiarized yourselves with the tunnels too?"

"I don't even know if that's possible. They're as expansive as the city itself. We're making an effort. It's safer down here while the flying Dragons are attacking, that's for sure."

"We can't have millions of people comin' down here for shelter every day," said Edom. "That's the truth of it."

"All the leaders should know about it," said Azure.

"What, you're not gonna argue 'bout it?"

"We still have our force field batteries taking a beating up there. We'll use these tunnels as Autumn suggested to mobilize select forces. Guerrilla attacks. We'll hit them quickly, then we'll run. The Dragons will think we're everywhere."

"My hunters are awfully good at that," said Odhran.

"I know. That's why I want you to become most familiar. You and Delano's people. They can shoot now too."

"They're learning to."

"They're making good progress. I'll tell them they can use the stadium for target practice again. The Dragons are done with it for now."

"Big Blue, you really think we can do it?" said Edom. "Take on two Dragon armies with what we got? I mean, we've got numbers. We've got weapons now. But we ain't no Union army."

"We defeated the PSF when our men were poorly armed and inexperienced. Now, we're packing. We've got these tunnels now too. The way I see it... we're gonna make it hard. We're gonna dig in. We're gonna force them to pry this city from our claws. Kill as much of them as we can. Make them pay for every inch they take with their blood."

"And win?"

"Yes, and win."

"You really expect the city to survive this?" asked Odhran.

"No," said Azure. "God willing there'll be enough of us left to rebuild it."

Someone called Azure up to the surface to take a look at something. To his delight, he saw Union starships in the sky. General Eridanus, Neela's father, was beamed down alongside a hologram of the fleet Vice-Admiral. He marched straight up to Azure and stared him in the eyes. Azure held out his hand. General Eridanus took it and immediately pulled him in for a hug, as if he were a long-lost son. Both of them began to tear. "Son, thank you for watching over her when I couldn't," he said. "It means the universe to me."

"I'm sure she's watching over us now," said Azure. "And she's loving this moment."

Eridanus pulled away and put his hands on Azure's arms. "You'd surely have my blessing, son," he said. "Oh, God, I wish… I could walk her down the aisle. She would've made such a beautiful bride."

"Yes, she would've. She was."

"Yeah…" Eridanus cleared his throat and wiped his tears. "We're all here to help you defend Malkuth. We're here to kill Dragons."

"Yeah? So are we."

"LEARNING TO FLY"

Azure rushed over to the northern neighborhoods which were coming under attack by flying Dragons. The allied Union starfleet stayed in the upper atmosphere, avoiding being caught in the crossfire by Azurite anti-aircraft weaponry while contributing to defense with homing missiles. General Eridanus and his officers used this opportunity to correct gunnery and artillery mistakes on the ground.

Some of Edom's men stopped to offer Azure a ride, and he hopped in the back of their truck. Wyverns and Leviathans streaked overhead. He tried to muster up enough concentration to affect them and eventually sent a dozen of them careening and spiraling out of the air as if caught in a twister. He pulled the twister along the sky as the vehicle traveled. More and more Dragons were pulled into the vortex until the beautiful colors of the Dragons formed something like a spiraling rainbow of scales and fur. When he saw solar panels and parts of roofs being lifted up, Azure panicked and released his psychic attack, letting the bodies of the Dragons fall.

In the northern neighborhoods, Azure helped pull debris off of more victims. One victim in particular, a middle-aged male Tyrannosaur, was impaled all over his body with glass. He was losing blood quickly. Azure was afraid that pulling the glass out would cause him to bleed to death. "You've gotta hold on and be strong ok?" said Azure.

"That means a lot coming from you, Ramatkal," said the man, shaking. "I never thought… a Tyrannosaur…" He rattled, feeling a surge of pain.

"Try not to look at it."

"Ok. If you say so, I'll try."

Autumn appeared with two of her Wraiths. They scanned the man's body and tried to determine the best way to go about helping him. They sent an emergency signal to the nearest medical personnel. That's when Azure realized she'd been the anonymous person who'd called the ambulance the day that Neela had blacked out. When the EMTs arrived, they were better able to prepare the man for treatment, and Azure was finally able to release his hand. "I would've needed more blood on hand for the Wraiths to have attempted surgery. You can't just produce that in a lab. We need to encourage people to donate blood."

"Right," Azure agreed. Both of them made some calls on their communicators to push the new initiative. Autumn even gave him control of the city's loudspeakers to encourage people to donate at the remaining hospitals, including the arena and St. Sargas High School, which had become makeshift hospitals overnight. She then broadcast a recording of his PSA, recorded with the smoke and rubble in the background for a grittier effect.

They both made their way to North Park which had become a tent town of Azurites, many who'd flown in from other worlds. "I saw whatcha did back there!" said Autumn in a sing-songy way.

"I tried, kiddo…"

"Well, we gave it our 110%, and that's what matters." Autumn threw a right-uppercut in the air.

"Heeeheeeheeehaaaw!" Loki appeared in front of them.

"Heeeheeeheeheee," Autumn mocked him, rolling her eyes back, contorting her arms, and letting her tongue hang out of her mouth.

"Tsk, tsk, tsk, dearie, it's poor form to mock disabled people," said Loki.

"I'm not mocking disabled people, I'm mocking you, Loki!" She then summoned up the remainder of her orange war-suit, which she called the *Psycho Suit*.

Azure took up a fighting stance as well.

"Oh, goody! Look at you!" said Loki, pretending to fawn over them. "Mary Sue and Gary Stu! Don't worry, the people behind you can't see me. I have an Invisibility spell cast. I don't need no dark lord's ring or helmet or cloak to do that. You can learn it too-hooooo!"

"Oh, yeah? Cool," said Autumn. With a thought, she and her suit became cloaked. "I can do a lot of things too, A-hole."

"It's just not the same. Technology. Magic." Loki pretended he was balancing two separate things in his two hands. He shrugged.

"I need you to teach me—" Azure began.

"NO!" Autumn interrupted, pushing Azure behind her. "Loki, you're gonna take back the deal you made with Azure! You're not turning him into another one of us. Another Antares. We're not playing your games."

"Well, he has free-will doesn't he? Azure, what if you could have healed that Tyrannosaur back there? Don't you want the power to save people? Hoohoohooohooo! Yes. You made a deal with the Autumn-Bomb here too. You do seem to have a thing for the horny ones."

"Hey! I resent that!" said Autumn.

Loki tapped his nose, and she realized he meant her nose-horn.

"Oh, god, you're such an insufferable jerk," said Autumn.

"Well, I'm the god of many things, dearie." He turned back to Azure. "She's becoming like a daughter to you, isn't she? You want to protect her. Make sure nothing bad ever happens to her like it did with Neela. Well, I have all the cheat codes waiting right here for you. And Azure, don't forget…I know, I know, I told you so. And I know, you know what I know…"

Azure gulped.

"What's he talking about?" asked Autumn.

Azure looked behind him at the camp to see if anyone was listening. "The holes in his story, dearie," said Loki. "The Catastrophe. The origin of life on this planet."

"He thinks he has dirt on me," said Azure. "He's the god of blackmail. And a liar!"

"Now, now, let's not be racist. It's called *gray*mail these days. But I am a liar sometimes, I'll give you that. I'll tell you what, Azure: scratch that deal for now. You're an important enough customer. I want to give you a free sample. Absolutely free. No strings attached."

"What is it?"

"Flight. I can teach you to fly. And if you're not completely satisfied, you can keep it. I'll even refund the shipping & handling."

"I can just lift myself with telekinesis, can't I?"

"Yes, you can. But it's a waste of energy. Very inefficient. Ask your super genius over there. Energy efficiency is everything in the cosmos. Even Athena rarely flies that way. She'd rather transform herself into an owl or a moth or something else dull and stupid. You should be able to fly as fast as you can fight, and at will."

"Azure…" said Autumn. "Nothing's free with Loki. There's always a catch, and it's always to ensure he wins in the end."

"I can use the power for good," said Azure. "I won't become like him or your dad."

"That's what everyone says before they get a taste of it."

"I promise, kiddo. I'm not strong enough to defeat these Dragons yet. I'm not strong enough to protect everyone, not strong enough to protect you. I should be."

Loki formed a portal. "I suggest we go somewhere more to discrete: to Alfheim, former home of the Light Elves. Don't worry, it'll only take about an hour of Malkuthian time."

Autumn pulled on his arm. She looked like she was about to cry.

"Oh, Autumn dearie," said Loki. "I'm not here to awaken old childhood traumas…"

"Shut up!"

"I've known you since you were just an itty-bitty egg, and then an itty-bitty little nose-horned girl baby already solving top-tier puzzles. I'm a little sentimental, I have to admit. I want to assure you: I'll return him promptly and in one piece, better than I found him."

"You bring him back, or I'll find you. I'll hunt you down to the edge of creation!"

Azure touched her shoulders and looked her in the eyes, which rested behind the visor of her suit. "I promise. I'll come back here to you no matter what. I'll rip the universe apart if I have to if it means keeping my promise."

Alfheim was a barren wasteland. Thousands of stakes stuck out of the ground with the skeletal remains of Light Elves on them. "I hate to say it," said Loki. "But they had it coming."

"Dragons did this…"

"They did this to just about every realm under Asgardian jurisdiction. I was to rule over them before the Dragons took that from me. Even their magic and magical weapons couldn't save them. But you and me… we exist on another plane of existence. You… oh, God, you… you have the potential to cast spells that I could never hope to cast. I tell you: if you truly want to defeat power, you need more power. Take it."

"Can I bring Neela back from the dead?"

"Things like that and time travel… that's up for you to discover. I can guide you. I can take you closer to that realization."

"Yeshua, Jesus, did it on Earth. He raised a widow's child."

"Yeah, well, that's *him*. He's the son of the most-high God, what do you expect? But he's guided by principles. He's guided by scruples. To do something like that… something *selfish*…you need to become like me. Ruthless. Lawless. Uncontrolled.

Unbridled. Unchecked. Set aside things like good & evil and focus on doing what's right for you."

"Neela deserved to live."

Loki pointed to the skeletons on the stakes. "I'm sure they felt the same way."

"Show me how to do this. Tell me whatever magic words I need to say, and I'll say them."

"Heeheeheeheeheeee! Magic words? Puh-lease," Loki flicked his wrist. "I'm no second-rate witch. Non-verbal spells are where it's at. Just do as I say… are you ready?"

"Yeah."

"Hold down L2 & R2 and toggle the right analog stick. Then, when your gauge is full…"

"What?"

Loki burst out laughing. "Oh, I just couldn't help it. Just fucking with you." He conjured a bag in his hands and spilled its golden powdery contents in his hand. He threw it at Azure who sneezed in response. "Pixie dust. Now, close your eyes…"

"Ok."

"And imagine what makes you happiest. What do you see?"

"I see…"

"Trees of green and clouds of white?" Loki whacked him in the head with his Elder Staff and sent a concussive blast that knocked him over.

Azure came to, growling with anger. "You!"

"There it is… that fury. That feeling like your expectations have been upset. You won't always have pixie dust. You won't always have happy thoughts. And in the vacuum of space, most of us can't make a sound, so what good is an incantation there? You will always have your expectations. You will always have your feelings. You feel foolish now, don't you? It pisses you off."

Azure came to his feet.

"Focus that anger. Make your wants become reality. Come at me. Come at me!"

Azure's body launched his body through space and crashed through the remnants of an Elvin tree village, becoming panicked as he found himself unable to stop. He tumbled over and struck some statues which toppled on top of him. Loki's laughter taunted him from the sky. "Up here, dearie," he said, wiggling his fingers.

In a blink of an eye, Azure found himself directly in front of Loki.

"That's IT!" said Loki.

Azure summoned up his sword and looked to strike but then stopped himself. He looked around and saw that he was hovering.

"What the hell did I just do?"

"You just learned to teleport."

"That doesn't count as a second spell, Loki! I wasn't in control of it! It just happened!"

"Oh, I know. I know. I know. I know. See, this is what happens, Azure. You think you can stop at just one bite, but no one can. They eat the whole donut and then the box."

"I can't…"

"It's ok, Azure. You can't help it. You're just like all of us. You are like us. You're an Asgardian, Azure, and not just any Asgardian, you're an Aesir. That's why you have such an affinity for magic."

Azure's eyes grew wide with surprise. "What?"

"Yes, an Aesir like me, and Thor, and Odin, and, hell, you could even make an argument for Hel. We all have the gift of magic within us. I just happened to dedicate my life to mastering it for my own ends. And look at me now. Look at you."

"Why am I floating here? Why am I not falling?"

"You're levitating. That's the power of thought. You're so used to that hocus pocus, abra kadabra, crouching tiger hidden bullshit. No, you and I are better than that. This magic we use is wish fulfillment. You're essentially a wish-granting blue genie with full autonomy. You think 'fly' and you fly, 'fall' and you fall. Now, disclaimer, kids: don't try this at home. Azure is a super-powerful-dinosaurian-creature with an affinity for this type of magic. Try this and death or serious injury might occur. Parts and accessories sold separately. Some assembly required."

"Why are you talking so fast? What are you saying?"

"Oh, nothing. It's an old habit of mine. Go on with your questions."

"Loki, you've been around a long time. You've seen a lot. You know a lot. What am I?"

"Heeeheeheee… you? You're an amalgamation of the very best and worst of the cosmos. You're an anomaly. The result of a billion, billion, billion coincidences as if the God of gods himself set everything in motion just to form you. I am rarely jealous, but I must say…"

"Do I have a mother? A father? What is my purpose? Why am I here?"

"Another story for another time. Go buy the supplementary material."

"Answer me! Please! Am I just a mistake? An accident of chance? Tell me!"

"Not knowing hurts, doesn't it? I was like you once. My family withheld some pretty important information from me. I felt betrayed. I'd lost my place in the world, in the universe. I questioned my own sanity then, and that went out the window a long, long time ago. I asked the same questions you're asking now."

Loki began to fly, and Azure tried to follow. Like an inexperienced skater on an ice rink, he began to slip and panic, flailing his arms around to keep himself upright. He breathed a sigh of relief once he did, coasting across the sky. "Ask yourself, Azure: does it really matter? Well, does it? Will you be a slave to fate or some higher power for the rest of your existence? Or, will you take control of that fate and become that higher power?"

The river below was murky and dark. In a flash to the past, Azure saw that it had glowed white like opals when the Light Elves were around.

"The Dragons will turn your world, your universe into this if you let them," said Loki. "Say goodbye to Edom. Say goodbye to Autumn. Say goodbye to everything you know and everything you cherish. She loves you, you know? The idea of you. She worships the ground you walk on. She believes in the idea of Azure—the perfect powerful man who can do no wrong."

A spark flew around Azure as he clenched his fists. For a second, the river glowed white before returning to its murky state.

"But you know she's wrong, don't you? You know you're incomplete. Unfinished. Disappointing. You can't protect them. You can't protect her. You can't save anyone."

A psionic blast left him, throwing Loki around until he caught himself. And just as Azure did this, a barrage of fireballs came his way, and he was forced to block it with a Mystic Shield spell. Loki's cackled.

Azure's hands smoked and he looked at them with surprise. The forest below had caught fire and the fire spread quickly. Little woodland creatures fled from it. "I've been angry before," said Azure. "Sad before. Frustrated. But why now, Loki? Why can I do these things now?"

Just as he thought about putting out the fire, a clump of water collected in a ball in the air and a waterfall flowed from it and down into the forest. Some of the animals who had survived the fire were now washed away and drowned. Azure realized this and was troubled.

"Before, your mind was fractured. You could not weave these kinds of thoughts together. But you are still limited by one thing: your conscience. The use of magic comes with consequences, some small and some not-so-small. You need to accept that people and things are going to get broken. Things will be destroyed, and lives will end. It's ok. Sacrifices must be made."

"I don't want to be that kind of person." Azure felt faint and was breathing heavily. He swept sweat from his head.

"Then you'll struggle to wield this power."

Azure began to tumble out of the sky and crashed to the ground in apparent exhaustion. Loki stood over the crater and chuckled to himself as Azure's body pieced itself back together. "Oh, Azure! Don't get too far ahead of yourself. Remember, there's still someone I want you to meet first. The one final piece in this great, big, glorious puzzle." Loki formed a portal and knocked Azure through with a concussive attack. "Thanks for stopping by! Toodalooo!"

When Azure returned, he was greeted with a hug from Autumn who'd returned to the spot an hour later to wait for him. He was very tired and went to sleep in the underground. Autumn scolded him and prodded him with questions, but he felt too weak to respond. Something inside of him reached out desperately, like a drowning victim seeking air. The lights on that portion of the tunnel flickered, and Autumn's generators there began to display higher outputs of energy. This happened intermittently throughout the night. And it was a terrible night. The Azurites had rioted and resorted to looting. Even businesses that had supported the movement fell victim. They did all this even while carrying portraits of Neela and Azure and chanting. Edom called Azure on the communicator, but Autumn needed to talk for him, telling him that she thought Azure might be sick. Delano and his tribe acted to put out some of the fires that had started.

Finally, Autumn took the initiative to denounce the rioting and looting, saying that "Malkuthians shouldn't take from Malkuthians."

Azure weakly reached out to use the microphone, and he said, "We mustn't destroy our own city. We mustn't destroy ourselves."

The two looked at the surveillance footage and realized that their words didn't have the effect they'd hoped for. "Let them go," said Azure, his eyes glazing over. "I'm done. I'm just done. I'm done fighting with them. I'm done arguing with them. I'm done pulling their leash. If they want to kill, then let them kill. If they want to steal, then let them steal."

"Azure?"

"I'm tired. So tired."

The next morning, Azure was feeling well enough to move around. He went with Autumn to the surface and they surveyed some of the damage. Owners of stores that had fallen victim to the looting and destruction eyed Azure as he passed. Some of them openly shouted at him.

Azure bent his head and Autumn could tell that the guilt and pressure was killing him. She thought of how she might cheer him up. "Heya!" she said. "You never showed me the flying spell Loki taught you! I wanna see! I wanna see it! Can I?"

Azure closed his eyes and began to levitate. "There."

"What do you mean 'there'? That's freakin' AWESOME! You should do that, then say a cool one-liner like, 'Time to die!' or at least something triumphant like, 'Tada!'"

"Heh, maybe you're right."

"Of course I am, I'm always right."

"It feels like I'm jogging the whole time."

"Heya, Azure... This Psycho Suit I'm wearing can fly too. I've seen it in computer simulations, and I've tried it out in the tunnels, but I've never actually done it out here. I'm pretty nervous, I know I shouldn't be."

"So... in a sense, you're kinda learning to fly too?" Azure realized.

"You wanna fly to the arena with me? Maybe get some footage of you helping the wounded? It'd make me really happy."

"And what if you fall and die? Your AI will be gone, and your dad will destroy us."

"That's why you'll be up there with me, silly. You'll catch me. C'mon, whaddya say?"

"Well, ok, kiddo. But be careful up there."

Autumn smiled. She marched in place. "Ok, here it goes!" Her propulsion system brought her to about 20 feet, hovering above Azure. "Wha-wha-wha-whoaaaa!" she said nervously as she gained altitude. "Azure, are you there?"

"I'm here, kiddo!" he readied his palms to catch her. "Nice and slow! Focus on your breathing."

Autumn closed her eyes and tried to compose her breathing. "Oh, my gosh!"

"What? What's wrong?"

"I'm flying, Azure! I'm really doing it! It's really happening!"

"You're doing great, kiddo!'

"Whoooohoooo!" she cheered, flying forward at the speed of a ground vehicle in neutral.

Azure flew to keep pace with her. "Easy… steady…"

"Azure!" Autumn called again.

"What?"

"Are you still there?"

"Yeah!"

"Azure!"

"I'm here! What is it?"

"I think I can really do this!"

"Good!"

"I can do this! I'm not afraid! I want to try to go faster…"

"Take it easy now! Be careful!" Azure insisted.

Autumn picked up speed little by little toward the Arena.

"Slow down!" said Azure, the wind resistance striking him like pins and needles. "Autumn, wait!" He swallowed some bad air and coughed.

"C'mon, Azure! Keep up!" Autumn began traveling as fast as a plane. "I'm *really* gonna go… race ya!"

"Kid!"

Autumn flew off like a jet toward the Arena. Azure instinctively launched himself in that direction. "Kid, where'd you go?!"

"I'm right here!" said Autumn, but too late. Azure tried to stop but he didn't know how. He managed to slow himself down but still ran into Autumn, knocking her out of the sky. "Azure! Help!" she cried, plummeting at terminal velocity.

Azure teleported under her and caught her. "Hahaha!" she laughed. "Gotcha!"

"Crazy! You gotta stop doing that!"

"I sorta like this. Knowing you'll always come and save me." She winked.

"Right… Please stop pressing your luck."

"I'll try," she said, knowing full-well her Psycho Suit could survive a fall. "Hey, when did you learn to do that?"

"By accident, while learning to fly with Loki."

"Did he trick you into accepting the deal?"

"No. I don't think so. He said that these things would happen naturally while learning magic. It's like a drug, I guess. Flying was the gateway. I managed to conjure fire and water too."

"Oooooh, can I see?"

"Maybe later."

"Awwww... but I wanna see it now..."

"Later. I'm already juggling here. I don't want to drop you."

"You couldn't live with yourself if something happened to me, could you?"

"No."

The Arena floor was filled with the wounded and dying. Azure and Autumn were pleased to see that people were donating blood. They came to the donors and thanked them personally. Autumn activated her suit camera and started to film. Azure walked down the aisles and watched the medics at work. There was so much blood and such a stench. There was also zero privacy for the bed-bound patients as they had to do their business in containers out in the open. Most of the patients lay on makeshift mats and blankets because of the shortage in beds.

When Azure would pass, the patients and medics would often cheer, raising their claws in the air to salute him. He visited some of the more critically wounded and did his best to encourage them. Some of them were clearly dying and there was very little they could do but make them comfortable.

As he continued to walk, he came across Aphrodite in her Helm of Darkness. She was healing one of the women. Azure asked Autumn to wait. "Hey," he whispered to Aphrodite. "It's nice to see you. Where's Susanoo?"

"You can, like, see me, Azure?"

"I believe I can see in dimensions that others can't. Something like that."

"Like, Su has his Ku-shi-na," Aphrodite rolled her eyes. "So, like, I took half of his cloud and came here to wait for my sister. Cause, like, why not?"

"I'm sorry to hear that."

"Don't be. His loss." Aphrodite looked to Autumn.

"You're beautiful, Aphrodite, everyone thinks that," said Azure.

Aphrodite's eyes watered. "You totally just made my day!"

"I'd say, just try to lay off other girls' guys and try not to be so in-your-face about everything. You gotta make a man work."

"Hey! Like, are *you* the goddess of romance or am I?"

"I'd like to think Neela woke up some of my common sense, that's all."

Aphrodite looked over at Autumn, who was busy comforting a patient. "Hmm... she's a cutie. Like, are you guys..."

"No. She's a friend. She's like a daughter or a little sister to me."

"Eww, gross…"

"Hey! I'm serious, it's nothing."

"You know, like, pretty much all of my boyfriends, girlfriends, beast friends, and in-between friends are, like, dead. You're not, like, over Neela yet are you? Like, I totally get it."

"I loved Neela. I still do. I always will."

"Yeah… well, like, my arrows are pretty potent. I can, like, hit her with one if you want."

"Don't you dare. Just save your magic for healing these people. Thank you."

"Yeah, yeah… Hey, like, Azure… I have, like, a favor to ask you."

"What is it?"

"If you see Malevant would you, like, make him hurt? Make him hurt, like, real bad."

"Absolutely."

"I want him to, like, feel some of the hurt and pain he caused us. I want you to, like, make it last."

"Oh, I intend to."

"And if you, like, run into my sister, would you make sure nothing happens to her?"

"I'll try my best," said Azure.

"Thanks."

"No, thank you. You guys stuck it out with me and Neela. I'll never forget it."

"BLACK HOLE"

The building shook as flying Dragons reappeared. Just as Azure was leaving with Autumn to confront the threat, he noticed that all of the patients now had pillows and that he'd conjured them.

Azure and Autumn levitated up into the sky to try to defend the Arena hospital. "We can't afford to lose you! Go back to the tunnels! I got this!" said Azure.

"Nuh-uh!" Autumn focused an energy-ball in her chest and fired it out in the form of a ray. It caught a dozen Dragons in it and fried them. "Howdya like my *Twilight Beam*?"

Azure focused on killing as many of the Dragons as he could with a combination of his techniques, and the two engaged in an informal competition for who could kill the most Dragons. Autumn's suit unleashed a combination of Twilight Beams, repulsor blasts from her hands, shoulder-mounted miniguns, and homing missiles that fired from its back. Even the finger-portions could be fired like missiles or shoot lasers in multiple directions. "I think I'm win-ning!"

Azure focused on trying to form a particularly large fireball but accidentally created a black spiraling vortex in the sky. "Oh, shit! Oh, shit! Oh, shit!" he exclaimed as the void appeared to grow larger.

"Holy moly, did you just create a black hole? So freakin' cool!"

"What do I do?!"

"Well, they don't suck you in. Just don't go near it and you should be fine. That's perfect, actually. It's forming an unsurpassable obstacle and forcing the Dragons to come in low."

What if I do something like this again around others? I'll kill them all.

"Autumn, please go back! I can't control these powers. I could hurt you."

"You'd never do that," she said. Unloading another volley of missiles and lasers. Her AI alerted her, "Power at 15%." She slapped her thigh. "I'm gonna need to recharge and slow down for a bit."

Azure spread his arms and grasped all the Dragons around him in mid-air. He crushed their heads and made them combust. "Autumn!" he said. "Get out of here now! I'm draining your suit! It's me! I can't control this! Go now! Please!"

Autumn finally returned to the ground and made her way underground. As Azure concentrated on another attack, fireballs and lightning bolts rained down from him, igniting some Malkuthian buildings on the ground including the Arena hospital. "NO!" he cried.

He landed on the ground and ran to the Arena to help evacuate it, afraid to use any more of his powers. He then saw a cloud sweep by, and Susanoo appeared, forming a rain cloud that helped to quell the fire. Sparks still flew from Azure, and he clenched his head, feeling as though he were going mad. A fatigue washed over him again, and he dropped to his knees, clutching his head. Azurites ran to his aid. He saw the black hole close like a wound sewn shut.

"Artist's Interpretation of Autumn Antares" by Lucas Lopez

"FINAL MEETING"

When he came to, he was in the Arena hospital. The smell of smoke was still present. Holograms of many of the Azurite leaders had formed around him, looking with concern. When they saw that he was awake, they started to clap. The patients and medics clapped for their hero. Autumn had played select cuts of his heroic deeds for all to see as propaganda. But while his spirits lifted for a moment, the truth loomed over him: he was dangerous, a threat to everyone; he had to use restraint with his powers. In the coming days, he watched feeling helpless as the flying Dragons attacked the city, unwilling to risk using his powers to any great extent,

He assuaged this by getting involved in the military planning for defense of the city. "It reminds me of the siege of Astrabad," he told the leaders.

"The bloodiest battle in pre-colonial history," said General Eridanus. "3 million people died. The Southerners refused to surrender for months."

"They dug in. I fought them. I was there. These Dragons have a strategist from another world named Athena. She's wise, but I'm wise to her plans. She's a bit of a turncoat. She'll try to use misdirection to create gaps in our defenses. The lines in front approach normally, deceptively, before flaring outwards just before the point of contact, allowing a second line to dash forward and rush any gaps that form. They expect gaps to form. We won't let them."

"Put my men up front, they won't let that happen," said General Eridanus.

"General, your men should form in the second rank," said Autumn. "To fill the gaps and keep the less experienced troops from fleeing."

"My men will hold," said the PSF Colonel. "You won't need to worry about that."

"They'll have irregular militia with them, Colonel," said Azure. "You'll need to keep them under control."

"Yes, sir. I intend to."

"You ain't gotta worry 'bout none of my boys runnin'," said Edom. "They know I'll put a boot up 'der ass."

"Same here," said Odhran. "My Raptors will pick off the bastards from the rooftops. The only retreat they make will be strategic."

"My people aren't cowards either," said Delano. "They've got the blood of warriors in 'em. We'll be at the front. I can use my abilities better that way anyway. As long as they've got metal on 'em, I can pull the rug out from under 'em."

"My men can help to hold the interior positions," said the Police Commissioner.

"And we'll try to keep the flying Dragons off your heads," said the Union Vice-Admiral.

"We'd appreciate that," said Azure. "Let the flak guns take effect first. They've had a lot of practice recently."

"And my peeps and I will try not to fuckin' die," said Glaucon.

Quite a few of the leaders chuckled at this.

"What?" Glaucon continued. "50% of 'em are on white rocks. 20% of 'em are on black rocks. 40% of 'em are on white rocks *and* black rocks. 50% of 'em are alcoholics. 90% of 'em don't remember what happened yesterday. I don't know where I was going with the math, but I'm sure it adds up to we're pretty much fucked."

"Yeah?" said Edom. "Tell 'em my boys will hook 'em up after the fight. All the rocks and booze they can ask for. Just tell 'em to shoot Dragons, nothing else."

"Shit, they might go for that. Ok."

Azure looked around at the collection of people around him. "Look at this. All of you. How great is this?"

Autumn began recording.

"All of these different people from all these different walks of life," said Azure. "I'm at a loss for words."

"We believe in you, Ramatkal," said the Union Vice-Admiral. "We believe in your cause."

"My daughter believed in you with all her heart. There's nowhere else in the universe I'd rather be," said General Eridanus. "Hail the Ramatkal!" he saluted.

"Hail the Ramatkal!" they all saluted.

"Thank you all. I should be at the front," said Azure.

"What?" Eridanus objected.

"To set an example for the people. I've been in many battles, fought in many wars. In the old days, brigadier generals like yourself fought at the front with everyone else. True, it was more practical back then, but it meant something to soldiers like me to see that my leader was there with me, risking everything with me. Kings and emperors, presidents and premiers, they all sat in the back, in relative comfort and safety. They gave out orders carelessly, knowing full well that they were sending many to their deaths. They didn't care one bit as long as it meant achieving their goals. I have an opportunity to change that picture. From now on, the

Ramatkal leads from the front with his men. When they see me standing there, fighting with everything I've got, they'll know what to do. They'll stand and fight too."

Autumn pointed to the red dot on her suit, indicating that he was being broadcast.

"WE'RE ALL MALKUTHIANS"

Azure began speaking to the Union over the broadcast. "I hate to say it, but I'm a bit on the spot right now. I guess I'm supposed to say something thrilling and inspirational. These are dark times. People are dying. People are homeless tonight, living in camps in the streets and in the parks because of these relentless Dragon assaults. People are orphaned. Widowed. You know my story. You know my journey. You know my pain. We've all lost something, haven't we? We all have pain. But I've been thinking… I've been thinking about how much we've gained. Everyone here: the rich, the poor, the upstanding citizen, the criminal, the soldier… Everyone out there: Tyrannosaurs like me, Ceratosaurs like Neela, Carnotaurs like Boss Edom, Daspletosaurs like Chief Delano, Raptors like Odhran, Allosaurs like Glaucon here… all other races and creeds… we're all Malkuthians.

I remember that conversation Neela and I had on that sky train about what makes us all so different. We're all Theropods. We all walk on two legs. We all have two arms, two hands, a big head and sharp teeth. We're all Malkuthians. Every single last one of us, from the biggest to the smallest, from the red and the blue to the white and the black to the orange and the green; from those of us with one horn, two horns, or no horns; from the Public Security Force and Union soldiers who've joined us and the police who've lent us their support… we're all Malkuthians. Those titles, those labels, they become secondary in the face of that one universal truth: we are all Malkuthians. Fierce. Free. Strong. United. Exactly like she wanted. Exactly like she envisioned. Tomorrow, we stand for Neela's city. Tomorrow we stand for Malkuth. Tomorrow, we stand as one."

"DRAGON CALL TO BATTLE"

General Malevant received word about what the flying scouts had seen on Malkuth: that there'd been a being who'd created a dark void of his own, who summoned fire and lightning from his body, who pulled them out of the sky and crushed them with a thought. "It seems this Azure you spoke of is truly on the other side," he spoke to Athena's mind. "You've made me wait too long for this, Athena."

"Wisdom says that good things come to those who wait," she replied.

"I may spare you punishment today should this battle plan work and this Azure not disappointment me. Form your legions!"

Athena raised her spear. "Cyclops! Centaurs! Form your cohorts!"

They obeyed.

Separately, Amaterasu marched forward, her flaming hand up in the air. "Creatures of Ame-Tsuchi! Prepare for battle!"

"Oni, I call you forward!" King Yama, Izanami at his side, commanded his fearsome demonic ogres.

Malevant's beta-generals ordered the Dragon heavy-infantry and flying-cavalry to form. There were millions of them on Bhumi, an absolutely terrifying and battle-hardened force. Lord Zeon hovered just above the atmosphere, watching as his forces gathered for this long-anticipated invasion. He channeled his energy to the Dragon mages so they could open their Black Gates.

General Deem kissed the top of Princess Darna's right-hand and knelt. "What I do, I do for you and for the Queen. For the future of our people."

"Arise," she said. She craned her head and closed her eyes, kissing him. It was a sloppy kiss but one nonetheless. Deem was surprised by this. "You've taught me a lot," she said. "Like how to do that. And how to dance. I hope we can do it again sometime. Come back to me when the fighting is over."

"I will."

"Go on and conquer," she said, channeling her energy into the waiting Dragon mages who prepared to open Black Gates. Legions of Deem's forces formed behind the mages, awaiting their time—columns and rows of fierce Dragon warriors, the very same who'd conquered Asgard.

There were armies of Fire Giants, Ice Giants, Elves, Dwarves, and Trolls.

"Go and be all I know you to be," said the Princess to Deem. "the greatest general in all of Dragon history."

"WHERE IS GENERAL DEEM?" Lord Mortimer, the serpentine Dragon who could coil around whole worlds, demanded to know. Mortimer's other generals reported that they'd lost contact with Deem and that his entire army was absent, having followed him in an apparent mutiny. "INCONCEIVABLE… NO MATTER. I WILL DEAL WITH HIM LATER. WE MUST NOT ALLOW LORD ZEON THE TIME TO STEAL THIS GLORIOUS VICTORY FROM US! WE COMMENCE THE INVASION!"

Loki signaled behind him to Diamond who stood from his meditation. "Steady, steady, and make ready…"

Thor picked up his hammer.

PART V
ALL OUT WAR

"THE GREAT BATTLE OF MALKUTH"

Black Gates appeared by the dozens, boxing-in the entire metropolitan area. Azure had foreseen this very moment and this very time. His army and its allies stood ready, arranged in layers of circular lines behind layers of forcefields and physical barricades. Before the Dragons could even begin to march from the gates, the allied Union starships began to blast them with their beam cannons as Autumn had suggested, exploding on the other side into waiting Dragon formations.

Vortexes formed in the skies and thousands of Wyverns and Leviathans flew in. They began to assault the starships whose shields managed to tank them initially but were now sparsely able to fire. The flying Dragons then flew down and began to attack the Malkuthian positions on the ground. Azure used his telekinesis to drag dozens of them at a time from the air and crash them down below to the cheering of all who witnessed this. Anti-artillery ordinances fired at the Dragons. Storms of bullets, blasts, beams, and lasers galore crossed the Dragons' own attacks.

Then, as the towering, imposing Dragon heavy-infantry emerged from the Black Gates, the Malkuthians focused their attacks on them. It appeared to be a familiar scene, with the Malkuthian weapons struggling to make a dent in the Dragon adamantine armor and hide, but they managed to kill enough of them to slow and hinder their advance.

As the Dragons crossed over North Park and into the remnants of a residential area, Autumn triggered the hundreds of explosives that her Wraiths had placed there. The explosions blew off Dragon limbs and killed hundreds of them. They sent a few remaining buildings falling on top of their formations. Similar explosives went off around the perimeters, catching Dragons in their midsts and creating obstacles for the columns behind them.

Still, the Dragon presence was becoming increasingly fearful. Their numbers were in the hundreds of thousands and only growing.

Some inexperienced Malkuthians either froze without firing their weapons or stood in the line of fire, being mowed down by it. "Dammit! Stay the hell down!" General Eridanus tried to keep order, pulling one such incompetent soldier down. "Stay low to the ground and pour it on! Keep it hot!"

Azure spoke to Odhran and his Raptor gunners with his developing telepathy. "Aim for the mages, the ones with the orbs, staffs, and robes. Take them out!"

Odhran and the Raptors obliged, beginning to snipe the Dragon mages from the rooftops. The surviving mages, of which there were still many, cast defensive spells that made the approaching tidal wave of Dragons even more invulnerable. Odhran put armor-piercing rounds through the heads of five mages, opening up their battalions to a hail of projectiles.

Delano tried to focus on bending the Dragon lances. He was able to do this with some success, bending the weapons of dozens and rendering them useless, but this took great effort. Adamantine proved to be much more resistant to his ferrokinetic powers than any other metal by far. He tried to see if he could cave in the thinner helmets of the Dragons, crushing the adamantine over even the thick skulls of the Dragons.

"THE GREAT BATTLE OF HOD"

An army of Dragons had appeared on the surface of Hod!

Supreme Chancellor Antares took up his war-suit and came to the situation room with the chiefs of staff to survey what was happening. A battle had already broken out around the Capital. The military on Hod was the largest and most powerful in the Union, but they were caught by surprise. Hod was believed to be an impenetrable planetary fortress—a sanctuary. Now, the largest concentration of wealth and political power in the Union was under siege.

"How the bloody hell did they get in?" Antares seethed. "This is preposterous! Not even the Collective and all their cubes could get through!"

"Our force fields are fully operational, sir," said the Chief of the Army. "The Dragons must have found a way to get under them."

"They must have known the supply route," said the Chief of the Navy, the former PSF admiral. "You think they followed our cloaked freighters?"

"I think they were informed," Antares growled. "Loki…"

He looked at the projections of the ongoing battle as the situation room itself shook from what was happening around it. Antares recognized the leader of the Dragon forces as the same one he'd disputed with: General Deem. "Loki… Loki… Loki…." he repeated maddeningly. He now knew that the Asgardian imp had pit the two of them against each other.

"Sir?" asked the Chief of the Army. "Our numbers and our weapons are greater than theirs. We should be able to stand."

"That Dragon general is worth a hundred battalions," Antares answered. Deem, on the projection, was seen rushing and destroying Union artillery and taking out Grand Fortress Mechs. With a thought, Antares signaled to the Watcher AI to "shut the hatch" on the perimeter of the city. A line of electrified force fields raised, running from the ground all the way to the main force field in the sky. It created a cage around the city, trapping retreating troops and civilians between it and the approaching Dragons. Even a few senators were trapped. They summoned the Watcher AIs and demanded that they be let through, but to their horror the Watchers simply said, "Sorry, I can't do that. Chancellor's orders."

"Elderly machines…" said Antares regarding the Grand Fortress Mechs. "Let's see how you fare against my Omega Mechs and special forces."

The Watcher AI deployed dozens of the top-of-the-line new Omega Mechs. These had devastating Omega Cannons that not only tore through the Dragon formations but also leveled city blocks, killing hundreds and causing septillions of BN in damage.

General Deem took on the Omega Mechs who proved resilient against his physical attacks. They revealed an impressive arsenal of beams, rays, lasers, and missiles that Deem managed to weather. The Union special forces then flew in behind him, wearing war-suits similar to those of the Antares and firing "Death Rays." Deem dodged these and fought them off, but as he was distracted, the Omega Mechs continued to attack his men. Deem turned to energy attacks to counter them.

Antares seemed pleased with these results. Just then, the Watcher AI in the likeness of Autumn informed him of another serious issue. "Master Antares, a Dragon lord and its army has appeared in the Deep Core. It is attacking the Cosmic Wall and is causing substantial damage."

Antares looked at the projection. It was Lord Mortimer, the great serpent, holding a moon-sized orb up in front of the Cosmic Wall which was causing the Wall to begin to rupture. "Master Antares, I have already initiated the defense protocol."

Millions of drones attacked Lord Mortimer and his army with little effect. The great serpent sneered and glanced back. His orb glowed red and many of the drones were destroyed. No less than 20 World Enders and three Resolvers came within striking distance of him. They all fired their super lasers at once. Mortimer turned himself intangible, and the super lasers passed through him. They struck the Cosmic Wall and blew a large hole through it, doing much of Mortimer's work for him. The AI ordered the weapons to hold their fire. Repair droids and replicators went to work repairing the Wall, but it seemed to be too little too late. Mortimer conjured up his destructive magic again as three Union fleets attacked him from all sides.

Antares summoned another suit, this one rounder and more bulky. This was his *Chrono Suit*, inspired by Davron technology. It was resistant to the effects of time manipulation. "Get your suits on too or I'm leaving you *all* here to die!" he said to the Chiefs of Staff.

"But, my men, sir... are we leaving the Capital?" asked the Chief of the Army.

"Our gambit has failed, we're cheating now, we'll force them to lose on time," he answered. "No one outthinks me! No one outmaneuvers me! I'll annihilate them! I'll obliterate them!"

Back on Malkuth, the Dragons infantry grew nearer to the Azurite front-lines. They released their Gravirah Blasts and fire attacks from their mouths. The Malkuthians began to take casualties. A Gravirah Blast struck near Edom and he watched as it tore three men next to him apart. Their screams were blood-curdling. All Edom could do from this distance was fire his beam-rifle and contribute to the barrage of projectiles that lit up the city perimeter. Many of the Malkuthians had gone temporarily deaf from the constant firing. Some became panicked and ran. Many who did this were caught again by friendly fire.

Azure spoke to the minds of all Malkuthians in the city, encouraging them to hold their ground. The Dragon mages cast their Mystic Shield spells, rendering the Malkuthian bombardment less effective. Azure told the Malkuthians to wait for the defensive spells to wear off and then open fire again.

Seeing as how the Wyverns and Leviathans were continuing to bombard Malkuthian positions, Autumn played a melody over the loudspeakers, thus summoning her vermilion birds to join the struggle for control of the skies. They wrestled and grappled in the air with the flying Dragons, pecking and clawing at them.

This seemed to go on for an hour or so and the Dragon heavy-infantry was stalled, having to wait to fill the growing gaps in their lines. More vortexes formed and out from them flew the Dragon flying-cavalry who began to break down Malkuthian obstructions with the elemental attacks from their mouths.

Azure flew forward and began hacking down a cluster of flying-cavalry with his holy sword. From that height, he saw more Black Gates open near the Warehouse District, and out from them came the forces from Gaia led by Athena: Cyclops and Centaurs who sprinted forward as the Dragon heavy-infantry fanned outward, forming a pincer. The Centaurs let loose an arched volley of arrows down onto the city as the Cyclops charged forward.

On the other side of the city, more Black Gates opened making way for the forces of Ame-Tsuchi led by Amaterasu, King Yama, and Izanami. Their Oni, Tokai, and Tengu rumbled forward and were met by enfilade fire from all sides. However, this drew fire away from the Dragons who began to make progress again. The allied Union and PSF mechs, including some Grand Fortress Mechs, advanced to help repulse the approaching Dragons.

Still, the front lines began to flee as the Dragons extended their lances and continued to devastate the front with their attacks. Malkuthian casualties were growing.

Azure continued to hack down flying-cavalry in plain view of both armies. "Disappear!" he roared, fanning out his hands and crushing dozens of flying-cavalry with a thought. He dashed through the formation, slicing many in half. He stabbed through the mouth of one Dragon, withdrew, and hacked down six in one swing. But he was struck by something: one of his own anti-artillery shells. It had blown off half his body. As he regenerated, the flying-cavalry came at him with their lances. With one arm, he sent them all flying as if hit by a shockwave from a nuclear blast. As he roared, another black hole formed, and the flying-cavalry were pushed into it. Azure completely regenerated and continued on the attack.

After an hour, the Dragon heavy-infantry had just about closed the distance with the front lines. They faced fire at point-blank range from the Malkuthians, but they also skewered and killed thousands of them. Delano pulled quite a few heavy-infantry off-balance by tugging their lances aside. This dampened their attack on his people and allowed the Daspletosaurs to fire directly at them while they were exposed.

At such a close distance, Edom jumped at the opportunity to join the fray. He wrestled lances away from even the huge heavy-infantry and decked them with punches and swings of his tail. Headbutts proved misguided against their armor though and he was pierced by several adamantine swords while stunned. Bloodied, he retreated back, trying to buy time to recover. The heavy-infantry were too quick upon him and trampled him like the terrain. He grabbed one of their legs and threw them down upon the others nearby. He was stabbed several more times, and the situation became desperate. Azure dropped down on them like a meteorite and slashed through their armor and weapons, protecting his friend, who he helped up by the hand. "I got you, Big Red!"

"Like better days, Big Blue!" Edom responded.

They looked in the distance as tornadoes had formed, attacking the Dragons. Azure knew this was the work of Susanoo. "Front-lines, fall back," he told the Azurites telepathically. Edom, clutching his wounds, waved his men away. Delano gave the order to his people as well.

"Azure," General Eridanus growled. "Dammit, son, you need to give me more time to react. Our shields are still up."

The allied Union fleet jumped back into action, firing down at the Dragon columns. By this point, the casualties on both sides were already in the tens of thousands. The outer city neighborhoods were destroyed, turned into smoldering cobwebs of rubble. The Azurites reformed on the second defensive lines. Dragon flying-cavalry, Wyverns, and Leviathans chased after them. It was a horrific sight as fleeing men and women were burned, skewered, and mutilated.

Incensed, Azure swooped down and fought off as many of the legionnaires as he could. Despite all of this, the swarm never seemed to end. A perimeter of gold-plated armor glistened under the Malkuthian suns, closing within three blocks of the second defensive line.

By that point, it seemed everyone was out of breath and there was no time to catch it. It seemed like for every Dragon they killed, five more appeared in its place. For every phalanx formation they destroyed, more marched over the corpses of the old.

Several cohorts of General Deem's army had marched through the Casino District of the Capital and approached the crowd of fleeing civilians trapped on the other side of the force field. They began to slaughter them.

Deem continued to fight off the Omega Mechs and special forces, matching them blow for blow. Seeing as though his army had stalled and he was caught in this stalemate, Deem focused his energies and began to transform again, taking up his larger and more powerful multi-armed form. He took out the special forces members one by one, moving much faster than any of them could keep up with. He attempted to fire a Brahmastra attack at one of the Omega Mechs but was met with a series of Omega Cannon Beams from the others surrounding it, forcing him into a beam struggle.

A shockwave toppled everything within several city blocks as the attacks met. Wanting to end this quicker, he asked Shiva and Vishnu to fuse together to grant him additional strength. "Allow me to fulfill my dharma," he said. Even more arms grew from his back and sides, wielding even more divine weapons. His eyes burned, his teeth grew longer and more fearsome, and he began to cackle. This was his Durga form. The size of the Brahmastra Beam grew and annihilated the Omega Mechs in front of him. The attack struck the force field, and an explosion engulfed that portion of the city. As Antares and company were leaving the situation room, the entire place shook. It shook the whole world. The sky seemed to roll up like a scroll, having its axis changed. The ground shot up, forming a small mountain that cut the Capital in two.

Least of all, the force field fell.

Deem in this monstrous form had lost much of his usual composure, mercy, and sanity, and pounced upon the opportunity to slaughter Union soldiers by the thousands. They screamed and fled in terror. He appeared to enjoy it as much as Malevant did in that moment. Then, slowly, he composed himself and he returned to his senses. He returned to his suppressed form, standing atop a mountain of Malkuthian bodies.

Azure returned to the ground, his weight distributed across a mountain of Dragon corpses. He saw one still writhing, trying to lift its weapon, and he stabbed it through the throat. Blood and gore covered him. His body spat up splintered lances, arrows from Centaurs, and shrapnel from his people's own artillery. "You think you can stop me?!" he shouted at the approaching heavy-infantry. He dashed forward and slashed through them three by three, six by six, and nine by nine. Hundreds of them piled up around him. Edom rejoined the fray and hurled a bus at a column of Dragons before charging-in after it.

Delano levitated the adamantine lances and swords of fallen Dragons and hurled it at the others. But just as he was gaining success at this, a fireball from a Dragon legionnaire caught him by surprise. He caught fire, and many of those around him tried desperately to smother the flames. But more fireballs came and ravished them as well. "No!" Azure called down to him.

An incredible explosion rocked the sky, larger, louder and brighter than the artillery or Wyvern blasts. An allied Union sky-carrier had been struck by this incredible blast, and it was falling in fragments to the lower city. Then, out of the smoke and fire, an especially large and fearsome Dragon appeared, flaring out his huge bat-like wings: General Malevant!

Malevant fired an energy attack from his mouth that took down another capital starship. Azure knew that he had to stop this most serious of threats, a cruel beast that he'd seen in his nightmares for centuries. *"Make him bleed,"* said Athena. *"Make him suffer for all the pain he's caused! Give it back to him tenfold!"*

"SHOWDOWN: AZURE .VS. MALEVANT"

Azure gripped the handle of his ethereal sword tightly and launched himself at Malevant. With a swoosh of his hand, Malevant sent Azure flying through a 40-story building. Glass had embedded itself in his body as he crashed through to the other side. Before he could even get up, Malevant had flown to within a sword's length of him. Azure blocked the Blade of Olympus and slashed the Terror Sword in half as it came toward him. Malevant, unfazed by this, caught Azure in one of his feet and smashed him into the concrete again and again. He then lifted him higher and plunged him onto an overturned bus, smashing him through it as if it were an aluminum can. Azure, desperate, bit him on the leg with the full-force of a Tyrannosaur's bite. He then executed a death-roll like a crocodilian, tearing a chunk off of the Dragon's leg. Malevant groaned.

Azure dashed at him again, backing him up over a burning building. Malevant revealed his sharp claws and slashed Azure over the face with them. They cut like knives. Azure swung his tail and struck the Dragon in the gut, knocking him into a semi-truck.

Malevant levitated several vehicles and crashed them over Azure's head and body, leaving him a bloody pulp. "Are you truly HIM? The one I've waited all this time for?" asked Malevant. "I'm disappointed."

Azure regenerated and sent a dozen vehicles barreling toward Malevant. The Dragon disintegrated them with beams from his eyes, but Azure got behind him and looked to cut him in half. Malevant wrapped his tail around Azure's neck and threw him aside. He knocked over a fire-hydrant, which began to spray water before crashing and rolling into an old familiar playground. It was where he and Neela had discussed the afterlife. Azure pulled himself up on the rail of the still-creaky merry-go-round. Exhaustion was setting in and he fought to stay conscious.

"Ok, Azure, you can stop, I'm getting dizzy again," he heard Neela say. He could see her face. A ghost of yesterday. *"Get up! You can support SOME weight, can't you?"*

Malevant came down and drove him through the piece of equipment, grinding his face into the metal as it bled. It smashed teeth out. His skull flattened. Somehow, a part of his consciousness seemed to linger—a spiritual consciousness—of which he was aware. Malevant drew the Black Sword and prepared to drive it into Azure's chest. Azure's body sparked, and an aura shot out briefly. He pushed himself up to his hands and knees despite the pressure Malevant applied. Malevant plunged the Black Sword into him but very little energy was drawn. He growled in frustration and withdrew the sword. "You're weak! You're nothing! You've wasted my time!"

Malevant struck Athena mid-battle with a psionic attack that grounded her. Cyclops accidentally fell over her as she writhed on the ground.

"Stop!" Athena cried.

"YOU! You've wasted my time! You lied to me! This Azure of yours is weak! He's powerless! All of this was for nothing!"

Azure crawled away and fell upon the yellow slide. Tears came from his eyes.

"I'll make you both suffer for this," said Malevant. "You look like you'll last a long, long time, Malkuthian. I'll make sure of it."

Malevant grabbed him by the tail and pulled him down the slide, drawing the Blade of Olympus with nefarious intentions as Azure kicked at him weakly.

"Leave him alone!" Autumn flew in with her war-suit. She fired a Twilight Beam at Malevant, which managed to stagger him. She circle-strafed as she'd learned in simulations, unloading every attack she had on the Dragon, who staggered back and groaned. Autumn screamed and cried.

Malevant struck her with a series of powerful eye beams, then one from his mouth. She went flying and tumbling through the air. Azure got to his feet and slashed Malevant in the back with the Sword of Heaven before falling forward again from exhaustion.

Autumn flew up and focused energy into the silos on her palms, chest, and feet. The beams merged and spiraled toward Malevant, who laughed. Malevant threw Azure aside and gathered energy in one palm, preparing for the Oblivion Beam to counter Autumn's attack.

"No!" Azure cried. The energy for the Oblivion Beam disappeared to Malevant's surprise, absorbed by Azure. The spiraling beam blasted Malevant, creating a cloud of smoke and debris.

Malevant dashed out of the smoke and crashed into Autumn, smashing part of her suit and knocking the wind out of her. He threw her to the ground, but Azure caught her. Azure had managed to recover by stealing some of the energy from the Oblivion Beam, though he didn't understand how. The nanomachines in Autumn's suit went about repairing it.

Malevant looked down at the two of them, bloodied and furious. His wings had been damaged blocking that attack. He tensed his fists and his body. His muscles engorged. Electricity and a purple aura spread out all around him for a city block. When the aura condensed, there stood Malevant in his mountainous *Giga-Malevant* form, towering over them. Autumn began to hyperventilate, her green eyes wide with terror as she grasped Azure's arm frightfully.

"It's ok, it's ok, it's ok," Azure comforted her. "Just close your eyes and count to ten."

"Sh-sh-sh-sh-shut up," she said, her cheeks puffing and fluttered with each sound.

The sight of Giga-Malevant protruding out of the skyline caught the attention of the Malkuthians, but they hardly had time to react as the other Dragons continued to bear down on their positions. The second line began to break despite General Eridanus issuing the order to hold. Some of the starships and artillery began taking shots at Giga-Malevant. He'd been hit by several large rail-cannons, causing him to stagger.

Azure took this opportunity to try to bring Autumn somewhere safer. Malevant caught him and began to carry the two of them up into the air. Azure slashed him on the arm with the holy sword, causing him to flinch and drop Autumn. Furious,

Malevant squeezed Azure all around his body and threw him through a skyscraper. He then pushed the skyscraper on top of him. The debris cloud blanketed the city. When Azure crawled out of the rubble, he found himself beside Neela's old thrift store. A green Wyvern fire burned on its roof. "Autumn," he tried to reach her telekinetically. "Autumn, are you there?"

"I... can... hear you..." she said, still struggling to catch her breath.

Before he could continue, there was a creaking sound, like a large metal object being bent. Then, there was a sound like an explosion. Another tall building was taken down by Malevant, again deliberately intended to crush Azure. Rebar punctured Azure's body in six places, and he howled in agony, struggling to pull it out. But some of the rebar was particularly long. Malevant once again came upon him and grabbed him, still impaled, flying up into the sky. He held his face up against the side of a sky district and dragged it there. He then threw Azure like a mere bean bag onto the surface.

The sky district was a ghost town, leveled by the flying Dragons. Charcoaled skeletons littered the white streets. Azure crawled to the edge: a familiar site. He looked on over the city as fire burned all around. Smoke. Dragons of various kinds streaked through the air in combat with starships. A chain of gold armor choked the city from all sides. Malkuthian weapons lit up every block. There were holes in the ground—holes where buildings had been.

Each time Malevant would reach down to grab or step on Azure, the Tyrannosaur would swing at him with his sword, occasionally nicking him. Malevant laughed and began levitating the remnants of homes to throw at him.

Just then, the Trident of Poseidon—a weapon that caused quakes and had killed Hades—plunged itself in Malevant's back. He roared in pain. Athena transformed from a Griffin to her normal form, her face like that of a woman scorned. She levitated the Blade of Olympus from Malevant's scabbard and plunged it into him as well. She spat on him as he fell to one knee. She double-backflipped to a safe landing. "Athena!" said Malevant.

"No more, Malevant! I'll not be yours to use and abuse anymore!" She took out her Epirus Bow and charged it to its maximum power, firing it at Malevant and hitting him in the hand as he attempted to block it.

Autumn reappeared in her war-suit and rained down a hail of missiles that opened up bloody wounds in the beast's body. Malevant struck her and Athena with Zeus's lightning bolts, causing Autumn's suit to overheat and bringing Athena to the ground. As Azure charged, he was hit with a combination of elemental attacks until he finally fell to the ground in a bloody pulp. Malevant came up to Athena first. When she tried to levitate her weapons, he levitated her and slammed her until she coughed up golden blood onto her white garment. He took a bolt of Zeus's lightning and prepared to hurl it at her.

Just then, a bolt of lightning struck him from the side. Thor had arrived through a portal that closed behind him. "Thou shall not harm the lady of Thor Odinson!" he declared. He swung his hammer and decked Malevant in the face.

Thor came next to Athena who looked up at him in relief.

"You! You came!" said Athena. "You idiot!"

"'Twas the least I could do."

Autumn fired a Twilight Beam at Malevant. Thor fired his lightning bolts. Athena fired her Epirus Bow. Azure slashed at him with his sword, opening deep cuts in his flesh. For a while, the group looked as though they might take down the beast, but Malevant fought back with a fury. He released a burst of giga-energy from his aura that swept the combatants away. He then pulled the weapons from his body as though they were mere splinters.

Malevant was still greatly weakened and began to move as if injured, likely in multiple places. He came to the nearest of the fallen: Autumn Antares. "Warning: energy at 10%" her suit warned. She crawled away from him desperately, activating the cloaking feature of her suit. "Warning: energy at 8% and falling rapidly." It had run out of power for cloaking.

"I hunger," he said, drooling, the gluttony of Gigatheta's taking over. He grabbed her and picked her up, trying to pull off her suit like the shell of an oyster. He then spread her out and tried to break off her limbs like the limbs of a crab. Despite the durability of her suit, it would be little obstacle for a being the size and power of Malevant. "Let me goooo!" Autumn cried, her scratchy voice breaking. The hinges of the suit buzzed and whirred as they fought to keep the suit together.

"I'LL KILL YOU!" Azure roared, slashing at Malevant's right hand and cutting it off. Malevant howled, catching Autumn in his opposite hand. Azure looked to come down one final time on Malevant's head, knowing that it would be the killing blow, but just then a black portal opened in front of him. Strong, inescapable arms reached out from it and pulled him through.

Chancellor Antares disintegrated the debris that had buried him on the way to the bunker. He activated a Time Mine, this time bringing all activity within the Capital to a halt. Only those with special suits like himself were able to move to any significant degree.

General Deem was shocked as his body was frozen in time, however, some of his consciousness remained. His army and the enemy had frozen in place as well. A hologram of the Chancellor appeared in front of him. "Dragon, you came to my front porch uninvited and expected just to walk away?" he said. "You continue to fail to adapt. You continue to underestimate our technology. The arrow of time in this city has stopped. Even now, the other Union armies on this planet are closing in around your position. You Dragons are now the ones encircled and under siege."

Deem shook, trying to escape the time trap.

Azure fell upon a patch of snow. "Nooooo!" he roared, running back to the portal behind him. It closed. What confronted him was a cold, mountainous world: Jotunheim, the realm of the Frost Giants. "I need to get back! I need to go back to them!"

"If you want to get back to them, you'll need to kill me first," said a voice from behind him. He turned and found Diamond, his plasma saber drawn. "Hello, brother," said the legendary killing machine in his white cybernetic armor. "Or should I say… father?"

"YOU!" said Azure, his body shaking.

Loki's laughter cackled in the sky. "I told you so. I told you so. One more piece of this pu-zzle!" Azure pleaded with Loki to return him to Malkuth so he could protect his friends and defeat Malevant. "I told you there was one last person I wanted you to meet. Don't you recognize him?"

"I don't fuckin' care anymore," Azure replied.

"Oh, but you should," said Loki. "This is it: the final key to the final lock to the final door to your powers. Kill him, and I will send you back to your friends."

Azure drew the Sword of Heaven and dashed at Diamond who used a combination of force shields and the plasma saber to counter his initial assault. Diamond seemed to know each move he'd make next. He fired a blast from his mouth that sent Azure skidding through the snow and some rocks.

"Fool!" Diamond scolded. "You remember that the Angel taught you the ways of the sword, but do you remember him teaching you anything else? Or have you suppressed those memories too?"

The enraged Tyrannosaur charged and dodged a series of energy balls before being hit by a super-heated beam that melted half his body. "How much of your story did you hide from her?" said Diamond.

Azure screamed in pain and grit his teeth, growling furiously and firing bolts of electricity at Diamond. Diamond slapped him in the back with his heavy armor-plated tail. "Did you tell her about me? Did you tell her that I'm here because of you? I exist because of you? That I'm a prisoner in this cage for the rest of eternity because of you? Did you tell her that?!"

Diamond charged his tail-laser. Azure swung at him wildly with his sword, forcing Diamond back but hitting nothing.

"Take me back to them!" Azure cried.

"Then kill me!" Diamond fired his tail laser and annihilated Azure, melting the snow for a mile and creating a crater. Azure's body reformed in the crater. "The Catastrophe, Azure. Did you forget to mention the truth?"

"I'll kill you!!!" Azure flew up to meet Diamond in the air and the two had a vicious exchange. Diamond allowed himself to be struck by the sword and held Azure in place to demonstrate that he could regenerate too in exactly the same way.

"You caused it, Azure. The powers-that-be thought the other side had launched first. It was YOU and YOUR lack of control, Azure! You killed billions! You ended the world! You're a murderer! A mass-murderer!"

"No!" Azure swung, Diamond intercepted his arm and headbutted him. "That was a long, long time ago…" Azure cried. "It wasn't my fault."

"Are you willing to let that happen again? Don't you fear your powers? The damage it can cause? Tell me, you've felt it."

He was right. Azure knew it.

"You're as much a threat to your civilization as the Dragons. You're a killer!"

Azure lowered his sword. "No," he shook his head.

"You're cruel and sick and bloodthirsty and power hungry—everything Neela hated!"

"No!"

"What more did you lie about? What other secrets did you keep from her?"

"STOP IT!" Azure hurled a stream of fire at him, but Diamond blocked it easily.

"This petty magic is beneath you, Azure. It's holding you back. It's blinding you. It's drawing you further and further from the truth of what you are!" Azure hurled a series of fireballs and lightning bolts at Diamond who avoided each one with above-light-speed. Diamond hit him with another blast from one of his shoulder cannons. It launched him into a snowy mountain and exploded, cutting the mountain range in half.

Diamond hovered over the damage.

"Send me back! Please!" Azure begged. "I can't let her die! I can't let them all down!"

"You promised someone else you'd protect them. But you can't. You're too weak. Everything you do saps your strength."

Azure created a small avalanche with his telekinesis, but Diamond easily avoided it. Azure tumbled down the side of the mountain, crashing on the rocks. He breathed heavily.

"Hold your breath. You don't need to breathe, you fool! You don't even need to drink or eat or sleep! You've learned these things. You've learned to be weak. You've learned to be mortal. You've learned to be limited. You should be anything but. If only you'd known sooner… you could've saved Bekah, and Enif, and Neela…"

Azure tensed his body and electricity shot out in all directions. A huge pulsating ball of energy formed in his hand and he plunged it directly into Diamond's body. It exploded in both of their faces. The mountains themselves crumbled.

Now with only one-hand, the towering Malevant bit into Autumn's suit. Desperate, Autumn flipped a plasma grenade into Malevant's mouth. It exploded. Burning his tongue, throat, and knocking out several of his sharp teeth. Thor leapt up with his hammer, but Malevant smacked it away with his handless forearm, then hit the god of thunder with his eye-beams.

"Critical: power at 3%," said Autumn's AI. She huffed and puffed nervously.

Malevant stomped forward toward Autumn, shaking the whole sky district. Thor flew up and brought the hammer down on the center of Malevant's left-foot. He howled. Just then, Athena dove down from behind the Dragon and planted the Black Sword directly into his back. He wrenched and writhed as the energy began to leave his body. He dropped down and began to thrash around. Athena was forced to withdraw the sword for a moment to avoid being crushed, but quickly plunged it between his scales again.

Autumn fired a sustained repulsor-beam from her hand at Malevant's head, burning off a chunk of his face. Thor struck him again and again in the arm with the hammer until the arm broke. Malevant spread his wings and attempted to fly away. Athena stayed on top of him, burying the sword deeper and continuing to draw energy. "Athena, stop this!" said Malevant.

"Never! Suffer and die, you bastard!" she screamed. He shrunk and he fluttered like a dying moth in the sky.

Aphrodite saw this from the ground and cheered.

Malevant crashed down, a fraction of his previous size but creating a shockwave in his wake nonetheless. "Reflect on my people, remember my world, feel all of the pain and suffering you caused us! All you stole from us!" Athena twisted the blade. Malevant groaned. Aphrodite flew up and began kicking Malevant's barely-living body, but hurt her foot in the process. Malevant rattled one last time before falling limp. His body began to turn to dust.

Athena, in a new ethereal form, stood in the middle of the crater. She was twice her previous size. Her eyes glowed. She began to laugh maniacally.

"My lady?" said Thor, hovering down.

"Uh, like, are you feeling ok, sis?" asked Aphrodite.

"The Dragons," she said with a raspy voice. "Let me tear off their wings!"

Azure and Diamond exchanged energy attacks. Snow melted in mid-air. "Neela used to bring home stray animals," said Diamond. "Are you another one of those? Another one of her projects? Just another poor, lost stray animal caught in the rain?"

Azure generated another energy ball, but it dissipated. Diamond struck him with his heavy armored tail. "Do you not realize what you are?"

"I need to save them!"

"From who? From General Malevant? And what do you plan to do against the Dragon lords? Against their Queen? Are you going to save your people from them too? You can't even beat me. You don't even know your potential! You failure!"

"You! You're a damn traitor, Diamond! You should be there with them! You should've been there with her! But you left us! You hypocrite! You left us!" Azure powered up an attack.

Diamond powered his Diamond Salvo Beam. "Bring it out!!!"

Their attacks met, shaking the entire realm. A mushroom cloud comparable to that of twelve hydrogen bombs rose, pushing aside the clouds for miles.

Despite the death of General Malevant, the Dragons legions continued to march deeper into Atlanta City, coming up on the third line of defense in the West while the second line held in the East where Dragons, Cyclops, and Centaurs lay piled on top of each other.

In the West, the Malkuthians were faced with the huge and vicious Oni who sprinted toward their lines. They tore apart those who straggled. A wounded Edom wrestled with King Yama, who proved to be a formidable opponent. With a club to the stomach, Edom spat out blood. Edom was able to stagger Yama with an uppercut, but he received a hook in return. Izanami appeared, revealing an ofuda (ritual strip of paper) with the word, "Darkness" written on it in Kanji script. She hit him with it, and it exploded in a puff of black mist that began choking him like mustard gas.

Yama swung his club downward, and Edom struggled for control of it. His energy and healing factor had reached their limits, and now he was struggling to breathe. Desperate, Edom speared Yama in the gut with his two horns, opening a wound there. Izanami prepared another ofuda, which stiffened, reading, "Fire." Just as she was about to hurl it, a beam from a Grand Fortress Mech burned her up, and the explosion threw Edom and Yama aside. Edom had ceased healing, and his strength was greatly decreased. Yama came upon him with both hands, choking him. Edom grabbed control of his right arm and put his shin in the Oni's throat. He leaned his body outward, using the weight of his tail to hold the Kami of the Underworld in place. Greenish-blue blood dripped from his mouth and the blade of his shin crushed the beast's throat.

Edom threw him aside and tried to crawl back to the lines. He remembered setting the record for the yoke walk and many other such endurance-strength challenges, but he wasn't severely wounded then. His vision was fading, and he could taste his own blood. The People's Square and the third line of defense awaited him in the distance as his men tried to cover his escape.

"SUSANOO .VS. AMATERASU"

A Starfire Blast hit Susanoo, throwing him into a light post and causing his targeted tornadoes to dissipate. When he came to, Amaterasu stood over him, trying to snatch his sword from his hand. Susanoo clinched the weapon, saving it, but Amaterasu used this opportunity to snatch the comb from his hair.

"What the bloody hell are you doing, Ame?!" Susanoo exclaimed, grabbing for the comb. Amaterasu withdrew.

"I'm doing what must be done, Su. What daddy taught me."

"We made our peace back on Bhumi! You fought beside me. You accepted Kushina into our family!"

"She'll never truly be a part of our family. She'll always be just another dirty human. Our father, the love of my life, is my true family. The only one who has always been there for me and trusted me. Now, daddy's life is at stake and you're the price."

"You fool! You bargained with those devil Dragons again?!"

"I had no choice."

"Foolish wench! You're wrong! You always have a choice!"

"Silence, brother! Give me your sword!"

Susanoo dashed at her and tried to snatch the comb from her, but she nimbly evaded him. "Enough with this foolishness!" He grabbed for it again, but each time Amaterasu held it away. "Stop acting like a child!"

Amaterasu hit him with another Starfire Blast, knocking him down. "Give up the sword!"

"Like hell I will!" Susanoo hurled a series of windstorms at her, and one of them swept the comb out of Amaterasu's hand. Both of them gasped, scrambling for it. Amaterasu got to it first and shoved him away.

"Give me the sword!" she demanded. "Give it to me or I'll melt this! You'll never see your foolish human girl again!"

Susanoo was just about to surrender when Aphrodite swooped in and snatched the comb from Amaterasu's hand. Furious, Amaterasu clipped her with a Starfire Blast, causing the goddess of love to crash down into the rubble below. Susanoo rushed to Aphrodite's aid, but his sister intercepted him, drawing a katana of her own. It was a katana that glowed like yellow fire. She slashed at him. Susanoo parried the strike. She stabbed at him, and he counter-attacked. The siblings had a dozen of these exchanges, having learned the ways of the sword from their father, Izanagi. It was a stalemate.

Knowing she couldn't out-duel Susanoo, Amaterasu transformed the comb back into Kushina who lay confused next to the injured Aphrodite. "Maybe this will convince you!" Amaterasu aimed an extra-powerful Starfire Blast at both Kushina and Aphrodite, who both gasped frightfully.

"Wait!" said Susanoo. "You don't have to do this, Ame! General Malevant is dead."

"He has already given the order. It can't be rescinded"

"Then we can go back to Bhumi together and save father!"

"Our time is too short. I need to kill you! I must kill you no matter what! I'm sorry. Lay down and give up the Totsuga-no-Tsurugi! Then, we can say our goodbyes. Please, brother... don't make this so hard." She held the Starfire closer to Kushina and Aphrodite who both screamed from the increased heat.

Susanoo flipped the sword with the handle facing away from him. Just as it was thought he'd merely surrender the sword, he plunged it into his stomach and cut it open. All three women screamed and cried, "NO! SU!"

"I've saved you the guilt, Ame," said Susanoo. He turned to Kushina and Aphrodite, who were in tears, saying, "I've always been selfish. You found a way to calm my storm." He fell dead.

Kushina and Aphrodite hugged his body and wept. A Wyvern scout flew down, seeing that Susanoo was dead and went back through the portal to report it. The two lovers of Susanoo looked up at Amaterasu with angry, teary, accusatory eyes.

Amaterasu backed away and fell to her knees. She took her sword and gutted herself, additionally sending a Starfire Blast into her own gut and immolating her insides. She reached out to Susanoo and held his hand. Soon, the Queen of the Kami was no more.

"Sis!" Athena called to Aphrodite's mind. "Sis! Listen to me! I'm not thinking straight. I'm losing control."

"Like, not now," said the goddess of love, trying to wipe the tears that kept falling.

"Yes, now! You want me to die today too? I need you to pull yourself together and remember where you hid Medusa's head. It may be our only chance!"

"THE DYING DAY"

By that point, the Malkuthians who weren't dead were either exhausted, wounded, or at least temporarily deafened. Their arms and trigger-fingers had gone numb from the constant firing. People choked and coughed on the soot and smoke. A large portion of the city was smoldering. The casualties were in excess of a million.

Among the dead was Chief Delano, whom the tribe hastily performed a burial ceremony for. As Edom reached the People's Square, he saw the charred body of old Glaucon lying there, having been struck by a fireball. "Rest in peace, you damn fool," said Edom. "I pray you'll be laughing wherever you end up."

In the East, the city's defenders fell back to the University campus. The retreating Malkuthians found the statue of Neela fallen on its side and broken, the melted bowls of ice cream offered to her were shattered and many of the candles scattered across the steps. The library behind it burned. There were burnt corpses everywhere. Some still clung to life, though barely. There was little that could be done for them.

The battle had reached its 13th hour, and the Dragons had penetrated about eight miles into the city. They'd lost their leader, but so had the Malkuthians. The Dragons held their ground and began to round up hundreds of Malkuthians in areas they controlled. They prepared stakes they'd brought with them through the Black Gates and began impaling the pleading prisoners on them in view of the Malkuthian lines. The screams of the victims were spine-chilling. "The hell with that, I ain't watching that shit," said Edom, laying down and favoring his wounds as a medic placed an oxygen mask over his face.

Autumn had made her way to the tunnels and was likewise horrified at the sight of this cruelty. She had her AI conjure up a holographic army to try to draw the Dragons away from the captives. The ploy worked for only a few minutes before the Dragons realized the fakery. Most of her vermilion birds had been killed, so they too proved useless. She tried to deploy some of her Wraiths to the surface to harass the Dragons with their lasers and mini grenades.

"Shoot them," General Eridanus, having seen the Dragons do this multiple times in the past, gave the order. "It's what Azure would want. Put the poor bastards out of their misery. Shoot them!"

The gunners took aim and fired at the Malkuthians who'd been impaled on the stakes and also at those who'd simply been captured. They opened fire, breaking the brief silence. At least, they thought, death would come quickly. It was a horrendous and tragic sight nonetheless. Whenever the Dragons would emerge with a new batch of victims, they were shot and killed as soon as possible, robbing the Dragons of the deed.

"Pathetic, Azure!" Diamond howled as the mushroom cloud continued to grow into the atmosphere. A hatch in his armor opened and red energy appeared to spiral rapidly from the distant sun that peaked through the hole in the clouds. The mushroom cloud itself appeared to spiral around the area and envelope Diamond.

Then, there was darkness. Complete darkness, save for the stars over Jotunheim. Azure was overcome with anxiety as he stumbled blindly through the cold darkness. He realized that he could sense something: Diamond's energy. "I'll find you! I'll crush you!" he roared.

"You've become married to your sight, Azure. You're a Kami. Can't you sense my energy?"

"Enough of these tricks! Enough of these games!" Azure began to form another pulse of energy in his palms, the light from it illuminated the area around him like a torch. He thought he saw Diamond pass, and he hurled the energy blindly. It exploded, and for a brief moment he saw Diamond in the light created by the blast. "I *SEE* YOU!" Azure unloaded a barrage of energy attacks at him, which he dodged.

"You don't even comprehend the power you're tapping into. It's the same as mine."

"I don't have time for this, coward! I need to be there with my people!"

Diamond formed a huge ball of white energy even larger than him, it illuminated about a quarter of a mile. Azure was astonished. "Can you form one of these?" said Diamond.

Azure growled, focusing all of his energy into his palms. "Let's test the myth of your invincibility, Diamond!" he said, firing another green pulse of energy. Diamond met the attack with his energy ball and the resulting explosion was even larger than the first, perhaps as powerful as 30 hydrogen bombs.

The mushroom cloud illuminated the area for some time in an orange glow. Azure was caught up in the shockwave and tumbled for many miles before finally resting on a patch of ice. He was so exhausted, he could hardly move. Diamond swept down and crashed him through the ice, into the chilly water below. He struggled to breathe but remembered he could do without it. Diamond threw him back up to the surface. "What good is having all this power if you don't use it, Azure?"

"Take me… back…"

Diamond kicked him over. "Aren't you listening, you fool?!"

"I need to… get back to them…."

"You can't even defend yourself," said Diamond, slamming his armored tail down on top of him.

"AZURE'S POWER"

Azure was a bloody, pulverized mess. Diamond again opened the hatch in his back and again the energy from the mushroom cloud spiraled around him until the world had gone dark again. Diamond formed yet another energy ball to light the darkness. "It's called *Qi*, Azure," Diamond lectured. "Life-force. Life-energy. The power that's in you and in me. It's in everyone. In everything. It's never destroyed. It flows. It changes. It transfers. Thanks to you and the Symbiote in my heart, I am a reactor. Just like a damn bomb. A weapon. You're a reactor too. You have an affinity to life-energy that's second to none. You can convert anything from anywhere without limit, something not even I am capable of. You could drain the whole cosmos if you wanted to, kill everything."

"H-h-how?…"

"Loki believes that you came into contact with two great powers at the beginning of your creation: the God of gods and Ain, the Queen of the Dragons. You are the result of their greatest expenditures of energy meeting at the genesis of New Heaven, in the landfill of creation. An unprecedented anomaly in all of space and time. But look at you now… a pathetic disappointment. All of us believed in you—Loki, Thor, Athena, Aphrodite, and Neela… You've disappointed all of them! You've disappointed her!"

"No…"

Loki displayed some scenes from what was happening back on Malkuth. Azure saw Delano and Glaucon burn to death. He watched as hundreds were impaled. He saw Edom, wounded and exhausted, returning to Vegas and the moon pup. He saw as Susanoo sacrificed his life to save Kushina and Aphrodite.

He saw as Odhran intercept Autumn in the tunnel at gun-point just as she shed her suit. He shot her in the leg and spat on her as the other Raptors tied her up, threw a noose around her neck, and dragged her away.

"NO!" Azure cried.

"You said you'd protect her. But can you? Remember feeling so small and helpless as hundreds of innocent people died around you? Remember being a slave? Being a prisoner in that asylum, unable to help your blind-deaf girl?"

Sparks flew from Azure and his green aura shot out and sustained itself.

"Don't you remember feeling so small and helpless as the PSF took Neela away and locked her in that gibbet cage? Remember as Nusakan taunted her and twirled her around as you hid and watched? Remember as you watched her die, slowly, progressively, painfully. Helpless to do anything to stop it! Helpless and WEAK!"

Azure roared. He stood to his feet. The ground shook. It began to splinter. The ice shelves broke but he hovered over the cold water that revealed itself from underneath. Ripples became waves that shot out in all directions from him. Azure's eyes became like green fires. His mouth smoked like that of a Dragon.

"Remember their betrayal. Remember their deception. Remember finding her, cradling her limp body in your arms. So fragile. Remember what broke inside of you!"

The kaleidoscope of visions in Azure's mind shattered like broken glass and coalesced into one single point of light. Azure's aura reached out for miles and rapidly grew until it covered the whole hemisphere. It was like a green sun had risen over the realm and swept the darkness away. The energy from stars flowed to him until the stars themselves vanished. His roar tore apart the fabric of space-time. Hundreds upon hundreds of holes formed in the sky. Other worlds in other universes shook. The world beneath him turned black as a clump of coal and disintegrated. Jotunheim was no more. Nearby Alfheim was no more. Helheim was no more.

As he cackled with excitement, Loki realized that his Nether Dimension was crumbling around him, and he quickly fled.

Lord Mortimer, as he was attacking the Cosmic Wall, felt this surge of power and was momentarily distracted.

Lord Zeon, preparing to tear a portal over Malkuth, also felt Azure's power.

Queen Ain noticed the streams of energy that flowed to her bending ever so slightly.

Two pairs of wings sprouted from Azure's back: two wings like a Dragon and two like those of an Angel. New arms sprouted from under his other ones.

"Now, contain it, Azure! Bring it to your center like jelly to a glass jar. Gather it into your center and shut the lid! Don't let it escape! Don't let it go!" Diamond realized that Azure couldn't hear him over the chaos, and he asked Loki to transfer the message. "Don't let it explode!"

Azure growled as he focused on drawing the power in and containing it. There was a blinding explosion of light. As it cleared, there hovered Azure, sparkling, glowing, and pulsating with immense energy like a neutron star sitting alone in the dark. At long last, Azure's true power had been realized.

"STRUGGLE FOR THE COSMOS"

Satan had rallied his Demons on the Earth facing the Gates of Heaven, prepared to invade at the ideal time, once the Cosmic Wall in New Heaven had fallen. Then, he hoped to invade Heaven itself from two sides with the help of the Dragons.

Lord Mortimer continued to wear away at the Cosmic Wall in the Deep Core, the lifeblood of the Malkuthians and the center of this cosmic conflict as it was a back gate of Heaven. The invasion of all other worlds including Malkuth and Hod was intended to draw the Union defenses away from the Wall. The Resolvers, World Enders, and fleets that remained managed to hamper their efforts, but the Dragons, as always, were numerous and resilient. Lord Mortimer himself proved to be powerful enough to deal with these superweapons, using gravity-based magic to begin destroying them while simultaneously wearing down the Wall.

As the hole became large enough to allow energy to spill out like water from a broken dam, an army of Angels emerged from it led by the Arch-Angels Uriel and

Raphael. They fought the Dragons and harassed Lord Mortimer, forcing him to turn his powers away from the Union superweapons and the Wall.

Lord Zeon tore open a portal over Malkuth. The jaded Malkuthians in Atlanta City looked up in horror, having seen Dragon lords in broadcasts and knowing one was making its way to their world. So far, only the Resolver superweapons had managed to kill the lords, and Zeon had survived multiple Resolver and World Ender attacks in the past. Edom, seeing this, reeled Vegas and the moon pup in, preparing for the worse. Even he couldn't hope to overpower something like that, especially in his state. The moon pup whimpered in Vegas's arms.

"Don't do it, please!" Autumn cried as the Raptors looped the noose around a pipe overlooking a drainage trench. They handcuffed her to a pipe forward of it, teetering over the edge on her one good leg. "Why? Why are you doing this to me?"

Odhran slapped her. She barely kept from falling over and hanging herself. "I want to make sure that no matter what happens to us, your bloodline is erased! Your family killed mine. You killed thousands of us around the Union every day because you're all racist fucks!"

"No…"

Odhran slapped her again, bruising her face. She gasped as she almost slipped again. "Huh? You're still in denial, bitch?!"

"I'm not him. I'm not my dad!" said Autumn, tears, snot, and blood running from her face. "I'm not responsible for what my dad or my ancestors did! Please, stop it!"

"Your blood is your guilt. You're all bastards. You're all complicit in murder. Your blood's all the proof I need." He aimed his rifle at her lone healthy leg.

"My AI will stop working!" she said. "If I'm dead, the Empress Amber AI will die too. My dad will be able to kill you all. He won't hesitate! He'll send a World Ender or a Resolver to erase Malkuth. If I'm dead, there's nothing to stop that!"

"She's right, sir," said one of the Raptor lieutenants.

Odhran withdrew his rifle. "Then you best not lose your balance, sweetie," he said, pushing her gently but enough to force her to catch herself from falling again. She used her tail to try to anchor herself. "You're smart, aren't you? You know how gravity works. One little slip, and there's no coming back. I've watched quite a few hangings. It can take 10-20 minutes to die as all the air from your little lungs leaves your body and what little oxygen is left in your blood struggles to reach your brain. See, I know a thing or two too."

"Please… It hurts. My leg hurts! I can't hold this position! I feel faint!"

"Then, it's 'perfect,' just like your daddy always says. You Antares love this sort of thing—games involving life and death, putting everyone in peril for your own gain. It's a game. It's always been a damn game to you! Well, I'll play. Hang around, bitch."

"Please! Please don't leave me like this!" Autumn cried. "Please!"

As Odhran left, leaving sentries to guard her, Autumn wept into her shoulder. She had no idea where Azure was, the battle on the surface was getting worse, and she found herself in this predicament: persecuted by the very people she tried to help. Once again, she felt alone. So alone.

"BATTLE WITH LORD ZEON"

Athena, in her new cosmic form, had almost single-handedly halted the bombardment by the flying Dragons. She telekinetically pried the wings from their backs and appeared to enjoy doing this, smiling and laughing. Malevant's malicious spirit had begun to warp her personality. She came down on top of a wingless and still-living Wyvern and tore a chunk of its leg off to eat. Gigatheta's voracious spirit had also started to possess her.

"Ewww…. sis!" Aphrodite resisted the urge to puke.

"My lady?" said Thor, crushing the head of the Wyvern with Mjolnir. Athena took a bite of the leg. "You ought to roast that over a fire first!"

Athena threw the leg aside and clutched her head, screaming. "Have I gone mad?!"

Thor ignited a fire with some lightning and skewered the leg on some wood to cook it on.

"Just what we need right now, you idiot!" Athena shouted. "More fire!"

"I thought only of thy health, my lady."

Athena looked up at the sky as colossal Lord Zeon appeared there. "Thor, I heard you fought Giants non-stop for centuries."

"Why, yes, my lady. 'Twas the summer of—"

"Great! Go fight that giant Dragon up there for as long as you can to draw its attention. I'll try to get behind him. Do that for me, and I might consider you a worthy partner."

Thor smiled.

"Please get that stupid look off your face and just go already…"

"Does thou get a kiss?" said Thor.

"Yeah, sis," said Aphrodite. "It's, like, customary before, like, the guys go off to battle."

Athena closed her eyes and held her breath. She quickly nipped Thor on his bearded lips and immediately withdrew, coughing like someone who'd been underwater for too long. She spat out some of Thor's beard-hairs.

Thor flew up to confront Zeon, who was in the process of swatting Union starships out of the sky. He laughed. "HEAR ME, MALKUTHIANS! I AM LORD ZEON, THE GOD OF MIGHT! YOU SHALL ALL YIELD TO MY POWER!" His heads exhaled thick beams of energy that all but destroyed the remainder of the allied Union fleet. The flagship of the fleet was destroyed, killing the Vice-Admiral on board. With a sweep of his hand, he knocked one of the sky carriers over. It crashed down to the city below, killing tens of thousands instantly and blanketing a fourth of the city in soot.

"Dragon! You shall taste the wrath of the god of thunder!" Thor struck Zeon with the hammer. His left-hand fractured from the impact. Zeon laughed. Thor hastily grabbed the hammer in his right and threw it with all his might. It bounced off like a rubber ball from the pavement. Thor was stunned. He unleashed a flurry of lightning bolts at Zeon who continued to laugh before flicking him out of the air with a finger.

Athena snuck up on Zeon and plunged the Black Sword into his back, repeating what she'd done to Malevant. Zeon flinched briefly, but another head appeared from where Athena stood and swallowed her whole.

"NO, sis!" Aphrodite cried.

The jaws of the head were pushed open as Athena in her cosmic form was just barely able to hold it open with her back on one end and her sandals at the other. Aphrodite flew up and tried to pry her free, but it wasn't enough. Another head came up and barely missed snagging her too. Thor came up and struck that head, then helped to pry Athena free. They worked together and finally succeeded, but more heads and more arms sprouted from Zeon's back. Athena looked to Thor, and he nodded. They flew up together to fight for their very lives against overwhelming odds.

The appearance of Zeon created mass confusion that the Dragon legions exploited to advance as Malkuthians desperately tried to find whatever shelter they could. Both sides had lost most of their air support, but the situation now seemed to favor the Dragons. If Zeon were to make landfall on the city, there would be no city to speak of. He could erase the continent and perhaps ruin the whole planet just by landing on it with his immense size.

General Eridanus, Edom, and the other leaders did their best to encourage the troops to hold their positions and continue firing on the approaching Dragon columns. It was all they could do. In that hour, the Dragons had taken nearly twice the land of the previous 13. They marched over the People's Square, through the Warehouse District, over the University. A small contingent of Malkuthians desperately tried to defend the Arena and other hospitals as patients were evacuated. Stretchers and beds fell on their sides in the panic. Oxygen tanks and IV poles fell. Patients died or were left behind in the chaos. St. Sargas High School, one of the largest makeshift hospitals, was completely taken by the Dragons who began executing people there.

Out of nowhere, Diamond swooped in and struck the Dragons with his vast arsenal of attacks. Those who saw him were shocked and elated. They cheered. Their old hero had returned!

Diamond flew up and fired a Diamond Salvo Beam at Lord Zeon's side and opened a warehouse-sized wound in him. "You two!" Diamond called to Athena and Thor. "To me!"

Athena knew what he was up to and waved Thor toward her. The three flew around Zeon's main heads and away from the city, catching his attention. Zeon recognized Diamond as the one who'd fought his generals and destroyed several of his armies. He flew to pursue him. His frame eclipsed the suns like a massive dark storm cloud that stretched across the hemisphere. Diamond led Zeon up out of the atmosphere and into space, firing energy blasts at him intermittently to keep his attention. Athena took some shots at him with her bow. Thor took shots with his lightning, amped thousands of times the power of normal lightning. All of these had little effect.

"We should scatter," Athena communicated to the others.

"You read my mind," said Diamond.

The three went in separate directions, and Zeon's heads fired at them. One of the blasts broke one of the moons apart like a ball of chalk dashed against a wall. Diamond used this opportunity to charge an even more powerful Diamond Salvo Beam and fired it directly at his center head. It knocked off two of Zeon's crowns, but the head itself had survived the attack, an attack capable of destroying planets and countering Deem & Malevant in the past. "THIS IS… POETIC! AN OLYMPIAN. AN ASGARDIAN. A MALKUTHIAN. YOUR THREE PATHETIC RACES SHALL ALL PERISH TOGETHER!" said Zeon, collecting red sparking energy between his mouths.

"It's his Mass Extinction Attack!" Athena exclaimed. "He destroyed half of our universe with it. We have to stop him!"

"Lay it on him!" said Diamond. He unloaded multiple bursts of his Atomic Cannons, each attack exploding with the force of a nuclear blast. All this did was mildly annoy Zeon who revealed more heads and limbs to lay down counter-fire while his Mass Extinction Attack charged.

"Sis!" Aphrodite shouted, finally arriving. "I totally found it!" She tossed a bag to Athena who quickly took out its contents. It was the head of Medusa. She held it up in front of Zeon. His three central heads saw it and began to turn to stone. Zeon's attack stopped charging and his other heads looked away, realizing what was happening. Zeon swatted Athena out of the air, forcing her to revert to her original form. Thor rushed to catch her but ended up colliding with her. Zeon shed the heads that had turned to stone and regrew them with only the loss of their crowns.

Loki showed Azure the great conflict that was engulfing the cosmos. With his powers unleashed, Azure could now make sense of his clairvoyance. It troubled him greatly.

"Oh, don't worry! That Autumn is a smart girl," said Loki. "She'll find a way to survive. The Antares are like cockroaches, you see."

"She's in pain! Edom, Athena, Aphrodite, Thor, and the others. They're all in so much pain! I need to be there with them! I need to save them!"

"Just one last thing, Azure," said Loki. He showed him scaled down images of thousands of different universes. "You want to defeat that Dragon lord? The Dragon lord who survived a direct hit from a Resolver. The so-called 'god of might.' If you want to do the deed, then I know, I know, just what you need… choose one of these universes. Drain it."

"Will they—"

"Will they die? Oh, yes, of course. People always die. We play a zero-sum game, Azure. You'll need to choose: *your* people or *their* people—the future of the Malkuthians or the future of God-knows-whatever-they're-called. I'll make it easier for you…" he flashed his hand and zoomed in on one particular universe of moderate size. "You need just enough power to defeat Lord Zeon. Of all the ones you could choose to accomplish that daunting feat, this one is the least populated.

"I can feel them… life… everywhere… billions…"

"Yes, yes, yes, we're short on time. Hurry, hurry. Do you want to save your people or not?"

Azure watched as Autumn teetered over the edge in tears, her consciousness fading from the blood-loss. He watched as Satan and his Demons rushed the front gates of Heaven. He watched as Lord Mortimer and his Dragons did battle with the Angels in the center of New Heaven. He watched as Lord Zeon knocked Athena out of the way as Diamond and Thor tried desperately and in vain to keep Zeon from charging his ultimate attack. He watched as the Dragon heavy-infantry took more ground on Malkuth and continued to execute whoever they captured.

"For the greater good, Azure… do it," said Loki.

Azure relented and siphoned the energy from the universe Loki had shown him. He could hear the surprised and anguished screams of the creatures who were dying there. He could see them all turning to ashes. He could see their whole worlds and all their stars becoming black as coal before vanishing. He hardened his heart like a trained soldier. Just as Edom had once told him, he knew what he needed to do, and he did it. It was just business. It was nothing personal. But it still hurt. The screams and the sight of foreign creatures clinging to one another seared themselves like a brand on his conscience. A tear the size of a comet streaked down Azure's face.

And all the while, Loki laughed.

———

Satan and the Demons charged for the gates of Heaven. Michael led the counter-charge of Angels. The two armies clashed.

Terra and Laurel grappled, and Laurel quickly gained the upper-hand due to Terra's deterioration. "Tarrol, stop this, please!" cried Laurel. "Turn away from this vain pursuit! I don't want to hurt you!"

"Then, darling, allow me to hurt *you*!" Terra splashed her with the contents of her conjured goblet, burning Laurel's chest and arms like acid. Terra grabbed her by the hair and tugged it back. "Oh, does that hurt, Laurel, darling? Does that burn?"

"What has become of you, Tarrol? What happened to the friend I knew? The one who disregarded her rank to play with me in the garden."

"I killed her, darling. Because she wasn't good enough. She was *never* good enough. Great enough. Important enough. I am."

"She was all of those things to me," said Laurel. "You were."

Terra's face contorted and she placed her hands around Laurel's throat, choking her with all of her might. "You were always lesser than me!" she screeched.

Laurel scratched her over the face and arms with her nails until the Demoness pulled away. Laurel readied a pulse of angelic fire. "Wait, darling!" said Terra. "I'll go. I'll go away. I need to protect this baby!"

He's an unholy abomination, Tarrol

"He's mine, darling! We made him together… Samael & I…" she shouted back.

"Tarrol… stop…"

"I can't! I won't! If you want the prophecies to be fulfilled, darling, you need me! We need this child!" Terra fled, glimpsing back only once.

Laurel looked on. "I hope you're happy…" she said.

Samael and Michael, the ancient rivals, collided.

Before their weapons even met, they both sensed what Azure had just done. Satan sneered with satisfaction, even as Michael began to best him in combat. Michael felt something like a punch to the gut. An unfathomable darkness had come upon his old pupil, the one he'd named and raised for several lifetimes. Michael parried Satan's attack and slashed him over the wing. This caused the king of the devils to fall. "I've already won!" said Satan. "Even if you defeat me here, I've already won. Azure's mine. I'll tempt and corrupt the son of God the same way on Earth. It's *the flesh*, Michael! These creatures that Yahweh made, they'll always obey their flesh! They're all selfish! They'll always choose to save themselves, even at the expense of everyone else!"

Michael looked to stab him.

"Oh, are you going to seal my fate before the appointed time? Are you going to turn your God into a liar? That would be my greatest victory of all!"

Michael nicked him on the arm and coaxed him to stand back up.

Satan summoned back his sword and the two enemies older than time itself clashed once more.

General Deem managed to move despite the time trap, but he was brought to a snail's pace. The Union armies on Hod closed in on his warriors who remained frozen in time. "Dragon, these soldiers are armed with adamantine bullets made from your very weapons and armor," said Antares. "They'll shred you to pieces. You have zero chance of survival."

These Union armies came with new mechs as well, the X-Mechs, large and spider-like in appearance. There were Omega Mechs and Grand Fortress Mechs in their ranks as well. Even to the Dragons, this show of force was overwhelming.

"It would appear that Loki hasn't failed me after all," said Antares.

"Lo...ki..."

"He led you straight to your doom. Good show. I will enjoy watching the slaughter."

"You..." Deem seethed. Deem began to enter his fearsome Durga form again.

The time trap ended, and the Union forces swarmed in from behind, firing adamantine rounds which broke even the armor and hide of the Dragons. Deem rushed into battle, butchering thousands of Union soldiers as if they were fruits caught in a blender. The Union soldiers, however, got the upper-hand on Deem's warriors. Dragon bodies piled up at the edge of the Capital.

Deem tangled with the mechs and managed to take several of them down, but the Malkuthian numbers were just too great. He could only think of one other option: to destroy the capital planet itself and leave a hole in the Union high command.

He went up into the sky, just below the dome of the force field and began to collect energy for his most powerful and destructive attack: the *Brahmashirsha Astra*.

It eclipsed the power of his Brahmastra but could likely destroy him along with it. Chancellor Antares saw the energy readings on this attack and became gravely concerned, knowing that even trying to counter it would result in Hod's destruction. He immediately deployed another Time Mine, bringing Deem to a crawl and freezing the rest of the battlefield. He made his way to his escape ship, leaving the Capital to its fate.

Bizarrely, there was cheering in the tunnels. Word went around among the Malkuthians that the capital planet, Hod, had been completely destroyed by a Dragon attack. Not only was the planet destroyed but the entire sub-region had been erased from existence.

"You hear that, you little brat-bitch?" one of the Raptors taunted Autumn. "Daddy and all his friends are dead."

"Your turn is coming up, sweetheart," said another.

"Why are we waiting? If her dad's dead, then he can't hurt us anymore. We can do whatever we want to her. How's that, brat-bitch?"

"Look at yourselves in the mirror!" Autumn retorted. "You don't even understand what you're doing! You blame my family for all your problems, but you've become just as bad! You've become racist, bigoted killers!"

One of the Raptors kicked her in her one good leg and she fell over the ledge. The loose caught her throat and strangled her as she swung forward and back. She was able to pull up against the cuffs to take the pressure off her neck. She'd never managed to do a chin-up in her life but in this scenario, she was fighting to live. She swung her tail back and managed to catch herself on the ledge, gasping for air.

"Say that one more time, brat-bitch," said the Raptor.

As the blurriness in her vision subsided, she started to whistle a tune. There was a rumble through the tunnel and about a dozen of her remaining vermilion birds swooped in and attacked the Raptors who were guarding her. One of the birds snatched the keys to the cuffs and gave it to Autumn. She freed herself. She fell down and grabbed one of the rifles the guards had dropped and shot them. "Shotgun mode," she commanded the rifle, and finished the guards with scattered shot. Using the rifle as a crutch, she made her way back to her quarters. Using her visor, mic, and wrist device the Raptors had previously taken from her, she summoned the Empress Amber AI. "Acquire targets: Raptors," Autumn instructed. "Order: eliminate."

One of the Raptors pulled on her pant-leg. "Do it… prove us right…" he said.

She switched the gun to stun and knocked him out.

Odhran and the Raptors had assassinated the allied PSF Colonel and the Police Commissioner. The Raptors then dropped back into the tunnels in hopes that they could get to General Eridanus's position and assassinate him as well. One of the Raptor lieutenants ran into a laser trap on the way that cut him to pieces. "That bitch reactivated them…" Odhran realized. "Go around and find another way!" The Raptors broke into separate groups, each heading to a different outpost from which they hoped to snipe the general. The lights went off in their section of the tunnel.

"You're in my domain, Odhran," said Autumn over the tunnel's speaker system, her voice distorted. "And you've overstayed your welcome. Raptors, I am not your enemy. Turn your weapons away from your fellow Malkuthians and back toward the Dragons!"

"This is a trick by that damn Antares brat! Don't listen to her!" said Odhran, cleverly activating the pulse feature of his rifle to produce light. One by one, the Raptor lieutenants dropped, killed in the darkness by Autumn's Wraiths. Odhran activated the shotgun feature of his rifle and fired at whatever moved, accidentally gunning down some of his own people. More of the Raptors accidentally fired on each other in the confusion as the Wraiths passed in and out of sight. The lights began to flicker on and off, increasing the feeling of anxiety among the Raptors.

"Antares!" Odhran growled before he stumbled on a laser trap which pierced him in 22 different places, killing him. Autumn reactivated the lights in the tunnel, revealing Odhran and over a dozen Raptors lying dead. She resisted the urge to set off lasers across the entire tunnel way, potentially killing them all.

She summoned one of her medic Wraiths to her to work on her badly wounded leg. She shoved a soft cloth in her mouth and bit down on it, trying to grit through the pain as the Wraiths removed bullet fragments and patched the wound. The AI updated her about what was happening on the surface and abroad. "Dad…" she said, letting the cloth fall.

The Malkuthians in the city were holding on by a thread, huddled around the downtown area. Autumn's voice crackled over the city's remaining loudspeakers: "Malkuthians… I'm bleeding. I bleed with you. Malkuthians, I'm hurting. I hurt with you. Malkuthians, I'm struggling. I struggle with you. It's true, Hod has been destroyed. Malkuth is the last major stronghold still standing. With that said, the outcome of this battle will decide the future of our Union. This is the new Capital of our civilization."

Autumn projected videos of Azure slaying thousands of Dragons. "I believe that Azure will return. He would never leave us without reason. He would never let us down. I know. I believe in Azure. All we can do now is stand. Stand and fight. Malkuthians, many of you think of me as an Antares, and I may never be able to change that. But right now, I am a Malkuthian just like you, a proud Malkuthian. The enemy looks not only to take our lives but to erase our civilization, erase our history, erase the memory of our very existence. That means that all of those who've died in the past, everything we worked for, everything we fought for, everything we sacrificed for is at stake here and now. I tell you, we are hurting, we are bleeding, we are struggling, but so are the Dragons. They've come to our home. They've come to our yard to play. We've proven to them what a serious mistake that was. Their casualties are catastrophic. Their generals are dead. And what's more: they fight for an inferior cause. They fight to conquer and kill. They fight for power. They fight because their leaders told them to. WE fight for each other. We fight because we believe that our civilization—as flawed as it may be—is something worth saving. It's something worth holding on to. Hold on, Malkuthians. Fight, and fight, and fight until there's nothing left. Show these darn Dragons just who exactly they're messing with. We are Malkuthians, proud Malkuthians. We will not be extinguished."

And with that, the city's defenders huddled together shoulder-to-shoulder and fought throughout the night and into the morning.

"AZURE .VS. ZEON"

Thor held Athena in his arms and tried his best to avoid the constant attacks from Zeon's sporadically growing limbs and heads. With his hand broken, he was forced to hold Athena under one arm. He was eventually struck by Zeon. The two went flying through space.

Diamond continued to lay down blasts from his Atomic Cannons, and then charged another Diamond Salvo Beam. He launched himself at many times the speed of light directly into one of Zeon's mouths and fired the beam down its throat. It exploded and burst out from Zeon's skin, but the damage was still minimal.

Diamond retreated back to load another attack. Zeon continued to charge his Mass Extinction Attack, which surpassed the suns in the intensity of its brightness.

Just then, a large moon-sized tear appeared nearby, and colossal reptilian hands reached out from it followed by a snout, a body, two pairs of wings, and a tail. The being glowed with a spectacular green aura, and his eyes were like flames.

"Azure!" Diamond, Athena, and Thor exclaimed.

The scene was broadcast Union-wide, and a great cheer went out across the universe. Nowhere was it more pronounced than on Malkuth itself as they saw the figure of Azure appear in the sky opposite of Zeon and the glow of his attack. Autumn spat out the juice she'd just drank. "Azure!" she exclaimed. "You're freakin' freaky & huge!"

Zeon fired the Mass Extinction Beam, and Azure caught it in his hand and absorbed it. "WHAT?!" said Zeon. "WHO ARE YOU?"

"The end of your story," said Azure.

All of Zeon's main heads launched their attacks and Azure nullified them all. Zeon then lunged at Azure and swung with his right-claws. Azure caught his hand and held it back. With a thought, he threw Zeon's entire body into a moon, destroying it. Zeon stopped himself just shy of an asteroid field. He grabbed some of the asteroids and hurled them at Azure who swatted them away, breaking them into pieces. Azure clinched the planet-sized monstrosity like a wrestler and flew him further and further toward the center of the solar system. Zeon's heads all bit and grabbed hold of his neck and arms, but Azure remained unfazed, flying further and further at many times lightspeed. They came to the blue sun, a supergiant, and Azure threw Zeon into it.

Autumn struggled to keep track of the conflict using the Union surveillance she hacked around the solar system. She broadcast what she could and displayed it for even the Dragons in the city to see. To them, to everyone there, it was an unbelievable sight. Lord Zeon, one of the most powerful Dragon lords and one who'd taken direct hits from the Union's best weapons, emerged from the blue sun with his wings tattered. He swung wildly at Azure and lunged at him with his teeth, Azure simply evaded every attack, seeing them ahead of time. He grabbed one of Zeon's heads and tore it off like it was made of paper mache. When one of the heads tried to charge a beam, Azure shut its jaws and the beam exploded inside the head. Azure used the many arms he had in this new form to combat the attacks of the many heads of Zeon. Finally, he got hold of one of Zeon's wings—a wing the size of a large continent—and tore it off. Zeon careened. Azure caught him. "Order your armies to leave this universe and never come back!" Azure demanded.

Zeon's main head bit Azure in the face. Azure pried his jaws apart and twisted the head, breaking it off at the stump. Zeon retreated back and tore open a portal. "YOU! HOW?! HOW ARE YOU EVEN POSSIBLE?!"

"Tell Queen Ain: I'm the end result of her crimes, and they're all coming back to haunt her. Tell her that if her armies don't leave this universe and all other universes they've invaded, I will come for her next."

Zeon threw himself pell-mell through the portal and returned to the universe of the Dragons.

"AFTERMATH"

The Dragons on Malkuth paused, not able to comprehend what they'd just seen. Azure opened portals to the Dragon universe behind them and spoke to their heads, "Your leaders, General Malevant and Lord Zeon, are defeated. Leave this place or suffer their fate." The Dragons had no concept of retreat and they refused to return without an order from their leaders. With a thought, Azure reduced the remaining Dragons to ashes. Even the Dragon corpses faded out of existence. Only their armor and weapons remained.

An avatar of Azure, normal in size and appearance, appeared in the People's Square. He was deaf to the cheering of the crowds. His heart was filled with regrets. "I'm sorry," he said. "I'm so sorry I couldn't be here with you."

The crowd ignored his muttered words and rallied around him, chanting, "We pledge to Ramatkal! Our hearts! Our lives!"

Azure passed the thousands of Malkuthian bodies including those who'd been executed on stakes. "I'm too late," he said.

Edom dragged himself over to Azure. They shook hands and hugged. "Where you was, bro?" said Edom.

"Needing to become stronger, like you."

Hundreds of hands, many numb and bloody from the fighting, grabbed at him. Azure touched as many as he could, and he progressed through them. Eventually, he came to General Eridanus, who saluted him and eventually came in for a hug as well. "We did it, son," he said. "What's more: we're on the right side of history." These words comforted Azure, who nodded.

Azure came upon the charred bodies of Delano and Glaucon and he sat between them. "I'm sorry, old fool," he said. "I'm sorry, Chief. Can you ever forgive me?"

Azure teleported down into the tunnel and stood by Odhran's body. He shook his head. "I hope you get to see your dad again. Sleep peacefully, Odhran."

Finally, he made his way to the last person he was dying to see. "Autumn!" he called.

Autumn summoned a hoverboard and used it as a walker to meet Azure. "Azure!" she cried as she caught sight of him. Azure picked up speed and embraced her. "I knew you'd come," she said. "I knew."

"Thank you, kiddo," he said. "Thank you for believing in me. Thank you for not giving up on me. I'm sorry. I'm sorry. I'm so sorry."

"What are you sorry about, silly? You killed that big, huge Dragon lord! You saved us!"

"I should've done more. I should've done it sooner. You and Edom got hurt. Delano and Glaucon got killed. A lot of people..."

"Hey," she stroked his face. Her big green eyes comforted him. "Look at me, Azure... It is what it is. You did what you had to do. You did all you could in my eyes. You're a hero, Azure. A hero. And what's more, you're *my* hero and I'm proud of you." She kissed him on the cheek as tears ran down them.

"I'm proud of you too, kiddo," he hugged her tighter. "You are one scrappy little gal."

Autumn giggled. "You're crushing me."

"I-I-I'm sorry!" Azure withdrew.

"So, what now? Is it over?"

"A Dragon lord and his armies are still attacking the Cosmic Wall in the Deep Core. The Dragon Queen, Ain, is still out there. And your father... he's still out there too."

"What? My-my dad? He survived the destruction of Hod?"

"He abandoned everyone, and now he's alone. Alone with his thoughts. Alone with his guilt. He's lost just about everything important to him."

"I see..."

Azure knelt and looked at the gunshot wound on her leg. He kissed it. "There, all better," he said.

"My dad used to do that," said Autumn. "He used to always give my 'ouchies' a kiss and say that exact same thing." Suddenly, Autumn realized that all the pain in her leg was gone. When she looked down, the wound itself and all the stitching was gone as well. "Oh, my gosh, no freakin' way!"

"Kiddo, I want you to come to the surface with me. I want to show you something."

On the surface, the stench of death and smoke was still strong. Millions of tons of rubble were hidden by the darkness. Like prehistoric people, the Malkuthians lit torches and lamps to be able to see. Azure raised the Sword of Heaven, which illuminated the area around him like a lighthouse on the stormy sea. A crowd rushed to him, chanting and cheering. But there were still some who were crying and mourning. Autumn retreated behind Azure and tucked herself under his arm like a baby chick under its mother's wing. Azure waved the sword as though it were a wand. Just then, the building began to rapidly rebuild themselves out of the rubble. People who were in the way of the reconstruction were gently moved out of the way. The people gasped with astonishment as the entire city appeared to be rebuilt in under a minute.

"Wow! So freakin' cool!" Autumn exclaimed, laughing with delight as she leaned against him.

The wounded, including Edom, were healed. Food and water appeared for everyone. Even diapers and blankets appeared for the surviving mothers and their babies. Athena, Aphrodite, and Thor looked on amused by this display of power and charity.

However, the bodies of well over a million people still lay in neat rows lined up along the roads. A Preservation spell was placed over them to keep them from decaying any further.

There were cries from the crowd:

"Bring them back too!"

"My son!"

"My wife!"

"My husband!"

"My brother!"

"My family!"

"My daughter!"

"My baby!"

"Please, Ramatkal!"

Azure shut his eyes tightly and shook his head.

"Azure, what's the matter?" asked Autumn. "You can't raise the dead?"

"The consequences are more than I can bear," said Azure. "I cannot raise your loved ones from the dead, I'm sorry," he explained to the crowd. In that moment, many went from joyful to angry and demanding. They berated him as he walked away, eventually teleporting with Autumn back to the tunnels.

"Azure… I think I understand," said Autumn. "What you did was incredible, and it's incredibly ungrateful of them to demand that of you."

"It's not their fault. I don't blame them. They've all lost someone. Like you. Like me. We all want it back."

"You said the cost was too great… If you don't mind me asking, what's the cost for raising the dead?"

"...The living…" said Azure. "If I bring back someone's daughter, it might mean the mother or brother will have to die. If I want to bring back Neela, it might mean sacrificing you."

Autumn gasped and retreated back. "What?"

"I can't… And she wouldn't want that anyway. It would make her complicit in murder, and I could never do that to her. Look at me… I have the potential for unlimited power, and yet using it is a burden I'm struggling to bear. Everything good I do here will take its toll somewhere else. It's like dropping a rock in the ocean."

"Displacement," said Autumn. "You could drop an ice shelf off of one continent and create a tidal wave on another. It's a zero-sum game."

"Yes, exactly. So, this is why God is the way he is…"

"Leaders have to make tough decisions, Azure. As much as I rag on my dad, he helped to keep the Union together for hundreds of years and built a military that could hold off the Dragons for this long. Everyone wanted him to divert more funds toward poor neighborhoods, but my dad would say it'd only encourage generations to be stuck there and never make an effort to climb out. I'm not saying he was right, but… the truth is sometimes very ugly and very inconvenient. The truth doesn't care about how we feel. It just is what it is. My dad invested in the military because the military meant security. Without security, everything else would fall apart. You're choosing to not use your powers for a seemingly reputable cause because you know that there's more to it than just waving your hand and making everything fine-and-dandy. You know that there are profound costs and consequences. You're doing the responsible thing."

"But if you died... what would you have me do?"

"I believe that Heaven is full of moon pups, and I'd be pretty mad that you took me away from all of them. Heheh..." Autumn smiled.

Azure's eyes and lips rose slightly. "Neela's haunting us," he said.

"You mean like a ghost?"

"Yeah, in a sense... I can still feel a familiar part of her around."

Autumn leaned on him and hugged him. "So, ghosts exist... I always thought they were like people trapped in a parallel universe or another dimension just passing through."

"All things have a spiritual essence, and the essence travels and changes like water to vapor to snow to ice. They're all still water. Likewise, there's still a part of the person left. I can sense her, but it's like she's in two pieces. It's strange."

"Is she in pain?"

"No. She's at peace."

"Hey, Azure... "

"What's up, kiddo?"

"Is my mom out there somewhere too? Do you know? Do you think I can talk to her?"

"She's sleeping. Give it 14 years."

"Why 14?"

"Something's going to happen that'll wake her soul." Azure took both her hands and clasped them together as if in prayer. "Then, you can talk to her landlord anytime you want. That's a start."

"AZURE .VS. MORTIMER"

Lord Mortimer had all but obliterated the Cosmic Wall in the Deep Core, but his armies were heavily engaged with Angels and could not readily proceed with the invasion of Heaven. The Angels Uriel and Raphael specifically targeted Mortimer's orb. Growing annoyed, he activated its power, blowing them light-years away. "AWAY WITH YOU, PUNY FLIES!" said Mortimer.

Azure's cosmic body made its way to confront Mortimer, teleporting within striking distance of him, but Loki intercepted him. "Ehem, *excusez moi*. Need I remind you that you absorbed only enough energy to defeat Lord Zeon, and you've more than done that. Are you going to rush into battle with another Dragon lord at half strength?"

"I absorbed Lord Zeon's strongest attack."

"Yes, but this is Lord Mortimer we're dealing with now, the doom of Odin and Surtur. His brute-force power may not be as great as Zeon's but his magic skills are second only to yours truly. He's a dangerous foe, especially to you at half strength. Take the energy of these galaxies…" Loki opened portals to over a hundred different galaxies.

"I don't want to kill anymore."

"Ohoho, no worries, dearie. These are uninhabited, save for some bacteria and the like. Think of it as… washing your hands."

Azure again relented and drained the galaxies of their energy.

This didn't go without notice from Lord Mortimer who was astonished by the sight of another colossal being who now glowed like a thousand supernovae. "DON'T TELL ME…" said Mortimer. "YOU'RE THE ONE WHO DEFEATED LORD ZEON. I MUST SAY I'M IMPRESSED…"

"You should be terrified," said Azure.

"LORD ZEON RELIED TOO HEAVILY ON HIS RAW POWER. I FEAR NO ONE BUT THE GOD-QUEEN. SHE HAS ENDOWED ME WITH ABILITIES BEYOND YOUR WILDEST IMAGINATIONS."

"I'll crush you." Azure concentrated on eliminating the enemy Dragons with a thought. This worked to some extent, but Mortimer conjured a Mystic Shield the size of six solar systems that blocked the influence of Azure's spell.

"HAHAHAHAHAAA! AMATEUR. DID LOKI TEACH YOU THAT?"

Azure teleported forward and slashed his sword at the massive serpent, but the blade passed through Mortimer harmlessly. Mortimer teleported behind him and hit him with a Gravity spell that crushed him like the weight of a hundred suns. Stunned by this, Azure fought to escape the path of the attack like a drowning swimmer from a rip current. "I'll kill you!" Azure howled, firing off Qi attacks as thick and powerful as Zeon's heads. Mortimer's serpentine body twisted and turned through space, avoiding them.

"WHAT DO YOU FEAR? I WONDER..." Mortimer conjured up a dozen centipedes as long as he was, thicker than moons, that slithered toward him. Azure frantically fired Qi at them all, trying to keep them at bay, but Mortimer had cast a Mystic Shield on each of them. Azure retreated back.

Azure's avatar back on Malkuth jumped back and began to hug itself, experiencing the terror that his cosmic form was experiencing.

"Are you ok, Azure?" asked Autumn.

"My *real self* is fighting the Dragon lord in the Deep Core. He conjured giant, long bugs."

"Wait, what? You mean like you can be in multiple places all at the same time? Holy moly. What the heck?"

"They're so big... so many... legs... no eyes..." he shivered.

Autumn rubbed his back. "Azure, close your eyes and breathe. Slow and controlled. Count with me... 1... 2... 3.... 4...."

"5... 6..." Azure counted, facing down the zig-zagging swarm of giant centipedes, and fighting to think clearly. He formed planet-sized containment fields and trapped them all inside of them. He then started to crush the containment fields. "7... 8..."

Mortimer teleported behind him and wrapped his body around Azure's, beginning to constrict him like a snake. He bit into Azure's neck and began to drain energy from him. Azure teleported away, but Mortimer simply teleported with him and repeated the process. The bright white glow from the Deep Core tempted him. He reached out to it, considering siphoning energy from it, but then sensed something that changed his mind. "Neela?"

Azure diverted energy into his arms, and he pried Mortimer's jaws away. He fired a Qi blast from his mouth directly at Mortimer's orb and knocked it out of his hand. Mortimer left Azure to retrieve it, and just as he was distracted, Azure came down with his sword and cut the great serpent into pieces. Mortimer's head and neck, gasping, crashed upon the remnants of the Cosmic Wall.

Before Azure could act, Loki appeared near Lord Mortimer's head. "Well, well, well, behold the supposed 'god of all magic,'" said Loki, "the conqueror and destroyer of Asgard."

Mortimer grit his teeth angrily.

"Fuckethed art thou who fuckethed with me!" Cackling, Loki revealed a sharp end to his Elder Staff and plunged it into Mortimer's head as his body wiggled and twitched. He began to drain the remaining energy from the Dragon lord.

As the surviving Dragons attempted to intervene, Azure wished them out of existence. Mortimer's body turned to dust. Loki had grown and now glowed with newfound power of his own.

Azure's avatar fell back against the wall of the tunnel, appearing exhausted. "I beat him," he said.

"Hooray! Whoohooo!" Autumn cheered, jumping up and down on her now-healthy leg. "We should announce it to everyone. Oh, we should show 'em the footage!"

"Yeah… we should. But please don't show them what happens after."

The Demons led by Samael retreated from the Gates of Heaven, back into the realm of the Earth. They'd sensed the defeat of Lord Mortimer, Lord Zeon, and the Dragon armies. They'd also been overwhelmed themselves. Satan glanced back angrily at Michael who stood firmly in front of the gate at the head of the heavenly host. Satan hurled a dart, which Michael caught.

"He will bow to me and worship me, or I will kill him!" Satan shouted. "I will make him bleed! I will make him suffer! You will hear his screams even here!"

"The Lord, our God, is not deaf to the suffering or the dying," said Michael. "You may kill the body, but you are nothing to the soul, Samael. He will fulfill his plan and his word."

"And the Lord of Hosts shall reign forever and ever," said Ariel, another Arch-Angel, wielding an ethereal axe.

"Amen," the Angel Gabriel concluded.

"WEDDING?"

Loki continued to marvel at his newfound powers. He hurled fireballs the size of asteroids all around and began to juggle them.

"There was a soul so discontent
Who preyed upon the innocent…" he sang.

He opened a portal and coaxed his brother, Thor, through it. With him came Athena and Aphrodite. "Azure!" said Athena. "How could you allow this sociopath to absorb all of this power?"

"Brother," said Thor, "are you going to rebuild Asgard as you promised?"

"Heeeheeeheeeheeeehaaaaw! Do I lie, brother?" Loki aimed his staff at a nearby star and began to form a planet there, a new Asgard and a new Midgard. He changed his appearance to that of a male whose attractiveness rivaled Thor's. Even Aphrodite's eyes sparkled with interest. "And now… because I'm tired of sleeping with fucking disgusting Giantesses…" Loki surrounded Aphrodite in flowers and dressed her in the most elaborate and over-the-top wedding dress imaginable. He made one for Athena as well and placed himself and Thor in regal Aesir attire, the type reserved for special occasions. "Shall we have ourselves a great and glorious dual-wedding? OH, even better! An inter-racial dual-wedding!"

Athena assumed her cosmic form and grabbed Loki by the collar. "Listen to me, Loki… Your appearance may have changed but I know that you're ugly inside."

"And you, with the spirit of Malevant and Gigatheta both? Heeeheeeheee!"

Athena snapped his middle-finger. "Silence! I know you let your wife, Sigyn, suffer with you for 10,000 years only to die alone! I know that you only slept with your Giantesses to form abominations like Fenrir and Hel. You will not use my sister!"

"Oh, but Athena, aren't all creatures capable of having a change of heart?"

"You have no heart!"

"That's not true," said Azure. "It was brief, but I know that he regretted what happened to Sigyn. He mourned even. He'll never admit it."

"Uh… so, like, do I get a say in any of this?" asked Aphrodite. The others acknowledged. "You're like totally suuuuper hawt now but, like, what do you really want, Loki?"

"The same thing that you all want: a second chance at life, free of the Dragons. Second chance, second chance, cakes and flowers, a final dance."

"You *had* a second chance, Loki!" said Athena. "And a third, and a fourth, and a fifth—you're a scheming, untrustworthy snake, and you'll always be a scheming, untrustworthy snake!"

Loki pushed Athena away with a spell. Thor caught her. "Brother! Don't!"

Athena pushed Thor away and rocketed toward Loki. "I'll castrate you! I'll tear you apart!"

Aphrodite threw her body between Athena and Loki, and they both stopped to avoid hurting her. She turned to Loki and said, "I'll totally marry you as long as you, like, remake Olympus and Gaia too. And as long as you keep looking like that."

"Heeeeheeheee! You've got it, dearie."

"Sis!" Athena scolded. "Do you have any idea what you're doing?!"

"I've been, like, thinking…"

"You're supposed to leave the thinking to me!"

"I'm tired of being, like a third flute—"

"You mean 'third fiddle.'"

"Yes, like, a third fiddle. I'm, like a goddess, and a heroine too. I saw what Susanoo did. I want to, like, make a sacrifice. I want to be the one to, like, save our world."

"Not like this, sis."

Loki snapped his finger and a buffet of the most delectable food imaginable appeared before Athena. The Dragon in her was triggered and she began to scarf down food. "Don't think this changes anything, Loki!" said Athena, her mouth full of food.

Just then, another portal opened, and out of it came Samael-Satan and a collection of his battle-damaged Arch-Demons. "What great timing," said the devil. "It's almost as if it were meant to be."

"AZURE'S FATEFUL CHOICE"

"I don't remember inviting you, Sammy," said Loki. "Would you kindly see yourself out? Yes, thank you very much."

"Here I thought I'd be treated as a guest of honor, Loki. You're all forgetting one very big detail. Nothing you do matters so long as the Dragon Queen is alive to raise new armies. Any new world you attempt to build will be threatened with destruction."

"We're all much more powerful now, Samael," said Athena. "We can kill her."

"You have no idea... her power is second only to the God of gods. Now, with that said, I gave you all a little fetch quest to address this very problem. And I see you've succeeded." Samael faced Azure. "How are you feeling in your new body, Azure?"

"I should obliterate you."

"Oh, yes, perhaps you should. But I have a few things to get off my chest first. I'm sorry, Azure. I acted out in anger. I was intemperate and hasty in earlier days, and I'm sorry."

"I'll believe nothing you say."

"Oh? Well, you better. You think the God of gods really wants something as powerful and dangerous as you to challenge his power? Furthermore, I'm the only one here with your best interest in mind. I'm the only one here who is willing to tell you the truth. Don't you want to know the truth, Azure?"

Azure simply remained stern-faced.

"I know what you did. I know that all the Malkuthians are your seed, the seed of a rather embarrassing event in your younger years."

"Be quiet!"

"You became curious in your wandering and inseminated a hapless little creature... you became the father of a new race, a race of killers, thieves, rapists, and murderers. You, Azure. They all inherited it from you: the desire to dominate, and conquer, and kill. The desire to commit genocide on a scale rivaled only by the Dragons. That was you. Because of you."

"What do you want?"

"I just want to share some critical information before you make your next major decision. After all, the fate of your universe, and mine, are both equally at stake. The Dragon Queen, Ain, will want to come here eventually, and even you are no match for her in your present state. No, you would need to drain the energy from billions of universes to become nearly as powerful as her. 93% of the life in the cosmos, that's what you'd need."

"Why so much?"

"The God of gods slept for a Heaven's day from the expenditure of energy that formed her and began the cosmos as we know it. If you want to defeat her, it will cost just as much."

"I can't… I can still hear the screams of the people I've drained. I can still see their faces. I can see them turning to ashes."

"And what do you see in the future, Azure? What is the alternative?"

Azure saw Ain entering into New Heaven and destroying it, killing all Malkuthians. "Loki," said Azure. "Have you seen a future like that too? Where Ain destroys this universe?"

"I hate to admit it, but yes, oh yes, I've seen a future like this."

"I have an alternative for you, Azure," said Samael. "Look past this Cosmic Wall. Do you know what that is?"

"The back gate to Heaven," said Azure.

"Drain that instead. Go ahead. What good has God done for you? He left you. He abandoned you. He let Neela and everyone you loved and cared about to die, often horribly. Now it's his turn to feel the pain. Now it's his turn to suffer." Samael guided Azure's right arm toward the glowing white light. "Punish the tyrant! Take his throne and recreate the cosmos as you see fit! Set us all free."

"We're all free…" said Azure, lowering his hand. "That's precisely why we suffer. It's the price we pay. And it's a price worth paying."

"Azure… if we are truly free then why do tyrants like Antares and Ain rule over us? Why are we always beholden to the whims of fate?"

"There will always be tyrants. One replaces the next. It's the cyclical nature of power."

"But you're different, aren't you? When you recreate the cosmos, you'll rule it well. You won't let people suffer. You won't let people die. You'll provide for everyone richly, like a generous father. The people will never have to toil or work, ever. They'll always be happy!"

"But will they truly know happiness if they never know the alternative, if they never experience despair?"

"What a nihilist you are. The right answer is staring you right in the face. It's easy. Drain it. Erase the tyrant and take your place as the benevolent ruler of the cosmos. This is *good*."

Azure shook his head. "No, I feel her… I feel her in there…" Azure withdrew his hand again. "Neela's there. I feel it. I can't. I can't erase her."

"Neela's there? Are you sure it's her?"

"That essence I'm sensing, it's what I always sensed when I was with her. I couldn't miss it anywhere. That's her."

Samael looked downward, feigning sadness. "I didn't want to have to do this…" Samael opened another portal behind him and waved his hand forward. "Come now, show yourself." From the portal stepped a Demoness. The others parted to make way for her to walk. She was a magnificent sight even despite the bruises and scratches from the previous battle. "This is Terra, my wife. A former duchess in Heaven, now the Queen of Hell. She is talented in many ways, but her favorite hobby is impersonating people."

"No!" Athena shouted at Azure. "Don't listen to him! He's lying!"

"Like, it can't be…" said Aphrodite.

"You're lying, Satan!" Azure roared.

"Ask Aphrodite. She was with you both most of the time. Be my guest."

"Aphrodite, what's he talking about?" asked Azure.

"Like, when Susanoo and I were with you and Neela, we, like, always sensed a second being inside of Neela. Susanoo thought she was, like, Kami-possessed."

"It was the Symbiote. The thing living in her head! I'm not a fool!" Azure shouted at Satan.

"Oh? Then use your incredible intellect and riddle me the following: where were her biological mother and father? Did you ever see them in person?"

"No…"

"Azure!" Athena urged. "Neela was real! She was a real person who truly loved you! Don't listen to him!"

"If that were true, then where is the body?" said Satan. "I don't see one here or there or anywhere. And did you two ever argue? No? What couple always gets along? What couple never fights? Don't you think any of that was just too good to be true?"

Terra transformed herself into Neela and smiled at him. "Hello, Azure. I missed you," she said, touching him on the face as he cried. "It's ok, don't cry. I'm not hurting anymore. I'm not in pain anymore."

"You're not real…"

"I *can* be real, and I can be at your side forever. We can have kids. We can have a palace and a castle the size of a star. We can rule the world—no, the cosmos—together. King and queen. You and me. There can be no happier ending than that. Just do this one last thing for me… end the age of the tyrants. Drain it. Set us all free."

Azure reached out to the heavenly light. "We can do it together, you see?" Terra-Neela guided his arm and interlocked her hand with his. "It's not so big and scary now, is it?"

"I've seen this… I've seen the light from this drain away and everyone dies. Everyone! Heaven is the root of the tree. Killing it kills everyone."

"Don't worry, it's no big deal. You can recreate it. We can start anew."

Azure pulled away from Terra-Neela. "Neela would never want that to happen. You're a sham, and I see right through you."

"Why are you saying such mean things to me, Azure?" Terra-Neela reached out for him. "Come back! I love you! Don't you love me?"

"Go away, Terra!" Azure cried. "Whatever you are… whoever you are… you're not her…"

"Regardless of how you feel, Azure," said Satan. "The Dragon Queen will come here and erase everything you know and love. Even your precious little Autumn Antares. You are not powerful enough. You have to drain something if you want to stand a chance!"

Azure looked to Athena and Loki who nodded. "I hate to admit it, but Sam-I-Am is right," said Loki.

"Yes," said Athena. "It's a necessary evil."

Azure shut his eyes and tried to escape to a simpler time.

… … …

"You want some, Azure?" said Neela, holding up the tub of ice cream.

"N-no th-th-thank you," he said with his block of cheese.

"Shucks, you're missing out! It's cookies & cream. There's nothing better. You've got a little bit of vanilla and a little bit of chocolate cookie bits all mixed in together. Perfect imperfection."

"H-huh?"

"Perfect imperfection... I'm saying it's impure. Sometimes the best things are impure. Plain vanilla is so creamy and smooth, but it's also really boring. There's something about those added chocolate cookie bits. It's rougher, it's coarser, it's sweeter, it's darker." Neela took a huge spoonful to the head. "Ooh, and it's so good! There's something about that little bit of darkness. That little something different. That variety. I think it's kinda like us, you know? We're not perfect. We're not pure. But it's ok, you know? It's that little bit of darkness that lets us do more and become who we are. It lets us be a little naughty, a little mischievous, or even a little stoic when the going gets tough. It lets us take a chance on things, you know?"

... ...

"...you knew it was wrong." said Azure to Edom.

"Right and wrong are perspectives, Big Blue. We gotta do what we gotta do. It's a job. It's a business. It's nothing personal, you know? If God wants to stop us, I'm sure he will.

... ...

"Do it, Azure!" Satan demanded. "Take all the power! Become the most powerful being in all the cosmos! Make everything right!"

... ...

"Ain't you even listening to a word I said?" said Edom. "God puts us where we need to be. Ain't no room for regretting it. Your motives be right. Your conscience be clear."

... ...

"Azure, you have no other choice!" Athena urged. "Do it! Do it quickly!

... ...

"Leaders have to make tough decisions, Azure," said Autumn.

… … …

"Azure," said Jesus. "That's what the kings before me did and all of them failed."

"Being captured and killed by the enemy is failing," said Azure.

"No. In time, the belief in me will conquer even this great and powerful Roman Empire. And in time, just as they embrace these beliefs, Satan will discard the empire like an old toy. It will fall like all human kingdoms before it. I will not have lifted a sword, yet it will come to pass."

"I don't have that luxury. I'm forced to fight. I'm forced to kill. If you send me enemies, I will slaughter them all until their bodies pile up to the sky!"

"And who is your enemy, Azure? Is it Antares? Is it the Dragons? Is it Ain? And when they're all gone, will everything truly be right?"

"I'll make it right."

"All kings say that. I was not intended by my father to be such a king."

"...I'm not like you. I won't become like you! You're weak! I'm strong. I'm powerful. I can fight this! I'll save this universe! I'll make it great! I'll make my own heaven where no one will need to die anymore! No one will need to suffer!"

"So be it. Azure… I leave you with this for now: what's happening isn't just a war for your power, it's a war for your conscience. It always has been. It always will be. Don't let anyone tell you differently. I say this not to brag but to inform: I have laid down my divinity, my crown, my power, and my life for others. Others have clung to those things selfishly. Who will you listen to? Who will you trust?"

"I want to decide that for myself."

… … …

"Da ba dee da ba daa…" Loki sang. "The choice is easy. Da ba dee da ba daa."

… … …

"It's ok. It's ok. It's ok, Azure," said Neela. "Life's just that way sometimes. It's like you said, there's a 'transience' to things. The highs and lows. The ebbs and flows. Like the weather. Like the tide. Ever changing. Ever moving. On and on and on it goes."

"THE GREAT DYING"

Azure outstretched his arms and wings as he began to siphon energy from billions of universes. The stars disappeared. The nebulae blackened. Plants and vegetation withered away. The waters dried up. Planets turned to nothingness. The screams of the dying reached him.

Azure's avatar on Malkuth began to thrash and scream as the guilt consumed him. Autumn summoned her suit and clinched him, holding him as tight as she could. "Azure! It's ok! It's ok!"

"So much death… so much suffering… I can't stop… I can't slow down… I need to keep going!"

"How much are you taking?"

"71…71%."

"But I thought you needed 93% to kill the Dragon Queen?"

"I'll only take what I need to hold her off…" Azure placed his hands on her upper-arms and looked her in the eyes. "Kiddo, forgive me. Please."

It was the deadliest single hour in the history of the Omniverse, and at the center of it all stood Azure.

The deities berated him.

"You were supposed to take more!" said Samael.

"Why stoppy now?" said Loki. "With just a little more energy, you could blink the Queen out of existence!"

"Azure, what are you doing?!" said Athena.

"I've taken the minimum amount of energy I need to hold off Ain. No more, no less. She can't kill me, and I've starved her of most of her food. I need only to survive the fight."

"You fool!" said Samael. "At this level, you'll be fighting her for decades or centuries! Who knows what death and destruction she could wreak in that time!"

"Why do you care? You nearly had me destroy your universe and your Earth. But I saw how populated it is. You didn't care a moment ago. I believe you don't care about anyone but yourself, Samael. You never did."

Samael opened another portal and walked toward it. "I can see now that things between us will never work out." Just then, he turned and hurled a dart at Azure's head, striking him there like he did all those years before.

But this time, Azure was unaffected and unfazed. "You think that'll work this time?" he said. He tore open several portals in space-time and tore Samael into several different versions of himself. He then pushed them all into separate portals.

Suddenly, Athena came down from behind Azure and plunged the Black Sword into his back! "Athena!" he exclaimed.

"If you won't use that power, then I will!" said Athena.

"Sis, like, what the hell are you doing?!" said Aphrodite. "Stop it!"

Loki teleported under Azure's stomach and stabbed him with the end of the Elder Staff. "Time to pay the bank!" said Loki.

"Have the two of you, like, totally lost your minds?!" said Aphrodite. "We need to work together!"

As Azure felt the sting of these twin betrayals, he realized that Jesus had been right. The ultimate war had always been for his conscience, and all his life had prepared him for this moment. Azure's body absorbed the energy from the Black Sword and the Elder Staff as their wielders howled in shock and anger at having lost their cosmic powers. He thrashed and sent Athena and Loki some distance away. "You two allowed these new powers to change you, to warp who you really were," said Azure. "This Omniverse requires a mixture of both chaos and order. Darkness along with the light. If the son chooses to represent Heaven's mercy, then I choose to represent its wrath, justly dealt."

Azure opened a multitude of portals to various alternate timelines and separated Athena, Loki, Aphrodite, and Thor into various different versions of themselves.

"Like, wait, why me?!" Aphrodite's original body protested. "I totally didn't do anything!"

"Don't be afraid, Aphrodite. I don't intend to punish any of you. Think of this as you getting exactly what you deserve."

"Don't be hasty now!" said Loki.

"Azure, you're not thinking clearly!" said Athena.

"Good luck to you all, and take care," said Azure, pushing them just gently enough to have them fall into the portals. "I hope you all find what you were looking for."

PART VI
WARPING REALITY

"ATHENA'S TIMELINES"

Athena found herself in her old temple on Gaia. She looked up at the giant statue of herself with a strange mixture of pride and guilt. Such statues had inspired General Malevant to build statues in his likeness, and it represented a time in her life when she and the other Olympians felt untouchable. Behind the feet of the statue sat Terra, the Demoness. "You!" Athena shouted.

Terra sneered at her, raising her cup and saying, "Cheers, darling."

Before Athena could attack, she heard the shrieking screams of a human woman. It was the Priestess Medusa being held down by Poseidon on her altar. Athena remembered this event. She remembered not being willing to act, not being willing to confront her uncle from committing such a deplorable, abhorrent act. She remembered that rather than feel compassion for Medusa, she'd displaced her rage by transforming Medusa into the terrible snake-haired monster she'd become famous for.

However, something had changed in Athena. She remembered being dominated and abused by General Malevant, and those experiences had transformed her. Without another moment's hesitation, she ran to Medusa's aid and shoved Poseidon off of her.

"Athena!?! How dare you!" Poseidon shouted.

"How dare *you*! This is *my* temple, that is *my* altar, and she is *my* priestess! I forbid you from touching her ever again!"

"Forbid me by what authority? You're beneath me, Athena!"

"By the authority of basic decency," said Athena. "Are you going to fight me over that? There's nothing you can do to me that'll change my mind."

Poseidon raised his trident, looked at it, then lowered it after giving it a second thought. "As you wish, Athena, there are plenty of others," he said, turning his back and leaving, slamming the doors as he did.

Medusa clutched Athena's wrist and cried. Athena stroked her hair.

In another timeline, Athena prevented the rape of Cassandra in her temple in Troy, impaling the would-be assailant, Ajax the Lesser, with her spear. She fought off Apollo as he attempted to assault Daphne. She was even able to calm the uncontrolled rage of Odysseus upon his disloyal servant women, preventing their hanging following the deaths of the suitors.

Most fulfilling of all, Athena was also able to prevent the accidental death of her dearest friend, Pallas—a death that had haunted her all her life and made her afraid of forming attachments.

In yet another timeline, Athena found herself on Olympus. Her father, Zeus, hurled down lightning bolts on anyone who displeased him. He scouted the land for human women he desired. Sometimes, the victims of his lightning bolts were the husbands or suitors of these women. Hera, on the throne next to him, looked away, displeased, but too afraid to say so. Zeus handed her a crystal ball, saying, "Here's some entertainment for you."

The crystal ball played a scene in which Prometheus, bound to a rock, had his liver pecked out by an eagle for the thousandth day in a row. Zeus laughed, pointing out that the eagle had completed the deed quicker this time around and that he ought to tell the eagle to slow down.

"Do you not comprehend the pain you're causing, father?" said Athena.

A gasp went out through the throne room. Hera bolted up in her seat, looking around to find where the voice came from.

"What did you say, Athena?" asked Zeus.

"I said, do you even realize how much pain and suffering you're inflicting on others?"

Zeus looked to Hera, saying, "Can you believe what a mouth she's got on her?"

"She's right," said Hera.

"What? You damn hypocrite, Hera," said Zeus. "You've tormented my poor son, Hercules, for years!"

"Because he's the result of your incessant infidelity!" Hera shot back.

Zeus raised his hand to strike her, but Athena blocked his strike. After the initial shock of this, Zeus began to overpower her, but Hera joined in. They matched him. "Both of you should be punished for your insolence! I'll hang you both from the sky!"

The Black Sword pierced his back. Hades had done the deed. "It seemed like such a good time to pay you a visit, brother," he said with a wheezing voice. "Goodnight, little brother." Zeus's body vanished and Hades stood in his place, having absorbed his energy. Athena prepared her bow, prepared for a fight. "You can put that down," said Hades. "I came not to fight but to petition for my realm. I was fortunate to find him so distracted."

"What happens now?" said Athena.

"Your human students talk of something called 'democracy' don't they? They say it's a new way of doing things. I must say, it sounds appealing right now. I haven't the time to govern everything on my own. I want to enjoy my time with Persephone."

"You're not planning to plunge us all into an eternal winter, are you?" said Hera. "That edict and agreement with Demeter still stands."

"Of course," said Hades. "Call Demeter here, and Poseidon, Apollo, Ares, and the others. It's about time we discuss a new system of governance. Athena, as the wisest of us all, I'd like to make you the new regent of Olympus. I trust you'll rule fairly and justly in my stead." He conjured a golden tiara on a pillow. Athena grabbed it and placed it on her head.

Aphrodite and the other Olympians applauded.

"I swear I will," she said. *Azure, what have you done? This is too easy. Too easy.*

"LOKI'S TIMELINES"

Loki found himself in the royal court of the Asgardians including Thor, Sif, Heimdall, Tyr, Freyr, Hodr, and Baldur. He knew by the sight of them that this was surely before Ragnarok, before the arrival of the Dragons. He chuckled with glee until he realized what day this was: it was the day Baldur, the most beloved son of Odin and Frigg, would die.

Queen Frigg had asked everything living and non-living in all the realms to swear an oath not to harm Baldur, even the stones and the dirt. However, Loki had disguised himself and learned from Frigg that there was one thing that hadn't sworn this oath: mistletoe, which until this point had a tree of its own. Frigg had thought that mistletoe was too young to swear such an oath. *Oh, go figure! You are all so fucking stupid, I swear! This is why I should be in charge.* Loki had crafted an arrow from the mistletoe tree and given it to the blind god, Hodr.

Now, the Asgardian Aesir had a game they'd play that had become a court tradition. The game was to hurl different things at Baldur, testing his invulnerability. Even the sword of Tyr and Thor's hammer couldn't harm him. Loki had known this and snuck Hodr the mistletoe-laced arrow specifically for this reason.

Loki jumped into this timeline and watched as Hodr prepared to loose the arrow. Knowing the consequences of this action and its repercussions for millennia to come in a way even his clairvoyance had missed, Loki stopped the arrow just before it hit Baldur.

"Loki! What art thou doing?" Thor complained, pushing him aside. "Thou art spoiling the game for everyone. Get thee out of the way!"

"Don't you presume to push me, brother," said Loki, hitting him with a magical push.

"How dare you!" shouted Sif. "Thor will smash you like a bug, you stupid little imp!"

"I just saved dear Baldur's life," said Loki.

There was laughter throughout the court as it was still assumed that nothing could harm Baldur. Queen Frigg wandered out of the throne room, curious as to why everyone was laughing. She picked up the arrow and inspected it. "Loki is right," she said.

Everyone gasped.

"Aren't I always?" said Loki.

"If this arrow would have hit Baldur, he would surely have died. Loki, what's your game? It's not in your nature to act with such altruism."

"Heeeheeheeee… altruism? I'm just saving my own ass as always. I know what the death of Baldur would bring. A thing, a thing, an awful thing."

"Ragnarok…" said Odin, walking from the throne room. "The twilight of the gods. Loki, you have saved our beloved Baldur and possibly postponed our fated end."

"I can stop it," said Loki. "I can prevent Ragnarok. Fate and the Norns have no power here anymore. I have seen further than Mimir. Further even than you, great king."

"How is that possible?"

"Some gruesome details involving the eating of brains and tearing out my own eyes, it's not important right now. Just know… I can, I can, I am your man. In time, in time, you'll under-stand."

"You're acting funny, Loki," said Tyr. "I don't trust him."

"Here, here!" many of the others agreed.

"Wait," said Thor. He grabbed Loki by the upper arms and stared into his eyes. "I am not the sharpest tool in the outhouse, but I know thee, bother. Something has changed. Those eyes are not jealous nor hateful nor resentful eyes."

"Why, thank you for that acute observation, Nephew-Brother-Doctor Thor." Loki conjured a psychiatrist's couch and lay down on it, twiddling his thumbs and talking to the ceiling. "And then… when I was a little ole' icicle baby…" he said.

This managed to get a laugh out of everyone.

"Come now, 'tis time for the feast," said Odin. "You're free to join us, Loki."

Odin patted him on the back and went off to the dining hall with the others. Loki felt a great deal of satisfaction he was not accustomed to.

In another reality, Loki faced his daughter, Hel, and instead of petrifying her and taking over Helheim, he presented her a gift: a basket of golden apples from Yggdrasil. He also came to the Nether Realm that Fenrir was trapped in and transformed it into a more pleasant place. He even pet Fenrir.

In another reality, he found himself on the verge of cutting Sif's golden blonde hair as she slept, but stopped himself, knowing that story ended with him almost losing his head and his mouth sewn shut. Thor threw open the bedroom door and was shocked to find Loki. "What art thou doing, Loki?" Thor roared. "Why art thou here?"

"Why the bloody devil do you talk like that?… Anyway, I've taken up a hobby. Yes, yes, a hobby for hairdressing. I wanted to give your wife, Sif, a haircut as a gift. Yes, yes, because it's her birthday coming up, you see? Or did you forget?"

Thor looked down in embarrassment.

Loki shook his finger, "Naughty, naughty husband. You would have incurred the wrath of a woman had it not been for me. Have you even considered what you might get her?"

"Uh, no…"

"Well, why don't you ask the Dwarves! I know two families in particular who are the greatest craftsmen in all the realms. They'll do it for the price of some golden apples. Tell them to make three gifts each, and then award the title of "The Greatest Craftsman in All the Realms" to the winner! The other Aesir can be the judges. They could make, I don't know… a folding ship, a head of wicked-ass-locks, and a hammer, perhaps. What do you say?"

"Thou hath lost me, Loki. Say that again."

"Never mind, I'll explain it to them myself."

Sif, groggy, began to mumble, "What are you two dodo-heads doing talking so late at night? I'm trying to sleep!"

Loki and Thor apologized and backed away cautiously toward the door.

In another reality, Loki reunited with his wife, Sigyn, who toiled wringing out some clothes in a river. Loki waved his hand and the clothes hung on a line in the trees, all washed. Sigyn looked surprised to see him. "Such work is beneath you, dearie," said Loki. "Have you forgotten you're an Aesir?"

"Not after all the crimes you've committed, and all of the cheating you've done to create your abominations. I am disgraced. Have you come back just to mock your pitiful wife in her disgrace?"

"No," said Loki. "I've come to say… I'm sorry, sorry, very sorry. I can explain. I'll tell the story."

"What?"

"Did I st-st-stutter?"

"Well, you sang. That's usually how I know you're full of crap. What did you say? Tell me, in plain and simple words. No singing."

Loki rolled his eyes and sighed. "Fine. I'm sorry, dearie. I'm sorry for sleeping around with hideous creatures who are nowhere near as gorgeous as you."

"And?"

"I'm sorry for all the crimes I've committed that disgraced our family name and honor."

"And?"

"Dear goodness, woman, do you want my arms and legs too?"

"Keep going…"

"Ok, ok, I'm sorry for being a shitty husband and neglecting you all these years."

"And if it happens again?"

"I'll chop my own nuts off."

"You should leave me in charge of that."

"Fine. Deal." Loki extended his hand.

Sigyn looked at it, then knocked it away. She hugged him. Loki held his hands out to his sides, not knowing what to do. "Hug me back, you dummy," said Sigyn. "And get used to it."

Loki relented and embraced the wife who he now knew had been willing to suffer with him in the depths of Helheim for 10,000 years. "Say, did I ever tell you I cast a love spell on you a while back to achieve my goals?"

"Don't you dare ruin this moment for me!"

"Ok, ok, do what you say…"

"APHRODITE'S TIMELINES"

Aphrodite found herself next to her husband, Hephaestus, with some green grapes in her hands. They were all gathered around a great banquet hall with the nymph Thetis and the hero-king Peleus at the center, having just married.

The great door to the hall swung open and crashed against the nearby wall as if hurricane-force winds had blown it open. An angry female voice screeched into the hall: "Why the bloody fucking hell did no one bother to fucking tell me about this bloody fucking wedding?!"

Everyone knew: it was Eris, the goddess of discord.

"Listen to yourself, Eris!" said Dionysus.

"Shut the fuck up, you fucking drunk fucking cocksucking motherfucker! I'm older than most of you motherfucking cocksuckers! That means that ALL you motherfucking cocksuckers owe me an explanation. I should've been the FIRST person you fucking invited!"

Apollo covered his head, "Oh, here we go again. Why can I never predict when she'll show up?"

Ares stood and tried to guide her to the table. "Now, now, come on. Perhaps there's been a misunderstanding, Eris. We don't gotta fight a war over it or anything."

"Don't fucking try to fucking patronize me, you shit-stirring red-faced fuck!"

"Eris!" Zeus scolded. "That's quite enough out of you. The bride & groom are free to invite and not invite whomever they like. And, of course, as their king, I am free to make some alterations."

"Oh, I'm so fucking sorry, my lord, I'll try not to fucking throw up on your fucking shitty robes. Here's a shitty wedding gift I fucking found," Eris said, throwing a golden apple which rolled to the center of the table. "It's fucking special. May it go to the fairest of you all."

Eris left, slamming the door behind her.

"Hmmph," said Aphrodite, surprisingly going along with the moment despite knowing the outcome. She picked up the apple. "Like, she's clearly, totally talking about me, the sexiest of them all."

"Ehem, right…" Apollo cleared his throat. "Sexiest."

Athena snatched the apple from her. "Physical attractiveness is not the only determiner of fairness. You need wisdom, cunning, and intellect as well."

Hera snatched the apple from Athena. "Oh, is that so? Well, all of that pales in comparison to plain, old, good-fashioned power. As the Queen of the Olympians, I should claim this prize for myself."

"Nu-uh!" said Aphrodite, hastily covering her mouth, trying to hold back the impulse.

Poor Thetis sat silent at her own wedding party, not even vouching for her own wedding gift. She was still humiliated by all that had gone on before this to coax her to marry Peleus.

As Hera walked away with the apple, Athena swiped it from her. "The nerve of you!" said Hera.

"Let Zeus decide," said Athena, taking off her helmet. "My lord, who would you say is the fairest between me, Aphrodite, and Hera? I, of course, am the wisest and the most balanced in brains and brawn. Aphrodite here is beautiful, yes, but is lacking in other key areas."

"Heya!" Aphrodite objected. *You were such a titanic bitch back then, sis.*

"And Hera, while your wife and Queen, is not exactly a looker nor is she a fighter."

Zeus laughed. Hera elbowed him. He shrugged. "What? Fine. I'm not going to be the judge in this petty little squabble. I'll find someone else to judge this… hmm… I've got it! An impartial human prince from a foreign land! He has already seen Olympians before, it will not frighten him." He brought Athena, Aphrodite, and Hera to a meadow. There, a Trojan prince named Paris was practicing his archery and doing rather poorly at it.

"Oh, Uranus, save us," said Athena, rolling her eyes. "You're holding the bow upside down!" Prince Paris was embarrassed by this and blushed, correcting his mistake. "Please tell me you're not letting this scrawny dumbass judge us, dad." Zeus was nowhere to be found. "Dad?"

"Zeus!" Hera called.

"Hell-oooo?" Aphrodite called. "Ohhh, like, let's just get this over with. Hey, Prince Paris, who'd you say is, like, the fairest of the three of us? Like, clearly, I'm the hottest, right?"

Athena and Hera made similar appeals as they had at the banquet hall.

Hera then cheated by offering to make Paris "the ruler of a great kingdom" if he awarded her the victory.

Athena responded by offering Paris "wisdom and victory in battle" if he chose her.

Aphrodite was next, and everyone stared a hole into her. She remembered her mistake in her original timeline and never wanted to make it again. "Like...I totally got nothing."

"Well, then, I guess it's settled," said Paris. He brandished the Apple of Discord and handed it to Hera. "Make me the ruler of a great kingdom, Queen of Olympus."

"Gladly," said Hera, taking a bite of the apple.

Athena and Aphrodite looked on with envy. But Aphrodite caught herself and convinced herself she'd made the right choice.

In the coming months, Prince Hector, Paris's older brother and heir to the throne of Troy, died under mysterious circumstances. King Priam was also killed, quite obviously poisoned by Paris, who was losing his sanity. Paris was made king. He was a blundering and incompetent king who managed to upset both the Greeks and his own people. Paranoid and xenophobic, Paris had an arrow-launching contraption built to fire upon any approaching ships who could not be identified as Trojan. This resulted in them firing upon a Greek ship seeking shelter following a storm. The Trojans then killed all on board. When the Greeks invaded, triggering a new Trojan War anyway, Troy was greatly weakened by its own corrupt king, who had executed or imprisoned his best military leaders. Its only saving grace was having the famed walls built by Poseidon, but Odysseus had a plan for that.

Troy still burned, and thousands still died, but at least Aphrodite's hands were clean. Hera had grown as mad as Paris after the pageant and consuming the apple, becoming a tyrant in her own right whom not even Zeus would dare not question. Hercules was killed, as were many of Zeus's illegitimate children. Aphrodite did her best to stay far away from the seat of power and not get involved.

In a separate timeline, Aphrodite brought Cupid and Psyche together rather than opposing their union as she had in the past.

In another scenario, Aphrodite watched over Aeneas of Troy. Aeneas and his Trojan soldiers wandered after their defeat at the hands of the Greeks. She guided Aeneas to Carthage, the domain of the widowed queen, Dido. The two fell madly in love with Aphrodite's help, and in this scenario, Zeus did not demand that Aeneas leave Carthage to found his new home (which would become Rome). Hermes, the messenger, simply asked Aphrodite what her evaluation of the situation was. The onus fell on Aphrodite herself. "It's, like, perfect the way it is," she said, knowing that Aeneas's descendants would become a conquering people akin to the Dragons she'd suffered under. "Like, tell dad I think we should totally just let them settle down."

"Of course you'd say that," said Hermes.

"Ok, ok, like… tell him I think we'd cause a lot less damage this way. We don't need, like, more humans conquering other humans. How can they, like, stop to worship us if they're always killing each other?"

Still, despite this, Zeus intervened and killed Dido himself as Aphrodite and Aeneas looked on in horror. He then forced Aeneas on his journey by ravishing Carthage with a storm. But at least Aphrodite's hands were clean.

In a final timeline, Aphrodite's husband, Hephaestus, traveled to the underworld to retrieve some exotic metals to craft weapons with. He got stranded there after eating the food there and spent his time there crafting weapons for Hades and his growing army of the dead. In his absence, Aphrodite began an uninterrupted affair with the greatest of her loves, Ares, the god of war. He even taught her to fight, and even Athena was impressed. Athena and Aphrodite would often spar with Aphrodite holding her own. When the army of the dead led by Hades came to take over Olympus, Aphrodite, Ares, and Athena worked together to combat them and eventually win. The three eventually overthrew Zeus himself and Aphrodite became queen beside her new husband, Ares. They even made the underworld more hospitable for Hephaestus and the others stuck there with Azure's help.

"SAMAEL'S TIMELINES"

Samael sat on a great throne in a room that burned with unearthly flames. Believing that his grand desire had been fulfilled, he began to celebrate, boasting: "I have ascended to the throne of Heaven! I have ascended about the stars and the clouds! I have become like the Most High!"

Rapidly, the golden light around him turned to darkness, and the throne itself disappeared. He began to feel the energy being sucked from him. He experienced a feeling similar to hunger and thirst. Still, he celebrated his apparent victory, ignoring even his diminishing state. Then, he heard voices behind him and around him. Red eyes stared through the darkness. Samael recognized them. These were his followers, the ones who'd fought for him. They looked sick and emaciated. They begged him to help them, but he couldn't, and he wouldn't. "Help yourselves!" Samael shouted. "Must I do everything for everyone?"

"You promised us!" General Moloch cried.

"You said you'd be better than the tyrant!" said General Mammon. "At least the tyrant fed us!"

Samael heard an angry growl behind him, but before he could react, a dagger pierced his back. He turned, wide-eyed, and saw Be'elzebul there. "Be'elzebul?" he stroked his face. "Not you... Not you!"

"I'm sick of the lies, Samael. I'm sick of you saying you care about us when the only one you care about is yourself!" Be'elzebul shouted at him, twisting the dagger.

Another dagger pierced Samael. This time, it was Terra's. "Azure showed me what you were going to do to me, Samael! He showed me my city burning at your hands! He showed me my statues destroyed and replaced by your son's!"

"You useless bitch!" Samael shoved her away, but she came again and stabbed him. More daggers stabbed him again and again. "You're all ungrateful! I was to become a god! None of you deserve to be in the presence of my splendor!"

Be'elzebul stabbed him in the back of the head, and Terra stabbed him again in the chest. They all deteriorated like wilting leaves in a flame.

"Samael," said Azure. "With your dart, you sentenced me to a life of meandering and confusion. I would forget who I was. I would forget my very purpose. You tried to take meaning from my life, to render it futile. Now, I give you justice: to see and experience what will be, to know your fate and that of your son."

"THE END OF THE EARTH"

In a separate timeline, Samael watched a handsome young politician named Hod Emmanuel Romiti. Romiti was hiking uphill with his beautiful girlfriend, Carna, debating the afterlife. "And what happens to the billions of people who die without believing in Christ or whatever?" she said. "What happens to Atheists like me? Or you? Or like 99% of the people in China and India? You don't believe in that shit, right? I mean, we're not bad people. We don't deserve to go to Hell just because we don't believe exactly what the Christians do. That's bullshit."

"Yeah," Romiti agreed. "If I was their God, things would be a lot different, believe me."

"Well, if you were God, I might not believe in you at all," Carna smiled.

Romiti chuckled. "Right. But at least I'd have the ability to make things right."

"Ah, 'Hod the god,' has a nice ring to it."

The two came to the peak overlooking the city of Rome. Just as the sun was beginning to set. "Would you look at that…" said Carna. When she turned, she found Romiti holding out a box with a ring in it. "What's this, Hod?"

"What do you think? I want you to marry me. I want us to take on the world together."

Carna nodded with tears in her eyes, hugging him.

"Let me tell you about this place," said Romiti. "I was led here as a teenager, led here by a voice that kept calling me. It called to me all of my life. It said, 'Hod Emmanuel Romiti, you will be the greatest of men. You will do what Alexander, Napoleon, Hitler, Ghenghis Khan, and all the others failed to do: you will conquer the entire Earth.'"

"Hod… you're starting to scare me…"

"Don't be scared. Just listen. The voice was that of an Angel named Jibril. He said that as long as I bowed down to him, I could rule the whole world in his place."

"And did you?"

"I did. And afterwards, through all my schooling and my political career, I have never failed. My destiny is to rule this world and lead it into a new age. I want you to rule it with me."

"Rule the world? Don't you think that sounds a little crazy."

"You've seen my magic, haven't you? You've seen all I can do. You've seen me win again and again. I've never failed. I can never fail."

"You're still human."

"I shouldn't be. I should be more than that. I should be a god, and you should be my goddess, Carna. There would be no more nations or kingdoms, only one nation, one kingdom. There would be no more division between religions, only one religion, our religion."

"I'd rather do away with religion altogether, Hod."

"Ok, maybe we can work that out. But for now… now you know my secret. My deep dark secret. What do you think of me now?"

"…Hod, I don't know. You sound a little… crazy…" Carna hugged herself and walked down the hill, still wearing the ring.

"Don't turn your back to me, Carna!" Carna began to walk faster, beginning to cry. "Come back here now!"

Carna took off her ring and threw it at him. Carna lost her footing. She fell, tumbling down the hill. She hit her head on a stone at the bottom. "Carna!?" Romiti climbed down the hill. "Carna! Carna, are you alright? Carna!"

Samael laughed.

As Romiti got to Carna, he saw that her eyes were still open. She was dead. Her words echoed in his head, *"What happens to Atheists like me?"* Those words haunted him for the rest of his life.

"Will she go to Hell, father?" Romiti asked Samael.

"Why, yes, of course she will. Unless we win."

"You swear to me you're telling the truth?"

"I swear upon the ground upon which you stand, son."

"This is my fault. My pride. My arrogance."

"It's natural for someone as successful as you to have such traits. It is not to your detriment. It is your strength. But consider this: if it is your fault, then only you can make it right, right?"

"What do I do, father? What do I do?"

"Exactly what I tell you," said Samael.

At her funeral, Romiti's version of Carna's death was far different. He claimed that he had grabbed her as she began to fall, but that her hand slipped from his, leaving him only with her ring. "We will be married forever nonetheless. Even death cannot part us," he said. "I will dedicate the rest of my life to realizing our dream, the dream of a united world."

The media ate up this tragic and romantic story. Hod Emmanuel Romiti was not just popular with the people, now he had their sympathy. By his 30s, he was already the secretary general of the world's most powerful intergovernmental organization.

For a while, the world improved. There was less war, less poverty, and less starvation. It seemed like Romiti had worked a miracle. There was a new global religion and a new global government supposedly built on the principle of "Equality for All!" But "All" did not include Romiti or his elites who were above the law of any country. But few fought it. It was like the world was under a spell, entranced by this charismatic leader. Whatever he said had to be true. Whatever he ordered had to be obeyed. What's more: whatever his enemies said was wrong. Not only was it wrong, it was paramount to blasphemy in the general public's eyes.

Romiti even managed to do the seemingly impossible: secure a seven-year peace treaty between Israel, the Palestinians, and most of the Arab powers overseen by his Global Union. The Middle East actually enjoyed a period of relative peace. No shots were fired and no bombs exploded for months. Then, an explosion destroyed the Dome of the Rock. Peace in the Middle East was lost in a single instant. Israel was attacked by a hastily thrown-together collection of its enemies. However, the attack failed miserably. Their jets, missiles, and bombers exploded in the sky. Their tanks stalled at the border. God had saved the nation of Israel from certain destruction, but Romiti claimed that his defenses were responsible. He claimed that his anti-aircraft missiles knocked the enemy out of the sky and that an EMP pulse had taken out the tanks.

Israel's enemies and their powerful funders were infuriated, and the world took sides in a growing world-wide conflict.

Three separate governments formed a coalition to resist the Global Union. A world war ignited, eventually becoming a nuclear war that resulted in 1.2 billion deaths. Romiti and the Global Union stood victorious. However, the remainder of the population was in for much worse. A famine followed, which even Romiti failed to adequately address.

A range of supernatural plagues rained down on the Earth. A global earthquake ravished the planet. A meteorite named Wormwood scattered a chemical that contaminated a third of the world's fresh water. Another meteorite killed a third of the sea life and destroyed a third of the ships in the sea. There were giant hornet locusts called *Apollyons* that went about stinging the followers of Romiti. Their leader was named Abaddon. Perhaps most terrifying of all, four monstrosities from out of the Euphrates led an army of 200 million demonic creatures to kill a third of the remaining life on Earth.

It should have been more than apparent to everyone that Hod E. Romiti, a mere human, could not possibly save them from these plagues. However, they flocked to him anyway and begged him to solve these problems. While giving one his speeches at the headquarters of the Global Union, he was shot in the head and killed. Samael himself guided the assassin's aim. As his head bled, his last vision was of Carna's wide blue eyes staring lifelessly back at him as a puddle of blood formed under her head, soiling her luscious blonde hair. *"What happens to Atheists like me?"*

Then it was black.

Hysteria ensued. The world mourned the loss of its greatest and most beloved leader.

Hod Emmanuel Romiti, Secretary General of the Global Union, lay in state in the middle of the rotunda of the new Capitol building. Samael began to merge himself with his corpse and his consciousness. Then, on the third day, he reanimated it. On the third day, in plain view of cameras and hundreds of people, Romiti sat up. The world, even after having seen so many supernatural events over the previous three and a half years, was astonished by this.

Romiti went to the front of the building and began to give a speech for all to hear. He claimed to know the culprits for his assassination. "The same old culprits who point the finger at us and tell us we are unworthy and unrighteous. The same old culprits who've stood in the way of our union from the beginning, who've fought me every step of the way, who've accused me of the very evils their God has been committing against us since the end of the war. You know them. You see them. They're among us. Rats. Vermin. Wolves among us. The ones with the 'seals' on their head. The ones who wear those crosses around their necks. The ones who were exempt from the torment inflicted on us by the Apollyons. The ones who were spared the massacre by the 200 million demonic beasts. Those people. You know the ones. Find them. Find them and rat them out, just as they rat you out to their God. They've called down this darkness and death upon us! They've done so because we are different. We are not like them. We have no room in our peaceful world for such a divisive, discriminatory, xenophobic, and racist lot! I say: exterminate them! Wipe them out before they can wipe us out! These are the most divisive of people. The ones who say it's either their way or no way. Well, I will make a way: over their bodies!"

Christians, Jews, Muslims, and those of nearly any other religion that would not conform to *Romitism* were rounded up and killed, many in large gas chambers. The Pope denounced the actions of Romiti and his followers, finally declaring him the Antichrist, but Romiti had him executed with the rest. Churches and cathedrals burned, many times with their attendees inside them. They destroyed all religious iconography, statues, and even paintings depicting religious themes that were contrary to Romitism.

"Samael, darling!" Terra shouted at Romiti. "What are you doing? What have you done? You promised me! You promised me all those centuries ago you wouldn't let this happen!"

Romiti shoved her out of the way. "My promises are worth as much as my words, Terra *darling*. I simply don't need you anymore," he said. He conjured a fireball and incinerated Terra, leaving her to burn along with some of her icons. The *City on Seven Hills* caught fire and many ships in the Mediterranean watched with horror as the great city burned in the distance.

Romiti went to the newly rebuilt Temple of Solomon in Jerusalem, built over the remnants of the old temple and the Dome of the Rock. There, he declared to the whole world that he was god.

Romiti's cousin, Noren Raseak, became the high priest of this new religion that had formed around Romiti. He had giant golden statues of him built, which could interact with worshipers like an automaton. They could also kill those who argued with them or otherwise displeased them with fire.

Romiti and Raseak instituted an easier way to weed out the Christians and other dissenters. They required that every follower of Romiti and member of the Global Union receive a mark on their forehead or hand identifying them as such. The mark consisted of a number: 666. The Christians, who had been warned about this in their Bible, rejected the mark and thus were executed. In less than a year, Romiti's genocide exceeded even the Holocaust.

The God of gods, Yahweh, mourned the deaths of his faithful followers. It filled him up with a great wrath, a wrath that was collected into seven bowls. The first bowl was poured out over the Earth, and all of Romiti's followers suffered from loathsome sores that broke out over the entirety of their bodies. Rather than repent, the followers listened to Romiti as he continued to rally them against God and his believers. "These Christians are the most intolerant among us," said Romiti. "They damn us, they accuse us, they slander us. They say that we are immoral. They say that we are paramount to criminals. They tell us that we've broken the laws. They tell us that we're wrong. They tell us what's right, what to think, what to believe. No more! Now, they will kneel, or they will bleed."

The genocide intensified. Guillotines were introduced by the thousands, and heads rolled. In response, another bowl was poured out on the Earth, and it turned all the salt water on Earth into blood. A third bowl was poured out and it turned all of the rivers and springs on Earth into blood as well, meaning that the supply of safe drinking water was all but eliminated. It was as if God was saying, "if you are so bloodthirsty, then here, have some blood."

A fourth bowl brought a global heatwave that exacerbated the thirst. And a fifth brought darkness upon the world. A sixth dried up the river Euphrates, allowing the armies of the Earth to gather for battle in Israel in the valley of Megiddo, also known as Armageddon. Hod Romiti, Noren Raseak, and Samael called the armies of the world there, claiming that they would finally confront the God of gods and end the "tyranny of Heaven." They brought millions of men, tanks, and APVs. It was the largest military force ever assembled on Earth.

It had been three and a half years since Romiti had risen from the dead. It had been seven years since he'd signed the covenant with Israel and started this Tribulation period.

A blinding light appeared in the sky, and a familiar figure rode out on a white horse. He held no weapons and wore no armor. Samael, still possessing the body of Romiti, recognized him as the carpenter, Jesus. *"HIM!"* Samael realized. *"I should've killed him! What happened?! How is he still alive?!"*

Jesus spoke, and all of the armies of the Earth fell dead.

Samael tore himself away from Romiti's body and tried to escape. Romiti fell from the white horse he'd brought for show. His body looked as though he were decaying. Noren Reseak, the False Prophet, fell to his knees before Jesus, making excuses for his actions. The Angels apprehended him. Jesus and Romiti, Christ and Antichrist, then came face-to-face. Without a word spoken, Romiti kneeled. The battle was won, the war was over without a shot fired or a sword drawn.

Samael felt like vomiting his spiritual essence. He was incensed with rage.

The Angels apprehended Romiti and Raseak, hurling them into the Lake of Fire. In the end, they had been responsible for more deaths than any other humans in recorded history.

Jesus went to individual survivors of those horrible seven years and embraced them. He reminded the many who'd lost loved ones that they would see them again as he was ready to raise the dead and rapture his elect to Heaven. He would create a new Heaven and a new Earth as well as a new Jerusalem.

Samael continued to use this time to scurry away.

The Arch-Angel, Michael, came from the sky with an army behind him. Samael tried to draw his sword, but Michael overpowered him. He bound the devil in a strong chain and hurled him into the Abyss where the Apollyons had come from, there he would stay until the conclusion of the 1,000-year reign of Jesus, after which the devil would make a final futile attempt to turn the world against God.

Azure allowed him to have a glimpse of this Millennial Kingdom, to see the perfect reign of Jesus over the Earth in his absence. There was total peace and happiness.

Samael grew ever more annoyed and angry at the sight of this. "They came from the mud of the ground. They're dirt! I am a son of fire!"

"Out of everyone who I've sent to redeem themselves, you refuse to change, Samael," said Azure. **"You refuse to accept fault. You refuse to turn from your ways."**

"Don't you dare presume to patronize me!" said Samael. "I know I can stop this. I know I can prevent this!"

"Let's see."

Samael watched as Jesus, looking to be in his late 20s or early 30s perhaps, was baptized by John the Baptist and acknowledged by the voice of God as his son. He went into the desert to fast and pray. Samael knew this was the perfect opportunity. If he could not kill him, he could at least corrupt him.

First, he challenged the famished Jesus to turn the rocks of the Judaean desert into bread to eat. Jesus refused. Second, he challenged Jesus to throw himself from the top of the temple, using a literal reading of Psalm 91:12. Jesus refused, seeing the verse as poetic and retorting with Deuteronomy 6:16. Third, Samael took Jesus to the top of a mountain and offered him all authority over the kingdoms of the world as long as he bowed down and worshipped him. These three temptations would ensnare Hod Emmanuel Romiti and he would give into all of them. However, Jesus again refused, saying that only God was worthy of worship. "Get away, Satan!" he said. Samael departed, frustrated that his scheme had failed. As Jesus fell in exhaustion, the Angels caught him and tended to him, fulfilling Psalm 91:12.

"I underestimated him. This man, this king is not like you or me," said Azure. **"He doesn't take, he gives. He doesn't demand sacrifice, he is a sacrifice. He conquers not by the sword, but by virtue of his words and actions. I feel... if I am to become a great king and lead the universe of the Malkuthians, I should become like him."**

"You have more in common with my son, Romiti, than you do with God's son. Tell me: haven't you ever wanted to be God? Haven't you wanted to make the Omniverse as you see fit? You could make things the way you want them to be. You could make people behave the way you want them to behave. The Omniverse could be perfect, a utopia for everyone, and everyone would thank and praise you for it."

"Not like that. I will not create love slaves. I will not turn everyone into automatons as Antares hoped to. I will be like the son of God. I will not rob people of their freedom to choose."

"If you'll be like the son of God, then you will suffer like him too, Azure! Queen Ain will tear you limb from limb weak as you are now!"

"Yes, for a while. But I am prepared. I have suffered before, and I will suffer again and again and again. And it'll be ok in the end."

"You're fooling yourself. Ain is at least four times as powerful as you are! No, you've wasted so much of your energy sending us to these foolish timelines, she's probably ten times stronger now! You should've taken it all. You should've drained everything. You could blink her out of existence! Make the whole cosmos as you see fit!"

"And kill everything? Everyone? I am as powerful as I need to be for the task I must undertake. If I need more, then I will take more."

"I am disappointed, Azure. Neela would be too. You've gone soft. She loved a knight, a warrior of a man."

"Yes and no, Samael. She loved a knight, but I was no warrior. She loved my heart. She loved my spirit. She loved a man who was kind and loving and gentle."

"Ha! Is *that* what you believe…"

"It's my truth."

"Your truth doesn't erase the fact that you're as deep in blood as I am. You're just like Ain, and you won't admit it. No, you're even worse. 71% of the Omniverse—billions of universes are gone—all because of you. And to think their harrowing sacrifice will prove to be in vain when you submit to Ain's magnificent power."

"I will not submit. I will not quit. I will fight and fight and fight just as Neela did—to the very last. With every ounce of my strength and every last bit of my being. And I will never stop fighting until the fighting is done."

"So be it. You will lose, Azure. I guarantee it."

"And you? Having seen your future?"

"I refuse to accept that future. I'll kill him. I'll end the so-called 'Christ' before he can accomplish any of that. I will stand victorious in that hour."

"So be it." Azure snapped his fingers and returned his focus to the present.

"THE WEDDING"

Azure had formed a new planet Gaia with a new floating palace of Olympus. He formed a new Midgard and a new Asgard. They held their original splendor but lacked a population. "I leave that to you all," Azure explained, changing Athena and Thor along with Aphrodite and Loki into formal wedding attire. He even transformed Loki into the handsome form he'd previously held.

"Like, does this make me look fat?" said Aphrodite.

"Oh, no, you look ravishing, dearie!" said Loki.

"'Tis good for a woman to have some meat and marbling on her bones," said Thor.

"Gee, thanks, Thor! I needed to hear that," said Aphrodite. *See, like, this is why we didn't end up together.*

"If only father and mother were here to see thee," said Thor. "To behold thy strong, wise, and beautiful wife!"

"Yes… I know what you mean…" said Athena. "Azure, why did you make us see all of that? Why did you torment us with the past? Why did you tantalize us with what we had?"

"You have it still," said Azure's voice from the sky. "In here," he pointed an olive branch to her head, "and in here," he pointed it to her heart. "And somewhere out there… in some time, in some distant place, in some alternate reality that exists in the pocket of existence. You'll always have it. But now we're here together. Let's make the best of what we have. Now, it's up to us to build a better future. To start from the beginning again."

Azure formed an aisle lined with the most beautiful of flowers from the many universes leading to an arch. He positioned Loki and Thor there, and an avatar of him walked both Athena and Aphrodite to the front. He conjured a priest to do a little marriage ceremony. And just like that, the Asgardian Aesir and the Olympians were wed. Azure provided a great feast for them, and this time there was no Eris to ruin it.

They had several children, but the first of Aphrodite's children was very special. She named him "Su" after his father. So, even the Kami bloodline was preserved.

And of course, both she and Loki slept around, causing all sorts of mischief for their people in spite of all they'd learned but also populating and diversifying their world.

Athena and Thor had children too, and many of them became warriors and teachers. Athena and Thor became the rulers of Olympus and Asgard, causing great friction with Loki, who would once again stir trouble. Thor and Loki would once again be at odds, but their wives would always fight to remind them the importance of family, and Loki reminded Thor of his oath, forcing him to relinquish the throne. And so, ultimately, Athena and Loki ruled as co-regents.

"THE FUTURE OF THE MALKUTHIANS"

The people rallied around Diamond, and he finally shed his cybernetic armor, revealing himself to be Aohdfionn. Edom caught sight of his old friend and rival. "Come here, you son of a bitch," he said, reeling him in.

"You still have that death grip, 'Dom," said Diamond.

"Always will, bro. Forever strong."

"Forever strong."

The initial days after the Battle of Malkuth and the destruction of Hod were awkward. Despite the damage being undone, and the wounded being healed by Azure, the businesses and schools remained closed on the planet. The dead had to be claimed and buried.

Worst of all, there was great confusion and uncertainty across the Union. Azure, Autumn, Diamond, and the others made announcements for how the Union would now be governed. There would be new elections on every world. There would be a new Senate. However, Azure would remain a figurehead while leaving most of the governance to the elected leaders. Autumn was given the option of taking her father's ceremonial place on this new Senate, but she surprisingly refused. She told Azure that she'd be too busy expanding the influence of her Empress Amber AI, an AI she promised would do a better job at fairly managing the flow of information, supplies, and money.

"AZURE'S GOODBYES"

Azure's avatar came upon a new statue of Neela in front of the now-active Senate House. He sat at her feet and touched it. He cried. "I miss you," he said. "I'll always love you. You'll always be with me."

Autumn came to pay her respects as well, leaving a pink flower there and humming the tune to Losty.

A fleet of Union starships appeared in the sky, bringing both of them to their feet. Autumn's visor alerted her, "Chancellor George Antares detected on board."

Azure already knew. Autumn summoned her new Psycho Suit Mk. II and retreated to Azure's side. The capital ship hovered in the middle of the People's Square, and a company of Union soldiers were beamed down. In the middle of them was the old chancellor, George Antares, yet to be deposed, and looking determined to retake his empire. He was wearing his war-suit and wielded a large beam rifle intended for taking out mechs. "Lucky me," he said. "I rolled the dice and found you both here."

"Dad…" Autumn said under her breath.

Antares aimed his rifle at Azure, who drew his holy sword.

"Stop!" Autumn ran between them, her arms and palms outstretched. "Stop it, the both of you!"

"Get out of the way, Autumn!" shouted Antares.

"No. I won't move until you put that down," she said. "And you too," she said to Azure.

"He's as responsible for Neela's death as Nusakan!" said Azure.

"You killed my son," Antares seethed. "You corrupted my daughter! My people! You stole my empire! You stole… everything from me!"

"No!" said Autumn. "I left on my own accord. I left because of the way you are! The way you toy with people's lives!"

"This demoniac beat your brother to death in front of the whole Union! He'll do the same to you in time, I swear it!"

"He would never hurt me, daddy. Azure's my protector, my guardian. Isn't that right, Azure?" She winked at him.

Azure lowered the sword and it disappeared.

"This is your last chance, baby girl," said Antares, "move out of the way, and I'll shoot."

"Then you'll have to shoot me too," Autumn called away the protection of her suit.

Antares lowered the gun and threw it down. He called away his suit as well and fell to his knees. Autumn ran to him and embraced her father for the first time in ten years. Without the drugs and hyperbaric chambers on Hod, Antares had grown older and weaker.

"Thank you, daddy," she said.

"I'm sorry, baby girl. I can't cry in front of all these people."

"You can cry, daddy. It's ok. It's ok to cry sometimes."

And so, the two of them wept.

Another crowd had gathered, and they started to berate the two Antares. Guns were drawn on both sides. Azure guided the weapons down telekinetically. Autumn looked up to Azure, tears in her eyes and clinging to her now-elderly dad, "Please don't let them kill him. I know he's done a lot wrong, but he's the only family I have left."

"We should put him on trial!" said one of the Azurites.

Azure cast a protective spell on both Autumn and her father. "From now on, no one will harm this man. Nature will take its course." Azure walked up to the statue of Neela and placed his hand on her knee. "George Antares, do you remember her name?"

"...Neela," he answered in a raspy voice. "The girl's name was Neela."

Azure smiled with satisfaction. "Make good use of the time you have left, George," said Azure. "Don't waste it on scheming and hate. Everything you've been searching for is right in front of you."

As the days passed, Azure could sense Queen Ain's immense power and knew that it was coming time to finally face her—Death itself. Azure planned for his avatar to stay with the people of Malkuth for as long as possible, helping to lead and guide them. But his original body, his cosmic body, would go on to confront Ain. He explained the situation to his friends and followers, entrusting the governing of the Union to them and saying that he may vanish at any moment and not return.

He invited Autumn to see him in his cosmic form, encapsulating her in an atmosphere bubble, and summoning her to him. She stood in his palm, gazing in awe at the colossal multi-armed, multi-winged Azure. "Don't be afraid," said Azure. "I know I may look frightening now, but I'm still me, I'm still Azure."

"I'm not afraid, silly," said Autumn. "I'm impressed."

"I'm going off to fight a battle I know I may not win. I have chosen to accept a disadvantage in exchange for preserving the lives contained in a multitude of universes. My enemy is powerful and more experienced than I am. In a sense, you could say that she's my mother. I was formed in the midst of one of her greatest explosions. It merged with the Void Brightening, the Big Bang, and so I was born. Ain is the greatest threat to all the Omniverse. She is Death itself, the mother of all

Dragons, and I cannot let her continue to threaten us. I'm the only one who can face her and hope to survive."

Autumn reached out to him but could not touch him through the atmosphere bubble. She knelt down and placed her hand at the edge of it, just short of the skin of his hand. "I believe in you, Azure," she said. "I know it's cliche to say, but it's no less true. I believe in you, and I will always believe in you."

Part VII
AIN .VS. AZURE

"EONS IN THE MAKING"

It is said that in the beginning, the God of gods spoke, saying, "Let there be light," and there was light. And God saw the light and saw that it was good. And he separated the light from the darkness. He called the light "day" and the darkness he called "night." Two diametrically opposing forces of nature shared both the universe and the hearts of its inhabitants. So began the greatest story in history.

In that instant, when the daughter universe was born from the womb of Heaven, the cosmic Dragon, Ain, was born along with it. Ain, then nameless, possessed a malicious streak. She destroyed even the largest of galaxies and clusters like an angry child would destroy a porcelain vase. In doing so, she unintentionally formed many new universes.

Once, she destroyed a cluster of galaxies, leaving one of many great holes in the daughter universe and creating a cold spot. The energy from the blast expanded into a realm called New Heaven, a universe formed by the Demons during the Angel War.

New Heaven had become a landfill that gathered debris from many of the other universes. There was a remnant of the Big Bang inside of it, and it joined with Ain's explosion along with a host of other debris from other realms. By some miracle, that chaotic collection of energy and matter found order. It condensed into a singular point and gained sentience. Soon, it became self-aware. That being became known as Azure.

While Ain would become the mother of the Dragons, Azure would father the Malkuthians.

Ain's power grew exponentially for billions of years as her Dragons terrorized and ravished worlds across the cosmos. Her food was life-energy, and so she had become the very personification of Death itself. Death had come close to conquering most of the cosmos. The universes and their worlds trembled in fear at the sound of her name and at the sight of her armies.

Meanwhile, Azure wandered his world as a vagabond, weak, confused, and practically powerless. He trudged on hopelessly, experiencing the effects of death and suffering first-hand. He experienced love as well, and the pain of loss. It was these experiences, the good with the bad, that shaped him into something different.

As fate would have it, a simple Malkuthian girl named Neela restored his mind. With his mind restored, he had an epiphany, finally realizing that he was special somehow. But he had no time to revel in this realization as the love of his life, Neela, fell terminally ill. This was the direct result of having healed him. Pulled here and there, between the tug of good and the tug of evil, he was deceived and betrayed by those who held great power. The love of his life was taken from him, and he allowed it to happen. Familiar feelings came over him—desperation, helplessness, hopelessness, and powerlessness. Neela was killed as a result of this deception, and with her death, Azure's power of powers was finally awakened.

Many things had brought him to this point. Many people had touched his life along the way, and he had touched theirs. As had happened throughout history, there had been a revolution, and there had been a war. Both Azure and Ain had continued to grow in power.

It had all been leading to this.

"THE POWER OF AIN"

Ain erased the ailing Lord Zeon from existence to the shock and horror of General Deem and Princess Darna who witnessed this. "IT'S OK, DARLING," said Ain. "HE WAS FINISHED, YOU SEE?"

Deem and Darna approached the Queen and knelt to her. "My Queen," said General Deem, "I have destroyed the capital world of the Malkuthians and their best armies."

"Mom, I think he should be promoted," said Darna, looking at

him and smiling. "He is the greatest of our generals and the greatest of our warriors. No one has bested him in battle, not even the Malkuthians. I think he should replace either Mortimer, Zeon, or Gigatheta as a lord."

"WHY DO YOU LOOK AT HIM LIKE THAT, DAUGHTER?"

"Well, mom, it's because… I admire him."

"ADMIRE?"

"I love him, mom."

"LOVE?"

"Yeah… General Deem here told me that in the worlds he conquered, there were people who cared about each other a lot. Just like you care about me, mom. There's a word for it: it's called love."

"DOES LOVE DRIVE YOU AND DEEM TO DISOBEDIENCE?"

"Mom? No, what do you mean?"

"I SEARCHED FOR YOU, DAUGHTER. I WAS PLANNING THIS INVASION OF HEAVEN FOR LONGER THAN YOU'VE BEEN ALIVE TO KNOW IT. LORD MORTIMER WENT SEARCHING FOR YOU, GENERAL DEEM, AND YOU WERE NOWHERE TO BE FOUND. BOTH OF YOU. NEXT I LEARNED THAT MY OWN DAUGHTER HAD OPENED A TEAR TO THE HOMEWORLD OF THE MALKUTHIANS."

"My Queen, my apologies, I can explain…" said Deem.

"DON'T. FROM THE BEGINNING, DEEM, YOU'VE POSSESSED TRAITS THAT TROUBLED ME. IT'S ONLY YOUR SUCCESS THAT HAS KEPT YOU FROM MY WRATH."

"No, mom! Please don't hurt him!" Darna latched onto him and hugged him. "He was only trying to help you! The war was dragging on. He wanted to end it quickly! He succeeded!"

"MY TWO BEST WARLORDS ARE DEAD NOW, AND WORST YET HE HAS CORRUPTED MY DAUGHTER."

"My Queen!" Deem spoke up. "I believe I've done no such thing. I've sought only to serve you honorably. I respect your daughter dearly. I love her. And she loves me too. I played no such tricks. I told her only what I knew. Please understand!"

"I UNDERSTAND." Ain levitated Deem up into the air and crashed him into one of the colossal planets she'd crafted.

"Please, mom, no!" Darna cried, running to intervene. Ain trapped her in a prism that electrocuted her.

Deem transformed himself into his ultimate cosmic form, evoking the power of all the deities who'd volunteered to guide him. Without hesitation, he charged his Brahmashirsha Astra attack, the one that had destroyed the entire Hodian system, and fired it at Ain. He'd angled it so that the Princess would be out of the blast radius. The attack—the most powerful in Deem's entire arsenal—didn't even scratch Ain. She smacked him aside and sent him crashing into another of her worlds. He reverted back to his original form. The Dragon legionaries first inspected the crater, then fled from it as the Queen approached to finish him off. She began to torment him.

Princess Darna again flew over to him and threw herself over his broken body. "No, mom!" she cried. "Stop hurting him, please! I love him, mom. It's the greatest feeling I've ever felt!" She held his left-hand. "He taught me that. He taught me to kiss. He taught me about music. He taught me how to dance. Deem is the most amazing, incredible being I've ever known in my life, and I love him!"

Never before had a Dragon cried. Ain was astonished by this phenomenon, but her rage won over. "YOU'RE A DISGRACE, DARNA, JUST LIKE HIM." She fired an enormous and refined beam from one of her eyes. It struck the teary-eyed Princess and her champion, Deem, killing them both and sending shockwaves further than the effects of any gamma-ray burst.

"AIN!" Azure roared, arriving through a tear just in time to witness this. He weathered the shockwave of the blast.

Ain twisted her serpentine body and faced Azure. "ARE YOU THE ONE CALLED AZURE? THE ONE THAT SAMAEL TOLD ME WOULD COME? THE ONE WHO DEFEATED LORD ZEON AND LORD MORTIMER?"

"I am," he said. "How could you do such a thing, Ain? She was your daughter!"

"NO CHILD OF MINE SHOULD SHOW FEELINGS LIKE SHE DID. IT WOULD CONTAMINATE OUR RACE. MAKE THEM SOFT AND WEAK LIKE THE OTHER SPECIES. DRAGONS SHOULD SEEK JUST ONE THING: TO SERVE ME."

"You're wrong about that. Everything you said was wrong. It doesn't make one weak to care about another person. To care—to love—is not a weakness. There's no greater strength."

"CLASH OF WILLS"

Ain fired another enormous beam from her right-eye, the same that had killed Deem and Darna. Azure stopped it and nullified it with a thought. He then siphoned energy from Ain, appearing as a stream of red light. Ain responded by siphoning his life energy, which appeared as a stream of green light. This phenomenon formed a circular cycle of energy that flowed from one to the other and back again. Meanwhile, millions of other streams of energy flowed to Ain from all the inhabited worlds in the cosmos.

Loki created a crystal ball, which Athena, Aphrodite, and Thor could use to watch the long-awaited duel with him. Autumn did something she hadn't done before: she prayed for Azure, even as her father watched and asked her what she was doing, telling her it was pointless.

Azure tried to grab Ain with telekinesis, but she simply scoffed at his pathetic attempt. She countered and sent him hurtling over a thousand light-years away. As he careened through space, he saw that the Dragon worlds were inhabited with many warriors training for battle. He stopped himself and tried to regain his focus. Finding Ain again was not hard. She was the largest, brightest, most obvious thing in the universe, and the life-energy that left Azure led him directly back to her, and she to him.

Rather than teleporting, he made his way back to her manually, gradually gaining incredible speeds as he did. Ain saw this large streak of white and green light flying toward her and formed a tear, which he mistakenly flew through. He ended up in another universe entirely.

Ain appeared and pulled the planets and stars out of orbit, hurling them at Azure. They flew at him and pelted him like a handful of stones. The stars seared him slightly like a match against the skin of any mortal. He grabbed planets of his own, using his many new arms and hurled them back at Ain who broke them apart with a swipe of her hand one by one.

"General Deem was intelligent and noble," shouted Azure. "He was a far greater leader than you will ever be."

"HE WAS AKIN TO A TRAITOR, AND I ERASED HIM FOR IT. I WILL SOON ERASE YOU!" Ain gathered a massive amount of Qi energy into her palms, molding it into a refined shape like a potter. This was a Mass Extinction Attack similar to Zeon's but amped up a thousand times. Azure knew and waited for her to gather her attack, then, just as she was about to fire, he tore a hole into another universe and got away. "WHY RUN, COWARD?" Not wanting to squander the preparation for the attack, she released it anyway and destroyed the universe they'd been fighting in as well as several others that rubbed faces with it.

After seeking him out through the darkness, she could sense his aura elsewhere. She tore another hole through space and found him waiting with a Mass Extinction Attack of his own. She encased him in a rectangular containment field with the idea being that if he released the attack it would blow up in his face. Azure teleported out of the containment field and released the attack directly on top of Ain.

The explosion sent ripples that were felt in every universe and through dimensions.

Ain, however, had only suffered a small burn that healed quickly as life-energy continued to flow to her. They were in yet another universe, one that was nearly starless

The two titanic beings lit up the dark universe, each gathering the energy necessary for their ultimate energy attacks. Surprisingly, Ain did not prepare a Mass Extinction Attack, but a special surprise she called the "ANNIHILATION RAY," the very same attack that had helped to birth Azure billions of years in the past.

Azure had been formulating an attack of his own that he'd briefly practiced with Diamond. This was the Cosmic Ray, gathered between all of his arms with even his mouth and the tips of his wings contributing to the harnessing of energy. Neither of the two cosmic monstrosities was budging from their spot. Their auras could eclipse the light of a hundred trillion supernovae. "I AM DONE WITH YOU!" Ain roared, firing the Annihilation Ray, a ray of terrific golden light and devastating power.

Azure unleashed the power of his Cosmic Ray, a white ray of light with a terrific force of its own. When the two unfathomable attacks met, the shockwaves destroyed every asteroid, every planetesimal, and every star in that universe. It sent ripples through every universe once more, but the effects were pronounced this time. There were quakes on planets in other universes that were so powerful, they could not be scaled by the existing means. Some planets and stars were turned on their side or pushed out of orbit depending on their nearness.

Even Malkuth was hit with the most devastating quake in the recorded history of the planet. Edom, Diamond, Autumn, General Eridanus and the others sprang into action to save as many lives as possible. Even George Antares offered to help if it meant spending the rest of his rapidly-diminishing life with his daughter. Vegas put the moon pup on a pillow in the tunnels and told him to "stay and be good." She too went to help with the recovery efforts.

Azure was aware of these effects, but he didn't have the luxury of holding back.

"Heeeheeeheeehaaaaw!" Loki cackled, communicating with him. *"We've got ourselves a classic beam-struggle! The will, the will, it will until. The will, the will, leads to the kill."*

"You're tougher than she is, Azure!" said Athena. *"Stick it out!"*

"You, like, totally got this!" said Aphrodite.

In a flash, he thought of Neela and everyone he'd known on Malkuth, trying to encourage himself as even his ethereal cosmic body strained. Then, he remembered a little trick that Bekah had taught him centuries ago. She had shown him that the presence of certain plants in the prairie lands indicated that there was a source of water beneath them.

"Down yonder there be a patch of ole' shrubs that fall asleep when you touch them," she said. "You ain't never gonna guess, but poke some holes in them there roots and you've got yourself a spring!" When they came upon the place, Azure asked her to show him. She grabbed a hatchet from her pack and began to hack away at the ground. She punctured a sack of some sort between the roots. Little by little water began to squirt out as if from a small fountain. "You'd never guessed if I didn't tell you so," said Bekah as Azure drank. "Some things be there that you ain't never seen or known about. That don't mean that they ain't there. The Lord Almighty, he loves to hide himself some surprises. You best be digging to find 'em."

Azure tried to think of where he may be able to find more energy without it leading to more deaths. He sensed an energy that he could not see in that darkness of that universe, but that existed nonetheless. He began to draw from it. The energy was immense. Ain looked surprised to see Azure's ray grow thicker and more powerful, beginning to overwhelm hers. "YOU HAVE NO IDEA THE DEPTHS OF MY POWER! THE POWER TO TEAR EVEN THE MULTIVERSE ASUNDER!" Ain channeled more energy into her attack and matched Azure.

"Do you have any idea the depths of mine?" Azure continued to funnel the unseen energy into the Cosmic Ray. It began again to overpower Ain's Annihilation Ray. "You say you despise feelings like love. My love, Neela, gave her life to set my mind and my powers free! And you're going to taste every last bit of it!"

The Cosmic Ray had clearly won out and was gaining momentum toward Ain, taking her attack with it. It struck Ain and the subsequent explosion tore a massive hole through that universe and created a whole other one. Ain was knocked through it to the other side and Azure followed. Again, all Azure had to do was follow the cyclical stream of energy that ran from him to Ain and back again.

The great cosmic Dragon had never been so overwhelmed in her entire existence, but she quickly recovered, elongating her enormous serpentine body to appear even larger and more intimidating. The explosion had decorated the new universe with gaseous nebulae and magnificent colors as if someone had rolled an entire cart of various paint cans into a blank canvas, splattering colors all over it. Azure was briefly reminded of watching the sunsets from the sky district with Neela resting her head on his shoulder, eager to point out every distinct thing she saw. This thought calmed his nerves as Ain towered over him.

"DUEL OF THE REALITY WARPERS"

A year had passed in Malkuthian time since the commencement of the duel. While the Union sprinted toward democratic reforms, Azure and Ain continued to hurl attacks of inconceivable power at each other, eclipsing even the power of World Enders and Resolvers. With Azure demonstrating his superior use of Qi, Ain engaged him in another of her specialties: reality warping.

The two had ended up in a highly populated universe, and Azure tried to tear a hole to lead Ain away, but Ain closed the hole and sewed it shut. Each time he tried to do this, Ain would do the same thing. When he tried to simply teleport to another universe or dimension, he was stopped. Ain had erected a magical barrier that encircled the entire universe. When Azure would destroy the barrier, Ain would simply recreate it. Frustrated, Azure formed his Sword of Heaven and tried to cut through it, but when he did, Ain released the next phase of her plan. The fragments he broke off became like broken glass and darted at him like metal filings to a magnet, stabbing him all over his body, including his head and eyes. Ain shattered more of the barrier with a thought and it all came barreling toward him, tragically crashing through and destroying populated worlds. Azure erected a Mystic Shield that deflected the shards, but Ain took this time to begin moving populated worlds closer to their suns to begin scorching them or further away to begin freezing them to death. She knew this would likely lure out Azure who would try to reverse her effects. He did, but the trauma of this sudden change in orbital position killed nearly everyone on these worlds anyway, and Azure was still fighting to protect himself from the barrage of spacial shards that Ain now orchestrated at will.

Ain then began to deteriorate Azure's body simply by thinking it, but he regenerated from it just as rapidly. Azure did the same to her with identical results. "YOU ARE OUTMATCHED," said Ain. "I HAVE BEEN DOING THIS FOR A LONG, LONG TIME. ANYTHING I DESIRE TO HAPPEN WILL HAPPEN."

All the bodies of those who'd died in that universe began to gather in her hand, crashing and merging in a clump of gore as she relished Azure's horrified reaction at the sight. She threw the ball of bodies at him only to see him shrink away. Ain waved her hand, and the entire universe went from darkness to bright red! It disoriented Azure for a while. Ain teleported behind him, lassoed his neck with her serpentine body, and applied pressure. She formed a mountain that covered a whole corner of that red universe and forced Azure face-first into it, grinding it there and scraping off his flesh. Azure drew the Sword of Heaven and cut her tail away, forcing her to relinquish her hold. She reformed her tail and was furious. "HOW DARE YOU!"

Azure formed energy balls that were essentially giant stars. He surrounded Ain in them, bringing them down on her with all their heat and mass. Ain wished them away, and they faded. Months passed, and then years. The universe they were fighting in had become a gigantic warped mess akin to Loki's Nether Dimension, flickering from red to yellow to white as debris from their fighting swirled around chaotically.

Frustrated with the disorienting colors, Azure wished, and the entire universe became solid blue, complete with calming white clouds, replicating the Malkuthian sky on many times the scale. Ain darkened the clouds and made lightning spark all around—essentially creating a bastardized thunderstorm thousands and thousands of light-years in width. Rain fell from them, not of quenching water but of pure green acid. It burned away at Azure's skin.

In that chaos, the Dragon Queen had disappeared. In the past, all Azure had to do was follow the bright cycle of energy, but it had seemingly vanished along with her. He thought she might have escaped to another universe as both had done in the past, but he was occasionally struck by her Qi attacks. He guessed that she might be passing in and out of dimensions and attacking him intermittently, but he wasn't sure. "Show yourself, Ain!"

Suddenly, all became dark. The universe became completely black and he couldn't even make out his own hands. He began to panic, wondering if she had trapped him in a void or pocket dimension of some sort. Remembering that New Heaven had once been such a place, he knew he could still make it livable. Azure formed star-rich galaxies to try to act as torches to light his way. He created over 50,000 galaxies before they were all extinguished. *She must be here somewhere.*

From time to time, something would hit him or even stab him, but he couldn't see it or hear it. It was so unsettling that he began to miss Ain facing him out in the open, as large and terrifying as she appeared.

He remembered the mental asylum he'd been held at with Enif. He remembered that though she couldn't see or hear, she could still feel his breath when he'd blow short messages onto her fingers or when he had her feel his jaw as he spoke to make out the words he was trying to say.

He knew that he needed to close his eyes and concentrate on feeling Ain's movements as she snuck behind and around him to strike. He felt the attack coming and immediately intercepted it with his sword. It cut Ain, causing her to shriek. She healed and disappeared again.

He chased her for several more years. The two managed to find and strike each other in scattered incidents in that time. These essentially became blind skirmishes. Ain was realizing that her strategy was no longer working as well as it had. With that, Ain lit up like a giant blinding lantern in the middle of a dark closet and Azure could see himself again, his light also returning. The cycle of energy between them resumed. The two became reacquainted, staring each other down. "AZURE!" Ain roared.

"AIN!" he responded.

"I'LL BRING ALL YOUR NIGHTMARES BACK AT ONCE!" she threatened. She closed her right-hand and when she opened it, she conjured a new Lord Zeon. When she did the same with her left-hand, she conjured a new Lord Mortimer. She did this again and again, forming dozens of copies of the Dragon lords, sometimes three or four at a time. She formed over a hundred copies of Zeon, Mortimer, Gigatheta, Baladan, and a host of other Dragon lords. Azure formed duplicates of himself to fight off the swarm of Dragon lords who attacked with a barrage of unique attacks: the Zeons with their Mass Extinction attacks, the Mortimers with their galaxy-destroying magic, the Gigathetas with their volley of elemental attacks, and more.

Azure and his duplicates fought them off until he realized it would be a better use of his energy to wish them away. All the Dragons lords were reduced to ether. But even as Azure did this, Ain was conjuring more clones. She had formed an army of General Malevants who swarmed Azure and attacked him with thousands of Oblivion Beams, each powerful enough to destroy a large planet. Azure drained them all of their energy and drained the energy that remained from the Dragon lords before Ain could think to do it.

A million, million interdimensional portals opened, and Azure formed a vice with the fabric of space to forced Ain through one of them. They returned to the universe of the Dragons, Ain's own creation. Ain ripped her own planets out of orbit—some appearing like stalactites, crystals, gems, spheres adorned with spikes, pyramids, and other odd shapes. Some of them were inhabited by her own soldiers. She hurled them at Azure, and they broke upon his force fields.

More years passed, and their epic duel continued.

"PSYCHOLOGICAL WARFARE"

They'd fought each other for 13 years, destroying numerous universes in the process. The shockwaves of their conflict were felt throughout all of creation. The universe of the Dragons, one of the largest in all of the cosmos, was in shambles. The Dragon Queen hardly seemed concerned, believing that she could simply recreate it and the rest of her Dragons after the fight.

As the battle dragged on, both began to develop unique and interesting ways to attack each other using their reality warping abilities. When one would try to manipulate time, the other would simply undo the effects. When one would conjure up any kind of advantage, the other would counter it with an advantage of their own.

Over time, the two had each thought up a similar strategy. Azure made his wish, and Ain made hers.

Azure found himself in Atlanta City, back to his normal physical self, but still with all his memories. He was hiding behind the bushes on one end of State Street, across from a gibbet cage that held Neela. Her eyes reached out to him and a wave of guilt hit him. She raised her hand weakly to wave at him, and he waved back, his heart torn between acting and hiding. He watched as Nusakan Antares and some PSF troops walked by the hanging bodies and cages. Neela waved Azure away, but he shook his head. Nusakan came to Neela's cage and mocked her. "Nusakan!" Azure shouted, emerging from his hiding spot. The Chief of Public Security turned, shocked to hear his first-name called. "Go to hell!"

With a thought, Azure turned the PSF troops around him to ashes. Nusakan looked left and right, seeing those around him vanish. Azure summoned his sword and hacked off both of Nusakan's legs. The Chancellor's son tried to crawl away. More PSF troops came, and Azure diced them. When two mechs responded, Azure opened two tears and pushed them through. "Azure, what are you doing? Stop!" Neela tried to say through her bit. Azure released her by thinking it, and she found herself seated at the edge of the sidewalk.

Nusakan continued to crawl away, but Azure conjured a spike and hammered his tail in place, preventing his escape. When Nusakan raised his hand and pleaded, Azure sliced his hand off. He grabbed the son of Antares by the collar of his shirt, lifted him and bashed him again and again into the asphalt as Neela screamed. He could hear Autumn's screams too as she watched this from the tunnels. He continued to bash Nusakan long past the point of death. He remembered what Nusakan had done in his timeline, remembered the suffering, the pain, the loss.

When an army of PSF arrived, Azure swept his hand through the air and every soldier was cut into pieces, their bodies collapsing in piles of gore, their intestines and stomachs spilling out. At the end of all this, a blood-covered Azure turned and stared back at Neela who was backed up against the corner of the street, her eyes looking up at him with fear and horror. "I did it, Neela!" Azure roared. "Aren't you happy?! Huh? Aren't you pleased?! No more! No more will we have to be afraid! No more will we have to live like this! You and I can be in charge! You and I can change things!"

"Who... who are you?" said Neela.

"I'm Azure."

Neela looked at all of the bodies and then back at him. She squinted through her gun-metal glasses and shook her head. "No. No you're not."

Azure gasped at this response.

In another timeline, Azure found himself at Neela's bedside as she awoke in the morning. He'd apparently made breakfast for her, some eggs and sausage. She yawned and outstretched her arms in a morning stretch. Azure immediately reached over and hugged her, soaking up every bit of her. He couldn't help it. "Good morning to you too, hon," she said. "Sheez, it must've been a long night, huh?"

Azure cried. "Are you real?"

"That's a stupid question. Are you?"

"What day is it? What year?"

Neela answered, indicating that it was over ten years past her death in the original timeline. "Why are you acting so weird? Are you ok? Are the kids up yet?"

"The-the kids?!"

Azure rushed out to find that they had a boy and a girl, both around seven, and a baby in a crib. He was overwhelmed with joy. "What's wrong with you, dad?" his daughter said as he hugged her voraciously. "Why'd you wake me up? There's no school today! I'm trying to sleep!"

"Amber," said Neela from the doorway. "Be nice. Your dad just wanted a hug. I hope you're not already going through one of those phases. God knows I know all about that."

Azure met his older son, Michael. He was into sports but falling behind in school. "Can we throw ball today, dad?" he asked.

"Of course, son," said Azure, tears in his eyes, "anything, anything at all."

"Really? Can we go to the toy store today too?"

"Hey now, lil' Mike!" Neela objected. "You have enough toys as it is, and we keep tripping over 'em. Money's not gonna buy you happiness. I don't wanna get you started."

"Maybe we should listen to mommy," Azure told the child.

"Awe…"

Azure looked around at all of Michael's toys. There were knight figurines, superheroes, and monsters. There were even what appeared to be Dragons. He picked one of them up and inspected it. Its wings were life-like and its face was fearsome, complete with sharp teeth and red eyes. "You better be careful of these things in real life. If you see one, come tell daddy. I'll deal with it."

"Silly dad!" said Michael. "There are no such thing as Dragons! They're not real!"

Azure gasped. He turned to Neela and asked, "Are we at war?"

"What? Is this a joke? The Union's always fighting someone."

"Who are we at war with?"

"Uh… the Hekans. They're like space pirates who linger around the Binah region. They look like walking toilet plungers turned upside down."

"And what about Chancellor Antares?"

"He stepped down like six years ago. Did you hit your head again or something? I'm starting to worry."

"I think I must've fallen…"

"Oh, dear!" Neela knelt down beside him and inspected his head, looking into his teary eyes. "Do we need to go see a doctor?"

"No. Can I… can I just hug you for a minute?"

"Yeah, sure."

Neela and Azure embraced and he couldn't hold back the tears. As he cried, there was the sound of a baby crying in the next room. They went together to check on him. He had the large snout of a Tyrannosaur and the horn of a Ceratosaur. He was blue with pink stripes and speckles. "Hey, Starflower, what's wrong?"

"You named him Starflower?"

"We already had this conversation, I'm not getting into another argument with you. His egg came out of my body, I get to name him. End of story. Here, would you hold him for a little while?" She handed him off. He smelled like powder and pee. He had Neela's eyes.

She got a fresh diaper and some wipes. They went through the changing process.

Afterward, Azure sat on the couch, speechless and wide-eyed.

"Are you sure you're ok?" asked Neela.

"Yeah…"

"Are you sure-sure?"

"This… this life… it's just too good to be true. It seems too easy."

"Oh, bullshit, we worked our asses off to afford this. Sorry, I should probably watch my language with the kids around, I'm trying." She put a coin in a "swear jar" and washed her hands.

They took strolls outside like they used to. Many of the problems they'd known were gone now. There was no pollution in the waterway, no homeless camps, no redlight district. There were no hangings or public humiliations on State or Main. Even the playground was fixed. Azure pushed Neela on the swings as well as the kids. "Whoohooo!" his daughter cheered. "I'm gonna touch the sky!"

They took turns going down the slide together, hand in hand. Azure looked at the merry-go-round and spun it around. It was smooth and there was no creaking. "What's going to happen when the cancer comes back?" sprouted Neela.

"The cancer?"

"Don't frickin' joke around about that, Azure. I'm being serious. The cancer. The frickin' thing growing in my head. What's going to happen to them all when I'm gone?"

"How long do you have?"

"A year, maybe two at most."

It was like a punch to Azure's gut. Neela rolled the baby carriage closer and cleaned off Starflower's face with a damp napkin. "It's happening… again…" said Azure.

"Yeah, well, I'll fight it again. I'll fight it again and again and again with everything I've got if it means seeing you and the kids a bit longer. But Azure… I need you to promise me something…"

"Anything."

"When I can't fight, I need you to fight harder. When I can't be strong anymore, I need you to be stronger. You'll need to be both a mother and a father all wrapped into one, you understand me?"

"I will. I promise." He held her hand tightly but couldn't bear to look at her. "I love you, Neela."

"I know," she said. "And I love you too, Azure. I'll always love you. And I'll always be with you, no matter what."

"THE FIGHT MUST GO ON"

Both Athena and Loki harassed him in his head, telling him that none of what he was seeing and experiencing was real. "This is just an elaborate fantasy of yours come to life, you of all people should realize that," said Athena. "You've created these very same things!"

"I didn't create fantasies for you all. I created and showed you alternate realities separate from the one you're living in. If Ain is doing the same to me, then this is as real as anything. Neela and my family need me."

"But the whole Multiverse needs you here! Ain is recreating the Dragon universe and reforming her armies. It's all happening again, and you're sitting on your ass enjoying yourself!"

"Azure dear," said Loki. "Oh, Azure dear, your cosmic form has been gone for a year. It's only a matter of time before Ain comes... here."

"We're running out of time," said Athena. "If you don't come back. If you don't finish the fight, it'll all be for nothing. Malkuth, the Union, New Heaven—they'll be torn apart. And it'll all be on *your* conscience."

"My conscience? Don't I deserve to be happy too?"

"Uh, you're the most powerful reality warper in the Omniverse!" said Loki. "You can just hit the pause button. Recreate and relive this fantasy later. Why, it's like adult films now that I think of it!"

"...Right..." said Athena.

"I have a better idea." Azure split himself in two, creating another avatar of himself with his memories, personality, and essence. He put his hands on the shoulders of the avatar. "You're a lucky man. A lucky, lucky, lucky man. Love her. Take care of her. I'll be back when it's all done. I'll live and relive your life a million, million times. I'll give her all the kisses you've stolen."

"What about all the kisses you've given away to me?" said the avatar, indicating Azure's lingering guilt. The avatar shook his head. "Don't worry about it, they're yours too. You're still me and I'm still you. I'll love her as you would. Protect and defend her as you would. But I want you to do something in return… I want you to fight as I would. To protect and defend as I would. Do these things, and WE will win."

Azure nodded and tore a path out of the timeline. He hesitated at the mouth of the tear but heard Neela's footsteps approaching. Closing his eyes tightly, he walked through and closed the tear behind him.

"Loki," he said. "How many years has it been since I began fighting Ain?"

"Why, my blue bomber, by the time you get there it will have been 13 years and 343 days in Malkuthian time."

"Perfect."

"HAUNTING"

Ironically, Ain had been knocked into an alternate timeline by Azure as well. She found herself in a flower field the size of a whole universe, one of her earliest creations. She'd heard that there'd been flowers on other planets. Terra had shown her some in her efforts to play the ambassador between Ain and the Demons. Ain tried to replicate the flowers on a cosmic scale and ended up blanketing her universe in them. But the flowers failed to satiate her interest, and she let them all die. She focused instead on forming magnificent creatures like her: Dragons. She created armies of them, all of them loyal but very few of them with personalities of their own. This pleased her much more than the flowers did, and she began to build odd worlds to house her Dragon warriors.

However, because she'd given her creations so little autonomy, she was never fully satisfied with her relationship to them. There was always a disconnect and an emptiness she felt for them. This allowed her to feel fine about sending them to die by the millions, but it also left a hole in her dark heart. She wanted to create beings like the ones she'd heard about from Samael and Terra: genuine beings with emotions and minds of their own. The thought of this terrified her at first. What if they grew to hate her and no longer obeyed her commands? But she made a compromise: she would create one such being and shelter her from the rest. Rather than create this being in her normal way, she impregnated herself and gave birth to this being in the old field of withering, dying flowers. She gave birth to Princess Darna, her one and only daughter.

At any moment, Ain—having her memories from the future—could have chosen to change this course of events, but she refused to. She wanted to relive it, as much as it haunted her and hurt. As she held the newborn Darna in her arms, a feeling she'd never felt before came over her: a feeling like grief. For a moment, she made the flowers bloom to life again in honor of this child, but as her emotions became confused, she swept her hand and the field of flowers vanished.

Only then did she realize the ripple effects of her actions in birthing Darna. The Dragon lords and generals she formed after that point had sprinklings of her own latent emotions and personality: the hunger, the drive, the cunning, the ruthlessness, the sadism, the aggressiveness, and in the case of rare Dragons like General Deem, even a little light.

She had killed that light, and she knew it now.

Seeing the baby Darna, she hugged it and then began to crush it until the blood covered her hands, arms, and chest. "AZURE!" she roared into space. "HOW DARE YOU! HOW DARE YOU TRY TO TRICK ME! HOW DARE YOU TRY TO MAKE ME FEEL THIS FEELING! THIS... HAUNTING... LIKE THE MORTALS DO. I AM ABOVE THEM! ABOVE EVEN YOU! I'LL NEVER BE DISTRACTED AGAIN! I'LL DO WHAT I SHOULD HAVE DONE ALL ALONG!"

She tore a hole through the timeline and returned to her own. Then, she began to rebuild her universe, creating new worlds and raising new armies on them. These Dragons were even fiercer, faster, and harder to kill. They no longer needed armor because their hides were as tough as adamantine. All of them were given the ability to fly. If such a force were to start up a second war with the Malkuthians a decade into their rebuilding, the results could be much different. This was Ain's intent.

A new invasion force was poised for the worlds of the Malkuthians, led by a new collection of Dragon lords and generals, each as cruel and sadistic as Malevant. They didn't march. Rather, they flew and ran through the portals like an unruly mob. Ain had lost her patience. Azure's people would suffer, and she would regain her power.

"A NEW GENERATION"

It had been over a decade since the conclusion of the Dragon-Malkuthian War, the bloodiest war in the history of the cosmos by a huge margin. Now, it was like deja vu all over again. However, many of the invading Dragon armies faced a problem: Autumn Antares had designed new force fields that stretched out over whole star systems, similar to the force fields that had made Hod all but impenetrable in the past. She'd advocated for the continued importance of a strong military and security, and she was proven right.

Without the leadership of wise generals like Deem, the Dragons sent to invade these worlds struggled to find a way through these force fields. However, like water finds its way through the smallest of holes and creates a leak, the innumerable Dragons finally found the gaps intended for cargo ships.

However, Autumn Antares had a solution for that, knowing the Dragons would choose the path of least resistance. The guns of the Union starfleets were always aimed right at these gaps, and they became shooting lanes. What's more: the Malkuthians had melted down the leftover Dragon adamantine armor and lances, forming munitions and armor of their own from them. It was now much easier to kill a Dragon, even with their increased toughness, and it was now much harder to destroy a Union starship or mech, at least the newer models.

Still, not all worlds had these force fields or upgrades. Some governors of planets had actually opted out of them, wanting to demilitarize and also believing it might hurt the economy by limiting trade routes. Their concerns were justified, but these worlds were now under attack from an enemy they'd thought they'd left behind.

Diamond was now the Commander-in-Chief of the entire Union military. General Eridanus, Neela's step-father, was the Chief-of-Staff of the Army. Together, they helped lead the defense of these planets. They proved to be much more capable military commanders than their predecessors and were also leaders by example. Diamond proved that he was still a nigh-unstoppable killing machine in battle, devastating the Dragons as they charged.

His old friend, Edom, had made himself a trillionaire through Union-wide smuggling and criminal activity. *The Raised-Claw*, as his criminal syndicate was called, sold weapons to Malkuthians which were turned on the invading Dragons. Edom had a go with them and clobbered them with his hands, tail, feet, and fists like he always had.

Azure's avatar, though constrained in that state, was still able to manipulate space-time on a planetary scale. He teleported from world to world, devastating Dragon armies in each he appeared.

Athena, Aphrodite, Loki, and Thor had to work together to once again protect their worlds from Dragons. Azure had earlier restored to Athena the Black Sword and to Loki the Elder Staff, allowing them to regain their cosmic forms which greatly aided in their combat. However, Athena had to be particularly careful to cull her addiction to the power of the Black Sword as the spirits of Malevant and Gigatheta inside of it wore away at her famed sanity. She asked Aphrodite, her trusted sister, to be in charge of reeling her back when she'd gone too far and even allowed her to seize and hide the Black Sword when necessary. Once again, Athena got to fight alongside her sister and her husband.

Athena and Thor acted as the front-line brawlers. With the Elder Staff back and it having absorbed Lord Mortimer's essence, Loki now had arch-mage level powers that he used to combat even the stronger Dragons. Aphrodite used her incredible speed and healing abilities to serve as a sort of white mage, a role she'd become proficient at, having accumulated so much experience in previous battles. All of their children, even young Susanoo, fought alongside them in the struggle to save their worlds. Young Susanoo wielded his father's old sword.

"There's a beauty in struggle," Neela had once said. "As awful as it may sound at first. It's the friction that creates fire. It creates bonds stronger than steel. It pushes people—it forces people—together. If life were so perfect, there would be no reason or purpose at all. If there was no conflict, there'd be no journey. Without a mountain, there'd be no climb. That's the beauty of it. Azure, do you know what I mean?"

"THE DUEL CONTINUES"

Ain tore a portal into New Heaven and appeared in the Malkuth region. From the planet Malkuth, the outline and glow of her colossal body dominated both the day and night sky. The people shrieked in terror as the creature appeared to move toward them.

Autumn shook her head. She knew that even the solar-system-wide force field could not stop something like that. But like her father, she was always several steps ahead and was prepared to unleash a Time Mine if the Dragon Queen breached the force field, perhaps snagging a part of her.

Ain retracted her hand to smash through the barrier with a single strike, but Azure appeared and shoved her away, sending her careening toward the Cosmic Wall in the Deep Core. The Queen caught herself and threw a populated world at Azure along with all its moons. With Azure distracted, she fired a red Qi ball at him the size of a hundred red giant stars. Azure instinctively dodged it, but it barreled toward several more populated worlds in the Yesod region. Catching his mistake, Azure grabbed the Qi ball and held it in place like a dog by the leash. While he was distracted, Ain formed an identical Qi ball and hurled it the opposite direction toward the Netzach region. Azure literally duplicated himself and bilocated with his duplicate blocking the other Qi ball. Both versions of Azure absorbed the energy of the Qi balls, nullifying them and saving countless Malkuthian lives.

However, this gave the Queen an idea. She duplicated herself nine times. All ten versions of her flew off to attack each of the ten regions of New Heaven. Azure had no other choice. He duplicated himself nine times as well, and all versions of himself intercepted the other versions of Ain. They clashed again, but Azure was very hesitant to use any Qi for fear that it might kill Malkuthians. He and his duplicates took up a defensive disposition as Ain's duplicates did all they could to destroy Malkuthian worlds, even charging up Annihilation Rays all at the same time.

Athena, Aphrodite, Loki, and Thor saw a quasar-like light glowing in the sky in front of the imposing figure of one of Ain's duplicates. The power contained in one of those blasts was thousands of times what even they could conjure.

People on Malkuth were blinded by the bright light from Ain's attack. The heat, even at that distance, was searing. They braced for the very worse. There was nothing they could do but hope and pray.

Azure watched in horror and clutched his head. He'd burned through too much energy for the time being to counter ten Annihilation Rays, each capable of destroying multiple universes. Trying to calm himself, he did something he hadn't done in a long time: something compelled him to say Bekah's prayer, and so he did, over and over and over again like a professional athlete whose livelihood hinged on one play, making deals with God. He'd seen this moment play out before. He'd anticipated a miracle, a miracle that hadn't come.

Yet.

And then it came.

It came at the best of times.

Queen Ain's Annihilation Rays flickered before vanishing like burned out lightbulbs. Then, all of Ain's duplicates disappeared, leaving only her original self.

The millions and millions of streams of life-energy that flowed to her vanished as if someone had suddenly pulled the plug on creation's most elaborate Christmas lights display. Ain looked around, dumbfounded and confused. "WHAT? WHAT'S HAPPENING? WHAT DID YOU DO?!"

"I trusted and waited," said Azure.

"IT IS FINISHED"

On Earth, Samael-Satan clutched his head. All day, he'd gloated and celebrated, licking his lips as royal and holy blood was shed in Jerusalem. He'd gotten a taste of his future from Azure and looked to make good on his promise: he would make sure that this Jesus was killed before he could thwart Satan's dominance over the Earth. In making good of this promise, he now realized his enormous error. He now remembered the prophecies and the deal he'd made with the God of gods before the Angel War and before the beginning of the Omniverse.

God had addressed Samael's concerns about losing his power by stating that spiritual beings such as the Angels would continue to have access to the streams of spirit-energy until God's own blood was shed and his own life given. Satan believed this to be a sarcastic statement, thinking, *How can your blood ever be shed and your life ever be taken? God Yahweh always keeps his word! What a big old fool! This is a sure bet!*

There was a large earthquake that shook Palestine and tore the curtain in the Holy of holies into two, symbolizing that God's separation from his creations had ended. A darkness came upon the whole world.

One of the centurions guarding the execution commented that the death seemed unusual. "It was like something came at him howling and crushing him all at once! I could hear it! I could feel it even! Over a hundred crucifixions, and I've never experienced anything like that. That's not the wind, I tell you. There are powers at work here, and I don't want to stick around to see what they do!" The centurion took up a spear and aimed it at the lifeless victim hanging there. He passed it to the next man. "Here! You do it. Make sure he's dead. Pilate will want a record to be sure of it."

The soldier took the spear and plunged it into the victim's side. Blood and water spilled out from his heart and lungs onto the soldier's face. The soldier fell to his knees and cleared his eyes.

The centurion looked up at the body on the cross after having seen all of this and said, "Surely this was a righteous man. Truly, this man was the son of God."

Samael came to the feet of the cross as Mary wept. The blood dripped from Jesus' feet, it streaked down the wooden cross like the lamb's blood had done on the Hebrew doorways during the first Passover in Egypt. And like the first Passover, this blood was a deterrent to him, he flinched from it as if it were made of fire.

Frightfully, he retreated back. He looked up to the broken, bloody, and torn-up body that hung there. Although he relished in the pain and suffering he'd helped to inflict, Samael's thoughts were now running with what the consequences for this would be. But he knew. In truth, he knew.

As Ain looked around in confusion, Azure began to explain what had happened to her. "A long time ago, your benefactor, Samael-Satan, made an agreement with the God of gods. God's own blood would be shed before Samael and spiritual beings like him were to be stripped of their access to the life-force. You became Death, gifted with the ability to gather and harness the energy of all the dead in the Omniverse. But that ability was ultimately not contingent on you. It was contingent on Samael's agreement with the Almighty. God's son is an extension of him just as my avatars are an extension of me. Moments ago, he bled and died on a planet called Earth. He fulfilled his end of the agreement. Now the life-force has been stripped away from us. The power over Death will now fall into new hands, neither mine nor yours, and most certainly not into Samael's. It will fall into the hands of a selfless king."

Ain tensed her fists and her body. She rattled with infernal rage. She formed a great sparking red aura.

"Stop this, Ain."

"NO! NO, I WON'T STOP! I'LL KILL YOU! I'LL KILL EVERYONE!"

"A DESPERATE FIGHT"

Ain spread her arms and wings, unleashing thousands of smaller planet-sized Qi balls that flew to inhabited worlds around the Union.

Azure reached out his hand and stopped them all with a thought, drawing them all to him, converting them, and absorbing their energy. Ain bull-rushed him with the top of her horns. Azure's instinct was to sidestep her and redirect her momentum, a grappling technique that Edom had taught him. In this stage of the fight, Edom's fighting philosophy and Azure's combat experience would serve him well. Ain slashed at him, conjuring razor-sharp blades in her hands. She hurled them and stabbed him with them, conjuring more blades at will, sometimes dozens at a time. She levitated the blades and hurled them in volleys. Azure managed to stop and deflect most of these attacks.

Ain charged again, and Azure got under her and clinched her. In response, she wrapped her serpentine body around his enormous frame and began to constrict him with enough pressure to crush galaxies. His four wings were bent back and his many arms fought the entanglement. He bent his head forward and bit her. Shrieking and furious, she bit him too. She then dragged him toward the Cosmic Wall in the Deep Core, which had been rebuilt. With raw might, she plunged both herself and Azure into it, breaking through it and falling into the white void.

They crashed through together to the back gate of Heaven, landing on streets of gold. There'd been nowhere on Earth, Malkuth, Hod, Midgar, or Gaia as glamorous. It was almost indescribable. Angels, like a flock of birds, scattered. Both Azure and Ain suffered burns from the transition. Ain continued to try to pin Azure down. She slashed and punched at him with her plain old claws and fists. One of the blows knocked the back of Azure's head into the street. Azure tried to gain a hold on at least one of her arms and with the aid of his many arms, he did. He then wrapped his legs around her head and clamped down on it in a triangle hold Edom had taught him.

Ain fired Qi blasts from her eyes and mouth, forcing Azure to release the hold and roll away. Ain grabbed hold of him again and tried to impale him on the top of the pearly gate. When that wasn't enough, she came at him with her two horns. Azure pried her hands away and kept her horns at bay with his many arms. He headbutted her, and she stumbled back. Rushing at her with raw physical speed, he tackled her through the void and back into New Heaven.

Spiraling through light-years of space, the two cosmic beings wrestled, scratched, and clawed. They growled and roared and howled like beasts.

Autumn broadcast their struggle for the whole Union to see via hologram. This went on for months.

"AZURE!" Ain screeched. 'WHY WON'T YOU DIE?!"

"I have too much! Too much to live for!"

"I... I HAVE NOTHING! AND YOU... YOU SHOULD HAVE NOTHING TOO!" She aimed and fired a flickering Oblivion Beam directly at Malkuth. "EVERYONE DIES!"

"No!" Azure reached out and bent the Oblivion Beam away with a thought and sent it crashing back into Ain.

The Dragon Queen and Azure had clearly diminished during the course of the fight. While Azure could siphon energy at will, Ain no longer could. Her remaining energy went into either her attacks, recovery, or directly to Azure. Her aura disappeared and so did her glow. She lunged at Azure, and he let her. Finally, he hugged her. Even then, she punched and clawed at his ribs until her arms became too tired. Azure rubbed her back and head to comfort her. "Mercy. We should learn mercy. No more fighting. No more pain. No more suffering. No more death. It's over, Ain," he said. "It's ok. It's ok. It's ok. Close your eyes."

Ain rested her twitching, rattling hand on his side and closed her eyes.

"Goodnight and sweet dreams, mother," said Azure.

Ain faded away and was no more.

"NEW BEGINNINGS"

Azure sat beside the pond where Neela had spoken her last words. *"Do good, you hear me? There's enough evil and cruelty and wickedness in the world. In the cosmos. It doesn't need any more of that. No matter what happens, always love, always, always be kind, and always do good. Do good, my darling. Do good. And never lose your **self**."*

Amidst the cheerful swimming birds and fish, the water reflected the blue and magenta sky. The sister suns were rising on a new dawn.

There was crunching of the fallen leaves nearby and Autumn came, stepping through them. She hugged him from behind. "Heya," she said, resting her chipmunk cheek on his shoulder. "Whatcha up to?"

"Getting some fresh air. Are you holding up ok, kiddo?" Her father, the man who had once ruled the Union with an iron fist, had finally passed from old age. A private funeral was held.

"Yeah... You know, before dad passed, he asked me to show you something. A secret surprise." She led him away to a new laboratory in the city. "When you heal people, Azure, it hurts other people, right?

"Yes. There's always a trade. That's why I don't like to do it."

"That's partly why I think this thing is so special..."

Behind several layers of glass and other safety compartments there was a special stasis chamber. In it floated a large black worm-like creature attached to a clump of tissue. Azure looked away, disgusted at first.

Autumn rubbed his shoulder. "Hey, I'm sorry. I promise it's not bad."

"Is this it?"

"Yes. This is the Symbiote that was killing her and the last remnant of her: a part of her brain."

Azure placed his hand to the glass and cried. He sank down to a seated position. Autumn squatted down with him and hugged him. "Hey... don't you want to hear the good news?"

"What?"

"We're creating a sort of panacea from it—a cure for a whole range of diseases! Because of her, many more people and lives can be saved. We're gonna name the medicine after her. She'll be a hero!"

"She already is a hero," said Azure.

Autumn smiled. "Yes. And you're mine."

Azure sent his consciousness and avatars back to many different timelines, fixing and undoing many of the things he'd experienced in those timelines. He saved the people who'd starved in the cold. He rescued prisoners and fellow slaves. He prevented the burning deaths of the kind family that had adopted him. He thwarted the eviction of Delano and his tribe. He overthrew tyrants. He spared those abused by his gang. He proposed to Bekah and helped to contribute to the survival of her caravan with his powers, terrifying the superstitious lot.

He helped Diamond, then Aohdfionn, cope with life alone with his powers. He taught him how to use it constructively and raised him like a son. By some coincidence, they ran into little Neela and her mother along the way. Neela and Aohdfionn became friends, then more than friends.

Azure went back to the asylum, bringing with him the medicine that Autumn was talking about. He gave it to Enif. In days, it restored her sight and her hearing. How magnificent it was when the pupils of her eyes gained a bright brown color, and she could see him at last! Though she couldn't talk well, she tried. The people in lab coats were amazed by this sudden development. When they tried to apprehend her, kicking and screaming, Azure rendered them unconscious and lay them down gently. He escaped with Enif and explored the world with her, even building them a house. The Catastrophe did not occur. The universe was not colonized.

But in Azure's favorite timeline, he visited Neela and their little family. He brought the panacea to her as well, and the cancer went into remission, then shrank, and then vanished. They lived a full life together, and their kids grew old. Neela grew old, though Azure never aged. He took care of her all through the rest of her life and was at her bedside when she died. "Goodnight, Neela, my love," he said. "Sweet dreams 'til tomorrow, whenever tomorrow comes."

And tomorrow always came. Again and again and again. It marched on to infinity. It went on without end.

Printed in Great Britain
by Amazon